into the endless mountains

into the endless mountains

Norman K. Clark

This is a work of fiction. All the characters in this book are fictitious or, if they are historic characters, used fictitiously. References to, and descriptions of, locations and historic events may have been invented or modified to facilitate and enhance the telling of the story.

ISBN 978-1-67690-816-6

for Lisa

A Registered Letter

Russell Poe was almost asleep.

Reclining back in his desk chair, staring out his office window on the thirtieth floor, all he could see above the winter fog were the tops of the few buildings that rivaled his. Even William Penn, atop the Philadelphia City Hall just across the street, had submerged as fog slowly moved up the building all morning. Now only Penn's head occasionally poked up for a moment before ducking down again into the opaque mists.

Far away along the thickly carpeted, painting ornamented corridor, telephones rang discretely. Had the fog muffled all sounds and sensations this afternoon? Staring outside, he noticed the faint gray swirls of the fog, churned up by drafts caused by unseen forces and objects below. This must be what it would be like to live on another planet.

Russell's secretary came in. He could see her dim reflection in the window as she hesitated, probably thinking that, as usual, he had dozed off after lunch.

"Russ," she said quietly. Russell hated to be called Russ, but she persisted even after the four years that they had worked together. He spun around in his chair. She jumped slightly.

She had a thick registered letter from a law firm in Wellsboro, Pennsylvania.

"Wow, we never see these anymore," he commented. "I didn't know the post office still used registered letters. I wonder who's suing us up there in Wellsboro."

The letter was from an attorney in a two-lawyer firm. He was handling the estate of Simon Poe, who had been the older brother of Russell's father. He enclosed photocopies of an old will and a deed.

Russell could not recall ever having any contact with his uncle. The only thing that Russell knew about him were the stories he had heard while growing up: how Simon had made his fortune as a young man working in the Persian Gulf oil fields and, upon returning to the States, went into semi-retirement somewhere; how he was living in a commune somewhere in the Rockies; or was in prison in South America; or ran a charter fishing boat in Florida while smuggling guns to Cuba on the side. Russell assumed that he had died years ago.

The letter summarized the main points of the will. Except for specific bequests to two other people and some charitable gifts, the residue of the estate was left to Russell's father. The letter explained that the law firm had already determined that Russell was his father's only surviving heir. Could he please contact the undersigned at his earliest convenience to take care of the necessary documentation and to discuss his desires with respect to the deposition of the estate? The letter went on to describe how the principal asset in the estate was the decedent's house and land in northern Pennsylvania.

"Swell," Russell muttered. "Just what I need: a shack out in the sticks to worry about."

Russell sighed and started to draft a reply that instructed the firm to sell everything and send him the money. But he stopped in mid-sentence and spun his chair to look out over the city, now submerging even deeper into the mist.

Russell's telephone rang. He asked his secretary to take a message.

Simon Poe, he thought. His mythical uncle. Or was *legendary* the right word? What was he doing all those years, living so nearby and yet so remote? At least the rumors about South America appear to have been untrue.

Russell picked up the phone and dialed the number on the firm's letterhead. The lawyer who wrote the letter, Gus Weed, answered. He confirmed that his firm was handling the estate assets in Tioga County, Pennsylvania, on referral from a firm in Arizona, where Simon had resided when he died.

"I never knew Mr. Poe," Weed said. "He lived here for a number of years, but up in the mountains just east of here, not in Wellsboro.

When he moved to Arizona about three or four years ago – nobody knows for sure exactly when that was – he kept the house here and might have occasionally come back in the summer for a few weeks each year. We don't know when he was there last.

"The will was executed almost forty-three years ago, back in 1940, by a lawyer in Pittsburgh who used to write wills for employees of Gulf Oil Company before they would go out to work in the Middle East. The lawyer passed away in 1951, and the investigator that we hired out there in Pittsburgh couldn't find out whatever happened to his client files.

"Gulf Oil was able to confirm his employment dates from 1932 to 1952 and that he was stationed at the corporate headquarters in Pittsburgh from 1932 to 1940 and in Kuwait from 1940 until he retired in 1952. We know that he moved to Tioga County sometime between 1952 and 1953, when he bought the house here. Most importantly to us, the Gulf Oil people confirmed that he drew a fairly substantial company pension from 1952 until he passed away last year, but that there are no survivors' benefits.

"While the Arizona firm was helping Mr. Poe's companion get your uncle's affairs in order, they found the will and the deed to the property in Pennsylvania in his safe deposit box. As far as they have been able to determine, there's never been a subsequent will or codicil. There's not much more that I can tell you. As you know from the copy that I sent to you, the will was properly executed under Pennsylvania law and meets the requirements for probate in Arizona, as well.

"At the request of the Arizona firm, I checked the title to the property here in Tioga County. In most of these cases, where there's an old deed or a copy of it in the personal effects, the decedent sold the property long ago. In Mr. Poe's case, however, he still had clear title to it: no mortgages, no liens, and even the property taxes were paid up to date by a recurring payment from his bank in Arizona. So, it's yours, if you want it."

"What would we need to do to get the place ready to sell?" Russell asked.

"Basically, just put a for-sale sign in front of it," Weed replied. "You'll find everything in good shape, pretty much as Mr. Poe left it the last time he was there.

"We haven't done much to the house, except put new locks on the doors. The late Simon Poe apparently was very well organized, a probate lawyer's dream come true. The electric company confirmed that he had set up the electric bills to be paid automatically, so the power is still on. It also looks like he had arranged for his well and septic tank to be serviced within the last year or so.

"When he moved to Arizona, he apparently took everything he wanted. He didn't leave any clothes, food in the refrigerator, or canned goods in the cupboards from when he was there last time, whenever that was. You'll see what looks like all his furniture and a collection of old books. There's an old oak filing cabinet in the bedroom that's locked, and it's too heavy to tell whether there is anything in it or not just by hefting it. Also, we didn't want to try to break the lock and risk damaging the piece or anything inside.

"In any event, the filing cabinet and any of its contents are yours. So, if you find anything of value in it, just tell me about it, so that we can include it when we file the estate inventory with the court here."

"What about the estate assets in Arizona?" Russell asked.

"I can send you a copy of the inventory prepared by the firm in Arizona. Other than a savings account in Arizona and a few personal items there, like the furniture in his apartment, which he rented, there aren't any. Mr. Poe took care of his companion with a small life insurance policy and a rather sizable joint CD, which is more than she would otherwise receive under Arizona law. The Arizona lawyers say that she is content with that.

"So, the only major asset in the estate is the property here in Pennsylvania. The other assets – his personal effects in Arizona and the balance in his savings and checking accounts there – are more than enough to handle the charitable gifts and the specific bequests, which, fortunately for you, are not worth very much due to inflation since 1940.

"Now that I've made contact with you, the Arizona firm should be contacting you soon about the probate proceedings out there. Based on what they told me on the phone, I expect that your uncle's savings account will cover their fees and costs as well as ours. So, my advice would be to liquidate the remaining assets in Arizona to pay the probate expenses and keep or sell the house and the other stuff that he left here in Pennsylvania. We can help you with whatever you decide to do."

Russell made an appointment to meet Gus Weed and visit the property the following Tuesday afternoon. He might as well take a look, to conduct a little "due diligence" on the matter. It was only prudent.

The drive from Philadelphia into the mountains of northern Pennsylvania took five hours. The day started with a brilliant blue sky and the type of blinding winter sunlight that occurs only, but rarely, in January. By midday, however, heavy clouds had drifted in from the west and settled lower as he drove into the afternoon.

Russell arrived at the law firm, a small office in a handsomely converted storefront in the center of Wellsboro, shortly before two o'clock. The receptionist apologized that Mr. Weed had been unavoidably detained at a hearing in Scranton but had left instructions that Russell should be given the keys and directions to Simon's house. She told Russell that he could keep the keys, as the firm had a duplicate set. When Russell had made his decision concerning the property, he should advise the firm of his desires, which they would carry out quickly and economically. She also offered to reserve a room in a local hotel, should he decide to stay overnight.

"I know that the directions look a little complicated at the end, with the references to barns and the exact distances between turns," she explained. "It's only about sixteen miles from here but the last part is tricky. The first part is a straight shot out of town, but you will have to follow the directions carefully once you turn off Route 6. Eventually you'll be going up an old fire tower road for a couple of miles. The entry to the property is a dirt road going off into the woods on the right side. Look for a small mailbox with *Poe* on it. The mailbox is partially hidden by a bush and the name is faded, so it's easy to miss. I miss it all the time. But then just follow the dirt road for about one-third of a mile into the woods and you will come to the house."

As Russell started out the door, she called to him. "If you start seeing a lot of New York license plates, you'll know you've gone a little too far."

His plan was to do a quick inspection and then head back to Philadelphia. Depending on traffic, he could be home before midnight. He took the main highway out of Wellsboro and soon came to the intersection with a county road headed north. He passed quilts of open fields and chunks of dense woods. Occasionally, at some distance from the road, the first evening lights from a farmhouse would twinkle through the late afternoon haze. The colors of the day faded into a premature gray, almost like a black and white photograph. There seemed to be no sound except the strangely muffled rumble from the engine and a faint hiss of tires on wet asphalt.

The directions were precise, and, in the late afternoon mist, had he not followed them exactly, he might have never gotten close to his destination. Each turn took him onto a smaller and more uncertainly paved road. None of these half-hidden intersections had road signs. In England during World War II, they removed all the road signs to confound the Germans if they invaded. What invasions did people here anticipate? Or was it merely a matter of there being nothing worth pointing out to strangers in this misty, gray-green land? If you know where you're going, fine. If not, you really shouldn't be here.

The final two miles were under a dense canopy of bare trees, the road seeming to become narrower as he made a long ascent into the forest. Even driving slowly and watching for any opening in the forest on the right side of the road, he missed the mailbox the first time he passed it. Turning around, he found it and followed what was little more than a wide path, curving uphill into the woods and then down into a small clearing surrounded by forest. Simon's house appeared suddenly at the end.

The house rested at the back of a clearing with dense trees marking the wandering boundaries of the clearing. Small patches of old snow clung to the shadows at the edges. There had been an unsuccessful attempt at a small lawn in front of the house, centered around an oak tree, hundreds of years old, possibly a survivor of the virgin forest.

Russell walked slowly around the perimeter of the house. It was T-shaped and two stories high, much different from the simple cabin that he had expected. The wooden siding once might have been a brilliant white, but now had faded with time and had a soft gray-red appearance in the late afternoon light. Looking at differences in the styles of the windows and in the texture of the siding, Russell guessed that the house originally was one story, with only a short rear wing that was later extended further back. Then the second floor must have been added, extending over the central wing from almost the front of the house to the rear. A chimney was on each end of the front section of the house. The bottom parts of the chimneys looked original, stone to just above the apex of the first-floor roof, with brick extensions that probably had been added when the second story was built. The full-length front porch appeared to have been added last.

Standing outside the back wing of the house, Russell looked into the woods, which came to within twenty feet of the house on all three sides of the back wing. There was no borderland of brush or shrubs, just a cleared path wide enough to keep, with constant effort, the tree limbs from encroaching on the house. Beyond that there was nothing but forest, climbing the mountain, dark, gray, and misty, with random patches of snow, as far as the eye could see, up to where it dissolved into the low gray sky.

Before going inside, Russell looked at the copy of the deed that Weed had sent him with his first letter about the estate. Judging from the old-fashioned surveyor's description, the property started at the mailbox and continued in an irregularly shaped expanding wedge beyond the ridge behind the house, for 1,096 acres "more or less."

Inside, two large identically sized rooms flanked a small foyer. The walls and ceilings appeared creamy white in the late afternoon light. Large, faintly patterned, predominantly beige rugs of unidentifiable origin almost completely covered a dark hardwood floor. The room on the left had a small stone fireplace and was set up as a living room, with a brown leather chair and a matching sofa. There was no television, radio, or telephone, nor any pictures or books.

The room on the right was set up as a dining room, with a similar fireplace into which a wood stove had been installed. It had a small table, four straight-back oak chairs, a small sideboard, and a pie safe in the corner. The pieces were old, heavy, and rustic, possibly handmade one hundred years ago or more, but in good condition, as if they had been used only occasionally. Even the green and gray striped upholstery on the seats of the dining room chairs looked relatively new.

A short, narrow corridor led from the front rooms, past a staircase on the left side, leading to the second floor. There was a large bathroom on the right with old fixtures and a free standing, claw-footed tub. Behind the tub were two bare windows opening onto the strip of grass between the house and the forest. A vertical pipe, obviously added later, ran up to a simple shower head. An oblong shower curtain rod hung from the ceiling. Russell looked into the oak medicine cabinet, which had no mirror. It was empty.

Just beyond the bathroom, there was a single step up into the kitchen, which was at the end of the first-floor hallway. It was large, covering possibly one-third of the total floor space on the first floor. With windows on three sides and white walls and ceiling, the room glowed in the dim light.

A large painted table, its top covered with tacked-down red and white checkered oilcloth, dominated the center of the room. Two old, heavily painted, white wooden chairs were centered together in the middle, facing a back door that opened directly onto the small cleared area at the back of the house.

The appliances were like the ones Russell remembered from his childhood, when he would watch his aunt bake pies and cookies. The refrigerator had its coil on the top of the box, and the gas range was a clumsy Art Deco vision of a future that never materialized except in the science fiction comics he read as a kid. Opening the refrigerator door, Russell was surprised to see that it was running, although empty. He looked behind the stove to confirm that a gas line led through the wall to small propane tanks outside, which looked as if they had been recently replaced.

The white wooden cupboards above the kitchen sink and the stove were empty except for a few odd pieces of china and glassware. The drawers in the small cabinet to the right of the sink held an assortment of mismatched utensils and knives, probably just enough for four complete place settings. A small hand-cranked grindstone was clamped to the right side of the top of the cabinet. He tested the water, which had a faint, but not unpleasant, mineral taste and acceptable pressure.

Russell left the kitchen and opened a door next to the stairs leading to the second floor. He had assumed that it was a closet door, but instead it led four steps down a narrow staircase to a landing with pantry shelves and then around to the right, under the kitchen, and into a small cellar. Russell had to stoop to avoid hitting his head on the beams, which allowed no more than five and a half feet of clearance. There was a small electric hot water heater, which looked relatively new. There was no furnace, nor any signs that one had ever been installed. Apparently, Simon had relied on the wood stove in the dining room and the fireplace in the living room whenever he needed heat. This explained the ventilating grates that Russell had noticed in the ceiling between the first and second floors.

The second floor had two bedrooms at either side at the top of the stairs. The smaller one, in the front of the house, was completely empty except for two tall oak bookcases, which were filled with books. There also were some low bookshelves, built from bricks and warped pine boards, also packed with books. The room looked as if it had not been used for many years, except as a book repository, with no signs of furniture on the floor or pictures that had hung on the walls.

Russell noticed the pull-down stairs in the ceiling of the upstairs hall. They led to an attic that, in the dim light of a single light bulb, revealed itself to be completely empty, except for pads of fiberglass insulation on the floor and two pieces of plywood on either side, front and back, of the ladder opening.

The larger bedroom was at the rear of the second floor, built over the kitchen. Simon's roll-top oak desk was next to the rear wall, centered between two windows that looked out onto the woods behind the house. The top center drawer still contained a small collection of pens, pencils, and paper clips. The other drawers were empty.

A double bed, still made up with sheets, a gray wool blanket, and two pillows, was positioned perpendicular to the right wall. Russell walked over to the low two-drawer oak filing cabinet, which Simon had used as a bedside table. It had a lock in each drawer, but no key. A small table lamp was centered on it, on top of an ancient-looking lace-trimmed circular cloth. He resisted the momentary temptation to try to lift and shake the cabinet to listen for objects inside. It would be better to have a locksmith or antique expert try to open it later.

Two empty large wardrobes, without even a single coat hanger, almost entirely covered the wall on either side of the door. With windows on the remaining three sides of the bedroom, there was little space for pictures, but Russell saw that there were many discrete nail holes, indicating that Simon had made use of almost all the available wall space. The pictures, or whatever else was on the walls, were gone, probably taken by Simon to Arizona.

There was an old Regulator railroad depot clock on the back wall, between the two rear windows and centered above the desk. Russell opened the glass cover of the clock and reset the hands. As he guessed, the key was in the lower compartment with the pendulum. He slowly wound the mainspring, not sure whether the clock had run in years, but it started ticking as soon as he tapped the pendulum.

With the clock quietly ticking now, for the first time since Simon Poe left his bedroom forever, Russell returned to the desk and sat down, swiveling the chair slowly from side to side, studying the forest on all three sides, watching it grow slowly darker and even more endless as daylight crept away, almost from tree to tree, slowly up the mountainsides behind and beside the house.

Soon he realized that he was sitting in the dark. He made one final inspection of the rooms, lingering for a few minutes like the last visitor in a museum at closing time, and then walked out onto the front porch, double checking the lock on the front door.

Russell had intended to go back to Wellsboro and return the keys with a note saying, "Sell the place." It would be a simple matter. Just stuff the envelope containing the keys and his note into the mail slot in the front door to the law firm's office on his way out of town. They could send him the necessary papers consenting to the sale, and he then could just wait for the check.

Yet, even before he reached the mailbox at the main road, Russell realized not only that he would keep the house, but he began to think about how strange it was that what he had wanted, for so many years it seemed, without even knowing anything about Simon Poe, the existence of the house, or the mountains around it, was to move in.

He thought for a moment about going back to retrieve the clock but continued on to Philadelphia.

Russell Moves In

It took Russell six months to wind up most of his law practice in Philadelphia. All his life he had been cautious and deliberate, taking risks only when the odds were clearly on his side. These habits had their benefits. He kept his small row house near the Society Hill section of Philadelphia. The rental income, the buy-out of his partnership interest in the law firm, and his savings and other investments would produce enough income to support a modest lifestyle. If finances became tight, he could practice law on the side, taking only simple local matters that would produce a reliable fee. If things really got bad financially, he could move back to Philadelphia and go back to work full-time. Maybe, he thought, as he looked out the bedroom windows, feeling a gentle warm breeze rushing along the hallway from the front of the house, and listening to the ticking of his uncle's clock, this wasn't such a leap of faith after all.

He could now devote more time to his interest in history. Although he had published one short book and a few magazine articles, his interest in the history of the seventeenth and eighteenth-century American frontier had been just a hobby. Now he had decamped to the forests and mountains of northern Pennsylvania, without a clue as to what he would do and only just enough money to do it.

Russell moved in on a hot July day. He had visited the property twice during the spring, but he was not prepared for the wall of rich, multi-toned greens that overwhelmed him when he crested the small hill and drove down into the clearing. The forest seemed much larger, much more impenetrable, than before. The ancient oak on the front lawn appeared to have spread its canopy over half of the area in front of the house, almost completely obscuring it.

The noise of the place surprised him. On that first winter day, and even during his subsequent visits in the spring, the house and its clearing had been utterly soundless. During his previous visits, he couldn't even hear the occasional car or truck passing by on the road just a few hundred yards away. Now the breeze roared through the woods, even though he could only faintly feel it on his face when he got out of his car and stepped up onto the porch. The trees seemed to be loaded with singing birds.

Standing in Simon's old bedroom, with the windows open and high summer flowing through the house, Russell thought about that afternoon just six months to the day before, when he had first stood in that room. So much in his life had changed since then, but on this Monday afternoon in July, just as on that cold Tuesday afternoon in January, he knew that he had made the right decision.

His first priority was to set up his study in the vacant front room on the second floor. A locksmith drove out from Wellsboro late that afternoon to unlock the oak filing cabinet and give Russell keys that would work in it. It was a quick, easy job, and Russell and the locksmith moved the cabinet into the front room. Russell then prevailed on the locksmith's apparent good nature to help him move the oak desk there. After dinner, he worked late into that first evening, going through the contents of the cabinet by the light of a green glass shaded banker's lamp that had sat on his desk at the law firm from his first day there as an associate.

The probate, at least the part in Pennsylvania, would be simple. At first glance, Simon Poe seemed to have saved everything: pay stubs from the 1930s through his last job in Kuwait in 1952, as well as every utility bill and receipts for every repair from the day he moved into the house in 1953 until, Russell assumed, he moved to Arizona twenty-five years later. As the evening grew later, Russell became puzzled, however, by what Simon hadn't saved. He could not find a diary or journal. The meticulousness with which Simon had kept the house and his papers strongly suggested that he was the type of person to keep a journal. Nor were there any bank statements, cancelled checks, credit card bills, letters, or newspaper clippings – any of the other documents that one would expect to be kept by a string-saver operating just on the healthy side of hoarding. Simon might have taken them with him to Arizona, but Gus Weed reported that none of those things, nor any photographs nor other family documents, were among his personal effects at his apartment.

It was almost midnight when Russell found the map of the property, in an old, dark manila envelope taped to the back of the inside of the cabinet. He had to pull out the top drawer entirely to remove the envelope. It was not just a surveyor's plat. He already had one of those. Instead, this was a true map, apparently hand drawn, with more than a hundred small notations, some in black ink and some in pencil.

Russell already knew the metes and bounds of the property: 1,080 acres, more or less, situated in the Township of Richmond, and an adjacent 16 acres, more or less, situated in the Township of Tioga, County of Tioga, Commonwealth of Pennsylvania, with a two-story frame and stone dwelling house and sundry outbuildings. Other than the house itself and the "sundry outbuildings" (which apparently had been torn down sometime after Simon bought the property), he was not aware of many of the details of the property, all of which, except the clearing around the house, he assumed to be heavily wooded. On a previous visit in the spring, he had walked partway up an old, overgrown path leading up the mountain behind the house, but he was still ignorant of most of the land that had now become his home, especially the part that stretched east beyond the ridge almost to the river.

The paper on which the map was drawn was heavy and did not appear to be very old, even allowing for it having been stored away in the filing cabinet for an unknown length of time. Judging from the way that it was drawn, it might have been a copy of an older document. It was rich with detail, almost like the elaborately illustrated maps of the New World drawn by European cartographers, based on the unsure and sometimes fanciful accounts of the earliest explorers. He could easily understand the indications for the house, where the sheds had been, and paths that crossed the woods. However, most of the map was filled with tiny numbers, symbols, and other notations that had been added by hand over many years. Some appeared to be dates, such as *5-7-72*. Others seemed to note the location of various features such as *the Indian Rocks, the Wolf Pit,* and *Roanoke Campsite*. Others were just symbols: crosses, stars, and triangles, mostly.

Although the forested area of his property was almost entirely filled with these symbols and notations, they seemed thickest around a feature labeled *the Indian Rocks*. This appeared to be about four hundred feet up the mountain, just beyond the ridge, which ran from the northwest corner of the property to the southeast. There were also symbols clustered along a dotted line, labeled *Old Indian Trail*, which followed the ridge.

Russell studied the map for a long time, occasionally walking into the bedroom and looking out the back windows, up and in the direction of the various features on it, as if he could somehow see the faintest hint of them even at midnight. As he sipped tea and thought about the map, his mind began to race. He had always considered himself to be an investigative historian, albeit amateur. He loved to solve historical puzzles. Was this one of them? Was there a book in this map?

A comical thought crossed his mind: What if his uncle had been a birdwatcher, and these were merely a record of his observations? He considered this thesis until he realized that he had found nothing in or near the house that suggested any interest whatsoever in birds.

Russell's old Seth Thomas mantle clock downstairs struck two o'clock in the morning. Simon's Regulator upstairs joined in seconds later, as if singing a round. Minutes later, just before turning off the light to go to sleep, Russell took one final look around his new bedroom. The shadows of his uncle's pictures remained on the wallpaper. The sunlight from the windows on three sides of the room would in time bleach them away.

Wanda

Russell had originally intended to celebrate his first morning in his new home with an authentic rustic breakfast of biscuits, omelet, and bacon, but the late night before convinced him to settle for coffee. Sitting in the kitchen, he was more inhaling the steamy coffee aroma than drinking, when he was startled by the rumble of what sounded like a tank coming down his driveway. By the time he reached the front door, Wanda Abrams had climbed out of what had to be the world's most beat-up Land Rover – as well as the loudest – and was coming onto his porch with a large basket swinging from the crook of her right elbow.

Russell's first impression of Wanda was that she belonged in the opening scene of *Macbeth*. She was a thin woman, just barely five feet tall, but she approached the front door with an energy that somehow made her appear taller. Her black and gray hair was pulled back into a ponytail, but strands escaped from the sides of her head, sticking out as if carrying a permanent static charge. She wore blue jeans, black sneakers, and a black tie-dyed t-shirt, as well as a denim jacket, even though the day was already beginning to become warm.

Russell's second impression was Wanda's eyes. They were a deep brown, almost black, and still very much the eyes of a young woman. The rest of her face looked tired, sad perhaps, but her eyes were alert and inquiring.

As soon as they sat down with coffee, Wanda introduced herself further. She was Russell's nearest neighbor, living on a small apple farm bordering on the south of Russell's property. She and her husband Jack moved to the area twenty years ago, where they ran what she described to Russell as a "one desk" insurance agency in Wellsboro. When Jack died five years ago, Wanda sold the insurance agency.

"I decided to keep the farm," Wanda explained, "because Jack and I had worked hard to make it a going concern, and, once we put all the sweat equity into it, keeping up a small orchard like ours is really not a lot of work. But living up here on the mountain, I was just far enough from town to feel isolated. So, I became the county's first and only Welcome Wagon lady."

Russell asked Wanda how well she had known Simon.

"Not very well," she replied. "Jack and I invited him to a housewarming at our place when we moved in, to meet our new neighbors. Simon was there for a couple of hours, but never returned the invitation. I invited him once or twice after that to stop for a drink or supper, but he usually had an excuse. So, I just figured that he wanted to be left alone.

"Other than that, I would bump into Simon every couple of months, and then only in town. Usually it was on Saturday mornings when I went shopping. He was always very cordial, but I don't think we ever exchanged more than a dozen words any of those times. Jack knew him a little better, and occasionally they would go hiking together up in the woods or go fishing in the reservoir over on the other side of the mountain. But Jack said that the two of them would just sit quietly fishing, not saying very much to each other. Boring damn way to drown a worm, fishing."

Wanda paused, and took a sip of coffee, her eyes not leaving Russell.

"No offense, Russell, but your uncle was sort of weird. He stayed mostly to himself," she continued. "He wasn't a nasty person or a hermit or anything like that. I hear he spent most of his days just tramping around in the woods. 'The forest,' he called it. Only most of it really isn't a forest, not anymore. Your land might have one of the last few patches of virgin forest left around here."

"What did Simon do, tramping around in the woods?" Russell asked.

Wanda sighed. "Oh, I don't know. Some people say he had a secret crop of sang up there. I sometimes thought he just had a patch of grass up there in a small clearing somewhere, and wouldn't share it with anyone, if you know what I mean."

"Sang?" Russell interrupted.

"Wild ginseng," Wanda replied. "They say these hills are full of it, although I've never seen any and probably wouldn't know it if I saw it. Some of the old-timers used to make a living harvesting the stuff for sale as a traditional medicine in China. They say that at one time it fetched a higher price there per ounce than gold, especially the sang from around here."

"Simon was into ginseng?"

"Well, I don't know that for a fact. But there's no other reason he'd spend all his time up in the woods. Except maybe for the marijuana," she smiled.

"Don't worry, Russell, just kidding. Your uncle never seemed to me to be much of a pothead."

"Is there still ginseng around here?"

"Maybe. I know that some of the old guys in town still talk about how they plan to strike it rich hunting sang. But that's mostly bar room talk. I've never heard of anyone finding any."

"Did Simon ever actually talk about hunting sang?"

"Hell, no. Like I told you, I never spoke much with your uncle, and Jack never mentioned Simon ever saying anything about it. Of course, I'm just speculating."

"So, you wouldn't know why he eventually left and went to Arizona."

"No, I don't know anything about that. I know it was a little after Jack died, and I realized that I hadn't seen Simon in a while. I came over a couple of times to check on him, but there was never anyone home. I never felt safe – no, I don't mean that – I never felt welcome coming here, so after a while I just realized that I had better things to do than annoy him."

"Did he ever come back for a visit?"

"Well, I never saw him again, not after the last time in town a few days before Jack died. He could have come back here now and then, but I wouldn't have known, not with his house set back and invisible from the road. Hell, I didn't even know that he had moved away for good and that you had moved in until I saw the new mailbox with *R. Poe* on it a couple of weeks ago at the end of your driveway. I've been kind of stalking you ever since, trying to catch you at home to say hello and give you all this stuff in my basket."

"Well, I really didn't move in until yesterday, but I'm glad you finally caught me," Russell smiled. "But, tell me, did Simon have any close friends?"

"Not really, not that I know of. If anyone was really close to Simon, it was probably Paul Levesque. He used to own that little blue house down the road from us near the crossroads, the one with the windmill in the back. Simon and Paul used to go fishing, I understand, about once or twice a month, and sometimes Jack would go with them."

Wanda paused, as if she was thinking about what else she should tell him. She looked out the kitchen window, toward the woods behind the house, and slowly sipped some coffee.

"I'm sorry it seems like I'm cross-examining you, Wanda," Russell said. "I just have so many questions about him. It was all a big surprise to me. I never had any contact with my uncle growing up. I never even really knew for sure that he existed."

"No, that's okay," Wanda replied. "But it won't do you much good to try to talk to Paul, though. He spent the last couple of years of his life in the VA Hospital down in Wilkes-Barre and died there almost six years ago, just a few months before my Jack. They say that he was gassed in France in World War I and was never quite right after that. He lived in that little blue house ever since he came back from the war, I guess. Then something happened to him. I don't know what; nobody does. He just snapped. They found him one morning on his porch in his underwear, shooting at passing cars. Didn't hit anyone, thank goodness, but they had to take him away to the VA Hospital and keep him there, I guess. He was in his eighties when he passed away.

"There's a couple of professors from the state university over in Mansfield that live there now, the Graybills. I'll introduce you to them. I know you guys would get along just great."

Russell excused himself, went upstairs, and returned with the map.

"Take a look at this. I found it upstairs last night among my uncle's papers. What do you make of it?" he said.

Wanda looked at it for a minute, her finger appearing to trace a path.

"Well, all I can say is that it must be some record of your uncle's wandering around the woods. That's all I can make of it, from the dates and all."

Wanda pointed to northeastern part of the map.

"The Indian Rocks," she murmured. She was silent for a minute.

"What about them?"

"Oh, nothing," Wanda quickly replied. "It's just that I knew they were supposed to be around here somewhere, but –" Her voice faded away, not completing the thought.

"I haven't been up that far into the woods yet," Russell explained. "What do you know about them?"

"Well, Russell, they're sort of a minor landmark around here. Most people just call them *the Rocks.* You might hear a few old-timers refer to them as *the White Indian Rocks.* But they're just a circle of boulders, mostly overgrown, out there in the woods. Just another local mystery."

"Another local mystery? How many of these local mysteries are there?"

This time Wanda had the look of someone who shouldn't have just let the cat out of the bag. "Sure. Just a bunch of old legends and ghost stories."

"Any ghost stories about the Rocks?"

"No, of course not," Wanda snapped. She paused for a second. "Sorry, that sounded abrupt."

"So, tell me about the Rocks. Are they a natural formation of some kind?"

Wanda laughed lightly. "Oh, of course they aren't, not laid out in a circle like that. You're not one of those flying saucer nuts, are you?"

Russell wasn't sure how to respond.

She quickly added, "No, just kidding. Really."

"About thirty or thirty-five years ago or so," she went on, "long before Jack and I moved here, some scientists from Penn State came up here to study them. They said that the rocks were from this area and had been cut out of the bedrock and arranged in a circle by someone. They couldn't say who or when. It probably was one of the early settlers for some reason or other. The Indians had better things to do back in those days than to go around arranging rocks in the woods.

"Still," Wanda continued, "you sometimes hear a bunch of nutty stories about ancient civilizations and so forth."

Wanda looked up at the clock on his kitchen wall.

"Good lord," she exclaimed. "I got to get going."

Wanda Abrams left in a flurry of coupons from her basket and a cloud of blue smoke from her Land Rover.

Funning the Flatlander

Most of Russell's first full day at his new home was spent unpacking boxes and setting up the necessities of life: stereo, typewriter, and his brass espresso machine. Throughout the day, however, whenever Russell went into his study, he found himself lingering over his uncle's map, already mentally planning expeditions to discover the meanings of the annotations.

Late that afternoon Russell drove into Wellsboro to buy a basic supply of groceries and cleaning supplies. Wanda had recommended two grocery stores: a small Red & White store on Main Street in the center of Wellsboro and a larger supermarket on the edge of town. Russell chose Kaiser's Red & White Market, Robert & Janice Kaiser, Proprietors.

Janice greeted him from behind the single cash register. Russell introduced himself and told her that he had just moved into Simon Poe's place and was one of Wanda's neighbors. Her smile seemed to dim for a moment.

"Oh," she said quietly, but then she quickly recovered with "That's lovely. You'll love it out there. And thank you so much for driving all the way into town to shop with us."

As Russell filled his cart, Janice was joined by her husband, Robert. Both appeared to be in their sixties, white-haired but otherwise seeming as youthful and energetic as people half their age. Robert Kaiser was tall and thin and wore thick rimmed glasses that concealed hearing aids in the earpieces. Standing next to Robert, Janice seemed only half his size, slightly plump, with a smile that took over every part of her face. They told Russell that Simon had been a regular customer.

"He always griped about our prices," Robert chuckled. "Always said he'd start shopping at that other place out on Route 6, the one that's closer to you. But I guess he never did."

"What sort of stuff did he eat?" Russell was surprised and horrified at the inanity of his question.

"Usual stuff," Janice replied, "nothing special."

"Man is what he eats," Russell laughed.

Robert and Janice looked at him with blank expressions. Finally, Robert broke the silence.

"I guess so."

"So, what are you planning to do, now that you're all moved in?" Janice broke in.

Russell said that he hadn't really made any plans yet.

"Simon took good care of the old Paxton place," Robert said. "That's what we still call it around here. Even though Simon lived there for what, thirty-some years? Our friend Tom, who owns the hardware store across the street, says that your uncle was always buying stuff to keep after the place."

"Were the Paxtons the people my uncle bought the house from?" Russell asked. He remembered another seller's name on the deed.

"Not exactly," Robert replied. "They had all moved away, all but one of them, by the time your uncle arrived. The Paxton family had lived there forever. They were one of the first settlers in this area, a little after the time of the American Revolution. When Old Man Paxton –"

"Walter," Janice interjected.

"Yeah, Walter," Robert continued. "Well, when Walter Paxton died, his son Wally didn't want the place, nor did any of Wally's cousins or anybody else in the family. It took nearly two years to sell it. But then your uncle heard about it somehow and came here and snapped it up. That was – when was that, Janice?"

Janice looked up, studying the ceiling as if she were looking for a leak.

"Oh, I'd say sometime in the early 1950s. We were in a recession here. The last mines were closing, and the good timber was all taken. Most of the young men were away fighting in Korea, which was just as well because there was no work for them here. Nobody could afford to buy anything."

"Yeah," Robert added. "by that time the Paxton house was too old and too small for most folks to live in year-round, and the land was worthless for farming. I remember hearing back then that even the state didn't want it to add to the State Game Lands. That was what was happening to most of those old places."

"Are there any Paxtons still around?" Russell asked.

"Only one that I know of," Janice responded. "Pastor Bill Paxton. He has a little church just outside town. He was Wally Paxton's boy. Wally was Walter's only child. We always called him Wally, but his real name was Wallace."

"I'm surprised that an old family like the Paxtons wouldn't try to keep the old family homestead," Russell commented. He had the strange sense that Bill Paxton was somehow a rival, the rightful heir to the usurped kingdom.

"Well," Janice continued, "Wally was a good-for-nothing, if you ask me. By the time the bank finally sold the old home place to your uncle, Wally had run off to California with his girlfriend and left his wife and little boy – that's Bill – high and dry. We hear that once he got his hands on his share of the money from the house, he went through it like a drunken sailor, and when the money ran out, his girlfriend took off. His poor wife and child never saw a penny of it. He ended up blowing his brains out."

"Wow," was all Russell could say.

"Well the Paxton place – your place," Janice quickly corrected herself and smiled, "is a beautiful old mountain-style home, small but in one of the nicest places in the whole state, surrounded by woods and mountains. You're very lucky, with that lovely little house and that big tract of old forest on your land. Living there must be like going back in time."

Russell mentioned that he wanted to get out into the forest and explore it. "Wanda Abrams was telling me about an interesting rock formation on my land." *My land*, it still sounded so strange.

Robert suddenly turned away.

"Forgot something. Excuse me," he mumbled as he disappeared quickly into the back of the store.

"Oh yes," Janice said. "The Indian Rocks. They're something of a curiosity around here, an old Indian site, some say. When I was a little girl, my father would take us up the old Indian trail to the Rocks for a picnic. He and Walter Paxton – Old Man Paxton, not that bum Wally – were in the Redmen together. We'd have the most fun running and hiding among those rocks."

"I still remember it like yesterday," she smiled. "We'd sit in the middle of the circle of stones, eating our lunch and telling ghost stories about the place. And there was an old friend of Mr. Paxton's, a real live mountain man, who would sometimes come by and join us. His stories were the best of all."

Janice laughed, "Imagine: ghost stories in broad daylight. But they were scary all the same, even scarier when he'd swear to us kids that every word was true."

Janice suddenly was silent for a moment. Her face momentarily looked sad, as if she was remembering a tragedy rather than a happy time from her childhood.

"I'm surprised that Wanda mentioned the Rocks to you," she said quietly.

"Why?" Russell asked.

"Well," Janice continued slowly, "it was near there where they found her husband Jack's body. He'd been attacked by wolves, the Coroner said."

"That's how Wanda's husband died?" For a second Russell wondered whether Janice was telling daytime ghost stories of her own.

"Are there wolves around here?" he continued. "I always assumed that they were extinct in Pennsylvania."

Robert came walking up the center aisle of the store. "That's what the Fish and Game Commission people have been saying for years," he said. "But there's lots of things up in that forest that aren't supposed to be there: wolves, panthers, and the like."

"Have you actually seen wolves around here?" Russell asked.

"Oh, Robert," Janice interjected. "Now you've got Russell here all worried."

"No, Russell, to be honest with you, I haven't actually seen any wolves." Robert said slowly, apparently choosing his words with great caution, "But I know they're up there. The bureaucrats down there in Harrisburg say they're not, but that's just to soothe people and keep them from being afraid to come to the state parks and so forth. But they're up there all the same. So, I wouldn't go up into those woods at night if I were you. Hell, I wouldn't even go up there in the broad daylight. And anyone around here can tell you that I'm not afraid of much, not after storming ashore under heavy Jap fire at Iwo Jima. But, no sir, I won't go up there."

With that, Robert stared at Russell and then turned and returned to the back of the store. Janice looked distressed, but she quickly turned back to Russell, and looked into his eyes and smiled. She put her hand lightly on his forearm.

"Oh, you must excuse Robert. He gets like that sometimes. We call it *funning the flatlander*."

"So, what about all that stuff about Wally Paxton killing himself and Wanda's husband being attacked by wolves?" Russell smiled. He had to ask.

Janice's smile disappeared. "Oh, that's all true, Russell. Every word, I'm afraid."

Russell's First Visit to the Indian Rocks

It was not until almost a month later that Russell began his exploration of what he now began to think of as his mountain, even though the ridge was only about two thousand feet above sea level. He no longer thought of it, or the woods, or the house as Simon's. During that interval, he had frequently resolved that each day would be the day he would visit the Indian Rocks, the Wolf Pit, and some of the other landmarks that his uncle had noted, but each day brought its own excuse.

Some of them were honest ones. He had to take three days to return to Philadelphia to attend to the leasing of his house there, and a few other short trips to consult with his former partners and clients about some left-over issues from some of the transactions he handled for his old firm. He hated to go back there, preferring to focus on what he thought of as his new life, but the hourly "of counsel" fees that he earned made it bearable.

There were also the demands of attending to the little eccentricities of his new home: replacing the old, cloth-insulated wiring and fuse box, and adding new electrical outlets; getting telephone service installed, which had been delayed for months by the need to run a telephone line up the road from where it ended at Wanda's farm; and replacing his old Mercedes sedan with a vehicle more suitable to the mountain roads around his new home and the rough winter that Robert Kaiser was already predicting.

During all those errands and projects, Russell's thoughts often would drift back to that spring day several months ago, before he moved in, when he conducted his "reconnaissance mission," as he liked to call it, climbing partway up the path behind his house. The woods and the mountain became like wrapped presents placed under a Christmas tree two weeks early. He admonished himself that when the time came for him to go all the way up the mountain, he needed to be prepared to do it properly, even respectfully, and not just like a tourist from the big city. Sometimes, at the end of the day, he would wonder whether his delay was due to some barely sensed fear that he couldn't put into words, or whether it was because he wanted to continue to build the anticipation, so that he would enjoy his first experiences even more.

Wanda came by once a week, usually on Thursdays. "Just to see if you needed anything," she said. Usually she stayed for only thirty minutes, sometimes mentioning local sights or events that she thought might interest Russell. One Thursday afternoon, about three weeks after her first visit, she brought a pie and stayed a little longer.

"Before you start getting all grateful, Russell," she said, "about me baking you a pie, the Baptist church up in Tioga was having one of their bake sales yesterday. You know, there is this beautiful old woman who makes the best pies, so I got four of them as little gifts for a couple of my neighbors. She says that the rhubarb is from her back yard."

Russell made some fresh coffee, and they sat in the kitchen enjoying the pie. As she got up to leave, she said "Oh, by the way, Russell. I was driving home along the river and I looked up to the right and realized that I was looking at the back side of your property, right across the river, and I wondered whether you had gotten a chance to go up there on the ridge. I'll bet there's a great view from up there."

"No, not yet. But I plan to as soon as I get settled in."

"Well, don't wait too long, Russell. Nobody ever really gets settled in until they settle you into the ground that last final time." Wanda gave a quick smile, but it seemed to Russell to be more like a grimace, a response to a flashing pain rather than humor.

As she drove away, Russell realized that she had not mentioned the woods, or the Rocks, or the markings on the map since her first visit. Likewise, Russell did not feel comfortable asking her about what Janice and Robert had told him about Jack's death. He would let all of it rest unless she brought it up again.

Sitting in the front porch that evening, flanked by two citronella candles, Russell listened to music and watched the brilliant splotches of the sunset filtering through the trees. He walked around to the back of the house and looked up to the ridge behind his house, in the direction of the river on the other side of the mountain. How strange it was to own so much that he had never seen. As he did almost every time he looked up into the forest, Russell imagined himself making his way through dense stands of birch and hemlock, and great hedges of rhododendron, to break into a sunny clearing where the Rocks stood majestically against a brilliant blue summer sky. Each time, they grew taller in his mind until they rivaled Stonehenge.

"This is crazy," Russell said aloud.

Early the next morning, Russell packed his "field work kit" into an old gym bag: a liter of water; three apples and a dark chocolate bar; three disposable cameras; a compass; his old 50-meter cloth tape measure; some pens and a small spiral notebook; a photocopy of Simon's map; and a cutout portion of a topographical map of the area. Even though it was still late August, the morning air had a soft crispness and the first few golden leaves of autumn had already fallen. Russell hesitated, thought about going back into the house for a jacket, but then crossed the small clearing behind his house and started up the path.

The lower part of the path was partially overgrown but was an easy climb. The grade became steeper however, and Russell had to push aside the branches from the low bushes that encroached from either side. He was embarrassed by how his heart pounded when he stopped for a moment at a brief level spot. How had he gotten so out of shape? As he caught his breath, he glanced back at his house, still partly visible through the trees. Did he want to make sure it was still there? Russell smiled to himself and resumed his assault up an even steeper part of the hill.

The steep grade and rough path forced him to walk slowly, so that he could take in sights, sounds, and smells of the forest – his forest, he thought with a smile – that he realized that he would have otherwise missed. After about twenty-five minutes, stopping frequently to look around, he arrived at the top of the ridge at the old Indian trail indicated on Simon's map. He looked up and down the trail. It was a grassy lane, perhaps three feet wide, and bordered with teaberry and mountain laurel, weaving gently between the trees as it followed the line of the ridge. After the Native Americans left this area, he thought, animals probably continued to use the trail up to the present day.

Russell took out Simon's map and looked in the direction where it indicated the Rocks were. This would be the first test of whether the map meant anything or was little more than a catalogue of fantasies. Using his compass, he oriented the map to the north, determined the direction of the Indian Rocks, and started down the other side of the mountain, zigzagging from tree to tree to keep his balance on the slope, and stopping every twenty feet or so to check his bearing. It was only when he came to a large, relatively level area about eighty feet down the slope that Russell realized that Simon's map had led him straight to the Rocks. He literally stumbled onto them, his ankle being caught by a low vine, causing him to lurch forward into the circle less than two feet from one of the partly buried stones that, with the others, formed the Rocks. He was standing among them before he realized that he had arrived.

His first reaction was disappointment. This was no Stonehenge. Russell got out his metric tape measure, notebook, and camera. Each of the eleven rocks that formed the circle was a thick slab, each approximately 2.10 meters wide and approximately 70 centimeters from front to back. Most of the rocks protruded between 1.08 meters to 1.85 meters above ground, but two of them were 2.20 and 2.61 meters high. The lower parts of all of them were partially covered by vines or brush, so much so that the smaller rocks were almost hidden. The variation in height appeared random and, Russell hypothesized, was probably due to them being placed over different substrata and settling at different rates. Over time, all the slabs had shifted or tilted forward or backward slightly.

Each of the slabs appeared to have come from a common source, each colored a dirty, flat gray. The exposed portions of the boulders were smooth, almost polished, and on the exposed portions, at least, there were no noticeable veins or internal mineral structure, nor any markings or inscriptions.

Russell then tried to calculate the size of the circle. This was difficult. Since there was an odd number of stone slabs, no two of them lay on a straight line through the center of the circle. The area enclosed by the stone circle sloped downward slightly. The uneven ground and the irregular levels of brush, leaves, and grass also contributed to significant variation in his measurement. Nonetheless, he estimated that the eleven rocks were arranged in a circle of remarkable regularity, with a diameter that averaged 43.8 meters after twenty measurements.

Russell also measured along the circumference of the circle. The slabs were spaced with uniform gaps of approximately 10.50 meters, plus or minus up to two centimeters. Looking toward the center of the circle as he walked its perimeter, it appeared that the slabs all faced a common center point at a uniform angle, but he probably would need surveyor's equipment to confirm this.

Having completed his survey, Russell sat down inside the circle, leaning against one of the small birch trees that had grown there. The area around the Rocks was dark and overgrown, covered by a dense canopy of trees through which only a dusty golden light filtered. Looking back up the hill he could barely see the ridge through the trees. Looking across the clearing, due east, the only prominent feature was a large tree, with a thick trunk and twisted branches reaching, he guessed, about seventy or eighty feet tall. He concluded that this must be the Ancient Yew that was marked on his uncle's map. Beyond the yew, he could see only green, with occasional patches of sky, shortly beyond which the mountainside dropped away in a much steeper slope. He wondered why his very first impulse had been to measure the Rocks, rather than to sit down and enjoy the cool, quiet forest. Perhaps the apparent precision of the formation, coupled with nature's failed attempt to obliterate it, had issued a challenge to him as soon as he entered the site.

In the weeks leading up to this first visit, Russell had sometimes imagined that he would intuit mystical insights or psychic communications here. He tried to spend most of that half-hour lunch break trying to think about what the Rocks meant in the context of the indescribably pleasant earliest promise of another glorious Appalachian autumn. The phrase *silent sentinels* kept running through his mind. But his thoughts always returned to the apparent precision and consistency with which the circle had been constructed. As he reviewed his measurements, he realized that they appeared to be based on ratios of prime numbers. The approximate ratio of the width to the thickness of each slab was consistently 3-to-1, allowing for some possible weathering over the years. The ratio of the gaps between the slabs to their width was 5-to-1. There were eleven slabs around the circle: 3, 5, 11 – all prime numbers.

The thoughts about prime numbers led him, for a while, to attempt to recite the prime numbers as high as he could. He abandoned this game in the 110s, having realized that he never studied multiplication tables above the nines when he was in elementary school forty years before. Besides, other than the plain fact that there were eleven exposed rocks, his measurements could only be approximate, due to the uneven ground, the underbrush, and the apparent erosion of some of the rocks. He also doubted that whoever constructed the Rocks used the metric system, but how likely was it that the prime-number ratios were due to chance?

The only other notable event during his lunch was the appearance of a small deer at the far side of the Rocks. Russell did not notice its arrival. It appeared silently, as deer often do. They stared at each other, each frozen in place. Not wanting to frighten the deer, and with the deer waiting for his next move, Russell remained still. After a minute, perhaps less, the deer turned and walked slowly back into the woods. It almost seemed to shrug before it turned away and quietly melted back into the forest.

In all, his first impression of the Rocks was unremarkable: an interesting formation, not likely one of those rare phenomena where nature imitates the manmade so precisely. It was a pleasant place to relax and enjoy a bag lunch on a sunny afternoon, but also a faintly melancholy one. The Rocks seemed like a long-forgotten place, someplace that once may have been special but to which people no longer came, of which people remembered nothing. How many decades, maybe even centuries, had they been sitting in this far corner of an obscure tract of forest in northern Pennsylvania?

Russell paid six more visits to the Rocks that autumn, usually on Sunday, each time to eat his lunch during an exploratory tour of some other portion of his property. On each occasion, the deer (for Russell assumed it was the same one) would make a brief appearance, always on the opposite side of the circle. Deer and man would stare at each other for a moment, and then the deer would silently and slowly walk back into the forest, as quietly and suddenly as it appeared.

Whitey

During this first autumn on the mountain, Russell began to pull together into a plan his long-deferred ambition to write a book on Braddock's campaign in the French and Indian War. Russell had always had a passion for the history of the "old" frontier in the seventeenth and eighteenth centuries, the land just beyond the Alleghenies. His only serious effort, a short book on the earliest exploration and settlement of western Pennsylvania, New York, and Maryland, received some critical notice and even sold a few hundred copies, almost all of them at college bookstores. One of Russell's goals, the thing that drove his decision to move to the mountains more than he had realized at the time, had been to pursue his research and writing more than he could have done practicing law in Philadelphia. Now he had the opportunity.

Fall came early that September, and the gently falling leaves became a red and gold avalanche before the end of the month. By early October, as colder weather made snow a very real possibility in a matter of weeks, Russell realized that his efforts to keep ahead of the mounting tide of fallen leaves were going to be futile. He had always enjoyed an afternoon of leaf raking: the crispness and clarity of the air; the brilliant colors against a deep blue sky; the soothing rustle of the leaves as the rake moved them into piles; and the secret fun of running across the yard – a middle-aged man propelled by a boy's heart – and jumping into a pile of leaves. And even though he considered himself an uncompromising environmentalist, Russell loved the enchanting aroma of burning leaves, now almost unknown in this era of air pollution laws and township ordinances.

Realizing that he would never be able to remove all the leaves by himself before the first snowfall, Russell looked for a handyman to finish the job. It didn't take long. The local newspaper had at least a dozen ads for handymen, each promising reliability and low cost. Suspicious of those who had to advertise in order to get work, Russell also sought the advice of Janice and Robert Kaiser, who seemed to know almost everyone within a thirty-mile radius. Russell narrowed his choices to two men, the only two who had bothered to return his phone calls. Janice sketched each one as "a good-natured drunk, but a hard worker when sober."

Russell picked Whitey Wentworth. As far as anyone knew, Whitey appeared to be his real first name; no one knew any other. What made him decide on Whitey was Janice's remark, "Whitey's a good man, but don't let him start telling stories. He'll waste the whole day just leaning on his shovel and telling the wildest tales. You keep him sober and quiet, and he'll do right by you."

As she was with almost everyone else, Janice was one hundred percent accurate in her assessment of Whitey. His name frequently appeared in the "Police Blotter" column in the local paper, usually linked to allegations of public drunkenness or disorderly conduct. Although Russell could usually depend on him to show up for work on a weekday, Whitey almost never appeared on weekend mornings. His absences were caused, Russell soon deduced, by his being detained by a hangover, the police, or both.

Janice was also right about Whitey's endless treasury of stories. Many of them were from Whitey's Navy days, and most ended either in a Navy brig or in a police lockup in some exotic port. Whitey was also an encyclopedist of the occult, and many of his stories were able to weave space aliens, the pyramids, the Shroud of Turin, and even Nicola Tesla, all into one rich but weird tapestry.

On the other hand, Whitey was a genuine student of local history, which instantly appealed to Russell. From him Russell quickly assimilated a lifetime of legends, events, and personalities of the region. It was Whitey, for example, who first told him the history of the ancient Susquehanna Forest, and how his land had one of the last virgin stands that remained in all of Pennsylvania. He spoke vividly of Indian commerce along the mountain trails, including the one on Russell's land, that crossed the forest, providing an avenue that stretched from Lake Ontario all the way down into Virginia.

It was a rare Indian-summer afternoon in late October. Whitey and Russell were sitting on the porch having iced tea and sandwiches, taking a break from what Russell hoped would be the last of fall cleanup. Their conversation drifted, like a small boat in a slow, meandering river, touching land at inconsequential points such as how hard the coming winter might be, good places to buy firewood, and stories of winter adventures long ago.

After a few moments of silence, Whitey suddenly asked, "Been up to the Rocks much, Russell?"

Russell said that it was becoming his favorite picnic spot whenever he took a walk in his woods.

"Strange place, isn't it?"

Russell agreed, "You don't see many rock formations like that."

Whitey was staring across the clearing, beyond the oak tree. He seemed to be looking at something. Russell looked at Whitey, to watch his reaction to the next thing he was going to say. "Nature can do some amazing things if you give her thousands of years."

"Naw, nature didn't do that." Whitey kept looking away, staring across the clearing. Russell wondered what had captured his attention.

"What did?" Russell asked, hoping for one of Whitey's baroque tales, perhaps one about space aliens and ancient alien landing sites.

"Nobody knows for sure," Whitey replied. "But they aren't natural. Maybe they were built a long time ago by people that this world has completely forgotten."

"They've been studied, haven't they?" Russell asked. "Surely geologists could tell one way or the other."

"Well," Whitey continued, "there were some college professors who wanted to study them right after the war, perhaps excavate up there and maybe take some samples back with them. But Old Man Paxton – he owned this place back then – he wouldn't let them. When they said they were going to dig the place up, he took his shotgun to them and told them to clear out."

"Why?" Russell pressed.

"Don't know," Whitey replied quickly. "Maybe Old Man Paxton just liked his privacy and didn't want strangers digging up his land."

Russell took the empty plates inside. When he returned, Whitey was still staring at the same spot across the clearing. He slowly got up from his chair, but still appeared to be looking at something in the woods.

"Honest, Russell. You watch out around the Rocks. There's a lot more there than any of us know."

"What do you mean?" Russell asked.

"I don't know. All I do know, Russell, is that folks here don't go to the Rocks, and don't even like to talk about them. People have seen strange things up there. Shadows of things that aren't there. Forest things."

"Like what?" Mentally, Russell began to settle in for another of Whitey's folk tales.

"Like voices, Russell. People have been hearing voices up there for years, maybe forever. People voices, animal voices –"

"You mean like howls?" Russell interrupted.

"No, like real voices. Like how animals would talk if they could. But all kinds of voices. Some talking, some laughing, some crying, some singing, some just talking like you and me right now."

Whitey turned his head to look directly at Russell.

"All kinds of voices, Russell. And I've heard them."

Russell tried to draw out more details of Whitey's experiences at the Rocks, but he would respond only in uncharacteristic monosyllables. The conversation quickly died, both men staring at each other. A few moments later, Whitey shook the last few ice cubes from his glass into his mouth, crunched them with his teeth, and swallowed.

"Listen," he said, setting his empty glass down, "All that stuff happened a long time ago. I'd likely been drinking. But I'll tell you this, and then I want to let it go. I heard those voices as clear as I hear you. Scared me shitless when I realized there wasn't a living soul there, at least not a human one."

Russell and Whitey spent the rest of the afternoon working quietly, exchanging words only when necessary to complete raking and hauling the leaves away, or when Whitey would say, about every ten minutes, it seemed, "Damn, Russell. You know, you really got to get yourself a leaf blower."

That night, Russell sat in his living room, reading by the fireplace, with the first fire of the autumn quietly glowing at the end of the evening. He got up, walked to the kitchen, and deposited his wine glass in the sink, and wondered what he would need to do to install a dishwasher. Before he was fully aware of it, he had walked out the back door and into the clearing behind the house. There was a new moon that night, and the black mass of the mountain stood out sharply against more stars than he had ever seen in his life. He visualized the Rocks at night, with their exposed tops glowing softly in the starlight. Maybe that was why people sometimes called them the *White Indian Rocks*. For a moment Russell almost believed that he could hear Whitey's "animal voices." He had a passing impulse to get a flashlight and go up and over the ridge to the Rocks, to sit in the starlight and listen to the night sounds until dawn.

Instead, Russell laughed softly as he went back inside and tried to return his attention to the book. First there had been Janice and Robert, with their "funning the flatlander." Now Whitey was adding his constant stream of utterly incredible tales, but each one with its own hook that kept it securely vivid in Russell's memory. He had inherited a ghost story.

The Wooly-Bear Caterpillar

Russell passed most of the rest of that first autumn either planning his research on his book on General Braddock or, for light reading, glancing through local histories, most of which were unremarkable. He found one description of the Rocks in a small book on the small dusty local history shelf at the back of the township library. From the library card in the pocket, the last time it had been borrowed apparently was in 1938. It was published, or more likely self-published, in Athens, Pennsylvania, in 1882, by one Robert Fiske, and titled *Curiosities and Wonders of the Northern Tier of Pennsylvania.*

Fiske described the Rocks as "an arrangement of partially buried boulders, in a perfect circle." The book continued:

This stone circle is of a type that is unknown outside the British Isles. It is fancifully believed by some local folklorists to have been used as an Indian ceremonial place long before the White Man first penetrated the region.

The eleven boulders are presumed to be of local origin; although no similar objects of comparable size, natural or artifacts, have been discovered anywhere else in the Commonwealth. They appear to have been quarried to almost perfectly uniform dimensions, allowing for the wear of many years of wind, storms, and the seasonal heating and contraction of the stone. The closest similar examples are the ancient stone ruins in New England, the most notable of these being the so-called "Mystery Hill" at North Salem, New Hampshire. Those and other New England formations are not as precisely arranged in a circle, nor any other geometric shape; and the rock slabs at those sites are smaller and more irregular than these eleven cyclopean stones, each estimated from observable measurements of their visible parts to weigh at least twenty tons, now partially buried, but still standing in the mountains of eastern Tioga County.

The earliest accounts of the Indian Rocks of Pennsylvania date from the middle of the eighteenth century, described in an undated diary of Zebulon Butler, who is known to have made two, or according to some accounts as many as four, expeditions from the Wyoming Valley north to the upper reaches of the Tioga River and into the Endless Mountains in the late 1760s. They are sometimes described in local oral tradition as the White Indian Rocks. The origin of this name is obscure, but probably relates to the propensity of these whitish-grey rocks to appear to glow in the moonlight.

Despite these romantic imaginings of pre-Columbian aboriginal origins, the formation is undoubtedly European, possibly constructed as part of a mission complex by the Culdees or some similar seafaring monastic order from Ireland during their legendary explorations to the New World in the ninth century; because the Indians who inhabited the area, lacking a written language, the rudiments of mathematics, or even the wheel, would have been incapable of excavating, shaping, and moving the dolmens into their present positions with such geometric precision, which would challenge the skills of even the master stone masons and surveyors of today.

Local legends recount that, in the early nineteenth century, the circle was a frequent venue for the meetings of certain metaphysical societies, some of whom reputedly believed the site to be a source of mystical or spiritual inspiration or, for the more easily susceptible minds, great supernatural powers. No written records nor living witnesses have been found to corroborate these stories.

Robert Kaiser predicted an early winter that year. One Saturday morning at the end of October, when Russell was checking out at the cash register at the Red & White, he noticed that Robert had a fuzzy black and brown caterpillar on his index finger.

"Just look at this little guy, Russell," he said. "He's telling us we're going to have a hard early part of the winter this year, just like I told you, but then it will get mild come February or March.

"Now, I don't know why this wooly-bear caterpillar thing is accurate," he continued before Russell could say anything. "It just doesn't make any sense to an educated person like you or me, Russell, but I have never known it to fail."

Janice wasn't in the store just then, so Russell knew that she would not rescue him from another of Robert's "fun the flatlander" sessions. He tried to look respectfully doubtful, while also admiring Robert's ability to turn even a caterpillar into a tall tale.

"Now just to be clear, this is the caterpillar speaking and not me, Russell. But we should get ready for a nasty early part of winter, starting any day now. The winter will lighten up a little in February and early March, but then we'll get hit with one last cold spell in March right before it turns to spring. Why, you can even go week-by-week with these wooly bear caterpillars. They have thirteen segments in their bodies. Some say that's one for each week of winter.

"See, here's December 21st to 28th," he continued, pointing in the general direction of the caterpillar's head. "He says it looks like we'll have a white Christmas."

Russell pretended to look with intense interest at the caterpillar, which was still wandering up and down Robert's long fingers.

"Look, Russell, I know that you think that it's just an old folk tale," Robert said, lightly stroking the caterpillar with his finger. "Most folks do. But Professor Curran at the American Museum of Natural History in New York once did a famous study up on Bear Mountain, up the Hudson about forty miles north of the city, maybe about four hours from here. He studied the same species that we have here, the *Phyrrhartia isabella*. This was back in the late forties, and his findings have never been disproved. They were even published in the old *Herald-Tribune*. Now, nobody can explain how they predict the winter, not even Professor Curran. But they just do."

With or without the intervention of Robert Kaiser's caterpillars, constant rain, ice, and occasional snow flurries began the first week in November. Each week the generally foul weather was punctuated by a day with two or three hours of mild, weak sunshine. Whenever Russell made plans to explore another part of his property, with the now customary picnic lunch at the Rocks, he would awake to a cold, windy, discouraging day. As a result, his next visit to the Rocks was not until Christmas Day. The term *cabin fever* took on a new intensely personal meaning.

Christmas dawned mild and sunny, with the temperature in the high fifties. The last patches of snow from a recent snowstorm had melted. As had been his habit since childhood, Russell was up at dawn. With no family or close friends, this first Christmas in his new home started as they had for most of his adult life: sitting by himself, sipping coffee, reading one of the books that he had bought and wrapped as Santa's presents to himself. Baroque holiday music, but not too overwhelmingly religious, hummed in the background.

After his first coffee, Russell considered the same question he asked every year: *Why did he bother?* He went to church with his aunt when he was a kid but didn't consider himself to be Christian, at least not in anything more than a vaguely ethical sense. As an adult, he had never set up a Christmas tree, maybe, he admitted to himself, because it brought back happy, but now also painfully sorrowful, faint memories of his early childhood with his parents.

Aside from his annual charitable contributions, the few presents that he exchanged with others had been only out of a sense of courtesy or not wanting to hurt the other person's feelings.

His aunt had always observed the basic cultural elements of the holiday, but there was always a sadness that made Christmas the worst day of the year for both of them. Each year, Christmas reminded his aunt of her late husband. She would get out her photo album, play old 78-r.p.m. records of big band music from the early 1940s music on her phonograph, and talk about the plans that they had made before the War and how much better her life would have been had her husband not been killed in it. The stoic pain that she released through the house each Christmas Day made Russell feel like an unwelcome intruder on her sorrow and an unexpected burden that prevented her from getting on with her life. At the same time, he knew that she loved him very much. Even today, he could not listen to big band music without feeling profoundly sad.

The first year that Russell moved out of his aunt's house to take his job at the law firm in Philadelphia, he donated his bonus from the law firm to the Salvation Army and, declining all invitations, spent Christmas Day alone, except for a ten-minute call to his aunt, habits which over the years had become his Christmas tradition.

About ten o'clock Wanda Abrams knocked at the front door. She thrust a bundle toward him, wrapped in gold foil and tied with a metallic red ribbon.

"Just a tradition of mine, to take one of my fruitcakes to all the new families I welcomed during the year. I love the surprise and smiles on their faces – especially from the ones who hate fruit cake."

"Actually, I like fruit cake," Russell replied.

"Then you'll love this one," she replied. "It's been soaking in brandy for three weeks."

Russell asked Wanda to stay for coffee. She started to decline, saying that she had some other cakes to deliver. Then she hesitated for a moment and accepted.

"How long have you been alone, Russell?" she asked as Russell fussed with the espresso machine.

"Well, I'm never really alone, Wanda. At least I don't feel lonely," Russell replied. She did not look convinced.

"But you don't have any family?" She looked away. "I'm sorry, Russell. I shouldn't pry."

"No, that's okay. Really." Russell replied. "I have some second cousins on my mother's side, but I haven't had any real contact with them for thirty years, at least. One of them showed up for my aunt's funeral a couple of years ago, but she's a lot older than I am, and we didn't stay in touch. But it's no big deal, honestly."

"Well, maybe I know a little of what it's like, Russell," Wanda said. 'The first couple of years after I lost Jack were awful. Every holiday – even Labor Day, for Christ's sake – I went into a deep depression. But Christmas was always worst, and we weren't at all religious. Hell, Jack wasn't even a Christian, but we'd still do Christmas, I guess mostly for me."

"You don't have any close relatives, either?" Russell asked quietly.

"Well, a couple of sisters. One lives in Boca Raton, but frankly I can't really afford to go down to Florida very often. She's got her own family, and is busy enough at Christmas without her big sister barging in. Spending a week with her is enough to drive me nuts, Russell. Elaine's a nice person in many respects, but very self-absorbed with her lifestyle, her too-perfect kids, and her big fake Mediterranean style house – 'the villa,' as she always calls it. My other sister still lives in the old neighborhood in Queens, the last I heard. We haven't had much to do with each other for twenty years or so – family problems, you know. So, I like to get out and about on Christmas and add a little something extra to other people's holiday.

"Which is what I've got to get back to doing," Wanda said, getting up suddenly. Russell's thanks for the fruitcake and the company were lost in a swirling South American style wool poncho and jangling silver as Wanda roared out the door. She stopped on the porch and turned around.

"Thanks for the coffee, Russell. And Russell –"

"Yes?"

"Never mind."

"No, go ahead. What were you going to say?"

"I don't know of any way to say this without it sounding the wrong way, so take it as coming from a friend, Russell. You really need to get a life. Merry Christmas!"

Wanda and her Land Rover, louder than ever, rumbled and rattled up out of the clearing and out of sight, and Russell could still hear it as she turned onto the road and drove down the hill toward town.

Russell admitted to himself that, even if he didn't need to "get a life," he needed to get out of the house. Why not a Christmas picnic? The day was warming nicely. The sun was shining and there wasn't any wind. He wrapped up three slices of Wanda's fruitcake, poured a thermos of coffee, and headed up the path into the woods.

It was only noon, and he had a vague plan to investigate some of his uncle's markings on the eastern side of the map, about a half-mile from the house. So far, none of the marks had led to anything unusual. Two or three had turned out to be ancient oak trees, hidden by younger birches and occasional hemlocks. From their girth, Russell estimated that they must have been saplings long before the American Revolution, perhaps even before the arrival of Europeans. Russell had developed a special affinity with the old oaks, almost a friendship. In his mind, he started to give the oldest ones the names of figures from the eighteenth-century American frontier: Forbes, Bouquet, Wolfe, Montcalm; as well as native Americans from the period: Joseph Brant, Canaqueese, and Cornplanter. Three names, however, he kept in reserve for the most monumental trees, which he had yet to discover: Aliquippa, Washington, and, of course, Braddock. Except for these ancient landmarks, most of the notations on the map, particularly the ones that appeared to be dates, left Russell standing in the woods, looking around, and wondering.

Tramping up the old path behind his house, Russell was surprised to find himself humming the old Christmas carol "I Saw Three Ships" and almost stepping and swinging his shoulders in time to the music. He was delighted to notice that he made the climb easily, without the shortness of breath and muscle aches of only a few months ago. The sun, surprisingly powerful for late December, filtered through the network of limbs and branches overhead. Being out and doing something, especially on such a beautiful day, lifted his spirits.

It's corny, he thought, but it really is good to be alive.

After about a fifteen-minute march, he turned southeast along the old Indian trail at the ridge, walked about ten minutes, and arrived close to what he believed to be the first mark he had planned to explore: a small triangle with the numbers *6-26-61* beside it. He was certain that he was very close to the spot, for Simon's map, although small, had proven so far to be remarkably to scale. Most of the marks, particularly the apparent dates, were close to a physical feature, such as a boulder, an unusual grouping of trees, or, in this instance, a sharp bend in the path. Yet, as before, looking around, he saw nothing remarkable. Obviously, Simon Poe had seen something or done something here on June 26, 1961, but what? As with most of the other marks, he could find no clues upon which he could even begin to speculate.

The old Indian trail climbed gently up along the ridge. Looking to the left through the woods, Russell could see the river through the occasional spaces between the bare tree limbs. The next mark was somewhat unusual: a circle with the letter G in it. There were only two others on the map, deep in the woods. This was the only one near a path. Looking at the map and the path ahead, Circle-G, as he began to think of it, could be no more than one hundred yards ahead, and right in, or very near to, the trail. Just before reaching the spot that he believed Circle-G marked, the path turned sharply to the right to avoid an old oak. Once past it, the ridge flattened and widened on either side of the trail. The surrounding brush appeared different from that further back from the path. It looked as if an area, roughly circular and about fifty feet across, had at one time been cleared, and had since been retaken by new growth. Also, unlike the woods further back, there were isolated grassy patches. Had there once been a lawn here? If so, why? Did Circle-G refer to a grassy patch?

Poking around in the new growth, he slowly explored the area, step by step moving outward in a spiral pattern. The only other thing out of the ordinary that he found were short slivers of slate, as if someone had been working on slate shingles there once. It must have been a long time ago, since the edges were dull, not razor-sharp as slate can be. Those slivers, and the skeleton of a small animal, probably a possum or raccoon, were the only artifacts in the area. He cursed quietly to himself. As with most of his explorations so far, this one seemed headed in the same direction: toward yet another riddle.

The last of the three marks near that spot looked like another date: *10-2-63*. As with the first mark that afternoon, there was nothing extraordinary about the area on the map, just a woodland path meandering through the forest along the top of the ridge.

Having discovered nothing noteworthy and wondering why his uncle had bothered to note them, Russell began to give more credence to his bird-watching hypothesis about the map. He returned to the Rocks, which had become his favorite lunch spot in the forest. A gentle breeze rustled the tree branches back and forth.

He thought that he probably would never decipher Simon's curious markings on the map. They might have been nothing more than the manifestation of some mild mental illness or harmless delusion. In the half-year that Russell had lived on the mountain, nobody had been able to tell him much about his uncle, other than the superficial observations from occasional contacts. People would make one or two polite but inconsequential remarks and then change the subject.

At first, Russell believed that they were trying to be evasive, to hide some dark secrets that could hurt his feelings. Over time, however, Russell began to accept that the truth was that people just did not know much about Simon Poe. Just as Simon had withdrawn and virtually disappeared from his family for most of his adult life, he had also revealed little of himself to his neighbors.

Standing on the trail, looking for something that obviously was no longer there, Russell told himself that Wanda was right. He really did need to get a life. He needed to quit hunting down marks on maps and chasing the ghosts of his uncle's idiosyncrasies, most of which he feared were becoming embedded in his own imagination. He retired from the law and moved here to start a new productive life. Russell stopped and looked around. My god, he thought, I'm becoming like my uncle: a weird hermit tramping through my forest retreat muttering to myself.

As soon as Russell arrived at the Rocks and entered the stone circle, he noticed that it looked as if it had been visited recently, perhaps within the past three or four days. The brown-green grass and small brush were freshly trampled in the very center of the circle. By crouching down and looking across the circle at an angle, he could also detect a path leading out of the center to the far side and past the old yew tree. Other than the trampled grass and brush, there were no signs of disturbance.

This was puzzling. Russell didn't care if people hiked across his land and enjoyed his forest. Tiny scraps of paper and cellophane along the old Indian trail, which had escaped otherwise commendable efforts to clean up, also spoke of unknown visitors, probably picnickers like himself. Russell didn't object, so long as nothing was disturbed. Unlike some of his neighbors, he didn't post his land against trespassers although, at the start of hunting season, he had put up about twenty no-hunting signs, mostly for his own protection. His land was one of the last remnants of an ancient commons, of which he was merely the latest caretaker. He did not feel that he had the right to exclude anyone of good will who wanted to experience it.

He sat down at his favorite spot and started nibbling on Wanda's fruitcake. It was dark, moist, and almost sickeningly rich. As he lunched, he noticed that the trampled area was confined very tightly to the center of the circle.

A number of people, certainly more than two or three, had entered the circle together. The trampled entrance path was so narrow that they must have entered in single file. They had diverted in unison around small trees that prevented them from walking in a straight line, and then stood or sat in the center for some time. There were no signs that, as most visitors would, they had spread out and wandered around inspecting the various rocks. Most amazing of all, they had left along exactly the same path, almost step by step, by which they had entered.

The visitors had entered and exited near the yew tree. As far as Russell knew, there was no path anywhere near that side of the Rocks. To reach the Rocks from that side, they would have had to enter the woods from near the river, and traversed heavy brush, mostly witch hazel and raspberry bushes, on a very steep uphill climb. Even in early winter it would have been a dense, prickly thicket. He went to the area just to the southeast of the circle and looked beyond the rough path that circled the entire formation. The thick brush to the northwest was completely undisturbed. The visitors had evidently circled the outside of the Rocks, and then entered and left along exactly the same narrow way from the southeast.

Russell sat down again and opened his Thermos of coffee. The walk in the woods, the warmth of the sun, and Wanda's high-octane fruitcake soon overpowered the effects of the coffee. He spent the next hour dozing off into a series of shallow naps, but quickly awakening at the sound of a bird or an animal. When he fully awoke, his back aching from leaning against one of the boulders, it was almost five o'clock. Across the circle, his friend the deer was looking at him, its coat rich in the long wavelengths of rapidly reddening light. Quietly getting up, so as not to scare the deer, Russell descended the ridge in gathering twilight.

He was surprised by how quickly night was falling around him. The path ahead, the woods off to either side, were all changing, minute by minute, from a washed out green-gray monochrome to halftone to black and white. He was walking faster but didn't know why. He had been out before on the paths at twilight, and even after. He would reach his house before dark, or, at worst, only a few minutes after. This time, however, he had the feeling that he was being watched.

He sensed that some animal, maybe his deer, was silently watching him pass by, assuring itself that he was leaving for the night and posed no threat. No, it wasn't so simple. It wasn't just a deer or a raccoon. Maybe his imagination was merely responding to the shapes and shadows of dusk, but he also sensed something else. It wasn't immediate danger but more like a potential menace. He felt that he was being – *evaluated* was the only word that came to mind. Something was watching, deciding what to do about him.

He wasn't afraid. To the contrary, he worried more about scaring whatever it was that was watching him. He was mildly thrilled by the analytical challenge posed by the situation. For a moment, he was tempted to leave the path to find out what was following him, but he also sensed that, if he did, the animal would bolt deeper into the forest. He was enjoying the debate between reason and imagination, while an older animal sense deep inside him seemed to sharpen his alertness and sensitivity to levels that he could not remember having ever experienced before.

After about five minutes, Russell was certain he was being followed. There could be no doubt. It was not his imagination. Off to his right, perhaps fifty yards away, maybe closer, he could almost see someone or something quietly paralleling his path. Whoever or whatever it was, it carefully kept out of sight, just beyond his range of clear vision in the deep wells of darkness in the woods at nightfall. He could also sense that it was large, too large for a raccoon, too bulky to be a deer.

He stopped frequently, held his breath, and listened, but he heard only what he assumed was his own heart pounding. Once he impulsively veered off the path and went charging a few feet into the underbrush, hoping to flush out his stalker, but all he could perceive was the impression of shadow moving against the backdrop of all the other shadows and half-heard sounds of a twilight forest.

He arrived home just as the last redness faded from the western sky. Eating his dinner at his kitchen table, he laughed aloud at himself for allowing his imagination to run so wild.

"Get a life. I guess I have." he said to himself, "Probably not good enough for Wanda, but good enough for me, at least for now."

Russell put his dishes in the sink, picked up a book that he had left on the kitchen table that morning, and walked along the short hallway to the darkened living room. The old blue Hallicrafters shortwave radio in the living room, which had been his mother's and which he had had since he was a boy, was tuned to the BBC World Service and softly playing the last few minutes of the annual Christmas night concert by the Choir of King's College, Cambridge.

Snowbound

What Janice Kaiser later described as the first "real" snow of the winter, eight inches deep, started falling on Christmas night. The electricity went out sometime after midnight and was not restored until late the next day. The telephone service was out until the day after that.

Snow then piled upon snow, two or three inches almost every day, until there was almost two feet of it in Russell Poe's front yard by sunset on New Year's Eve. Russell's life that last week of the year was as unvaried as the winter sky. His one attempt to drive to the road and into town, two days after Christmas, had ended with his car irretrievably stuck in the snow only twenty feet from his house. So, he resigned himself to spend most of the time indoors, reading and listening to music, and occasionally reviewing his notes for his book on General Braddock.

Each afternoon Russell found himself looking out a window and quietly reciting part of Whittier's poem, "Snow-Bound," which his Aunt Rachel would recite at the first snowfall of each winter. He could remember only the opening lines:

The sun that brief December day
Rose cheerless over hills of gray,
And, darkly circled, gave at noon
A sadder light than waning moon.
Slow tracing down the thickening sky
Its mute and ominous prophecy,
A portent seeming less than threat,
It sank from sight before it set.

Wanda Abrams was his only outside contact between Christmas and New Year's Day. Russell called her twice, once service was restored, to see whether she needed anything, and both times left messages on her answering machine. She returned his calls on December 29th, to wish him an early happy New Year and to tell him that she would be leaving the next day to visit her sister in Florida.

"I thought you couldn't stand her," Russell commented.

"Oh, she's okay, I guess. I just need a break, Russell, from all the bleakness. Right about now, I could put up even with Elaine and all her pretensions, just to get away from here for a couple of weeks."

"Is there anything I can do, like checking on your place?"

"No, Russell, but thanks for asking. There's nothing that needs to be done with the orchard this time of year, and my foreman will stop by every three or four days. He has Elaine's number, so he can call me if I need to get back in a hurry."

Russell mentioned that he had tried to call Whitey to find someone to plow his driveway, but nobody had answered.

"No big surprise there," Wanda snorted. "He's probably still enjoying the Christmas spirits, if you know what I mean. Whitey used to work for me – odd jobs every now and then – but he was just too unreliable. He's basically a good person and a hard worker when he wants to be, but too unsteady, maybe a little mentally disturbed, I think. But don't worry; he will resurface after the holidays when he's out of money. He always does. That part of him is very reliable."

Wanda promised to call somebody to plow Russell's driveway. "You're a newcomer, Russell, so if you call, you'd be at the bottom of anyone's list, and when they do show up, they'll rip you off. I'll have someone reliable call you and set up the time and date."

Even with Wanda's intercession, it would take until the third of January, plus one hundred dollars and Russell's last bottle of Scotch, to get a narrow lane plowed more or less along his driveway to the road and his car shoveled out. Now reconnected to the world, but already set into his comfortable snowbound routine, Russell was surprised that he had no compelling desire to go out except only when necessary. So, he spent most of January inside, reading and writing, except for a three-day trip to Philadelphia to attend to a leftover issue with a former client and his weekly Saturday expeditions to the Red & White in Wellsboro.

"Well, if it isn't the abominable snowman in person," Robert Kaiser called out as Russell entered the Red & White on his first shopping trip in January, trying to brush the snow off his jacket so that it all fell on the flattened cardboard boxes placed inside the front door.

"Hadn't seen you since before Christmas," he continued. "Janice and I thought we'd have to send up a St. Bernard dog to deliver a keg of brandy to you."

"No," Russell replied, stuffing his gloves into his jacket pocket. "It just took a little while to dig out."

"Well, it sure looks like another Winter of '88," Robert replied.

"Don't pay any attention to him, Russell," Janice said, smiling as she waved from the cash register. "We don't have a dog, and you'll have to get your brandy at the State Store. Besides, he wasn't here in 1888."

"No, but my grandfather remembered it, living back then on the old family place on what was then the outskirts of Wellsboro," Robert continued. "He told me about it when I was about ten or eleven, right before he passed away." He rolled a shopping cart in Russell's direction, took another for himself, and started walking along the aisles with him.

"Well, it started snowing on Thanksgiving night of 1887 and continued off and on until the middle of February. It got so bad up in the mountains that the wolves came down out of the forest and were prowling around the farms and came right into Wellsboro looking for anything they could find to eat. They even attacked the family carriage horse – his name was Chief – that got out of his stall early one morning and wandered out into the paddock."

"They attacked a horse?" Russell tried not to sound disbelieving, but only as if asking for clarification.

"Sure. Well, old Chief killed two of them – kicked them to death – by the time Granddad got out there with his shotgun and scared the others off. I remember seeing those wolf heads stuffed and mounted side by side on a wall in the living room. They used to scare the bejesus out of me whenever I would go there to visit Granddad, hanging up there on the wall with their eyes glowing red reflecting the light from the fireplace, like they were still alive and just waiting for their chance to get even with the old man."

"What happened to the horse?"

"Oh, Chief was all torn up and bleeding all over. Granddad had to put him out of his misery."

"So, your grandfather — well, his horse actually — killed two and scared the other wolves away. How many were there in all?" Russell asked.

"Granddad said it was a pack of ten or eleven gray wolves – not counting the two that Chief killed – but by the time he told me the story, he was more than eighty. So, the number might have grown a little over the years. But when he told the story, it was just like you were there."

"But you said that it was an early spring that year, in the middle of February? What happened? Didn't the groundhog see his shadow?" Russell chuckled, trying to get the image of the wounded horse out of his mind.

"Nope, and he fooled all of us." Robert said as he frowned at the expiration dates on some boxes of macaroni and tossed them into his cart. He made a notation on a little notepad that he had secured with rubber bands to the inside of his left forearm.

"We had a little thaw that year, around the middle of February. The old-timers said the crocuses had even begun to appear. But then in early March, ka-bam!" He reached toward the back of a shelf and used his arm to sweep some cans of spinach to the front with such vigor that Russell went into a half-crouch to be prepared to catch them if they flew off the shelf.

"No," Robert continued. "Then we got hit with what they still call the Great Blizzard of '88, four days of non-stop snow. New York City got hardest hit, with almost five feet of the stuff. It killed more than four hundred people. We only got the tail end of it out here, but we still got four feet, so Grandad said."

"He said that on the ridges, like up where you live, there were still patches of snow on the Fourth of July. The Tioga River was frozen solid. They say folks were still ice-skating on it on Memorial Day, or Decoration Day as they called it back then."

Russell and Robert pushed their carts to the front of the store. Robert helped Russell unload his cart onto the counter.

"Thanks, Robert," Russell said.

"You just watch him closely," Janice said. "He'll probably try to sneak some of that out-of-date macaroni into your order."

Screams from the Mountain

The weather finally cleared on the tenth of January, as a high-pressure area pushed down from Canada, across New York and Pennsylvania, bringing clear skies and cold temperatures. The bright sun hurt Russell's eyes to look at the trees outside, the tops of their branches a blinding white in the morning sun, brighter than the deep blue sky behind and above them. During the night, the wind had shifted to the northwest and had drifted snow up onto the front porch and almost three feet deep against the front door. He grabbed his snow shovel, which he kept in the kitchen. This had been Robert's suggestion: "You never know when you might have to actually dig yourself out your own door, just to get to the snow that you want to shovel." Russell trudged around to the front of the house and started to excavate.

The scream almost froze him to the spot. It sounded like an animal in extreme agony, but it also had a human quality to it. There was an elemental fear in the scream, but it also seemed to express a reasoning understanding of great danger. It was coming from the forest behind the house.

Russell felt sick. Throughout his life, the thought of an animal suffering, even the smallest insect, had been unbearable to him. He knew he couldn't find, much less try to rescue, an animal that was in so much fear and pain. He turned to go inside, to escape the horrible cries that were echoing off the hills. He reasoned that the animal's suffering would probably be brief, that it would either attract a predator or drift off into frozen, painless death. Either would come soon and would be merciful, but he didn't want to stay outside and listen for the end.

It screamed again. This time its howl was lower, more pleading than terrified. It seemed to have a human quality. Russell went back inside, a dozen rescue scenarios rushing into his mind at once. He grabbed supplies without consciously assigning them to a rescue plan: an old Navy surplus woolen blanket, some rope, and a half-liter bottle of water. Remembering snowy rescue scenes from old movies, he poured out the water and refilled it with the last of his

Spanish brandy. Turning his shovel upside down and using it as a staff, he walked around to the back of the house and started plowing his way through the snow up the mountain, the blanket draped around him like an enormous scarf and the rope loosely coiled around his neck. Fortunately, the wind had cleared much of the snow from the path, leaving no more than six or seven inches except where snow had been blown down from the trees.

Even with few obstacles, it seemed to Russell to take almost an hour to reach the top of the ridge. He was breathing heavily but enjoyed the sensation of icy air spreading through his lungs. He was moving as quickly as he could uphill in the snow, but it seemed to him as if he were moving into a slowly changing two-dimensional pattern of black and white against the deep blue sky.

Russell told himself that he was crazy. He would never find the animal. With the snow muffling the sound, he couldn't be certain of the direction of its cries. Even if he did find it, it would probably attack him out of fear. He would spend the whole day tramping around in the snow, determined to search the forest for as long as he believed that he could hear the animal, but growing more frustrated as it seemed more apparent with each step that he had no chance of rescuing it. He imagined himself standing alone in the woods in the late afternoon, shovel in his hand, tears streaming down his face in frustration as he heard the last piteous moans, then silence.

Russell kept trudging up the hill, following the path and the sound as best he could. Sometimes there was a soul-ripping scream of terror, although not as loud as it had seemed at the bottom of the hill. Sometimes it was just a whimper. It sometimes sounded human, pleading, trying to communicate with anyone out there.

By the time Russell reached the ridge line, he was certain that the cries were coming from the Rocks. He started down the eastern slope toward them, grabbing one tree then the next for stability as he pushed a plume of snow ahead of him. There was nothing, animal or human there, but someone had been there recently. Fresh human footprints in the snow followed almost the same path that he had seen on Christmas, leading into the center, where the snow was trampled down in a rough circle about ten feet in diameter.

Someone had been there recently, but they left no traces other than footprints fast filling in as the wind shifted to the northeast and began to blow the sharp, dry snow crystals uphill, almost perfectly in alignment with the path. The only sound was the wind rattling the tree limbs overhead.

Russell was about to turn around to go home, reluctantly and with a heavy sadness, when he heard the whimpering sound again, very close to him. Moving quietly so as not to scare the wounded animal, he followed the sound along the trampled path out of the Rocks and down the eastern slope. He had to be cautious, because the snow hid a sudden drop that he knew was no more than twenty yards beyond.

Only five or six feet to the right of the path, a young man, perhaps in his mid-twenties, sat leaning against a tree. He wore only a cotton sweat suit. His feet, hands, and head were bare. He shivered visibly and rolled his shoulders from side to side against the tree trunk. As Russell approached him, he looked in Russell's direction, but his eyes appeared to be unfocused or perhaps looking beyond Russell deep into the forest. He made a sound that was half-scream, half-howl, short but sharp enough and loud enough to echo faintly even against the snow-covered mountains. At first, Russell could not tell whether it was from fear or pain, but the yellow stain on the snowy residue underneath the young man seemed to confirm mortal fright.

Russell stopped, waited a few moments, and then approached him more slowly, speaking softly, trying to assure the young man that he would help him. The young man gave no sign that he understood, but he allowed Russell to come closer. Russell slowly squatted down and placed the blanket over him. The young man's only reactions were to startle and then sit perfectly still for a moment. Then he resumed his rocking side to side.

Russell asked him who he was, what had happened, and where he was in pain. The young man responded in low guttural sounds that sounded like attempts at words, but which Russell couldn't understand. Russell was not even sure that the young man understood Russell's questions. Russell offered the young man a sip of brandy. He took a sip and then turned his face away, pushing the bottle away with his hand.

Russell looked around for any clues, perhaps a second set of footprints, but, except for his own footprints, all he could see were the traces of what he assumed to be the young man's, almost completely obscured by the drifting snow. They appeared to have come downhill from the Rocks but disappeared only eight or ten feet away.

Russell tried to examine the young man for signs of injury. He didn't resist but didn't cooperate. His fingertips, toes, and nose were pale white with a faint reddish-blue tone that Russell assumed to be the first signs of frostbite. Other than what looked like occasional shivering, the young man gave no other signs of being cold. The only fresh marks that Russell could see on him were some abrasions around his wrists, as if they had been tied by a coarse rope, and bruises on his feet.

Russell assumed that the young man couldn't have been exposed to the elements for more than a few hours, or he would have been dead, and, unless he got inside soon, he would be. Even in the sun and protected from the wind, the temperature was still well below freezing, and he needed more than a wool blanket to survive.

Russell doubted that he could manage to get the young man to the warmth of his house safely by himself. However, if Russell left him alone while he sought help, the young man would almost certainly die before Russell could return. Russell put his gloves on the young man's hands and his knit watch cap on the young man's head. He then quickly took off his boots and socks, and put the socks on the young man's feet, and placed his own feet back in the boots. Taking the young man firmly by the forearm, Russell pulled him to his feet. The blanket fell off, so Russell took off his own jacket and put it on the young man, then replaced the blanket around his shoulders. These measures, Russell hoped, would arrest the loss of body heat somewhat, maybe enough to save him.

The young man offered no resistance on the way back down the hill in the snow. He seemed completely unaware of his surroundings, not even shivering as his feet, clad only in rapidly dampening socks, waded through snowdrifts. Nor did he respond to any of Russell's questions with anything more than a few low, slurred mumbles. Instead he just trudged alongside, frequently stumbling and slipping, as Russell kept his arm tightly around him. Sometimes the young man would stop and look around. Russell, worried about the need to get down the mountain and inside, would have to pull him to get him moving again.

As soon as Russell had him covered with blankets on the sofa, he called the police. Within fifteen minutes the township police and the volunteer fire department ambulance arrived. The paramedics confirmed second-degree frostbite, which they said was treatable, although the young man might eventually lose a toe or two. Their best estimate from his body temperature was that he had been exposed for about six hours, possibly since before sunrise, and had been near death when Russell found him. They said that the stupor was typical in severe hypothermia cases, but they couldn't rule out drugs as a possible contributing factor.

The police officer seemed skeptical about Russell's story.

"What made you go up into the woods like that?" he asked.

"As I said, I heard those hideous animal-like sounds. I thought that an animal was in trouble."

"And the source of the sounds was the kid? Are you sure?" the officer responded.

"No doubt about it. I even saw him scream when I first approached him." Russell was beginning to get annoyed. Wasn't the cop listening to what he said?

"But, I mean, did you hear or see anything else that could have been making those sounds?"

"What else could have made noises like that?" Russell asked.

"Well, nothing else in these parts, I suppose," the officer replied. "I was just wondering, that's all. It's not important."

The next day a State Police officer, Bob Patterson, visited. Over coffee, Russell provided the same information, and told him that he had not remembered anything new. Patterson reported that the young man still was not communicating, except in gibberish, and was unidentified. Moreover, there were no missing person reports anywhere in the state for anyone matching his description.

"We're checking with New York and New Jersey, because their kids come out here sometimes, but my hunch is that he is from around here. We have some people out showing his picture over at Mansfield State, and we're putting up some posters in Wellsboro. So far nobody's identified him," Patterson said.

"Well, I don't recall ever seeing him before, but I've only lived here for about six months," Russell replied.

"The good news about all this," Patterson continued, "is that the kid isn't dead. Even after you warmed him up taking him down the mountain, and with what the EMT guys did for him, his body temperature was still only 88 degrees. When you found him, he should have been dead. They now think he might have been up on your mountain almost all night."

"So maybe I didn't save his life," Russell commented. "but he just had a tough constitution or –"

"No, no. I don't want to take any credit away from you, Mr. Poe," Patterson interrupted. "Had you not gone up and made him walk back with you, he definitely would have died."

"So, do a lot of people around here die of hypothermia?" Russell asked.

"No, but it can sneak up on someone pretty fast," Patterson continued. "Some people are more resistant than others, but it's deadly for anyone. The doctors tell me that this was an unusual case. I personally have only seen one case that was worse than this one, and it was really strange."

"How so?" Russell asked.

"Well," Patterson hesitated, "I know that you're going to find this hard to believe, Mr. Poe, but I pulled an old man out of the Tioga River several winters ago. We found him sitting slumped over in the shallows just off the riverbank. Well, he was pronounced dead at the scene, an obvious case of hypothermia, we thought. So, we covered him up and took him away, and when we were unloading him at the hospital morgue, the old boy came to, sat up, and thanked us kindly for the ride into town." Patterson laughed.

"That's quite a practical joke," Russell replied. "How did he fake being dead?"

"No, he wasn't faking. There is no doubt that he was dead when we pulled him out, and he possibly had been dead for a couple of hours. He wasn't breathing, had no pulse, and his pupils were fixed and dilated. The medics tried to resuscitate him but couldn't. One of the doctors at the hospital said that there have been a few cases like that one reported in the literature. Apparently, the warmth in the ambulance and the motion of the ride somehow brought him back."

"Officer Patterson," Russell asked. "is there any evidence about what caused the young man I found to be up there on the mountain? I couldn't find anything where I found him that suggested how he got there, except maybe that his hands had been tied and maybe he was led there."

"As best as we can tell, the rope burns that you saw were three or four days old, maybe a week," Patterson replied. "The other odd thing is that the toxicology report came back completely clean. Sometimes when kids wander off and get into trouble like that, they're under the influence of something. But this kid was clean: no alcohol, no drugs, nothing, at least nothing at a level that could be detected."

"What happens now?" Russell asked.

"Nothing," the policeman replied. "They've taken the kid to the state hospital down in Danville to try to bring him back to reality. We still don't know who he is. Maybe we can find out something then, if he remembers any of it. Maybe he will think it was all just a bad dream."

Stewardship Sunday

It was Pastor Bill Paxton's habit to say a short prayer each morning as soon as he realized that he was awake. It was early Sunday morning. Long ago he had thrown his alarm clock away, and even now he would always take off his wristwatch before entering his bedroom. Looking outside into the darkness, Bill reckoned that it was shortly after six o'clock.

Before he could allow any other thoughts into his mind, Bill closed his eyes again and listened for guidance this Sunday. He hated Stewardship Sunday. Even after fifteen years of building the Mountain View Chapel up from a Bible study group in someone's living room, he still was embarrassed to ask his congregation, the third Sunday every January, to dig down deeper to support the church, just to support him. Those folks could barely make ends meet, let alone follow the Bible's injunction to tithe ten percent.

Bill had modified that years ago. "What it really means," he would tell his congregation each year, "is that after you've bought your groceries, and put clothes on your kids' backs, and paid all the rest of your bills, and helped others who are in need, you give the Lord ten percent of what's left. If all you got left on Saturday night is one thin dime, the Lord will be happy with a penny on Sunday morning. He wants you to have a little left over to enjoy life." But he never felt that he sounded very convincing.

Well, he thought as he finished his prayer and rolled out of bed, at least there won't be a big crowd today. Stewardship Sunday kept people away. Even on Christmas and Easter, the most he could expect would be about one hundred. Today he would do well to draw thirty. But the rest of them would come around, one by one, to make their pledges.

Bill thought about the meeting that he had the previous evening with Cathy Wallace. She had said that she might want to meet with him briefly today, after the services.

Cathy was one of the most faithful members, and one of the very few young adults in his church. Most were in their forties and older.

A few brought their children with them, but the kids would usually stop coming once they were in their teens. When Bill would ask their parents about how their children were doing and whether they might come to church someday soon, the parents would usually mumble excuses and look at the ground.

Cathy was in her late twenties and still single. Why did he say *still*? Things have changed. Kids are marrying later, or not at all. This generation is so different from young people twenty years ago, even ten years ago. So many of the old ways are crumbling. Good riddance to some of them.

Cathy seemed different from most of the young people that Bill knew, more serious and maybe a little old-fashioned. She lived in a Victorian house in the center of Wellsboro, where she cared for her 78-year old grandmother. She worked in the advertising department of the local paper, the *Wellsboro Bulletin*. In fact, Cathy Wallace *was* the advertising department. She once told Bill that her boss, Ed, spent most of the day across the street at the bar, "schmoozing customers" he'd tell her.

Bill picked up his bedside Bible to start his morning scripture reading, opening the book, as he always did, at random. Cathy's grandmother gave him that Bible more than thirty years ago, when he was twelve. Agnes Grogan taught the Communicants Class that he had to take before joining the First Presbyterian Church and taking communion for the first time. He had never told Cathy that, nor asked to visit "Aggie" as she insisted that the kids call her. He never understood why not. Bill flipped through the heavily notated pages, recording decades of Bible study. On some pages Bill's notes almost obliterated the printed text. The thin black leather binding rubbed particles of fine dust in his hands.

"I have recorded my whole life's journey and hold it in my hands," he said quietly as he turned the pages, remembering when he made some of the notes and what he was thinking at the time. He suddenly felt old.

Bill thought about the night he met Cathy. He was conducting the service one night during the annual Old-Time Tent Meeting that his church held every July. It was a serious ministry, not a bunch of fake faith healing and other scams, and it brought scores of people to Jesus, although most probably drifted away right after Christmas. The good home-cooked food, brightly colored tent, and upbeat Gospel music brought people from as far away as New Jersey and Maryland. Bill wanted people to know that religion could be fun.

The Tent Meetings never produced many new members for Bill's church. Most of the folks in the area who were inclined to join Mountain View had probably already done so. The people who came forward at the end of the evening usually already had churches of their own and merely wanted to rededicate themselves, rather than be saved for the first time. Some of them came forward without thinking, only because they found themselves overwhelmed by emotion triggered by some word, the notes of a hymn, or some faint memory from long ago. None of that mattered, however. Bill always told himself that if he helped create an hour's meaningful spiritual experience for each of them, it really didn't matter whether they joined Mountain View or returned to another church, or simply drifted away from God and back into their day-to-day lives. All Bill hoped for was that the experience of that moment would mean something that stayed with them.

More tangibly, the offerings and the food and beverage sales at the Tent Meetings raised more money in those five nights than the congregation contributed in five months. Every year Bill would fight a friendly battle with the church board about how to spend the Tent Meeting money. Each year they would recommend that, after the expenses were paid, he should keep half of the proceeds and put the rest into the church's operating fund. But they always gave in to Bill's insistence that all the money go anonymously to charities that Bill would select.

"That's not our money," Bill would say. "We collected it but are only its stewards. It belongs to the people who need it more than we do." He would always say that he was happy to live on his share of the Sunday offerings from the members, even when it was only a few dollars.

Bill stood up and walked to his bedroom window. The sun had just risen but cast only a faint red smear across a gray sky. He looked at the thermometer outside: nineteen degrees. It would be a cloudy day today, possibly with snow. That would keep the attendance down at church. Maybe that was a good thing.

Bill felt frustrated and ashamed. He had allowed thoughts of money to disrupt the first moments of the day, the time that was so important to him. He needed to get his priorities straight. Stewardship Sunday would take care of itself. He needed to refocus on Cathy Wallace and their conversation the night before.

Cathy had come forward to receive Jesus at the end of his sermon on the last night of the Tent Meeting two years ago. Friday usually drew the largest congregation. Bill remembered how the tears on her cheeks sparkled as she slowly walked up the center aisle, while the two hundred or so people – many of them African Americans who had come up in two buses from a church in Scranton – softly sang "Just as I Am." He asked her afterwards if she belonged to any church, and she had said First Presbyterian. He gave her the little tract about Mountain View Chapel and told her that she was welcome to come to the services without any expectation that she should join. So, he was pleasantly surprised when she attended his service the next Sunday morning, signed the membership book that Bill always kept open in the front of the sanctuary, and then came to the mid-week Bible Study Class on Wednesday night. Since then, Cathy attended almost every week and always was one of the first to volunteer to help with the Tent Meeting and other church events.

Last Sunday, while Bill stood by the door greeting people after the service, Cathy asked if she could talk to him later. He offered to meet with her that afternoon, but she said that she wasn't ready yet. She would call when she was ready. Bill had gone through the week's routine, wondering what problem Cathy had, but feeling more confident as the week progressed that she had solved it. He was surprised when he came home from his errands on Saturday evening to see her sitting on his doorstep.

"I called, Pastor," Cathy said as she stood up and brushed the bottom of her skirt, "but you weren't home."

"I hope you weren't waiting long," he said.

"No, I just got here." Bill suspected she was lying.

They went into Bill's study. Cathy declined a soda or herbal tea. She seemed to want to get to the point, at last.

"It's about my boyfriend, Kenny," Cathy began.

Bill quickly ran the name through his mental card file. Kenny Kelso. Nickname: Spook. Scrawny kid in his mid-twenties. Long stringy hair. Scraggly mustache. Loner. Usually unemployed. Never had amounted to much but had never really been given a chance. Bill wondered how a beautiful mature girl like Cathy had gotten involved with him.

"I need your advice about him," she continued.

Bill went to his mental filing cabinet. Romantic issue? Possibly pregnancy? He started mentally rehearsing what he would tell Cathy, even as she continued speaking. The Scriptures have a lot to say about love and marriage. Couples who follow the Bible enjoy long and happy relationships. We can love each other only if we are united in our love of God. Bill disapproved of the way relationships were carried out these days. People miss so much when they are not committed to each other for life.

He realized suddenly that he hadn't paid attention to anything that Cathy had said for the last thirty seconds. He assumed he hadn't missed much, probably just how much she loved Kenny but wasn't sure she wanted to marry him. The next sentence that Bill paid attention to made him sit up straight.

"So," Cathy continued slowly, "have you ever heard of a pagan god named Bel?"

She seemed to cringe back in her chair as soon as she completed the sentence, as if she expected to be hit.

"Baal?" Bill asked. He shuddered slightly but hoped that Cathy hadn't noticed. He could never think of Baal without picturing the babies being tossed into a furnace, burned alive as love offerings to Baal.

"No," Cathy replied. "Not the Baal from the Old Testament. No, I mean Bel. It's spelled B-E-L."

Bill paused, selecting his words carefully. He didn't want to scare her. "Well, I'm not really an expert, Cathy, but I think Bel is an old Celtic form of Baal. You know, like Jupiter was the Roman name for the Greek god Zeus?

"Celtic – like Irish?" Cathy asked.

"Yes," Bill replied, "but the Celtic people lived all over: Spain, France, and England, as well as Ireland. They probably learned about Baal from Phoenician traders who traveled all over the known world back before the time of Christ."

"Were the Phoenicians those ancient people from what's Lebanon now?" Cathy asked.

"That's right. They are believed to be the same people that are called the Philistines in the Old Testament," Bill said. "You might remember their great cities, Tyre and Sidon, which sold King Solomon the cedar trees for his Temple in Jerusalem. They traveled all over the Mediterranean and founded great cities like Carthage in North Africa and Cadiz in Spain. We know that they traded for tin with the people in the British Isles. Some scholars believe that they even got as far as Brazil. And they took their gods, including Baal, with them."

"So, Bel was simply the Celtic version of Baal, which they took from the Phoenicians, or Philistines," Cathy said quietly, looking down at her hands folded in her lap.

"Well, again, I'm not an expert on all of this, but from what I understand, the Celtic god Bel was not nearly as bad as the Philistines' Baal," Bill smiled, hoping to reassure her. "He was like a sun god to them, a source of life."

"So, Bel is a false god?" she said. It sounded more like a conclusion that she had reached on her own, rather than a question.

"Yes," Bill went on. "It's not like where we Christians and the Jews and the Muslims all worship the same God, but in our own ways." Stop parading your knowledge, Bill scolded himself. You'll only make it worse.

"Is Bel evil?" she asked quietly.

Bill sensed where this was leading. He reached over and took Cathy's hand.

"Cathy," he said quietly. "Bel or Baal or any of those false gods are not real. They were ideas – sometimes evil, wicked, strange ideas – that people used to try to understand life, nothing more.

"Anything that keeps us from the love of the one true God is evil. It doesn't matter whether it's a god called Bel, or Baal, or whatever. It can be our own pride – thinking that we have all the answers and don't need help from God – that keeps us from God's love. It doesn't have to be a scary stone idol. So, yes, in that sense, Cathy, yes, Bel is evil if he keeps you from God's love."

Cathy reached beside her, into the pocket of her jacket, which she had so carefully draped over the arm of the chair, declining Bill's offer to hang it up. She carefully pulled out four pieces of notebook paper, grasping them at the edges with her fingertips.

"I found these on the floor in Kenny's bedroom," she said.

Bill instantaneously regretted his wincing visibly at the word *bedroom*. Cathy's face reddened and she looked down at her feet. Remember, Bill, he told himself, kids are different today, even religious girls like Cathy, and they have been for a long time. They're not always going to do as you expect.

"They look like some sort of list of weird names and sayings," she said. "Some of them I recognize from the Bible, but some of them I've never seen before."

She handed the papers across the coffee table to Bill. As he glanced at them, she reached over and pointed.

"See, there's Bel – 'the great god Bel' it says. Right there."

"Did you ask Kenny about these?" Bill asked.

"Oh yes," she said. "At first, I was just curious, like whether they were something that he needed to keep or if I could throw them away. But then I saw all this pagan and other weird stuff on them. So, I asked him."

"Kenny's got a past," she continued. "I mean I love him like anything, and the past is the past, but I was afraid he was getting into Satanism or something."

"What did he say?" Bill asked.

Cathy drew in a breath.

"Well," she said, "first he said it was just some scribbling. I didn't believe him, so I told him so. I said, 'Kenny, are you getting mixed up in some sort of cult or something.' And he goes, 'No, nothing like that'."

"What happened next?" Bill prompted.

"Well, then he says that it's just some stuff he had to memorize for a lodge that he was joining. So, I ask him which one, and he says that I wouldn't have ever heard of it. 'It's just like the Masons,' he said.

"Well, then I knew he was lying, Pastor," she continued. There was a note of triumph in her voice. "Because my Uncle Jack is a Mason and he never talks about any stuff like that.

"So, I tell Kenny that I know he's lying, and that it's not Masonic. And he said it was *like* the Masons, but different."

"And then?"

"Well then, Kenny got serious. And he says, 'Please Cathy. Forget you ever saw that stuff. I want to join this lodge, and if they find out that I let out their lodge secrets, they won't let me in'."

Bill looked again at the four pages, torn from a small notebook. They looked like lists, but there was no apparent order to them.

"Do you know for sure whether Kenny wrote this? Is this his handwriting?" Bill asked.

"Oh, definitely," Cathy responded, "but I didn't know that Kenny knew anything about the Bible or those pagan things."

Cathy was right. A few of the items on the list were from the Bible: Anti-Christ, Magog, the Seven Seals, the end of days. Some were familiar but appeared to be Celtic references: Bel, Children of Bel, the White Goddess, sacred oaks, Sulis, Artio. Most of the words, however, could have referred to anything.

There were a few phrases on the second page. They looked as if they had been dictated and copied. Some of them were disturbing:

We are older than the world.

Satan is a lie.

Jesus is a lie.

Only one of us speaks as God, and only in his time.

Death is the highest beauty of Nature.

We must die so that we may be raised up.
The purest of us all may reign only 900 years.

"Pastor?" Cathy asked quietly. "Is Kenny involved in Satanism? Should I leave him?"

"Well," Bill started, but paused. What do I tell her?

"Well," he repeated, "I can't say for sure about Satanism. It comes in many forms, but Satan is real. The Bible reminds us that, in the last days, many false prophets will appear. Many people will raise up false gods."

"Like Bel?" Cathy asked.

"Yes, like Bel and dozens of other ancient false gods, Cathy, but also some modern gods."

"Like money and success and fame," Cathy finished the thought, nodding her head in agreement.

"And you see, Cathy," Bill continued, "What makes it hard for the faithful is that we believe that we should love all of God's children. But some of them, even ones who call themselves Christian, may actually be serving the Anti-Christ, the last form that Satan will take.

"A lot of good people will be fooled in the last days, Cathy, even people who believe that they are good Christians. The Bible tells us that Satan was the most beautiful of all the angels, and he will appear to us in a beautiful form, so compelling that many of us will believe that we are looking into the eyes of Jesus himself.

"This is why the Apostle Paul advised us not to be yoked to unbelievers. In the last days, it will be very hard for even the most faithful Christians to tell good from evil. It will be even harder if we are pulled down by an unbeliever, no matter how much we love him or her."

Bill thought he could see tears in Cathy's eyes. He wondered whether he had pushed the last days references too far.

"Cathy," he said quietly. "I remember one night two summers ago, the last time I saw tears in your eyes. Do you remember?"

She nodded.

"Remember the night you came forward for Jesus. It wasn't an easy step to take, in front of all those people, was it?"

She shook her head.

"Well, Cathy, Jesus sometimes needs for us to take other steps, sometimes, that are just as hard as that first step you took for Him."

"So, I should leave Kenny? But I love him, Pastor. He's good to me."

Bill paused. It's probably better if she stays with Kenny. He chose his words very carefully, speaking them very softly, very deliberately. He wanted to leave no mistaken impressions. Cathy already had absorbed a lot tonight.

"Cathy, I can't tell you what to do. Only God can do that through prayer. So be sure that you've heard God's voice before you make any decisions. That might mean a different type of prayer, when you just open your mind and heart and listen to God, rather than spend the time telling Him what you want. But God will help you, Cathy. Whether you stay with Kenny or leave him, you should tell him that you want nothing to do with his lodge, or whatever it is."

Cathy smiled and sighed. She seemed relieved.

"Pray for him, Cathy. If you love him, pray with all your heart. That's important. Maybe the Lord will speak to him," Bill continued.

"But, Pastor, Kenny's not religious. I'm sure he doesn't pray," Cathy interrupted.

"That's okay, Cathy. God can speak to any of us, even an unbeliever, in ways other than prayer, like in the majesty of a sunset or the beauty of a flower or the smile of a child. Kenny doesn't have to pray to hear God.

"But, whatever you do, Cathy, don't confront Kenny any more over this. That won't help. And keep me informed of how it's going. I'll remember both of you in my prayers every day until you and Kenny have gotten through this."

Bill took Cathy's hand and said a short prayer. As they got up and started toward the front door, Cathy turned and looked up into Bill's eyes.

"Pastor, we're truly in the last days, aren't we?" It was more of a statement than a question. "I'm so afraid."

"I don't know," Bill replied as he wished her good night. "Just trust in the Lord and try to do the right thing. That's all any of us can do."

And now early on Stewardship Sunday, Bill Paxton stared at the coffee grounds in the bottom of his mug. The words and phrases on Kenny's lists marched in front of him. Despite his problems, Kenny had seemed so promising. Cathy could have been such a good influence on him.

Bill put the mug in the sink and looked at the dingy cream-colored phone on the kitchen wall. Tony was an early riser, and probably had been up for hours already. Bill had met him in prison in Lewisburg, where Tony was doing Federal time for getting wrapped up in a drug ring. Tony had been at rock bottom. His promising career in pro football had been wrecked during his very first exhibition season, even before he had played a single down for the Eagles.

When Tony was eligible for parole, Bill set him up with a job in Wellsboro, as far as possible from the old influences in Tony's life. A few people in the congregation were uncomfortable at first with a convicted felon in their midst, because Tony told everyone his whole story the first Sunday he attended. But they soon learned about Tony's basic good qualities: his willingness to sacrifice to achieve a goal, his patience, his good humor. In time, Tony was elected a deacon in the church.

Tony answered the phone on the first ring.

Bill didn't identify himself, but said only softly, "We have a problem."

Kenny

Kenny Kelso wanted to get drunk and forget his evening with Cathy. He walked alone in the cool night air. Walking was a bitch, but he'd had his license taken away for points. At least he could get good and loaded at Shannon's Pub and walk home without having to worry about the cops picking him up for DUI.

When Kenny arrived at Cathy's house for their date earlier that evening, she wasn't home. Her grandmother invited Kenny in and said he could wait in the living room. She didn't seem to understand Kenny's questions about where Cathy was or when she was expected home.

"She'll be here presently," was all the old lady said before she nodded her head in the direction of the sofa and silently disappeared into the back of the house.

Kenny waited for a half hour, listening to a clock ticking in another room and looking at the framed, faded photographs on the coffee table. He stood and was headed to the front door to leave when Cathy entered.

"Where have you been?" he asked, trying to hide his annoyance.

"Sunday night prayer service at the church, just like every other Sunday. You know that." she said. "It ran a little late tonight. I left as soon as I could."

"Why didn't you leave early? You knew we had a date."

"I'm sorry, Kenny, but Pastor Bill had only seven people there tonight, and I couldn't just get up and leave. Thanks for being so patient." She gave him a quick kiss on the cheek.

"Well, it's just that sometimes I feel like that goddamned church means more to you than I do."

"Quiet!" Cathy grabbed his arm. "You know I don't want Grandma to hear that kind of language, especially from you. It's bad enough the lies that I tell her so I can be with you. And yes, my 'goddamned church,' as you put it, does mean a lot to me. So, quit making me feel like I have to choose."

"Okay, I'm sorry."

Cathy went to the back of the house and spoke quietly with her grandmother. Kenny couldn't quite hear what the two women said to each other. She came back into the front hallway, picking up her purse and putting on her gloves. She threw the end of her knit scarf over her shoulder.

"Let's go," she said, "or we'll be late."

As if it was my fault, Kenny thought, but he didn't want to get into a fight with Cathy, not tonight. They had planned that, after a movie, they would go back to Kenny's apartment, where they would spend the night together. Kenny didn't have any work scheduled for the next day, and Cathy didn't have to be at her office until noon. Kenny had spent all day cleaning the place, even getting some food so that he could cook her a special breakfast.

When they were in Cathy's car on their way to the theater, Kenny asked, "So, where did you tell her you were going tonight?"

"Oh, pretty much the usual, that I'm going to visit a girlfriend down in Williamsport and will stay the night, rather than drive home so late. And then I'll drive back home in the morning, look in on her, change for work, and go into the office."

"Doesn't she ever get a little suspicious about your staying out all night?"

"No, sometimes I'm not sure that it registers with her, so I leave her a note. But I really don't think that she really cares, just so long as she knows I'll be home the next day. You know that I always call her around her bedtime, just to make sure she's okay."

"Why don't you just tell her the truth about us? That we want to move in together. Are you ashamed of me?" Kenny said quietly.

Cathy stopped the car along the curb.

"Look," she said, turning to him, "you know I'm not ashamed of you. But she's a kind old lady who's no longer in her right mind all the time. Things take time with her, Kenny. I've got to wait for the right time, so she will accept the idea that her little Cathy is all grown up and that I have a life of my own, even before I try to tell her how serious I am about you. But the idea of us living together would freak her out right now.

"And besides, you know I don't want to move in with you, and you know why. We've gone over this a hundred times. You also know that I'm responsible for her. She's got nobody else left to take care of her. So please don't make things harder. Just trust me."

Cathy fell silent and they did not exchange more than a few words at the movie. As they were driving to Kenny's apartment afterwards, Kenny had the sense that she was somehow forcing herself to go with him, that she really didn't want to spend the night with him, at least not this night.

"What's wrong, Cathy?" he finally asked as they pulled into the gravel parking area beside his building. "You haven't said more than three words to me all evening. Are you mad at me about something?" As soon as he spoke, he had a feeling that somehow it was the wrong thing to say.

Cathy said nothing as they got out of the car. She walked around to the passenger door, where Kenny was leaning, lighting a cigarette. She stopped five feet from him, pulled four crumpled pieces of paper from her jacket pocket, and thrust them at him.

"It's this," she said quietly, walking slowly toward him, waving the papers up and down in time to the words.

Kenny took the papers and looked at them.

"Well, what about it?" Kenny said. He leaned his head back and exhaled a column of smoke straight up into the darkness. He started to walk toward the steps leading up the side of the building to his second-floor apartment.

"What are you getting yourself into, Kenny?" Cathy followed, grabbing his arm hard and pulling him back just as he was about to take the first step up the stairs. She quickly moved up onto the first step, turned, and was at eye level with him. She blocked the stairs, her back to the dim bare light bulb by Kenny's door at the top. Kenny couldn't see her face, and he couldn't tell whether she was worried or angry.

"Jesus Christ, Cath, will you let it go? I told you, it's just some stuff from that lodge I'm thinking of joining. It don't mean nothing. Just let it go."

"I know," she replied calmly. "You told me that. But I saw my pastor yesterday, Kenny. He confirmed that this is Satanic writing. Evil. So, don't try to bullshit me about it being some kind of lodge. I'm not an idiot."

"No, it ain't evil." He tried to be just as calm as she was.

"Yes, it is, Kenny. Please. Believe me about this. If you don't believe me, then believe Pastor Paxton. This is about your soul, Kenny, not just some social club." She seemed to be choking on each word.

Kenny wondered if Cathy was getting ready to cry. He shifted his body to the left, but she followed him, keeping her back to the light at the top of the stairs, blocking him from retreating up to his apartment, and keeping her face in the dark.

"Well, Kenny, you and I both know the truth about this, so quit trying to bullshit me. I love you, Kenny, but I can't have anything to do with this. You have to choose."

"Aw, Cath, this is silly. Lighten up."

"No, Kenny. It's not silly, and I'm not going to lighten up. I think we both need to do a lot of thinking. Apart. When you're ready to admit to me what's going on, you can call me. I love you. I'll be here for you. I'll even try to get you help.

"But, Kenny, I can't have a life where I don't know what's true and what's a bunch of lies."

Cathy suddenly kissed him on the cheek, pulled away quickly from his attempted embrace, and got back into her car. Without saying another word, she drove away. Kenny stood at the foot of the stairs to his apartment, watching until her taillights disappeared.

Like a big green Irish lighthouse, the neon shamrock at Shannon's Pub came into view as soon as Kenny rounded the corner. Walking fast, partly because of the cold and partly because of his anger, it still took him longer than he had expected to arrive at the door.

Shannon's was almost empty, as it was every Sunday night. Four guys were standing around one of the two pool tables, watching Angel and her girlfriend shooting pool. The guys weren't from around here, but they had their eyes on Angel's girlfriend. She looked hot and kept looking at all four of them. They were going to be disappointed, Kenny thought.

Jill the bartender smiled at him as he sat at the bar. Kenny ordered a draft, chugged half of it, and then set it down.

"Rough night, Kenny?" Jill asked.

"Just some shit, that's all," Kenny replied. One of the four guys at the pool table came up to the end of the bar with four empty mugs. Jill went to refill them, leaving Kenny staring at himself in the mirror behind the bar.

Maybe it's time to move away, he thought, maybe to California. There's no future here, working construction the rest of my life, only ten days a month even when things are good.

Kenny watched the reflections of Angel and her girlfriend shooting pool. There's another reason, he thought. Things are just too tangled up right now. Cathy's all over you about joining the Children of Bel. Christ, was she pissed about it! And those guys from the Children are leaning on you because you're not sure yet. Hell, you had thought it was a motorcycle club at first, you stupid bastard.

The four guys at the first pool table stared at Angel's girlfriend as she racked up a game of eight ball. Angel leaned on the cigarette machine behind her and looked, too. One of the guys, the tall one with the blond beard came up to say something to Angel's girlfriend, but Angel moved in, too.

Jill came back to check on Kenny's half-empty glass.

"Hey, Jill," Kenny smiled. "Those guys don't seriously think they're going to get any action over there, do they?"

Jill smiled. "Hey, it looks like everything's nice and friendly over there." She nodded in the direction of the pool tables. Angel was smiling at another of the guys.

"I don't know," Kenny said. "I wouldn't want to try to move in on Angel. She's pretty tough."

Jill smiled and leaned over the bar, her face just inches from Kenny. For a second, Kenny thought Jill was going to kiss him.

"Angel likes to watch," she whispered. "It'll be just fine. Everybody will get what they want."

Jill patted Kenny's arm and moved down the bar. She paused, glanced over her shoulder, and winked at Kenny. Kenny smiled.

I was probably sitting on this very barstool that Thursday night last September, Kenny remembered, when I met Willy and Claw and first got hooked up with the Children of Bel. It had been about four months ago. Cathy was away that weekend visiting relatives somewhere, so he was free for the evening. He had just finished a construction job and had earned some overtime — paid in cash, the best way — he decided to have a sandwich and fries at Shannon's and hang out there for the evening.

Kenny usually kept to himself. He'd join in conversation, if invited, but he preferred to sit and slowly drink his beer and think about things. He had seen Willy and Claw on their motorcycles once or twice before in town. They came into Shannon's about nine o'clock. Willy was at least fifty years old, maybe closer to sixty, with a heavily lined face. He was short, wiry, with long gray hair and a short scruffy beard that looked like he hadn't shaved for about a week. Claw was younger, maybe just a few years older than Kenny. Claw was built like a bear: tall, massive, and dark. His black hair merged into a black beard, but his eyes seemed gentle to Kenny.

Willy and Claw had been shooting pool for about an hour, when Kenny noticed Willy standing behind him. Willy tapped his shoulder.

"Want to shoot some eight ball with us?" Willy asked. "I'm getting sort of bored beating my buddy all the time."

"I'm not too good," Kenny replied. "You'd get bored pretty fast playing against me. But sure, why not?"

Willy, Claw, and Kenny spent the next two hours taking turns playing eight ball and drinking. Willy asked Kenny a lot of questions about what he did, where he lived, what friends he had. At first Kenny was on guard, but later assumed that Willy and Claw were just trying to be friendly. However, Willy and Claw didn't reveal much of themselves in response to Kenny's questions. They vaguely said they both lived "out in the sticks," as Willy described it, but liked to come into town for a change of scenery every now and then. Claw said he worked as a mechanic. Willy said he worked only occasionally, because he'd been messed up in Vietnam and couldn't work regular hours ever since. When Kenny asked about how he had gotten hurt, Claw gave Kenny a look that clearly said, "Don't go there."

Shortly before midnight, Claw put his cue back in the rack, finished his beer, and told Kenny, "Well, man, we got to split."

"Hey, it's still early," Kenny replied.

"Well, we got an appointment," Willy replied.

"Yeah," Claw chuckled, "we're going to a picnic."

"At midnight?" Kenny asked. Willy and Claw exchanged glances.

"No," Willy laughed, "Claw's just messing with you. It's just a bunch of our friends. We get together sometimes for a late party. When the weather's nice we get together outside."

"Sounds like fun," Kenny said hopefully.

Willy and Claw exchanged glances again. Willy stared at Kenny for a moment.

"Would you like to come along?" Willy asked quietly.

Kenny had heard about biker parties. He'd like the wild sex he'd heard about, but he wasn't too sure about the drugs.

"Sounds great," he said. "So, it's some kind of a biker party?"

Claw laughed.

"No," Willy said. "They're not bikers or anything like that. Claw and me, we just like to hang around some with these guys. They're pretty straight."

"Yeah," Claw added, "some of them even drive cars." All three of them laughed.

"Tell you what," Willy continued, "I got to take a leak before we go. We'll meet you outside. You can follow us in your car."

"I ain't got wheels," Kenny interrupted.

Claw looked at him like he was some kind of freak.

"I mean, I got a car," Kenny continued. "But my license got suspended. I can't drive."

"Well, you could ride with me," Claw said. "I got a spare helmet. But me and Willy are heading straight home after the party. We can't bring you all the way back here."

Kenny realized that he really wanted to go with Claw and Willy.

"How about this?" Kenny suggested. "How about I walk home and get my car? I only live about four blocks from here. I'll be back in ten minutes tops, if you can wait for me."

"I don't know," Willy said. "I mean, if you get caught by the cops. Shit. Driving drunk on a suspended license. Man, you'd be in deep shit."

"I'll be careful," Kenny replied. "There's only two town cops on duty this time on a Friday night, and one of them's at the station. If we keep to the back streets until we get out of town, the other guy will never see us. The Staties don't know me. It'll be okay."

"Okay, man." Willy agreed. "We'll meet you out in the lot in about ten minutes. But we can't wait very long for you, okay?"

"And one other thing," Willy continued. "Everything you see and hear from this point on you got to keep secret, okay?"

"There's not anything illegal going on, is there?" Kenny asked, thinking about drugs. "I mean, I'm still on probation for a possession with intent charge from a couple of years ago."

"No, it's cool. Don't worry," Will replied. "We promise you. There's nothing illegal that's going to happen."

"Shit," Claw interjected, "I still have another two years of fucking parole or it's back to prison for me. You can be sure I ain't going to take no chances."

"It's just that some of our friends are a little uncomfortable with outsiders," Willy continued, "so Claw and I will have to sort of vouch for you, that you're okay and can be trusted."

"Sure, I'll be there. Thanks, guys." Kenny quickly grabbed his coat and almost ran out the door.

Driving back to Shannon's parking lot, Kenny was sure Willy and Claw would be gone. They'll ditch me, he thought. They don't want a dork like me along. He was surprised when, just as he got out of his car in the parking lot behind the tavern, Willy and Claw came out the side door. They appeared to be arguing about something. He could only hear a few words before they saw him there and stopped suddenly.

"Man, this is the craziest thing you've done yet," he thought he heard Claw say. "We don't even know this kid."

"It's okay," Willy responded. "It'll be fine."

Claw noticed Kenny and walked over, clapped him on the shoulder, smiled, and said, "You came back. Good. Just follow us. It won't be far."

Willy and Claw drove their motorcycles out of town, east toward Mansfield, scrupulously observing the speed limits and waiting until all the stop lights turned green. As he followed them, Kenny realized that he had a little too much to drink, not enough, he was sure, to be legally drunk, but enough to slow down his reflexes. So, he just concentrated on following the taillights of the two motorcycles and not doing anything erratic. His thoughts kept bouncing from "this could be dangerous" to "I'm going to get laid."

After about twenty minutes, Willy and Claw turned off the highway onto a back road and drove, more slowly now, for about another five minutes. Just before the road curved to the right, Willy and Claw suddenly slowed and turned off the road to the left and began to cross a grassy area toward a row of trees at the base of a mountain.

"Shit," he said aloud, "There's nothing up there. Where the hell are these guys taking me?" He realized that, with the tire iron in the trunk, he would be defenseless if they tried to mug him and steal his car. But if he turned around and tried to head back to town, they would chase him and catch him.

"They know that I can identify them," he almost shouted. "Shit, if they mug me, they'd have to kill me." He pounded the steering wheel, angry at himself for being so stupid as to get set up so easily.

Kenny stopped on the road, his turn signal clicking while he wondered whether he should follow Willy and Claw. He knew that he was somewhere near Mansfield, probably just a couple of miles from the police station. If he followed the road around to the right, he could be out of sight before they noticed he was gone and could turn around and get back on the road to chase him.

Kenny was about to drive off, but he first looked to the left to see whether Willy and Claw were still in sight. They were only about ten yards off the road, stopped at the edge of the trees. They had switched off their headlights. He could see their dark forms turned around, as if they were watching him. Claw waved his arm to motion Kenny toward them. He thought he heard one of the motorcycles beep. For the first time that he could remember, Kenny had felt panic. He had never in his life been this scared or uncertain about what to do, but something deep inside him was overriding his fear and forcing him to turn and follow them, like a stray dog instinctively following what it thought was a kind person.

Driving by the light of his parking lights, Kenny followed Willy and Claw through a gap between two trees, just wide enough for his car. He heard the branches softly scrape against the roof. They then followed a broad flat grassy area that ran along the base of the mountain, gradually curving to the left, for about a hundred feet. There were eight cars and trucks, along with a roughly equal number of motorcycles, parked at the far edge of the field where the trees began again. Kenny parked beside a pickup truck and, looking around for other people, he walked over to where Willy and Claw were taking off their helmets and jackets and stowing them on their bikes. Kenny could hear the water rushing in a creek on the other side of a thick row of trees, perhaps only ten yards away. He felt himself calming down. If they had wanted to mug him, they would have done it before now, and not where all these other people have parked and were nearby. Maybe this was going to be okay.

Nobody else was there, and the only sounds that Kenny could hear were a soft wind, the water, and his feet shuffling in the fallen leaves as he approached Willy and Claw. At first, he could see only their shapes waiting for him by their motorcycles, and a momentary sparkling from the silver cross earring dangling from Willy's left ear. Willy walked toward him, his face emerging from the dark, like a silver mask glowing in the moonlight.

"Now we walk," was all he said.

The Children of Bel

Kenny followed Willy up a steep narrow path leading off to the left. Claw walked about four feet behind him. The bushes brushed lightly against either side of Kenny's body, making a faint rushing sound. He could hear Claw's footsteps almost matching his own, but faint for such a large man walking on a carpet of newly fallen leaves. The sky had cleared, and the full moon overhead, glowing through the first bare tree branches of late September, was brighter than Kenny had ever seen. Willy was silent, silver, and ghostlike, not looking back.

Claw spoke quietly to Kenny, in a low rumbling voice that Kenny felt more than heard.

"You need to know some stuff. This group, we have some rules that we always follow. You're a visitor, but you got to follow them, too, if you want to stay."

Kenny simply nodded.

"First of all," Claw continued, "when we get where we're going, we enter the area in a single file, okay? The ground is a little tricky up there, even in the moonlight, with some old rocks sticking up out of the ground."

"Old rocks? I've heard about them."

"No, you haven't. Now shut the fuck up and listen," Claw hissed.

"As I said, we enter silent and in single file. Besides keeping you from falling on your face, it's a way of showing respect to the place. Just stay in line behind Willy, and I'll stay behind you. Just follow Willy and do what he does.

"Also, we don't use our real names. You told us your real name back at the bar, and that's okay, because we won't tell anyone else. Some of us know each other from our daytime lives. You might even see people here tonight that you know, or maybe not. But when we're together or doing stuff for the group, we use what we call our Old Names. Like my real name isn't Claw, and his isn't Willy."

Kenny began to feel alarmed, but Claw's low rumbling whisper seemed reassuring.

"So, like I said," Claw continued, "we know your real name because you told us already back at the bar, but from now on we'll call you something else. So, what do you want us to call you tonight?"

Kenny thought for a moment.

"Come on, man," Claw's voice sounded urgent. "We're almost there. We got to introduce you to the others."

"Back when I went to college, they called me Spook," Kenny said. "Would that be okay?"

"Sure, for now," Claw replied. "If we decide to take you into our group, we may learn that your true Old Name is something else. But Spook's okay for now."

Spook was the first thing that came into Kenny's mind. That one semester when he tried to go to Mansfield State, he lived in a room in an old hotel above a bar on Main Street. It was all he could afford: twenty-eight dollars a week for a barely furnished ten by ten room without a bath. He felt out of place there, nineteen years old, poor, and trying to make it on his own in college. He would quietly leave the hotel, unseen he hoped, at six each morning to walk to the campus. He went to classes and spent the rest of the day in the library, not returning until after dark, when the bar would be too busy for anyone to notice him slip in the door and go upstairs. The other guys that lived there, students like himself and old men on welfare, called him "the Spook."

"Take me in?" Kenny whispered over his shoulder to Claw. "Is this some kind of club?"

"Keep looking where you're going," Claw growled.

"Don't worry about that now," Claw continued in a friendlier voice. "When the time is right, we'll explain everything to you. I mean, if we feel that you'd be right for our group and it's something you'd like to do. But tonight, you're Willy's guest. So just be cool and you'll have a good time."

For the first time during their climb, Willy looked back at Kenny and Claw. He seemed to be frowning.

"Listen, Spook," Claw said. "We're almost there. So, no more questions for now, okay? Just listen up and follow our lead."

Up ahead the woods seemed to thin out. Kenny thought he could hear faint voices, but he wasn't sure.

"You're going to meet some people," Claw continued. He was speaking faster now, but still not above a whisper. "They'll tell you their Old Names. Like I said, you might know some of them. But you got to remember that anything you see and hear stays here, okay? I mean it, man. This is serious."

The slope was a little less steep now. Willy had slowed the pace slightly but kept looking straight ahead.

"We don't usually invite people to come up here unless we've known them for a long time," Claw said. "But if Willy says you're okay, that'll be good enough. But even if you never get invited back, or even if you decide that you don't want to come back or be one of us, you got to keep this stuff to yourself.

"There's some heavy shit that goes down sometimes at these things. I mean really heavy spiritual stuff, Spook." Claw's voice seemed a little worried. "If you talk – I mean like to anyone at all – we'll find out. And it could be very bad, man, very bad.

"So just keep your mouth shut, listen, watch, and learn. Speak only if someone speaks to you."

Claw paused for a moment, and then returned to his friendlier voice, "Don't worry, man. This will be good. It could change your life."

Willy stopped suddenly. The three of them stood silently in single file. The voices were still faint, but a little more distinct now. Willy turned around. Kenny could make out beads of sweat softly glowing in the moonlight.

Willy said softly, "Okay, Spook. We're here.

"Don't let Claw scare you, and don't scare yourself," he continued.

Kenny was surprised that Willy had heard him and Claw whispering as they climbed the hill. He now felt more puzzled than scared.

"Nobody's going to get hurt, and you're not going to have to do anything you don't want to do," Willy said. "I brought you here because I can read people's souls. I believe that you are one of us, in your soul. You always have been, for longer than you can ever know.

"But don't forget what Claw said. If you decide, or we decide, that you don't belong here, we'll part as friends. But if you ever reveal anything that you see or hear tonight, or even ever tell anyone that you were here, we'll find out. And you will pay for it, and in ways that you can't even imagine."

Willy's face was expressionless as he stared at Kenny, like the faint silver mask he had seen earlier in the moonlight. He then silently turned and led them, still in single file, as they climbed the last few yards to a clearing just below the top of the mountain. Willy led them in a circle around the outside of the clearing. At first, Kenny wanted to giggle at the thought of him and these two tough guys walking around in a circle in the woods after midnight, but didn't know whether he feared Claw behind him, or Willy in front of him, more. So, he suppressed his laughter. After they circled the clearing three times, they stepped into the middle.

Kenny had expected a campfire of some type, but there were no lights. There were people, perhaps fifteen or eighteen, lying silently on their backs on the ground, some of their bodies hidden by tufts of tall grass. They were in a circular pattern, like the spokes of a wheel. Their heads pointed to the center of the circle and were about two feet apart.

Willy whispered something, too softly and suddenly for Kenny to understand. Silently, the people in the circle rose and slowly walked over to where the three of them were standing, encircling the three of them, but far enough away that Kenny could not see their faces. A tall woman stepped forward from the rest of the group. She wore a dark hooded sweatshirt and a long skirt. Her right hand reached up and lightly touched Willy's left shoulder as she kissed him on his right cheek. The gesture was so graceful that it was over before Kenny fully noticed it.

She then stepped past Kenny, as if he were invisible, and greeted Claw in the same way. Kenny felt Willy's arm reach out and pull him alongside. Willy's arm was around Kenny's waist. He felt uncomfortable.

"Laurel," Willy said quietly. "This is Spook. He bears the Sign but does not know yet that he is a Child. Do not be deceived by his outward appearance, for I perceive him to be very old."

Laurel stepped in front of Kenny. She gently took his face in her hands. Kenny closed his eyes, expecting a kiss. Instead she just stared at his face. Kenny opened his eyes to see her dark eyes, looking unblinking into his. Kenny couldn't make out any of the features of her face, which remained shaded by the hood of her sweatshirt. He could only see the points of light, reflecting the moon, one in each of her eyes. As they looked at each other, the forest became more silent than Kenny had ever known.

Finally, Laurel said, quietly, "You are welcome here, Spook. Come into our circle if you desire." She lightly took his hand. Turning to Willy, she said, "All is ready."

Another woman lit a small burner. The light smoke was musty, but not unpleasant. The others gathered around Laurel, Kenny, Willy, and Claw. Men and women both greeted Willy and Claw with the light touch to the shoulder and the kiss on the cheek. Some gave a slight nod in Kenny's direction. Others merely stared at him, as if searching his face for something, and then moved away. Kenny began to feel uncomfortable again.

Still holding his hand, Laurel spoke to the group. Her voice was less quiet now.

"Children, this is Spook. Our brother Willy, who can read souls, discerns the Sign in Spook. We welcome him into our circle on this special equinox, an equinox of the full moon. There will not be another night like this for many years."

There was no reaction from anyone. Instead, people seemed to float down into the wagon wheel formation, like leaves falling to the ground. The incense burned at its center, filling the clearing with a heavy aroma. Kenny could almost feel it on his face. It smelled like leaves that his father would burn on a cold Saturday afternoon in late autumn, after they had already begun to rot in thin damp layers on the ground.

"Come be with me, Spook," Laurel said. She took Kenny's hand and led him to the formation. He lay down, clumsily, noisily, he thought. How could the others move so quietly, so gracefully? Laurel silently lay on his right and Claw on his left. Willy lay on the other side of Laurel. There was silence for what seemed like many minutes. Kenny began to wonder whether the sun would be coming up soon.

Kenny felt drowsy almost at once. The crisp September night air, the memories summoned by the smoke from the burner, all that beer he had drunk earlier – it all started working against him. He knew that it would look bad if he fell asleep. Stay awake, he told himself. These people are really freaky, like the hippies of the 1960s he'd heard about. Stay awake. Laurel likes you. Stay awake. Maybe later everyone will pair up and go off into the woods. He looked over at Laurel. The hood of her sweatshirt had dropped back revealing her face, which glowed faintly silver.

No, Kenny thought, she's too old to be interested in you. But he could not escape the strong attraction that he was beginning to feel.

He wasn't sure whether he dozed off. Suddenly a man's voice from behind him started reciting something that sounded like it came from the Bible. The sounds were like music, but he could not quite make out the words. It sounded a little like a foreign language, but one so beautiful that the meaning of the words didn't matter. Then Laurel recited a poem that he could not quite hear clearly. Her voice was hypnotic, and he caught himself dozing off again. He seemed to wake up as she finished:

We are all but children, even John Bard,
Who has ruled this forest for these countless years.
We live forever but must die many times.
We alone are the Children of Bel.

Laurel stopped. Kenny thought that he could hear the footsteps of the tiniest creatures of the forest gathering at the end of the circle, watching them. Laurel then said quietly, "None of us are here of our own free will, but only because each of us has been chosen."

Kenny felt like he was beginning to fit in. Nobody had ever chosen him for anything.

"We see things that other people cannot see," Laurel continued. "We hear the soft whispers of the universe, the voices that others ignore. We preserve the ancient wisdom. Lying here, we are embraced by the White Goddess, the mother of us all, as we look out into her universe tonight, midway between summer and winter, each of us a link between the eternal and the earthly. Let us be one."

At that word, Kenny felt Laurel reach over and silently take his hand. Hers was cool, almost cold, and damp with dew. Claw also reached over and took Kenny's other hand. On the other side of the circle, another woman sang quietly, just a few words in a foreign language.

The group lay on the ground, a wagon wheel of joined hands, silent for many minutes. Kenny looked at the patches of sky beyond the trees and then over at Laurel, but he found his gaze always returning to the sky. He saw a shooting star streak down to the tree line. He thought he could hear its faint shrill whistle pierce the night. That was the first time he ever saw a shooting star.

To his right, Laurel was whispering something he couldn't understand, almost like a chant. On his other side, Claw was breathing slowly, heavily, his eyes wide open, moonlight making the tears running down his cheeks sparkle. Kenny looked upward again, fixing his gaze in hopes of seeing another shooting star.

Willy's voice rumbled along the ground, so low that he didn't recognize it at first.

"Blessed be. Tonight, another of our ancient brothers has been found and has come home to us." It took Kenny a moment to realize that Willy was speaking about him. He felt Laurel gently squeeze his hand. "Blessed be, Spook," she whispered.

Willy's voice continued. It almost seemed to be coming from underground.

"For thousands of years we have kept the wisdom. Soon Bel will summon us to cleanse the world, to make it new again. We shall emerge from our sacred groves and circles, quietly retaking our place in the world. For thousands of years through so many lives, we have waited for the hour that is almost at hand. It will not be tonight. It will not be tomorrow. But it will be soon, as the great wheel turns into its next cycle."

"Now let us each draw our power from the earth and moon and the stars," Laurel said. "Let us become one with them."

A low hum arose from the circle. Kenny joined in. He didn't understand what anyone had said. He had never heard of Bel or the White Goddess. It was probably just what these people called God. But he liked the idea of belonging, and of drawing power from the moon and the stars.

As if by some secret signal, the humming stopped. Everyone stood up silently. Some of the group said goodbye to each other with the shoulder touch and kiss Kenny had seen earlier. Each person came up to Kenny and lightly touched his shoulder. Each one stared again into his eyes for a moment. Some simply said, "Spook." Others said nothing. Kenny didn't know what to say, so he remained silent, only slightly nodding to each person and trying to look reverent.

The group then walked single file from the clearing. Kenny simply followed Willy. Kenny was not surprised when the group circled the clearing three times before slowly, carefully, descending the path in the dark to where their vehicles were parked. Everyone was silent. Kenny could hear only footsteps.

At the bottom of the hill, everyone silently got into their cars or trucks, or onto their motorcycles, and drove out between the trees and onto the road, one by one.

Kenny looked at his watch. It was almost four o'clock in the morning. Claw had already left. Even Laurel had left without saying another word to him or even looking in his direction. When he looked up, he realized that only he and Willy remained. Willy was standing by his motorcycle, looking at the sky. Kenny walked over to him and looked up, too.

Without looking down, Willy said, "Your questions will be answered in time. You will be visited."

Willy then put on his helmet, and without saying another word to Kenny, rode off. Kenny made many wrong turns finding his way home. When he arrived, he climbed the stairs to his apartment feeling as tired as an old man, but at the same time full of a kind of energy he had never felt before. He made some coffee and stayed up until seven o'clock, when he called the construction company and told his boss that he was sick and couldn't come to work. Then he went to bed.

"You okay?" Jill touched his forearm as she as she wiped away the potato chip crumbs and moisture from the zinc top of the bar. "You seem to be a hundred miles away tonight."

"Yeah, or like a hundred years," Kenny said. "I'm just thinking about stuff."

"Problems?"

"No, just stuff."

Kenny looked at himself in the mirror behind the bar. Maybe I should get rid of the ratty mustache, he thought, and maybe get a haircut. Get cleaned up a little.

Just stuff, but good stuff. Kenny wanted to tell Jill, tell anyone who even pretended to care about him for a moment, about all the new things in his life. She would understand even if Cathy didn't. But he couldn't tell her. Everyone had made that clear.

Since that September night, there had been no contact with Willy, Claw, or any of the others, not until about two weeks ago, when Laurel and Brendan showed up at his apartment door on a Saturday afternoon. He had heard nothing from them since, and Kenny wondered whether they had decided somehow that he was unworthy. But wouldn't they tell him, so that they could part as friends, like Willy said?

"So, Jill," he said when she passed by him the next time. Jill stopped.

"You need something, hon?"

"No, I just was wondering how you're doing. That's all."

"Same old, same old," she smiled. "Working my ass off with this and my day job and trying to be a mom to my two kids. Not too bad, overall. I've got a lot to be thankful for. But how about you?

Something seems to be on your mind tonight. Problems with Cathy?"

"No," Kenny replied. He was sure Jill didn't believe him. "I'm just thinking about what to do with my life."

"Ain't we all, Kenny" Jill took another vigorous swipe with her rag. "Ain't we all."

She walked over to Kenny and leaned forward, her face just a few inches from his. She looked around the bar and then at Kenny.

"But you know, Kenny, if you ever need a friend –"

"Yeah?"

"You'll always find plenty of them here at Shannon's." Jill smiled, lightly touched his hand with the rag, and moved on down the bar.

Higher Education

Kenny laughed as Jill walked away.

"I'll keep that in mind, Jill," he called out to her.

Kenny studied how the beer sloshed foamlessly in his mug as he moved it around in tight circles, first clockwise then counterclockwise. He followed his drifting thoughts back to the second time he had seen Laurel. He was surprised when she showed up at his front door Saturday afternoon two weeks ago. He hadn't seen her since that night on the mountain last September. He was too surprised even to ask how she knew where he lived.

"Hi, Spook," Laurel said when he opened the door. "Remember me?"

For a second, Kenny didn't remember. "Oh, yeah. So, how've you been?" he asked, stalling for time.

"It's Laurel. Can we come in?" She didn't introduce the man that was standing behind her and to her right, just out of Kenny's sight when he looked out the partially opened door.

Kenny still didn't recognize the woman in the doorway, wearing jeans and a black sweatshirt under a blue parka: Laurel, from that weird night on the mountain. She looked different now, darker, less shiny than she did that night.

"Uh, sure. Please. Come in."

Laurel and her companion stamped their feet to shake loose the snow and then went directly to the small couch in Kenny's small living area and sat down. Laurel dropped the hood of her parka and shook her hair, freeing it from the folds.

"Sorry if we tracked in any snow," Laurel said.

"Can I get you guys anything?" Kenny asked as he went into the kitchen area, grabbing an empty pizza carton from off the top of the television as he went by. He returned with one of his two kitchen chairs, the one without the duct tape patching the cuts, and positioned it opposite his two visitors.

Laurel looked at Kenny for a few seconds before speaking.

"Spook," she said, "this is my friend Brendan. We need to talk with you about a few things."

Kenny looked closely at Brendan. He didn't remember him from the night on the mountain when he met Laurel. At first Kenny thought that he had seen Brendan before, maybe in town, or perhaps when he was working an odd job somewhere. But Brendan could have been anyone, just another average middle-aged white guy, of average height and weight, maybe a few years older than Laurel. Kenny gave up trying to place him.

"Spook," Brendan said, with a large smile, "I know that you're trying to figure out who we are and where you have seen us before. That doesn't matter, because our everyday identities, the names our parents gave us and what we do in our physical lives, are not important. But even if you think you know any of us, not just Laurel or me, by any other name or from any other association that you might have had with us before, all that has to be a total secret, not known to us or to anyone else."

"I know that Willy and Claw told you the same thing that first night," Laurel said, "and you agreed then."

"After today we will not remind you of this again." Brendan continued. "So, if you are not willing to commit to absolute secrecy about everything that happens with us during our visit – and to commit to it right here and now – Laurel and I will thank you for your time and leave."

"As you were told at the equinox back in September," Laurel said, "if you don't want to continue with us and can't make this commitment, we will part as friends and not have anything more to do with you. But from this point there really is no turning back. Do you understand?"

"The equinox?" Kenny asked.

"The time you were with us up on the mountain," Laurel replied.

"And please do not ask us what would happen if you ever broke your promise." Brendan added, stopping Kenny just as he was about to ask.

Kenny was silent, trying to make sense of what Laurel and Brendan were telling him. He looked at Laurel. She said nothing, but just looked at him as she had done the first time they met, as if she were looking for some sign in Kenny's expression. Kenny nodded, but said nothing. Brendan seemed to be looking past Kenny, as if he were staring out the grimy window overlooking the parking lot. There was complete silence in the room, not even the sounds of cars and trucks passing by on the road. Kenny could only hear his own breathing.

He hadn't really understood anything that he saw or heard that night on the mountain, except that it made him feel good. He didn't really understand much of what they had said during the first few minutes of their visit. How could he commit to any of it, when he didn't understand a word of it? But he wanted to commit, to belong, to be part of something that was bigger and better than he had ever experienced.

Kenny nodded silently, trying to look as serious and committed as he could.

"Okay, Spook," Laurel said. "Relax. Come over here and sit beside me, while we explain some things." Brendan got up and took Kenny's seat, pulling the chair closer to the couch.

Brendan and Laurel took turns telling him about the Children of Bel. Kenny did not recognize most of the references to ancient peoples and beliefs, but he didn't want to look stupid, so he didn't ask any questions.

After about thirty minutes, Laurel stopped in mid-sentence.

"Spook, are you getting all this? Don't you have any questions?"

"No questions, but would it be okay if I took some notes?"

"No, I'm sorry," Brendan said, smiling. "I guess that Laurel and I sometimes get carried away when we talk about these things. It is a lot to take in all at once, but we can't risk any of this being put down on paper."

"We trust you, Spook, and trust you with our knowledge," Laurel said, briefly taking his hand. "But notes and papers have a way of getting lost or misplaced and ending up in the wrong hands."

"And don't worry if you don't understand it all right now," Brendan added. "There will be plenty of time later. We just want to give you a little introduction, so you are informed about the commitment that you are making today."

"But, remember," Laurel said, "These are secrets that only we know and now you know. You must never discuss this with any outsiders, not even your girlfriend."

"You know about Cathy?" Kenny asked, trying to hide his surprise.

"Let's just say that we checked you out a little," Brendan replied, "to make sure that you're a serious person who can be trusted with important knowledge."

"What else did you find out about me?"

"Don't worry," Laurel replied, lightly touching Kenny on the arm. "Had we found out anything unsuitable about you, we never would have come here." They checked me out and I passed, Kenny thought. He felt more relaxed now.

"So, have you been thinking about your experience with us that night?" Laurel asked.

"Yeah," was all he said.

Laurel looked at Brendan, just for a second, and then back at Kenny. Her dark brown eyes burned into his. She looked angry.

"And –?" she said after a few seconds of staring at Kenny.

"I mean," he continued, searching for the right words, "it was a wonderful time. I felt like I really belonged, you know. I felt like, for the first time in my life, here was something I could really believe in. I haven't thought about much of anything else."

He tried to stare back at Laurel but couldn't. She continued to look at him silently, now without any expression.

"We've been thinking about you, too, Spook," Laurel said slowly. "We believe that there is something special in you. Willy referred to it. We call it the Sign, but it's not really something that anyone can see. We think you have it."

"What exactly does having the Sign mean?" Kenny asked. "I mean, what does the Sign – what's it a sign of?"

"It's very complicated, Spook," Laurel replied. "In time, you will understand why it can't really be explained in words. For now, let's just say that the Sign means that you are one of a very few souls who are destined to live very special lives, special in ways that you can't understand now. It means that you are one of us."

"You mean you want me to join?" Kenny asked.

For the first time that evening, Laurel smiled. She lightly patted his arm.

"Whoa," she laughed. "It's not that fast. What we mean is that we believe that, in your soul, you may already be a Child of Bel. You don't really join us, Spook. You already are one of us or you aren't. You may remember how Willy said he could read souls?"

"I think so," Kenny replied. He was quickly becoming confused.

"Well, all that means is that Willy and some of the rest of us can tell a person's true nature. Willy believes you have the Sign. Willy is a Reader. He has been reading people's souls for thousands of years. But even the wisest person sometimes can be mistaken. So, we need to be sure, as do you. Because there is no turning back, Spook. Not for you. Not for us."

Laurel paused, waiting for Kenny to reply. He took a moment. This was really heavy. He had to be sure.

"So, what do I have to do? Some sort of test?" he asked finally.

Laurel and Brendan were silent for what seemed to Kenny like two or three minutes. They just looked at him. Finally, Kenny broke the silence.

"I mean, like, is Willy really thousands of years old? Do you guys really believe that?" Kenny asked.

"We don't just believe it, Spook; we know it to be true in a way that most people will never understand. It's as real as that special place on the mountain and the full moon and stars that were in the sky that night," Laurel said quietly.

Brendan said, "Let me tell you a little bit more about us. It might help you answer some of the questions that you have."

Brendan's voice gradually became quieter and deeper, almost like the voice of a hypnotist Kenny had once seen perform. He wondered if Brendan would try to hypnotize him. Kenny had heard that you couldn't be made to do anything against your will under hypnosis, but he began to hear alarm bells go off in his head. Brendan seemed to sense that Kenny was uneasy, so he paused for a second and then continued, his voice only slightly more animated.

"Spook, I want to tell you about us," he resumed. "I have to warn you again, though. You must never ever reveal anything we tell you to any other person. You can't even tell anyone we were here. Even if you decide that you are not truly one of us, you must keep these things secret for the rest of your life. Do you understand?"

"Sure," Kenny replied.

"I mean it," Brendan continued. "If you reveal any of this – even one little detail – we will know it. Don't ask how we'll know. Just accept it. It's a fact. And, believe me, others will visit you to deal with it."

Kenny glanced at Laurel. He wanted her to say something less frightening. She remained silent, looking into his eyes.

"Look at me, Spook. Do you understand?" Brendan repeated.

"Yes, I understand," Kenny replied hoarsely. "I promise, I won't tell anyone anything. I swear."

Laurel and Brendan exchanged a glance. Laurel reached over and took his hand.

"Listen, Spook," she said. "We don't want to scare you. We just want to make sure that you know the score. This is serious business. We trust you. If we didn't trust you, we would never have come here. But if this is uncomfortable for you, we can go. Think about it."

Kenny replied immediately, "No. No, I want to join – I mean, I want to be one of you very much. You can trust me."

Laurel smiled. "Good," she said. "That makes me very happy."

For the next half hour Brendan spoke almost without interruption. Whenever Kenny would look at Laurel, she would just nod her head in agreement. When he tried to ask a question, Brendan would stop, without the slightest trace of irritation at being interrupted. Laurel would lean over and softly say, "Let us finish our work, Spook. All will be clear to you in time."

Kenny had trouble following what Brendan said. The Children of Bel, Brendan told him, was a very old group. They believed that God was everywhere in the world and took many different forms. To Christians and Jews, God took the form of Yahweh or God the Father. To Muslims, God manifested as Allah. Every religion, Brendan explained, and every people had their own concept of God, but it was essentially the same God. Their God took both female and male forms. The much older form that was shown to humans was female, whom they called the White Goddess. The male form they called Bel.

"Why aren't you called the Children of the White Goddess?" Kenny asked.

Laurel laughed and started to respond, but Brendan held up his hand.

"No, Laurel," he said. "That's a very wise question. We have kept the name of Bel because when we established our family thousands of years ago, the form of God that we understood, that was revealed to us at that time, was that of Bel. We keep Bel's name to honor our spiritual ancestors. We understand now, however, that knowledge of Bel is just one avenue to the older entity, the Goddess. And she leads us to the purest essence of everything that exists, or has existed, or will ever exist in the future."

Kenny was now thoroughly confused. A hundred questions seemed to churn through his mind, but he couldn't form the words to ask any of them. So, he decided to sit quietly and try to understand whatever he could.

Brendan then explained what it means to have the Sign.

"You'll remember that Laurel told you earlier that you can't join us. You are already one of us or you aren't?"

Kenny nodded.

"Well, in this world, we calculate that there are only eleven thousand Children of Bel. We who have the Sign have always been Children of Bel, in all our past phases of our lives and always will be. You are old, Spook, countless thousands of years old. You have always been one of us, even though you may not realize it yet in this life. We want you to come home, Spook. But as with any long-lost relative, we need to make sure that you are truly a member of the family."

"This is important to us," Laurel added. "Because when all of us have been gathered together, a new age will begin. The old evil world as we know it will be transformed."

"I think that's enough for today, Spook," she concluded. "We have only touched the surface, but before you make the commitment that we are asking from you, we feel that you are entitled to know some of the basics."

"Spook," Brendan continued. "I know that we have said this already, but it's important. Do not try to locate us until we come back for you. If you see either of us during your daily activities, you must not approach us, must not show any sign of recognition, not even a glance or a smile. Remember what I told you about respecting our trust in you. If you reveal any of this, even the fact that our group exists or that we visited you, we will find out."

"That would tell us more than anything else that we were mistaken about you. We have made mistakes in the past, not many, but some," Laurel interjected, reaching across and touching Kenny's hand again, tugging on it gently.

"And it would be very bad for you," Brendan added. "We had to correct one of our little mistakes just a couple of weeks ago. We took no pleasure in it."

There was a moment of silence, then Laurel and Brendan stood up.

"That's enough for the first time, Spook," Laurel said, taking his hand. "Do you have any questions for us?"

"No," Kenny replied after thinking for a few seconds. If he asked any questions about what he had just heard, he would only appear stupid. The best thing was to take it step by step, trusting that, as Brendan had said, "all will be revealed to you in time."

"So, what's the next step?" Kenny said as they walked to the door.

Brendan opened the door for Laurel. It was late afternoon. A deep overcast had settled in. Brendan turned around and put his hand on Kenny's chest, just as Kenny was about to step outside with them. He gently pushed Kenny back inside. Laurel followed Brendan back into the apartment and gently closed the door.

"It's better if we're not seen together," Brendan said. "As I thought we mentioned earlier, one of us will contact you to continue your Higher Education. When you have completed that –"

"Wait a minute, you guys know that I went to Mansfield for a semester. Do I need to go back to school?"

"We know that, Spook," Laurel replied. "Brendan is talking about your true education about the higher powers that govern the universe."

"Oh, yeah." Kenny still didn't understand.

"Well, after you have completed your Higher Education," Brendan continued, "you will be recognized as your true self."

"That's when we formally welcome you home, Spook," Laurel said. "It might take you only a few months or it might take many earthly lifetimes. Each of us is different. But, while you continue your Higher Education, you will still be our brother and welcome at our gatherings."

"We'll go now," she continued. "Please do not try to follow us, or even watch us once we step outside. We will contact you again in the fullness of time."

Kenny expected Laurel to repeat the gesture that she had used to greet Willy and the others at the gathering on the mountain, the touch on the shoulder and the kiss on the cheek. Instead, Laurel and Brendan, said nothing more and left, not even responding when Kenny said goodbye through the closing door. He didn't watch them leave.

Brendan and Laurel had talked non-stop for over an hour about things that Kenny had never heard of – not in this life, not in any life. He needed to write them down, what he could remember, before he forgot it all. He would only keep the notes for a couple of days, just to help him learn. He was sure that Laurel would understand. He went into the bedroom and returned with a handful of pages of notebook paper. He began writing down anything he could remember, mostly just words and phrases.

Kenny went to the public library two days later, to look up some of the names and other words in his notes and maybe get a head start on his Higher Education. Some of the names came from ancient myths and legends. He found one book, *The White Goddess* by Robert Graves, but it was too dense, too complicated, for him to understand easily. After two hours, he left, concluding that his Higher Education would take a long time.

"Higher Education," he murmured aloud as he sat at the bar at Shannon's, looking into his empty glass. Jill heard him and came over.

She silently picked up Kenny's empty glass, wiped the bar, and set down a full one in front of him. It looked like one smooth, continuous motion. The full glass thumping on the bar made him look up.

"Still a hundred miles away with all that stuff?" she asked.

"Yeah," Kenny replied. "There's been a lot of stuff in my life recently, good stuff. And I think Cathy dumped me earlier tonight."

"I'm sorry," Jill said.

Jill pointed at the full glass and nodded in the direction of two men at the far end of the bar.

It was Willy and Claw. Kenny raised his glass to them. Claw smiled back. After taking a sip, Kenny looked back in their direction, but they had left. He realized that he was alone in the bar. Jill came over to him.

"Friends of yours?" she asked.

"No," he shrugged.

"That's funny," Jill said, "because the big guy, when he bought you that drink said, 'Give my friend there another round on me'."

"No," Kenny repeated. "Honest, Jill, I don't think I ever saw those guys in my life."

"Well, maybe you're famous," Jill smiled. "Or maybe this is just your lucky night after all. Come on, how about drinking up and letting me close a little early?"

"Sure, Jill."

Kenny drained his glass. On his way out, he went into the men's room. Standing at the long porcelain trough, almost overpowered by the smell of the disinfectant cubes, he smiled as the pressure on his bladder diminished. This had been a good night after all. He stood up to Cathy. It's too bad she found his notes from the meeting with Laurel and Brendan, and he was sorry that he had to lie to her about it. He loved her as much as ever, but he didn't need her running his life, keeping him from being himself. Maybe she will come back, maybe not. He thought about Laurel and the strange attraction he had to a woman who must be twenty years older. He wondered what it would be like to be with her all the time. He thought about the others he met at the equinox that night on the mountain, how they all wanted to accept him and value him and even love him as he is.

Jill already had the stools up on the bar and the chairs on the tables. She returned from the kitchen with a push broom.

"You still here?" It sounded like an accusation. Kenny felt a little hurt.

"No, Jill," Kenny replied. "Just on my way out. I can stay and help you clean up if you want."

Jill laughed. "Thanks, hon, but I can handle it. I've been closing this place most every night for the past five years. Besides, I'm too old to take you home with me."

Kenny laughed as he said good night and crossed the bar. He looked back over his shoulder as he pushed the door open. Jill might not be so bad, he thought. She can't be more than thirty-five, is by herself, and still looks pretty hot. He felt ashamed of the thought. It seemed disloyal to Laurel.

Outside the night was heavy with a cold humidity, but Kenny enjoyed being out of the stale air of the bar. He put his hands on his hips and bent back, eyes closed, feeling the faint throbbing in his forehead that comes only when he had one beer – not two or three, but just one – too many. He inhaled as much of the cold air as he could, holding his breath, and then letting it out.

It wasn't until after he had exhaled for the third time that he noticed Willy and Claw standing in front of him, waiting patiently.

"Hey, thanks again for –" Kenny started to say.

"Spook," Claw interrupted.

"Spook," he said again quietly, his voice friendly but all business. The neon sign cast a sick-looking greenish glow on his dark skin. Suddenly, as Jill turned off the sign, his features vanished into the dark.

"Spook," he repeated, "We need to talk."

Kenny's Lesson in the Forest

His own shivering shook Kenny awake. He opened his eyes suddenly and saw only tree branches and patches of red-gray sky. The early morning dampness dug deep into the core of his body like cold iron pincers almost meeting in the center of his guts. Still curled up in a ball, he looked around the forest clearing where he lay. Patches of snow surrounded him, but he lay on an area where the snow had been cleared away. He had almost convinced himself he was dreaming when his temples started to throb, proving that he wasn't.

Kenny's mouth was dry and had a bitter taste in it. He started to get up but tripped over the gray woolen blanket that covered him, lost his balance and fell forward, twisting to try to keep his balance. His right shoulder struck a large tree branch on the ground. He couldn't decide whether the pain in his shoulder or the pounding in his head was worse. Trying to get up, every muscle in his body protested any movement, however slight.

Kneeling on the ground, Kenny realized he was naked, and had been covered only by a damp smelly gray woolen blanket as he slept. He had no idea where he was. The first memory of the previous night – he assumed it was last night – was of meeting Willy and Claw in the parking lot outside the bar. At least, he believed it was Willy and Claw. His mind was so foggy he couldn't be sure.

Kenny managed to sit up and inspect his body, very gently moving his arms, legs, and neck to minimize the pain. He couldn't see any cuts or bruises. He tried again to get up, confusedly untangling his feet from the blanket, but he fell back down to the mulch floor of the forest, too dizzy to stand. These guys were good, he thought. They beat the shit out of me, almost killed me so I can't even stand up, and they didn't leave a mark.

Eyes closed, wrapping the blanket around him as closely as he could, shivering in the forest dawn, Kenny could see film clips running across his mind from the night before, memory fragments that faded in and out of focus, sometimes silent and sometimes with distorted sound. He remembered leaving Shannon's with Willy and

Claw. He hadn't wanted to go with them, tried to make excuses, but Willy unzipped his jacket just enough so that Kenny could see the pistol.

"You have disappointed us, Spook," Willy said. "We're your best friends – the only real friends you have in the world – and you've let us down." His voice was calm, almost friendly, but also vaguely sad.

"What did I do?" Kenny asked. "I haven't done anything. What did I do? If I did something wrong, I'm really sorry."

Claw walked over from an old pickup truck, where he had been standing. His bulk blocked out all the light.

"Come on, man," he hissed from the darkness, his face just inches from Kenny's. "You must think we're awful fucking stupid. We know all about you talking to your lady. Half the fucking town probably knows about us by now, thanks to you, asshole."

Claw put his hand on Kenny's left shoulder. He patted it and then squeezed with the strongest grip Kenny had ever felt. "And now, Spook, we need to show you the error of your ways," he said, firmly guiding Kenny to the truck.

"Honest, guys, I never told anyone. There's got to be a mistake." Kenny said, trying to keep his voice from trembling.

"Just shut the fuck up and get in the goddamned truck," Willy said. He pushed Kenny against the door, and Kenny yelped as the handle dug into his stomach. Claw grabbed him by the collar of his jacket as Willy opened the door and then threw Kenny onto the seat.

All that Kenny could remember about the truck was that it was old and had New York plates, and the inside smelled like rotting fish. Kenny sat between the two men as they drove out of town. Willy drove, reaching across Kenny to fiddle with the radio. Claw continuously looked out the side window, as if he was searching the roadside for something. Kenny tried to talk to them, plead with them, convince them that there had been a misunderstanding, that he hadn't broken his promise of secrecy, but both of them ignored him, remaining silent as an oldies station faded in and out on the radio.

They drove for almost an hour, turning frequently. Finally, Willy broke the silence. "We're almost there."

Claw turned from the window, reached into the glove compartment, and pulled out a small flask, which he handed to Kenny.

"You need to drink this, Spook," he said, "It will make things easier for you."

Oh, Jesus God, Kenny thought. They're going to kill me. Oh, Christ Jesus, no! They're going to fucking kill me!

He tried to turn his head away from the flask. Willy stopped the truck, turned, and quietly pulled out his gun. Holding it in his right hand, he gently prodded the side of Kenny's head with the barrel.

"You just will not do what we tell you, will you, Spook?" he said. "Do I have to persuade you? Or maybe I should just blow your fucking brains out right here and dump you in the woods."

Kenny drank. It was a thick, sweet syrup. He liked it and wanted more, but the drugs in it took effect in less than a minute. He half-remembered half-dreamed taking what seemed like a very long walk through the forest. At one point he tried to run away into the night, but his feet wouldn't move fast enough. The next thing that he remembered, he was standing naked in a clearing somewhere. His hands were tied loosely behind his back. The ropes were loose around his wrists. He could have wiggled out of them, but his arms wouldn't move. He could feel the textures of the leaves and twigs on the soles of his feet, and a breeze blowing across his body, but he wasn't cold even though the temperature had to have been below freezing. What had happened to his clothes?

There were other people there, but how many? Sometimes there were just Willy and Claw, sometimes he saw eight or ten people surrounding him. Sometimes it seemed like a hundred, always moving in circles, one way then the other. He could see their dark shapes moving against the background of trees, but he couldn't see their faces or even their clothes. They were just black shapes, but they were real. He could feel many hands pushing him from one side of the circle to another. He felt himself being hit again and again, not hard and not painfully, but each blow seemed to suck what little strength he had left from him.

He had a cloudy, silent memory of lying on his back on a bed of fresh cut branches. He could feel the cool, smooth leaves against his skin. Where did they get green leaves at this time of the year? He tried to move but couldn't. He looked down his body and saw his erection, the largest he could ever remember. Is this what happens to you when you know you're going to die?

Somebody came to him carrying a torch. Oh, Jesus save me, they're going to burn me alive! He tried to speak, tried to beg, to plead for his life. He couldn't speak. He tried to tell them he was sorry. He tried to scream for Laurel. But none of the words, none of the things he wanted to say in the last seconds of his life, would come out. He couldn't even whimper.

Strong hands pinned his shoulders against the ground. Leaves were stuffed into his mouth. He gagged, spitting them out, but they were replaced. He could feel them vibrate and hear the soft humming noise they made as he breathed. He saw a torch lifted up and a long knife passed through the flame. He closed his eyes, waiting for the knife to go into him, to end it all. He heard voices but couldn't understand the words. He opened his eyes to be sure that he was still alive. He saw the long, curved blade glistening in the light of the flame, just inches above him. He heard what he thought was Willy's voice, distant above him, but clear.

"And now Bel shall have his gift."

It seemed to echo through the surrounding forest – gift gift gift – again and again, compounding itself into a buzz, increasing in pitch and intensity until a sharp deep pain drilled into Kenny's skull through his ears.

This is it, Kenny thought. He tried to close his eyes but couldn't. This isn't a dream; this isn't a joke. They're really going to kill me. An arm draped in white, holding the knife reached down. He felt a hand gently lifting his balls, another holding the head of his penis pulled to its full length. He wanted to close his eyes forever and let it happen, but something inside him forced him to look. He felt the knife cut deep into him, but it was painless, almost pleasurable.

Able only to raise his head slightly, he watched, his mouth open in a voiceless scream, the leaves falling from his mouth onto his chest, as his severed penis, bloody but still erect was lifted to the blackest sky he had ever seen, with a few snowflakes swirling in the torchlight before they melted. Before he passed out, Kenny felt the bile erupt in his throat.

Now still lying on the forest floor, still not able to get up, Kenny began to feel the first rays of the sun warming him, drying him. His last memory of the night made him check his body again. He felt his crotch. I'm intact, alive, he thought. It was just a bad trip on those drugs they gave me. He knelt, and then gradually pushed himself to his feet.

As he brushed off the bits of grass and leaves, he noticed his clothing, neatly folded and in a pile at the base of a tree. They had left his wallet and keys undisturbed in his pockets.

There was a note pinned to his shirt:

Spook.

Your worst dreams can come true.

Your best dreams can come true.

We are watching.

Kenny quickly dressed. Dragging the gray blanket behind him, he slowly, stiffly walked downhill, hoping to find his way home.

Histories

The setting sun cast long shadow stripes across the road, their darkness deepened by the contrast with the sparkling ice crust on the snow. Russell was driving slowly up the fire tower road, trying to detect the icy patches, as he returned from a week in Philadelphia. It had been, he hoped, his final visit to his former law firm to help complete, after many attempts over the previous nine months, a complex corporate acquisition by one of his former clients. He hadn't minded the diversion from his everyday routine, which in the short days of a northern Pennsylvania winter, was becoming a little bit claustrophobic.

Up ahead of him, he saw – and heard – Wanda's unmistakable Land Rover rattling downhill toward him. It turned off onto the gravel road to her house. Russell hadn't seen Wanda since Christmas. On an impulse, he turned right and followed her.

"Hey, Russell. So, you've come to help me unload the groceries?" was her only greeting.

Russell picked up what appeared to be the two heaviest bags and followed Wanda through a side door directly into the kitchen.

"Just dump them on the counter anywhere," she said, "I'll put them away later.

The two of them silently shuttled bags of groceries from the back of Wanda's car to her kitchen. When they had finished, Wanda said, "Well, the least that I can do is to offer you some coffee. Can you stay for a few minutes?"

Russell sat on one of the oak chairs at the round kitchen table while Wanda ground some coffee and poured water into the coffee maker.

"I hope you like Colombian," she said. "At least it's made from beans and doesn't come from a can. I know that you're something of a coffee expert, with that espresso machine of yours, so I hope it's okay."

"That will be fine," he replied. "You know, I haven't seen you for almost two months. I was beginning to wonder what had happened to you. When I hadn't heard from you, I came by a couple of times, but you weren't home. So, when I saw you on the road just now, I thought that I could stop by and just say hello and see how you were doing." He was irritated with himself that his voice sounded apologetic.

"Well, I just got back from Florida two days ago and have been running around like a crazy woman ever since."

"I know what that can be like," Russell said.

"What? Being a crazy woman?" Wanda laughed.

"Not exactly, but I've known a few," he replied.

"I'll bet you have, Russell. I'll bet that you have."

Wanda brought two mugs of coffee to the table and sat opposite Russell. He studied the faded Towanda Diner logo, a group of brown bears standing around a coffee urn, each improbably holding a coffee mug in its paw.

"See," Wanda said, "I saved the fine china for you. As I recall, you take your coffee black?"

"That's right, Wanda. Always black after 11 a.m."

They silently sipped their coffee for a few moments. Russell looked around the kitchen. This was the first time he had ever been in Wanda's house. The kitchen was white with golden oak cabinets, chairs, and table. A collection of copper pans and skillets, too clean to have ever been used, hung from a wooden rack suspended over the sink. Another rack held six large wine glasses, one of them sparkling and the other five with slight traces of dust on them. Two bottles of red wine, their labels turned to the wall, stood on one of the counters. He noticed a long, rectangular wooden plaque over the door to what appeared to be the dining room. It had a small painting of a road leading into distant, blue misty hills, and said *Bíonn blas ar an mbeagán.*

"Is that Gaelic?" he asked.

"It is," Wanda said, "It's an old Irish proverb. My Gaelic isn't what it once was, but it says that it's a long road that has no bends in it – basically, things are never all good or all bad."

"I didn't know that you were Irish. I thought that with a name like Abrams –"

"That I was Jewish? Well, my husband Jack came from a Jewish family – their family name was Abramowitz in the old country – but none of his people were observant," Wanda explained. "and he himself was an uncompromising heathen. But I am as Irish as a shamrock. My maiden name was O'Malley."

"Wanda O'Malley," Russell tried it out.

"We all came over from Ulster during the Great Hunger in the 1840s, and settled in New York, where I was born."

"How did you and Jack meet?"

"I grew up in Crown Heights, Brooklyn. You know Brooklyn?"

"A little. I had a partner in my old law firm from there and went with her to visit her family one weekend."

"Ooh-la-la," Wanda replied, with what struck Russell as an unexpectedly sexy laugh.

"It wasn't what you think, believe me," Russell said.

Wanda nodded her head slowly. "Well, maybe we'll explore that later. I learned a long time ago that most things are exactly what I think.

"Anyhow, getting back to my family, I think we had been there in Crown Heights for at least three generations: 1333 Carroll Street. But by the time I was born, we O'Malleys were probably the last Irish family left in the neighborhood.

"Jack was almost the boy next door. He lived at 1339, just up the street. We played together for as long as I can remember. I never really had any other boyfriends. So, when we were older, it just seemed natural to me that we'd get together. But not to my parents.

"Starting when I was twelve or thirteen, my mother would tell me that it's okay for Jack and me to be friends, but we couldn't ever get serious. She would try everything she could to keep us apart. And when we got married –"

"A good Irish Catholic girl marrying a Jewish boy?" Russell asked.

"Even worse, my family was Northern Irish Presbyterian, real Bible-pounding Calvinists, the worst type of Irish with all of the narrow-mindedness and none of the gentleness. But there was nothing they could do after Jack and I eloped on them. We drove one morning down to Maryland and got married by a justice of the peace. But my folks never got over it.

"When we came back two days later and told them, my mother quietly got up and left the room. She didn't speak to me from that moment for the rest of her life – literally. My dad gave me fifty bucks, probably all he had on him, and told me it was best if I left. I would sometimes see them on the street – Jack and I were living with his parents for the first six months or so – but they would cross the street or turn around and walk away. I would call out to them, but they never gave any indication that I was even there.

"Neither of them ever said another word to me – never – except the only time I heard from my dad was when he called to tell me that Mom had passed away and that it was better if I didn't go to the funeral. He died a couple of years later without ever speaking to me again.

"Well, Jack's family welcomed me like I had been their daughter all my life. My sisters and I have since reconciled. I see Elaine – the one down in Florida – from time to time, although my sister in New York and I still aren't very close. But all that was years ago."

"Still, it must have been hard on you, to be shut out like that."

"It was. It still is. But it also was the first brave thing I ever did."

Wanda wiped a single tear from her left eye. She sipped her coffee and then looked at the plaque above the door.

"So, how was Florida?" Russell asked. "From what you told me about your sister, I didn't expect you to stay there so long."

"Well, Russell, as I said when I decided to go there after Christmas, I just couldn't face all the bad weather here. It was worse than having to deal with Elaine and all her pretensions. And once I got there, I started to think seriously about not ever coming back. There were times that I almost called you to ask you to help me sell this place and have all this stuff moved down to Florida."

"The weather was that good?"

Wanda stared into her coffee mug. The rising steam almost reached her nose.

"No, it's not really that. Russell, I can't really tell you what it's like for me to be here by myself, trying to continue the dream that

Jack and I had together. I try so hard to keep busy with all the community stuff, like Welcome Wagon and volunteering at the library, but everything I see or hear around here reminds me so much of Jack and what I have lost.

"You can't imagine what it's like. Maybe I need therapy or something. For instance, last December, the Saturday right before I left to go to Florida, I went into the library to do my shift as a volunteer in the children's section. When I went through the door, I could have sworn that I saw Jack sitting in his favorite chair in the corner, reading a magazine with the afternoon sun coming through the window over his shoulder. He'd always do that while I did my shift. He even looked up and smiled at me as he always used to do. I closed my eyes, and when I opened them, I realized that no one was there. They had even moved his chair to another part of the building months ago. I just couldn't do my shift and had to come home."

"Wanda, I am so sorry," was all Russell could say.

"You know, Russell, when I was making the coffee just now, I heard a noise when you scooted your chair on the floor, and you remember that I looked around at you?"

"Yes."

"Well, when I did that, I expected to see Jack coming in from the dining room there and sitting down."

Russell grasped for something to say, but before he could reply, Wanda continued.

"I feel like I have to get away from here, Russell, and at the same time I can't bear the thought of leaving, of abandoning –"

Wanda set down her mug and looked across the table at Russell.

"This place is haunted, Russell, not just the house, but everything around here. And I am still desperately in love with the ghost."

Wanda wiped another single tear from her eye. She coughed once and cleared her voice.

"Well, enough about me and my problems. Like that sign says, my road is not always easy or always hard." She smiled.

"So, Russell, what have you been up to?"

Russell told Wanda that he was on his way home from a week working in Philadelphia.

"Aren't they ever going let you retire, Russell? I thought that you had just about quit being a lawyer."

"No," he replied. "You never can quit. It's a terminal condition.

"When you're a partner and leave your law firm – or, at least, when I left my firm – there are always a few loose ends, and you have to make sure that your former clients are taken care of," he continued. "Besides, it gave me a couple of days to do some research at the library of the University of Pennsylvania. For me, it was like being a kid in a toy store.

"They have probably the best collection of primary sources on the French and Indian War anywhere in the world. I found two soldiers' diaries; I don't think that they had been looked at for more than a hundred years.

"The first one was written by a soldier who had been on Braddock's campaign. He claims that he was captured and taken to Fort Duquesne but escaped and made his way by himself back to Cumberland, Maryland."

"Fort Duquesne? Where was that? I don't know much about the history back then," Wanda interjected, raising her hand.

"It was at what was the Forks of the Ohio back then; today it's Pittsburgh. Fort Duquesne was a French fort that was a key strategic point for the control of the lands beyond the Allegheny Mountains. So, it was a major objective for the British." Russell had to stop himself. He sounded like he was beginning to give a lecture.

"Oh," Wanda replied and sat back in her chair, nodding. "Pittsburgh."

"Well, back to the book," Russell continued. "It had a scrap of paper between two pages, which some researcher had left behind. He – or she – probably left it to mark the page, but never came back. The note was dated August 2, 1881."

"What did it say?" Wanda asked.

"It was only a reference to another book that was supposedly in the library. But the second book wasn't in the catalogue. Two of the staff in the rare books room and I searched for a whole day, until we finally found it misplaced behind other books in a bookcase, literally covered with a quarter inch of dust. Since the card catalogue was installed in the 1920s, the book had probably been lost since before then, sometime after that unknown researcher used it in 1881. Or maybe he or she hid it, so a rival couldn't use it. It was an 1810 reprint of a diary of a Scottish soldier who survived Braddock's expedition and then returned later when Fort Duquesne was finally captured by General Forbes in 1758."

"And this is part of your research for the book about the French and Indian War," Wanda said. "You mentioned that to me before. How is it coming?"

"Well, the book is about only a small part of the war, General Braddock's disastrous campaign from Virginia to try to capture Fort Duquesne. I have spent most of the past few months just organizing my notes and some of the references that I already have here. Maybe this spring I will start doing some field work, visiting some of the historic sites, and then begin writing.

"But, to tell the truth, Wanda, I am getting a little distracted by the local history around here. Some of it is pretty mysterious."

"Oh, you mean the Indian Rocks?" Wanda interrupted.

Russell was surprised that she mentioned that example. "Well," he said slowly, "they are part of it, but there seems to be a treasure trove of legends around here."

"You have obviously been talking to Robert Kaiser at the grocery store," Wanda laughed.

"Well, he's been more talking to me. But a lot of his stories, or at least parts of them, check out historically."

"Be careful, Russell," Wanda said. She got up and returned with the coffee pot. "It's so hard to tell how much of that stuff is true, if any of it, and how much is just a bunch of ghost stories and tall tales. It will drive a smart person like yourself nuts, if you let it."

"I'm sure there's no risk of that," Russell replied.

"Don't be so sure, Russell." Wanda sat down and took a sip of coffee, her eyes continuing to look at Russell. "You've probably heard that they sometimes call this part of the state the Endless Mountains, from here east to the Delaware River and up to the

Catskills. In the old days they said that you could get lost forever in them only a mile or two from home. The same is true of some of the stories that you'll hear from the old-timers like Robert Kaiser. You will start following one of them and find yourself lost forever. They're endless just like the mountains."

Russell was surprised. "It sounds like you know more than you're letting on, Wanda."

"Me?" she laughed, her right hand making a little dismissive gesture, the coffee sloshing over the edge of the cup and onto the table. She dabbed at the drops with the end of her sleeve.

"No, Russell, I'm just another flatlander like you. But Jack got interested in some of the old stories. He and a friend of his, a guy named Paul Levesque – I think I might have mentioned him to you before – they used to sit around, right here at this table, and drink Scotch, and swap some of the stories they'd heard."

"What kinds of stories?" Russell asked.

"Oh, Russell, I never really paid much attention to them. But they were like a hobby for Jack. And Paul was a great storyteller, at least before he got ill and had to be hospitalized.

"Any more coffee for you?" Wanda said, standing up. Russell took this as a signal that it was time for him to leave. He started to stand up, and Wanda waved him back into his chair.

"No?" she said. "Then stay put. I'll just clear the table. I just hate to have dirty dishes setting around." She picked up Russell's mug and hers, hooking them both on her right index finger in one smooth motion. She grabbed the coffee pot and took them to the sink and begin to rinse them.

Russell joined her at the sink. "The least I can do to thank you for that great coffee is to help you clean up," he said.

Wanda washed the mugs with a vigor that was almost an attack. Russell found a dish towel and stood by ready to dry them, but Wanda continued to scrub as she spoke.

"So," she asked, "just how did a successful lawyer like yourself ever get interested in local history?"

"It's a long story," he began.

"As most of them are, but I have time," Wanda responded.

"When I was younger, I was too self-absorbed, I suppose, to have been a very interesting person. I even bored myself. Maybe that is one of the reasons why the few serious relationships that I had always failed after just a few months. Looking back at it all, I think that I was looking for someone who didn't mind my single-minded obsession with work, because she was that way herself. I know now that it would have never worked.

"So, I sort of gave up on that part of life and just burrowed deeper into my work. Five years in a row, I was the top biller in my firm: more than twenty-five hundred billable hours per year as only an associate. I kept up that pace after I made partner, working harder than anyone else and bringing in the biggest fees. But, after one of my partners dropped dead of a heart attack at his desk at age forty-five, I realized that I was literally going to work myself to death, and, worse yet, nobody would come to the funeral, at least not anyone that I cared about. So, I started looking for a hobby. I tried a lot of them, ones that would get me completely away from the law: jogging, painting, tennis, even fly fishing."

Wanda laughed, "You? Fly fishing? That's hysterical."

"Why?" Russell responded, pretending that his dignity had been assaulted.

"Oh, Russell. The thought of you in a funny hat with lures sticking to it, and a flannel shirt, standing waste deep in some ice-cold stream trying to outsmart a fish – it's just too funny." Wanda finally handed him a mug to dry.

"I guess you're right, at least about the fly fishing," Russell said, nodding in agreement.

"But," he continued, "none of them satisfied me, not even fly fishing. With all of them, I'd quickly reach a point where I realized that I was as good at it as I was ever going to get, or I'd just get bored." He held up the dried mug. Wanda took it and put it in a cupboard.

"I'd always been interested in history, especially local history," Russell said, picking up the second mug to dry. "I'm one of those guys who will stop and pull off the road to read every historical marker."

This can't be interesting to her, he thought. I barged in here uninvited, and now she's just being polite. He looked out the window behind the kitchen sink. It was dark.

"I'm sorry to have taken up so much of your time, Wanda," he said. "And I haven't been home yet to unpack or anything. I really should let you get on with your evening."

He put on his coat and began to walk to the outside door.

"That's no problem, Russell," Wanda said. "I know you have a lot of things to do. I hope I didn't keep you too long." She put her hand on his arm.

"Thanks for coming by," she said.

"I'm sorry if I brought back any bad memories, Wanda."

"No, you didn't bring them back. They are always with me, almost like friends sometimes." She looked out through the window in the kitchen door, toward the forest, as she put her hand on the doorknob.

"But before you go, tell me the rest of the long story," she said, still looking out the window.

"Well," Russell continued, "To try to make the long story short, there was this time about ten years ago when two of my associates and I had to drive up to Chambersburg to do a deposition for one of our client's deals that had gone south on him. Ever since I was a little kid, I had heard about the Lincoln Highway, the first transcontinental highway in America. It was almost like an obsession with me. Sometimes, driving out to Western Pennsylvania to visit my aunt, I would take U.S. 30 instead of the Turnpike, just to be on it.

"So, on this trip, as we drove out Route 30 to Chambersburg, I'd slow down or stop and read to my traveling companions all the historic markers along the way – Paoli, Lancaster, York, Gettysburg, and all the little towns in-between – Columbia, Abbottstown, New Oxford – you get the picture. Since I was the senior guy in the car, no one said anything. But the trip took almost six hours."

"Russell, why you're nothing but a flatland tourist," Wanda laughed.

"Guilty as charged," Russell smiled. "Well, at the firm's Christmas party six months later – after I had completely forgotten about the trip to Chambersburg – I was presented with a full-sized replica of one of those big blue state historical markers, with the state seal and perfect in every detail. But it simply said, 'On this spot in 1698, nothing happened.'

"But that gag gift told me what I really should be doing with my life."

"And the rest is history," Wanda said. They both laughed as Russell walked out into the crisp evening air. As he walked to his car, he could still hear her laughing after she closed the door.

Messing with the Rocks

By mid-March the crocuses were poking up among the remaining patches of brownish gray snow. Russell resisted the temptations of the first warm afternoons to resume his explorations of his property, even though he felt vaguely unsettled by the realization that in the nearly nine months since he moved in, he had located and deciphered not even a twentieth of the markings on his uncle's map.

Now that the last bits of his former law practice in Philadelphia appeared to be wrapped up for good, Russell also resisted the temptations of what he had always envisioned as a semi-retired lifestyle in the country. He continued to get up at six-thirty each weekday morning, would shower and get dressed, and would listen to the news on National Public Radio while having a leisurely light breakfast at the kitchen table and planning his day. Unless he had identified any errands or chores for the morning, he would return upstairs to report to his study in the front room promptly at nine o'clock, where he would work on research for his book or, occasionally, handle a few minor legal matters for his old firm. Sometimes he would get so involved in what he was doing that he skipped lunch. Evenings usually were devoted to listening to music and reading for pleasure, often from one of the hundreds of old books that Simon had left.

One crisp, sunny Monday morning in the third week of March, while Russell was finishing his breakfast, Whitey returned, trudging around to the kitchen door, carrying a long-handled rusty rake and an axe over his shoulder. He looked thinner and older than he had when Russell last saw him before Christmas.

"I'm back, Russell, just like the robins," he said, grinning. Russell noticed that Whitey appeared to have lost one of his lower front teeth, but he thought that it was best not to ask Whitey about it.

"I sure could use a cup of coffee before I get to work on your yard," he continued nodding at the coffee maker, "if you got any left."

Russell poured a cup and handed it to Whitey. Whitey nodded his thanks, then took a long sip.

"I didn't hear you drive up," Russell said. "But I'm glad to see you."

"Nah, Russell," Whitey replied. "I hitched a ride part way and then just walked up the road the last mile or so. My truck busted an axle a couple of weeks ago, and I ain't had the time nor money to get it fixed.

"So, I said to myself, I bet old Russell Poe's got some work for me up at his place. And here I am."

"Well, that's good, Whitey," Russell said. "As you saw when you walked back here, the yard could use some work, and we need to fix some places in the driveway."

"Then I'd best get to it," Whitey replied, as he drained the last drops from his cup, rinsed it in the kitchen sink, and then carefully set it on the drainboard. He started toward the door, then stopped and turned back to look at Russell.

"Been up to them Rocks recently?" he asked.

"No," Russell replied. "I've been too busy here at the house."

"Busy?" Whitey laughed. "Doing what? I thought you were a rich old retired lawyer, enjoying the good life."

"Well, I guess I'm enjoying life, Whitey, but I'm not completely retired and definitely not rich. But no, it's been a while since I was up there. Why do you ask?"

"Oh, no reason, Russell. Just curious. Ain't nothing. Well, I'd best get to work. Three bucks per hour cash like before?"

"Sure," Russell replied as Whitey left the kitchen, picked up his rake and axe, and, whistling to himself, started toward a large fallen branch at the edge of the woods.

Whitey's question about the Rocks teased the edges of Russell's mind all day, and by that evening he had concluded that there was some reason why Whitey thought that he should go there.

Tuesday morning was sunny, a true first day of spring. It would be a good day for Russell to continue to explore the Rocks. Although he had measured the size of the stone circle and the distance between the rocks, he also wanted to determine the true height of the stones. Did he have a buried American Stonehenge on his property, or was it, as he suspected, something more modest?

He arrived at the Rocks shortly before noon. Starting with the northernmost stone, which was one of the ones that protruded from the ground more than the others, Russell used a small folding spade to probe beneath the surface and to dig away the dirt at the base, being careful not to strike the stone with the shovel. After digging a narrow hole to a depth of two feet, it became apparent that the stone was sunk much deeper and was much taller than he had supposed. He probed several other stones and found that they also appeared to be sunk deep into the ground.

Russell returned the next day with a long-handled fence pole digger and continued to probe downward, but it became progressively difficult due to the roots and rocky soil. At a depth of about four feet, or 1.20 meters as he measured later, he hit what appeared to be solid rock.

On his knees, bending over before the stone to reach down into the hole to pull up rocks and flying handfuls of dirt, Russell discovered a flagstone-like pavement that appeared to stretch for some distance away from the stone. With his right shoulder reaching as far as he could below the surface, beyond the point of pain, Russell used the edge of the shovel blade to probe the area where the pavement intersected with the upright stone. He thought that he could feel a tight seam, suggesting that the bottom of the upright stone might be buried many feet below the pavement.

Russell straightened up and rubbed his right shoulder. There could no longer be any doubt. The Rocks were a construction, precisely designed and erected. They probably had been partially buried deliberately at some point. He did some quick mental math. Even if the tallest upright slab he had measured ended where it intersected with the pavement, it was at least three meters tall, almost ten feet. Natural forces could not have covered them to such a depth near the summit of a wooded mountain in this part of Pennsylvania in anything less than a thousand years.

Russell's first thought was to lease a small earth mover to continue excavations, but he quickly realized that he would have to construct a road to get it to the Rocks. He then considered taking borings at various points inside the circle, digging post holes down until he hit pavement. The rocky soil would make that very difficult. There appeared to be little alternative but to continue digging by hand, but he would need help.

That evening he telephoned Whitey to offer him a job helping excavate the site.

"Why do you want to dig up the Rocks, Russell?" was his only reply.

"We're not going to dig them up, Whitey. I just want to excavate here and there to see what we can find." Russell explained. "So, Whitey, are you up for a little archeology?"

Whitey was quiet for a moment.

"You mean like where they dug up old tombs?" he continued.

"Well, something like that, Whitey, but not as big. We'll just gradually excavate small areas down to about three feet. We'll work very slowly and carefully. I don't want to do the whole area. We just need to do a little bit of it to learn what we need to know."

"You shouldn't mess with the Rocks, Russell," Whitey said flatly. His voice bore no traces of warning or menace, only of a statement of fact.

"Why not?" Russell asked, half hoping for another of Whitey's tales.

"You just shouldn't," Whitey replied. "There are just some things in the mountains that you shouldn't mess with. Nobody should. Just leave them be."

Eventually Russell was able to overcome Whitey's reluctance with pay that was double the usual rate. They began work together on a sunny Friday afternoon. The sun shone through the still bare branches, creating dancing patches of light on the path as they carried small shovels, a sieve, string, a bag of iron spikes, and other smaller tools up to the ridge.

Along the way, Whitey pointed to a clump of fresh green shoots.

"Sang's up already, Russell."

"We have ginseng growing here?" Russell asked.

"Sure, Russell," Whitey responded. "Ginseng. Only we call it 'sang' around here. A hundred, hundred fifty, years ago these mountains were loaded with it."

"That's what I've heard," Russell commented. "Ginseng is still popular, Whitey. Lots of people use it as an herbal supplement. Do people around here still grow it?"

"No, the cultivated stuff is shit, Russell, if you'll pardon my French. We just used to harvest only the wild sang. Best kind had roots that looked like a man. Center part with two arms and two legs. The old folks said that just a little bit of it, ground up in a drink, could keep you and your lady going in bed all night, if you know what I mean."

Whitey went over to the young shoots and bent over them. For a moment Russell thought he was going to pull one up. Instead, he just ran his fingertip along the shoot, almost contemptuously.

"No," he continued, "This stuff is definitely inferior, and there's not enough of even this poor grade stuff left in these hills to be worth a man's while."

"It sounds like you're an expert," Russell said as he continued up the path. "You seem to know a lot about it."

"Sure, all my family's been sangmen," Whitey replied. "My father and grandfather and their fathers before them, far back as anyone knows. They say that my great great great granddaddy is the sangman's ghost that some folks say haunts these parts."

"Your great grandfather is a ghost?" Russell asked, getting ready to enjoy another of Whitey's tales.

"My great *great great* grandfather. Yes sir, that's what some folks say."

"Do you believe it, Whitey?"

"Sure. Why not? I've even seen him once or twice. Never up close, but I've seen him off in the distance, hiking along the trail, wearing his old buckskins, and sometimes a blue coat like George Washington used to wear, and carrying his old Pennsylvania long rifle."

Russell smiled to himself. This was going to be one of Whitey's best ones yet.

"Buckskins *and* a blue coat?"

"Well different times, Russell, different times. The old boy doesn't wear the same thing all the time.

"Anyhow," Whitey continued, "They say Great Great Great Granddaddy was one of the top sangmen ever," Whitey continued, looking ahead up the trail. "He had himself a whole number of secret stands of sang all over these mountains. Made himself rich, too.

"But that was long ago, Russell. By the time my old man got into the sang business, it had really just about died out. He probably was the last one. All the same, he and Granddaddy worked all over these mountains back during the Depression. There was nothing else to do back in those days, just odd jobs. They never made a lot of money from it, neither one of them. And it eventually put Dad in his wheelchair."

"How'd that happen?" Russell asked.

Whitey stopped for a second and sighed.

"Oh, the two of them was out harvesting sang, just a few miles from here. And the guy who owned the land took offense. Shot at them with his 12-gauge. It just gave Granddaddy a butt full of buckshot, but Dad got his in the spine. Paralyzed him from the waist down. I was just a baby then. Glad he waited a while to get himself shot up or I wouldn't be here, likely."

"Did they prosecute the guy who shot them?"

"No, they were trespassers," Whitey replied.

"Still," Russell said, "A landowner isn't allowed to shoot even trespassers. Not unless they threaten him. That's the law in Pennsylvania."

"Well, that may be, Russell." Whitey paused for a moment, as if to process this new bit of information. "That may be, but things are a little different up here, you know. The guy whose sang they were taking was one of those guys you don't mess with. Even if they had sued him in court, they would've lost and just gotten in bigger trouble."

Russell and Whitey had arrived at the Rocks. After they dropped their loads, Russell reached into the small cooler and tossed Whitey a cold soda. He looked at it, like a wine steward who had just been handed a jug of cheap, coarse red.

It was obvious that no amount of logic would change Whitey's views on the legal system. Russell thought the conversation would drift off to other topics. But, after Whitey sat down and took a gulp of his soda, he continued.

"Yes sir, Russell, it was a damn shame. My Granddaddy lost interest in being a sangman. Never went out harvesting again, as far as I know. He and Dad were probably the last of the sangmen around here. Haven't heard of anyone going out harvesting for years, except maybe as a hobby or something. Who knows, maybe the sang has come back since then. But I don't think so. No, I don't think so based on what we saw coming up the trail."

Whitey helped Russell stake out an area five meters square to begin the excavations, about three meters inside the circle, just opposite the North Stone, as Russell now thought of it. Setting up the excavation well inside the circle would reduce the risk that they might accidentally undermine the slab and cause it to come crashing down on them. He then checked his compass and plastic protractor several times, adjusting the spikes and lines to align the grid as closely as he could to a north-south line.

As Russell adjusted the alignment of the strings, Whitey commented, "This seems like a lot of extra work just to dig up the place, but I guess you know what you're doing."

"This is one of the most important parts, Whitey," Russell replied. "We have to get our alignment as exact as we can, so that we can record precisely where we find artifacts."

Russell and Whitey then used the twine and spikes to divide the square into sections of exactly one meter by one meter, for a total of twenty-five sections to the grid.

"Like laying out a big garden," Whitey observed. "Now that makes sense to me."

Russell explained that caution and thoroughness, not speed, were what mattered. If they found anything, it would not be touched until it was photographed exactly where they found it and its exact position was measured and noted.

Whitey just nodded slightly and said, "Sounds okay to me. I usually dig *for* something. Here you say you don't know what we're digging for. Well, that's okay. Sounds like a treasure hunt. Might be fun, and besides it's your money.

"Only one question, though, Russell."

"What's that, Whitey?"

"Well, why are we using meters and centimeters and the like, instead of inches and feet? Is that because you're thinking about writing up what we find and maybe getting it published somewhere?"

Russell replied, "Maybe. It depends on what we find, if anything.

"But don't worry, Whitey," Russell chuckled. "I'm going to mention your help when I do."

Whitey nodded, his face taking on a serious expression.

"Oh, I'd rather you didn't mention me, Russell. That's okay. I'm happy to be just the hired man on this. I don't need nothing else."

Each spade of dirt was to be sifted. They started in the northwest corner of the square, uncovering the first section to a depth of approximately ten centimeters before moving on to the next section. The digging went very slowly as they had to break through tangles of weeds and roots; but, by the end of the first day, they had excavated twelve sections to a depth of ten centimeters, but without finding anything other than ordinary stones and an occasional animal bone.

The second day's work was similarly unproductive, but they had learned an efficient rhythm that made it go faster. At first Russell had insisted on sifting and Whitey seemed content to do the digging. As it turned out, the sifting – moving spadesful of dirt and stones around a flat, somewhat awkward frame – proved every bit as physically taxing as the digging. So, Russell suggested that he and Whitey should switch jobs every hour. Whitey surprised Russell as he undertook the sifting with a care and precision that produced items, mostly bone fragments, that Russell would have probably overlooked.

During the second day, Russell noticed that, as they gradually dug deeper into the grid, Whitey seemed to become quieter and more serious about their work. While Russell was taking his turn at shoveling, he would glance over at Whitey. Sometimes, Whitey would be staring intently at the spade as Russell lifted up the soil, as if Whitey was anxious to be the first to spot whatever was unearthed. When it was Whitey's turn to dig, Russell noticed that Whitey's work seemed to become tentative, almost timid. Russell told himself that Whitey was merely trying to be careful, but he couldn't shake the feeling that Whitey was also worried about what they might find.

Russell's suspicions became stronger on the third day, a chilly gray Sunday. Whitey didn't show up, so Russell assumed he was still sleeping off Saturday night somewhere. Working alone at the Rocks, Russell again had the feeling that he was being watched intently, but this time definitely by a person, not an animal. At one point, Russell suddenly dropped his shovel and walked quickly in the direction from which he thought he had heard movement. He thought that he saw a momentary flash of blue moving behind the tree trunks, but then saw nothing else. He heard only a soft rustle in the brush.

When he arrived at the spot where he believed the person had been standing, silently watching, there was no one there. But he saw on the ground a small ball of what he assumed, from its texture and smell, was pipe tobacco, still smoldering.

Notebooks in the Attic

Sitting alone in her attic, Wanda stared at the golden rectangles of light produced by the afternoon sun as it filtered through the window and spotlighted the floor. The mantle clock downstairs ticked away an otherwise timeless day. One of Jack's stenographer's notebooks rested in her lap. It had taken her almost two years after his death to bring herself to store them and Jack's journals, removing them from the small bookcase on his side of their bed and taking them up into the attic. She could not even bear to look at the covers, each one of which Jack had numbered in black marker, to be sure that she was packing them in order. She had looked away from them as she gently placed each notebook or journal into one of two cardboard filing boxes.

Since Jack died, she had visited the attic from time to time, intending to retrieve one or two of the journals to read how Jack had transcribed his notes into narratives of the legends that he had collected. Each time, however, she could not open the journal in her hands. Holding it was enough. Sitting on the attic floor, sometimes sobbing in short, quiet bursts, she would try to reassure herself that the notebooks and journals were there always for her to read when she was ready. They kept a part of Jack alive in the house. That had been enough.

But it did not give her the strength she needed. The thought of opening one of the notebooks or journals still frightened her somehow. She feared the pain that she knew would come flooding back when she saw Jack's handwriting. How many times had she climbed the rickety pull-down stairs to the attic, determined to open, to read, to commune with Jack once again? Yet, when the time came for her to open the book she held in her hands, she could not bring herself to do it.

Somehow today was different. Thinking about Jack, Wanda felt again, for the first time since his death, that energetic joy that she used to see on Jack's face when he shared one of the mysterious legends or implausible tall tales with her, and, with that joy, courage had returned, without the pain or fear. Today it all seemed right.

Today she could face these remains of Jack's work and all that it had meant to her.

Jack's project had started about seven years after she and Jack moved to Wellsboro from New York to take over the insurance agency from Jack's cousin. One evening after work, as Wanda and Jack sat in their tiny living room in their old place in Wellsboro, half-watching television, Jack entertained her, as he frequently did, with another story that a customer had told him.

"Jack," she said, "With all those stories that you're hearing, you could write a book."

"Maybe someday I will," he replied.

That was the beginning of it. When he returned home the next evening, he waved a small tan stenographer's notebook above his head as he almost ran through the front door. Its first page was already filled with notes.

Even now, more than fourteen years later, Wanda could still hear Jack's laugh when he described one of his first interviews with the local "coots," as he called the people who contributed to his project. It was more than a project, though. Jack's fascination with the local folklore became almost his other life, so different from the bottom-line hustling of insurance, but in some ways similar, too. She remembered how Jack would sometimes work late into the night, but never too late, transferring his "field notes," as he called them, from his notebooks and organizing them in a small green cloth-bound journal. Once, when Wanda teased him about doubling his work, he explained that transcribing his field notes helped fix the information in his mind and relate it to the rest of the material he had collected.

"And as bad as my handwriting is," Jack laughed, "if I don't do it right away, even I won't be able to decipher them tomorrow."

Sometimes he would work almost every night on his notebooks and journals. Then he wouldn't touch the project for weeks or, one time, for almost a year. Jack never lived long enough to write his book. He even had a working title for it, *The Sangman's Ghost*, but maybe he never would have gotten around to writing it. There always seemed to be just one more legend to track down, one more "coot" to visit on some remote farm or in a nursing home, one more variation on a theme that he wanted to explore.

Jack was passionate about his work. Wanda recalled a conversation that they had over drinks one summer evening shortly before he died. They had been silent for several minutes, each of them looking out at the sunset. "Even if I never write the book," Jack said suddenly but quietly, "I will have saved so much. So many of these old stories are dying out with our grandparents' generation. That's what's really important; that's why I'm doing it."

Cold air penetrated an invisible crack somewhere in the attic wall, bringing Wanda back to the present. She closed her eyes and opened the notebook on her lap. Her fingertips lightly moved across the page, feeling the faint ridge of graphite from Jack's pencil, set down so long ago. She wondered if she was doing the right thing, giving away so intimate a part of her life to a stranger. But through her fingertips she could also sense Jack's joyful presence telling her that he wanted his work to continue.

Wanda opened her eyes and looked at the notebook in her lap. It was the last one, Number 39, the one Jack had been working on when he died. A crude pencil drawing, in Jack's hand, of "The Indian Rocks as They Originally Appeared," was on the first page. Eleven large boulders circled a stone floor, with a large tree growing on one side. Dotted lines radiated from near the center, some of them extending beyond the stone circle. Underneath the sketch were the words *as described by Paul Levesque.*

As Wanda flipped through the pages of that final notebook, she found isolated phrases, references to sacred groves of trees, ceremonies with strange names, and even what sounded like human sacrifice. These were so unlike the rest of the material that Jack had shared with her. Most of the entries in the notebook were rambling and disjointed, unlike the ones that filled up most of the other notebooks that she had seen. Jack's rough notes had lost their precision, and whole pages contained nothing but sentence fragments, so unlike Jack's careful attention to detail. Many of them were undated. What had caused the change? And then, all too soon, Wanda saw page after page of blank paper, the pages that Jack never got to fill.

Sitting in the dusty afternoon sunlight in her attic, Wanda could not recall exactly when or how she decided that day to offer Russell all of Jack's work. Immediately after Jack's death, she had offered the notebooks and journals to the state university in Mansfield and to the county historical society. She thought at the time that it was the right thing to do, but she was relieved when they declined. The historical society would accept the notes "for archival purposes" but said that they had no capability to organize them or publish them. The college library said, "We greatly admire the dedication and hard work that your late husband devoted to this project, but we regret that we currently have no plans to expand our collection to include this line of folkloric research."

So, she kept them all these years, and let their constant presence in the attic keep Jack near. But this morning, when she woke up and saw the empty bookcase by Jack's side of the bed, she realized that someone had to finish Jack's work, that she owed it to Jack, and that Russell Poe was the person to do it. Jack would have approved of him. There was something that connected Russell and Jack, something more than their relationships with her.

Wanda had lingered over breakfast, wondering whether she should tell Russell about his other connection to Jack, how it was Russell's uncle who had found Jack's body? Wanda had never completely understood Jack's death. There was no reason for him to be up in the forest, certainly not on Simon Poe's land. The crime scene investigation left no doubt that Jack had died there. Why could she not shake the faint suspicion that Simon Poe had known more about Jack's death than he ever disclosed? Was Jack on his way to the Rocks? Why else would he be on Simon's property? He would have never gone there without asking Simon's permission first, yet Simon claimed he knew nothing about Jack being there.

Nor was Wanda satisfied with the reported cause of death. The Coroner concluded that Jack probably had been attacked and killed by a wolf or wolves. She had heard that there still are a few wolves in the forest, but all of them are miles to the west, further up in the mountains, and they almost never come that close to civilization. They had never been known to attack a human, even in the wild.

"I'll just never know for sure," Wanda murmured, "I'll never know."

Her mind drifted back to the day that Jack's body was found. Jack had left the insurance office that morning, shortly after he and Wanda opened it, saying that he needed to interview "another old coot, but someone who might actually know something."

Jack had promised to be back by one o'clock for lunch, but when he hadn't returned by two, Wanda simply envisioned Jack sitting at a kitchen table in somebody's home while his host spun one long tall tale after another. Jack could be like that, losing track of time when he got caught up in a good story. She didn't suspect at first that anything was wrong when Chief Davis and a woman officer from the Wellsboro Police quietly entered the office shortly before five o'clock to tell her that Jack's body had been found in the forest near their home in Richmond Township. The township had asked the Wellsboro police to notify her and, because of the "uncertain circumstances," to assist Richmond Township in the investigation.

Things moved too quickly for her to remember, and yet that evening seemed to last forever. Wanda had no clear recollection of closing the office or how she got home. She assumed that the police drove her. An auxiliary policewoman from Richmond Township was waiting for her when she arrived home and stayed with her until late evening, but Wanda could not remember anything of their conversation, not even the officer's name. Jack's sister, Denise, arrived from New York shortly after midnight to stay with her. Wanda did not remember whether she or the police had called Denise and asked her to come. She had no memory of calling her sisters. Like Denise, they simply appeared two days later.

Her only clear memory of that evening was when Chief Davis arrived at her home at sundown. She remembered how thin his silhouette looked, standing at her front door with the red sunset behind him. The red light seemed to envelope him, almost making him invisible. It was like talking to a ghost.

"You don't need to identify the body, Mrs. Abrams," he had said softly. "Your neighbor, Mr. Poe, has taken care of that."

"When can I see Jack?" Wanda had asked.

"Mrs. Abrams," Chief Davis paused. "Wanda," he continued, "I know that want you to remember Jack as he was, and not as we found him. I can tell you, though, that he passed away quickly and felt no pain at all. Please don't ask me for more than that." Chief Davis cleared his throat and looked down.

After the autopsy in Wellsboro, Jack's body was sent directly to the funeral home. The funeral director advised that there should be no public viewing and the funeral should be with a closed casket. Wanda agreed, and moved through the funeral rituals like a robot, moving precisely and when expected, but unable to feel anything and remembering almost none of it. She felt almost nothing, only numb disbelief.

It took a long time for feeling to return to Wanda. She remembered the day it happened. It was the day she had taken Jack's research to the attic. After she had carried the thirty-nine notebooks and five journals upstairs and had packed them in the two boxes, she stood looking at them. They looked so small, so lonely, in the mostly empty attic. She dropped to her knees, wanting so badly to look at Jack's notes one last time, but she knew that she couldn't. That was when, for the first time, she truly felt the loss of Jack. She had ended that day, kneeling beside Jack's boxes, not overcome by the familiar grief that she had felt every hour since Jack's death, but by a new gripping apprehension that she might never know why Jack was taken from her, and a sickening feeling that she should have done more to find out why.

Ever since that day, Wanda had assumed that Jack's last notebooks or the last journal might contain some clue that would explain what was happening, what it was he wouldn't share with her, in those last few weeks of his life. There might even be a clue to his death, she had hoped. Many times, usually in the late afternoon after a day of working up her courage and resolve, she pulled down the stairway ladder to the attic and went upstairs. Sometimes she would even take one of the green journals, reaching in the cardboard box at random, and bring it downstairs. She would fix a pot of tea, turn on some quiet Chopin or Beethoven, and sit down on the couch. But she could never bring herself to open the journal and read. She would sit there, in the late afternoon silence, thinking about Jack, crying quietly as she tried to sip her tea with a shaking hand. Then she would take a deep breath and take the green journal back up to the attic. Sometimes the moisture from her hand made a faint damp mark on the green cloth binding.

"It's not time yet," she would always whisper as she put the journal back in the box. "I'm sorry, Jack, but it's just not time."

Today was different. After a late breakfast, she telephoned Russell, but there was no answer. Remembering that Russell had once told her that he detested answering machines, she assumed that he had turned if off for some reason. She drove to his place and noticed that Russell's car was gone. So, she taped a note to his door, asking him to call.

Returning from her errand, and before she went inside her house, Wanda spent almost an hour walking through her apple orchard, caressing each tree as she passed it. She thought about all the hours she and Jack had labored together there, the dreams that they had shared, and how the orchard had become almost a sacred grove for her. Knowing that she was doing the right thing, what Jack wanted, she walked back to the house and immediately went to the attic to prepare the notebooks and journals for Russell. Now, two hours later she was still sitting on a box, with Notebook 39 on her lap and her right hand absently stroking its cover.

Wanda thought that she heard one of the clocks downstairs chiming and confirmed the time with her watch: three o'clock. She removed all the notebooks, arranged them in numerical order, and repacked them: the five journals in one box and the thirty-nine stenographer's notebooks in the other. As she began to try to carry the box containing the thirty-nine notebooks down the pull-down attic stairs, the weight of the box reminded her of the finality of what she was doing, that this part of Jack was leaving home possibly for the last time. The box was too heavy and cumbersome for her to manage. Fearing that she would fall, she made the transfer of the notebooks and journals in six trips, trembling from a coldness that seemed to come from nowhere. She repacked the two cardboard boxes on the kitchen table and sat there, forcing herself to regain her composure. She couldn't bring herself to look in a mirror, but she did not want Russell to see her the way that she knew that she must have looked.

Wanda sat quietly at the kitchen table looking at the two boxes. After about ten minutes, she stood and spoke in a loud voice, which she wanted to reach every corner of the house: "Jack, we can do this."

She was reaching into a cupboard for a bottle of white wine to put in the refrigerator when the mantle clock that had been a wedding present from Jack's grandparents chimed four o'clock. She heard a thumping on her front door. That might be Russell, she hoped.

"Poor Jack," she whispered as she walked to the door. "Maybe now we can both be at peace."

Legends and Dreams

Russell was still unsure precisely why Wanda had invited him. The note that Russell had found taped to his front door a few minutes before, when he returned from two days of field research on his book in southern Pennsylvania, had said only:

Dear Russell

Please come over.

Anytime.

Wanda

Russell noticed another note, this one taped over the doorbell on Wanda's front door, which read:

Bell Broken.

Please Knock.

HARD!

Russell thumped the door six times with the side of his fist. He was still massaging his hand when, a few seconds later, Wanda opened it.

Wanda immediately began by exchanging pleasantries. Russell, tired from the long drive home, finally had to interrupt.

"Your note sounded urgent, Wanda. What's up?"

"Urgent?"

"Sure. You stuck the note on my front door. You asked me to come over anytime. I thought there was some sort of an emergency."

"Heavens no, Russell. I meant you could come over or call me anytime you liked. There was no hurry, but I'm glad you're here. Come on in."

Russell wanted to argue the small point, but before he could say anything, Wanda smiled and quickly turned away, walking through to the kitchen.

"I hauled these down from the attic," she said, pointing to the two cardboard boxes. "They meant a lot to Jack, and to me too. But they're not doing anyone any good gathering dust up there. I don't want to part with them, Russell, but Jack would want them to be of use to someone."

Russell opened one of the boxes and looked inside. It was filled with notebooks. Russell picked one and glanced at several of its pages. "It looks as if Jack was doing a lot of research. Are they all like this?"

"Basically," Wanda replied.

"Was he planning to write a book?" Russell asked quietly, still flipping through the pages.

"Well he was, and he wasn't," Wanda replied. "Ever since we moved here from New York, Jack was fascinated by the stories he'd hear. Being an insurance salesman, he got to meet almost everybody, sooner or later. So, he just started asking questions and taking notes.

"Pretty soon he was going out into the country and up into the mountains to track down people who supposedly knew about these things. He'd also try to get them to come into Wellsboro so he could advise them on their insurance needs, but they'd usually be as poor as mud. He'd take notes in those old brown notebooks.

"Then he'd come home," she continued, "and sometimes sit up half the night organizing and transferring his notes into those green books in that other box there.

"You asked about a book. Well, Jack sometimes talked about writing a book of all the folk legends and stories he collected. He even had a title for it, *The Sangman's Ghost.* But just when you'd think he had collected them all, he'd hear of one more twist on an old story and head off into the mountains to track it down. 'Visiting the coots,' he called it. I think he enjoyed that more than he ever would actually sitting down to write a book about them."

"Coots?"

"Yeah, 'coots and characters,' that's what Jack called them. The coots were the old-timers who told him the legends; and the characters were the ones who weren't old enough yet to be coots."

"What's behind the title, *The Sangman's Ghost*? How did the sangmen fit into it?"

"Oh, so you've already heard about sang," Wanda said, staring at him for a moment.

"Well, actually, I first heard about it from you, Wanda, that first day that we met. Remember?"

"No, not really, Russell, but I guess it's possible, if you say so."

"Well, maybe you just mentioned it briefly, Wanda," Russell, replied. "Other than that, Wanda, I've heard a few old stories from Whitey and the Kaisers at the Red & White about how people supposedly used to make a fortune harvesting wild ginseng."

"Well, I really don't know about how it all fit together in Jack's mind." Wanda looked down into the box containing the five journals and paused. "Jack would sometimes share some of the better stories with me, but I don't know if he ever had a big picture, so to speak, about how it all fit together into a book.

"I do remember," she continued, raising her eyes again to look at Russell, "that Jack was almost obsessed by an old tale about the ghost of a sangman, who supposedly still haunts the mountains. There was also some sort of hidden treasure involved in some of those stories. You can't have a good ghost story, I guess, without a buried treasure somewhere."

Wanda sighed and ran her finger along the wire spiral binding of one of the notebooks in the box.

"But he never got around to putting anything together. It's a shame. Maybe he never would've. Some people are like that, Russell. The treasure hunt is more fun than actually finding anything. We'll never know."

"Wanda, are you sure?" Russell asked. "These mean so much to you. I can't take them. Maybe you could continue and finish Jack's work."

"Me? No way," Wanda interjected. "I really don't know the first thing about what Jack was doing. I just helped him now and then.

"I'll be honest with you," she continued." I do feel like I'm ripping a part of my life right out of me, Russell, giving these papers to you. But it hurts me even more to see all of Jack's work just setting up there in the attic from year to year, just gathering dust. You might be able to put Jack's work to good use somehow. Please take them."

"Well," Russell hesitated for a moment. "If you're sure. I'll have finished my book on the French and Indian War soon, and I'll be looking for another project. I'll edit and publish them under Jack's name, if that's all right with you."

Wanda smiled. The clock on the living room mantle struck four-thirty.

"Only if you stay for dinner," she said. "Then I'll help you load all this stuff into your car."

Over a dinner of microwaved chicken and vegetable chili, with a reasonably decent New York white wine, Wanda entertained Russell with stories about the neighbors, local politics, and the changes and adjustments that she and Jack experienced when they moved from Wellsboro into the country and took up apple farming as a second business.

"You know, Russell," she said as she filled a third tall glass for each of them, "I'm supposed to know everyone and everything that goes on around here, but I don't know anything about you, except that you were a successful lawyer down in Philly. And then I guess there's that great story of yours about your law partners giving you that fake historic roadside sign, and how you took up history as your hobby and then chucked it all to come up here. So, what's the rest of your story?"

"My story?" Russell asked.

"Sure," Wanda replied. "Everybody's got a story. It's who they think they are. What's yours? What brought a flatlander like you up here?"

"Basically, my uncle died."

"I know that already," Wanda said, grimacing slightly. "I mean, what caused you to give it all up and keep Simon's place? Everyone here was sure you'd just sell the place, take the cash, and stay down there in Philly. A couple of people even had their eyes on it. I heard that Bill Paxton was really interested in buying it. One of his friends is the lawyer in Wellsboro handling your uncle's estate. It was the old Paxton homestead, you know. Reverend Bill grew up there."

"It was just one of those happy coincidences, I guess, Wanda. I no longer liked what I was doing with the law, saw no point to it. It was no longer fun; perhaps it never was. All I had to look forward to was another twenty years of the same old drudgery, unless I was lucky enough to work myself to death before that. I had made a few reasonably good investments over the years, had nothing else to spend the money on, I suppose. So, when the opportunity came, I was able to take it."

"Did you know your uncle well?"

"Not at all, Wanda. I knew vaguely that he existed, but I don't know that he ever knew that I did. I inherited the place because he willed it to my father many years ago. My father died before he did, and I was my father's only heir. But you and Jack knew him better than I did."

"Well, Jack knew him better than I did," she replied. "Like I think I told you before, I saw him only once in a while.

"So, let me fix us a little desert," Wanda said, quietly getting up. "Should I open another bottle of wine, or would you like anything a little stronger?" she called from the kitchen.

"No, thanks," Russell called back. "I'm fine. Maybe some coffee later."

Wanda returned with two slices of apple pie.

"Right from our orchard. The last of last year's crop, which was one of our best ever," she said.

"Oh Russell," she said as she sat down, "You know it's evenings like this that I do so miss Jack. I guess my getting down those boxes of his has made me think a lot about the old days. And we're having this early spring, I think, which makes me remember how we'd sit out there on the porch on those first warm spring evenings. The only sounds would be from the breeze in the trees and the last birds settling in for the night.

"And we'd talk and talk, talk about everything and anything long into the night, sometimes past midnight. Or sometimes we would just look at the stars."

"You must miss him very much."

"Oh God, yes," Wanda said, looking at her lap and shaking her head almost imperceptibly. "I still can't believe he's gone," she said slowly, pausing for a second after each word.

"I'm sorry."

"You know how he died, don't you?" she asked.

"I've heard something about his dying up in the forest above my house."

"That's true, but have you heard how?"

"Uh, no." Russell instantly regretted the lie, but he still didn't entirely believe the tale Robert and Janice Kaiser had told him.

"They say he was attacked by wolves, Russell. Or a wolf." Wanda paused, as if waiting for Russell's reaction.

"But you don't believe that," Russell guessed.

"No, I don't." Wanda sighed. "That's the problem, I just don't believe it."

Russell wanted desperately to change the subject. Instead, he was horrified to hear himself ask, almost automatically, "Why not?"

"It just doesn't make sense," Wanda said. "Wolves don't attack grown men, at least they've never been known to do it around here. Hell, people say the wolves in these parts were all killed off more than a hundred years ago.

"And all those strange happenings right before he died," Wanda continued. Clearly, she wants to talk about this, Russell thought. I should let her.

"What kind of strange things?" Russell asked.

"Oh, that's the problem, Russell," Wanda said, tracing the edge of her plate with the left-most tine of her dessert fork. "Nothing by itself means anything. But we started getting a lot of wrong numbers. The phone would ring and when I answered, they'd just hang up. When Jack answered, he'd listen for a moment or two and then hang up and say it was just a wrong number. I think someone was calling Jack and telling him something he didn't want me to hear. But what was it?"

"Had anyone been threatening him? Had he had any disagreements with anyone?" Russell asked.

"No. Who'd want to threaten Jack? Everybody liked him. That's what makes the wolf story so –" She paused, as if looking for the right word. "So believable," she finished. "I mean, I want to believe that's what happened, that nobody would have wanted to harm a gentle soul like Jack.

"And you know what the worst part was?" Wanda continued.

"You don't need to tell me."

"No, I do, Russell. I do need to tell you. The worst part is that they wouldn't even let me see him at the funeral home. Everyone said it had to be a closed casket. 'You want to remember him alive,' they told me."

"I'm so sorry," Russell said so quietly he wasn't sure that Wanda heard him.

Wanda took a final sip of her wine. Russell watched as she held the wine in her mouth for five or ten seconds before slowly swallowing. She exhaled, quietly but forcefully, as if she had drunk something stronger, and turned to look at Russell.

"Russell, you're a lawyer," she began.

"Was, Wanda," Russell interrupted. "I used to be a lawyer." He realized that this was the first time that he ever had thought of his practice of law in the past tense.

"Well, you still are, Russell," Wanda replied, "even if you aren't practicing."

"But," Russell began.

"Russell," Wanda continued, "I always wanted someone to look into Jack's death, to dig beneath the surface, to get to the truth. I was too stunned at the time, I guess, to ask any really smart questions. And ever since, well, I guess I've been afraid of what I'd find out, that his death really was senseless – attacked by wolves in broad daylight, just like they said, or whether it was murder. I can't go on not knowing."

Wanda lightly put her hand on Russell's wrist.

"Russell, could you do it for me?"

"Gee, Wanda. I am – was – a commercial lawyer. You know, contracts and financial transactions. I haven't investigated a criminal case since right after I got out of law school. You need someone with some forensic medicine background and investigative resources. I can refer you to some people."

"No, I need you." Wanda's voice was flat, emotionless, and firm. "I trust you. Besides, you lawyers all think alike." She smiled.

"Well, I can look into it, I suppose – look at the records, talk to the police if you want me to. But I can't promise you anything Wanda. This really isn't my line of work, never was."

"Don't worry about it, Russell. I'm satisfied. I'll pay you what I can."

"Christ, no," Russell laughed. "I'll get disbarred if I take your money for something that I'm not competent to do."

"I'd never tell," Wanda grinned. "Seriously, though, it would be a tremendous favor. I don't expect much, really. I just want someone to help me put my mind to rest."

"No, Wanda," Russell said firmly, "It would be wrong for me to take your money. I want to do this for you as a friend."

The evening wound down quickly with a second piece of pie and Wanda's strong black coffee. Standing by Russell's car to say good night, Wanda kept staring at the two cardboard boxes on the back seat. The yellow porch light turned the gray strands of her hair into faint yellow stripes, and the features of her face into a relief map of a life of great hope now reduced to daily coping. Russell thanked Wanda for entrusting him with Jack's notes, and vaguely alluded to enthusiastic plans to finish Jack's book. But Wanda didn't appear to be listening. She just seemed to be staring silently into the back seat of the car, her lips silently whispering something that Russell was unable to hear clearly.

Wanda then turned to Russell and quietly said only, "Thank you, Russell." She then quickly turned away and walked back into her house, not looking back.

Russell admonished himself all the way on the short drive home. How could he have made such a commitment to Wanda? Jack had filled two full boxes with his research. It's one thing to write a book from one's own notes, quite another to try to organize someone else's, especially when the researcher is dead and therefore can't be consulted. But Russell was committed now. He couldn't let Wanda down. And then there was the promise to investigate Jack's death. He must have been crazy to make such a foolish commitment. And what, actually, had he promised to do?

Russell drove up to his house, turned off the engine, and sat in the car for several minutes. Okay, he thought. We're over the first phase of "panic and purge." Panic and purge had been Russell's way of meeting problems all his adult life. It's okay to push the panic button. Get it out of your system. Run around like a chicken with its head off. The sky is falling.

The panic phase allowed emotions to run free, to exaggerate the problem way out of proportion, to the point of being ludicrous. And then, when it is so ludicrous you can no longer take it seriously, sit back and brainstorm how you're going to overcome the challenge.

After all, Russell thought, organizing Jack's material won't be that much different from what he was doing writing his own book. Jack's notes probably were neater than the unsteady stacks of yellow sheets from legal pads and note cards that towered from Russell's desk. Russell had no formal training in historical research. He just wanted to write about the colonial frontier, so he just did it. With no training in archeology, Russell was spending three or four days each month tramping all over southern Pennsylvania and western Maryland looking for the traces of Braddock's camps. Yes, he thought, I can do it. Jack has given me a foundation. I'm not starting from zero.

He smiled to himself. He was like Tigger in the Winnie the Pooh stories his aunt used to read to him. Tiggers could do anything.

He recalled the sadness in Wanda's eyes when she told of her husband's death. He could make some inquiries; he was committed to do that at least. Wanda's a smart woman. If she wanted a detective, she would have hired one. She has the money. What she wants most is a sympathetic person, but one whom she also can trust to remain objective.

The last traces of the sunset had disappeared. Russell got out of the car. He looked at the boxes on the back seat, considering whether to haul them into the house tonight or leave them for morning. As he did, he thought about how Wanda had stood by his car a few minutes ago, looking in at the same boxes, filled with legends and dreams.

Grave Robber

Russell was up early the next morning but saw that his plans to spend a productive Saturday at the Rocks would probably be ruined by a cool drizzle that seemed to seep from the clouds. Russell called Whitey to tell him that he would not be needed, but there was no answer. So, still in his bathrobe, he went into the kitchen and switched on his coffee maker.

Russell had left the two boxes with Jack's research unopened on his kitchen table, because he knew that if he had started to look at them last night, he probably would not have gone to bed before morning. He was glad that he had brought the boxes inside from the car the night before. The dampness outside seemed to permeate everything and probably would not have been good for them. He thought about buying a dehumidifier for his study to protect them.

He sat on one of his white wooden kitchen chairs. Holding his cup of coffee between his hands, he stared at the boxes. After a few moments almost in a trance, he realized that he making excuses to himself to postpone opening them, to avoid disturbing – the word *desecrating* flashed first in his mind – the way that Wanda had so carefully packed them, almost as if she had intended that they never be opened, like the last adjustments to the hair of a loved one before the coffin is closed the final time. Did he really want to open these cardboard caskets, to see what was inside, to venture deep into the weird tangle of myths, tall tales, and oral history that he knew awaited him? His reluctance made no sense to him at all, especially the voice, inside him he thought, hissing at him: *grave robber*.

"I pretend to be a historian," he said quietly, "but maybe that's all that I really am, a grave robber."

He stood up and, coffee cup in hand, walked to the back door and looked out the window into the gray morning. Those words reminded him of the time he went to an estate sale outside Philadelphia. He had never been to one of those weekend sales that had become an obsession for many people, especially his secretary.

"You really have to go, Russ," she would tell him every Monday morning, in response to his polite question about how her weekend had been. She would describe all the odd items she had bought, usually ending by saying, "They're fun, and you never know what you'll find."

A delay on the Broad Street line on his way to work one rainy Friday morning had forced him to turn to the classified section of the *Inquirer*, which another passenger had left on the seat. A large boxed ad, stretching across three columns, announced an estate sale the next day at what was described as a Main Line mansion of a prominent but unnamed family. The promise of hundreds of old books, including some first editions, and early American manuscripts tempted him. He had nothing better to do on Saturday. "Who knows what I'll find," he said to himself.

The "mansion" turned out to be a slightly larger than average late Victorian house with faded blue paint on a leafy street in Wayne. He arrived at the announced opening time but had to stand in line under a colorful canopy of linked umbrellas for almost an hour. Russell was let into the house by the front door and almost at once was enveloped, almost smothered, by an invisible but palpable atmosphere that he thought smelled and felt like death. But it was more than death. It was also deep remorse and final dissolution. What had been someone's home only weeks before had become a disorganized warehouse, with all personal traces expunged.

The walls were empty, with only dozens of unfaded rectangles in the wallpaper telling about the pictures that once hung there. He quickly walked through the entry and living room, past the odd pieces of furniture lined up along the walls and into what once had been the dining room. Three large folding tables held the books that had survived being picked over by collectors. He could find none of the manuscripts that were for sale, and nobody remembered seeing any.

"These estate sale guys always let their buddies in early, so they can get the best stuff," said a large, jolly-looking woman whom he asked. Her laugh blended resigned good humor with bitterness, like someone who had lost their last quarter in a slot machine in Atlantic City. "We peasants get to pick over the junk." She laughed as she picked up two books, opening a formidable gap between her thumb and fingers to grasp them, and stuffed them into a cloth mesh bag.

Russell smiled at her and picked up a small green leather-bound copy of Emerson's essays that stuck out halfway down one of the stacks of books on the table. The price penciled inside the cover was five dollars. The inscription simply said, "To Betty from Father, on your Graduation Day – June 1, 1923." He turned the pages looking at random at annotations carefully entered obviously at different times by the same hand, now dead. He could see the handwriting age and could almost see Betty age with it. Some of the older, faded notes were crossed out. He tried to imagine who the book's owner had been, what she liked, what she feared, what stimulation or comfort she received from Emerson. He wondered what it was like to have a lifetime relationship with a long dead author. For a moment, he felt grief, knowing that the book still waited faithfully, as it had done for so many years, for Betty's hand, which would never return.

"Well, are you going to buy it?" a young man, standing beside him said. His tone was friendly and encouraging. The young man smiled and hefted an armful of small books. The dust from them clung to his Temple University sweatshirt.

"Because, if not," he smiled, "could I have it? I'm into the Transcendentalists, you know, sort of one myself." Russell nodded and silently handed the book to the young man, who tucked it into the stack under his arm, grinned again, said "Thanks and good luck" and hustled over to the cashier's table by the back door.

Russell stared for a moment where the Emerson book had been and quietly left, walking past the cashier's table, nodding at the young Transcendentalist, and returning the smiles of the two old ladies who were tallying up his purchases. The sun came out momentarily when he emerged from the back door of the house, onto an old brick patio, almost covered by the uncut tufts of grass growing out from between the bricks. A small deeply weathered cement statue of a cat was overturned on the short weedy terrace that rose behind the patio. He wondered if it was the grave marker for Betty's pet, which she lost long ago and whose name was now forgotten forever. He stepped up onto the terrace and reset the statue, patting the dirt around it, before he left.

Looking out his kitchen window, for a moment Russell imagined that he saw the cat's grave marker in his back yard. "Enough of this," he said to himself and returned to the table. He carefully started unpacking the box that held the stenographer's pads with Jack's original notes. Each pad was numbered sequentially, with its number in black marker on the cover. Wanda had packed them in numerical order in three stacks of thirteen notebooks each, with the earliest ones on top of each column. Most of the notebooks were badly worn and stained. Some had almost half of their pages missing. The first notes were dated 1970, which Russell estimated to be several years before Jack and Wanda moved from Wellsboro out to the apple farm.

Jack had written his notes in pencil, but the pages had no signs of erasures or corrections. Curious about what Jack had been researching right before his death, Russell found the last notebook, Number 39, at the bottom of the box. It was dated 1978. It looked as if about half of the sheets had been torn out, some of them leaving their top edges in the wire spiral binding. Most of the remaining pages, at the end of the notebook, were blank.

As he glanced through the last notebook, Russell noticed that, unlike the first notebook, which appeared to contain contemporaneous notes of Jack's research and interviews, many of the entries in Number 39 were little more than words and phrases, with only an occasional narrative or paragraph. There appeared to be no order or logical structure to them, unlike in some of the other notebooks. His eyes were drawn to several mentions of the Rocks, but there was no apparent context or connection to these entries. The last pages were blank.

Russell opened the box containing the five green journals. The earliest one was on top. As he glanced through its first pages, it appeared to be, as Wanda had said, an almost verbatim transcription in ink of various parts of the first few notebooks, with the addition of summaries of some of the legends that had multiple sources, as well as a few pen-and-ink sketches of various places in the region. There were large gaps of empty pages in all of the journals, as if Jack had an organization or structure in mind for the journals and, accordingly, had left space for material to be added later. Jack had cross-referenced some of the journal entries to their source notebooks, but, at first glance, it appeared that many of the shorter entries in the notebooks did not make it into the journals.

He looked for material from Notebook 39 in the fifth and final journal but did not notice any. Russell wondered whether Jack had died before he could transcribe any of his final notes.

The clock in the living room struck ten.

I've got too much to do today, Russell thought. He needed to make his Saturday grocery expedition into Wellsboro. This would probably mean at least a half hour chatting with Robert Kaiser. He had also planned to repaint the stairwell leading to the basement, hoping that a fresh coat of white paint would make the stairs better lit and less dangerous. He also would stop at the hardware store to see whether he could buy a dehumidifier.

He replaced the notebooks and journals in the boxes and carried them upstairs to his study, carefully placing them on the floor in front of one of the bookcases.

No, he thought as he closed the door to the study. I just can't get into all that today. Maybe I'm just not ready.

Russell returned at two thirty, earlier than expected due to Robert Kaiser not being at the Red & White. The last thing that he had wanted to hear today was another of Robert's tall tales, so he quickly did his shopping, and exchanged a few pleasant words with Janice, who said that Robert would be so disappointed to have missed him. Fearing Janice's prediction that Robert would return at any moment, he made his urgent excuses and quickly left. Catching himself looking up and down the street as he left the store, in case Robert might be on his way back, he momentarily felt a little ashamed of himself, for he enjoyed talking with Robert and Janice and usually looked forward to his visits to their store.

By the time that Russell returned home, the drizzle had stopped, and patches of blue had appeared in the sky. Reckoning that he still had several hours of daylight left, he grabbed his "archeology kit," contained in an old leather mailbag that he had just bought for fifteen dollars in an antique store during his most recent trip to Philadelphia, slung it over his shoulder, and hiked up the path to the Rocks. He hadn't really intended to do any serious explorations at the site that day. There wouldn't be enough time. But a walk in the quiet crisp air would help him clear his mind. It had been a busy, challenging week.

As he crossed the trail at the crest of the mountain and walked downhill into the stone circle, Russell again had the strange sense that someone or something was nearby watching him. He scanned the surrounding woods, looking for even the faintest sign of movement. There was none.

The pipe tobacco that he had previously found just off the path, and the momentary glimpse of what looked like a blue coat or jeans, suggested that it was someone rather than something that was following him just out of sight. Whitey was an obvious suspect. As far as Russell knew, Whitey was the only person who knew about his research at the site and appeared to be worried about what he might find. On the other hand, if Whitey was the presence Russell had sensed in the woods, how could he have disappeared so quickly and silently? Stealth did not seem to be one of Whitey's talents, and he had never seen Whitey smoke a pipe. Maybe it might have just been a curious passerby hiking along the trail, who realized that he was a trespasser and was embarrassed to be confronted.

By four o'clock, the skies had become a low sheet of battleship gray. It was colder and a few snow flurries drifted down. Working alone on the final square that had not been previously excavated, Russell wondered whether his labors were pointless. Whitey was right about one thing: Russell didn't have the faintest idea what he was hunting, what he might find, or what he would do with it if he did find it. Russell could hear what Janice Kaiser would say to all of her customers about that foolish flatlander digging up the Rocks and how everybody knew that there was nothing up there. No, Russell thought as he stood up and stretched, this is nothing but the sore muscles talking.

He knelt to go back to work, determined to finish the first layer of the entire grid before dark. He felt a faint *thunk* as the tip of his trowel hit a solid object. Assuming that he had struck yet another stone, he cursed the futility of his day as he started to dig it out. His frustration quickly turned to delight. It wasn't a rock, but a curved flat object. Too eager to stand up and walk back to his kit bag to retrieve a soft brush, he used his fingers to push away the tiny clumps of dirt, some of them still stuck by frost to the blade of an old-fashioned sickle about ten inches in diameter.

He stood up and walked back to get his bag, glancing back to look at the sickle blade on the ground. After brushing a few final specks of dirt off it, he photographed the blade exactly as he found it and logged it in his notebook. Then he picked it up. It was surprisingly light in his hand. It must have been discarded decades ago, or more, to be so deep beneath what appeared to be an undisturbed surface. It was remarkably well-preserved, unlike the Civil War bayonets he had seen on display in museums. His research at French and Indian War sites was always a great triumph for him when he found even an unidentifiable misshapen metal fragment.

Russell looked in vain, and without a realistic expectation, for a handle; but he did find eight small glass beads, each about a third of a centimeter in diameter, made of a brilliant blue glass. They were found at approximately the same depth in a five-centimeter square area about ten centimeters east of the blade.

By the time he had finished labeling and logging everything, it was after five o'clock. Night was quickly advancing up from the valley. Walking down the path to his house, he had the same sharp feeling of being followed and watched. This time, however, he was sure he could hear faint rustlings, just to his right and perhaps fifty yards into the woods. At that distance, he should have been able to see the shape of his stalker, but, as before, nothing was visible.

When he arrived home, he found a note taped to the back door.

Russell:

Knocked but you weren't here.

Sorry. Not able to work this weekend.

Maybe Tuesday.

Whitey.

This probably would be the last weekend that Russell would be available to work at the site for at least the next month. He was beginning to feel frustrated that the work was taking longer than he had expected, and that, without being able to depend on Whitey's help, it could take months to complete the grid, perhaps even longer if he started finding more artifacts. Russell telephoned Whitey, hoping that he could entice Whitey to change his mind and work with him on Sunday, but he was not surprised when there was no answer.

Sunday was a perfect day for physical labor outdoors. A light dusting of spring snow had fallen during the night, but by midday it was gone. The air was clear, crisp, and stimulating, but the sun kept the temperature mild. Before setting off at noon, Russell telephoned Whitey one final time, but there still was no answer. So, he filled a Thermos bottle with strong black coffee, put it in his kit bag, and went up the hill.

Progress was very slow. Russell found twenty-three more glassy beads, which took him over an hour to photograph and record. He had just stepped back outside the grid and was walking toward the yew tree, where he planned to have lunch, when he felt a very deep, almost subsonic rumble beneath his feet. He thought that it might be one of the occasional freight trains passing by on the old Tioga Central line in the river valley at the bottom of the mountain. He reached down and picked up his Thermos of coffee. Just as he took a sip, the ground beneath him cracked, with the sound of wood splintering, and then simply dissolved. He dropped, still sipping his coffee.

Under the Indian Rocks

Russell found himself sitting in the dark on a low pile of loose dirt and wood fragments, clutching the Thermos bottle to his chest. He had to laugh, realizing that his first thought had been to protect the coffee and feeling so satisfied that he hadn't spilled any of it. He then moved his arms and legs to test for broken bones and, amazed that he hadn't detected any, he stood up. He felt no pain at that moment, but he knew that the aches would come later.

He looked up. A small opening appeared to be at least eight or nine feet above him. The parts of the sky that he could see through the tree branches were almost dark.

He realized that he needed to escape, but he was too surprised and too pleased by this discovery to be worried. He wanted to explore the situation. He would figure a way out soon enough.

As his eyes adjusted to the faint light still filtering down from the surface, Russell saw that he was in a small roughly circular subterranean chamber. He paced the diameter, which was roughly thirteen feet. The walls and floors both appeared to be covered with smooth, irregularly shaped stone tiles about two feet across. To one side, a triangular opening in the wall suggested an entrance to a tunnel. He picked up and tried to examine in the quickly fading light some of the pieces of broken wood around him on the floor. These were probably parts of a hatch in the ceiling, which was rotten and gave way when he stepped on it. Except for the bits of wood and some dirt that fell with him, the room was empty. He wondered why he hadn't fallen through it sooner.

He bent down and peered into the tunnel opening but could see nothing. The entrance was almost a perfect equilateral triangle, about four feet on each side. A faint odor, sickeningly sweet and faintly putrid, like rotting fruit, came from the tunnel on a faint breeze.

The discovery of the tunnel and the odor coming from it triggered a quiet panic. Visions of a slow hungry death from exposure appeared. He could see his rotting skeleton trapped forever down there. Perhaps, if he was lucky, the mysterious visitors to the Rocks would come back and would notice the hole. His body would at least have a decent burial, although he doubted that few would bother to attend. Maybe the whole thing was a trap, and the excavation above would be covered up quickly by those who wanted some awful secret of the Rocks buried forever along with him. Someone had gone to a great deal of effort to dig and conceal the underground chamber. They could have constructed the hatch and this underground room not for any ceremonial purpose, but only as a trap for any intruder – grave robber – who tried to excavate in hopes of discovering dark secrets.

His disappearance would eventually become part of the folklore of the Endless Mountains. Maybe future generations would claim to see his ghost prowling in the forest, glowing faintly like Whitey's sangman ancestor. Maybe he would appear in the notebooks of some future Jack Abrams.

Russell knew that he was beginning to panic. He welcomed it. Panic helped to flush the irrational fear from his mind. He closed his eyes and took a deep breath. He held it until he could hear his heart. Then he let it out, trying to force every molecule of air out of his body. Then he inhaled again. He repeated this until he had calmed down.

He sat down on the stone floor to try to regain control. He realized that he was not likely to die from exposure. It was already April and he was underground, where the temperature would remain cool, but relatively constant, uncomfortable but survivable in the clothes he was wearing. The chamber was large enough that he could dedicate a small area along the wall as his toilet. He would get used to the smell. After his coffee ran out, the hole in the ceiling would provide some fresh rainwater, so he could probably avoid dying of thirst. Hunger would be a problem, but, being a little overweight, he was confident that he could live off his own body fat for at least two weeks, maybe longer. Eventually, if he hadn't escaped or been rescued within about ten days, he would have to find a food source. Perhaps his clothing was edible. He also recalled a grim story about a shipwrecked person who survived by eating his own flesh.

"Farewell to arms," he laughed aloud, pretending to take a bite out of his forearm. He realized that he had calmed to the point where he could again laugh at his predicament. He knew he would be all right.

Several essential facts emerged as he sat there as dusk deepened every minute. He was not in any immediate danger and had time to devise a solution. It was possible, but not likely, that Whitey might eventually wonder what had happened to him and guess where to come looking for him. But time was also his enemy. After several days, the lack of proper nutrition, more than hunger, would begin to take its toll, making it more difficult for him to carry out any plan that required physical exertion.

It was the final fact that seemed most important. He was in an underground, man-made room. Whoever constructed it must have had some way of ingress and egress other than dropping through the ceiling. The opening in the ceiling and the remains of the wooden door suggested one way in, at least, and possibly out: through the ceiling. The other obvious way was through the opening in the wall. It was obviously a tunnel leading someplace. The faint movement of air from it told him that there was an opening to the outside world somewhere in, or at the end of, it. He had no way to explore the tunnel safely. He could grope along in the darkness, but what would he do if he came to an intersection?

The thought of exploring the tunnel took Russell back to a weekend trip when his aunt and one of her neighbors took him to Luray Caverns in Virginia. He was ten years old and enchanted as they followed their guide zigzagging through the fantastic underworld of colorful rock formations. He wondered what it would have been like to have discovered the caverns, to be the first person to go deep into them, terrified and thrilled at the same time by the prospect of getting lost in them forever. As he peered beyond the brightly lit parts of the cave, he saw himself as he would have been hundreds of years before, the first human ever to grope his way along in utter darkness, without even the faintest trace of filtered light to which his eyes could adjust. Even better, what an exquisite torture it would be to confine your worst enemy here and then seal up the entrance, condemning him to wander in the dark until he died.

As his tour group passed the intersecting passages that faded away to the left and right, he would lag behind to look into each one, sometimes stepping with increased bravery a few steps behind a stalactite or stalagmite, each time to venture one step further away from the light.

Russell was behind a stalactite that reached almost to the floor, tracing its bands and swirls of faint colors. He could still hear the guide's singsong voice saying something about the discovery of the caverns. Then the lights went out. He heard the gasps and then the nervous laughter of the other people in the tour, but he lost all sense of the direction from which their voices were coming. They seemed to bounce at him from all directions. Even though he could hear the voices, he was convinced that he was dead. He felt the dark rock formations close around him, drawing him into them, sealing him up forever.

In those few seconds of darkness he flailed his arms around, trying to feel the passage back to where he had left the tour group. The pain from striking the rock vibrated up his arms. His head struck one of the stalactites. He tried to cry out, but no sound emerged. He had to get out of there. They would never find him, lost forever in a place so utterly dark and so beautiful.

The lights came back on and he quickly rejoined his aunt and the rest of the group. Apparently, they hadn't even known he was gone. He knew that the lights had been out for only a few seconds, but a voice deep inside him had told him that only a second was all that was needed for him to be dead forever, with no hope of ever coming back.

The sound of brush rustling overhead, a twig breaking, rescued Russell from his memories. He called out. Nobody answered. He heard the sound again, of something or someone slowly walking around his excavation site. He called out again. The footsteps stopped. Only silence answered. He listened as closely as he could but did not hear any more movement. The night became absolute darkness. There was no moon and the faint light of the stars could not seep down into this catacomb.

Russell paced in the dark chamber for what seemed like hours thinking, planning and then dismissing plans, and weighing alternatives. At one point, he found his situation so inexplicably funny that he laughed aloud. Just as he concluded that there was no alternative to going into the tunnel, he felt the shallow niches cut into one of the walls. Each one was about two inches deep, as if a wedge of stone had been cut out. They progressed up the wall at intervals of about two feet, staggered left and right.

Handholds! Someone, probably the people who built this chamber, had cut handholds into the wall. Russell immediately started climbing, but realized that once he easily reached the top, there was no way to reach the opening in the center of the ceiling. It was at least five feet away, too far to jump for it hoping to grab the edge of the opening and to pull himself up through it, even if his desperately clutching hands did not pull more dirt in on top of him.

Who would go to all the effort of constructing a way to climb up a stone wall, and then have it lead nowhere? Poking at the ceiling, he could detect what felt like heavy beams of stone or perhaps petrified wood. The space between them was filled with tree roots, rocks, and packed dirt. Some of it came loose as he probed it with his fingers and dropped to the floor. He continued poking at the ceiling near the top of the handholds but could reach only solid rock above the nearest beam. He wondered whether the ceiling was part of the original construction or had been added later to hide what originally had been a stone-lined pit.

The only other way out had to be through the tunnel. After climbing down, Russell sat motionless contemplating how to explore the tunnel without getting lost. Rather than try to take uniform steps while walking bent over almost double in the low tunnel, he would crawl counting his "handsteps" – the term came to him immediately – which would consist of moving each of his hands forward approximately one foot, one after the other. He practiced on his hands and knees, moving around the chamber, his eyes closed so that he could rely on feedback from his muscles and joints to assure uniformity in his measurements in the dark.

He decided that, if he reached an intersection in the tunnel, he would return to the chamber and draw a map before returning. His first plan was to use his Swiss Army knife to etch a crude map into the stone floor; but when he reached into his pants pocket for it, he realized that he had left it with his kit. Even if he had the knife with him, he would be unable to see what he was doing. He would have to etch a map of the tunnel into his mind. To keep his mental map at least roughly accurate, he needed to establish compass points, if only fictitious ones. He tried to orient the chamber to features on the surface, as he recalled them, but couldn't. So, he decided that the tunnel entrance would be his "north."

Russell wasn't satisfied that he had fully thought out his predicament. He considered waiting until morning, when there would be some light to illuminate part of the tunnel, but he also knew that if he waited, the memories of that afternoon in the caverns in Virginia would return to freeze him into inaction. He had to enter the tunnel now or he probably never would. Besides, without a light, it didn't really matter whether he explored the tunnel by night or day.

So, Russell crawled into the tunnel, counting his handsteps, and feeling the rough stone floor carefully as he went. He thought that he could feel shallow chisel marks in the floor, as well as in the walls, as if the tunnel was cut through solid rock. After eighty-seven feet, his outreached right hand smacked against rock, as the tunnel made a sharp turn to the right.

Russell followed the tunnel to the right. He moved ahead very slowly, partly from discomfort and partly due to caution. He had already fallen through one trap today. Much worse ones could be just ahead in the dark. At one point he lost count of his progress. A moment of alarm welled up inside him. He tried to remember the count but couldn't. So, he took off his belt, left it as a marker, crawled backward to the entrance, and started over again.

As he crawled deeper into the tunnel, the sweet smell got slightly stronger. Its source surely lay ahead. Russell shivered. Would he stumble over a decomposing body? Was it another involuntary explorer, like himself? Or was it someone deliberately put here to die alone in the dark, surrounded only by his own terrors? Russell took a deep breath, held it, and exhaled into the blackness surrounding him. He forced back the panic.

"If it is a body, it can't hurt you," he whispered slowly to himself, like explaining something to a scared child.

After slightly more than 181 feet after the first right turn, Russell arrived at an opening to the right. He reached for the left wall. It seemed to be blocked by debris. The path to the right was clear, so he turned right. He crawled a few feet to try to determine its slope and direction. It appeared to run to the "south," back in the general direction of the chamber, and he thought he detected a slight downward slope. He crawled backwards to the chamber to reorient himself and to study his mental map of what he had found.

As he lay on the stone floor the terrors from his childhood came creeping back. All these years he had forgotten, or perhaps simply suppressed, his terror of complete darkness. He was amazed by his will power now as he resisted the urge to go scrambling headlong through the tunnel, franticly looking for escape. He concentrated on his notes for his book, trying to recite encampments and dates during Braddock's campaign to Fort Duquesne.

Russell soon fell into a light sleep, awaking every hour or so. When he did, he experienced the same momentary panic that he frequently did in hotels when he was traveling on law firm business, awakening and not knowing where he was. The hard floor quickly reminded him.

The pre-dawn bird songs woke him on Monday. Sitting in the main chamber, leaning against the stone wall, he sipped a small ration of coffee, still slightly warm, and planned the day as he waited for dawn. Trying to escape through the opening in the ceiling would be too dangerous and probably impossible. He could return to the chamber and call out every hour or so, in case someone might be in the area.

He was now sure of three things. First, if he proceeded in the direction of the source of the faint breeze, he would eventually reach the surface. Second, he was unhurt, except for a few bruises and aching muscles, and time was on his side at least for a few more days. Most importantly, he realized that all day he must fight the urge to press forward, without stopping to go back to the beginning and reorient himself to his mental map. Hopeful assumptions that he was on the right way out, no matter how convincing they seemed, could lead to a fatal mistake.

Once daylight returned to the chamber, he reentered the tunnel. At the first turn, he waited motionless, trying to detect a breeze. There was none. He looked behind him at the daylight that was now seeping into the tunnel, almost to the right turn. He quickly turned right and continued. He paused at the next turn to poke with his fingers at the debris to his left, which he had felt the night before and which appeared to have been filled in to block access to a tunnel beyond. He turned right, and immediately beyond the intersection the tunnel seemed to begin a slight downgrade and then leveled after ninety feet, where he noticed a smaller tunnel branching to the right. He considered taking it. He thought that perhaps it might lead back to the first chamber, where he had fallen in, but then realized that there was only one opening into that room. So, Russell continued along the main tunnel for another 237 feet, where the tunnel ended abruptly at a T-intersection, with passages going off to the left and right at roughly ninety-degree angles. He again waited but could detect no breeze. He could not smell the sweet decaying odor, and he assumed that he had become accustomed to it. Resisting the urge to press onward, he made his way back to the first chamber to stand up, stretch his muscles, and use his finger to sketch an imaginary map out on the hard floor.

"This is crazy," he said aloud. "I could be down here for weeks without finding a way out. Or I could be just a couple of feet from an exit."

Russell reentered the tunnel. At the T-intersection, he decided to explore the passage to the right, to the "west" of his mental map. The tunnel went 119 feet, where the walls disappeared from his touch. He had entered another chamber.

Like the first chamber, where he had landed after falling through the ceiling, this room was roughly round. Feeling around the edges, it appeared to be about the same size as the chamber into which he had fallen. Standing up very slowly, his hands stretched above his head, Russell could not feel a ceiling. He could not feel any handholds cut into the walls. There were no other openings.

Russell crawled back to the first chamber. He had found that the trips back and forth had helped to strengthen his mental map of the tunnels. It also seemed to make the long crawls seem shorter. The discovery of the second chamber meant that the tunnels were probably not just a maze, but links in an underground network. The branch tunnels that he had discovered, but had not explored, probably led eventually to other underground chambers. Russell realized that he could spend days or weeks crawling through the catacombs under the Rocks, each turn into each new passage increasing the risk of his getting disoriented. He had to find the one tunnel that would lead him out; but he also had to force himself to remain calm and disciplined. He also had to stop more frequently, be as still as he could be, and try to detect a flow of air, which should eventually lead him outside. He felt more confident navigating through them in the dark, but he also kept reminding himself that over-confidence could be a greater danger than panic.

Judging from the brightness of the light coming through the opening in the ceiling of the first chamber, Russell believed that it had been close to noon when he entered the tunnel for the final time. He returned to the T-intersection and turned left, to his "east." After 717 feet he crawled into a third chamber, which was approximately the same size as the other two. It had three entrances: the one he had come through, and two more, each at roughly ninety-degree angles from the entrance. He could feel a slight cool breeze coming from the right side, so he selected that tunnel to explore first.

He scolded himself for not returning to the first chamber to reorient himself and fix his new discoveries in his mind, but he knew that he must be getting close to an exit and must follow the breeze before it faded again. The fresh breeze was stronger now, coming up and chilling Russell's face. This confirmed his sensation that the tunnel was descending more steeply; and he had difficulty keeping his handsteps uniform as he started to slide forward in the dark. The increased breeze was a good sign, he thought. His fall must have opened some sort of a natural chimney, which meant that there must be another opening below, where the air was entering.

He began to fear that he would not have the energy to climb back up. This might mean that he would have to spend another night underground in order to rest and regain some strength.

The best thing to do was to continue downward. "Onward and downward," Russell said aloud, chuckling at his ability to laugh in such a situation. He soon felt a quiet sense of satisfaction, however, almost a proud vindication, when his eyes, now used to absolute darkness, began to detect very faint shades of gray on the walls. After two hundred feet, he could see the outline of his hand in front of his face.

Russell continued scrambling downward as he tried to keep count of his handsteps. Soon the slope leveled, and the height and width of the tunnel decreased. He could see thin lines of daylight piercing a wall ahead. After another sixty feet, when his hand reached that wall, he felt a cracked wood panel, the source of the light. It gave slightly when he pushed on it, and apparently was not locked on the other side. Since he couldn't get his shoulder against what he assumed to be a wooden hatch, he spread his legs to brace his feet against the walls, his knees drawn up. Russell then sprang forward, amazed at the power of his legs driving his body and outstretched fists ramming the door. The door popped open, and he landed with his outstretched arms, head, and shoulders outside in heavy underbrush, looking down the hillside toward the river.

Squinting in bright sunlight, Russell looked around trying to orient himself. He knew, from his measurements underground, that he must be some distance from the Rocks, perhaps more than twelve hundred feet, not counting the turns. The entrance to the tunnel had been concealed well. Tangled bare stems of vines covered the wood panel. At first, he thought they were artificial, but when he looked more closely, he saw that the door panel was a shallow wooden planting frame, with the vegetation growing into it, the roots eventually weakening and cracking the bottom of the frame along the lines of the wood grain. About twenty feet away, on the other side of two oak trees, a steep path worked its way up to the old trail along the ridge. He knew where he was. Looking uphill, he could see the giant old yew tree in the distance, perhaps a thousand feet away, he guessed, and to the left of the path. He had hiked up and down that path several times before, between the river and the ridge, usually trying to locate Simon's strange map annotations, without any clue that the entrance to an underworld was just a few steps away. Even in winter, it would have been impossible to detect.

Arriving back at his excavation grid, Russell looked around the stone circle. His initial impression was correct: the tunnel entrance was at least a quarter mile from the stone circle, but further to the southeast than he had expected. His designation of the tunnel entrance in the first chamber as "north" had been almost exactly right.

Russell walked past the yew and carefully stepped inside the grid that he had been excavating to collect his gear and, if the raccoons hadn't stolen them, a couple of pears that he had taken along for his lunch. The bag had been opened and its contents scattered, but nothing except the pears was missing. He saw the hole through which he had fallen, just before he came to the grid, and wondered whether he should cover it. He tried to pull up and place some branches and brush over it, knowing that it wouldn't prevent falling into the hole, but hoping that the pile would deter an animal from approaching it. He could cover it more securely later.

As he left the stone circle, passing the upright stone on the north side of the circle, Russell smelled and then found a small pile of pipe tobacco, as if someone had recently tapped a pipe against the stone to eject the tobacco from the bowl. The trampled grass indicated that someone had stood there for several minutes, walking around in a small area, perhaps smoking the pipe and trying to determine whether Russell was still alive underground.

Walking down the hill to his home, Russell thought about what he should do next. Never before in his life had he felt so tired, physically or mentally. His thoughts were meandering wildly from notifying a university about his discovery to moving away immediately and selling the property. He thought about the boxes on the table in his study and, at the same time, wanted to plunge into them immediately and to return them unopened to Wanda. He wondered whether there was anyone in the world whom he could trust with what he had just experienced. By the time that he arrived at his back door, Russell's horror at the creeping paranoia in these ideas had convinced him that he couldn't trust his own thoughts, not until after a meal, a bath, and eight hours of good sleep. He would wait until tomorrow to sort through his discoveries, theories, and suspicions.

One last thought swirled through his mind before he fell into a twelve-hour sleep that evening. Two days before, when he found the sickle, he left it at the site. He didn't have proper materials to wrap it for safe transportation back to his house, and he didn't want to risk stumbling over a rock or root on his way down the trail at dusk and dropping or damaging the artifact. Fatigue could have been playing tricks on him, but he couldn't recall having seen it at the Rocks that afternoon after his escape.

The Paxton Circle

From *Research Journal 1,* transcribed by John S. Abrams from original notes in Notebook 3

<u>Researcher's note</u>: This narrative is based on an interview that I conducted on May 8, 1971, with Thomas Leplace Girty, age 65, of Tioga, Pennsylvania. He is a retired (due to disability) electrician and a life-long resident of this region. He insists on being addressed as "Tommy."

Tommy Girty stated that he needed to explain his family history first, which he said was tied up with many of the legends of the region. The relationship between his family and the Paxton family goes back to the earliest days of Tioga County. Tommy admitted that most of the information about his family was based on what he had been told growing up in the early twentieth century and that he might not have remembered all the details accurately. "I can't always say where the facts end and the legends begin," he said, "but it's all been kind of a hobby for me ever since I was a kid."

Tommy Girty claims to be a descendant of the infamous Simon Girty, who was a renegade Irish American who lived with the Seneca Nation and sided with the Indians during the Indian wars of the 1760s and with the British during the American Revolution. Simon Girty led bloody Indian attacks on early settlers in western Pennsylvania and the old Northwest Territory, in what are today parts of Ohio, Indiana, and Michigan. Simon Girty is a legendary villain in this region to this day.

Tommy Girty said that his family originally came to America from Ireland in the early 1700s and settled in Dauphin County, Pennsylvania, near Harris Ferry (now Harrisburg). Sometime toward the end of the American Revolution, Simon Girty married an Indian princess from the area near Fort Detroit and moved into Canada to escape pursuit by the Americans. An old family Bible records that their grandson, John Thomas Girty, was born in Ontario in 1818, the same year as Simon's death in Canada, where he is buried. By the early 1840s, John Thomas had moved back into Pennsylvania, settling on a small farm about two miles east of what is today the village of Lawrenceville, Pennsylvania. John Thomas and his wife Annie, who was half Mohawk, had three or four children, but only the youngest child, James Simon Girty, who was born in 1847, survived to adulthood. Annie died giving birth to James.

James Simon Girty was Tommy's grandfather. He never used his middle name, because of its bad connotations in this part of Pennsylvania, and preferred to be known simply as Jim Girty.

Jim Girty was a surveyor. According to Tommy, Jim Girty probably knew the geography of Tioga County and the neighboring areas across the state line in New York better than any other person before or since, from his tramping through the forests and fields as part of his surveying work. That made him one of the most successful sangmen in the region.

Jim married a distant cousin on his mother's side, Marie Munger Leplace, who was part French Canadian and part Indian (possibly Seneca). Tommy said that he was always told that Marie also was a descendent of Simon Girty. Jim continued his surveying business, while Marie managed a small herd of dairy cattle on the family farm.

Tommy Girty said that a "Girty family curse" began to come true around the time of World War I. William James Girty, who was Jim's and Marie's only surviving child and Tommy's father, was born in 1886. When the United States entered World War I, William enlisted and was later commissioned as an officer in the Army. He was killed in action in France early on the morning of November 11, 1918, just hours before the Armistice. The next month, on Christmas Day 1918, Tommy's younger sister Mary died in an influenza epidemic. Tommy was twelve years old at the time.

Tommy's mother, the former Sarah Kaiser, was devastated by these losses. "She was never in her right mind after that," Tommy remembered, "and my grandparents were afraid that she couldn't take care of herself." So, Jim Girty brought Tommy and his mother from their bungalow in Tioga out to the Girty family farm. Tommy and his mother lived with Jim and Marie until 1922, when they both died in their sleep during the same night. Tommy says that he suspects to this day that they were murdered in their sleep or had a suicide pact, but the undertaker, who also served as the Coroner in those days, ruled that it was death by natural causes in both cases.

Tommy inherited the Girty farm and sold the cattle and most of the land. "I never was a farmer," he said, "and we needed the money more." He and his mother lived there until 1928 when, at exactly 11:00 a.m. on the tenth anniversary of her husband's death, Sarah burned the house to the ground and disappeared while Tommy was at work. At first, people assumed that she had died in the fire, but no traces of her body were found. Tommy believes that she just "went crazy" and wandered off. He said that lots of people did that back then. There was nothing left of the Girty farm, so Tommy sold the ruins of the house and the remaining land and moved back into Tioga, where he worked until his retirement.

Tommy Girty claims to be the last of the Girty family in this part of the country. Except for Tommy's father, who is buried in France, and his mother, of whom no trace was ever found, the local members of the Girty family are buried in unmarked graves in a family plot on what was the Girty farm and now is part of the Middaugh Cemetery east of Lawrenceville. The gravesite is at the back of the cemetery, about one hundred yards from the remaining overgrown foundations of the old farmhouse. It is hard to find, with only a single flat stone marker in the ground, which simply says GIRTY. Tommy stated that he wanted to be buried there "to close the book on the Girty family curse." He refused to answer any questions about the nature of the curse.

A Legend of the Paxton Circle
as told by Tommy Girty

The mysterious stone circle in the forest above the Paxton family place used to be known as the Paxton Circle. People today just refer to it as the Rocks or the White Indian Rocks. When I was a boy, growing up just a few miles away, we called it the Paxton Circle because of Noah Paxton and the strange happenings there.

Noah Paxton was the first member of the Paxton clan in this part of the state. He moved here from the Harrisburg area around 1820 or 1821, with his young wife Ruth and their infant son

Samuel. The area was still pretty wild, even as late as the 1820s. Only fifty or sixty years earlier, it had been considered to be beyond the frontier.

Samuel Paxton, who was just a baby when they moved into this area, later became a friend of my grandfather, James Girty. They were lodge brothers together in the Improved Order of Redmen. Most of what I know about the Paxton Place and the Paxton Circle was what Samuel told my grandfather shortly before Samuel died in 1898. When I was a boy, my grandfather told me parts of the story from time to time. What I am relating now is my best attempt to put all the parts together as best I remember them.

As soon as he arrived with his family, Noah bought the house that people still call the Paxton Place. It was a log cabin back then, already one of the oldest houses in the area having been built shortly after the American Revolution. I don't think much remains of the original log cabin except perhaps some timbers in the basement and one of the stone chimneys. Over the years, the Paxtons expanded the cabin and tore down most of the original logs.

The people who lived in the cabin before the Paxtons had suddenly moved out. Nobody knew where they went. Nobody still remembers their names. Some people say they headed west, but others said they just disappeared.

When folks came looking for them, they found the cabin still full of furniture and all the animals fed and cared for. Most of their clothes and their wagon were still there. The whole family – a man, his wife, and four children ages two to eleven – had vanished without a trace. My grandfather heard this part of the legend from Samuel Paxton, who was a baby at the time and heard it from his mother some years later, so some of the details might not be right. But the old family was gone, without so much as a goodbye. Noah Paxton was on the spot and had money in hand, so he bought the house and land – contents, livestock, and all – at a Sheriff's sale for ten dollars, which was a bargain even back then. This would have been in 1820 or 1821.

It was Noah who discovered the stone circle on his property shortly after they moved in. Samuel Paxton – the member of their family that my grandfather knew – was still a baby. The Paxtons had been living there for about a year. Before then nobody knew anything about the Rocks or if they did, they had never told anyone about it. One night, after supper, Noah and Ruth were sitting out back, reading by lantern light. It was a hot summer night, and they were enjoying the cool evening breeze coming off the mountain. They heard faint music, like chanting, up in the forest behind the house, and they thought they saw lights moving slowly through the forest. Then they heard a loud screech. Ruth later described it to Samuel as a half growl, half shriek.

Noah wanted to go up right then and there to investigate, but Ruth reminded him that it might be a hunting party of Indians come down from New York State, where a lot of them still lived. Ruth's family had come from Lebanon County, Pennsylvania, which was the scene of some of the worst Indian attacks in American history. Her grandmother had been in a raid on a neighbor's farmhouse and had escaped death or captivity only by hiding in a fruit cellar under the floorboards. Everyone else was killed on the spot or carried away. Samuel said that his mother could never forget her grandmother's stories. On top of Ruth's fears, there were still said to be Indians in these parts, and even though they were peaceful and kept to themselves, people were still a little jumpy about meeting up with them, especially after dark. Many of the folks who settled this area had come from downstate and, like Ruth, had heard family stories of the Indian wars only sixty or seventy years before. That was unfair to the Indians, but that's the way folks were around here back then.

So, the next afternoon, after his chores were done, Noah decided to go up the mountain to see what he could find. What with all his work down on the flat part of his property, close to the cabin, he hadn't had much chance to go up into the forest and explore his own land. At most, he'd hiked up the old Indian trail that ran along the ridge, across the property and went all the way to Lake Ontario, so they said. Ruth packed Noah a supper and he promised that he would be home by sundown, which at that time of the year would have been around nine o'clock.

When he returned that night, Noah told Ruth about an ancient circle of stones, some of them standing upright as tall as a man, that he had found in the forest, about thirty yards on the other side of the ridge. He was sure that this was the area where they had seen the lights the night before. Someone had been through there, because he could see where they had trampled down the low ground cover in the clearing. Ruth said that they should tell someone about the discovery. Although she hadn't much schooling, Ruth was an educated woman for those days, and remembered reading about the mysterious stone circles of England.

Noah said that he did not think it would be wise to tell people about the stone circle, not just yet. He said that he had a feeling while he was up at the circle that it was a sacred place and should be kept a secret. Ruth asked him why he felt that way, but he just replied that he just did and that was all that he could explain.

Noah strictly forbade his family to go to the Rocks and even into the woods, warning that he had seen signs of wolves, cougars, bears, and Indians. Samuel told my grandfather that, about when Samuel was ten years old, one day he ventured up to the Rocks and found them just as his father had described, but there was nothing else unusual. When Samuel asked him about the stone circle and what it meant, Noah said that he been mistaken the first time he went there, when he thought he saw a circle of stones. Noah insisted that there was no stone circle because the "stones" were just dead hemlock tree trunks that looked like tall stones from a distance. Then Noah whipped Samuel with his belt and warned him never to go there again.

From then on, about four times a year, summer or winter, Ruth would pack Noah a supper and he would take a lantern and go up into the forest and spend the evening there by himself, always returning around midnight. He did this for the rest of his life. Ruth would look out at the mountain and see his lantern twinkling in the distance as he moved among the trees. Sometimes she would see other lights, too; sometimes only Noah's lantern could be seen.

When Samuel told his mother about Noah's explanation, Ruth wondered why Noah would tell her one thing and everyone else something else. By that time, Noah's behavior had become so eccentric that she decided not to press the matter for fear of upsetting him. Noah was still a hard-working farmer and a good husband and father, but he started to spend more and more time going up onto the mountain, in addition to his night-time visits. When he wasn't on the mountain, Ruth would sometimes see him standing and staring in the direction of where he said the stone circle was, and she would notice his lips moving quietly. Sometimes, if he was holding a tool, Noah would move it in time to some secret rhythm that only he could feel.

Noah Paxton died in 1835. It was a night of the full moon in early November, a cold windy night with clouds racing across the sky like silver clipper ships bound for China. Ruth packed Noah his supper and he set off for the mountain. She watched him disappear into the forest and waited for a few minutes to see the light from his lantern go up the mountain. After a little while, Noah had still not lit his lantern, so Ruth went back inside. She figured that by now, Noah could find his way in the gathering dark without the need of a light.

During the night, shortly after Ruth had gone to bed, she heard that same screeching noise that she and Noah had heard that very first evening. She went to the window and saw what she believed was the light from Noah's lantern up near the ridge and slowly moving down the mountain toward the house. She believed that everything was all right, and that Noah would be back home just after midnight.

Noah didn't come home that night, or ever after. The next morning, Ruth got worried and sent Samuel into town to get help. Samuel wanted to just go up the mountain himself. He was almost sixteen at the time and felt he could take care of himself. Ruth was afraid that whatever had happened up on the mountain behind their home could be too much for Samuel to handle by himself. So, she made Samuel fetch the constable from Tioga, who rode out later that day. He and Samuel started searching up the old Indian trail, and about fifty yards on either side, figuring that Noah would not have gone too far off the trail in the dark. Several other men joined in the search, and one of them found Noah's body, laid out in the middle of a circle of standing stones east of the trail. A long shaft of highly polished oak pierced Noah's heart. They said that it was about the thickness of an arrow, but it didn't have any tail feathers or arrowhead. When they found him, Noah's eyes were closed and his face had a peaceful look on it, almost a smile.

The constable reported the death to the Coroner, but nothing ever resulted from it. The Coroner ruled the death a homicide "by a person or persons unknown." No clues, other than the oak shaft, were ever found.

Who killed Noah Paxton? Some say it was a renegade band of the Wolf Clan, but by 1835 all the Indians were pretty much gone from around here. Most of them were up north in New York State and they were peaceful, law-abiding people. Others said it was the mysterious White Indians. Samuel always thought that his father had somehow gotten mixed up with the White Indians, and that he somehow broke one of their laws and was punished. If that were true, why did he die with such a peaceful expression on his face?

After his father's death, Samuel posted "no trespassing" wooden signs at the two points where the Indian trail entered his property and threatened to shoot any trespassers "for their own good." Sometime after Samuel's death in 1898, another member of the Paxton family found the signs partly fallen over into the brush along the side of the trail. The wood was rotten, but you could still read parts of the warning.

Noah's death pretty much drove Ruth mad. Samuel stayed at home and took care of her. After she died, sometime around the start of the Civil War, he finally married and raised his family in the Paxton Place. But until she died, Ruth would spend every evening sitting on a stool outside the kitchen door, looking at the mountain behind her home. She did this every night, summer and winter, except on the coldest nights. She never said a word, but sometimes, the next morning, she would tell Samuel that she had seen two red glowing eyes, like those of a huge cat, staring at her from the hillside. She was sure they were coming from the area up near the top of the mountain, where she had last seen Noah's lantern. Samuel went up onto the mountain several times to investigate, but never found anything. After two or three of these trips, Samuel would only listen patiently, kindly, to his mother's reports.

He continued to visit the Rocks on the anniversary of his father's death until shortly before he died of old age in 1898. Although he never found anything unusual there, he would sometimes sense a presence that reminded him intensely of his father – so much so that he thought that he heard Noah Paxton speaking to him, urgently but in a soft deep voice that he could not understand. He knew it wasn't his father, but something beyond his imagination, something that could not die.

The Police Chief's Daughter

Whitey woke up suddenly on Tuesday morning, wondering where he was. The last thing he remembered from the night before was drinking shots and beer at Red's. The rest was blurry, with unconnected clear fragments coming to the surface every now and then. He looked around, and it took almost a minute for him to be sure that he was at home.

Whitey swung his feet out over the floor and sat up. As he tried to stand his temples started pounding, like his heart had been shifted up into his sinus cavities. He was tremendously thirsty. Slowly moving over to the bedroom window, he looked out first with alarm, and then with relief. His truck was nowhere to be seen. That's good, he thought. At least he hadn't tried to drive home.

Noises were coming from the kitchenette. The first aroma of strong coffee made its way into the bedroom. Whitey inhaled, hoping that the aroma would help clear his head and ease the pounding. Walking out of the bedroom, following the aroma, he noticed a pair of women's white sneakers and blue jeans on the floor by the couch. Still puzzled, but with a growing sense of smugness, Whitey stopped in the bathroom. While urinating, he wanted to look up into the mirror and grin but knew he shouldn't. Don't push your luck. You may have scored last night, but you're no prize in the looks department, and you got to look like roadkill this morning.

Just as he turned the corner into the small living room, and looked toward the kitchenette, the name came back to him: Sandy – Oh, shit! the Police Chief's daughter! Had she told him that she was divorced, or only separated and in the process of getting a divorce? She lived by herself in a trailer park about five miles outside town, one of the nicer ones.

Whitey had seen Sandy a lot recently in Red's. She would usually come in around nine or nine thirty, two or three nights each week. She would play some pinball with the guys and have a few drinks. Sometimes she'd get really shitfaced and they would have to call a taxi to take her home, but most of the time she'd keep herself under control. Sometimes she'd pick out some guy, hang all over him all night, and leave with him just at closing. Sometimes she'd leave early by herself. Whitey had no idea how she ended up with him. Usually she ignored him altogether. In fact, she had never before spoken more than two or three words to him.

Sandy was sitting at the kitchen table, staring down into a chipped mug of coffee which she held with both hands. Her long red hair fell in front of her face like a beaded curtain. Whitey walked behind her to the coffee maker and poured a cup for himself. She didn't look up as Whitey approached, just stared into the mug.

"Hey, Whitey," Sandy said, still not looking up.

"Hey," Whitey replied, smiling but not sure what to say.

"Some night last night," Sandy remarked.

"Sure was."

God, Whitey thought, if only I could remember any of it!

There were two or three seconds of silence, but it seemed to Whitey like minutes. Then Sandy looked up and grinned. Whitey noticed the dark circles under her eyes. She couldn't be more than thirty, but her face looked much older, like a woman who had lived some hard times.

"So, what are your plans for today, Whitey?" Sandy smiled, not a grin this time, but a full smile. It made her look young again.

"Stay in bed with you all day."

Sandy laughed. "Sorry, lover. Last night was great, but I take things only one night at a time."

Sandy nodded in the direction of the old electric range.

"That thing still work?" she asked, getting up quickly.

"The stove?"

"No, the clock on the stove. Is that the right time? Ten thirty?"

"Beats me," Whitey shrugged. "I never use it." He looked at his watch.

"It's a quarter to eight, if you got to know."

'Whew, that's a relief." Sandy got up, poured herself another mug of coffee.

"I don't have to be at work until ten, but if I'm late one more time, I'll get fired for sure."

"Same here. I've crapped out so many days on my job, it's a wonder I can still find one," Whitey said.

"I didn't know you had a steady job, Whitey."

"Well, not really. I'm still working odd jobs. I kind of like it that way, a little job here, a little job there, you know. But I've been working these days mostly for Russell Poe, the new guy out at the old Paxton place. He's got me doing handyman work and helping him do some excavation work. He pays me good money, every day and in cash."

"What kind of excavation work is he doing, Whitey? Putting in a swimming pool?"

"No," Whitey explained. "He's studying that old stone circle on his property, you know, the Indian Rocks. We carefully dig down a few inches, sift the dirt, and record and photograph anything we find." Whitey studied Sandy's face carefully, looking for some sign that she was impressed. See, I'm not just an ignorant drunken hick, he thought. She stared back at him.

"Wow," Sandy finally said, suddenly perking up. "That sounds interesting."

"Not really," Whitey shrugged. "We almost never find anything. But it's easy work and kind of nice being up there in the woods all day, even when it's cold."

"Well, what have you found?"

"Oh, just some old animal bones and a few beads. Probably old Indian wampum, being so close to the old Indian trail and all." Whitey wasn't sure how much he should be saying about the Rocks. Russell had not told him to keep the work a secret, but he probably would not like to hear that Whitey had been talking about it.

"Why's he doing it? Is there a treasure there?" Sandy topped off her cup. She pointed the coffee pot at Whitey.

"Want any more?"

"No thanks, I'm fine.

"I don't know why he's doing it," Whitey continued. "He hasn't told me. Just curiosity, I guess. He's also some kind of historian and is writing a book." At least that part is the truth, Whitey thought.

He realized he had no idea why Russell Poe had this sudden interest in digging around the Rocks.

"What's the book about?" Sandy asked.

Russell had talked about his book sometimes while he was working with Whitey, but Whitey hadn't paid attention.

"Something about the Indian wars or something," Whitey replied. "Maybe a battle was fought up at the Rocks. He said that George Washington was in it. I don't know anything about it, really."

"Well," Sandy pressed on, "How much of it have you dug up? Isn't that some kind of historic landmark or something? Won't you guys get into trouble?"

"I don't know nothing about all that," Whitey answered. "It's on his land, so I guess he can do what he wants with it. We've just done a little bit, just a little grid, as Russell calls it. I don't think he wants to dig up the whole thing. It'd take years. We're mostly doing it by hand, breaking the surface with a spade and then using little trowels, like you use in a garden, and hand brooms and little brushes. He probably just wants to take a sample to see if there's anything important there. Like I say, I don't know anything about it. I just help him out, that's all."

"Well," Sandy concluded, "I don't think that you guys should be messing with the Indian Rocks. There's a lot more to them than just a bunch of old stones. They mean something."

"Superstitious, ain't you?" Whitey grinned.

"No," Sandy replied. Her face showed that she didn't know Whitey was joking. There was annoyance in her voice. "I always heard that it was some sort of sacred ground or something. To the Indians. Maybe it's an old burial ground or something. It's not right for two white guys – who knows, hundreds of years later – to go messing it up. Let whatever's up there or whoever's up there rest in peace."

"Well, if I meet up with a ghost up there, I'll send him over to haunt you." Whitey chuckled.

Sandy still didn't smile. "Yeah. Well, I got to go. Christ, Monday mornings are always hell at work."

She stood up and kissed Whitey on the top of his head.

"Thanks for some great loving last night."

Whitey tried to pull Sandy down onto his lap, but she spun away, breaking his grip on her wrist.

"C'mon, Whitey. I ain't got any time for that." Sandy walked over to the couch. Whitey was amazed by how fast she got dressed. He followed her, but Sandy grabbed her sneakers and held them in one hand in front of her, like a shield.

Her voice dropped a half octave. "I mean it, Whitey. Back off."

Whitey raised his hands chest high, palms outward.

"Okay, honey. I was just fooling around."

As Sandy turned and walked out the door into the hallway, she looked back over her shoulder.

"By the way, your truck is still parked up at Red's." The door closed, not with a slam, but firmly.

As Whitey listened to Sandy drive off, he remembered that Red's was four miles away.

"Shit," he whispered, and walked over to the refrigerator.

"Shit and double shit," he muttered when he saw that all the beer was gone.

Pouring another mug of coffee, Whitey called Russell, hoping to get a ride to retrieve his truck.

"Hey, stranger," Russell greeted him. "Where the hell have you been? I really needed you on Saturday, and Sunday, too."

"Well, Russell," Whitey started. "It's a long story about the weekend and all, but all I got to do right now is go fetch my truck. It's parked a couple of miles from here. And then I'll come right over, maybe around noon or so, as soon as I get my truck. If you can pick me up and give me a lift –"

Russell cut him off.

"No, Whitey, I can't help you today." Russell's voice seemed distant to Whitey, as if Russell were talking to a stranger. "I'm not going to need you today."

"Okay," Whitey responded. "What time do you want me tomorrow?"

There was a pause. "Well, Whitey," Russell continued slowly, "I'm not sure when I'm going to get back to that project. I have a ton of other things to do, some of them out of town for a few days. So, I'm going to be tied up for the foreseeable future, but I'll call you the next time I need you."

Whitey started to ask if Russell needed any other work done around his place, but Russell continued.

"Whitey, listen, I hate to cut you off, but I have to go. Honest. I have a ton of stuff to do. I'll keep in touch. I promise." Russell hung up without saying goodbye.

Whitey stood looking at the phone. Russell had as good as fired him. He wondered what he had done that pissed off Russell against him. He didn't show up on Saturday like he had promised, but he took all the trouble to drive up to Russell's place to leave him a note that afternoon. And besides the weather was bad all Saturday morning. So, what had gone wrong between him and Russell?

He opened the refrigerator door again, before he remembered that he had checked for beer only a moment before.

"Shit, shit, and triple shit." He slammed the refrigerator door shut. The old bowl on top, where he sometimes kept fresh fruit, rattled and almost fell off.

Sandy and June

Sandy Davis drove slowly along the narrow blacktop road that was the main street of her trailer park, watching for silhouettes of children, dogs, toys, and bouncing balls against the bright morning sunlight. As soon as she turned the bend, she saw the police cruiser parked just beyond the short driveway by her trailer. Oh great, she thought.

The almost invisibly thin silhouette in the driver's seat could only be her father. Why can't he telephone like real people? She even had an answering machine. Instead he always had to drive out in that damned cop car, making everybody in the trailer park think she was a drug dealer or a hooker or worse.

Ray Davis unfolded from the car and walked slowly up to Sandy's old Volkswagen, looking around as he did. Ray had been thin all his life. Over six feet tall, he couldn't have weighed more than 150 pounds, even though he was in his mid-fifties. When Sandy was a teenager, she wondered if her father was anorexic, but he could eat enough for three people and never gain an ounce.

Sandy saw that her father had his "sad face" on today. It made him look so old and tired, like he was wondering whether it was worth it to draw even one more breath. He had probably come about her mother, who had been "sick" all of Sandy's adult life. *Nuts* was more like it.

Sandy remembered what her mother used to be like, not very long ago. *Full of life* was the only phrase she could think of that described it. That's what everybody said about her. June Davis used to be so happy, and their mother-daughter relationship was a real friendship, not the wars that Sandy's friends were always waging with their mothers. Then, about the time Sandy turned eighteen, June began to throw off her contacts with the outside world. It was like a movie Sandy once saw, where an airship was losing altitude over the Arctic Ocean. The crew was frantically throwing all excess weight overboard. Even as some of their most needed equipment and supplies crashed into the ice below, the airship continued to sink. Sandy had watched June sink the same way.

June used to love to drive. She would think nothing of getting into a car and driving all the way to King of Prussia, four hours each way, on a Saturday morning just to go shopping at the big mall there. Sandy lived for those trips, mother and daughter, just the two of them together. She would even give up the Friday night dance after the high school football games, so she could get a good night's sleep. They would get up and leave at six in the morning, tiptoeing and whispering their way out of the house, so as not to wake up her father. Riding together down Route 15, out of the night and into day, they would sip coffee and make plans about all the things they wanted to look for and where they thought they would find them.

The best part of those Saturday trips was lunch together. Sandy always envied the women she saw in the mall restaurants, sitting at their tables with shopping bags arranged at their feet like presents around a Christmas tree. Sandy and June never had that many packages, usually not even enough to fill a vacant chair at their table. Sandy wondered what it must be like not to have to agonize over every purchase, and sometimes having to come home without having bought anything except lunch.

On second thought, the best part wasn't lunch. The really best part was driving home, tired and happy. As soon as the sun went down, June would switch on the radio. Sandy was always amazed by June's ability to tune in AM radio stations from halfway across the country. It was magic, hearing *Grand Ole Opry* live on WSM all the way from Nashville or *Jamboree* on WWVA from the Capitol Music Hall in Wheeling, West Virginia. Listening together, exchanging words only between the songs, they would drive steadily north into the night, away from the foggy half-daylight of the parking lot at the King of Prussia mall at night, and toward home. After an hour or so, once they got away from the city, Sandy could see the stars and constellations out the car window, so bright that they looked like Christmas lights someone had hung. When the stars came out, she would arch her neck back and stare at the stars through the sunroof of her mother's car. Lost in her dreams of distant stars, she would almost always drift off to sleep long before they got home. Her last thought before home would always be the same: how much her mother sounded like Patsy Cline, singing softly as she drove them home in a dazzling starlit Pennsylvania night.

Shortly after Sandy graduated from high school, she began to notice little changes in her mother. June seemed quieter now, and noticeably shyer, preferring to spend her free time reading instead of visiting neighbors or going shopping. One by one, June dropped out of the clubs and social groups in which she had always been so active. Whenever Sandy would suggest an all-day shopping trip and lunch out of town, June would agree at first, but then, usually on the day before the trip, she would tell Sandy that she just didn't feel up to it. Eventually Sandy stopped suggesting the trips, and June never brought up the subject again.

The night of Sandy's twentieth birthday party, June surprised Sandy by announcing that she was no longer going to drive. It wasn't really a party, just her parents and the neighbors having cake and ice cream together, but June tried to make it special for her, with balloons and lots of little presents. After the neighbors had left, and as June and Sandy were doing the dishes, June told Sandy that driving had become too dangerous for her and she was going to quit.

"What is it, Mama? Are your eyes going bad?"

"No, Sandy, my eyes are fine. Maybe they're too fine. It's the people who are always following me, everywhere I go in the car. They make me so nervous, I'm afraid I'll cause an accident."

"They know what I know," June continued, "and they're afraid. That's why there's always a car behind me. Not always at first, of course. But they find me and follow me. First one will follow me, then he'll turn off and another one will pull in behind me and follow me some more."

"Who are they," Sandy asked. "Do you know any of them?"

"No, but it's awfully strange that it's always one person, then another, then another, always somebody following me.

"At first, I thought that maybe they're trying to get at your father for locking up one of them or one of their friends," June continued. "I told your father about them, and he said that I shouldn't worry. I don't think he's telling me all he knows because he doesn't want me to worry about him. But I do, all the same."

Soon afterward, June stopped altogether going out of the house by herself. She complained bitterly that the people who were watching her, following her, were spreading lies about her. She said that everyone would stare and talk about her whenever she walked down the street or went into a store.

June continued to love to shop, but now did it only by mail order. She would carefully select the items she wanted from the dozens of catalogs that arrived every month. Then Sandy would order the items in her own name.

"You should never order personal things in your own name, Sandra," June would always lecture her. "The companies turn all that information over to the government. And you know who really runs the government." June would then quietly, calmly outline for Sandy how there are hidden forces that control the government, not the people that are elected. They were watching all of us and we had to be careful. There was never any fear in June's voice as she would recite her speech, which Sandy had heard a hundred times. Just the opposite: June was always calm and sounded rational. She didn't sound like the crazy person that Sandy knew she had become.

Of course, June Davis never used a credit card. "There are enough people who know what you're doing, Sandra," June always warned. "You don't want the banks involved, too. Above all, not the banks. Always order COD." Sandy had to admit that this made sense, to keep to a budget.

When the merchandise arrived, if Sandy was home she would take the money from the envelope hidden behind the mantle clock and pay the delivery man, while her mother watched from the landing on the stairway to the second floor, or from the kitchen table, where she was able to watch the transaction without being noticed.

Inspecting the packages was like looking for a bomb, Sandy recalled. Sandy or her father would have to open or unfold each item and look at it closely. Sandy never knew what they were looking for. "We're looking for signs," June would say when asked. "I'll know them when I see them."

Once Sandy asked her father why June insisted on the careful inspection of the packages that she ordered.

"Oh, Sandy, it was a silly thing," Ray replied, sighing and shaking his head. "Once your mother claimed that someone had put a note in with the clothing she ordered."

"What did it say?"

"I don't know for sure. Your mother snatched it out of my hand, looked at it, and then tore it up. I told her that if it was threatening or obscene, I'd take it over to the post office so that it could be investigated, but she refused to give me the pieces."

"The funny thing," Ray continued, "was that several days later, I was doing the laundry. When I put the sheets in the washing machine, a scrap of the note fell out. At least, I assume it was from the note. It looked like a signature. Someone named Brendan."

"Who was Brendan?" Way to go, girl, Sandy thought. Mama has a secret admirer.

"Beats me. Probably some lonely guy working in the warehouse. Your mother claims she never knew anyone named Brendan. But as scared as she seemed to be from the appearance of the note, she probably did. Maybe it was someone in her past.

"Well she was obviously agitated about it, so I told her that I took the scrap of paper over to the post office, but I never really did. I just wanted to calm her down, reassure her a little. Please don't ever tell her that."

Ray hadn't waited for Sandy's promise. There was no question about it.

"Mama knew who this Brendan was, didn't she? Why else would she keep the note hidden in the bed?"

"A good cop never jumps to conclusions, Sandy. We can't say for sure that she deliberately kept that scrap of paper, or whether maybe it had just got attached to her robe. Static electricity, you know. Then it got transferred from her robe to the sheets the same way."

"Did you ever ask her again about it?"

"No. It really upset her. I wanted her to let it go."

Whenever Sandy would try to talk to Ray about her mother's condition, he would dismiss it as "one of your mother's little eccentricities." The discussion always ended in an argument, with Ray and Sandy each saying things they regretted.

"I know the signs to look for," Ray would say. "And you can be sure that at the first sign of really serious mental illness, if I thought for a moment that she was a danger to herself, I'll get her seen by somebody right away."

Then, on Thanksgiving morning five years ago, June just didn't get up. She was too weak, she said. When she didn't feel better the next day, Ray called the doctor to the house, and, on his recommendation, took her up to Syracuse for an evaluation at the university medical center. Ray obtained several opinions, but they were all the same: There was nothing physically wrong with June. She was a perfectly healthy, although slightly underweight, woman. Quietly, gently, they told Ray that June was undoubtedly mentally ill, with a preliminary diagnosis of paranoid schizophrenia. They recommended immediate hospitalization, at least long enough to start treatment and medication based on further observation.

June refused to remain at the psychiatric unit at Syracuse, pointing out how the doctors were part of the group watching her. She rejected medication as being part of their conspiracy to control her mind. The social worker who was assigned to June advised that, because June did not appear to be in danger of harming herself or others, an involuntary commitment was not an option. Ray could not bring himself to have June put away against her will, even if only for a few weeks.

"It wouldn't have been respectful of her," Ray later told Sandy. "I love your mother, but even more importantly, I respect her. I know what those psychiatric units are like, and I just couldn't do it, not unless her life was in danger."

So, Ray brought June home to Wellsboro, back to the small house that had been Ray's home since birth and helped her back into bed. One of the nurses taught Ray how to pretend to take June's medication before she did, to assure her that it was safe, but Ray suspected that June sometimes only pretended to swallow the pill and later spat it out. He refused the suggestion to hide it in her food.

From that time on, except for Sunday mornings, June Davis preferred to spend most of the day in her bedroom. She carefully maintained her appearance, neither gaining nor losing weight despite her refusal to eat more than two tiny meals each day and of any suggestion of any exercise whatsoever. Each morning she got up, walked slowly to the bathroom and bathed. She put on fresh makeup and a clean nightgown and came downstairs for breakfast with Ray before he left for work. After cleaning up after breakfast, she usually returned to the bedroom, where she would spend the rest of the morning in bed reading or humming quietly to herself. She would spend the afternoons sitting in an old white wicker chair that Ray had brought up from the porch to the bedroom and positioned it so that she could watch television or simply look out the window at the old sycamore trees in the front yard. Perhaps, Sandy liked to think, June's imagination would put aside her shadowy stalkers long enough to let her play in those trees once again, just as she and Sandy had done when Sandy was a little girl. By eight o'clock, June usually was back in bed, having finished a light supper that Ray or Sandy brought to her on a tray. She always was asleep by nine.

Sometimes Sandy felt that the mother whom she had known and admired and needed so much had died – no, been allowed to die – and had been replaced by an imposter who lived in her own world now, fooling nobody except Ray Davis, who still lived in his own little dream world with his beautiful, vivacious wife and his loving, dutiful daughter. Why hadn't he tried to stop it – whatever or whoever caused her deterioration – when it all began years ago? Maybe he didn't want to. Maybe he couldn't. Maybe Sandy would never know whether she should hate her father or feel compassion for him, but she knew that she didn't have the strength to do both.

The impatient shuffle of Ray's shoes in the gravel parking area broke into Sandy's memories and interrupted her building rage. She did not know how long he had been standing by the door to her car, making no move to open the door or even tap on the window. He waited silently as Sandy slowly got out of her car. She was furious at his making a spectacle of himself and her once again in front of her neighbors. He looked so sad, so beaten down. She had to force her voice to communicate her annoyance, not pity.

"Dad, why do you always have to come in that goddamned cop car? The neighbors must think I'm some sort of a crook with a cop car hanging around here waiting for me all the time."

"No, it's not all the time, Sandy, and they know it's only me, and they all know I don't have any jurisdiction outside the borough." Her father could be so obtuse at times.

"Besides, honey, you know I like to talk to you face to face, father to daughter."

Bullshit, Sandy thought. He probably just gets off riding around in the cruiser scaring people. It's a macho cop thing.

"I came by several times last night, Sandy, but –"

"Jesus Christ, Dad, are you spying on me?"

"But you weren't home," Ray continued after pausing for a second. "Are you just getting home now?"

"No, Dad, I was at church until sunrise, praying for my sins and your soul. It's none of your goddamned business where I was at last night."

"Well, you were probably hanging around Red's again last night. That's okay, honey."

Sandy closed her eyes. Her temples pounded. She ached. She shuddered as she pictured last night, in bed with Whitey Wentworth. She had actually let him, actually *wanted* him.

"I'm sorry, Dad. I had a really bad night, I feel like shit, and I'm going to be late for work. Can't this wait until tonight or tomorrow sometime? I really have to hurry. I've got to get ready for work and get back into town in less than an hour."

"It's your mother," Ray continued, almost whispering. "She's having spells again. All last night and all this morning she's just lying in bed, humming what she calls the Old Song, again and again. It's driving me crazy, honey, and I don't know what to do. She wouldn't even come down for breakfast like she always does.

"Can't you please come over, just for a few hours? I can square things with your boss, if you need me to. But sometimes you're the only one who can reach her and calm her down, Sandy. I can't anymore. She just looks at me with those suspicious eyes of hers and won't say anything. She just keeps looking at me and humming, looking and humming. I'm afraid she's going to hurt herself."

Sandy closed her eyes and tried to block out the image.

"Dad," she said, her eyes remaining closed, "We have been through this before. She's away in her own world now. She'll come back to reality just like she always does. She's not going to hurt herself, at least not seriously, and she never has before. You said that even the doctors up at Syracuse told you that."

"Sandy?" Ray asked quietly. "Are you okay?"

The question surprised her. Sandy opened her eyes. Her father had walked a few steps back toward the police car. He turned away for a moment then turned back to face Sandy. He raised his hands slightly, palms upward.

"You've got to help me with her, Sandy."

She closed her eyes again. Thoughts of waking up with Whitey crowded out memories of her mother. Filthy, stupid, Whitey. Waking up with the town drunk. She shuddered. She could feel acid backing up in her throat.

"Dad, I just can't handle this right now. Not today." She opened her eyes.

"It's nothing to do with you or with us. I just can't deal with it right now. Mama's going to be okay. So, please go home and just take care of her. That's all any of us can do for her now.

"But, I'm sorry, Dad. I know I'm letting you down. I'm really truly sorry, but I just can't get involved in this right now. It's too much for me."

As she ran past her father into her mobile home, she glanced into the mirror opposite the door. She could see Ray still standing outside, turned toward her door now, his face looking surprised and hurt and bewildered and worried all at once. But looking back at him through the window of her door, Sandy saw something that she had never seen in her father before. His shoulders were slumped, and his hands hung by his side in complete defeat.

Sandy watched her father take a deep breath, then turn around and walk slowly back to his police car. He got in without looking back or waving, as he usually did, and slowly drove away.

The Dead Deer

Russell carefully placed the wine glass on an envelope from a long-paid and forgotten electric bill that he found stuffed behind the electric meter on the side of his house. The red ring from its base had slowly spread through the paper fibers into the old cardboard coaster beneath it.

This is crazy, he thought. I've been reading Jack's notes all evening, and now, well past midnight, I'm still looking for something that I should already know is not there. Even that last thought doesn't make any sense, he scolded himself.

Earlier that day, Russell had returned to the Rocks for the first time since he escaped the chamber six days before. The pile of brush concealing the hole appeared to be undisturbed, as had the entrance from the path down the mountain. After hiking back up to the rocks, he spent almost two hours napping lightly as he leaned against the old yew tree and looking slightly up into the center of the circle and the grid that he and Whitey had so carefully excavated. Plants were already beginning to grow in it. As he walked down the path to his house, he concluded that he had accomplished nothing except another pleasant walk in the forest.

After dinner, Russell took the notebooks and journals downstairs and spread them out on the kitchen table. After having skimmed through each one, by midnight, he concluded that there was no clear reference in Jack's notes to any network of underground chambers and tunnels under the Rocks, such as he had discovered. He saw one entry in Notebook 7 that described how a manitou, a forest spirit that once had been a man, could rise out of the ground and suddenly appear, but he dismissed any logical link between that legend and his underground experience as being too remote. Moreover, if there supposedly were spirits rising up out of the ground in the forest, certainly more than one person would have mentioned it. There also were isolated references in the later notebooks to "things that cannot be entrusted to pen and paper" and "discoveries for which the world is not ready." These weren't in any context and could have referred to almost anything. Russell thought that, at about the time he made those entries, Jack must have been reading some of the same H.P. Lovecraft stories that Russell loved as a teenager, and that Jack might have been influenced by Lovecraft's style.

The clock struck one o'clock. Russell realized that he had fallen asleep. He sighed and decided to look one last time in the last green journal. It was different from the other four, which were full of carefully transcribed notes and Jack's narrative recounting of the legends that he had recorded, with what looked like carefully planned gaps for entries that Jack had intended to add later. All the other journals had a coherence to them, which seemed to be the product of a careful, almost painstaking, attempt by Jack to organize the thoughts spread across his thirty-nine notebooks. The last journal started that way, but several pages into it, the tone of the narrative changed suddenly.

Judging from references in the green journals, Russell estimated that Jack's last entries in Notebook 38 and the few coherent ones at the beginning of Notebook 39 were made during the three or four months before his death. The journal entries, however, seemed to continue beyond the items recorded in the last two notebooks. Unlike all the previous journal entries, the ones in the final journal, except for the first four pages, were not like the careful summaries of interviews, stories, and transcriptions of other items from the notebooks. Russell could not find any related entries in any of the notebooks from approximately the same time. Jack's final entries in the journal were more like epistles from Jack to whomever might find and read the journals in the future, with a testamentary quality that disturbed Russell and made him read them again and again, searching for clues to hidden meanings.

Before turning out the light and going upstairs to bed, Russell read, for the ninth or tenth time that night, Jack's last three entries in the fifth journal. There was something haunting about it that drew Russell back to them again and again. Unlike the rest of the journals, there were no introductory comments like the researcher's notes that began most of the other journal entries.

March 3, 1978: As I look back upon all this work, all I ask is to be judged faithful to the histories and respectful of those who related them to me. By recording them, I honor both the core truth in each one and those who held it in their hearts, a precious gift from parent to child, over all these hundreds and hundreds of years.

The next entry was almost two weeks later.

March 13, 1978: We had an ice storm yesterday afternoon. Walking out to the road to get the mail, I found myself in a silent silver world, the peace broken only by the rifle crack of a branch breaking away from a tree off in the distance. I have never felt such beauty and, at the same time, such fear. What if this crystal wonderland would be my last memory of life, just before a tree fell on me? I heard a groaning noise in the branches, somewhere above me. I walked along faster.

The final entry was one of the strangest of all.

March 14, 1978: We had another ice storm during the night. When I went out this morning, I saw the deer. The tree, my tree, the one that I loved to lean against on a hot Sunday summer afternoon and read the books that Wanda and I had just brought back from the library, had fallen during the night, and now lay across the body of the deer. It looked like the tree had fallen on its neck. I hope it did.

But as I approached, praying to whatever god looks after deer in late winter, I saw the note. It had been torn from a brown paper grocery bag. Someone nailed it to the deer's still warm neck. Blood had seeped from beneath the note and dried in a reddish-brown line leading to the ground. Trying hard not to be sick, I knew that I couldn't touch it. So, I bent over and looked at the note. It had only three words on it, written neatly in black marker:

Jack. We know.

The next morning Russell telephoned Wanda.

"Can I come over for a little while this afternoon?" he asked. "I have a couple of questions about Jack's final journal, if you would be all right talking about it."

"Sure," Wanda replied. "You know you're always welcome here. You don't need to call first."

Russell was at Wanda's front door at noon. After accepting a cup of coffee, Russell sat at Wanda's kitchen table. She brought out some apple strudel and sat across the table from him.

"Homemade from the orchard. I picked these apples after the end of the harvest; but it's been frozen since at least last October," she said, without any trace of apology in her voice.

After a few minutes light conversation about the weather and Wanda's hilarious story about making a Welcome Wagon call and having a goat answer the door, which almost made Wanda fall off her chair with laughter, Russell became quiet for a moment, hoping that he signaled the need for a change in mood.

"Wanda, I need to ask you about Jack's last journal, and some of the last entries he made," Russell said quietly. "I don't want to get into anything that's too painful for you to talk about, so if you'd rather not discuss it, don't worry. I'm just curious about how the last notebook and the last journal had changed so much at the end."

"How do you mean?" Wanda asked. She turned away for a minute and seemed to look past Russell into the living room, as if distracted by a noise there.

"Well, first of all, Wanda," Russell said quietly, "before I go into details, have you ever seen the fifth journal, or did Jack ever tell you what was in it?"

"No," Wanda replied, equally quietly. "I could never bring myself to look at the last journal, because I know that Jack was working on it just before he died."

Russell paused, wondering how to proceed. He decided that the direct way was best.

"Well, all of the other four journals, and even the first few pages of the last one, were transcriptions of interviews, or his versions of the legends, or summaries of his notes," Russell said. "But, except for the first few pages, the fifth journal was like Jack was starting a personal diary. I wonder what had changed."

Russell read aloud the last entries, ending with the one about the dead deer. Wanda sipped her coffee but said nothing until Russell had finished. When he read the final words, about the note that had been nailed to the deer's body, Wanda's hand jerked, rattling the cup and splashing coffee onto her saucer.

"A note," she said. It sounded more like a comment than a question. "I remember that day – I wish that I didn't – and this is the first that I've ever heard about a note."

"Wanda," Russell asked, "At that point in time, how much was Jack sharing with you about his research?"

"Well, I don't really know much about what he wrote in those journals," Wanda said abruptly. "Even when he was still with me, I don't think that I ever looked at those notes or the journals more than five or six times," Wanda said in firm, almost emphatic, way that surprised Russell. "Oh, maybe a few more times than five or six, but not many and not at all toward the end.

"Sometimes, in the early days, he would tell me some of the background behind one of his journal entries and ask me to read it to be sure it was clear. But, after a while, he stopped showing me the notebooks and the journals. He'd still sometimes tell me the stories, but he stopped showing me the versions in the journals. I guess I just assumed that he was waiting until he had the whole thing finished and was going to show it all to me then."

"But you didn't ever ask to see them?" Russell asked.

"No, because that was Jack's special thing," Wanda replied. "Maybe other couples aren't like this, but we always respected each other's privacy. And, like I said, I just assumed that Jack was waiting to show me the finished product all at once. He wasn't hiding anything from me. We weren't like that. I knew that I'd see everything when he was satisfied with it, that it was as good as he could make it. Jack was like that."

"No, I never meant that Jack was hiding –" Russell began, but Wanda continued.

"Since then, I haven't really been able to open any of them," Wanda said more softly. "I tried more times than I can remember to sit down and read them all, to honor Jack because he had worked so hard on his project. But I just couldn't. I think that I told you all that when I gave you Jack's notes."

"So, what happened about the deer?" Russell asked quietly.

"I remember the incident with the deer," Wanda said. "But I didn't know that Jack wrote about it, or anything about the note. Like I said, I wish I didn't remember anything about that day, and now with what you've told me about a note, I don't think I will ever get that day completely out of my mind, not ever."

Wanda picked up her cup and saucer, got up suddenly, and went to the window over the kitchen sink. She kept her back turned to Russell. The cup and saucer trembled in her hands.

"Are you okay, Wanda?" Russell asked. "We can talk about this some other time."

"No, Russell, it's okay. It upset me a little because the memory is so vivid, and this is the first that I ever heard about the note that was pinned – nailed – to that poor creature. Not knowing about it, that's what upset me. Jack had never mentioned a note. Maybe he just didn't want to upset me, but that wasn't the way we were with each other."

Wanda continued to look out the window as she recounted the day. At times Russell had to strain to hear her, but he didn't want to interrupt.

Jack had come in from the cold. He looked like a little boy who had just seen his puppy get run over by a car. A large tear hung to the outer corner of each eye.

"What is it, Jack?" she asked. She looked up from a two-week old *New Yorker*.

"Oh, nothing, dear," Jack replied. His voice trembled, ever so slightly. "Nothing at all. Just some poor deer that got hit by a falling tree."

Wanda started to go outside to look.

"No," Jack said. "Please, don't go out. You don't want to see it."

Wanda went to the kitchen and poured Jack some coffee. He and Wanda sat in the living room. Wanda sensed that Jack was very upset and was not ready to talk about it. Wanda resumed her reading. Jack sat with a book in his lap, but obviously not reading it. He occasionally glanced outside.

Later that afternoon Whitey Wentworth came by with his truck. Jack answered the door. He didn't come in. Wanda stayed in the living room but heard him standing at the front door, talking to Jack.

"Just passing by," Whitey said. "I was just passing by and saw that poor doe under your tree. Want me to take her away?"

Later that afternoon, over tea, Jack had mentioned something about how strange it was that Whitey had come by.

"I haven't seen Whitey around here in ages," Jack said.

"Oh, it was just a coincidence, I'm sure," Wanda replied. "Whitey will probably butcher the carcass, freeze the meat, and live off it for months."

Jack changed the subject to something else, and the deer was never mentioned again.

"And, you know, Russell," Wanda said as she sipped her coffee, still looking out the window, "I had almost put that day out of my mind until you read Jack's journal to me just now."

"I'm sorry, Wanda," Russell replied. "I assumed that you knew everything about the deer."

Wanda said nothing in response. She returned to the kitchen table and sat down.

"Actually, Whitey had been here a couple of times in the previous fall for day work in the orchard," Wanda said suddenly. "Jack was probably out somewhere at the time or maybe he had just forgotten."

"That could be," Russell murmured, nodding.

"But, you know, Russell," she continued. "I don't think I will ever forget that day. Maybe it was a premonition of some sort about Jack. And I still think about that poor creature, and what it must be like to be a deer on a crisp March morning, walking in – how did Jack describe it?"

"A crystal wonderland," Russell said quietly.

"In a crystal wonderland, that's right," Wanda continued. "Walking in that crystal wonderland, hungry and looking for food, walking across the same patch of forest that it had crossed every day of its life. And then –"

Tears gathered in Wanda's eyes. One of them slowly flowed down her left cheek. She looked away from Russell.

"And then in the middle of such beauty and such safety, a blow to your neck, a moment that flooded your brain more with surprise than pain, and then nothing, nothing but the cold, icy, grass drawing your warmth from you."

Russell waited quietly, watching Wanda until she turned her face back toward him.

"And so I guess that's about all there is to the story about the dead deer, Russell," she sighed. "Whitey hauled the poor animal away. Jack stayed indoors for the rest of the day and the day after that, except when he went out to get the mail. And then, two days later, he left and never came back."

"Do you have any idea who could have put that note on the deer?" Russell asked.

"No, Russell, I don't."

Wanda paused for a second, as if she were searching her memory again.

"Who wrote that note and what it is that they knew about Jack," she said deliberately, "I have no idea."

"Another thing, Wanda, that I need to ask you about, and I don't know how to say it best. So, please forgive me if it sounds cruel, but was Jack well in the weeks before he passed away?"

"Why would you ask that?" Wanda said. Russell thought that he detected a hint of defensiveness in her voice.

"Well," Russell replied, "It's probably nothing; but I noticed – how should I put this – I noticed that his notes, the ones in Notebook 39 specifically, had become sort of vague and disorganized, like he was writing something down to help him remember it, but he didn't want to write down the thing itself. They are just words and phrases that don't seem to relate to anything else in his research, and there's none of the care that I saw in the other notebooks."

Wanda picked up her coffee and took a slow, quiet sip. She brushed another tear away with a brisk single movement of the thumb of her hand holding the cup. She cleared her throat and took another sip.

"You know," she continued as she set the cup down, "Jack had changed in the final six months or so before he died." It's funny, Russell thought. Wanda always describes it as *died,* not *was killed.*

"He became quieter and withdrew from other people, except maybe me, and I'm not even sure that he wasn't beginning to drift away even from me. Jack had always been the same outgoing guy, everybody's pal – you know the type – typical insurance salesman."

"Was there anything that happened in those last six months that could explain why he changed so much?" Russell asked.

"If anything, and I'm not saying that it was, I know that Jack was really shaken by Paul Levesque's death."

Russell opened to Jack's last mention of Paul in the final journal.

December 19, 1977: I went to visit Paul Levesque today at the VA Hospital in Wilkes-Barre. He telephoned me yesterday and said he had several things that he wanted to tell me about the White Indians, the "Children" as he called them. This was to be a breakthrough! For months Paul had played games with me each time I visited him. At first, I supposed that it was part of his mental illness. But part of his delight in dangling little bits of information in front of me was very deliberate. He wanted to see how I would react, and how far he could trust me.

When I arrived at the Reception Desk, they informed me that Paul had died earlier that morning of natural causes. They were not allowed to give out details.

"That's a real tragedy, that he passed away before Jack could interview him that last time," Russell said. "I would have liked to have talked to the old boy myself. From what you told me, and from what I read in Jack's notes, he must have been an interesting character."

"A coot?" Wanda attempted a laugh.

"Yeah, something like that. But his name appears a lot in the notebooks."

Wanda continued, "Paul's death shook Jack badly. Sure, it looks like Paul took with him something that Jack had been looking for, some key piece of information that would have tied Jack's research together. But there was more to it than that, I think.

"I don't know what it was. I do recall Jack telling me once that Paul knew a lot more about the so-called White Indians than he let on. But, then again, it could have been just a crazy old man having some fun with someone who was willing to sit and listen to him spin stories, just like Jack said in that entry you just read to me from the journal. I really don't know."

Wanda described how she and Jack had attended Paul's funeral at St. Peter's. Jack had been one of the pall bearers, discretely pulled aside by the funeral director when the hearse drove up alone, as Paul had died without any known family and only a few friends. Fewer than a dozen people attended. Wanda didn't know most of them but had been surprised to see Whitey Wentworth at the funeral, the squeak of the heavy door at the back of the small church announcing his arrival ten minutes after the mass had started. He stood behind the last row of pews, as if he was undecided about whether he would stay. Finally, he took a seat at the far-right corner of the last row.

Wanda remembered how small and lonely Paul's casket looked, even under the flag that draped it. Just before the mass began, two men in dark suits approached the funeral director and talked quietly to him. They handed the funeral director a small black case, which he opened and gently placed on top of the flag, just over where Wanda supposed Paul's heart would be. Wanda noticed the inverted star shaped medal on a blue ribbon with tiny white stars.

When the priest offered communion, no one came forward at first. Wanda told Russell how Jack had whispered in her ear, "Father Girard and Paul are the only two Catholics in the place." Finally, the funeral director came forward and knelt at the rail.

When it was all over, Jack, the funeral director, and the two men who had brought the medal escorted Paul's flag-draped casket along the aisle to the back of the church, the priest following, and then Wanda and the other mourners. Whitey had already left. Just outside the doorway, the two men in dark suits, now wearing Veterans of Foreign Wars caps, came to attention and saluted.

After the hearse was loaded, most of the people got in their cars and drove away. Only the priest, the two VFW men, and Jack and Wanda remained. They formed Paul's cortege.

Wanda had not wanted to go to the cemetery. She was catching a cold and didn't want to make it worse in the chilling drizzle of that late December afternoon. But Jack said that they had to go, because almost no one else was. She agreed. It was the right thing to do.

The priest and four mourners huddled under umbrellas over Paul's grave. The priest read from his Bible and said a short prayer. Wanda held on to Jack's arm, looking down at the beads of water on the toes of her shoes, feeling Jack shivering.

Then, when it was over, the two VFW men stepped even closer to the grave. One knelt down on one knee, the blue wool of his suit attracting small clumps of mud. He produced a small cassette player and pushed the play button. He and his companion took up positions at either end of the casket. In a moment, the faint sound of a bugle playing *Taps* struggled upward in the heavy, chilled air, each note sounding like a sob. Wanda marveled at how clear and majestic such sadness could sound. When the last note faded, one man carefully picked up the medal case, which had been closed against the rain, and placed it in the pocket of his raincoat. Then, together and with obvious practice, the two men folded the flag into a tight triangle. They handed it to the funeral director.

Just as the two men were getting in their car to leave, Jack and Wanda approached them.

"Hi," Jack said. "Did you guys know Paul well? Did he belong to your club?"

The younger man, getting into the passenger side, winced noticeably at the word *club*. The older man smiled. The two men walked over to Jack and Wanda.

"No," the younger man said. "This is just something our post does whenever a veteran from one of the wars passes on. If we find out about it in time, we always send someone to the funeral."

"That's really a wonderful thing," Wanda remarked. "That medal you placed on his casket, what was it?"

"The Medal of Honor," he answered. "We don't see those very often. We had to borrow this medal from one of our members down in Scranton."

"Do you know what Paul earned it for?" Wanda asked.

"We tried to find out, but there wasn't that much time," the younger man explained. "It was something in the First World War in France, but we don't know what. It had to have been something pretty heroic. This is the first time I've ever been at the services for a Medal of Honor recipient.

"Our Post Commander got a message at work the other day, saying that a Corporal Paul Levesque had just died at the VA Hospital, and that he was a Medal of Honor recipient from World War I," the older VFW man continued. "We checked it out with the Army, as we always do. They confirmed that he was awarded the Medal of Honor for heroism in the Meuse-Argonne Offensive in 1918 – that was the deadliest single battle in American history, more than twenty-six thousand of our boys died – but they were unable to locate a copy of the citation. I was in France back in 1918 myself, and I would have given anything to know how he earned it, so that we could have really honored him like he deserved, and I could have said thank you properly."

"The citation?" Wanda asked.

"That's the document that describes what he got the Medal of Honor for," the younger man explained. "It's not unusual for the paperwork to be missing after all these years, especially from the First World War."

"Jesus," Jack said softly, "In all those war stories he told me, he never mentioned anything like that."

The men from the VFW smiled.

"You'd be surprised," the older man said. "A lot of us veterans remember combat better than anything else. For some of us, it was the biggest thing in our lives, before or since: to have risked your life, see your buddies get killed just inches away, and come out of it alive and for the rest of your life wonder why you survived and so many good people were killed. But when it comes time to tell other people about it, some of us want to keep it to ourselves; 'just doing my job,' most combat vets will say if asked about it. I guess maybe I'm a little like that, but I can tell you that I never did anything half as heroic as what Corporal Levesque must have done to earn the Medal of Honor."

Wanda told Russell how, after the two VFW men drove away, Jack asked her to wait for a minute, while he said a final goodbye to Paul. His voice was trembling, and his eyes were filled with tears. Wanda waited by their car as Jack walked quickly back to Paul's grave. Wanda could see the two grave diggers about twenty yards away, discretely turned away from the grave site, waiting to do their work after everyone had left. One looked over his shoulder and nodded quickly in Jack's direction, and then he and the other worker quickly turned back around to face the woods and the mountains in the misty distance.

Jack stood by Paul's grave for two or three minutes. He seemed to be saying something, but the wind rushing through the trees carried the sound away in the opposite direction. He then tossed something into the grave. When he came back, he appeared to be in control of his emotions, but Wanda sensed that he didn't want to talk. Neither of them said anything all the way back home and Wanda never asked him about it, assuming that if Jack wanted to share it with her, he would do so at the time that was right for him.

"Can you tell me more about how Jack was, after Paul passed away and before he –" Russell couldn't finish the sentence.

"Oh, please, Russell," Wanda said. "Please, please don't make me relive those months. The thing with the deer was bad enough. Maybe someday I can talk about it, but not yet, and maybe never."

"I understand. I'm sorry," Russell replied. "I shouldn't pry. I won't bring it up again."

"No, it's not that. It's just that after Paul passed away, something just went out of Jack."

"In what way?" Russell caught himself. "No, forget that. I'm sorry. You asked me not to –"

"It's okay, Russell. I have to face up to it eventually."

Wanda got up and poured another cup of coffee for herself.

"Can I freshen you up?" she asked.

"No, thanks."

Wanda returned and sat down. She looked down into her cup, said something that Russell could not hear, and then looked into Russell's eyes.

"It's okay." Wanda took a deep breath.

"If you don't want –"

"No," Wanda interrupted. "No, goddamn it. I said it's okay."

They sat together for a moment in silence. Wanda looked down and ran her right index finger around the rim, counterclockwise. She didn't look up, and Russell almost had to stop breathing to hear her voice.

"You know, Russell, we never made love after Paul's funeral, not even on New Year's Eve, like we always did. Jack became so quiet. I thought that it was something that I had done, or hadn't done, but I also knew, somewhere inside me, that it wasn't me.

"Jack started having bad dreams. They weren't nightmares really, but in the middle of the night I'd wake up, sensing that something was wrong. And Jack would be all huddled up in a ball on the other side of the bed. I'd reach over, and I could feel him trembling in his sleep. I'd ask him about it the next morning and he'd say, 'Don't worry. It was just a bad dream'."

"Did Jack tell you anything about how his research was going?"

"No, in fact after Paul died, Jack never spoke of it again. Oh, I knew he was writing in his notebooks and journals every now and then, but not like before. But he never shared it with me, not like before – not like when sometimes he'd come back from interviewing someone that was really interesting, and we'd pour a glass of wine, and he'd tell me all about the latest piece of folklore he'd uncovered."

Wanda smiled down at her coffee mug, but Russell could see her eyes glisten with tears.

"No, Russell. My Jack just drifted away from life."

The White Indians

From *Research Journal 3,* transcribed by John S. Abrams from original notes in Notebooks 18 and 19

Researcher's note: This account is based on several sources and references, primarily the notes of two interviews, on November 1, 1973, and December 5, 1973, with Frances McNabb, age 68, and Dorothy White, who said that she believed that she also was 68 years old.

Miss McNabb is a life-long resident of Wellsboro and lives in her family home, with Miss White, in the west end of the town. She is the last surviving daughter of Judge William R. McNabb, III, and Bertha Paxton McNabb, both of whom died in an automobile accident on the U.S. Route 6 in 1948. Miss McNabb, who was riding in the back seat of the car, stated that it was a "freakish accident," in that Judge McNabb swerved to avoid a large animal that was crossing the road. She remembers that it was not big enough to be a bear but was too large to be a dog. The Judge lost control of the car, which left the road and went down an embankment into a large tree. Miss McNabb volunteered that her only other memory of the accident was of an old man who apparently was nearby, who came down the hill and helped her out of the car and back up the hill to the road and then disappeared into the forest on the other side. She suffered only minor injuries, but her parents apparently were killed instantly.

Miss White was born on a small farm outside of Parrott, Georgia, at a time when births of African-American children were seldom registered in Georgia. She never married, but moved with her family to Bethlehem, Pennsylvania, in the early 1920s, where her father worked in a steel mill. After his death in 1929, Miss White and her mother worked as cleaning women and learned through church connections of an opening for a cook and housekeeper in the McNabb household. They moved together to Wellsboro in 1931. Her mother died in 1936, and Miss White remained and has worked ever since in the McNabb household, taking over her mother's responsibilities as cook and also serving as housekeeper for the family. She remained in Miss McNabb's employment after her parents' death in 1948. As Miss McNabb has been in poor health in recent years and seldom leaves the house, she also serves as Miss McNabb's caretaker and companion.

Because most of this information came from Miss McNabb and Miss White during my two interviews with then, I have organized it as a continuous narrative by both of them. Miss McNabb recalled stories and parts of stories she heard from her parents when she was young. Her mother was "something of a student" of Native American folklore and history. Miss McNabb apologized for being "a little vague" about some details, which she said that she had forgotten over the years. Some of them were filled in and corroborated in part by other research that I did at the Tioga County Historical Society, as well as from two sources who have insisted that they remain anonymous and that their information must never be published.

Miss White was unable to corroborate any significant parts of Miss McNabb's accounts, explaining that "The Judge and Mrs. McNabb never spoke with the help about things like that." However, Miss White stated that she occasionally overheard the McNabbs and their guests talk about the White Indians before the Judge and Mrs. McNabb died in 1948, and that the details that Frances McNabb related were consistent with what she had overheard in the McNabb household. Miss White also added some details that Miss McNabb said that she had forgotten. Both ladies emphasized many times that they were sure that the stories that Miss McNabb had been told by her mother, when she was a girl and as an adult, were true. "Mrs. Bertha McNabb was the most truthful person I ever knew," Miss White said several times during the interviews.

I was unable to corroborate the accounts of the ritual sacrifices, or of the summer solstice ceremony that was supposedly witnessed by an outsider in 1885, which Miss McNabb described during the interviews, and which are related at the end of this summary.

The White Indians
as told by Frances McNabb and Dorothy White

The last Indians to live in this area were the Wolf Clan of the Delaware Nation. Actually, the band that lived in northern Pennsylvania were an offshoot of the main Wolf Clan. Unlike the other bands of the Delawares of eastern Pennsylvania, they never acknowledged the authority of the Iroquois Confederation, and they would never accept being "women" to their neighbors to the north and west, except when they had to. Most of the time they just went their own way, and the Iroquois left them alone.

The last of the Wolf Clan were gone from Pennsylvania by 1840. They were forced off the land by the farms and the timber industry had destroyed their way of life. So, one by one they left. A few settled on the Cornplanter Reservation along the Allegheny River in the northwestern part of the state, and some of their descendants might still live in that area. Some eventually rejoined the main body of the Delawares, or what was left of them, out in Oklahoma. But by the 1850s they were all gone from these parts, or so most of us assumed.

About the same time that the last of the Wolf Clan had supposedly left, just before the Civil War, people in northern Pennsylvania started talking about a small band of Indians that still lived in the mountains in this region. They were called the White Indians, because their skin was as fair as any white person's and many of them had blue eyes. The chief was a mysterious fellow called John Oakman.

There were many wild tales about John Oakman, such as that he had fought in the American Revolution, or that he had been educated at Harvard, or that he was nothing more than the ringleader of a gang of moonshiners and bandits. Some people claimed that they had seen him up in the mountains, hiking along one of the old Indian trails, but no two descriptions of him ever matched. Kids were told never to go up into the forest alone, because John Oakman liked to kidnap children and raise them as his own.

Nobody knew much about the White Indians. From time to time, a hunter or woodsman would come upon one of their camps. They didn't have a fixed village like most of the Eastern Indians normally used to have, like Tioga Point or Conestoga further down the

Susquehanna. Instead, they were completely nomadic, moving from place to place up in the mountains. They would camp in a clearing in the forest and set up a medicine circle of stones to mark its boundaries. The only trace of their camps would be a small circle of stones and the remains of some campfires, but nothing else.

Nobody knew where the White Indians came from or when. Most people believe that they had been here long before William Penn founded Pennsylvania. Some people say that they were descendants of the Vikings, who wandered down into the area from Vinland, through New England, and lived peacefully alongside the Indians. Others say that they were the remnants of Walter Raleigh's Lost Colony in North Carolina, who escaped when the Indians wiped it out and fled inland, making their way up the Chesapeake Bay and the Susquehanna River eventually to what we call the Endless Mountains. Still others say that they were just a bunch of damn fool Connecticut Yankees who tried to steal the northern half of Pennsylvania during the Yankee-Pennamite Wars in the 1790s and got kicked off their land.

Another legend was that the so-called White Indians were really a lost remnant of the Allegewi, the native American nation that first inhabited this region, even before the Susquehannocks, Delawares, and the ancestors of the Iroquois tribes crossed the Mississippi River and migrated into Pennsylvania thousands of years ago. Some scholars think that the Allegewi might have originally come from Mexico. The Allegewi supposedly disappeared a thousand years ago, being absorbed into some of the tribes that later migrated into Pennsylvania, but it is possible that some of them, like the Wolf Clan, kept themselves apart. Their name lives on in Pennsylvania, however, in the Allegheny Mountains and the beautiful Allegheny River.

Nobody knows the answers to these questions, because the White Indians were too dangerous to approach. Even the Senecas and the Shawnee left them alone. There is a story that once every eleven years they would sacrifice their king and eat his body. They would smoke the heads of their dead kings and keep them all in a row in a sacred underground cave up in the mountains, so they could ask the heads questions and get their wise advice. Twice a year, at the summer solstice and the winter solstice, they would bring the kings' heads to one of their circles and the heads would talk.

This custom supposedly continued well into the 1800s. There even was one person who claimed to have seen the ceremony at the summer solstice of 1885, but no written record of his report remains. That person, whose name apparently has been lost to history, supposedly disappeared shortly thereafter.

If you were an outsider who stumbled into their camp, and went inside their stone medicine circle, and they learned about it, you were a dead man. Even if they didn't see you violate their sacred space, they somehow would know about it and hunt you down. But if you were just out in the woods and not bothering anybody, they'd let you alone. They'd even help you if you were in trouble. But if you entered one of their circles, you'd find yourself tied onto a stone altar where they would stuff leaves into your mouth to keep you quiet, and then slit your throat, just a little, and leave you in the forest to die slowly.

What happened to the White Indians? One story is that they were members of the Wolf Clan, who left Pennsylvania before the Civil War. Another story is that some of them stayed around longer. Still another theory is that they were another, much older, group who stayed long after the Indians left. We stopped hearing new stories about them around the turn of the century, but nobody really knows for sure whether or not they're still up there in the mountains.

Queen Lizbeth Mistletoe

From *Research Journal 3,* transcribed by John S. Abrams from original notes in Notebooks 18 and 19

Researcher's Note: Most of the people who mentioned the legend of Queen Lizbeth Mistletoe were unable to provide much detail, although their stories were generally consistent. An eccentric young woman ran away from home in the 1880s to live as a recluse in the mountains, and she returned to civilization an old woman some seventy years later.

This account comes principally from multiple interviews in January 1973 of Robert Costello, who, until his recent retirement, taught English at the Williamson High School in Tioga, Pennsylvania. His grandfather, Peter Costello, was one of the physicians who attended to the old woman in the years before her death and who attempted to corroborate her story. He died in 1971, just two years after the old woman. Robert Costello's younger brother, John, now lives in Sandusky, Ohio. He was interviewed by telephone in July 1973 and corroborated Robert's basic story about their grandfather and the woman who claimed to be Lizbeth Mistletoe, but he could add no significant details. John added that he has sold the shotgun mentioned in this account to a collector.

In addition to matters of public record, the family history of Bertha Wilcox was provided by Martha Munroe Fulton, of Westfield, Pennsylvania, who is a daughter of a younger sister of Esther Wilcox, Bertha's mother. Ms. Fulton was interviewed briefly on three occasions in May and June 1973. Notwithstanding the legend, Martha Fulton does not believe that the old woman was, in fact, her great aunt.

Queen Lizbeth Mistletoe
as told by Robert Costello

Queen Lizbeth Mistletoe was 104 years old when she died. She had gone to live with the White Indians back in 1886 and came back off the mountain an old lady in the 1950s. The last two decades of her life, she stayed in the State Hospital because all those years in the woods had made her crazy and there was no one who would care for her. She was born on April 9, 1865, on the very day the Civil War ended; and she died on July 20, 1969, on the day of the first landing on the moon.

Lizbeth Mistletoe wasn't her real name. It was Bertha Wilcox. Bertha was the only child of old Judge Bayard Wilcox and Esther Munroe Wilcox and grew up in Wellsboro with the best of everything. Judge Wilcox even sent her down to college in Philadelphia. In the 1880s that was unusual for a girl; most just stayed at home, got married, and had children.

Bertha was a wild girl in many ways. She returned home after her first year in college and announced that she wasn't going back. The Judge didn't push the issue, because he knew that Bertha was going to do whatever she wanted. So, Bertha settled back into life in Wellsboro.

There were no young men in Bertha's life. Her father and mother would introduce some of the area's most eligible bachelors to her, but she simply was not interested in any of them. Instead, she would spend all her time tramping around in the mountains, wearing pants and carrying one of her father's shotguns for protection. On a summer morning, Bertha would be up at sunrise and wouldn't come home until sunset. Even on the coldest days of winter, Bertha would bundle up and go out. There was something about her that just had to be outdoors.

Bertha Wilcox was tough. One summer day, Bertha was walking through the woods and tripped over a tree root, badly spraining her ankle. She thought it was broken, but it was only a very bad sprain. Still, she knew what to do. She knew she couldn't get back to town unless she crawled all the way, and it might be days before anyone came along the old Indian trail she was on. So, she dragged herself over to a fallen branch, took out her hunting knife, and started making herself a crutch.

As she worked on her crutch, and as it was starting to get dusk, along came John Oakman and his band of White Indians, moving from their camp at Spanish Hill to another camp further west in the mountains. When Bertha saw them, she was sure she was a goner; because she had heard all the stories about the White Indians. But

John Oakman himself picked her up and put her over his shoulder like a sack of potatoes and commenced to carry her off. Well, Bertha screamed and pounded on him with her fists, and kicked at him with her good leg. But John told her not to worry, that they would not harm her.

When Bertha didn't come home, the Judge set up a search party the next morning. They scoured the forest between Wellsboro and the Tioga River to the east, because that was where Bertha said she liked to go. The search party looked behind every rock and up every tree, but they couldn't find any trace of Bertha Wilcox. They had just about given her up and figured that a bear or a wolf pack had gotten her, because there were still lots of those animals running wild in northern Pennsylvania in the 1880s. Then, after she had been gone for almost a week, one evening she just strolled back into town, as good as new.

Bertha told her father that she had stayed with the White Indians while her ankle got better. When her father asked for details about the White Indians, Bertha refused, and told him that she had promised not to give away any of their secrets. So, everyone just figured that Bertha had made up the story.

For the rest of 1886, Bertha would go off for weeks on end in all types of weather. She would sometimes be spotted with an old man sitting in a camp on top of Spanish Hill more than fifty miles away as the crow flies, or sometimes by herself at the White Indian Rocks above the Tioga River. People would occasionally see her, always by herself, as they took short-cuts through the forest along the old Indian trails.

Folks claimed that she had married one of the White Indians and that her husband had several camps up in the mountains, each one at a place sacred to the Indians, where she would visit him from time to time or move with him from camp to camp. Some other people claimed that the White Indian story was just a cover-up for the fact that she had a secret lover that she visited in another town.

Most people, though, just assumed that Bertha was going crazy and would just go up into the mountains and wander around. She knew how to take care of herself in the wild, so nobody really worried that much. Finally, on a day in early November in 1899, as the first snows were falling, Bertha left for good. She left Judge Wilcox and her mother a short note when she left. It just said that she was going off to live in the mountains and that they shouldn't worry. She would be all right, she said, and would be with good people who would take care of her. That was the last that the Judge and his wife ever saw or heard from their daughter.

When Bertha didn't come home after a week or so, the Judge began to worry. Winter was closing in fast, and even an experienced outdoorsman would have trouble surviving out in the woods all winter. The Judge almost went broke paying for people to search the mountains. They had to break off the search by mid-December because of the weather, but they resumed it early the next spring and searched all summer.

For the rest of his life, Judge Wilcox offered a reward of ten thousand dollars, a fortune in those days, for the safe return of his daughter. He paid some smaller rewards to people who claimed that they had information, but none of it ever proved to be true. Nobody ever found a trace of Bertha. This killed the Judge. He died unexpectedly on Christmas Day 1900 of a broken heart, they said. His wife passed away the following spring. When she died, the house was sold and the estate assets were held in trust for Bertha, the sole heir, by the Orphans Court for the required seven years, after which Bertha was declared legally dead and the funds were distributed to relatives of the late Mrs. Wilcox and several charities mentioned in the Judge's will.

What really happened was that Bertha had gone off to join the White Indians. John Oakman had taken Bertha as one of his queens. The White Indians named her Lizbeth Mistletoe, Lizbeth after John Oakman's mother, and Mistletoe after the mistletoe plant, which was sacred to the White Indians. She and John Oakman ruled over the tribe for many years, living far up in the mountains.

On a summer day in 1951, an old lady came walking into town, carrying an old sack and an old shotgun. She went straight to the Courthouse and asked to see Judge Wilcox, whom she claimed was her father. At first everyone was confused, and nobody knew who Judge Wilcox was. But, as the Courthouse guard was trying to gently escort her from the premises, the old woman saw an old painting of the Judge at the end of a hallway, right outside the restrooms by the back door. The Courthouse staff knew whom she wanted. Of course, the Judge had been dead for more than fifty years.

So, after she stayed for a few days for observation at the Soldiers and Sailors Memorial Hospital in Wellsboro, they took the old lady to the psychiatric unit at the Danville State Hospital, over in Montour County. There she told the doctors that she was Queen Lizbeth Mistletoe, and that she was the queen of the White Indians. She had decided to come home to Wellsboro to visit her "other family," as she called them, before they all died. However, when they asked her questions about her other family and her early life, she said that she didn't remember anything about it, other than she was the daughter of Judge Wilcox and left to live in the mountains when she was young. Unfortunately, all the Wilcoxes had been dead for years, except for Martha Munroe Fulton, who was contacted but was not able to identify the old woman as possibly being her long-lost great aunt.

When the doctors told the old woman that they were unable to corroborate any part of her story, and that there was no one who wanted to visit her, the old woman tried to leave the hospital. She said that she couldn't stay because she had left her husband up in the mountains and he was waiting for her to come back. When the people at the hospital asked for her husband's name, she said, "His English name is John," and sometimes she would say only "My husband has many secret ancient names." When they asked for her address, she would say "We don't have none." But she kept insisting that she was a queen and that her children were all waiting for her to come back.

She refused to answer any more questions, and just started rocking back and forth and singing a little chant to herself in some foreign language. The doctors at the State Hospital were even more sure than ever that she was just a poor crazy old mountain woman, so they diagnosed her as having senile dementia and, since there was no place for her to go, obtained the court order for her permanent commitment.

Lizbeth lived for almost another eighteen years. The first few years she was in the hospital, she would insist every day that she needed to return to her husband and children up in the mountains. They kept her in a locked section of the hospital because, every month or so, she would try to escape, and once she almost succeeded, running all the way across the hospital grounds to the river, where she said that her family would be waiting to take her home in a canoe. They caught her just as she was beginning to wade out into the Susquehanna River.

After a few years, Lizbeth just quit talking and became docile. As far as anyone knows, she didn't say a single word for the last ten years of her life. She died in 1969, and they buried her in the potter's field adjacent to the Odd Fellows Cemetery in Danville.

I learned about Queen Lizbeth Mistletoe from my grandfather, who was one of her doctors at the State Hospital. He told me that he half-believed her story and tried to find out who she really was. The old woman resembled the few surviving old photographs of Bertha Wilcox in her teens and early twenties, but there was no one still living who could identify her. I remember him telling me that, until she stopped speaking, she sometimes appeared to be educated and well-spoken, but often she could not remember where she was or why she was there. He had some notes of his efforts to verify her story, but they were lost shortly after my grandfather passed away.

My grandfather told me about the bag she carried the day she arrived in town. It was an old-fashioned carpet bag, that had been patched in so many places that it was almost impossible to determine what was the original fabric. It was thrown out shortly after Bertha arrived at the hospital, because it was packed only with dried plants and roots. He kept her shotgun, however, because nobody else wanted it. My brother still has it. I hope that he never tries to use it.

My grandfather had heard about the old stories that had circulated for generations about the so-called White Indians, but he was unable to find a real live White Indian or even anyone who had ever met a White Indian. He concluded that even if some group that called themselves the White Indians were still in this area back in the 1880s, when Bertha Wilcox left home, they had long since vanished. He also was convinced, however, that even if he couldn't prove her identity, her story about living in the mountains all those years was probably true, based on her robust physical condition up to the day that she died.

My grandfather said that she died quietly in her sleep in her chair in the TV lounge, just after having watched the moon landing. Her heart simply stopped, and she quietly closed her eyes. He said that she was smiling.

Russell Meets the Police Chief

Russell Poe was surprised to discover that the thin, tired-looking man whom he had seen every now and then around Wellsboro was the Chief of Police. He had always assumed that Chief Davis was an auxiliary officer or a school crossing guard. Even at the last minute, just as Russell heard the lazy "Yeah, come on in" in response to his knock on the door to the Chief's inner office, Russell had expected a fat, doughnut-munching cop with a uniform shirt that was three sizes too small and who was half hidden behind an old oak desk piled with case folders and reports.

"Chief Davis?" he confirmed. "I'm Russell Poe. I called you yesterday about Jack Abrams."

"Sure, Mr. Poe," Ray replied standing and holding out his hand. "Please, make yourself comfortable." He smiled broadly, but his eyes looked flat somehow and very tired, even though it was only ten o'clock in the morning.

"I would offer you some of our station house coffee, but there are too many forms to fill out whenever a civilian gets sick on it."

Russell instantly liked Ray Davis. He sat down in a visitor's chair across the glass and steel desk from the Chief. His chair was identical to the Chief's. The room was lit entirely by daylight from the windows behind and on one side, with no curtains and their venetian blinds pulled all the way to the top. The modern, glass-top desk was almost empty, except for a single closed file folder almost perfectly centered on it and a sharpened pencil alongside it. Davis sat down and swiveled in his chair in one motion, turning to the telephone on the credenza behind his desk. The credenza was empty except for the telephone and photographs of two women, whom Russell assumed to be the Chief's wife and daughter. The only other decorations in the office were two diplomas on the wall above the credenza: a Bachelor of Arts degree from Cornell and a Master's Degree in Criminal Justice from Penn State.

"Sergeant Washington," he said. Russell assumed that he was speaking to the officer who occupied a desk by the front door and had greeted Russell when he arrived. "No calls or interruptions, please."

"With you in just a second." Davis stood up, walked over to a steel filing cabinet, placed the file folder in it, and returned to his desk, which was now completely empty, except for the pencil.

"Little rule of mine," he said, his voice seeming almost apologetic. "Never have anything on your desk to distract you from the matter at hand."

"That's a good rule," Russell said. "I wish I had your self-discipline."

"Believe me, Mr. Poe, it is not easy. If I gave into my natural personality, you wouldn't be able to see me across the desk because of all the paper I'd have piled on it."

"Mr. Poe," Chief Davis continued, "I guess I haven't had the chance to officially welcome you to the area. I understand from Mrs. Abrams that you took over your uncle's place some time ago. I can't say that I knew your uncle very well. He lived outside our department's jurisdiction, out there in Richmond Township, and pretty much kept to himself. But I never heard anyone say anything against him, so I guess that's pretty good.

"I also owe you a long-overdue apology for not getting in touch with you sooner to thank you for rescuing that boy back in January. I read the report on it. We get copies here in Wellsboro of any reports about any police activity anywhere in the county. You saved his life. I wish we had more folks like you."

"What became of him?"

"Last I heard, he was released from the hospital and just went away, disappeared. They're not even sure of his name, and they didn't have a verified address for him. But there was no legal reason to hold him against his will after he recovered."

"Did he ever say what happened to him?"

"Not a word. He claimed he had no idea how he ended up in the hospital, didn't even remember you rescuing him."

"That's unusual, isn't it, Chief."

"Not really. You'd be surprised.

"So, Mr. Poe," Chief Davis continued, pulling himself closer to his desk and folding his hands on it. "I understand from Mrs. Abrams that you want to talk about Jack Abrams' death. She called me several days ago about it."

"That's right, Chief, but my name is Russell."

"Mine's Ray, then."

"Well, Ray, I'm sort of glad you haven't had the opportunity to welcome me in any official capacity." The two men laughed. "Although I understand that a guy who does odd jobs on my property, Whitey Wentworth, is a regular customer of yours."

"Well, Russell, you know I can't really talk about that." Ray smiled and shook his head.

"No problem, Ray. He's always had good things to say about you."

"I'm glad to hear that. We always want satisfied customers here."

"So, to get to the point, I understand that your department investigated Jack Abrams' death."

"Yes," Ray said slowly. He glanced down. His smile disappeared.

"Did I say something wrong?"

"No, no. Of course not. As you might already know, we coordinated with the Richmond Township police, since Jack was – since it happened in their jurisdiction. At first, there was some question about that, because, as you know, the northern part of your property actually is in Tioga Township.

"So, we just supported them because of the need to involve the Coroner's office and we had a little more manpower to throw at it, especially on the crime scene investigation, than the two-officer department you have up there where you live."

"Weren't the State Police involved?" Russell interrupted. "I thought that they would automatically take jurisdiction in a suspected homicide in one of the smaller counties like Tioga."

"Not always," Ray answered quickly. "The State Police will assume jurisdiction only if there's clear evidence of foul play, so they left it to us to do the preliminary investigation. Chief Verona –

he's the Richmond Township Chief of Police – and I were pretty confident that we could handle it between our two departments, along with the County Coroner's office. We used the State Police crime lab, of course, but it didn't turn up anything unusual. And all those cops and a few volunteers from the community scoured that forest for a good hundred yards in every direction and found zilch, not even an old beer bottle.

"But before I go any further," he continued, "could I ask what your interest might be in Jack's death? I thought the estate had been probated years ago."

Russell was about to tell Ray that he was semi-retired from practice, but he decided not to mention it. For some reason he couldn't articulate to himself, he didn't want to give the Police Chief that assurance, not just now.

"That's true, Ray, and I'm not aware of any problems with the estate. But Wanda has asked me to help bring some closure for her about Jack's death – just as a friend, you understand."

"And as her attorney?" A trace of a smile appeared briefly at the corners of Ray's mouth. Russell had heard that tone and seen that smile before in his career. He had to act quickly before Davis started erecting defenses.

"No," Russell said, "I'm not acting as anyone's legal representative, not hers and not for the estate. At least not now."

"I see." Ray shifted in his chair. He looked at Russell for a moment and then glanced in the direction of the window to Russell's left. Russell followed Ray's eyes, wondering what Ray was looking at in the parking lot.

"I hadn't realized that you and Wanda are friends," Ray finally said after a few more seconds of silence.

Russell was surprised. "Well, *neighbors* is more accurate maybe, but, yes, I guess that she's a friend, too. Look, Ray, I'm just trying to tie up a few loose ends is all, trying to help her answer a few questions. I'm not trying to reopen the investigation."

"Well, let me tell you this right now, Russell. Even though we might no longer be actively investigating, we never actually close an investigation in a death case until we're satisfied that we know all the answers. The Coroner's report says that in Doc Murphy's opinion death was caused by an animal attack; 'consistent with wolves,' it says. But, you know, Russell, this case has never been closed in my mind, not beyond a reasonable doubt. I don't know what that doubt is, to be honest with you, but I still hope that somehow, someday, we'll find out what really happened up there at Simon Poe's place."

"My place."

"Right, your place."

There were several seconds of silence as the two men looked at each other across the empty desk. Russell noticed for the first time how the sunlight streaming in from the side windows was refracted somehow through the glass top of Ray's desk, making a faint spectrum pattern on the light gray carpet below. Looking back up at Ray, Russell began to think that he understood the tired look in Ray's eyes, a look of mental weariness, perhaps even moral tiredness, the look of a still relatively young man who felt that he had simply seen too much in his life.

"Ray, all I want are some facts and some objective perspectives. I mean I could track it all down, search the newspaper records and the files at the Coroner's office, talk to people who knew Jack, but that would be a little silly, wouldn't you say, since you've already done all that?"

"Not necessarily, Mr. Poe. That's always your right."

I'm losing him, Russell thought.

"Ray, it seems to me like you're getting a little defensive about this, and I don't understand why. I'm not suggesting that you or anyone else did an unprofessional investigation or even made any mistakes. And I really appreciate your candor about your own lingering thoughts."

"Lingering thoughts, as you call them, Russell, are part of good police work. Any cop who has no lingering thoughts about a case is a fool."

"So, Ray, please let me reiterate that I'm not interested in reopening an investigation or trying to make a big deal of it. I'm just trying to help a friend bring some closure to her tragedy."

"But what's Wanda's interest in all this? I know that she asked me to speak with you, and I guess that's good enough authorization for this conversation. But why – and I don't mean any disrespect, Russell – why would she want a lawyer to look into this?"

"That's between me and –" Russell had started to say *my client*. "Between me and Mrs. Abrams. But I can say this. She is still trying to make sense of it all, how it happened, and perhaps even why."

"Okay, Russell," Ray said. "I accept that you just want to help, and I accept that I might have been a little defensive back there a few moments ago. I'm sorry for that. But, being a lawyer, you must understand that we can't just talk about ongoing cases to just anyone."

"So, the case really is ongoing?"

Ray looked stunned for a moment. His voice had resumed its slow, cautious tone.

"Well, officially, it's still an open case, just like I said, unless Richmond Township closed it – technically it's their case. But they would have notified us since we're assisting, and Chief Verona and I have an understanding that until we can definitely rule out foul play, we're keeping it open.

"The reality, however, is that we exhausted every lead, we looked at every piece of evidence, we even spent almost two weeks scouring that mountain of your uncle's – I mean yours. I still have my doubts, but we could find not even what you lawyers call a scintilla of evidence of foul play. But if we turned up anything like that – today, next month, next year, even twenty years from now – we'd be on it in a heartbeat.

"But, let me ask you this, Russell. Does Wanda think we're still actively investigating it? That poor woman." Ray looked down.

"That's not the point, Ray. I'm just trying to assemble all the facts for her, not just a bunch of rumors."

"You mean the wolves?"

"So, it really was a wolf attack?"

"Well, that's not exactly what the Coroner's findings were. As I think I said before, the injuries were *consistent with* a wolf attack. He never said that it was a wolf attack."

"He couldn't rule out a wolf attack. I understand," Russell said.

The phone rang. Ray answered it.

"Yeah, just a minute." He put his hand on the mouthpiece and looked at Russell.

Before Ray said could say anything, Russell spoke up.

"Would you like me to let you take that? I can come back some other time."

"Not necessary," Ray gave a faint smile. "I'm sorry, but I have to take this in private. It will just take a minute. If you don't mind."

Russell waited outside Ray's office in the more traditionally furnished small-town police department reception area, studying the wanted posters on an ancient clipboard with two large metal loops at the top. Some of them dated back more than five years. Russell wondered how many of them were still at large.

He jumped slightly when he heard Ray's voice just behind him.

"See anyone you know?" Ray chuckled.

"I sure wouldn't want to know any of these guys," Russell replied, hanging the clipboard back up on the tarnished hook. It gave slightly under the clipboard's weight, so Russell kept his hand under the clipboard until he was sure it would hold.

"Listen, Russell." Ray's voice sounded friendlier again. "I don't want you to leave with any bad impressions. I'll be happy to answer any questions I can, but first I need to pull the full case file and check my notes. Like I say, there may be some things I can't tell you, either because I don't know or it's still confidential. But I'll do everything that I can.

"Since you're asking for official records and some of them are protected by privacy regulations, I'll need to get a written authorization from Mrs. Abrams – you know, paper for paper. I can have someone drop it off at her place – no, I'll run it out there myself. She deserves that, at least. Can we get back together in a couple of days?"

"When?"

"I'll need to check out a few things with my schedule and, of course, find the case file." Ray chuckled. "My desk might look neat, but you have no idea what our file room looks like. That's why some of us wear sidearms in the office, in case we ever have to go in there."

"I'll appreciate any help you can give me, Chief."

"I'll call you when I'm ready," Ray promised. "But I do need to dig out the file and check a few things."

"I'll appreciate any help you can give me, Ray," Russell repeated.

"Yeah, well, I guess you have a right to know, since it happened on your property."

Russell offered his hand to Ray to say goodbye, but Ray had already returned to his office and closed the door. Russell stared at the closed door for a moment, then turned and slowly walked past the desk sergeant, who smiled and said, "Have a great day." As Russell walked out into the afternoon sun, he wondered why it had seemed so much brighter in the Chief's office, even with the lights off.

Old Photographs and Memories at the Manse

"Over here, around the side."

Russell Poe heard what he assumed to be Bill Paxton's voice, but he looked around, unable to see where it was coming from. He stood by the red front door to the church, which he had already found locked. Paxton seemed to be calling from a side entrance, but which one?

A moment later, Bill Paxton appeared from behind a large rhododendron to Russell's left. The first buds of the coming spring's growth were already dotting the dark green leaves from previous years.

"Over here, Mr. Poe."

Russell grinned and walked quickly over to where Paxton was standing. At least, Russell assumed that the smiling middle-aged man in a cabled sweater and jeans was Bill Paxton, even though he was not what Russell had imagined. When he drew within two paces of the bush, Russell extended his right hand, expecting Paxton to come forward. Instead, he remained on the other side of the rhododendron.

"Hello, Reverend." Russell tried to drop his hand unobtrusively. Paxton didn't seem to notice. "Thanks for seeing me this afternoon. I know it's late in the day."

"Please, call me Bill. Everyone else does. Reverend is too churchy, like I'm better than anyone else and I hate *Pastor Bill* – it sounds like I should be hustling money on TV from little old ladies. Just plain Bill is good enough." Paxton smiled but stayed behind the bush.

"Hi, Bill. Pleased to meet you. My name's Russell."

"Yeah, I know. I'm glad to meet you at last. I had heard you moved into your uncle's old place some time ago. I had thought about paying a call on you, but never got around to it."

"To recruit me?" Russell asked, only half-joking.

"No, that's not our style. Since you had moved into my family's old place, I just wanted to come by and say a special hello. But I guess you beat me to it."

Russell stepped around to Paxton's side of the bush and they shook hands.

"Come on back to the Manse," Paxton said.

Bill Paxton turned and led Russell across the lawn along the eastern side of the small brick church. Russell glanced in through the tall, clear windows. The sunlight, streaming in the windows on the other side of the church and through the sanctuary, allowed only squared-off silhouettes – pews and pillars, Russell assumed – to be seen. All else was softly engulfed by the faint red tones of the late afternoon light. It reminded Russell of a picture he had once seen of the skyline of a medieval town in the hill country of Tuscany, where each petty noble tried to outdo his equally mad rivals by building the tallest tower, from which each could feel secure, watching for the approach of enemies, both real and imagined.

They entered what looked like it once had been the front door to a cottage. It was attached to the main church, which looked like a tumor that had grown from the house and eventually overwhelmed it.

"Here it is," Paxton glanced over his shoulder as he opened the door and stepped in ahead of Poe to turn on the lights. "We call it the Manse, but it's hardly what Nathaniel Hawthorne had in mind."

"Yeah," Russell responded. "No moss and not that old."

"Right." Paxton smiled. He seemed pleased that Russell caught his literary reference. "But it's home and more than enough room for me."

"No family?"

"Nope, I'm not really a confirmed bachelor. I just have never found a woman who will put up with me," Bill laughed.

"Me neither," Russell said as he followed Paxton into a small foyer, not much larger than a pantry. There was a cork bulletin board on the wall opposite the door, but it held only thumb tacks.

"The sanctuary's through there," Bill said, pointing to the right as he turned sharply to the left and into a large room with folding chairs stacked along one of the walls.

"Actually, this part that we're standing in right now was the original part of the church. It was just a two-bedroom bungalow that one of our founders left to the church. Until then we just met in our members' homes, including here.

"We were given this house about ten years ago and made it into our first permanent home. Edna Folkes, the lady who left us the property, said that she had come to think of her living room as a holy place, because she took her turn, just like all the others, hosting our services. In fact, back when this area was Mrs. Folkes' living room, we held services right in here. I don't know for sure, but this may have been where our church held its very first service."

"So, you haven't been the pastor for the whole time?" Russell asked. "For some reason I assumed that you were the founder of the church."

"Not exactly. I didn't become associated with them until after they had been meeting informally among themselves for some time. Mountain View Chapel started out as a Bible study group made up of people from several different churches in the area. I came along a little later, just when they were beginning to hold their first services on Sunday evenings. At that time, they took turns performing the various roles in the service: selecting the scripture reading, leading prayers, and giving short talks. They asked me to help them get things organized and more formal, so I sort of became their pastor by consensus, I guess.

"So, once Mrs. Folkes passed away" Bill continued, "and we took possession of her house, we tore out the wall between the old living room and the old dining room and made it into our first real sanctuary. We did all the work ourselves, on Saturdays and sometimes in the evening. We still use this area for Sunday School and small informal meetings.

"Eventually we raised enough money to add the new section in front, which now is our sanctuary. When we did that, the congregation invited me to move into the old part, which still had the living room, where we're standing now, and the original bathroom, kitchen, and two bedrooms."

Bill led Russell through a sliding wooden door into a small kitchen, crossed it, and entered a short hallway with a room on either side. At the end of the hallway, Russell could see through an open door into a bathroom with old fixtures.

Paxton paused at a doorway on the left side of the corridor. He reached into a room, and flipped a light switch, looked inside as if checking to see if anyone was there, and then entered.

Paxton's study was slightly smaller than Russell's bedroom. What used to be a heavy walnut dining room table served as a desk. Books were piled on it, as well as on the floor surrounding it on three sides. Almost every square inch of the walls was covered with photos and prints. Russell thought that he even saw several of his own house, taken a long time ago, with small groups of people in front.

"Here we go, Russell. Welcome, and God bless the mess."

Paxton turned around to face Russell, like a tour guide addressing a group that had just entered another room in the castle.

"This was Mrs. Folkes' bedroom, but now, as you can see, it's my study. I use the smaller bedroom."

Paxton headed for the other side of the table. Russell aimed for a chair just in front of the desk, but Paxton stopped suddenly, and waved his hand back and forth over the cluttered desktop. The wind from his hand shifted several sheets of paper off the neat piles where they had been stacked.

"No, we'd better sit over by the window." Paxton gestured toward a pale-yellow cane-back rocking chair along the left wall. Russell started toward it, and then paused, expecting Paxton to wheel his desk chair over. Instead, Bill picked up four or five books that were on a cushioned window seat, tossed the books onto the floor, and sat in the window.

"Well, enough of the two-cent tour, Russell. I just 'love to tell the story' as the old hymn goes."

"Well, you must be proud of all that you've accomplished."

"Hey, Russell, I'm not supposed to be proud. Ultimately, it was the Lord who gave us all these things. But I am proud of our stewardship of the Lord's gifts."

"So, how many people belong to your congregation?"

"We have just over a hundred on the rolls, and unlike too many churches today, most of them attend services more or less regularly. Oh, some can't come every week, I understand that. But we almost always have forty to sixty on a good Sunday, and some of those come back Sunday night for Vespers.

"But I'm monopolizing the conversation, Russell. I'm sorry. How can I help you? You said that it had to do with some historical research?"

"Well, partly, Bill. As you may not know, I'm interested in history. I've published one small book and am researching another one on the French and Indian War."

Paxton sat up, like someone who wanted to demonstrate how interested he was.

"Wow, the French and Indian War. You've certainly come to the right part of the country." He sounded impressed.

"I didn't really come here about that, though. You see, I am also doing some research on local history around Wellsboro, particularly some of the old folklore, sort of finishing the work that Jack Abrams started before he died. I've become simply fascinated by it."

"Well, Russell, we do have a lot of local history here. I really have never had that much to do with it, though. I've been too busy with the Chapel. Some of it, I have to tell you, is pretty wild for a sleepy place like Wellsboro. There used to be some pretty unsavory people around here. Still are, perhaps."

"Well, Bill, let's just say some of it is very colorful. And I didn't even know anything at all about this area until about a year ago, when I moved up here. Northern Pennsylvania was just a big blank space on my mental map."

"Well, we've been hiding up here in these mountains for some time now, Russell. I'm still not clear how I can help you, though. Have you checked with the county historical society?"

"Oh, I plan to stop by someday when I'm in town and they're open. But getting back to you, Bill, one of the things that interests me is what you could tell me about the house I live in. As you mentioned when we met outside, it's your family's old homestead. And I noticed several old photos of it on your wall."

Russell pointed as he got up and started to walk toward one of the photographs he noticed when he entered the room. Bill stood quickly and stepped behind him as he looked at the photograph.

"Yes, I was right. That's my place. How old is this picture, Bill?"

Russell turned around and was surprised to see Paxton standing so close behind him. Bill was smiling. Russell could almost see the memories playing across his face.

"Yes, that's the old home place," he said. His voice was almost a whisper. "It's yours now, of course, but that was home to my family for generations.

"The central part of the house was built sometime after the Revolutionary War. We bought it when we moved up here from downstate sometime in the 1820s. I once knew the date for sure, but, if you are interested, you might be able to look it up at the Courthouse. I think that it was just a log cabin when we bought it, and we added to it over the years.

"Now, I think that picture was taken around the turn of the century. I could be wrong. There's nothing there that really dates it."

"Well," Russell said, pointing to both pictures, "you can see wagon tracks alongside the house, right there."

"That's true, Russell, but wagon tracks around here don't mean very much. Some folks were still using horse-drawn wagons out in the country as late as thirty years ago. I remember that the road that our place – your place –is on wasn't even paved until around 1970 or so, and then only up to that bend at near the top of the hill, right beyond your driveway.

"But I think this picture was made around the turn of the century, judging from the clothing those two women are wearing; but, again, I could be mistaken. This area has never been a capital of high fashion." Bill chuckled and looked down at his feet, as if he were remembering a funny family story.

"So, is that your family, Bill?"

Paxton leaned over Russell's shoulder and peered at the picture, as if he had never really inspected it closely before. Russell moved sideways until Paxton was no longer standing directly behind him, then he walked back to the rocking chair.

Paxton stood in front of the wall of pictures, facing Russell. He took a pen from his shirt pocket to use as a pointer.

"I think that one of the two old gentlemen with long white beards is my great-grandfather, Samuel Paxton. I could be wrong about that, because he died in 1898. But, if I'm right, that would have to date these photos no later than 1898. You'll notice that both of these guys show up in one other picture.

Russell returned to the wall and peered at the two photos that Bill had pointed out.

"You're right, Bill," he said. "They're the same two guys. But you don't know which one is Samuel?"

"I have a hunch," Bill replied, "but only by process of elimination." Paxton pointed to the shorter of the two white-bearded men posing in front of the Paxton house.

"This old gent also shows up in this photo." Paxton pointed to a badly cracked photograph of a man wearing a knee-length overcoat and a knit cap. His beard was longer, but it looked like the same man. He carried what Russell guessed was an early nineteenth-century Pennsylvania long rifle. He carried two large sacks, one slung diagonally over each shoulder. He was standing by a river or a large stream. He had a surprised expression on his face.

"Now, I have a hunch that this picture was taken sometime well after the turn of the century. If you look very closely," Paxton tapped on the glass covering the picture, "you can see what looks like an old car on the bridge in the background.

"If it's the same man," Russell continued, "then it couldn't be your great-grandfather."

"Right, because we didn't have automobiles around here until at least 1910 or 1915," Bill said.

"So, your great-grandfather would have been gone by then."

"Yes, we know that he passed away in '98. That's why I think the other old bearded man in the older pictures at our house was my great-grandfather."

"Nice deductive reasoning, Bill. And these other people in the photos by the house, are they your family?"

"I don't think so, Russell." Bill moved the tip of his pen back and forth between the two photographs. "Except for the two old guys, they're all different.

"I can remember as a boy visiting my grandfather there – his name was Walter Paxton – and sometimes there were a lot of strangers there. Well, for a kid they seemed like a lot of people, but probably never more than eight or ten. My grandfather sometimes would introduce them as his friends, and sometimes he wouldn't introduce them at all. I was just a kid then, and I guess I was expected to play outside and not pester the grownups. Sometimes one or two of my cousins would be there and we'd all usually just go up into the woods and come back in when we heard my grandmother ring the old dinner bell she had outside the kitchen. Sometimes I'd just go by myself, which really was more fun.

"The family had a lot more land back in those days than what you have now. It used to stretch almost all the way to the New York state line," Paxton continued. "I can remember sometimes getting lost up in those woods, but I would always keep within hearing range of the dinner bell and just rely on it to lead me back.

"But my grandfather sold off most of the family's land to a timber company in the 1920s. He kept just the hills right behind the house, what you have now."

"Where the Rocks are."

"Yeah," Bill said slowly. "The Rocks. Well, the good news was that the timber company went bankrupt in the Crash of 1929 before it had a chance to cut a single tree. The state took over the land during the Depression, and it's been part of the State Game Lands ever since. Except for the recreational area that the Civilian Conservation Corps built during the Depression, and a couple of boat docks, most of it is still as it was when my grandfather sold it."

"Did your grandfather ever try to get the land back?"

"Not that I know of. I guess he felt that he'd gotten a fair price for land that he was never going to use, and as far as he was concerned, the state could keep it.

"I know that my mother always said that the land was more trouble than it was worth."

"Do you know what she meant by that?"

"Not really." Paxton turned and glanced out the window behind him. "Maybe she just had a lot of bad memories associated with the Paxton family.

"I'm sorry if I sound a little vague about this, Russell. One thing to keep in mind is that the Paxton family all fell apart when my grandfather died. My father inherited the family place but didn't want it. Instead, shortly after my grandfather's death, he abandoned my mother and me and went to California with his girlfriend. When the estate finally sold the place about two years later, the money went straight to him. My mother never saw a penny of it.

"But the last time I ever set foot in my grandfather's house was when my mother and I went to collect any personal items that we wanted. I was eleven at the time. All I really wanted was the old dinner bell, but it was already gone."

"You said that your grandfather sold off most of his land in the 1920s. Do you know why he kept the Rocks? They're a good half-mile from the house, up and over the ridge."

Paxton was silent for almost thirty seconds, his head down, his eyes staring at the floor. Finally, he looked up and shrugged.

"Don't know, Russell. Walter Paxton was a bit eccentric, I guess. Maybe he thought he could develop the Rocks into some kind of a tourist attraction. I don't know. What I do remember is that my mother was kind of obsessed with them. When we would visit my grandfather and I'd go out into the woods to explore, my mother always warned me to stay away from the Rocks. She would never say why."

"I can think of no stronger invitation –" Russell started to say.

"Than a prohibition?" Bill finished the sentence, smiling. "You're right, Russell. As soon as she said that, I'd be racing up that hill to the Rocks. But, you know, once I got there, I was always disappointed."

"How so?"

"Well, they were just a bunch of overgrown rocks in the woods. The romance quickly wore off."

Paxton slowly returned to the window seat. As he sat, he leaned back, spreading his arms out to either side along the windowsill. The branches of the oak trees outside the window had a faint green haze from the emerging leaves, trimmed with yellow from the afternoon sun. They surrounded Paxton's head in the window, almost like a crown. Paxton's face was hidden in shadow, gray and hard like a statue. His eyes were partly closed.

Russell broke the silence. "This is a great chair, Bill."

"Thanks. It belonged to my grandmother, Walter's wife." Paxton's eyes remained closed. Only his lips moved very slightly as he spoke. "In fact, it might have been her mother's before that. I don't know. It was always in my grandfather's house as long as I can remember."

"It's in great shape. Has it been restored?"

"Not as long as I've had it. Besides, that would destroy all the memories, somehow."

"The memories?"

Paxton finally opened his eyes.

"One of the earliest memories of my life is spending afternoons in that chair, sitting on my grandmother's lap after lunch on hot summer afternoons. Grandma would give me the best lemonade in the world, and then I'd climb up into her lap. She'd rock very slowly, very faintly, as she read me a story. I'd doze off and when I woke up, she would still be reading.

"Every time I sit in that chair, Russell, I go back to those hot summer afternoons, my very first memories, so long ago." Bill closed his eyes and slowly inhaled, holding his breath for several seconds before exhaling completely.

"Sorry," he said after a moment, "Sorry, I was having a Tao moment just then."

"A Tao moment?"

"It's a concept from Taoism – you know, the ancient Chinese religion. It's a moment when one is connected to the elemental forces of the universe, what they call the Tao. It's kind of like a prayer state, but you're listening, not pestering God with some problem or complaint. You're connected with something that the Chinese believe is even older and deeper than God."

Russell thought that this was an odd concept coming from someone whom he had assumed to be a Bible-thumping preacher. He thought about saying something but didn't want to get sidetracked into religion.

"Well, that's okay, Bill. Everyone should have memories like that. Sometimes it's memories like yours, Bill, that are the best realities. I wish I had more of them."

Bill rotated his shoulders, keeping his arms on the windowsill.

"So, Russell, getting back to business: You want to know all about the history of your place?"

"Well, yes. Of course, as I said, I was interested in your family's involvement, especially any family stories about the Rocks."

Paxton sat up erect, his arms dropping from the windowsill as he placed his hands on his thighs, the fingers pointing inward.

"That's easier said than done, Russell. I don't know what's history and what's just old ghost stories. As far as I know, they were there when the house was built, right after the Revolutionary War. That was before my family came here."

"I found one reference to the Rocks in an old book in the library."

"The library over at the state university?"

"No, the township library. The book was published in 1882. It concluded that they were made by European settlers, because the Indians were too primitive to have built anything like them."

Paxton leaned back and once again stretched out his arms along the windowsill behind him.

"Russell, you'll hear as many different stories around here as there are people in these mountains. All I know is that they're probably some sort of a more or less natural grouping that some old ridge-runner nudged around a little to make them look man-made, and therefore mysterious."

"Sounds like a lot of work just for a hoax."

"I can say this, Russell, because I was born and raised here. There are a lot of strange folks around here who would do just that, just for the sake of doing it and maybe someday fooling some educated stranger like yourself."

"I don't think it's as simple as that, do you, Bill? Really?"

Paxton got up and walked over to a battered barrister's bookcase. He peered through the glass doors as he spoke.

"Have you ever heard of the so-called Viking Mill up in Newport?"

"Rhode Island?"

"Yes, that's the one."

Russell paused for a second. "Sure. I think so. Isn't that the round stone tower that some people say was built by the Vikings hundreds of years before Columbus?"

"That's it, Russell. Now they've done excavations and researched the thing to death. There's not a shred of evidence that it was of Viking origin. There's a Norse influence, to be sure, but it's almost identical to seventeenth-century mills in northeastern England, which was the area that the Danes ruled for several hundred years in the Middle Ages. There's no artifact that's been found anywhere near it that is more than three hundred years old."

"So how does this relate to the Rocks, Bill? They're not Viking."

"No, they're not. But here's the point, Russell. Anyone who knows anything at all about the Viking Tower knows that it can't possibly have been built by the Vikings. But you can't convince the folks in Newport of that. And these aren't a bunch of ignorant rubes, Russell. But they still want to pretend that it's Viking because they want to believe that it's special, and that they're special because they live in a special place."

"I think I know what you mean, Bill. Instead of being able to prove that the stone tower is Viking, the true believers just say, 'Prove that it isn't.'"

Paxton returned to the window seat.

"I thought I had a book in the bookcase there about all these so-called ancient sites in America. I must have loaned it to someone.

Anyways, the Rocks are the same thing as the Viking Mill in Newport. They weren't built by the Indians, not unless the Indians had compasses and rulers."

"You're aware of the measurements?" Russell thought he was the only one who had ever bothered to measure the stone circle. Bill Paxton looked surprised.

"Well, not really," he said, "Just a lucky guess. Maybe I heard it somewhere."

Something is wrong, Russell thought. He decided to press on just a little further.

"From your family?"

"Must have been. Maybe from my grandfather. He was always going up to the Rocks. Maybe he had measured them and told me about it."

Paxton turned and glanced over his shoulder, out the window.

"Thought I heard someone," he explained, turning back to face Russell. "Listen, Russell, when I was a kid, I'd run around all over that mountain. My cousins and I sometimes would play hide and seek all around the stone circle. The Rocks are just a bunch of overgrown boulders that someone arranged in a circle. Who knows who did it or why? And who really cares?"

Paxton sounded annoyed. Russell responded in what he hoped was a conciliatory tone. He rose and walked over to a group of pictures on the wall. He looked at them intently as he spoke.

"I'm sorry to keep harping on it, Bill. It's just that a year ago, I didn't even know this place existed, and now I own some mysterious rock formation up in the woods. And every time I ask someone about them, I hear a slightly different story. You wouldn't believe what I've heard, or maybe you would, having grown up here. Some of it is pretty crazy, too: space aliens, ancient Egyptians, Druids."

"Druids? That's a new one."

When Russell turned to look at Paxton, he was surprised that Bill wasn't smiling.

"Where'd you hear that one, Russell? You're right. I've heard all sorts of tales, too, but never one about Druids."

"I don't remember exactly," Russell lied. "I think I came across it in Jack Abrams' stuff."

"Jack's stuff? Oh, you mean those notebooks he was collecting?"

"Yeah, you know about them?"

"Well, sure, Russell. Jack had talked to just about everyone in this part of the state over the years. He interviewed me several times. I didn't know that Wanda still had his notebooks."

"She still does. She let me borrow them recently."

"Interesting. I'd just assumed that Wanda had given them to a historical society or something after Jack died. I know she was really broken up over Jack's death."

"No, Bill. She kept them."

"Why would she give them to you? I mean, if you don't mind my asking. I'm just curious, is all."

"No problem. She knew I was interested in history and thought I might find Jack's work interesting. I'm going to try to get them organized. I may even try to track down some of the facts behind the legends. I want to get them published in Jack's name, posthumously."

"That's really nice of you, Russell. I know that will mean a lot to Wanda."

"You know Wanda well, then?"

Bill rubbed the tip of his index finger quickly back and forth across the grain of the fabric in the thigh of his jeans. It seemed loud, like a crosscut saw, in the quiet room.

"No, not really. She's not a member of our congregation, but everyone around here knows the Welcome Wagon lady. And I expect she probably knows more people than I do.

"But," Bill continued, "I think it's great what you're doing for Wanda, and for Jack's memory, of course. Let me know how I can help. It was a shame he never got to publish his book."

Both men sat quietly, looking past each other, for a moment. The greens in the leafy background behind Bill Paxton's head had turned darker; only the thinnest lines of reddish gold outlined each leaf. Bill's eyes were downcast, and for a moment Russell wondered if Bill was nodding off to sleep or praying.

"Well, Bill, I don't want to take much more of your time. I keep getting off the track."

"No problem. It's really interesting to get this chance to talk with you."

Bill stood up and stretched his arms straight above him.

"But first, Russell, I need to get to the kitchen and get us something to drink. I'm being a lousy host. It's an occupational hazard of being a bachelor preacher, I suppose."

"How's that?"

"I'm always the guest and never the host. What can I get you, though?"

"Whatever you're having is fine."

"Then it's a cold beer, okay?"

"But to get to the point, Bill," Russell continued after Bill returned and handed him a bottle of beer with a paper napkin wrapped around it. "Which is that I could really use any help you could give me about some of the recurring themes I hear around here – in the old legends, I mean."

"Why me, Russell? I'm glad to help however I can, but I'm no expert."

"That may be, Bill, but your family has been in this area as long as anyone's. You know a lot of people. A number of folks have told me that I should really talk to you. Maybe you can help me connect the dots, and, believe me, Jack left a lot of dots – thirty-nine notebooks full of them."

The conversation appeared to Russell to be drawing to a close, at least as far as Bill was concerned. The two men drank their beers silently. Russell, who hated beer, nonetheless commented on how refreshing it was.

"Well, Bill, thanks for your time. I really enjoyed meeting you."

"I did, too," Bill replied. Bill glanced out the kitchen window and said, "Let me walk you out to your car. I need to pick up the mail and would enjoy some fresh air. Sometimes sitting in that study with all those books and old pictures gets a little close, even for me."

Russell followed Bill to the parking area. As they shook hands, Russell looked beyond Bill toward the dark green mountains rising to the west.

"You really do have a mountain view," Russell commented as he got into his car, "just like in the name of your church."

"Yeah," Bill replied, clapping him on the shoulder, "no false advertising here. What you see is what you get."

Wanda's Suspicions

Wanda sipped her wine and looked over at Russell. The long red rays from the early evening light, filtered by the ancient azalea at the end of the porch, made Russell's hair seem to light up around the edges, turning his gray hairs a deep copper color. Russell had been quiet all afternoon, ever since he arrived a few hours before. He was pleasant as always, as he returned the tools that he had borrowed from Wanda the week before, but only a part of him seemed there. Now, sitting in the old wicker porch chair, Russell seemed miles away. Wanda wondered where.

Jack would sometimes get like that. Wanda used to watch Jack when he got into one of his quiet moods, trying to guess what he was thinking. Jack sat in the same chair and looked across their front yard, watching everything that happened and yet not seeming to be really paying attention. When they were first married, and still lived back on Long Island, Wanda used to worry that there was some problem that Jack didn't want to share, didn't want to burden her with. But there almost never was. When Jack was worried, he almost never held back, Wanda soon learned. Most of the time when it looked like Jack was watching the rust spread on the old iron gate at the front of their house, he probably was doing just that. But, at the same time, Jack's thoughts could be roaming the universe.

"What are you thinking about, Jack?" Wanda whispered to herself. She hoped that Russell hadn't heard her.

"Sorry? What did you say?" Russell murmured, still looking ahead, his eyes half-closed.

"Oh, nothing. Sorry, Russell. Just thinking out loud."

That's what Jack would say. If Wanda followed up with another question, Jack would take her on a wild ride through his mind. In those moments Wanda became a little girl again, holding her father's hand as he led her into the dinosaur hall in the natural history museum, into a world that was real, yet at the same time so distant as to not even be a memory.

Russell's eyes seemed to be fixed on a spot about half-way across the road, several hundred yards away. How many times had Jack stared at the same spot? Maybe it was one that only men could see. Wanda never understood the fascination with that invisible spot.

"Cars," Jack had responded one afternoon as he stared at the spot in the road. "I'm thinking about cars and the people in them."

"What about them?"

Wanda remembered how she had felt the same tingle that she had felt at the doorway to the dinosaur hall. It was a hot afternoon in the city, but even without air conditioning, the museum was cool and quiet. Just beyond the doorway everything was a damp gray color, inviting Wanda and scaring her at the same time.

"Just think," Jack had said. "Just think. When a stranger drives by, that may be our one chance ever, in all eternity, to link up with his universe. Each person is a universe unto himself, Wanda. Each person lives and dies right at the very center of his universe."

"I don't think that way. Not about you, not about us."

"That's different, Wanda. Love has shifted our universes, yours to make room for me and mine to make room for you. But most people sit smack in the center of the universe and watch it whirl all around them."

Jack fell silent as another car drove by. It was a convertible, with four teenage boys in it. A quick blast of music escaped as the car disappeared up the hill and around the bend.

"There go four universes, Wanda. Just think. Four entire universes."

"I've never really thought of it that way, Jack."

Actually, Wanda had thought of it that way, long ago and not exactly in those terms, but she had thought about it. When she was fourteen, she took her first airplane trip, a long sad flight to North Carolina to attend a favorite aunt's funeral. She had never flown before, her parents always preferring to travel by car or train. This time they had no choice if they wanted to be there in time.

Wanda thought it was funny that the passenger cabin sloped uphill toward the cockpit, and she was frightened when, as the plane started its takeoff roll, the tail lifted off the tailwheel, pitching her forward just before the plane became airborne. She forced herself to look out the window, just in time to see La Guardia Airport and, beyond that, Long Island stretching out to the east, into the glare of the morning haze.

Everything and everyone I know and love are down there, she thought.

Wanda had never seen a dead person before. That evening she stared into the coffin, trying to imagine that the waxy statue in it had once been her Aunt Mary.

The whole world, everything she knew, everything that existed for her, is gone. I'm gone, too.

For many nights after that, Wanda would lie awake wondering about the universe and whether it would survive after she died. In time, she realized that she didn't fear death, but ever after she felt incredibly sad about it. Now, so many years closer to the destruction of her universe, Wanda still thought about it.

"You seem a million miles away, Wanda."

Wanda looked up, startled. Russell even sounded a little like Jack. She turned her head and smiled.

"I guess I was. A whole universe away."

"Anything you'd care to share?"

Wanda hesitated.

"Or not," he smiled. Wanda had never seen that particular smile on Russell before. In fact, she couldn't remember having ever seen Russell smile, not a deep sincere smile that comes from inside. At most Russell would just flash a quick, shallow grin, now and then. This was the first time she had ever seen him truly smile.

"Oh, Russell, I was just sitting here thinking about things. Missing Jack, I suppose. We used to sit out here of an evening, a lot like you and I are doing now. We'd have a little snack, sometimes instead of supper, and sometimes a little wine, and watch night fall together."

The smile faded but didn't altogether disappear. Russell shifted in his chair, his eyes remaining fixed on Wanda. He nodded his head slightly, almost sadly.

"I'm sorry, Wanda," he said at last. "Maybe I should go, if you'd like to be alone."

Don't go, Wanda thought. But I'm afraid to allow you to stay. This is so nice, and it hurts so deeply at the same time.

"No, no." Wanda waved the hand holding the almost-empty glass of wine. The last few drops churned around the sides of the glass, magnifying the movement of her hand. It caught her eye.

"I'm just a little confused tonight, Russell," she said. "I guess I'm like the wine in the bottom of this glass."

Russell looked at her, his smile completely faded. He looked worried.

"I don't understand, Wanda."

"Never mind."

"But," she said as she reached over and slapped him on the forearm, "tell me about your work with Jack's material. How is it coming?"

"Well, this has been a busy week. As I told you on the phone, I stopped by the police station in town and saw Chief Davis. He seemed a little reluctant at first."

"Oh, he's okay, Russell. That's just the way Ray Davis is. They say that he has a lot on his mind, what with his wife a shut-in and that wild daughter of his. But he's a good man. He was awfully kind to me when Jack died, and when I spoke with him about talking to you, he seemed like he really wanted to help any way he could."

"I sensed a little defensiveness from him at first," Russell said. "Maybe he's a little professionally suspicious of lawyers. But, after we got to know each other a little, we had a good meeting. Like you said, he struck me as really wanting to help you. He said he was going to bring you a consent form to sign, authorizing him to share the police files and reports with me."

"Oh, yes, he came by this morning," Wanda said. "He said that he enjoyed meeting you."

"Did he say anything else about the case?"

"No, Russell. In fact, he didn't even come inside when I invited him in for coffee. He seemed a little uncomfortable being there. So, we just stood on the front porch. He explained the form to me and told me that I didn't have to consent. He asked me if had any questions and whether I was sure that I wanted you to see the files. I said that I was sure, and I signed the form. He said that he would pull together the documents as soon as possible and let you see anything that you wanted."

Russell nodded. "So maybe I will have something to tell you soon. By the way, I also finally met Reverend Paxton yesterday."

"Oh? Whatever the hell for?"

"His family keeps appearing in Jack's notes and in several of the entries he wrote up in the journals. You sound like you don't approve of him, Wanda."

Wanda leaned back in her chair and looked at the porch ceiling.

"Frankly, no. I don't have much use for him."

"Why is that? He seemed to me to be a nice guy."

"Stay away from him, Russell. He's no use to you either."

"Actually, I thought he might be of a lot of use. Like I said, I noticed in some of Jack's notes that the Paxton family is mentioned from time to time, and I do live in their ancestral home."

"Well, they are one of the oldest families in the area, although maybe I should say *were.* They're all dead or moved away by now. Bill Paxton is the only one left. He and Jack used to be sort of friends, or at least good acquaintances, I think. But about three years before Jack died, he and Bill Paxton went their separate ways. They must have had some disagreement."

"Over what?"

"I don't know, and I didn't ask. I don't have much use for preachers, Russell. All most of them ever do is preach division and hate. I don't know; maybe I think that because of my upbringing. But Jack was well off without him as a friend."

"Well, some clergy are all right," Russell responded mildly. "I don't have much use for organized religion either, Wanda, but I do recognize that there are some who are tolerant and don't preach hate. Besides, Bill seemed like an honest man to me. I've heard some of the stories about his family, but he seemed okay."

Wanda felt her arms and legs tensing, trying to hold in her anger. She felt more anger toward Russell than toward Bill Paxton. Russell could be so thick sometimes.

"I think Bill Paxton had something to do with Jack's death."

There, she had said it. Wanda waited for Russell's reaction. There didn't seem to be any. Maybe he was waiting for more from her.

"I can't really say how or why, but I just feel that Paxton was involved somehow. You know right before he died, Jack was getting strange phone calls and messages. He tried to keep them from me, but I knew all the same."

"There might be some references to them in his notes, Wanda, but they look like phone numbers, nothing else. I haven't tried to check any of them out."

"Well, when you get a chance, Russell, call them. I just know that they'll lead you back to Bill Paxton.

"In fact, just a week or so before Jack died, a stranger came by our office in town and said he'd like to talk to Jack in private. Jack was out right then, and I was minding the store, answering calls and watching the desk. I remember that it was a Friday afternoon, and things were usually slow in the afternoon. We never did figure out why. We'd be up to our necks in work all morning and then around one o'clock it would all drop off. So, because it was a Friday, I was thinking about closing the office a little early, as soon as Jack came back.

"But to get back to our visitor, I asked the stranger what it was about, and said that maybe I could help him. The man said he had a question about life insurance, and someone had suggested that he speak with Jack."

"Nothing unusual about that, was there, Wanda? What did he look like – old guy, younger guy? You said he was a stranger, so you'd never seen him before, maybe around town?"

"No, Russell, I would have remembered him had I seen him before. He was older, maybe 45 or 50 years old, and real thin. His face looked like he had lived a hard life. He had long gray hair tied back and wore scruffy old clothes, like he had just come from work.

"So, I told the stranger that Jack was out, but I expected him back soon. He asked if it would be all right for him to wait until Jack returned, and I said that would be fine. He sat down across the desk from me. I tried to be pleasant to him, but he didn't want to talk."

"So how does Bill Paxton fit into all of this?"

"Well, I asked who it was that had referred him to Jack. Jack and I would always send a little thank-you note, or sometimes maybe a coupon for a free car wash, or for a free desert at the Wellsboro Diner or something like that, if someone referred a new client to us. And he said that he was new in town and said again that his pastor had recommended that he talk to Jack.

"I asked him which church he was going to, again just to make polite small talk. He thought for a moment, like he was trying to come up with the name of a church really fast. Then he said, 'Oh, it's the Mountain Church.'

"So, I said, 'Oh. Reverend Paxton's church.' But I was a little suspicious, because everyone knows that it's Mountain View, not just Mountain, and it's called a chapel, not a church."

"And he stopped for a second, like he had never heard the Paxton name before, and then smiled, 'Yeah, Reverend Paxton'."

Wanda continued to stare at the ceiling. She didn't want to look at Russell Poe, not now, not as she was sharing this with him. She didn't want to see that lawyer's skeptical look that she was sure was on his face. She had said a terrible thing about Reverend Paxton and had to follow it through.

"And how does this fit in with Jack's death?" Russell prompted quietly.

"Just about that time, Jack came back to the office. The stranger jumped up like he already knew Jack. He even greeted Jack by name."

"Did Jack know the man?"

"I don't know. Jack looked surprised, like a long-lost acquaintance – but not a friend – had come to visit unexpectedly. But at the same time, it was like Jack couldn't exactly place the man, couldn't remember when or where they had met before.

"Jack asked the man how we could help him, but the stranger insisted that they step outside to talk. That was pretty strange for someone who wanted privacy, I mean, to want to discuss his business out on the street. But Jack went outside with the man."

"Did Jack say anything to you as he left?"

"No, he just looked at me, like he wanted to say something, but didn't know whether he should in front of the man.

"So, they went outside and around to the side of the building. There's a little walkway, between our old building and the next one, that leads back to the next street. I guess they went in there. About two or three minutes later, Jack came back in through the front door.

"I asked Jack what it was all about, but he said it was just some nut case that claimed that Paxton told him the world was going to end and he wanted to buy life insurance. But I didn't believe a word of it."

"Why not?"

Wanda laughed. "Oh, Russell, where have you been all these years? That's the oldest joke there is in the insurance game. If the world comes to an end, how is anyone going to collect?"

Wanda got up and offered Russell some more wine. As she went into the kitchen and poured them each another glass, she thought that the first time she told that joke to Jack, he didn't get it either. Just before returning to the porch, the wine glasses in her hands, Wanda paused for a second and looked at Russell through the filtered silvery light of the screen door.

After Wanda had sat down, Russell asked, "Did Jack ever tell you what the man really wanted?"

"No."

"Didn't you ask Jack at all about the guy's flimsy story?"

"No. But I could read Jack's face when he came back in the office. It was a mixture of anger and fear. I asked him what was wrong, but he said, 'Nothing at all. Just a little craziness.'

"I asked him at least two more times that day, because I could tell he was bothered by something. Finally, just before bedtime, we were sitting out here on the porch, in these same chairs. I said, 'Please, Jack. If there's some kind of trouble, please let me share it.'

"'No, Wanda,' he said. 'There's no trouble. There's nothing to talk about. Forget about it.'

"And a week later they found Jack dead."

"So, how do you think Bill Paxton fits into it?" Russell was being persistent. Sometimes, just like Jack, he seizes on something and just will not let it go.

"Oh, I don't know, Russell," Wanda said letting out a long sigh. "But I really think that the stranger really was sent by Paxton with some sort of message. Maybe it was a warning of some sort."

"Did you ever ask Paxton about it?"

"Oh, Lord's sakes no. I couldn't do that. It would seem like some sort of an accusation."

"Isn't that what you're doing now? Accusing him?"

"No, I know I don't have any evidence, at least not enough to try to talk to a lawyer like you about it. But it's damned peculiar, isn't it? That's what makes me so mad. I know, I just know, that Paxton was mixed up in Jack's death, but I don't have a shred of evidence.

"And just because you think he's a nice guy, you're sitting there discounting everything that I say."

Wanda wondered how to get out of this conversation. She was beginning to sound shrill and paranoid. But Russell kept pressing in.

"You say that you know Bill Paxton. What is it about him – what has he ever done to you or Jack – that makes you suspicious? I'm not discounting you or arguing with you, Wanda; I really want to know."

"Oh, I don't know," Wanda said. "I – I just get so damned mad at times."

Wanda suddenly stood up and threw her glass toward the road. A red plume flew up behind the glass, leaving small red spots on her arms and blouse. They felt cool and calming. The glass bounced in the grass but did not break.

She looked at Russell. Why didn't he at least stand up and hold her, just a friendly gesture, just for a second? Russell sat motionless, silent, looking away.

"Oh, God, Russell. I'm sorry."

"It's okay, Wanda. It's okay."

Russell was always so calm, so much in control. He was so much like Jack. Nothing ever fazed Jack. What must it be like to go through life so totally in control?

Wanda walked silently past Russell out into the yard. She picked up the glass and walked back to the porch, studying the way the facets in the glass broke up the patterns of green from the lawn.

When Wanda returned to the porch, Russell was already standing.

"Please don't think you have to go, Russell. Not yet."

"No, Wanda, I really do. I have some things to do yet this evening."

Russell took Wanda's hand.

"Don't worry, Wanda," he said as he started down the three porch steps, gradually letting go of her hand. "We'll find out what really happened. I promise."

Wanda watched as Russell drove away. It sounded like there was a hole in his muffler, because she could hear the popping sound from his car long after he had disappeared around the bend in the road. She picked up Russell's half-full wine glass and finished the contents in a single gulp, then walked into the house, shaking her head. She felt very old tonight.

Sunday Brunch with Connie and Dick

Russell sat on his front porch, enjoying the briskness of an early Sunday morning. He had already driven into Wellsboro to claim his copy of the *New York Times* at Polk's News. The *Times* was one of the last artifacts of what Russell Poe had come to think of as his "past life." Reading the Arts and Entertainment section, he promised himself to attend several of the plays and exhibits, but, at the same time, he realized that he would probably not find time for a trip to New York, at least not soon. There was just too much to do.

The ringing telephone made Russell spill a large slosh of his cappuccino. He was surprised to hear Connie Graybill's voice on the line when he picked up the phone, wiping his wet hand on his pants as he did so.

"Hi, Russell, it's your neighbor, Connie Graybill."

Neighbor was a slight exaggeration. Connie and her husband, Dick, lived at the bottom of Russell's road, about two miles away. Connie taught anthropology at the state university, where Dick taught English literature. Wanda had introduced Russell to Connie and Dick one day when they arrived at her house to buy some apples just as Russell was leaving. Since then Russell had only occasional contact with the Graybills. Like most academic couples that Russell had known over the years, they tended to travel in a small, somewhat cloistered circle of friends, mostly other academics like themselves. Russell had become something of an associate member of their group after he mentioned to Connie his research and occasional writing on colonial history.

As always, Connie seemed a little breathless as she spoke. Russell could see her, tall, slender, in her early forties, long dark brown hair usually tied back simply, wearing round tortoise shell glasses that made her eyes seem larger than normal, and gave her a look that alternated from perpetual surprise, when she spoke, to curiosity when she listened.

"Dick and I are having a few people over today for brunch. Can you come?" she asked.

Russell had attended several of the Graybills' affairs before, although none of the others in the group had ever invited him to one of their events. The group did not appear to plan them, at least none that they ever discussed in Russell's presence. The two times that the Graybills had previously invited Russell to their house, it had always been by means of one of Connie's breathless, last-minute phone calls: "Several people dropped by unexpectedly. Can you come over, too? I know they'd like to meet you."

Russell had not yet become close to either Dick or Connie. A football player in college, Dick was unable to break into the pros. He drifted into professional wrestling for several years, which gave him an endless inventory of colorful stories. He then went back to school for his master's degree, and was working on his Ph.D. He referred to himself as a "journeyman academic," moving from one school to another, usually on short-term contracts, until the state university hired him as a non-tenured assistant professor with a promise of tenure when he completed his doctorate. Dick had once told Russell that he suspected that Connie had made that promise part of the deal for her to accept her professorship.

"Being a college professor is a little tame, Russell, but getting tossed around the ring six nights a week gets old pretty fast," Dick said once, when Russell had confessed to his boyhood love of professional wrestling. "Most of what you see are just very well-practiced gymnastics and a lot of choreography, but when you hit the canvas, that's real. It wears you down, no matter how good a shape you're in."

When Russell had a serious conversation with Dick, they would usually spend the time talking about literature or history. Russell soon discovered that he had more gaps in his reading than he realized or cared to admit to Dick. Dick seemed genuinely interested in Russell's work on the French and Indian War, because he had written about James Fennimore Cooper's tales for his master's thesis and had been impressed by Cooper's vivid descriptions of the eighteenth-century settings in upstate New York.

On two occasions, Russell had asked Dick to accompany him on one of his field trips to research the Braddock book. Dick expressed interest, but would decline, citing other commitments. Russell sometimes had sensed that Dick saw little point to driving four or five hours each way, just to spend an hour or two poking around an obscure corner of a farm or woods. On both occasions, however, the weather was still cold, which might have been a reason for Dick's "perhaps next time."

Russell also thought it strange that, unlike Dick, Connie never showed any interest in any of his field trips. His invitations always included them both. He had thought that, being an anthropologist, Connie would be interested in his field work, but Dick would report that she always declined without giving an excuse.

Russell had no plans for that Sunday other than to read and sip cappuccino in the morning, tea in the afternoon, and wine in the evening. He told Connie that he would be glad to come and offered to bring some bagels and cream cheese with him.

"Oh, no, Russell," Connie demurred. "You'll have to drive all the way into town."

"No problem, Connie," he replied. "I'll just go over to that little deli in Mansfield. I'll be glad to do it."

Shortly after he turned onto the road into Mansfield, Russell was slowed by the presence of several state police cars and a fire department ambulance along the side of the road. About fifteen feet off the road, an old Volkswagen was parked, the doors open. About sixty feet further into the field, Russell saw two state troopers, wearing heavy vests and baseball caps, walking toward the road, shotguns over their arms. When he returned, thirty minutes later, the police were gone. A lone tow truck was hitching up the car and preparing to take it away.

The impromptu affair at the Graybills' was much like the previous ones Russell had attended. Russell noticed two people whom he hadn't met before, Clay and his sister Margaret. He never caught their last names. Given Connie's informal social style, it was highly probable that Connie never gave them when she introduced Russell. Margaret was tall, thin, perhaps in her early sixties, and could have been Connie Graybill's mother. Clay surprised Russell when he introduced himself as a retired attorney. Clay's long gray hair, gathered in a ponytail, and his scraggly gray beard made him look more like a country singer who had seen a few too many hard times.

Two hours into the party, Russell found himself on the Graybills' front porch sipping wine with Clay. They had tried unsuccessfully to connect by talking about their experiences as lawyers. Clay had been an attorney in the Marine Corps, a "regular Semper Fi jarhead who used big words," as he put it. After his disability retirement ten years ago, he was hired by a law firm in Wilkes-Barre but soon decided that it just wasn't for him. Since then, he had been living off his Marine pension, sharing a place with Margaret while she tried to get a career as a poet off the ground and working as an adjunct instructor at several colleges in the region. Margaret said that she planned to move to Oregon at the end of the summer, to take a full-time position as a poet-in-residence at a small college there.

"But what do you do now, Clay?" Russell asked.

"Me? Shit, Russell. I stay alive," Clay replied. "That's all I got to do, just stay alive and Uncle Sam kicks in fifteen hundred a month into my checking account. I have a couple of interests that keep me busy – such as the zoology of this area – but basically I can just be."

"That was my dream, too, Clay. To come up here and just be. No responsibilities, no clients, no worries. Just hang out up here in the woods."

"Yeah, I hear you," Clay said. "But, you know, Russell, sometimes I get so bored, I want to go out and commit a crime, just so I can have at least one client.

"You aren't still practicing, are you, Russell?"

"No, Clay, not really. I keep my license current, but I just occasionally give out a little free advice to friends and neighbors. And I still have one or two matters from my old firm that I sometimes get involved in, but my former partners have those pretty much under control.

"But you mentioned zoology –" Russell began.

Russell was interrupted by the appearance of a young woman, with short straight black hair and a blinding white smile, stepping out onto the porch.

"Oh, I'm not interrupting anything, am I?" she asked.

"No," Russell and Clay responded in unison.

"Oh, good." She held out her hand to Russell.

"I know Clay, but not you," she said. "I'm Susan Kline."

"And I'm thirsty," said Clay, slowly getting up. "Can I get you guys anything?" he asked, not waiting for an answer before he disappeared through the door.

Russell felt awkward. He hadn't noticed Susan before. Maybe she had arrived late, another of Connie's afterthought invitations to even out the numbers.

"So, Russell, is it?"

Russell nodded.

"Yeah, well," Susan looked down at her feet, then back up at Russell and smiled again.

"So, Russell," she continued, "like, what do you do?"

"I'm sort of semi-retired," Russell started.

"So, tell me about the *semi* part, then," she invited.

Russell recited his story, how he had inherited his uncle's place and, almost on a whim, decided to give up his law practice in Philadelphia, move up into the mountains, and devote himself full-time to "staying out of the rat race," as he put it, and doing some writing.

"What about?" Susan asked.

"Mostly history. It's always been an interest of mine," he said, "and now I have a chance to see whether I'm any good at it."

Susan listened quietly as Russell talked about the Pennsylvania frontier in the seventeenth and early eighteenth centuries, her eyes never shifting from his. After a few moments, Russell sensed he was beginning to bore her, and she was just being polite.

"Sorry," he said, "I've gone on too much."

"No, really," she protested, "It's interesting. Really."

"How about you, Susan?" he asked.

"Not much to tell," she shrugged. "I grew up in Camp Hill, right outside Harrisburg. When I was away at college, at Villanova, my folks sold the house and moved up here. Dad had been a journalism major and had worked for the *Philadelphia Bulletin,* the *Baltimore Sun,* the *Washington Evening Star,* and a couple others, but he always wanted to run his own newspaper. So, while I was in school and he was working as features editor for the *Harrisburg Patriot-News,* the managing editor job came open suddenly up here at the *Wellsboro Bulletin,* and he grabbed it. Honest to god, he and Mom were so excited about it that they actually forgot to tell me they had moved, until they called me at school the day before Christmas vacation began and told me to come up to Wellsboro instead of Camp Hill."

"So, after college you decided to come here instead of staying around Philly?" Russell asked.

"Not at first. I fell in love with this guy the last semester of my senior year. We got married the day after graduation, and I got a part-time job and started grad school – journalism at Temple University. Following in my father's footsteps, I guess.

"It lasted about a year before I caught him sneaking out of a cheap motel early one morning, right behind the station where I was waiting for the train into Center City. I mean, I could see that bastard actually walk out of her room."

"That must have been rough, I'm sorry," Russell said.

Susan smiled, looking down.

"No, it wasn't that bad."

"But all the hassle of a divorce."

"He didn't even bother with a divorce," Susan said. "He just split. We're still married, I suppose. I haven't gotten around to filing for divorce. I mean, why bother until I have to?"

"So, you moved here to be with your folks?" Russell prompted.

"I really didn't have any choice. That whole thing really messed me up. I quit my job, dropped out of school, and just got in my car one night and started driving."

"To Wellsboro?"

"No, the opposite direction. For some reason I decided to drive to Florida, as far as I could go, all the way to the Keys."

"How'd you like the Keys?"

Susan laughed. "Never got there. My car blew a rod in the middle of nowhere in North Carolina. Fortunately, the tow truck guy towed it to a junk yard, where I sold it for enough money for a bus ticket back. I arrived in Wellsboro with eighty-five cents."

Russell didn't know what to say. He was almost afraid to ask any more questions.

"But, Russell, you know what hurt most of all?"

"What?" Russell asked.

"Well, when I called my father and asked if I could come home, just until I got my feet on the ground," Susan started. She laughed quietly. Russell heard a quiet little catch in her voice.

"You don't have to tell me this," he said quietly.

"I know, Russell," she said. "But I've been drinking wine all afternoon, and frankly, good sir, I am slightly sloshed. And this is good for me. So why not?"

"Well, you don't," he repeated.

Susan seemed to ignore him. "Well, the hardest part of all was my father telling me, 'That's okay, Suzie. I always knew that Brett – that's my ex – that Brett would dump you. But you're our little girl, and you always have a home with us'."

"Why was that hard?" Russell asked. He really didn't know why.

"This place isn't my home. I came here because I was alone, and rejected, and a little scared, and couldn't face making it on my own. And on top of it all, I wasn't here two weeks before I found out I was pregnant." Susan's voice was raised.

"Did you tell Brett about it?"

"I wouldn't give that sack of shit the satisfaction of knowing that he could accomplish anything. He still doesn't know about my daughter and he never will."

Connie Graybill appeared at the door. She saw Susan and Russell talking and quickly went back inside.

What is going on here, Russell thought. A strange woman, although a very attractive one, comes out onto the porch. Clay who is rather strange himself, splits. And now here I am conducting psychotherapy.

Susan went on telling her life story, and Russell found himself quickly losing interest. Her father had hired her as a part-time reporter for the *Bulletin*. She hated working for her father, but it gave her spending money and helped her keep her self-respect, she told Russell. When her father left the paper, about a year ago, she stayed on full-time, but also still did freelance work.

"What type of pieces do you write?" Russell asked.

"Anything that I can sell" Susan replied. "But mostly, I collect people. I don't know why I'm telling you this, I never told anyone else."

"I appreciate that," Russell murmured. "I really do."

"Everyone is an island, Russell," Susan continued. "No, that's a cliché. Even the *Bulletin* wouldn't publish it. Each of us – you, me, Connie, Dick, all of us – we're each a complete continent – that's better – waiting to be explored. And I'm like an ancient mapmaker, Russell."

"The journalist as cartographer," Russell mused. "I've never thought of it that way."

"What would I write on your map, Russell?" Russell had expected a smile, but Susan's face was blank, serious, flatly and plainly confronting him.

"I don't know," Russell replied. "Here be dragons?"

They both laughed.

"So, what do you write, actually, Susan?" Russell's boredom had subsided. He was becoming sincerely interested again.

"Well, I suppose some people would refer to my pieces as human-interest stories. You know, short on action and long on personal insights. But I've done okay. Some of my pieces have been picked up by the *Inquirer* and the *Post-Gazette,* and I even sold one to the *Boston Globe* and another one to the *New York Post.*"

"Congratulations," Russell said flatly. He instantly regretted his lack of enthusiasm, but Susan didn't seem to catch it. If she did, she ignored it. She pulled a pack of cigarettes and a lighter out of the small purse slung over her shoulder.

"I've got to stay out here. Connie has decreed a slow, painful death to anyone caught smoking in her house: having to listen to a semester of her lectures."

Russell and Susan laughed. Susan's laughter made her cough while she tried to light her cigarette. She then took a deep drag and exhaled, blowing the smoke straight up.

Russell hoped that he hadn't visibly winced.

"So, it must be kind of dull for you up here," she continued, "I mean, after a life as a big-time Philadelphia lawyer."

"Not really," Russell replied. "Like I said, I have some things that keep me busy.

"Also, there's a lot of mysterious stuff around here," he continued. "at least for a city slicker like myself. And there always seems to be weird things happening. Hell, just driving over here, there was this abandoned car driven off the road. Cops were everywhere. I wonder what was going on."

"Let's find out," Susan doused her cigarette in a drink that someone had left on the porch, led Russell inside and, without asking permission, punched a memorized number on Connie's kitchen phone.

Susan turned her back momentarily, spoke a few hushed words into the phone, and then hung up. Russell only heard her say "Thanks." She turned back to Russell, half-smiling.

"Interesting story," she reported. "The Wellsboro police chief's daughter was driving home from somewhere early this morning. Probably drunk, but my contact won't say so. She apparently passed out at the wheel and drove off into the field. She got stuck and couldn't get out. She claims she saw a panther in the road and swerved to avoid it."

Dick walked up with a tall tumbler that was half full of red wine.

"Was she hurt?" he asked.

"Just banged up a bit," Susan continued. "The strange thing is that when she got stuck, she apparently came to and wandered up onto the hillside. When the tow truck arrived, Sandy came strolling down the hill as if nothing had happened."

"So, what's the story about panthers?" Russell asked. "I keep hearing about them and wolves, but they're all supposed to have been extinct in this part of Pennsylvania for almost two hundred years."

Dick started to speak, but Susan chimed in.

"Russell," she laughed. "That's the most common excuse around here for one-car crashes, either that or a bear. It's the oldest one in the book."

"Yeah," Dick laughed. "This would be the third or fourth panther that the chief's kid has seen in the past two years, wouldn't it, Susan?"

"The cops are just covering for her to protect her dad," Susan replied. "Chief Davis is a decent guy – a bit slow at times, but honest. He's helped me out with a couple of stories I was doing. He doesn't deserve all the problems he's got."

"I don't know why they try to cover up for Sandy Davis," Connie Graybill said quietly. Russell hadn't noticed her standing behind him, listening. "She's already got a reputation."

"What kind?" Russell turned around and asked.

Connie cleared her throat and started to clear away a few empty plates from the small table near where they were standing. "Drunken whore," she said as she walked away and into the kitchen.

Dick looked toward the front door and said, "Excuse me. I have to say goodbye to some folks." He left Susan and Russell standing together by themselves.

Susan stared at Russell, as if searching for his reaction. She nodded slightly in Connie's direction. Russell didn't want to get involved in whatever was going on with Susan, Connie, and the police chief's daughter, so he shifted the subject.

"Well, Susan, I am curious about all these stories of wolves and panthers and cougars, though," Russell said. "They seem to go back a long way, don't they? And I've just heard another one."

"You really have a thing about big scary wildlife, don't you, Russell?" Susan smiled.

"Not really," Russell said. "I'm trying to put together a book of area folk legends from the notes Jack Abrams collected, and wolves and panthers keep appearing in them."

"Wanda's husband?" Susan asked.

"You know Wanda?" Russell was surprised.

"I'm a reporter," was all that Susan replied.

"Wanda's given me all of Jack's notes," Russell continued. "I'm trying to organize them into a book that I'm going to try to get published posthumously in Jack's name. I haven't gotten very far into them, but there are some really wild tales around here."

Connie returned from the kitchen smiling. She put her arm through Russell's and squeezed it.

"That's true, Russell," she jumped in, laughing. "They've got legends about everything around here: ghosts, lost Indian tribes, giant panthers, even trees that eat people. But I wouldn't be too quick to discount them, not completely. Behind every legend there's a grain of truth."

"You seem to know a lot about the local folklore, Connie," Russell commented.

"Well, as an anthropologist, my ears perk up whenever I hear an old legend. But I've never really studied the local ones," Connie replied. "That's the problem with local folklore. If I started chasing every old tale, I'd get so far afield that I would never get back to serious research. One just leads to another with no way out."

Susan started to say something just as Connie's phone rang. Connie answered it, frowned, and handed it silently to Susan. Susan turned her back, spoke briefly into the phone, and handed it back to Connie.

"Sorry about that, Connie," she said.

"Well, gotta run," she continued. "Russell, keep in touch. I'd like to talk to you some more. Dick, Connie, thanks as always for a nice afternoon."

"Breaking story?" Dick asked, smiling.

"Yeah," Susan laughed. "A murder. Mine, if I don't pick up my kid from my mother soon."

Dick and Russell walked with Susan to her car. Just before she drove off, Susan lowered her window and handed Russell a card.

"Call me, Russell," she said. "Anytime. I'd like to help you."

A Box Full of Nothing Solid

By the time Russell Poe arrived at the police station, in response to Ray Davis's telephone call earlier that Monday morning, Ray had decided that the best way to handle Russell was to lay it all out, the dead-end leads, the weak corroboration of the witnesses' statements, the lack of any credible theory of the case. Russell Poe was smart, a real Philadelphia lawyer, Ray thought, chuckling to himself. He probably doesn't think much of us upstate cops. Ray was pretty sure that Russell would appreciate directness, and Ray wanted to be sure that he didn't seem insulting or condescending. Ray didn't want to seem to be saying, *Okay, Mr. Big-City Smart-Ass Lawyer, let's see if you can do any better*. No, that wouldn't be fair. Russell was just trying to help a widow who could never accept how her husband died, and probably would never know why.

After a quick greeting, Ray got to the point. Sitting across Ray's desk, Russell was looking intently at the faded, stained cardboard file box that was between them, the only item on Ray's desk. Russell seemed to be staring at the name and case number.

Ray pushed it across the desk.

"Go ahead, Russell," Ray said, hoping he sounded cordial. "Go ahead and look through it. Make copies if you like; you can use our copier. Mrs. Abrams said she wanted you to see everything, including some things – crime scene photos and such – that I haven't shown her. You understand, of course, why I didn't."

Ray watched silently for a few moments as Russell nodded in response and pulled out the documents and photographs and flipped through them.

"There's quite a lot here," Russell said, "more than I had expected, based on our previous conversation."

"There's nothing there, Russell. That's the problem. That box is full of nothing solid."

Russell held up a paper. Ray strained to see what it was. It looked like a typed witness statement.

"Whitey Wentworth was involved?"

"Only tangentially. And he turned out to be pretty worthless."

"So why did you take a formal statement?"

"To be honest, Russell, because I didn't believe him."

Russell nodded.

"Let me sketch out the only lead we ever had. I think you'll agree with me about Mr. Wentworth."

"Whitey seems always to be mixed up in everything that goes on around here, one way or the other," Russell said, "but I can't believe he'd be involved in something like this."

"Well, like I said, let me give you an overview of what we know for sure," Ray replied. "In the morning of the day he was killed, Jack Abrams was seen with Whitey and two unidentified men at the Pine Tree Inn. And that's about it."

"Pine Tree Inn? I don't think I've ever heard of it."

"I should hope not. The Liquor Control Board closed it down about three years ago. It was a roadhouse out on Route 6, about twenty-five miles west of here. Real low-life place.

"The fact that we developed this lead at all was an unbelievable stroke of luck. One of our officers, Larry Keller, was coming back from taking a prisoner over to Coudersport. Larry got caught short, if you know what I mean, so he stopped at the Pine Tree, just to relieve himself and maybe get a soda."

"Not anything a little stronger?" Russell was grinning. Ray was relieved that he obviously wasn't serious.

"Not Larry. Teetotaler. Doesn't care if others drink, but he won't.

"So, it was 10:48 a.m. when Larry radioed that he was leaving the cruiser, and he checked back in when he got back on the road at 10:54 a.m. He wasn't in the place more than five or six minutes. Then he came back to the station and checked out for the day.

"The next day – this was Friday, the seventeenth of March – when Larry came in at noon for his shift, I briefed him on Mr. Abrams' death and that we were coordinating the preliminary investigation with the Richmond PD. There was a recent photo of Jack Abrams attached to the incident report. That's when Larry told me that he'd seen Jack Abrams the previous morning, in the Pine Tree Inn with Whitey Wentworth and two other men. He said he couldn't say for sure that the four of them were together, but Wentworth was sitting on the end, to the right as you face the bar, with Jack to his left. The other two men were on the next two barstools to Jack's left. He remembers that Whitey and the other two men appeared to be doing most of the talking, and Jack was turning his head from one side to the other – like someone watching tennis, Larry said."

"That was a lucky break, Chief."

"Yeah, it was. Usually in police work you have to make your own breaks. You don't get stuff falling into your lap. But you know that already, being a lawyer."

"Well, I didn't do much criminal work when I practiced."

"Yeah, well, I'm sure it's the same with any branch of the law. It's not like TV, is it? Well, we went out to the Pine Tree and located a couple of local folks who remembered seeing Jack and the two men with Whitey.

"The most obvious witness, the bartender, vaguely remembered the four men at the bar, but couldn't say exactly when they entered or left. He says that it was just at the beginning of the lunch traffic – apparently most of the customers there took liquid lunches – and he was busy. All he could say is that there were a bunch of people sitting at the bar, just like any other weekday late in the morning. His name is Rob DiNapoli, and he's got a reputation of being the blindest bartender in the county, if you know what I mean. He'd notice if an elephant came into the bar but would only remember that it was big and gray and, maybe if you slipped him a twenty, that it ate all the peanuts.

"But there were two other witnesses who remembered the four men at the bar."

"I'll read their statements later, Chief," Russell interrupted. "You don't have to take time now to go over every one in detail."

"Well, that's part of the problem, Russell," Ray replied. "I really should give you the big picture, because there are some inconsistencies in the statements. It's hard to reconstruct exactly what happened, but it was just a few hours before Jack was killed."

Russell nodded. "Okay, Chief, you're the expert at this. I'm in your hands."

"Well," Ray continued, "There were only two witnesses who recalled anything definite. They were sitting at separate booths across the room from the bar, so they couldn't hear any conversation. But they agreed that Whitey arrived first, sometime shortly after ten o'clock, and Jack arrived around ten fifteen or ten thirty. The two other men at the bar arrived a few minutes later. The first witness in the booths, a guy named Andy Hollander, said that he was he was pretty sure that all four of them left together a little before noon.

"The second witness, Charlie Legrand, said that the four of them left a little bit later than that, but he couldn't really remember what time it was. He thought that it could have been as late as one o'clock, but he couldn't be sure. Legrand also wasn't sure that they left together as a group, as opposed to just leaving at the same time, if you what I mean."

"What did Whitey say?"

"Mr. Wentworth had an entirely different story. Whitey had heard somehow that we were looking for him and he turned up here at the station the next day – that would be two days after we found Jack. I let Larry run the interview, since he had actually been there at the time, but I had a couple of questions to ask him, so I sat in.

"Wentworth said that Jack contacted him a few days before to request an interview to clarify some points about some folklore material that Whitey had given him. Whitey said that he arrived sometime after ten o'clock, consistent with the statements of the other two witnesses. He thought that it was around ten fifteen because Jack was supposed to meet him at ten thirty. So, Whitey arrived a few minutes early. When Jack came in, they sat at the bar. Whitey said that he had a shot and a beer and Jack had a Pepsi."

"Ray, did Whitey say why they met so far out of town?"

"Yeah, I asked him that. He said he suggested the place, because he wanted to meet somewhere that he wasn't known. He gave me some bullshit about how he had to protect his identity because he was a confidential source for the book Jack was writing.

"Well," Ray continued, "Whitey said that he and Jack talked for a little more than an hour and then Jack said he had to go. And this is where Whitey's story diverges completely from the other witnesses. He said that Jack left sometime around twelve noon. Whitey walked out with Jack to say goodbye in the parking lot, and he saw Jack drive off, headed back toward Wellsboro. Wentworth said that he went back into the bar and moved to a table back in a far corner of the room, near the toilets. He stayed at the Pine Tree for about another two hours, drinking beer and playing the pinball machine, and then he left a little after two in the afternoon."

"What did Whitey say about the two other guys that sat with him and Jack at the bar?"

"Well, Russell, let me put Whitey's story in context. Our other two witnesses, Hollander and Legrand, said that the two other men arrived together about ten or fifteen minutes after Jack did. So that would be around ten forty or ten forty-five at the latest, because all four of them were seated at the bar when Officer Keller arrived at ten forty-eight. Hollander told us that Whitey appeared to know the two other men, said hello to them, and introduced Jack to them. Legrand didn't notice that."

"So, Whitey had set up a meeting between Jack and the other two guys?"

"No, counselor, you're jumping the gun. Whitey said that he was just being polite, saying hello and introducing his friend Jack to them. That's all."

"Okay, Ray, I could see Whitey doing that."

"So could I, Russell. But, to get back to the story, there were these four guys all sitting at the bar in row, left-to-right: the two unidentified men, Abrams, and Wentworth. Hollander and Legrand were seated in separate booths across from the bar, each a little more than twenty feet away. Hollander said that he didn't see Whitey ever talk to the two other guys directly. Legrand was pretty sure that he saw Whitey and the two guys exchange words several times, but he couldn't say that they were having a conversation. Their backs were turned to Legrand and Hollander."

"But did either Hollander or Legrand say anything about whether Jack, specifically, spoke with either of the two men?"

"We asked them that, Russell. It's all in their statements. Neither Hollander nor Legrand remembered one way or the other. Both of them said that the room was beginning to get a little noisy as people came in for lunch, so they probably couldn't have heard a normal conversation at the bar, even if they wanted to."

"But, Chief, let's look at what you already have," Russell said, placing both hands on the file.

"Jack and Whitey arrive within fifteen minutes of each other at a place that is twenty-five miles out of town, and not near where either of them lives or works. Then two other guys come in and sit at the bar next to Jack and Whitey, even though there probably are more comfortable seats at a table or in a booth. The four of them sit there for a while and exchange at least a few words, even if nobody else hears an actual conversation among them. That's what your officer saw when he stopped in a little before eleven. Then they all leave at the same time. And a couple of hours later Jack Abrams is dead.

"Sounds like Whitey set up Jack Abrams to meet the two men, doesn't it, Ray?"

"Sure, that's a good theory, Russell, but I have only one problem with that. There's no proof, not a bit of evidence to support anything beyond the fact that there were four guys sitting at the bar at the same time, and that they might have exchanged more than only a few words. And Whitey's testimony could be enough to raise reasonable doubt, given the weaknesses in the statements from Hollander and Legrand."

Russell's eyes opened wide and blinked.

"Or to convict him, if it is true that Whitey left with Jack and lured him to the place of the murder," Russell said.

Ray was amused by how the conversation was developing. Russell Poe had become the cop, trying to prove his case. Meanwhile, Ray was sitting back, judicious, lawyer-like, poking holes in Russell's theories.

"And both the witnesses say that Whitey and Jack left at the same time as the two unidentified men. Isn't that correct, Ray?"

"We pressed Hollander and Legrand on that, and they both were rock-solid that all four of them left at the same time, even though they disagreed about what that time was. You'll see the notes of the follow-up interviews in the file." Ray patted the file box.

"So, how does Whitey explain that discrepancy? Did you ask him about it?" Russell asked.

"We did, Russell. He insisted that the two other guys at the bar were still there when he and Jack left. Whitey says that after Jack drove away, he got a pack of smokes out of his truck and went back into the bar, and that Hollander and Legrand must not have noticed him return."

"And neither one of them noticed Whitey standing around the pinball machine for two hours?" Russell asked.

"I don't believe it, either," Ray said, smiling.

Russell continued, "Did you ever find out who the other two men at the bar were? I assume you got descriptions from Hollander or Legrand."

"Only partly, Russell." Ray replied. "Hollander was able to provide us the more detailed description. He remembers when the two unidentified men came in. He says he remembers thinking to himself, 'Oh shit. Just what we need. A couple of bikers.' Hollander says that one man was about five-nine or five-ten, thin, and in his late forties or fifties. His hair was turning silver, almost white, long and tied back in a ponytail. Hollander says he thinks that the man was wearing a single dangling silver earring and a silver chain around his neck. The other man was younger, maybe in his thirties, and was big – well over six feet tall and easily three hundred pounds, Hollander said – built like a pro football lineman. He had a dark complexion, and Hollander thought that he might have been part African American or maybe part Native American, and that he had short black hair and either hadn't shaved for a couple of days or had a close-trimmed beard."

"What did Legrand and Wentworth say about the descriptions?" Russell asked.

"Theirs aren't quite as detailed, Russell. Legrand agreed with the differences in age and size, but the rest of his descriptions don't quite match Hollander's. For example, Legrand said that the older guy had an old-fashioned crew cut and he didn't notice any jewelry. The big guy was white, but with a dark complexion, possibly suntanned, had no beard, and medium length black hair. Of the two men, Legrand was less certain of his descriptions and said that he really hadn't noticed or paid much attention to them."

"And Whitey?"

"Whitey said that other than saying hello to the two guys, he didn't notice anything about them: middle aged, average height, average weight, dressed in jeans and black T-shirts, no distinguishing marks or tattoos."

"It's interesting that Whitey was sitting almost next to them and could give you only a generic description, and two guys sitting across the room, who were not really paying attention to what was going on at the bar, were the ones who could give you some details, even if they're inconsistent," Russell remarked.

"As I'm sure you know, inconsistencies like that are common in eyewitness statements," Ray continued. "Bystanders like Hollander and Legrand seldom are paying close attention when something ordinary is going on and sometimes they tell us what they think must have happened, based on their incomplete or inaccurate memories.

"And as for Whitey, I'm sure that he's not telling us everything he knows about the two men at the bar. But it's all in the file there, all the details, all the discrepancies. And I might be leaving some small things out."

"That's okay, Ray. I just wanted to get a general idea of what you found out. I'll look these over later, if I may."

"Sure. I can't let you have the originals, but I'll have copies made for you. I'll have to ask you to sign for them, of course."

"No problem. I'll keep everything locked up."

"So," Ray said, pausing for a few seconds to collect his thoughts, "to sum it up, the big unsolved questions are what did the four men

– Whitey, Jack, and the two other guys sitting next to them at the bar – talk about, and did they all leave at the same time."

"And, in a nutshell, you have two witnesses that are firm that Whitey's answers to those two questions are incorrect," Russell commented.

"Incorrect," Chief Davis smiled. "I love the diplomatic way you lawyers put things. I would use a stronger word: *lie*."

Russell smiled and nodded.

"Did you check out the cash register tape, to see if that could help fix the times when Jack and Whitey paid their bills?" Russell asked.

"Good point, counselor," Ray smiled. "Maybe I should deputize you right here and now.

"But, yes, we asked to see the tapes and DiNapoli – he's the bartender – said that he uses the cash register basically to hold the cash. It's one of those old machines where you can only enter the total; it won't add up the items. But he said – and knowing what the Pine Tree Inn used to be like, I believe him – that they didn't bother with running a tape. I remember that he even made a big production of showing me how three of the keys didn't work."

"Credit card receipts, maybe?" Russell's smile signaled that he already knew the answer.

"At the Pine Tree?" Ray chuckled. "That was strictly a cash operation. DiNapoli would allow some of the regulars to run a tab, which he kept on a yellow pad, but the payments were strictly cash."

"So," Russell continued, "even if Jack didn't leave until one o'clock, like Legrand said, it still could have been theoretically possible for him to drive from the Pine Tree Inn, hike up onto the mountain, and be killed before two."

"Possible, but not likely. The fact that we know for sure is that Mr. Abrams was dead by three o'clock, plus or minus about thirty minutes. This means that Hollander's estimate – he's the one who said that Jack left around noon – is more likely. And had your uncle come along even thirty minutes earlier, he might have witnessed it."

"Or maybe even stopped it," Russell added.

"Or maybe gotten killed himself," Ray finished the thought.

"I'm also still a little unclear about the evidence about whether there was a conversation and, if there was, between which of the four men," Russell said. "You have Officer Keller's observation that Jack appeared to be listening to the other three men but not saying much himself. Did Hollander or Legrand observe Jack – not Whitey, but Jack – actually conversing with the two men?"

"No. Hollander said that he assumed they had been talking because they all left together. It's on the second page of his statement. He also told us that he didn't actually see them talking. He just assumed they were, but he admitted that he couldn't be sure. Legrand said essentially the same thing."

After a moment of silence, Russell asked, "So what do you think, Chief Davis? What's your hypothesis at this point?"

Ray reached behind himself, opened a drawer of the credenza, and pulled out a cigarette pack, a lighter, and an ashtray. He gestured at Russell with the cigarette pack.

"Want one?"

"No thanks, Ray."

"Mind if I do?"

"No, but thanks for asking. Go ahead. It doesn't bother me."

Ray lit the cigarette, took a deep breath of smoke, and exhaled toward the ceiling.

"What do I think?" Ray continued. "I don't think anything, Russell. There's just nothing solid enough to go on. We tracked down almost anyone who'd ever been anywhere near the Pine Tree anytime that whole month, to see if they could give us more on the two unidentified men. Nothing.

"But even if everybody agreed on everything, without knowing what was actually said, we have no solid connection whatsoever with Mr. Abrams' death just a few hours later, just speculation."

"And what do you think of Whitey's story?" Russell responded. "In your gut, Chief."

"In my gut? I think Whitey might be partly telling the truth, but not all that he knows. Whitey and I go back a long way. I don't trust him, never have. The problem with this case is that I don't have any reason to disbelieve the two witnesses who, as far as we could determine, were completely disinterested bystanders with no reason to be untruthful."

Ray paused. He had a lot of reasons to dislike Whitey. He noticed that he thought *dislike,* not *distrust.* He recognized an anger beginning to seep up inside. He had to control it, to stay professional. He took another long drag on the cigarette and stared at Russell. Russell showed no reaction.

"It's mostly a policeman's instinct, I guess, but I think that Whitey set up the meeting, not Jack. I also think that the purpose of the meeting was to set up Jack for the two strangers. Forget about what Whitey said about Jack leaving by himself. I think it's pretty clear that he walked out of the bar with the two men. As to where he went after that, and with whom, if anyone, we don't have a bit of evidence. And regardless of which version of when they left you believe, it was too close to the time of Jack's death, too close for comfort."

"But you had no luck finding them?"

"Not a bit. I had Wentworth, Legrand, and Hollander all do an identikit with the sketch guy from the State Police. You'll see the drawings in the file." Ray nodded at the file and waited. Russell flipped through the papers and found the drawings.

"At least two of them are a little similar," Russell observed. He held up the one sketch that was completely different. "And this one is obviously Whitey's."

"Obviously," Ray agreed.

"But these could be any one of a thousand men," Ray continued. "Sure, they're a couple of unusual looking guys, but nothing really distinguishing like *That's the man!* I see guys that look something like that almost every day.

"I took Hollander's drawing – his description is the most detailed – and circulated it through the State Police statewide and into the nearby counties in New York and New Jersey. You'll see the State Police flyer in there, listing the men only as possible witnesses."

"But no leads, Chief?"

"We had a few calls, but nothing to go on," Ray responded. "At best, all the callers could say was that they thought they had seen men who looked like this somewhere around Wellsboro sometime during the previous six months or so. That's about as specific as it got."

"Did any of them describe a vehicle?"

"That's another problem, Russell. We had several callers say that they saw one or both of them with a vehicle, but they were all different, ranging from two motorcycles, to two guys on one motorcycle, to an old Ford pickup with New York tags. Again, nothing really to go on."

"Getting back to Whitey, do you consider him a suspect?"

Davis mashed his cigarette out in the clean ashtray. "Not as a perpetrator. I did at first, but he could account for himself for most of that afternoon until 9:47 p.m."

"9:47 p.m.?"

"Yeah Russell, 9:47 p.m., when the Mansfield Borough police picked him up for DUI on U.S. 6 just on the west edge of the borough. Whitey was so blasted that he probably still doesn't remember how he got there. At the end of his statement there, you'll see he describes several places where he thinks he went after leaving the Pine Tree.

"During that time, he bar-hopped his way all the way from the Pine Tree Inn, fifteen miles west of town, probably followed Route 6 east past Wellsboro, and ended up about eleven miles east of here in Mansfield. We couldn't account for any time before three-thirty, when he rolled into the Junction Roadhouse up on 287 in Stokesdale, but from that point on, the ones he could remember all checked out.

"Whitey couldn't remember exact times, but people in the other places did, at least close enough to pretty much rule him out as actually having been involved in the act itself. It seems that Whitey made quite a memorable spectacle of himself."

"So, if Whitey was telling the truth, and he left the Pine Tree around two, it wouldn't have been possible," Russell said slowly, "that he could have driven at least forty miles to the crime scene on my property."

"Actually, 42.8 miles to the entrance to your driveway; we measured it," Ray interjected.

"Okay, 42.8 miles," Russell continued, "and then he had to hike up the mountain another twenty-five minutes or so to where Jack was killed. Then, after participating in the killing, he had to hike all the way back down, another twenty or twenty-five minutes, to his car and drive to the Junction Roadhouse."

"Another 11.2 miles back toward town. That's right, Russell. He couldn't have participated in a killing at or around three o'clock."

"But," Ray continued, "if he left earlier, around the time the other witnesses said that he did, it would have been a tight schedule, but possible. Let's say he left at one. He could have been at your place before two. He could have hiked up to the scene by two thirty. That would give time to participate in the killing, go back down to where he left his vehicle by three or three fifteen, and then drive the eleven miles to the Junction, arriving there easily around three thirty. If he left the Pine Tree as early as noon, it would have been even more probable.

"The problem with both theories is that we don't have solid evidence to support either one. Still, we haven't ruled Whitey out as a possible accessory or co-conspirator. He made sure that he was noticed every place he stopped that afternoon. That's consistent with someone who knows that something bad is going down and wants to establish an alibi. He wasn't a suspect when we interviewed him, but I think that we would have to give him his *Miranda* warnings if we talked to him again about this."

"So, you don't buy the wolf attack story?" Russell asked.

"To be honest, Russell, I just don't know. There's enough that went on at the Pine Tree to make anyone suspicious. But at the scene, where we found Jack's body, there were no signs of foul play."

"How do you mean?"

"As you probably know, he was found in a clearing on your property. There were no signs of a struggle or of anyone else being there. No brush disturbed, no stomped down paths through the brush leading to the scene. No divots in the soil. Whoever or whatever attacked Jack did it before he could react.

"Although I think that Mr. Abrams was killed quickly and without much struggle, there were a lot of signs of – well, let's say violence – but not foul play. Which leads me to that brown envelope in your hand."

Russell held it up. "This one? Autopsy photos?"

"Worse. Crime scene photos. This is something I'd rather you keep to yourself. I don't think it would do Mrs. Abrams any good. Let's just say Jack's body was pretty well mutilated when we got to him. As best as we could tell, he'd been dead no more than two hours. There were still pools of uncoagulated blood. And he'd been literally torn apart. Worse yet, most of the – the disrespect – to his body was post-mortem, like someone killed him quickly and then went berserk with his corpse. You might not want to look at those pictures."

Russell visibly swallowed and seemed to turn pale for a second. "Thanks. I probably don't. But the autopsy report, is it in the file?"

"About a quarter inch down, Russell. Don't worry, all the really gruesome photos are in the envelope marked *Crime Scene*. There are a couple of routine photos from the autopsy that are clipped to the Coroner's report, mostly close-ups of the wounds, but you might not want to look at those.

"But getting back to the crime scene, I still have nightmares about it. Even if you never want to see the crime scene photos in that envelope, I think you need to know how we found Mr. Abrams. He was lying face up on the trail. There were large gashes in his neck and on the top of his head. Almost all of the abdominal organs were gone. Both the arms had been dislocated from the shoulders, one of them completely detached. We found it a good thirty feet away. There were deep, broad gashes across the face, and the blood flow made him almost unrecognizable. In fact, we had to use his driver's license, which was still in his wallet in his pocket, to confirm your uncle's identification of him. Both legs were pretty well mangled, all the way down to the bone."

Russell's face turned pale and beads of sweat appeared on his forehead.

"Are you okay, Russell?" Ray asked quietly. "Jesus, I'm sorry. Maybe I shouldn't have told you that."

Russell didn't answer but bent his head over the file box and quickly found the autopsy report. He removed the photos that were clipped to it and replaced them face-down in the box. He picked up the report and slowly read aloud in a soft, clear voice:

> *There is no evidence from the incomplete organ set available of any natural disease that could have caused or contributed to death. The injuries to the neck, shoulders, back, and abdomen are consistent with an attack by a large, powerful animal or several such animals. The partial evacuation of the abdominal cavity, dismemberment, and deep broad wounds over most of the face and torso are likewise consistent with animal attacks and probably were postmortem.*
>
> *The cause of death was a sudden and catastrophic arterial blood loss due to a complete severing of both carotid arteries and secondary to the massive incisions into and partial evacuation of internal organs from the abdominal cavity.*

"My god," Russell said quietly. "No wonder people think it was a wolf attack."

"We didn't release all the details, just in case we did someday get a confession from someone and needed to verify it. But, yes, you can see why most folks believe the wolf attack story. Nobody wants to believe that someone around here could be capable of that."

The two men sat silently for a few moments. The telephones ringing in the outer office seemed far away. Ray watched as Russell flipped quietly, almost cautiously it seemed, through the file. He quickly passed over anything in an envelope.

"As I said, we can make copies of anything you like, Russell. I know that I already have your word, as an officer of the court, that you won't show them to anyone else."

"Sure, Chief. No problem there. I just need to learn all I can, so I can give Wanda my advice."

"Advice? Is she considering some sort of legal action?" Ray began to wonder if he had made a mistake, had told Russell too much.

"No. Nothing like that, Chief Davis. Sorry for the poor choice of words. What you told me is a little unsettling right now. No, I'm just trying to help her bring it all to closure."

Ray pointed to the brown envelope, which contained the crime scene photographs and which Russell had laid aside on the desk. "Do you need copies of any of that?"

"No, Chief. Thanks. Just the statements will be enough, and the Coroner's report. I don't need any pictures. I have already seen enough. I don't want to see more."

The Catacombs

"This is like 'The Cask of the Amontillado'," Russell remarked as he followed Susan Kline down the trembling wooden steps into the basement beneath the *Wellsboro Bulletin* offices.

Susan laughed and shined her flashlight on the stone walls that formed the foundation of the building. They twinkled as the beam of light struck the mineral deposits that had built up over more than a hundred years.

"See anyone you know?" she asked.

This is surreal, Russell thought. A few hours ago, he had been sitting in his study on a warm spring evening, wondering about when he should give Wanda a progress report on his inquiries – he tried to avoid the word *investigation* – about Jack's death. Wanda hadn't mentioned it to him after the day she accused Bill Paxton of having been involved in it somehow, but Russell knew that he owed her some information. He simply didn't know what he should tell her, or how, or when.

Russell had been surprised to answer the phone and find Susan on the other end of the line.

"Hi, Russell, it's me, Susan Kline. We met at Dick and Connie Graybill's brunch a couple of weekends ago." She had used the same fast, clipped voice that Russell had found a little annoying at first when he met her at the brunch, but then accepted and eventually found amusing after she mentioned that she was a reporter.

Before Russell could ask why she had called, Susan had jumped right into her explanation that after their conversation at the brunch, she had started thinking about Jack Abrams' death and decided to find out more about it.

"I'm always looking for a story, even a morbid one," she told Russell.

"I asked Claire – she's a part-time admin assistant who's been working at the paper forever and knows everything – I asked her if she remembered any coverage by the *Bulletin*. She said that by now the file probably had been taken to the catacombs, which is what we call the basement of our building. She even directed me to the right drawer in the old oak card catalog."

"Really? An oak card catalog?" Russell interrupted, "Like in the old libraries?"

"Yeah," Susan responded, "We're a little old-fashioned here, just got word processing about two years ago. Well, when I pulled the card for Abrams, John, it said *Restricted – See Mr. Kenyon for Access."*

"Kenyon? Who's he, the editor?" Russell asked.

"Only the grand old man of Wellsboro journalism," Susan had replied. "He published and edited the *Bulletin* for more than sixty years, right up until the day he died four years ago at age eighty-eight. The old guy came into the office every day, even on the day he died. He hired my father as Managing Editor."

"So, did you get the file?"

"That's the problem, Russell. When I asked Claire for the key to the basement, she said that I would still have to get permission."

"Not from Kenyon, obviously."

"No, from Kenyon's grandson, Greg, who took over when the old man died."

"Couldn't your father help you –," Russell started to say.

Susan interrupted. "No, he got into some sort of pissing contest with Greg about a year ago and quit – came into the office in the middle of the night and cleared out all his stuff. But Greg made a point of immediately asking me to stay on full-time.

"I asked him about the incident with Abrams, and he said that he remembered it but didn't recall any specifics. He basically told me what I knew already, that Abrams was supposedly killed by wolves in the woods. He didn't think that there was still anyone on the paper who worked that story and said that anything that the *Bulletin* developed would be in the file."

"Which was locked up and restricted," Russell added.

"Right," Susan responded.

"And, I take it, you didn't get permission from Greg to retrieve the file you needed."

"That's right, Russell. I called him at home and explained that I needed to get into the basement. He asked what for, so, like a dummy, I told him I was doing a piece on unsolved deaths in the area and wanted to see the file on Jack Abrams."

"And he refused?"

"Not right away. He said he needed to check something out and he'd call back. I asked him if there was any problem, and he said he didn't think there would be. But he just needed to check something first. He said he'd call back in ten minutes."

"Did he?"

"One thing about Greg Paxton is that he's punctual," Susan had slowed down long enough to chuckle. "Ten minutes on the nose. He said –"

"Wait a minute, his last name is Paxton?" Russell interrupted. "Any relationship to Reverend Bill Paxton and that family?"

"I think he's a cousin or something. It's a big family, or at least used to be, in this part of the state. They must have bred like rabbits. He lives down in Wilkes-Barre and only comes up here once in a while. I think Reverend Bill is the only one of the clan still left around here."

"Must be hard to edit a paper when you're never there."

"Not really. Greg owns a chain of small papers, including the *Bulletin*. We fax copy to him or have one of our interns from Mansfield State drive it to him. All the layout is done down there in Wilkes-Barre. About all that goes on here these days is selling advertising and providing a place for the local reporters to call their office."

"So, I'm sorry I interrupted you, Susan," Russell had said. "What did Greg say when he called back."

"He simply said that I couldn't have access to the file. End of story."

"Isn't that unusual in the newspaper business?" Russell realized that the name Paxton had caused him to become suspicious. He thought for a moment that maybe he was jumping to conclusions.

Susan continued, "I don't know about the rest of the newspaper business, Russell, but it's always been almost impossible for a reporter to have access to the old files here at the *Bulletin*. Old Man Kenyon kept a tight lid on everything. His grandson is just following family tradition."

"What could be so sensitive about the *Bulletin*'s files?" Russell was genuinely puzzled by the secrecy. "No offense, but it's just a small-town weekly."

"Semi-weekly," Susan corrected.

"Sorry," Russell said.

"No offense taken, Russell," Susan replied. "That's what it is now, but back in the old days, back when Kenyon ran the paper, it was a daily with a circulation of almost 35,000 over six counties. It ran real news back then, not just the garden-party stuff and used car ads you find in it now. There's almost a century of serious journalism locked up down there in our catacombs and probably a lot of stuff that some people still wouldn't want to become public."

"So, what's to prevent you from just going down into the catacombs and taking what you need?" Russell asked.

"Oh, nothing at all, Russell. But I always like to at least pretend to follow the rules before I break them."

Susan then invited Russell to join her in "a little burglary" at the newspaper office later that night. Russell demurred at first, but Susan assured him that nobody would find it suspicious if she were in the office after closing hours doing an interview of him. She revealed that she had already "borrowed" the key to the basement from Claire's desk after Claire had locked the basement door and gone home.

"Some of us work at the office in the evenings sometimes." she explained, when Russell arrived at the agreed time of 10:30 p.m. "We won't attract any attention, except possibly a cop stopping by to make sure everything's all right. Which it will be, because my cover story, if someone comes by, is that I'm interviewing you for one of my puff pieces."

Russell felt a little hurt by the phrase *puff pieces*, but he let it pass.

"But doesn't Greg Paxton realize how easy it is for you or anyone else at the paper to go downstairs and get whatever files they want, whether he approves or not?"

Susan laughed. "Greg is just like his grandfather, like most petty tyrants. The stupid bastard honestly believes that no one would ever disobey him. Claire is one of his spies here in the office, but it's easy to get around her, just like we're doing."

So now, flashlight in hand, Russell found himself in the catacombs with Susan. He had expected a cramped cellar with low beams challenging his head. Instead, the room had ceilings that were at least ten feet high. Dim light bulbs – some of them looked like they had been installed in Edison's day – dangled every twenty feet in rows above the canyons of document storage boxes closely stacked together and reaching almost to the ceiling. The wooden ones had dates going back into the late 1880s. The more recent ones were cardboard. Holding the index card in her hand and shifting her flashlight beam from the piled boxes to the card, Susan walked slowly, and then stopped suddenly, turned, and faced Russell.

"Old Man Kenyon gave each box an address with what he called 'avenues' – they run along the long dimension, from the front to the back of the basement – and 'streets' that run across. They're also stacked more or less in chronological order but based on when the papers were boxed up and brought down here, not when the stuff actually happened. But the address system helps."

"For a place that's supposedly off-limits to everyone, you seem to know your way around here," Russell commented.

"Well, I've been down here a few times before," Susan replied.

"With or without permission?" Russell asked, chuckling.

"Counselor, you know that I don't have to answer that question," Susan said, smiling. "Besides, Kenyon's system is really easy once you know it."

"We're looking for 1134 Fourth Street. That means that our box is in the fourth cross street and between First Avenue – that's the one that runs along the side over there to the left – and Second Avenue, which is the next one in. The middle two numbers tell us that the box will be in Stack 13. That's an odd number; the odd stack numbers face toward the back of the room, the even numbers to the front. And the final number tells us how far from the bottom of the stack the box is located; in our case, it's the fourth one up from the bottom."

"We should have brought breadcrumbs, so we can find our way out," Russell remarked. Susan appeared to ignore him.

"Ah, we're here," she said a moment later. "There should be a ladder over there by the wall somewhere."

Russell retrieved a tall stepladder, while Susan found 1134 Fourth Street. Russell climbed the ladder and handed down the five boxes that were stacked on top of it. Susan took each one and stacked them in reverse order on the floor. Russell then handed down the box they wanted. When he rejoined Susan, she was crouched on the floor, shining the flashlight on the top of the box and laughing.

"What's so funny?" Russell asked.

"Oh, just that poor Claire has been watching too many spy movies. She's taped the lid to the box and written her name and a date across it."

"So, we'll have to be very very careful with such impenetrable security," Russell laughed. "I don't suppose that you are adept at forging her signature?"

"Just like everyone else in the office," Susan replied. "Claire always brags about her perfect grade-school penmanship, which is the easiest to forge."

Holding his flashlight above the open box, Russell watched Susan peel back the masking tape and run her fingers expertly through the nine or ten manila folders in the box.

"Bingo," she said, extracting one of the folders. "Let's see what we have."

"If you don't mind," Russell said slowly, "do you think we could take it upstairs and look through it there? Frankly, this place gives me the creeps."

"Sure," Susan said. "Besides, with the lights on upstairs, we really should be up there and visible from the outside, because it's late and we don't want people to see the lights with nobody inside and call the cops."

Russell quickly replaced the boxes and the ladder. Susan led the way back to the stairs and up to the office. She locked the door and, detoured to the front of the office to drop the keys into the top center drawer of the desk closest to the front door. They then sat at a desk at the back of the office, but plainly visible from the street. Susan opened her purse, removed an unlabeled floppy disk, and inserted it into the computer.

"That way it will look like I'm interviewing you, if someone should come in."

Russell looked at the screen:

LOCAL AUTHOR EXPLORES WELLSBORO'S PAST

by Susan Kline

What's the best way to settle into a new community? According to Russell Poe, it's to get involved in the legends and folklore of his new home's colorful past.

Poe, a former partner in the Philadelphia law firm of Watkins, Spencer & Poe, retired to the Wellsboro area less than two years ago. Already a published author...

Susan nodded at the screen and smiled.

"Is that a real article?" Russell asked.

"No, but it could be," Susan replied. "We've got to make this look real if someone comes in. And if someone does, just follow my lead."

Susan opened the file and started handing papers to Russell.

"It looks like *The Bulletin* ran just three articles on the case," she said. "We had just converted from a daily to semi-weekly, publishing on Tuesdays and Fridays, so these cover —" she paused as she checked the dates.

"Yes," she continued, "the first two ran in two successive issues. Then the third one was published about a year later."

Wanda had shown Russell all three articles. The first announced the discovery of Jack's body in the woods above Russell's house.

MISSING WELLSBORO BUSINESSMAN
FOUND DEAD IN FOREST
by Kenneth Young

(Wellsboro, March 21, 1978) Mystery ended in tragedy when the body of John Abrams, age 47, of Richmond Township, was found in a remote section of forest near his home, approximately one mile from Lambs Creek Road late Thursday afternoon, March 16, 1978. Abrams, a co-owner of the Abrams Insurance Agency in Wellsboro, had been missing for most of the day, having failed to return home from a meeting. His body was found by the owner of the property, Simon Poe, who happened to be hiking nearby on one of the old Indian trails that traverse his property.

Police are withholding detailed comment on the case but are investigating further. "Whenever someone dies under mysterious circumstances like these, we always have to treat it as a possible homicide investigation, at least until we know more facts," said Wellsboro Borough Police Chief Raymond W. Davis. The Wellsboro Police are coordinating the investigation, at the request of the Richmond Township Police Department and the Pennsylvania State Police.

Sources close to the investigation, however, have disclosed that the apparent cause of death may have been an animal attack. Chief Davis has declined comment on this report. "Let's wait for the facts," he said. An autopsy was conducted yesterday, but the results have not been released.

The family has not completed funeral arrangements at this time. Mr. Abrams is survived by his wife, Wanda Abrams, and a sister, Denise Abrams, of White Plains, New York.

The rest of the article outlined Jack's business career and his activity in local business and charitable organizations. Russell put the old photocopy down softly on Susan's desk.

"This one appeared a few days later," Susan continued after Russell had finished reading the first article. "This was when Ray Davis tried to sell the wolf attack theory."

WOLF ATTACK POSSIBLE CAUSE OF DEATH IN ABRAMS CASE, CORONER SAYS

by Kenneth Young

(Wellsboro, March 24, 1978) The Tioga County Coroner's Office has determined that the death of Wellsboro businessman John Abrams was probably the result of an animal attack, possibly by a wolf or a pack of wolves. Abrams' body was found eight days ago in a secluded wooded spot twelve miles northeast of Wellsboro in Richmond Township. Sources close to the investigation had informed The Bulletin that the police had been unable to locate any witnesses or possible suspects.

Wellsboro Police Chief Raymond W. Davis announced the Coroner's findings at a press conference on Thursday morning, March 23. Reading from a prepared statement, he said:

"The Coroner's autopsy has determined that Mr. Abrams died from massive blood loss suffered as a result of large wounds to the neck and abdomen, consistent with an attack by a wolf or a pack of wolves, or some similar animal or animals."

"Every indication is that Mr. Abrams' passing was very quick and painless," Chief Davis added.

Davis refused to discuss autopsy details. "I'm not going to discuss any further details out of respect for the privacy of Mrs. Abrams, and I would ask the press to do the same. We have lost a valued member of our community and a good friend. I know that our thoughts and prayers are with Mrs. Abrams and the family."

Investigation to Remain Open

In response to a question, Chief Davis stated that, notwithstanding the Coroner's report, the investigation will remain open. "As some of you may already know, we have been unable so far to locate any reliable witnesses who can shed any light on this case. Several people saw Mr. Abrams on the day he disappeared, but we have been unable to find anyone who has any information about incidents that may have led to his death.

"Although the Coroner's report makes it pretty clear what happened to Mr. Abrams, we still don't know why. So, we're not

going to close this case until we know all the answers. We owe that to the memory of this fine gentleman and to Mrs. Abrams."

Chief Davis requested that anyone having any information about the incident should contact the Wellsboro Police Department at 555-9600, or the Pennsylvania State Police Criminal Investigation Division at 1-800-999-9000.

No Danger to Area Residents

Officials of the Pennsylvania State Fish and Game Commission have advised The Bulletin that there is no danger to area residents, despite the Coroner's findings.

"The Coroner's report in the Abrams case does not say definitively that he was attacked by wolves. It merely says that the injuries were similar to those that wolves might inflict," explained John Del Greco, FGC Public Affairs Coordinator for the North-Central Region.

"In fact, there have been no verified sightings of a wolf pack in Pennsylvania since 1853, and the last wild wolf known to be alive in the Commonwealth was shot in 1898. The closest wolf population is in Ontario."

Del Greco estimates that there are fewer than 5,000 wolves living in the wild in the continental United States at this time. The closest wolf population in the U.S. is in the Upper Peninsula of Michigan, where fewer than 600 are still living in the wild.

Del Greco described wolves as shy animals, which will usually run from humans.

"There has never – repeat never – been a documented case anywhere in North America of a normal, healthy wolf attacking a human," he said.

Del Greco refused to speculate about what type of animal might have caused Abrams' death. "It might have been a pack of wild dogs, but we don't have any reports of those in this part of the state."

Davis Appeals for Calm

Chief Davis urged area residents to remain calm, citing a recent rash of accidental shootings of dogs and other pets. He also commented on the recent increase of citations for firearms violations in the borough limits.

"Wellsboro has strict laws about carrying firearms in public, and we will enforce them. If anyone has any concern about their safety, they should contact the Police Department, and not try to take matters into their own hands."

"Now that people have the facts, they should realize that there is no need for alarm," he added.

"This Kenneth Young," Russell asked, "Is he still with the paper?"

"Well, in a way he never was," Susan replied. "That was one of Old Man Kenyon's pseudonyms, Kenneth Young – Ken Young – which might explain why the file was restricted.

"And this one appeared a year later," Susan said, handing Russell another photocopy. "You'll see that poor old Jack had slipped back to page 6 by then."

STILL NO LEADS IN YEAR-OLD "WOLF ATTACK" CASE

(Wellsboro, March 22, 1979) Wellsboro Police Chief Raymond W. Davis confirmed this week that there is no new evidence in the year-old mystery surrounding the disappearance and death of Wellsboro businessman John Abrams. Abrams' body was found in a remote wooded area northeast of Wellsboro. The Tioga County Coroner ruled that Abrams died of wounds consistent with an attack by a wild animal or group of animals.

"The only good news I have," Chief Davis reported during an exclusive interview with The Bulletin, "is that there have been no similar incidents since then. Whatever killed Mr. Abrams evidently left the area shortly thereafter."

The Fish and Game Commission confirmed last week that there have been no confirmed wolf sightings anywhere in Pennsylvania or New York State in the past year. An unnamed FGC spokesperson, who said that she was not authorized to comment publicly on the case, said:

"Even if Mr. Abrams was attacked and killed by a wolf, which is highly unlikely, it would have to have been a very sick animal, and, being sick, it probably died shortly thereafter. But I must reiterate that the gray wolf was extirpated from Pennsylvania and

neighboring New York State more than 80 years ago. There are no wolves in the wild anywhere within a 500-mile radius of the Commonwealth."

Chief Davis denied that the police have closed the investigation. He stated that the investigation has yet to find any witnesses to the incident, and he described the statements of witnesses who had seen Mr. Abrams earlier in the day as "inconclusive."

"We never close a death case," Davis said. "Not until we know all the answers. Never."

Anyone with any information that they believe would be helpful should contact the Wellsboro Police Department at 555-9600.

"There's no byline on this one. Do you know who wrote it?" Russell asked.

Susan shuffled through the remaining papers in the folder, nodding as she glanced at each one.

"No, this was probably a team piece, put together by several people. Dad began to shift from individual bylines to unsigned pieces around then. He said he wanted to build team spirit, but he pissed off a lot of reporters, and a bunch of them left around that time. I can ask around if anyone remembers."

Russell sensed that this might not be wise at this point.

"No," he said slowly, "let's hold off on that for a while. I'm not sure that you want people to know that you're nosing around this."

"Why, Russell," Susan smiled, "you really do have the makings of a good reporter."

She took another look at the other papers in the file folder, shaking her head this time as if in disbelief.

"The rest of this is just a bunch of old notes from the press conference a year later, but, what's odd is that there's no indication who took them. Old Man Kenyon was dead by then and –"

While she was speaking, Susan opened a plain brown vanilla envelope and started to extract what looked like photographs.

"Oh my god," she gasped, turning her head away and gagging. Russell thought she was going to be sick.

"Are you okay?" he asked.

"Yeah, just give me a minute and whatever you do, don't look at those pictures. They're –" She took three deep breaths and returned the envelope to the file. "They're of – they're of what – what was left of Mr. Abrams when he was found."

"I already heard about the condition of Jack's body from Chief Davis," Russell said quietly. "I don't need to look at them, at least not right now."

Susan looked away, took another deep breath, and returned to the file.

"Sorry about that, Russell. I guess I'm not as tough as I pretend."

Russell decided to say nothing.

"Now this is really interesting," Susan said, holding up a small piece of yellow paper. "It's a phone message from the Reverend Bill Paxton, dated the day after we ran the first article. 'Please do not attempt to contact Mrs. Abrams anymore.'"

Russell reached across the desk and picked up the phone message. "Have you ever seen anything like this?"

"Oh, all the time," Susan replied. "But then there's also this memo from Old Man Kenyon."

She read aloud while Russell looked over her shoulder:

Date: March 25, 1978

From: Kenyon

To: All City Desk Staff

"City Desk?" Poe asked, smiling, looking around. "Which one is it? I've always wanted to see a City Desk."

Susan rolled up the memo and swatted at Russell with it.

"The old man still had his dreams, I guess," Susan replied. She continued reading:

Subject: Abrams Case

In your coverage of the recent death of John Abrams, you are not to mention the following items:

1. The condition of Mr. Abrams body.

2. Mr. Abrams' avocation as a compiler of local folklore.

3. The recurrence of reported sightings of wolves, panthers, and other animals proven to be extinct in this region.

These requests are made to spare Mr. Abrams' family undue grief and invasion of privacy, and to maintain the standards of this newspaper for responsible journalism. Staff members who violate these policies will be held accountable.

"That's outrageous," Russell almost shouted.

"No, it's hilarious, Russell. Kenyon was putting a gag order on himself. This memo was just his attempt to cover his tracks with someone out in the community. Nobody here at the paper would have been fooled."

"Isn't that unusual?" Russell asked. "I mean, what about freedom of the press?"

"No, Russell," Susan replied, "that's editorial discretion. It happens more often than you might think, even at a little outfit like the *Bulletin*. He was before my time, but from everything I've heard, Old Man Kenyon ran a tight ship."

Russell fumed silently while Susan looked at the final piece of paper in the file.

"Hmm, I'd never thought of that," she said.

"Never thought of what?"

Susan handed the sheet of yellow legal paper across to Russell. Russell noticed that it had been written with a fountain pen. The blue ink had soaked through to the back.

"Like I said earlier, Russell: Anyone you know?"

Letters to the Editor
Wellsboro Bulletin
Wellsboro, Pennsylvania
Dear Sir:

As will become abundantly clear in the following paragraphs, this letter is not intended for publication in its entirety, and if you do publish it, I will trust you to edit out material that would be unsuitable for a community newspaper like the Wellsboro Bulletin.

I must take issue with your unthinking reporting of the irresponsible and dangerous speculations by the authorities in the case of the recent death of my neighbor John Abrams. Despite the Coroner's opinion – not a determination or finding as you reported, but an opinion – there is absolutely no evidence that Mr. Abrams was attacked by a wolf or even a pack of wolves.

I agree with the general theory of an animal attack, but no wolf could have done the damage that was done to Mr. Abrams' body. I will not go into detail, but since I discovered Mr. Abrams' body, I had the misfortune of seeing the state of his remains.

It is my belief that the police, as well as the State authorities, should seriously consider the possibility of an attack by a felis concolor azteca, or cougar, also sometimes known as a mountain lion or panther. The extensive damage to Mr. Abrams' neck, and the long cuts on his shoulders and upper back are consistent with the way a cougar attacks: from behind, biting the victim's neck or head and using the cougar's large forepaws to push the victim to the ground. The evisceration that I observed is also consistent with the actions of a cougar once the victim has been downed. Removal of limbs, although uncommon, is not unknown, especially when the cat is extraordinarily large and powerful enough to pull the limbs from the torso.

Cougars still exist in this area. The folklore that Mr. Abrams was studying at the time of his death is full of sightings of cougars, some of them very large. As large as a small man, or even larger, a single cougar could easily cause the massive injuries that Mr. Abrams suffered. I am astounded therefore that no one is willing to consider or discuss openly this obvious hypothesis.

Chief Raymond Davis says there is no cause for alarm. I respectfully disagree. If felis concolor azteca was the agent of Mr. Abrams' death, we can only expect that it will strike again.

Faithfully yours,
Simon Poe
April 3, 1978

All Russell could say was "holy shit." He looked at Susan. "Was this published? Do you remember? Can you find out?"

"No, I'm sure it never was. If it had been, this file would probably have had a photocopy of the actual printed copy, not just the original. No offense to the memory of your uncle, but this is what we sometimes call a tinfoil hat letter. We get dozens of them every week. Usually they take issue with something in the paper. Space aliens, communists, and conspiracy theories are the most popular themes."

Russell tried very hard to control his reaction to Susan's comments about tinfoil hats. He wasn't sure whether to laugh or be insulted on behalf of his uncle.

Susan paused, as if she were waiting for a reaction from Russell. She then quickly continued, "But it's not. This most definitely is not tinfoil hat material. I mean it looks like classic tinfoil hat – handwritten on a legal pad, advocating an unconventional theory – but anyone that knew anything about the case should have taken it seriously. But there doesn't appear to have been any follow up, not even a telephone call. Chief Davis is going on about wolves, and the state is saying that it couldn't have been wolves, and here is your uncle, the guy who found the body, making a case for a cougar. And nobody followed up."

Russell sat silently looking at his uncle's letter. He traced his index finger over some of the writing.

"Know any cougar experts, Susan?" he asked.

"Oddly enough, I do. So do you: Clay Collins."

"Clay Collins?"

"Yeah, the aging ex-Marine hippie you met at Dick and Connie's."

Cougars

The first thing Russell Poe noticed as he followed Clay Collins into his den was the small brass plate by the door:

PENNSYLVANIA COUGAR RESEARCH CENTER
C.Z. COLLINS, Director

The Center was a converted room in Clay's house, filled with books, pictures, maps, and piles of folders on the floor. Except for the large window behind the large walnut desk in the center of the room, the walls were completely covered with photographs of cougars and a large map of the United States and Canada, with multicolored pins stuck in it.

"This is fascinating, Clay," Russell said as he sat down in an easy chair that Clay had just cleared of old magazines. "Tell me about the Research Center. Where is it? How big is it?"

"You're sitting in the center of it, Russell," Clay replied. "Like King Louis XIV would have said, 'The Research Center is *moi*'.

"And here is my research assistant," Clay smiled, patting a small computer plugged into a small monitor on his desk."

"I've been thinking about getting one of those, Clay. I never felt the need for one, even when I was practicing law. Our secretaries had them, but I still used the good old yellow legal pad."

"Well, I don't know what I'd do without mine" Clay replied. "What I'm doing now is trying to summarize all the notes, documents, *et cetera*, that I've collected over the years and put them into some sort of order, so that I can retrieve the information I need without rummaging through all my files. You can put a hell of a lot more data on one of those floppy disks than you can in a whole box of paper."

"That's what I need, Clay. I have boxes and boxes of notepads, notebooks, loose notes, drafts. I can look around and tell that you know what I mean."

Clay simply smiled and nodded in agreement.

"Well," Russell continued. "I really appreciate you meeting me on a Sunday."

"No problem," Clay said. "It gives us a chance to get to know each other a little better. I enjoyed meeting you at Connie and Dick's a couple weekends ago. What can I do for you?"

"Well, Susan Kline says that you're the resident expert around here on cougars," Russell said.

"I guess so," Clay replied. "Basically, what we do – what I do – here is track sightings of cougars in Pennsylvania and other parts, mostly in the northeastern United States. I publish them in a newsletter that I send out each quarter, or whenever I have enough material to fill four pages. It also has some other information."

Clay handed Russell a four-page printed newsletter. Russell immediately noticed the fuzzy photograph of what looked like a big light brown dog – or it could have been a cat – partially hidden by bushes.

"The latest issue," he said. "I currently have more than a thousand readers on my mailing list. At least, I like to think that they're all actually reading it."

"So, you're really interested in cougars, trying to improve public understanding of them, things like that?" Russell asked.

Clay smiled. "Yeah, that's how it evolved, but I guess my main purpose is to counter all the lies that the Fish and Game Commission has been putting out all these years."

"That cougars are extinct in Pennsylvania?"

"Right. Come over here to the desk and have a look."

Clay pulled a large, white loose-leaf binder from a pile of papers. He opened it in front of Russell. The first ten pages were filled with photographs of cougars. He flipped through the other pages, which were mostly photocopies of newspaper articles.

"Very interesting," Russell said. He hoped that his voice didn't sound non-committal, but he saw nothing very convincing.

"That's just my talking-points book," Clay said, "what I show to visitors or possible donors."

Clay pointed over Russell's shoulder to a bank of four gray metal filing cabinets, with four drawers each.

"Back there behind you is where I keep the background materials: more clippings, some books, more photos, anything that you'd ever want to know."

Russell turned and looked.

"But don't get too impressed, Russell. Only two of those cabinets are full. I got a good deal at an auction of some old state property a couple of years ago."

"You mentioned donors, Clay. Do you get many?"

"No, not really. Sometimes somebody doing some research for a paper or an article might contact me and come up here. They're usually disappointed when they see the place, so I tell them about how I'd like someday to open a proper center, with a museum, library, gift shop, the whole works. Sometimes I can get them to cough up a few bucks."

"That's impressive, Clay. Remind me when I leave to get on your mailing list, and I'd be happy to donate a few bucks. You're doing worthwhile work." Russell hoped that he sounded sincere. "But I have really a basic question to start with. What are the differences among a cougar, a mountain lion, and a panther?"

Clay leaned back in his desk chair.

"In North America, there aren't any. The three names all refer to *felis concolor azteca.* In the West, they're mostly known as mountain lions. In the South, they call them panthers. Here in the Northeast, we usually call them cougars. But it's all the same cat, with the possible exception of the Florida panther, of course. Some zoologists say that the Florida panther is a distinct subspecies."

"So," Russell asked, "if I hear people around here talking about panthers, they're really referring to a cougar or mountain lion?"

"Well, not exactly, Russell. Folks around here don't usually use the term *mountain lion.* You will hear people around here sometimes talk about panthers. Generally, when they use the word *panther,* they're referring to a very large, very powerful cougar, maybe two hundred pounds or more."

"They get that big?"

Clay flipped the notebook pages about halfway to the back and pointed to a large cat standing in a clearing in a forest. This photograph seemed clearer than the others. Russell wondered whether it had been retouched.

"Imagine a short, compact, very powerful man. Normal size for a cougar is about one hundred thirty to one hundred fifty pounds. An adult will stand about twenty-six to thirty inches at the shoulder and will be anywhere from forty-three to fifty-four inches long, not counting the tail. That's normal for the North American cat, but there has been evidence of ones much larger, two hundred pounds or more."

"What kind of evidence?"

"Just look here." Clay turned the page and pointed to two pictures of paw print casts. "The top prints are from a pretty typical-sized adult cougar. We know it's a cougar because of its size and shape, as well as the absence of claw marks. Forepaws are about ten centimeters, or just under four inches, front to back, and 8.5 centimeters wide. We can get a pretty good estimate of weight from the size of the forepaw print. This cat probably weighed about seventy kilograms, or about 154 pounds. All in all, a pretty good-sized cat, but not unusually large. It could have been male or female, but the females usually run a little smaller than the males."

Clay pointed to the bottom picture on the page. "Now here's a print taken out in Minnesota about ten years ago. It measured thirteen centimeters by ten centimeters, more than an inch larger all around. The cat that made that print had to go at least ninety to a hundred kilos. That's more than two hundred pounds, maybe even a bit bigger."

"Where was the first print, the seventy-kilo cat, taken?"

"On the Cobbs Creek Golf Course, in Fairmount Park, Philadelphia."

"No way. It's got to be a hoax. I'm from Philadelphia, Clay."

Clay smiled. "It's no hoax, my friend. I took that cast myself. There were several prints, but this was the best. You must remember it, Russell. It was in the papers down there for almost two weeks. There was a steady string of sightings. The first one was on a golf course in Cobbs Creek Park, near the city line with Upper Darby Township. Then there were several in Delaware County, then a few in Chester County as the cougar moved west. The last one was on the bank of Octoraro Creek in southern Lancaster County about five weeks later. We tracked that cat for over sixty miles."

"We?"

"Me and a couple of people down in the Philadelphia area."

"From the universities?"

"The universities? Hell, no, Russell. We approached a couple of folks at Temple and Drexel, but it was clear that they thought we were a bunch of crackpots. One of the profs even made a smart-ass remark about the Loch Ness Monster having been sighted in the Schuylkill."

Russell returned to his chair. When he lived in Philadelphia, he seldom read the local newspapers, except for the front page and the business section, and he almost never watched television. It was entirely possible that something like that could have happened and he would have missed it. Still, it was so hard to believe.

"But what about up here, Clay? That might have been a cat that escaped from the zoo or from the home of somebody who keeps exotic pets. Have there been any confirmed sightings up here?"

"The official line, Russell, is that the last confirmed cougar sightings in Pennsylvania were in 1891, when one was killed over in Clinton County and another was killed in Clearfield County, further west of here. As late as 1903 there were sightings reported in twenty-three of the state's sixty-seven counties. Up in New York State, there was a confirmed kill of a cougar in 1908 at Elk Lake. Of course, the state won't confirm a sighting unless a state game warden actually sees the cat and positively identifies it."

"How often does that happen?"

"Never. At least not since 1891."

"Why won't the state admit at least the possibility that there are still cougars in the wild? I think that would be something they'd want to publicize."

"I don't know, Russell. To be fair, the state guys can't confirm what they don't see with their own eyes. Pawprints can be faked, but anyone who knows anything at all about cougars can usually spot a fake print right away. Also, a confirmed sighting could really cause a panic, especially if it involved an attack of some sort. The Cobbs Creek cougar scared people away from the golf course for months after that."

"Do cougars attack people? I always thought they tried to stay away from people?"

"They do try to stay away, but if people start crowding them out of their range, they will sometimes go a little crazy. That's what's happened out west as vacation homes and such have encroached into the wild. There have been a couple of cases of cougars having someone's pet dog for lunch.

"Keep in mind, Russell, that since 1890 there have been only ten confirmed fatal cougar attacks on people anywhere in the United States. Half of these have been in the past ten years. A couple of states have stopped enforcing their bans on cougar hunting in response to the hysteria, and that's even though two of the subspecies, the Eastern cougar and the Florida panther, are on the Federal Endangered Species List, which started about ten years ago.

"Let me show you something."

Clay rummaged around on his desk and found a note card clipped to a photocopy of a newspaper article.

"Here it is. This has got to be my all-time favorite cougar story. A friend of mine down in West Virginia sent it to me."

Clay handed it to Russell and continued. "Here's the story in a nutshell. Over the course of three or four days, the police in the Victoria, British Columbia, area had received about a half dozen reports of a mountain lion on the loose. Then, one fine September day, a cougar just strolled into an office building in downtown Victoria. The receptionist saw just its tail and thought it was a big dog, so she called the local dog catchers. They came and, after the initial shock, shot it with tranquilizer darts. It was a three-year old female, very malnourished. It had been a very dry summer in British Columbia, which was especially tough on the bigger wildlife, like bears and cougars. They caught another one further north, wandering around a park right in the middle of a Vancouver suburb."

"Yes, Clay, but that's out west. What about here in Pennsylvania? Have there been any other than the sightings down in the Philadelphia area?"

"My friend in West Virginia, the one that sent me that clipping, he runs a similar operation outside Morgantown. It's much bigger than mine and he gets some support from West Virginia University. Now, he tracks cougar sightings all over the East Coast. He says that just last year there was one actual sighting, confirmed by a couple sets of tracks down in the northeastern corner of Preston County, West Virginia, near where Pennsylvania, West Virginia, and Maryland meet. I guess that's almost Pennsylvania.

"But that's about the way it has been running in Pennsylvania, one or two credible sightings every two or three years, but nothing officially confirmed. Further south, down in western Virginia and West Virginia, and down into the southern Appalachians, however, there are dozens."

Russell sat silently for a moment, taking it all in.

"And I thought you were just a retired Marine."

Clay smiled. "Well, cryptozoology has always interested me, ever since I was in high school. Growing up around here you hear stories about birds and animals that once roamed these parts but have disappeared. I guess I just could never accept that, you know, and was always looking up in hopes of seeing a passenger pigeon or an ivory-billed woodpecker or running into one of the last eastern bison in some remote part of the forest. And then there's a really special link between the cougar and this area in particular."

"I know," Russell responded. "I've been editing some of the work that Jack Abrams did on the folklore of the region."

Clay's smile dimmed for a second. "Yes. Jack. Which is why you're really here."

"I originally had two questions when I came here, Clay. The first is whether there was any basis in fact for all the legends about giant panthers still roaming these mountains. You've answered that question. It appears that there is."

"Don't jump the gun, Russell. You and I have been talking about ordinary cougars, not the bigger cats like that one in Minnesota or some of the ones in the west. I don't have anything specific about what you'd call giant panthers around here."

"Good point, Clay. So, we're talking about what I guess you'd call ordinary cougars, then. The state says that even those are extinct around here."

"Agreed," Clay replied. "But actually, *extirpated* is the correct technical term – killed to extinction locally but not genetically extinct elsewhere.

"So, what's your second question, Russell?"

"It's about Jack's death."

"What's your interest in it?" Russell noticed a look of concern on Clay's face. Clay cleared his throat.

"Well, Clay, it has sort of a legendary quality to it. A successful businessman is set upon by wolves in the forest, the only problem being that there are supposedly no wolves at all anywhere for hundreds of miles."

"But we both know that wolves didn't kill Jack Abrams, don't we, Russell?" Clay had spun around in his chair to face Russell. The sunlight from the window refracted through his silver hair momentarily to create a rainbow aura around him. Russell closed his eyes and rubbed them.

"That's what his wife has asked me to find out." Russell regretted the words the instant he spoke them, but he needed some sort of moral authority. Surrounded by pictures of cougars and artifacts of their kills, he suddenly felt like prey himself.

Clay sat back in his chair. He blinked. "Oh."

"Well, I'll get to the point then, Russell. Jack Abrams was killed by a cougar. I'm sure of it. Right after they found his body, your uncle called me."

"You knew Simon?"

"No, in fact the only times I ever had any contact with him at all were just that one phone call and a visit to his place a couple of days later."

"What did he want?"

"He said that he was at the library and had seen the Research Center's phone number listed in the phone book. I was really surprised, because I don't think I get more than three or four calls per year on that line, other than wrong numbers. I use it mostly for my fax machine.

"Simon asked me if I had heard about how Jack Abrams had supposedly been attacked and killed by a wild animal. He said the body had been found on his property and that he had gotten a look at the remains before they took them away."

"What did he tell you?"

"Well, I don't remember all of the details, and to tell you the truth I'm just as glad that I don't. It was pretty gruesome. But what he described had classic signs of a cougar attack."

"Which were –?"

"Which were the bite marks and claw marks on the head, neck, and shoulders, for one thing. Cougars don't attack like wolves do. Wolves generally run their prey down. They'll go for the throat first and then just generally mutilate their prey.

Russell hoped that Clay wouldn't get too graphic.

"No, when a cougar attacks a larger prey, like elk, horse, or cattle, they will almost always attack from cover and from behind. Sometimes they actually jump on their prey from behind and force it to the ground. The cat will go for the head, back of the neck, and shoulders. The prey is usually surprised and doesn't have time to get away. What your uncle described to me was a typical cougar attack, probably by one animal, but a big one."

"Would you expect to see that a cougar attack on a man would be any different?"

Clay was silent for a moment, appearing to ponder his answer.

"No, I wouldn't, Russell." He said. He paused for another couple of seconds before continuing. "If anything, there would be fewer signs that a man tried to get away. Humans don't have the same instincts in the forest as other prey. We wouldn't smell or sense the presence of the cat. It would be on a man and probably kill him before he knew it."

"The damage to Mr. Abrams' stomach area was also typical of a cougar," Clay continued. "After they bring their prey down, the first area that the cougar eats will be the heart, liver, lungs, and so forth.

It's the easiest to get at. I understand that there was dismemberment, as well. If they are strong enough, big cougars might sometimes gnaw through the joints, rip off the limbs, and carry them away to hide. The big cats can do that easily, but that's a little unusual with something as big as a grown man."

Russell felt the cold sweat breaking out. "That's enough," he said weakly. "I get the picture."

Clay looked concerned. "Oh, shit, Russell. I'm sorry. I didn't mean to –"

"It's okay." Russell took a long drink of cola. "Are there any other signs that would point to a cougar attack?"

"Well, without going into any more detail, from what your uncle told me about the extent of the, uh, injuries, I'd have to say that if it was a cougar, it was a very large one. A typical sized cougar couldn't do that much damage to a man, especially not to the limbs. Neither could a wolf, not even a pack of them. No, it had to have been a cat, and a big one, that killed Jack Abrams.

"There are several other typical signs of a cougar attack. A cougar will almost always cover its kill, or part of it, with leaves, sticks, soil, whatever is loose. Even where there's nothing to bury the kill under, the cat will try to leave something on top, if only a twig or two.

"Cougars will also leave what we call *scrapes* or *scratches,* little mounds of dirt about six inches high, usually marked with urine or feces. This is how the cat marks the kill as his."

"I'm not sure if there were anything like that."

"Neither was your uncle. I'm sure I asked him about it. I think he said that the cops were walking all over the area. They didn't know what they should have been looking for, so I'm pretty sure any scrapes would have been trampled down. When I went to the scene a couple of days later with your uncle, it was impossible for me to know whether any of those signs had been there."

"Clay, did the police ever contact you about the case?"

"No."

"Doesn't that seem a little odd, given your expertise about large animals like cougars?"

"Not really, I'm known as the cougar nut, not the wolf nut. I don't think it ever occurred to the cops to ask my opinion."

"Didn't you want to set the record straight when Chief Davis started talking about a wolf attack?"

Clay drew in a deep breath. His face turned slightly redder. He seemed to choose his words with care. When he spoke, he seemed to be fighting to control some emotion that Russell couldn't identify.

"No, I didn't, Russell, and I'll tell you why. There were two good reasons. Reason number one: I don't volunteer to help the fucking cops. You can't trust them, even the so-called good cops. It's just a rule of mine, learned the hard way in the Corps, and remember this is a Marine lawyer talking here.

"Rule number two: The last thing we needed was a lot of hysteria about cougars. It was bad enough when the wolf story started circulating. It's a miracle no one was killed. There were folks who would shoot at anything that moved."

"That's what I've heard."

"So, I told your uncle two things, Russell. Thing number one: If an animal attacked poor old Jack Abrams, it had to have been a cougar, and probably the biggest fucking cougar that had ever lived in these parts. Thing number two: I told him to keep it to himself. The last thing we needed was for fucking Ray Davis to get up at a press conference and start talking about cougars. Like I said, his wolf scare was bad enough."

"Did you know that my uncle wrote a letter to the editor of the *Bulletin* arguing that it probably was a cougar, not wolves?" Russell asked.

"Oh, Christ. I was afraid that he'd do that. Was it published?"

"No, apparently the publisher of the paper killed any mention of a cougar theory and shut down any further reporting about the case."

Clay smiled faintly. "Well, no harm, no foul."

"I hope you don't take this wrong, Clay, but it sounds like you were on the cougar's side." Russell tried to reassure Clay with a big grin.

"Maybe I am, Russell. Maybe I am. And who knows? Maybe it wasn't the cat's fault. Maybe Jack Abrams did something to provoke it."

Russell thanked Clay for his time and the information.

"You've given me a lot to think about, Clay," Russell said as Clay showed him to the door and they shook hands. He started to walk toward his car, then stopped and turned around.

"One last question, Clay, which I forgot to ask you. Was there anything about Jack Abrams' death, based on what you were told about it – any little detail or circumstance –that would be inconsistent with it being a cougar?"

"Yes, now that you mention it, Russell, there was just one thing. It was the face."

"The face?"

"Yes, your uncle told me that his face had been – well, *mauled* isn't quite the right word – but it had been badly lacerated, with long, deep cuts across the face. Cougars don't do that."

John

It took Russell five weeks to return to the Rocks. He didn't understand why he kept postponing it. Three times recently he had started up the mountain path behind his house, but each time he turned back once he reached the ridge. It was not a matter of his not wanting to go further; he just felt that he wasn't prepared to do so. Russell sometimes caught himself looking down as he walked along the paths, searching for traces of large pawprints in the dirt. Any noise in the forest made him flinch. He told himself that he was letting his imagination overpower him, that it was all silly. Nonetheless, he kept thinking about Jack walking that ridge trail on a March afternoon in the last hour of his life, not knowing what was lying in wait for him.

Russell also felt that he hadn't thought things through enough to proceed further with his discovery of the underground chambers and tunnels. His first impulse had been to notify the County Historical Society and perhaps someone in the Archeology Department at Penn State, if there was one. However, he soon convinced himself that he should not tell anyone about the underground chambers, not yet. He needed to collect more evidence, photographs, maybe some artifacts, and definitely more precise measurements before he could credibly announce what he had found. After reading Jack's notes, and talking with Ray Davis and Clay Collins, he was beginning to feel that he really knew less about the Indian Rocks, not more, than he needed to know on another level, one that he couldn't quite define.

One time, about two weeks before, Wanda had casually asked about how his explorations around the Rocks were progressing. He replied that he had found "something really interesting," but she didn't ask for more details, and Russell quickly was relieved that she hadn't. Neither of them had mentioned the Rocks since.

A few days after he found the underground network under the Rocks, Russell had returned to confirm that the covered-up hole where he fell and the exit where he escaped had not been disturbed. But, even now, after having done so, he still couldn't escape a weird fear that his experience had been only a dream or a hallucination of some sort, even though he was convinced at a rational level that it all had been real. He sometimes even chuckled at the vision of himself proudly leading an intrepid group of investigators and scientists up to the Rocks only to be unable to find any trace of the entrance or exit. He imagined them staring at him, annoyed but also feeling sorry for him.

He could easily dismiss this as nonsense, but all these crazy thoughts suggested to him that he needed at least to check the site again, to reconfirm the precise location of the tunnel system, and to assure himself that it hadn't been disturbed since his last visit.

Monday morning dawned sunny and the weather forecast promised a warm spring day. Today's the day, Russell vowed.

He started to telephone Whitey. Whitey had worked with him at the Rocks, and it might be good to have a witness. Although he liked Whitey, he could not ignore his growing doubts about him: the incident with the dead deer and the meeting that Whitey had with Jack just hours before Jack was killed. But Whitey understood the excavation project at the Rocks. There wasn't any reason yet to rule out Whitey for future work, at least not yet.

Whitey had telephoned several times in the past five weeks to see whether Russell had any work for him. In the early days of spring, Russell really didn't have any major projects or chores that needed Whitey's help; except for one time in mid-April when Whitey helped him remove a tree that had fallen during a windstorm earlier and was partially blocking his driveway to the road.

There had been little conversation between the two men as they worked together during the failing hours of that gloomy Saturday afternoon. They wanted to get the debris cleared before dark. After they finished, and as Russell was paying Whitey, Whitey looked back at the mountain behind Russell's house.

"Been up to the Rocks, recently, Russell? Anything new going on up there?"

"No," Russell replied cautiously. "I really haven't had time and, besides, the weather has been lousy."

Russell's lawyer's instincts told him that he should not ask Whitey why he had asked about "anything new." Whitey immediately answered Russell's unspoken question.

"Just curious, is all. Wondering how your dig was getting along."

"No, Whitey. I just haven't had the time to do anything. I plan to get back to work up there maybe in a month or so, when the weather gets a little better."

Whitey looked silently at Russell for a second or two. Russell sensed that Whitey didn't believe him, but Whitey said nothing further about it. He just tugged at the bill of his ballcap, said, "Okay," and left.

Now, as he hiked up the path to the crest of the ridge, Russell again had that strange sense that someone was following him, just out of sight to the left. As before, he would stop suddenly, look, and listen, but detected nothing.

"Just my nerves," he said aloud as he continued up the path. "I've got to do something about this paranoia," he chuckled.

Russell noticed nothing unusual when he arrived at the Rocks. The brush that he had piled over the place where he had fallen into the chamber appeared to be undisturbed, except for the possible addition of a few more branches that must have fallen during the ice storm in March. He photographed the brush pile from several vantage points then went down the eastern slope to the exit. It was harder to find, but after a few minutes of retracing his steps when he escaped from the tunnel and probing the brush in the general area that he remembered, he found the brush-covered wooden door. New growth had covered most of it, blending it into the hillside. It, too, appeared not to have been touched since he put it back in place. He had to remove it carefully, so as not to uproot any of the new plants. He took some photographs of the area, with the door removed and in place.

It was now early afternoon. Sitting leaning against what had become his "favorite rock," Russell struggled to keep his eyes open. The surprisingly warm early spring sun, the cheese and half-bottle of wine he had brought along for lunch, and his relief at finding the site undisturbed combined to make him drowsy. His thoughts drifted to distant and long-ago places. The slight chill that lingered in the breeze made him think of autumn, not spring. The sunny, tingling air working its way through the forest transported sounds that he knew must have been so far away that he had to be dreaming about them, and about the sleepy Sunday afternoons in the back seat of his aunt's old Plymouth, riding into the mountains east of Pittsburgh to see autumn foliage.

Russell wondered if that special field was still there, just over the hill where U.S. Route 30 ran close alongside the Pennsylvania Turnpike, just a few yards apart. They had stopped for a moment to stretch their legs, and to look at the rolls of hay, perfectly spaced awaiting pickup, stretching before them in a hazy golden October afternoon. He was sure it was still there. He had passed it many times since. Why hadn't he ever stopped again?

Russell suddenly sensed the old man's presence without hearing him.

"Oh," the man announced. "I'm sorry. I didn't know you were napping."

Russell quickly got up, brushing the dried grass and leaves off his pants.

"Oh. Yeah. Well, hi there. Just daydreaming a little after lunch."

"Seemed to me more like real dreaming, sir."

"Well, maybe some of both." The two men chuckled, smiling at each other.

They regarded each other silently for a moment, each man continuing to smile. The old man was short and wiry, with a medium-length white beard and long white hair tied in a ponytail. No, Russell thought, it was more like a club, like they used to wear in the early nineteenth century. The old man wore a blue chambray shirt, faded almost to white, covered by a long blue jacket that drooped halfway to his knees. His blue jeans were tucked into high-top moccasins. He carried a bag over his shoulder. It looked like a laundry bag, but made of leather, with a rawhide drawstring at the top. It appeared full, but must have been light, because the old man handled it without strain. All that was missing was a coonskin cap and a Pennsylvania long rifle.

"Oh, I'm sorry. Forgetting my manners. Hope it's all right if I hike across your property."

Russell looked back. How does he know who I am?

"Oh, my," the stranger continued. "I do have the advantage of you, sir. I know your name, Mr. Russell Poe, and you don't know mine. Well, my name's John."

The two men shook hands, John bowing slightly as he did.

"Yes sir," John continued. I had heard that Simon had passed on and that his nephew had taken over his place. I had seen you down around your house, so I knew it was you."

"You come here often?" Russell asked.

"Well, not as much as I used to. Only every now and then. I hope you don't mind, because this is one of my favorite spots. Just like it is yours, I reckon. But if you have any objection to my trespassing, I'll –"

"Oh, no," Russell waved his hands. "No, it's okay. You're not trespassing. Just so there's no hunting and no litter. That's all I care about, really. These woods are too big for just me to enjoy. I don't mind sharing them. I know that people like to hike along the old Indian trail and come up here to the Rocks from time to time. You're welcome to come here whenever you want."

"Well, thank you, sir. That's very kind of you."

The old man again gave a funny little quarter bow and sat down, stretched out his legs and leaned back against one of the rocks. Rather than use the sack as a cushion, he dropped it to his side.

"Ah, that's better. These old bones are getting so tired that even a rock feels soft."

"So, where do you live, John? I don't think I've ever heard any of the neighbors mention you," Russell said as he sat down again.

"Not surprising. No, not surprising in the least. I sort of keep to myself," John said.

"But you come through here a lot?"

"Oh sure, I've been tramping around these mountains for more years than I can remember. Mind, I don't get over this far as much as I used to. But sometimes I just get a-wandering and end up all sorts of far places. Why just last evening I set out to take a little constitutional before bedtime and ended up spending the whole night out under the stars, just running the ridges, enjoying being out in the night. Watched the sunrise, took a little nap, and then decided I'd come over here on my way home and check things out."

"You were out all night? You must be in pretty good shape for a man of –" Russell paused. "Do you mind me asking?"

"You can ask, sir, but I ain't telling."

"Sorry. Forgive me for asking."

John threw his head back and laughed, a high, sharp laugh that sounded almost like a bird call.

"I ain't telling 'cause I don't rightly know. Back when I was born, they didn't keep good records. So, I just tell folks I'm as old as the hills."

"So, where do you live, John?"

"Oh, I have a little cabin, just an old one-room lean-to really, further up in the mountains, maybe twenty miles or so from here. That's twenty miles hiking up and down the mountains, not as the crow flies. It's just me and my cat. He wandered by one day. I don't know how he got clear up where I live, but he did. So, I fed him, and, being a cat, he decided to stay. I named him General Steuben. That must have been ten years ago."

"Do you have a phone? Electricity?"

"No, sir. I really don't need them. Never had them before, and I've gotten along all right. But that's just my winter home, where General Steuben and I hole up. When spring comes, I set out again and just sort of wander around the mountains. I got me some little camps here and there that I use from time to time, and I just move from one to the other, a couple nights here, maybe a week there. General Steuben, though, he's a homebody, so he always stays at the cabin. Strangest thing, though, is that General Steuben always knows when I'm coming back from one of my rambles, and he comes out into the forest, finds me, and escorts me the last mile or so home. What a cat, sir! Yes sir, there is something about cats that we'll never understand."

"So how do you support yourself?" Russell asked. "No, wait. I'm sorry John. I shouldn't be asking you all these questions."

"No, it's all right. Anything I don't want to answer, I won't. Anything I don't know, I usually make up. It's all right. After all, I'm the trespasser on your land, no matter how kind you are about it. Most people would make me look up the barrel of a shotgun when they asked me questions."

"It's not that, John. I really shouldn't be prying. But you've got to admit, you're a pretty interesting person. All my adult life I've always lived in big cities: Pittsburgh, Philadelphia, a little while in Washington. I've never met anyone like you before."

"Not many like me, sir. Not around here anymore. I just sort of live off the land. Do a few odd jobs now and then when I have to, but to tell the truth, I think my last odd job was longer ago than I can rightly remember. Catch most of my own food or grow it."

John laughed again, slapping his palm on his thigh.

"Pittsburgh and Philadelphia. Haven't thought of them in years. You may not believe it, sir, but the last time I was in Philadelphia, it took me the best part of three days to get there. Yes sir. Three whole days.

"First, I had to tramp from before nightfall until sunup, just to get down to Wellsboro Junction, where you could board a train back then. We didn't have any roads or railroad lines up where I lived that a fellow could walk along. No sir, I had to use the old Indian trails, what was left of them, or go cross country. Then it was an overnight railroad journey – actually three trains – down to Philadelphia. Yes sir, three days in all. And I hear that folks get there in just five hours now."

"What took you to Philadelphia?"

"Oh, back in those days, I still had a little business – a farming business I guess you could call it – up in the mountains and, every once in a while, I'd need to take my goods to market. Most times I'd just go over to Scranton, where I knew a man that would take the goods and sell them for me in New York, but sometimes I'd go to Philadelphia, wherever I got the better price."

"But that was a long time ago. I guess things have changed a lot down there since I was there."

"I'm afraid you're right, John. But you'd probably recognize some of the landmarks, like Independence Hall and the old Wanamaker store."

"Well, I don't rightly remember a Wanamaker store, but Independence Hall, back in my day, we still called it the Old State House."

"That's right. But it's a big tourist area now."

"And Pittsburgh, I believe you mentioned."

"Yes, and Washington."

"Oh now, I've never been to the Federal City. I understand it's a real pest hole, all swampy and disease-ridden and the like."

Russell laughed. "Well, I won't argue with you about the pests, but I wouldn't say it's swampy or that there's a lot of disease."

John nodded thoughtfully. "Well, that's good to know. I don't know why they had to move the capital around so much. I thought it was just fine down there in Philadelphia."

"Actually, I think I'd rather have the politicians further away." Russell was beginning to enjoy the conversation immensely.

"That is true, sir. I had not thought about it in that way."

The two men sat side by side for a few moments, each looking into the woods. John broke the silence first.

"Pittsburgh, you say?" he asked.

"What about Pittsburgh?"

"I believe you said that you have been to Pittsburgh."

"Oh yes," Russell replied. "I went to law school there. I also lived for about a year in Washington. Our law firm had an office in Washington, and I worked there for a while. When I said I had lived in big cities, I mentioned Philadelphia, Pittsburgh, and Washington. Most of my adult life, though, I've lived in Philadelphia. Until I moved here, of course."

"Well, that's what puzzles me, sir. I wouldn't consider Pittsburgh a big city, at least not the last time I was there."

"Well, it's not nearly as big as Philadelphia."

"But I have nothing against Pittsburgh, no sir. I was only there once. It was an agreeable little town all snug by its three rivers. I boarded a steamboat there, the *Washington* I believe she was called, a big stern wheeler – they say she was the biggest of her class in the country at the time, more than a hundred feet long, as I recall – for my journey all the way down to New Orleans."

"That must have been exciting. I think there still are one or two boats that go up and down the Ohio and Mississippi."

"Well, the *Washington,* she was more than a boat, sir. She was a floating palace, and we all lived like kings, we did. That was before the war, of course. I'm sure she's been scrapped for many years now.

"But Pittsburgh, sir. Pittsburgh impressed me as an agreeable little town. Yes sir, agreeable and with good prospects. A good place to board a floating palace like the *Washington*."

Russell could almost smell the black smoke from the boilers belching into a red evening sky.

"Now, it's my turn to ask you some questions," John chuckled.

"Sure."

"Well, I suppose the biggest question of all is why you moved here. I hear that you were a famous lawyer down there in Philadelphia. Why give all that up to move up here in the mountains?"

"Well, I wasn't famous, but thank you for the compliment. When my uncle, Simon Poe, died, I inherited the house."

"True, you did. But why did you decide to move up here? I'm sure you had a nice enough place in Philadelphia?"

"I did. In fact, John, I hadn't intended to keep my uncle's place. I drove up here one day to see it before I decided to sell it. But once I was here there was something about it, and about this area, that appealed to me. I sort of felt at home. I was well enough off from my law practice, so I really couldn't come up with any good reason not to move here."

John kept silent, looking at Russell with his deep blue eyes, waiting for more.

"Besides, it would give me a chance to do some writing."

"Oh, you're an author as well as a lawyer. What sort of writing do you do?"

"Not very much, I'm afraid. I've always been interested in regional history, and I've published a book and a few short pieces about it."

"Which region would that be, sir?"

"Oh, Pennsylvania mostly. My book was about life on the frontier in colonial Pennsylvania. Right now, I'm working on a project about the French and Indian War in Pennsylvania."

"Now that was one long, tiresome war, I can tell you, sir, especially around here. There weren't many white folks here back then, and we never knew what to expect from the Indians. First, they'd be on the side of the French and then they'd side with the English. There'd be great long periods of quiet, and then there'd be a raid or a skirmish somewhere. Most times, the French and the English did all the fighting. The Indians were smart. They'd just stand by and watch the white men kill each other. And by 1800 most all the Indians had cleared out, either gone west into the Ohio Country or up into New York. And most of the Frenchies high-tailed it back up into Canada, although a few of them settled around here, but not many.

"Can't say that I know why you'd want to write about it, sir. I guess everything that's worth saying about the war has been said already. Not a lot of it happened around here, though, mostly just an Indian raid every now and then."

"That's my understanding, too, John. So, I'm going to write mostly about Braddock's march to Fort Duquesne. That all took place in southern Pennsylvania and Maryland."

"Well, I've always thought there's enough other mysteries around here for a whole room full of books. Like these rocks here, sir. I'll wager that they've got your interest."

"Actually, I have wondered about them. What can you tell me about them?"

"Nothing to tell, sir. They've been here forever, as far as I know."

John stood up, rising without using his hands for support.

"Well, sir, I'd love to spend the afternoon talking with you, but I want to be back home before sundown if I can. I really don't want to spend a second night under the stars when I hadn't planned to spend even one. It's too early in the year for that, and General Steuben is probably hoping that I'm bringing something good for him in this bag."

Russell stood and shook hands with John, who again gave the curious little quarter bow.

"I've really enjoyed talking with you, John. And please feel welcome to come here any time. I hope we meet again."

"I enjoyed your company too, sir. I don't see folks much anymore. In fact, I guess I sort of try to stay away from them too much. Don't know why that is. So maybe we'll meet up again. I hope so.

"There's one other thing about this here stone circle, Russell," the old man said as he picked up the sack and tossed it over his shoulder. It struck his back with a soft thump. Russell realized that this was the first time the old man addressed him by his first name.

"Well, I don't know just how to say it right, Russell. But, if I were you, I wouldn't go poking around too much about these rocks."

"Why not?" Russell tried to look into the old man's eyes, but they remained fixed on the forest off to his left.

"That's what I can't tell you, Russell. Let us just say, sir, that there are some folks around here who feel mighty peculiar about this place. There's a lot that goes on up here in these parts that you'll never know, and that you don't want to know. And that's best, Russell."

Russell stared at the same spot the old man was watching. He didn't notice anything.

"I'm not sure I understand, John. What are you trying to tell me?"

The old man glanced in Russell's direction, and winked.

"Nothing is ever what it appears, sir."

Before Russell could reply, John turned and strode across the clearing. As he disappeared into the forest, Russell thought he heard the old man say something else, but he couldn't tell what it was. A few seconds later, Russell saw a flash of blue against the many shades of green – was it his jacket? – and he thought he heard the old man laughing in the forest.

What Can Seem Real Sometimes

Russell put down Jack's *Journal #4,* the page marked with a pencil from the small Mason jar that he kept on his desk. He stared out the window into the dark.

Had he actually met someone at the Rocks earlier that afternoon? Had it been an old, bearded, strangely dressed man? Or had it been one of those short dreams one often has while dozing after a quick lunch outdoors, half of it a dream and half wandering thoughts?

That had been Wanda's theory. Russell had just come down the mountain path and entered his house through the kitchen. By coincidence, Wanda had just come up onto the front porch. Her hand was raised, just about to knock, when Russell opened the front door. She made a little shriek of surprise and jumped back.

"Sweet Jesus, Russell, you almost scared me to death," she said after catching her breath. "Don't you have anything better to do than lurk behind your front door and scare people out of their wits?"

"No, it was just a happy coincidence, Wanda."

"Well, coincidence or not, I'm glad you're home. I had some of your mail delivered to me by mistake. Ruby's apparently out sick or something, and the substitute carrier got some of your things mixed up with mine."

Russell glanced at the three envelopes, all of which were bills. His impulse was to toss them onto the small table by the door, but he feared that Wanda would think that the gesture was somehow ungrateful or dismissive of her effort in bringing them. So, he set them down carefully in a neat stack, aligning the lower left corners of the three envelopes.

"Well, the least I can do is offer you some coffee. Can you stay a couple of minutes?" he said when he turned back to Wanda.

Wanda followed Russell back to the kitchen, sat at the table, and watched Russell prepare the coffee. She started to tell Russell about an offer she had received to buy her apple farm earlier that day.

"Grace Kennedy – you don't know her – she's a real estate agent Jack and I used to know in Wellsboro. She moved a couple of years ago down to Philly and opened an office out on the Main Line. She called me to say that a nice young couple she knew down there had driven past my place earlier this week and somehow fell in love with it, just by passing by along the road. They called Grace to ask her to see whether I might be interested in selling if the price was right.

"Grace said that she thought that I could easily get a half million for the place, with the value of the orchard thrown in."

"Well, you do have an attractive home, set back from the road at the base of the mountain, a nice parcel of land, and that beautiful orchard of yours to the side."

"Well, thanks, Russell for saying that. My crew and I do try to keep it up, so people won't think that Jack and I were a couple of flatlanders who didn't have any business trying to run an orchard. But, of course, I'm not interested. There isn't enough money in all the world to make me leave. And most of what Grace said was probably just realtor hype. You know how they are."

"I'm glad to hear that, Wanda."

"That it was all hype?"

"No, that you're not planning to sell."

"Well, I'm not, but it was flattering and a little tempting, I guess. I could take that money and move to Florida. It's a big enough state that I wouldn't have to deal all the time with my sister.

"Grace said that the couple were really curious about the immediate area around here. Are any of the adjacent properties for sale? What's up in the forest? Could they buy just a large tract of land on one of the mountains?"

"They probably just wanted to escape the rat race of living in the city," Russell said, pouring the coffee into two mugs. "I know the feeling." He set one of them and a small pitcher of milk in front of Wanda.

"Well, don't worry, Russell. I'm not going anywhere." She poured a generous amount of milk into her coffee and took a sip.

"Delicious, as always, sir.

"But this is where Jack and I lived and where we will die," she continued. "Jack's ashes are scattered out there in the orchard and when my time comes, I've made arrangements for my ashes to be mixed into the soil where his are; so, we'll always be here together until the end of the world."

Russell produced a small packet of German chocolate cookies and opened them onto a small china plate, which he set before Wanda.

"That is one of the most beautiful things I've ever heard," Russell said quietly and a little sadly as he sat down across the table from Wanda.

"I'm glad you came by, Wanda. I just had the weirdest experience up on the mountain this afternoon."

"I was wondering what was going on with you today, Russell. I thought you seemed a little preoccupied by something. Was it something bad?"

Russell told Wanda about meeting John at the Rocks. Wanda didn't interrupt with any comments or questions. She remained silent for a few moments after Russell completed his story. She nodded her head slightly.

"Interesting," was all she said.

"What is really weird, Wanda, aside from the way he was dressed, was that he reminded me of some photos of an old man that I saw in Bill Paxton's study."

Wanda grimaced.

"And then," he continued, "there are all those stories that Jack found, about an old man that wanders around in the mountain. Jack heard him referred to by several names: John Oakman, Old John, John Bard."

"Yeah, Russell. And there also was the lunch that you had, and the little bit of wine that you like to take up there with you, and the sunny afternoon. Just a couple of days ago you'd seen an old guy with a white beard in a couple of old photos. You had been reading Jack's notebooks. You dozed off after lunch and maybe heard a sound in your sleep, maybe an animal moving through the forest, and your mind turned that sound into an encounter with this John character. You were dreaming the whole thing. It sounds like a nice dream, by the way."

"You might be right, Wanda, "Russell replied, "but it seemed so real, so clear. There was nothing dreamlike about it, none of the distortions of reality that are part of dreams."

"I don't know, Russell. An old guy who looks and talks like he stepped out of a time machine from two hundred years ago – that sounds like a distortion of reality to me. But you'd be surprised what can seem real sometimes. I wouldn't worry about it."

Russell began to ask Wanda about whether Jack had ever mentioned to her any stories about Old John or anyone like him, but Wanda cut him off.

"Russell, those are just a bunch of old ghost stories. If you get all obsessed with them, you'll end up like –" she snapped, ending in mid-sentence. She turned and looked away. Her index finger quickly flicked at the corner of her right eye.

"Well, enough of this, Russell. I have to be going. I've stayed too long as it is," she said, getting up from the table. "Thanks for the snack."

"I'm sorry, Wanda, if I said anything that upset you."

Russell followed her to the front door, where she turned and reached up to put a hand on his shoulder.

"Don't worry about it," she said, quickly kissing Russell's cheek. Before he could react, Wanda turned and walked briskly to her car, waving at him as she walked away, not looking back.

Russell spent the rest of the evening searching Jack's notebooks for mentions of Old John. The name John Bard sometimes appeared by itself, once three times on a page by itself, one of those entries underlined and followed by three question marks.

Just before going to bed, Russell thought about the photographs of the old white-bearded man that he saw on the wall of Paxton's office. He could understand why Bill would have the two pictures that included the man he believed to have been his great-grandfather, but why was there the picture of the white-bearded man by himself, taken years later?

It was almost midnight. Before going to bed, he decided to return to the Rocks the next morning, to look for any traces of the visitor. He also made a note to telephone Bill Paxton.

The next morning was cold, with a steady rain that gave no signs of ending soon. By nine o'clock, Russell had decided to postpone his return to the Rocks. He telephoned Bill Paxton and left a message on Bill's answering machine.

"Bill, it's Russell Poe. I came across your name in Jack Abrams' notes as one of the sources for a legend about an old sangman called Old John. And then I had a rather strange encounter in the woods yesterday – or at least I think that I did. Could you call me back so we could arrange to get together again sometime soon? I need to pick your brain on a couple of points."

Bill returned the call within an hour.

"I need to stick around the Manse today," he said. "I have a counseling session this afternoon with a young couple that's getting married later this month, and I need to prepare for it. But I think that I can spend a half-hour or so with you sometime later this morning. If it's not too much trouble, could you come by before noon? I'll be in my office and you can pick what few brains I have to your heart's content."

Childhood Memories

When Russell arrived at the Manse, a note tacked to the door welcomed him:

Russell:

It's unlocked.

Come on in. I'm in my study.

Bill

Russell went back to Bill's office. Bill was on the telephone but hung up almost immediately when Russell appeared in the doorway. He rose, shook Russell's hand, and moved to the window seat, gesturing to Russell to take the rocking chair.

"How can I help you, Russell? You said you wanted to pick my brains."

"Well, it's nothing that important, Bill, but, as you know, as we discussed last time, I've been working with Jack Abrams' research."

Bill stood up again quickly. Russell thought for a moment that something was wrong.

"Sorry, Russell. I'm forgetting my manners. Can I offer you anything? Coffee? Soda? Water?"

"Thanks, Bill, but no thanks."

"You sure?" Bill asked, sitting down again.

"Positive, but thanks all the same, Bill."

"So," Bill said, "before I interrupted, you were mentioning Jack Abrams' project. How can I help?"

"Well, as I think I mentioned the last time I was here, Bill, you appear several places in Jack's notes as something of a local expert about some of these old stories, you and your family."

Bill smiled and nodded.

"Well, yes, we have been haunting these hills for a long time."

"Well, Bill, as you can imagine with material of this nature, there are lots of variations in the details, and some of the bits of the stories don't fit together at all. You know, it's like I'm trying to put together two or three jigsaw puzzles. They're all of the same picture, and a lot of the pieces look like they're the same general shape, but each one is cut differently."

"I know what you mean. The Bible is like that sometimes."

"But there are several things that keep appearing in Jack's research," Russell continued, trying to ignore the Bible comment, "and these themes are reasonably consistent over a very long span of time."

"I suppose the mysterious Indian Rocks are one of them," Bill said.

"They are," Russell replied, "and there's another dimension. All sorts of legends seem to be tied up with the Rocks in one way or the other."

"Isn't that to be expected, Russell? A prominent, mysterious location will always attract mysteries. In any event, I think that I've already told you – and Jack Abrams, of course – just about all I know, or at least all that I remember.

"But," Bill continued, "if you want my opinion – the pickings from my brain, as you put it – the Rocks are just some eighteenth- or nineteenth-century prank. But because they're mysterious, they get wrapped into a lot of the stories. If you want a legend to seem real, you have to link it to as many real things as you can. And if the kernel of truth is mysterious in and of itself, it's even better. And in this case, we've got eleven big kernels of truth up there on your mountain."

"That may be true," Russell said, "but I think there's a lot more there, Bill, things that some people might even know and not realize it."

Bill looked puzzled. "I'm not sure I understand what you mean," he said slowly. Bill stood up, retrieved a small notepad and a pen from his desk, and returned to the window seat.

"You mentioned consistent themes, Russell. What are some of those themes?" Bill asked as he resumed his seat in the window, with the pencil poised over the note pad. "There's the Rocks, of course. What else?"

"Well, in addition to the Rocks," Russell replied, "which I think are really a focal point for a lot of things, and maybe even some sort of a key to it all, there are all the legends about ginseng."

"Ah yes, the Sangman," Bill interjected.

"And his ghost and his treasure, *et cetera, et cetera,*" Russell continued. "I understand that about a hundred years ago, there really was a famous sangman in these parts who supposedly made a fortune from the ginseng trade. Or maybe more than one famous sangman, as the legend might be a composite of several real people. And Whitey Wentworth tells me that his father and grandfather were sangmen, at least part time."

"Well," Bill chuckled, "Whitey's a good man. I've known him off and on since we were kids. But don't go believing everything Whitey tells you about what goes on around here. He's one of the biggest practical jokers in the area, and nobody can tell a tall tale better than Whitey Wentworth."

"I'll keep that in mind," Russell said.

"Don't get me wrong," Bill protested. "No, I didn't mean that Whitey is dishonest or anything like that. All I meant was that he loves to tell stories.

"Especially," Bill grinned, "to slick Philadelphia lawyers."

"Oh, I've already been treated to some of his tales, Bill."

"And as far as the treasure stories go, Russell," Bill continued, "they have been circulating around here for generations. There actually are some elements of truth in them, I think, because some of those old-timers did get rich in the ginseng trade. There was even a stash of old coins and bills found in the walls of one of the mansions in the west side of Wellsboro. But I don't think you'll find any treasure chests filled with gold coins or anything like that."

"What else, Russell?" Bill made a few notes on his note pad.

"Well, there are the so-called White Indians."

Bill nodded. "Everyone's heard of them," he said.

"It's one of the most interesting legends of all," Russell continued. "It's persisted until very recently, certainly as late as thirty years ago. There are even some semi-documented cases of people who claimed to have lived with them."

"That's one that I can help you with a little, Russell. I can remember as a boy hearing my grandmother warn me to stay off the mountain behind your house on certain days. She'd tell me that the White Indians were supposedly coming through, moving on to their summer camp or winter camp or wherever."

"Who'd she say that they were?"

"I don't think she ever did." Bill's smile made Russell want to remember her fondly. "No, I don't think she ever did. She'd just tell me to stay away from the old Indian trail at the top of the mountain, because if the White Indians spotted me, they'd carry me off with them deep into the mountains and I'd never be found again."

"Wow," was the only reply Russell could think to make. He briefly envisioned himself as a sheltered eight-year-old boy hearing the warning. He could almost see ghostly white people, clad in Native American garb, silently filing along the old trail along the ridge.

"And, you know," Bill continued, "I actually thought it might be kind of fun to be captured and carried off to live with them up in the mountains, to move silently through the forests, to live free – real *Leatherstocking Tales* stuff."

Bill's face had the look of a man whose thoughts were far away in time. The traces of a smile tugging at the corners of his mouth faded.

"I can remember that my mother and grandmother would get into the most awful arguments. One time when my mother had come home from work to pick me up, just as my grandmother was warning me about the White Indians. My mom just went off on my grandmother like a stick of dynamite. And my grandmother started shouting back at her.

"I ran downstairs and hid in the cellar. I didn't know what would happen. Even with the door closed, I could hear them upstairs going at it.

"My mother shouted, 'Quit filling Billy's head with all that superstitious rubbish. You've driven Wally almost mad with your wicked tales, but you're not going to get my Billy'."

"Wally?"

"My father, Russell."

"That's what I thought."

"Yeah, his real name was Wallace, but he went by Wally.

"But, to get back to the White Indians," Bill continued, "the only other thing I definitely remember about that big fight between my mother and grandmother was Grandma shouting back. 'Hell's bells,' she shouted. That was the strongest language I ever heard her use. But 'Hell's bells,' she said. 'When are you going to grow up and learn that there are things out there that we should leave be unless we want to get ourselves hurt?' and 'The boy needs to learn about them, so he can protect himself when I'm gone.'"

"What was she referring to?"

"I don't know, Russell. Maybe she believed that the White Indians were real."

"That must have been some scene."

"There's one thing more, Russell. After my grandmother talked about leaving things be, my mother said, and I'll never forget this because it seemed so funny at the time. I almost laughed out loud at the picture it created in my mind. My mother said, 'Well, Belle, if you want to strip naked and go running around in the woods playing Pocahontas, you can do that. But leave Billy out of it.' I thought that was really funny, my grandmother running around naked and pretending to be Pocahontas, every now and then shouting, 'Hell's bells.'"

Russell chuckled softly.

"So, your mother thought that your grandmother was somehow connected to the White Indians?" he asked.

"I don't know, Russell. I was always afraid to ask her. All I remember was being down in the cellar, afraid that she would hurt Grandma. I could hear things being thrown around upstairs. So, after that I kept quiet about it. I didn't want to upset her."

"Your mother?"

"Either one of them."

"So, what do you think, Bill? Is there something to the old legend about the White Indians – with or without your grandmother as Pocahontas?"

Bill leaned over and rested his chin in the palm of his right hand, his right elbow on his knee. He seemed to linger in a bent over position for a moment too long to be comfortable. Then he straightened up slowly.

"The White Indians? Could be something to it. I think my grandmother really believed in them.

"You know how it is, though," Bill continued. He looked out the window for a few seconds as he spoke. "Most legends have that kernel of truth that you mentioned."

Bill turned around to face Russell again. He was smiling.

"Possibly," he continued, "the White Indians myth goes back to the days when the Onondagas and Cayugas would occasionally come down from New York and raid the few farms that were around here, back even before the French and Indian War. There are cases where they would kidnap settlers' children to raise as their own. When these kids grew up, they would take their place in their native communities, just like anyone else. Some of them would be rescued, only to run away back to their Indian homes and families.

"My own theory is that the White Indian stories originated from people of European origins – the kidnapped children and their descendants – having been seen fighting for the Indians during the frontier wars in the early 1700s.

"So, a legend was born, Russell. A few were supposedly re-captured by the English, or later by the Americans, and repatriated. They told their stories, but by that time the legend had taken on a life of its own."

"That's interesting, Bill," Russell replied. "In my research on the French and Indian War, I came across accounts like those. It was rare, but, you're right; it happened. And when it did, it stood out in people's minds, got talked about, and probably grew with each retelling. But, Bill, how does your theory explain how the legends persist until fairly recently?"

"How recently?"

"Well, your own childhood, for example."

"Same reason that I think you still hear about sightings of cougars and wolves around here, Russell. The cougars have been extinct in this part of the state since the early 1800s, but it seems like every year somebody swears he's seen one."

"What about the wolves that supposedly attacked Jack Abrams?"

Bill paused a moment, nodding.

"I can't explain that, Russell. Except, I don't believe it was wolves. Maybe it was a pack of feral dogs, but not wolves. The wolves went extinct around here before 1900. I hear that Wanda Abrams doesn't accept the wolf theory, neither do the cops, not really."

"I'm not sure I do either," Russell remarked, hoping that Bill would say more in response.

"Is that part of your research?" Bill asked quietly, "Jack's death?"

"No, that's something else that I am doing for Wanda. But you must admit that it has a legend-like quality to it. Poor old Jack probably will become part of the canon of local folklore eventually. A man walking along a well-traveled path in the forest, in broad daylight, is attacked and killed by a pack of wolves, which supposedly have been gone for the best part of a hundred years."

"So, I should add wolves to the list?" Bill chuckled.

Russell said nothing. He was about to tell Bill that he thought that anything connected with Jack's death was not a laughing matter, but the telephone on Bill's desk rang. Russell started to get up.

"No, stay put," Bill said. "I can take it in the kitchen."

After Bill left, Russell stood up and stretched. Jack's death was real, not some mountain tall tale. Russell was able to use the break to recover from the brief flash of anger he felt about Bill's remark about adding wolves to the list.

He noticed another old group photograph on the wall opposite the desk. They were sitting in three rows in what appeared to be a small clearing on a hillside. The picture hung at eye level for a person seated in Bill's chair behind the desk. Russell hadn't noticed it when he previously visited. He was still looking at it when Bill returned.

"You're really fascinated by those old photos, aren't you, Russell?" Bill said.

"Well, as you know by now, anything historical gets my attention. This photo, though, the one of the group of people in the clearing in the woods, who are they?"

"Those folks? I think that they're members of an old lodge of some sort that used to be active around here around the turn of the century. I'm not sure where this was taken, but I think that it might have been somewhere on your property. From the steepness of the slope it might be on the side of the mountain that overlooks the river, but I don't know exactly where.

"I don't recognize any of those folks. This was one of the old pictures, like most of the other ones here, that my father took when my grandmother died, but Mom wouldn't let him hang them anywhere in the house. After Dad left home, they just stayed packed away. For some reason she never got rid of them. I was surprised when she passed away and I found them in a box under her bed. So, I got them out and brought them here, at least most of them. Some were too badly damaged to save.

"I don't know anything else about that picture," Bill gestured at it. "I can make a good guess at the others, but this one is a mystery. You know, I've even pointed out this picture to people who visit my study, especially some of the older folks, to see if they know anyone in it or maybe more specifically where it was taken. Nobody ever does."

"What about this old guy in the back row, the one with the white Rip Van Winkle beard? Could he be the same man that's in the photo that was taken in front of your family's house and the one of the old man by the river?" Russell pointed across in their direction.

Bill walked over to look at the two photographs that Russell had indicated. He seemed to stare at them for about thirty seconds and then returned to stand by Russell and look again at the group photo on the hillside.

"What I would give for a really good magnifying glass!" he said, his nose only an inch from the picture. Russell could see his face reflected in the glass.

"You might be onto something there, Russell," Bill said, stepping back from the pictures. "I just don't know. Those images are awfully blurry. It could be, but I don't think that's likely. If it's the same guy, he doesn't appear to have aged very much. He already looks old in all three of them."

"But it could be," he repeated.

"Well, whoever he is, Bill," Russell said, "he reminds me of one other thing to add to your list: the legend of John Bard."

Bill turned and looked straight into Russell's eyes.

"Who's that, Russell? John who?"

"John Bard."

"Never heard of him."

"You must have, Bill. According to Jack Abrams' notes, John Bard – or what was probably the same guy but with a different name – was always showing up in legends of one sort or the other. I might not be remembering what I read accurately, but I think I recall that in Jack's notes you even mentioned John Bard by name."

"The only thing I ever discussed with Jack – at least about some old guy running around in the mountains – is that ghost story about the Sangman," Bill replied. "Honestly, Russell, I've lived here almost all of my life, and this is the first I've ever heard the name John Bard."

"How about Old John or John Oakman?"

"Nope. Sorry," Bill said.

Bill's eyes seemed fixed on Russell's face. Bill genuinely looked puzzled.

"He's linked to a number of the legends, Bill. Take the Sangman stories, for example. Some of them identify John Bard as the Sangman. Some of the White Indian legends have John Bard or someone with a similar name as their Chief. I've even read a story that says that John Bard is hundreds of years old and was an old man at the time of the American Revolution. I can't believe you've never heard of him."

Bill's face remained expressionless.

"If he is all those things, maybe you should interview him for your book.

"No, I'm sorry," Bill added quickly. "That didn't come out the way I meant. No – and this is the God-honest truth, Russell – I really never have heard of him. Maybe I've led a sheltered life. Like anyone else who grows up around here, I've heard all the Sangman stories and all about the White Indians, like I told you earlier. But Russell, this is the first time I've ever heard of someone named John Bard or any of those other names you mentioned."

"That's really weird, Bill," Russell said, returning to the rocker. Bill remained standing by the old group photograph, looking intently at it.

"His name, or variants of it, shows up again and again in Jack Abrams' materials."

"Well, Russell, I don't mean any disrespect to Jack Abrams." Bill said, resuming his place in the window seat. "I didn't know him well, but I know that he was a good honest man.

"But Jack Abrams also was a flatlander – even worse, from New York City. It was like he was walking around with a big sign that someone taped to his back: *FOOL ME HARD*. I think that maybe some of the folks he talked to might have been having some fun with him."

"But a conspiracy to create a legend, Bill? Do you really think so?"

"Well, nothing that sinister, Russell," Bill replied. "It's harmless. I'm not saying that's what happened, because I don't know. But it might have been just some harmless fun. It wouldn't be the first time an outsider got fished in."

"I don't buy that, Bill. For one thing, the mentions of John Bard in Jack's notes are spread over several years. And Jack was a careful researcher. From what I can tell from his notes, he would always try to corroborate what he was told. I can't imagine that he'd allow himself to be fooled. I suppose it's possible, but I just don't buy it."

"Russell, believe me, as someone who's lived here all his life. The stuff that's real here can be a whole lot stranger than the legends."

"What do you mean?"

"Well, for one thing, a lot of people around here are pretty private," Bill replied. "These mountains are filled with secrets. Some of them have been kept for generations. Some folks don't like a lot of poking around, especially by outsiders. And that's what Jack was, even though he lived here for years. And – I say this as your friend, Russell – that's what you will always be, an outsider, even after you've lived here even longer than Jack did."

"Can you give me some examples of the secrets?"

Bill smiled. "Come on, Russell. You know I can't betray a confidence. Let's just say that the very best secrets I have to keep to myself."

"What? The clergy-penitent privilege is involved in this?"

An owl hooted.

"Did you plan that?" Russell asked, laughing.

Bill smiled back.

"Nice effect for the end of a sermon, Russell. I've got to hire that bird. But, as we were saying, all I can tell you is to look for the kernel of truth. But, at the same time, don't be surprised if a lot of folks don't want you to get too close to it.

"For example, take the stories about the Sangman's treasure. There was a big ginseng trade up here, as you know, about a hundred or hundred fifty years ago. There are still some people who go up into the mountains, including some places where they really shouldn't be going, to look for sang. Fact. But a treasure? Of course, there's a treasure. Has to be one. Wouldn't be a good legend without a treasure."

"That's what I find so interesting, Bill: trying to find the treasure of fact."

"Well, I'm happy to help you find that treasure of fact any way I can." Bill stood and extended his hand to Russell. Russell took this as a sign that the meeting was over, so that Bill could prepare for his counseling session. As they shook hands, Bill reached up with his left hand and clasped Russell in a half hug.

"Thanks, Bill," Russell said, easing out of Bill's grasp and moving toward the door. "I know that you have another appointment coming up, and I don't want to keep you from it."

"Yeah, two kids from our church are getting married, so I always like to have some sessions with them about marriage. If you'll let me get a little religious on you, Russell, I believe that marriage is a Godly state, the highest expression of love. In our community, we believe that it has special spiritual significance, and it's a tragedy that so many marriages fail."

"Well, I never really came that close to marriage, Bill. But I have to say, as one professional person to another, that I really admire that you feel that you need to make special preparations for your meetings with the couple."

"I really do, Russell. It is so very important. And here I stand, as Martin Luther said. I'm just an ordinary guy to whom these kids look for guidance as they embark on the most important adventure of their lives. So, I owe it to them to do whatever I can to help them to prepare for it. I really do believe that it is the most important thing that I do in my ministry."

Bill paused and smiled. "Sorry, Russell. I get carried away sometimes," he said.

"Don't worry, Bill, you'll never convert me. But I am a little interested in your history, Bill. What drew you to a religious vocation? Maybe we can talk about it sometime."

Bill went to his desk and sat behind it.

"I have a minute or two before I really have to kick you out. So, let me give you the short version," Bill said, smiling. He motioned for Russell to return to the rocking chair.

"My story isn't that remarkable, Russell. As you know, I grew up around here. I was more or less raised in the church: First Presbyterian in Wellsboro. I guess my mother wanted to counteract what she thought was the heathen influence of my grandparents. But like most kids, I sort of drifted away from church. It just didn't seem relevant to me. After I graduated high school, I started college at Penn State. I stuck it out down there for three semesters trying to figure out what to major in, and I eventually decided that it just wasn't right for me, or I wasn't right for it, at least not yet.

"So, I came home and just knocked around these parts for about two years or so, working odd jobs here and there. I was going nowhere. And then one Sunday morning I was just walking up in the forest, up in the old State Game Lands, on my family's old land.

I liked to go back there from time to time and hike around up there – still do, in fact – just to think and remember my childhood a little. And one Sunday morning I just decided that my life needed changing."

"Simple as that?"

"Yeah, simple as that, Russell. No blinding light, no voices, none of that Road to Damascus stuff. Just an answer deep inside me. I knew then and there what was missing in my life: faith. So, I started going to church at First United Methodist in Mansfield, which was close to where I was living at the time. They were really so kind to me, helped me find a regular job, and a few of them even pooled their money to help pay for me to go to a small Christian college, down near Lancaster, and finish my degree. Then I just came back home to wait for the Lord's directions."

"Where did you go to seminary?"

"I didn't. I didn't feel the need. The Lord's calling to me was stronger. He needed me in the fields, not in school. I volunteered to help out, first at First United Methodist. The pastor, Carl Blakey, was spending half his Sundays circuit riding to minister to two tiny chapels out in the country, as well as leading the morning and evening services in town at First Methodist. Carl was already in his early seventies and not in great health, and it had become too hard for him to keep going back and forth all the time. So, I sort of took over responsibility for one of the chapels on the circuit, a little congregation out in the country west of Tioga – Elkhorn Chapel, it was called, but it's gone now – and started going up there every Sunday afternoon to hold worship services for them. It was an old congregation. Their chapel had been built by farmers back in the 1880s, because it took too long to go by horse and buggy into town for services. By the time I arrived on the scene, there were only seven families left, but they came all the time. Pretty soon I was spending most of my time up there with them."

"So, you became their pastor?"

"No." Russell was surprised at the sudden disgust in Bill's voice. "They wanted me to serve as their pastor, and even offered me a hundred bucks a month plus lodging in a trailer in back of one of the members' homes. That was a big sacrifice for them. But the Conference found out about it and killed the idea."

"The Conference?"

"Yeah, Russell. That's the regional governing body of the Methodist Church. They said that the chapel couldn't pay me unless I was ordained, and I couldn't be ordained unless I went to seminary."

"What did you do?"

"Nothing much really that we could do. I kept going on as before, working for free. I even would refuse money that some of the families tried to pass to me under the table. We actually grew the congregation to fourteen families – doubled the size in less than a year. After about a year the Conference found a retired ordained minister to take over. I stayed on and helped him for a couple of months, still working for free, but I could tell he wanted me out of the picture. Also, he started subtly turning the congregation against me."

"Really?" The idea of two clergymen fighting over a fourteen-family congregation seemed unbelievable at first.

"Nothing overt," Bill continued. "The new guy – Dr. Wayland Baxter was his name – was a pompous old guy. I was just known as Bill, but he insisted on being addressed as Dr. Baxter – not even Reverend Baxter. He would say things like, 'We all really owe Mr. Paxton a debt of gratitude for filling in' and 'Well, as an ordained minister, I think that –' Those sorts of things. Finally, one Sunday, after the service Dr. Baxter took me aside and said that starting next Sunday, he wanted the members to take turns leading the prayer or reading scripture. I had been doing those things, so I realized it was his way of firing me."

"What did you do then?" Russell asked.

Bill shrugged. "I just kept going to the Sunday service every now and then, sitting with the congregation, but gradually stopped going. I felt like a fifth wheel, and I wasn't doing any good for the people there. Baxter just shut me out.

"So, I came back to First Methodist and resumed helping out Carl as a deacon. Carl retired about a year after that, and they sent a younger guy to replace him, Jim Murray. He's still there, a real nice guy, but I think that, at first, he might have felt that I was some sort of competition for him. It was a little awkward for both of us. He really needed to get to know the congregation better, so I sort of backed out of some of the things that I was doing, you know, to signal that Jim was their spiritual leader, and I was just another member of the church, like the rest of them. It was perfectly amicable, and Jim and I still keep in touch.

"About that time, a couple of our members told me about a Bible study group that was meeting on its own and asked me to join them, not as their leader or anything like that, just as a member. There were folks from a number of different churches, including a family that had left Elkhorn Chapel, and some that had no church affiliation at all. So, we'd meet once a week at someone's home – including right here as I think I told you last time – to do a little Bible study, pray together, and sometimes just talk things over.

"After a while we decided to incorporate our own non-denominational congregation, we got our tax-exempt status, and they asked me formally to become their pastor. At first, I declined, but they eventually convinced me. We even had a little ordination ceremony, just fifteen of us standing around in a circle in the old living room over there. Jim Murray came over to preside, and he told me later that he took a little heat from his bishop for going outside the denomination and doing that. But that's the story.

"So, that's how Mountain View Chapel was formed, almost fifteen years ago now. We've grown, but there's always room for one more, Russell." Russell was relieved to see Bill grin, to assure Russell that he was, at most, only half-serious.

"If you've got just one more minute, Bill, there was one question that I forgot to ask you earlier," Russell said. "How was it that your family gave up the Paxton Place after it had been in your family for so many generations? I hope I'm not getting too personal."

"No problem, Russell. Basically, what happened was that my grandparents died within a couple of days of each other. Granddad went first, from a heart attack while he was splitting wood out back. One moment he was swinging the sledge, and a second later he was gone. They say he never could have known what happened, it was so quick.

"Then, on the evening after Granddad's funeral, Grandma just walked out the kitchen door and up the mountain a little bit and died. You might have noticed a little stone marker alongside the path where she passed away."

"No, I don't think I have," Russell said quietly. "But I'll find it and take care of it."

"Well, maybe it's been overgrown since then. She was still dressed from the funeral. She didn't say a word to anyone, just got up after most of the company had left and quietly slipped away."

Russell hoped his silence would encourage Bill to continue.

"My mother had taken me home," Bill said, "and Dad had stayed behind with his younger brother, my Uncle Woodrow, and a couple of neighbors. Dad said that they looked all over the house for Grandma. It was Uncle Woodrow – Uncle Woody we called him, what else? – who found her. Dad said that Woody had a hunch and started up the trail. He was in a hurry, Dad said, because it was almost dusk.

"Grandma would sometimes do that, just go up the mountain, sometimes all the way to the Rocks, just to be alone for a little while."

Bill looked beyond Russell and stared out the window for a moment. He was biting his lip and appeared to be fighting back tears. He took a deep breath and continued.

"Sorry, Russell. A ghost just walked across my grave.

"As I was saying, about twenty minutes or so later, Woody came back down the trail. Dad heard him coming and went out back to see if he knew anything. Dad said that tears were pouring down Woody's face, but he was smiling at the same time.

"'I found Mama,' my Uncle Woody told Dad. 'She's so beautiful, just sitting up on the mountain, about halfway to the top, looking like a queen, and I've never seen her look so happy. She just went up the trail, sat down, and died. She was holding this.'

"Woody handed Dad an old watch chain and fob. Grandma had given it to Granddad on their wedding day. I think it had been in her family for a long time before that. Dad and Uncle Woody had thought that it had been buried with Granddad earlier that day."

Bill stood up and walked to the window. Russell turned and noticed that dark storm clouds were forming to the west, the darkening sky blending with the distant outline of the mountains. Bill sat again in the window seat and looked out the window.

"I still have that old watch fob," he said, his voice trembling. "I never have used a pocket watch in my life, but I went out and bought one, just to have one to attach Granddad's chain to."

Russell quietly said, "Well, maybe the way they went, your grandparents, was the better way. Almost together."

"Yeah," Bill said. He was silent for a minute. Russell decided to wait for Bill to compose himself.

"I'm sorry," Bill finally said and sighed. "I guess I've never gotten over my grandparents dying so unexpectedly and almost on the same day.

"I get so wrapped up in myself sometimes, Russell. It's a real flaw in me, and a real liability for someone in my line of work. You know, I'm supposed to dedicate my life to caring for others and their problems, so I try not to think and talk about my own. Sometimes all the memories and pain and fears that have been backed up for all those years, like water behind a dam, they find a weak spot and break through. I know it's a flaw in me, Russell, one of many, but it's the only way that I keep from dragging myself down and failing the people who need me."

Bill was silent for a moment. He seemed to be looking beyond Russell and out the window.

"But what I was trying to say, Russell," Bill continued, "is that I will never forget those days. Granddad was an okay person and could be fun sometimes. I never really felt close to him until just before he died, and, unlike my Dad, he was always there for us. But, my God, how I loved my grandmother!

"Well, after the funeral, there was the question of what to do with the house and land. My grandmother's will left it to my father, but even though it had been his childhood home, he didn't want the responsibility, I guess, of keeping it up. Maybe he was already planning to dump us and go to California with his girlfriend; I don't know. Uncle Woody lived down in Wilkes-Barre and couldn't take care of it very well. He was content with whatever they had left to him. I don't know if it was very much, probably just the money in their savings account.

"And it was about that time, just after my grandparents passed away, that Dad suddenly decided to run away with his girlfriend. It was a complete surprise to my mother; she hadn't had a clue that he was cheating on her.

"After Dad left, Uncle Woody tried to persuade Mom to move into my grandparents' house, because we needed an affordable place to live. He even offered to buy the house from the estate and then sell it to her for one dollar, so that she would be the sole owner. But she refused.

"And then, when the bank that was the executor of my grandparents' estates sold the property, my father got all the proceeds of the sale, and my mother never saw a penny of it."

"I can understand why she felt that way, I guess," Russell said quietly. "Your mother wouldn't want to live in a place associated with a husband that had just deserted her."

"No, it was more than that," Bill responded. "She had an obsession about the house. I can remember one night, right before my Dad pulled his disappearing act, that my parents fought almost all night. I really was afraid that they were going to kill each other. They were both shoving and slapping each other around in the kitchen. I tried to call the police, but Mom caught me and ripped the phone off the wall and threw it at Dad. Mom said that she was glad that Dad's parents were dead, and she no longer wanted anything to do with them or their evil memory. Those words – "evil memory" – still ring in my ears. She said that the best thing Dad and Uncle Woody could do would be to burn the Paxton Place to the ground, preferably with both of them in it."

"Why would she say that?"

"I don't know, Russell. Remember I was just a kid. I might not be remembering everything accurately, but there's one part that really stands out."

"What was that, Bill?"

"During that big fight," Bill continued, "I remember my mother saying to my father something like, 'I've kept quiet all these years out of love for you. They were your parents, Wally, after all, but they were evil.'

"I didn't hear what Dad said. All I heard was the door slamming as he left. It was the loudest sound I had ever heard in my life. And I heard my mother shouting after him, 'Evil. Do you hear me? Evil. You can't walk away from it. They were evil and we're all better off that they're gone and burning in hell.'"

"Wow. I don't know what to say, Bill. What on earth did she mean by that?"

"Don't know, Russell. I never asked. And I never saw my father again.

"So," Bill continued, "since neither Woody nor my father nor my mother wanted the place, the bank ended up taking possession of it and selling it for the estate. I guess it took a couple of years for them to find a suitable buyer, because I think that I was about twelve or thirteen when they sold it to your uncle.

"I felt sad that it was going out of the family. There was a time, about fifteen years later, when I approached your uncle to see if he would be interested in selling the place to me, or at least some of the land up on the mountain. He wasn't interested at the time, and, even if he had been, there wasn't a bank that would give me financing based on what I was making as a pastor of a small church. When I casually mentioned to my mother, about that time, that someday I'd like to buy back the old family place, she just blew up and threw a book that she was reading at me. She said that I could do as I please, but she would never set foot in 'that evil place.'

"Sorry, Russell, but that's what she called what's now your home, all the rest of her life." Bill smiled and shrugged. "I have a friend who's a Catholic priest and might be able to do an exorcism for you."

Russell hoped that Bill was not serious.

"So, my father got all the proceeds from the sale," Bill continued. "Mom and I never saw a penny of it or anything else from my grandparents' estates, other than a couple sticks of furniture and my grandfather's watch fob. Uncle Woody even offered to give her half of what he had inherited, but Mom said it was tainted money and refused to take any of it. Even so, Woody would help us out every now and then by slipping me some money to help out with our expenses. I never told Mom where the money came from, so it all probably worked out for the best in the end."

"What did your mother have against the place?" Russell asked. "Your grandparents were gone. Your uncle was willing basically to give the place to her, free and clear. Was it just all her memories associated with them?"

"I don't know, Russell. Once again, I never asked. I've sometimes wondered whether it was mother who was the evil one, not Dad or my grandparents. Maybe she was just mentally ill, refused to get help, and eventually drove Dad away. But I never asked, so I'll never know. Maybe I never wanted to know."

"And both your parents are gone now?"

"Mom passed away from cancer five years ago. She was only sixty-two. Even as she was dying, I think that she hoped that somehow that my father would come back. But he didn't, and I got a letter about eighteen months later from his girlfriend telling me that he had committed suicide and his ashes were scattered over the Pacific Ocean at Big Sur. I wrote back to her asking if my father had ever mentioned me, or maybe left something of his for me. Did she need any financial help? Was there anything that I could do for her? But I never got a response. It was probably just as well. I didn't have a spare dime, but I would have tried to help all the same."

"What can I say, Bill, except that I am so very sorry for your losses."

"Thanks, Russell. I know you mean it, that you're not just being polite. I really appreciate that."

Russell stood up. Bill joined him.

"Bill, I know you have a lot of things to do," Russell said. "I mean it this time; I'd best be going and let you get on with them. But thanks a million for your time and for filling me in a little on some things."

"No, Russell, thank you for listening. I guess I carry a lot of baggage with me that I really hadn't felt.

"And, about your finishing Jack Abrams' research, I really want to help. Maybe I'll ask some of the older members of the congregation if they have any old stories they can share with you."

"Thanks, Bill. That would be great."

Bill walked Russell back to the car. They shook hands and promised to see each other again soon.

Just before Russell got into his car, Bill said, "Wait a minute. I almost forgot. You mentioned in your voice message something about a weird experience that you had and that you wanted to tell me about?"

"Don't worry, Bill. It was just a crazy dream that I had about meeting John Bard up in the woods. That's why I asked you about him."

Bill said, "Well, so long then. Please come over any time."

"You too, Bill."

As Russell drove away, he glanced to the right. Instead of returning to the open door at the side of the church, Bill Paxton was walking briskly, his head down and hands behind his back, across the small field behind the church that led to the woods. Russell wondered whether he noticed the darkening sky and the flash of lightning in the distance.

Uncle Johnny

Bill Paxton returned refreshed from his walk in the fields behind the church, but also very angry at himself. Why had he denied ever hearing of John Bard? He must have seemed evasive. He liked Russell Poe. He accepted Russell's explanation that he was asking questions about Jack Abrams' death simply as a favor for his friend Wanda. But, at the same time, Russell Poe was not a fool. Bill would have to explain his way out of his denial eventually.

When he entered the Manse, Bill went straight to his tiny bedroom and opened the old jewelry box. Here was the gold watch chain that had been his grandfather's. For many years, Bill just assumed that the tiny watch fob was a miniature of some ancient statue. Only later, he learned that it was the Celtic thunder god, Taranus, holding the solar wheel in his left hand, and a lightning bolt, garlanded with oak leaves, in his right. He picked the fob up gently, as if it were glass, and studied it closely. It must have been hundreds of years old.

When Bill was a little boy, his grandmother would invoke Tannus, as she called the god, to comfort him during summer afternoon thunderstorms. She would quietly sing songs about him in an old language that she spoke only when the two of them were alone together.

"Hush, Billy," she would whisper as she hugged him on her lap. "Hush now. It's only Tannus passing by. He is feared only by the evil. He protects us, though. He has protected our family for thousands of years and always will."

As he fingered the tiny thunder god, Bill wondered what he would tell Russell about John Bard the next time they met. Would he admit that he knew something of the John Bard of legend, the White Indian chief turned sangman, whose ghost still roamed the mountain? He could not reveal that John Bard was real and an ancient fiction – perhaps *fraud* was the better word – at the same time. He could not be sure that he understood it himself.

It had been two years since Bill had last seen John Bard. Sometimes, in the past, years would pass without any contact from him, not even the sign of a tree branch broken in a special way. But, just as Bill began to think that John Bard had died somewhere up there in the mountains, he would appear.

The Sangman's Ghost, was that what Russell was going to call Jack Abrams' book when he finished it? What would he say if he knew that the ghost was still very much alive?

John Bard had once told Bill that he was nine hundred years old. Bill didn't believe it but really had no basis to deny it either. For as long as the Paxtons had lived in the area, and for as far back in Bill's life as he could remember, John Bard – Uncle Johnny, as his grandmother called him – had been around, just out of sight back in the woods.

"Grandma, is Uncle Johnny really my uncle?"

"Yes, Billy, he really and truly is."

"Then why don't I ever see him? Why doesn't he give me presents on my birthday and Christmas like Uncle Woody does?"

"Billy, he gives you hidden presents, presents that you will discover only when you are a man."

"But why don't I see him, Grandma? Doesn't he like me?"

"He can see you, Billy. Uncle Johnny is always there. And sometime, some special time, if your eyes and heart are wide open, you'll see him way off in the woods. You'll see a flicker of blue from his coat as he walks through the woods. You might even hear him laughing or singing as he walks along."

He once asked his mother about Uncle Johnny. He was nine years old, and his mother had announced plans for the family to visit his great-aunt, his mother's aunt in Scranton.

"Is that where Uncle Johnny lives? With Aunt Bess?"

"Who's Uncle Johnny?" his mother asked. His father came into the room suddenly, a worried expression on his face.

"Let's not worry about Uncle Johnny right now," he said quickly.

Bill's mother turned to look at his father. "Okay, Wally, I'll ask you. Who is Uncle Johnny?"

"Just an old family story, Margaret."

"No, he's not," Bill Paxton had piped up. "No, he's real and he lives in the woods, and he can make it thunder. Grandma Paxton told me all about him."

His parents quickly went to their bedroom, his mother leading the way, his father following with his arms outstretched. The door closed, muffling raised voices. A few minutes later – but it had seemed like hours – Bill's father came out and knelt on one knee.

"Billy," he said, putting his arm around his son's shoulder, "We really shouldn't have any more talk about Uncle Johnny. It's just an old fairy tale that your grandmother likes to tell."

"But Grandma says he's real. Is she lying?"

"No, Grandma's not lying."

His father sat down on the floor and motioned for Bill to sit beside him.

"You know how you used to have an imaginary friend?"

"Yeah. His name was Jimmy."

Bill remembered how silly the imaginary friend seemed. One part of him had hated to admit that Jimmy was imaginary, and admitting it made him feel grown up. But he also felt what he now understood to be a feeling of guilt and betrayal for denying Jimmy's existence.

"He was pretty real to you in your imagination, wasn't he?" his father asked.

"Yeah."

"Well, Uncle Johnny is sort of our family's imaginary friend. He's not a real person like you or me. He lives in our family's imagination. He's real in our imagination, and he's been a part of our family for as long as I can remember. But he's not a real uncle like your Uncle Woody."

Bill's mother came out of the bedroom and knelt on the other side.

"You understand, now, sweetie?" she said softly. "You see, I get upset sometimes when I hear about Uncle Johnny, and some of the other things your Grandma Paxton says. Not because they're bad things. They're not bad because they are part of the Paxton side –

your father's side – of our family, and that makes them a part of you. But it's really important, honey, to always remember the difference between what's real and what's make-believe, because sometimes make-believe things can seem very real. But they're not, and not knowing the difference can sometimes get us into trouble.

"You understand what I'm trying to tell you, Billy?"

Bill looked at his father, who turned and walked out of the room, saying nothing.

"Yeah, I think so," Bill replied, but he didn't really understand.

From that day Bill Paxton never mentioned Uncle Johnny to his mother or father, but he still looked carefully for the flicker of blue in the deep woods. He knew that what his mother could not accept, and what his father falsely denied, was real nonetheless.

He could no longer deny John Bard, not to someone like Russell Poe, whom he genuinely liked and hoped he could keep on friendly terms. He also knew that Russell was too smart and probably didn't believe his flat denials at the Manse. Truth was always the best damage control, and Bill feared that he was sliding into a damage control situation. Besides, Russell would probably figure out the truth, at least as much of it as could be rationally figured out.

Bill decided to sleep on it. The next morning Bill awoke just at dawn. His morning devotions quickly became an internal debate. He had responsibilities to others to protect secrets that had been entrusted to him. But that did not justify lying to someone he might someday need as a friend, or at least not as an enemy.

He waited until after eight o'clock to be sure that Russell would be awake and then telephoned him. There was no answer, so Bill left a message on Russell's answering machine. He was relieved that Russell had not answered the phone. That would give him a little more time to finesse his way out of the lie about John Bard. His explanation had to be credible, or he could get sucked into a whirlpool of deception, one lie needing an even bigger one to explain it, that could only lead downward.

Confession

Russell set the telephone handset into its cradle on the small wooden stand in the downstairs hallway. He looked in the mirror above it. Yes, he thought, he really did look as puzzled as he felt. Bill Paxton's message on Russell's answering machine earlier that morning had been simple and mysterious.

"Russell, this is Bill Paxton. I got to thinking about our conversation yesterday over at the Manse, and there's something I really need to tell you right away. Please give me a call as soon as you can."

Despite what seemed to be an urgent tone in Bill Paxton's voice on the answering machine, he hadn't wanted to discuss the matter when Russell returned his call. Bill invited Russell to the Manse, but Russell insisted that he owed Bill the hospitality this time. Four hours later, as Russell checked to make sure that the beer that he had hurriedly purchased that afternoon was cold enough, he heard Bill's car slowly crunching the gravel in his driveway.

Bill ignored the three steps leading up to Russell's porch, taking them as one, his right hand already outstretched, smiling even before he said hello. His cheerfulness continued right through the pleasantries, comments about the weather, and Russell's delivery of a cold bottle of beer into Bill's hand.

"You said you had some news?" Russell started as they sat down in the living room. Bill looked around the room. "You've done a nice job fixing this place up, Russell. A definite improvement over the last time I was here."

"How long has it been?"

"Well, I did come by several times to see your uncle, but we always stayed outside on the porch. They weren't really 'come inside and chat' visits. So, I guess the last time I was inside the place, before it stopped being our family home, was the day of my grandmother's funeral. We came back here. Uncle Woody and his wife, my Aunt Helene, had laid out a little lunch for everyone.

During the funeral, my mother got a migraine headache – she got a lot of them when I was a kid – and didn't come back here for the lunch. I think that this one was just an excuse, however. But Dad dropped her off at home and then came here with me. I was sad about Mom not being there. I wanted her to share some of the sadness I was feeling about losing my grandmother, but I remember that, at the same time, I was a little relieved that she wasn't there. Had she come back here with the rest of us, I'm sure that she would have said something that would have caused a big fight with Uncle Woody or one of my grandparents' friends and would have ruined the day."

"I'm sorry," Russell said.

"Don't be. Many of my memories of this room are happy ones."

Bill smiled as he looked around the room, his head nodding.

"Well, it looks like you're having a good day today, Bill," Russell said after allowing Bill a moment to complete his reflections. "It must be good news."

Bill looked down into his glass for a moment.

"No, Russell," he said, "it's really not. It's just something about our conversation yesterday that I need to clear up with you. I think I might have misled you about something, and I really feel bad about it."

"I'm sure whatever it was, I'm sure it wasn't intentional, Bill. It can't be that serious. We were just talking about old ghost stories and legends and so forth. By the way, I really appreciate your offer to help me with Jack's research."

"Well, Russell," Bill said, looking at his beer bottle, gently swirling its contents. "I think it is serious, in a way. It's about the John Bard legend. And I did intentionally mislead you a little."

"How so?"

"Well, as you recall, Russell, I said that I had never heard of John Bard. That's not exactly true. After you left, I really thought about what I had told you, even prayed a little about it. But, after I tell you what I've got to say about it, you'll understand why I said what I did."

"Once again, Bill. It can't be that bad. Lots of people will deny something that seems silly to them. It's natural. Forget about it."

"Well, let me put it this way, Russell. To me, John Bard is pretty real."

"You mean that you believe in the legends?"

"Not all of them, of course, Russell. But let me explain."

Bill took a sip of beer.

"Can we keep this confidential?" Bill asked. "I don't believe in the Catholic sacrament of Confession, but I have something that I need to confess about this, and you're the person I trust most with it. Can you be my confessor about this?"

The outgoing, self-confident person that had bounded up Russell's front steps a few minutes ago seemed smaller now as he sat hunched over the drink in his hands.

"Jesus, Bill – oops, sorry about that – this sounds pretty serious. I don't do priestly things very well, so let's just say it's under the attorney-client privilege."

"You're not going to send me a bill, are you, Russell?" Bill's grin told Russell that he was joking. It also told Russell that Bill had put himself at ease. He straightened up in the chair, took a long drink, and set the bottle on a magazine on the table beside him. The tension in Bill's voice was gone. He smiled again and looked around the room.

"Well, Russell, my Grandmother Paxton evidently was pretty deep into a lot of superstition and folk legends and the like. I'm not even sure she was a Christian, even though we gave her a more-or-less Christian funeral. I don't know; she could even have been a bit of a pagan.

"When I was a kid, my grandparents would always talk about my Uncle Johnny, who I since have realized was supposedly this John Bard character that you mentioned."

"So, John Bard was a real person?" Russell hoped that his voice was hiding his excitement.

Bill smiled. "Well yes and no. I know it sounds nutty. You have to keep in mind that a lot of this is based on childhood memories. I was eight or nine when I first heard all these stories, so I might not be all that accurate, and I might have unconsciously repressed some of it."

"Bill, I appreciate this, but you don't have to go into anything personal. Maybe if you could just answer a couple of questions that I have about the legend. I really don't want to get involved with family matters."

"Thanks for saying that, Russell, but, you see, the legend and my family seem to be all mixed up together. Besides, I owe you the truth."

Russell got up from his chair and walked into the dining room to retrieve a yellow legal pad and a pencil from the old rustic pie safe that he used for auxiliary storage of his files.

"Well, if you're going to share this with me, do you mind if I take some notes?" he called back into the living room.

Bill's voice suddenly became flat and expressionless.

"Notes? Why? Why do you need to do that? I really don't have anything complicated to tell you."

"Nonetheless, Bill, it's just that I've really just begun to get into this folklore research, and I'm having trouble keeping it all straight in my own mind, as well as how the few additional things that I've learned relate to Jack Abrams' notes," Russell explained, looking back into the living room. "Maybe it's overkill, but it's how I do my historic research. I take lots of notes rather than rely on my memory, which really can be bad at times."

"Oh, well okay, Russell, but I thought that Jack Abrams had everything all written down in his notes."

"That's true, Bill. He did, at least an awful lot of it. But I've picked up a few things that Jack never got a chance to discover, I guess."

"What kind of things?" Bill asked, his voice seemed to be somewhere between interested and worried. "From what little I know of Jack Abrams, I assume that he probably had chased down just about every ghost story from here to Canada."

"True," Russell said, "but I've stumbled on a few additional pieces of evidence, especially about the Indian Rocks and their relationship to some of these old legends. As I think I mentioned the last time, I'm really focusing more on the factual basis for some of the material in Jack Abrams' notes rather than the legends themselves."

Russell expected Bill to respond, but Bill remained silent. Bill had partially turned away from Russell and appeared to be looking at the fireplace. Russell stood by the pie safe, his legal pad and two pencils in hand.

"If you'd rather I didn't take notes," he said, gesturing with the legal pad, "I'll honor your wishes. But if you let me take some notes, I promise you that I won't ever quote you or indicate that you were the source of the information, without first getting your consent."

Bill waved his hand. "No, no. That's okay. Fair enough, Russell. I was just curious. I didn't realize that you were enlarging on Jack's work."

"Well, there's not that much enlarging to do. He was pretty thorough. I wouldn't say that he tracked down every ghost story between here and Canada, but he probably collected most of the ones from around here."

When Russell returned to the living room, Bill was standing by the fireplace, feeling the stones that surrounded it. For a moment, Russell was afraid that he had changed his mind, and was getting ready to leave and taking one last look.

"I see that you've kept the old fireplace," Bill said. "I think that this might be the only surviving part of the original cabin that was on this site, possibly dating back to Revolutionary War times.

Bill gestured for Russell to join him at the fireplace and pointed to a spot in the mortar between the stones. "Come over here, Russell. Look at this."

"What is it?" Russell asked, peering at where Bill was pointing.

Against the dark gray mortar, still faintly visible in slightly lighter pencil marks, was the word BILLY.

"Is that you?" Russell asked.

"Yeah," Bill smiled. "I must have been only six or seven when I wrote that. I can't believe that it survived all these years." Bill's voice sounded choked up. He quickly brushed a tear from his right eye.

"All these years," Bill repeated. "Amazing."

"I'll make sure it doesn't get erased," Russell said, putting a hand on Bill's shoulder. "Not as long as I live here. I promise."

"That's not necessary," Bill said. "It's your home now, and you don't need any graffiti by some bratty kid from thirty-five years ago."

"Nonsense," said Russell. "It stays, for you and your family. I may have legal title to this property now, but it will always be the Paxton Place."

They returned to their seats, Russell sitting on the couch and Bill in the chair. Russell allowed Bill a couple of minutes to think about things and to recover his composure.

"So, tell me all about your Uncle Johnny," Russell said gently.

"Sure," he smiled, "Uncle Johnny.

"Let's start by my telling you what my grandmother used to tell me. Basically, John Bard was – or is, I guess, because some people evidently still believe he's alive – a mysterious figure who's lived in the mountains around here for as long as anyone can remember. My grandmother used to tell me that he was almost nine hundred years old; 'the real Methuselah' she used to call him. When I was a kid, she used to call him Uncle Johnny."

"Uncle Johnny. Her uncle or yours?"

"My uncle?" Bill looked directly at Russell for the first time in many minutes. He was slowly clenching and unclenching his left fist, something that Russell had never seen Bill do before.

"To tell you the truth," Bill continued, "I don't know. So, let's forget about the 'uncle' bullshit. None of them ever gave me a straight answer. I think there was one time that my Dad referred to Uncle Johnny as his uncle – my Grandmother Paxton's brother maybe – but I don't know for sure. On the other hand, whenever we'd talk about the family, like discussing whom to invite for a family picnic, they never mentioned Uncle Johnny, at least not in my presence. But I was just a little kid then, so maybe they were hiding something. It's also possible that he might have been just an honorary uncle of some sort.

"But except for my grandmother, nobody ever mentioned him except when they were arguing."

"Bill," Russell intervened. "This is obviously bothering you. All that uncertainty and conflict couldn't have been fun."

"Come on, Russell," Bill said sharply. "I came here to square some misconceptions that I gave you yesterday. I didn't come here for amateur psychotherapy from a Philadelphia lawyer."

Bill paused and smiled. "I just realized how stupid that must have sounded. I'm very sorry, Russell."

"No problem," Russell said. "We don't have to go into this any deeper if you –"

"There you go again, Russell," Bill interrupted, chuckling. "Where did you pick up all the psycho-babble: obviously bothering me, go into it deeper? Was that some elective you took in law school?"

"Listen, Bill," Russell said quietly, trying to hide his growing annoyance. Don't get hooked, he told himself. You've handled clients who were much more upset than Bill.

"Bill," Russell continued, "nobody's making you discuss anything. If you'd rather not, that's one hundred percent okay with me. You asked for the meeting, not me."

"No, I'm sorry, Russell. I really am. I guess the bottom line is that I was just a kid then. I'd believe anything my grandmother told me. She always seemed to me to be a loving, wise person – sort of a safe harbor from all the turmoil among my parents and grandparents. Maybe Grandma Paxton was just a crazy old dingbat, or maybe she was trying to confront a truth that everyone else wanted to deny. I don't know, Russell. I still don't know how I feel about all of it even today."

"Did you ever meet Uncle Johnny?"

Bill quickly answered, "No. Never did." He appeared to hold his breath for a few moments, then exhaled audibly. The clenching and unclenching of his fist had stopped.

"I'm really sorry, Russell," Bill said. "As you can see, this is bringing back some upsetting memories. But please, let's continue."

"Okay, Bill, do you have any idea why your grandmother referred to John Bard as your uncle?"

"Not really. I can only make a lot of wild guesses based on some things my mother told me."

"What types of things? Can you give me some specific examples?"

Bill waited a moment before answering. Russell wondered whether Bill was afraid that Russell was trying to trip him up somehow.

"Well," Bill said with a long sigh, "the important thing to remember, Russell, is that my mother probably was mentally ill. I don't know of any diagnosis or treatment of her at the time – it was the late 1940s – but looking back on it, I think that she had real problems. And, as you know, my mother and Grandma Paxton didn't get along.

"So, anything that Mom might have told me about my father's side of the family has to be taken with a big hunk of salt – not just a grain but a great big Lot's Wife size hunk. My mother was deeply religious, a staunch Bible-believing, fundamentalist Wesleyan Methodist. I don't know what Grandma Paxton's religion really was. Like I said, we gave her a superficially Christian funeral. I think Uncle Woody prevailed on a Unitarian minister he knew downstate to come up here and conduct the service as a personal favor – a celebration of her life, they called it. But religion really isn't a major part of all this.

"I seem to remember Mom once telling me that when my grandmother was young, before she met Granddad, my Grandma Paxton was involved in the White Indian cult and ran around in the woods and participated in White Indian ceremonies and even would go on what they called the 'spring and fall migrations' up into New York State and even into Ontario. But everyone knows there's no such thing as the White Indians; at least no educated person I know really believes in them. So, I think my Mom might have just used that old legend to get at my grandmother."

"But some folks around here believe in them," Russell interrupted. Bill momentarily looked annoyed. "Or, at least that they existed at some time in the past," Russell finished.

"But, Russell, like we talked about that first time you came over to the Manse, that's just Viking Mill thinking. Why, you have probably one of the biggest 'Viking towers' in the eastern United States right up the mountain behind us: those Rocks. But, anyways, I remember Mom telling me once – and this was some time before Grandma died – that Dad had told her once that Grandma claimed that she was John Bard's niece." Bill hesitated for a moment, looking Russell in the eyes.

"And also his daughter."

"That can't be true, Bill," Russell replied. "Besides, that's just triple hearsay – what your mother told you that your father told her that your grandmother told him – and none of the three of them are very reliable witnesses."

"Well, I don't know anything about triple hearsay, Russell, and I don't believe the story. But it's an old legend of some sort in our family. It has persisted, like old wood smoke in the curtains in a cabin. It caused a lot of tension in our family.

"But to cut away some of the layers of hearsay that you object to, I myself remember how Grandma would always sort of glory in being the daughter of her mother and her mother's brother. She'd say this weird stuff herself; I heard her. I even remember one time, at Thanksgiving dinner, just before she died, she announced that John Bard had even had relations with her – not just in the past but at every new moon – in the center of the Indian Rocks. Looking back on it now, I think that she might have just said this stuff to get a rise out of people, but I'll never know for sure."

Russell stifled simultaneous urges to gasp and to laugh.

"Nobody in our family believed it, of course," Bill said. "but it still caused a lot of pain in our family."

"Especially for your grandfather," Russell prompted.

"No, my grandfather seemed to ignore it. But stories like that, even things that you think are family secrets, somehow get around. When I was in grade school, I got a lot of teasing about it. I remember my best friend in fifth grade once saying that he had heard that I was part Indian because my real grandfather was the chief of the White Indians and that my grandmother was his whore and that she was servicing all the men in the tribe."

"That's really rough, Bill. Kids can be so cruel."

"Yeah, well, at age ten I didn't know what the word *whore* even meant. When I asked my Mom, she hit the roof.

"The rumors persisted into junior high school, after my grandparents were gone. But," Bill shrugged, "most of those kids – even my friends – were inbred ignorant hicks from up in the mountains themselves." His voice became louder. "They'd fuck their sisters, their mothers, their animals, anything that moved."

Russell was momentarily stunned by the sudden change in Bill's demeanor and the venom in his words. Bill fell silent. Russell decided that Bill would have to break the silence.

After about thirty seconds, Bill resumed quietly, "I'm sorry, Russell. That was unworthy of me. Please forgive me. Those poor kids didn't realize what they were saying or the hurt that they were causing. But, for all my childhood I had always felt like an outsider, like I just didn't belong. I was never good enough.

"Anyhow, Russell, all of that – that crap that I had to grow up with – that's why I reacted the way I did when you mentioned John Bard. The name just brought all of that back. It shut the better part of me down. I'm sorry."

"I understand, Bill."

"I felt the same thing when Jack Abrams interviewed me about the Sangman legends, but maybe I controlled it better. Of course, I never told Jack what I just told you. I guess that I never really trusted him. But, I'm really sorry I misled you, Russell."

"No problem, Bill. Don't worry about it. I would never include any of it in Jack's book."

"Oh, I'm not worried about that, Russell. I'm just sorry I'm so thin skinned about it and it still bothers me so much after all these years."

Bill Paxton seemed very uncomfortable for a man who had just pulled what Russell thought to be a relatively minor skeleton out of his closet.

"Yeah, well, I guess I'm probably one of the best sources of John Bard stories there is, Russell. I know I heard them all when I was a kid, from my Grandma Paxton."

"What sort of things did she tell you about John Bard, then?" Russell almost said *Uncle Johnny* but remembered that Bill still was very sensitive about the family relationship.

"Oh, you probably already know most of them already."

"I've read Jack's material, Bill, but I would sure like to hear some of them from you, from someone inside the family."

Paxton looked at his watch and jumped up.

"Oh, gosh, it's after three. I'm sorry, Russell. I've got an important call I have to make. Can I use your phone? It's local, but I've got to call one of our members about something really urgent. I promised to meet her in a little while to counsel her about it, and I'm running late."

Russell pointed to the phone and went to the kitchen to get two fresh beers, half-listening to Bill's whispered end of the conversation – he could not clearly make out any coherent words or phrases – to ensure that he did not return to the living room until Bill was finished. He thought that he heard Bill mention his name once or twice but could not be certain. After about three minutes, Russell noisily walked along the hallway connecting the kitchen from the front of the house. As he walked past the living room, he held up the two bottles of beer and gestured to the front porch. Bill stopped speaking, put his hand over the mouthpiece of the phone, nodded, and waited until Russell was outside before he resumed the phone conversation. About three minutes later, Bill came out onto the porch.

"I'm really sorry about that, Russell." Bill took a bottle from Russell. "One of our members had to go up to Corning for her mother's funeral, and I promised to call her when she got back. Poor woman, she was the only mourner there. It was just her and the undertaker and the minister and her mother."

"I was going to say, Bill, that I hope she's okay. But how can anyone be okay after something like that?"

"I don't know, Russell. Sometimes I just don't know."

"So," Russell tried to smile, picking up his note pad. "What do you know about John Bard?"

"Nine hundred years old?" Bill asked, smiling back.

"Is he?"

"Heck, no, Russell. Come on. Get real."

"But don't you believe the part in the Bible about Methuselah living to be nine hundred. Don't you believe that's possible?"

"Of course not," Bill said flatly.

"But, Russell," he continued, "getting back to my illustrious Uncle Johnny. Grandma's story was that John Bard was a Welshman who came up here in the nineteenth century. He lived up in the mountains and got rich on sang."

"So, John Bard and the legendary Sangman are one in the same?" Russell asked.

"Probably."

"What about the treasure?"

"Who knows, Russell? Could be. As I told you before, some of those old ridge runners made a lot of money about a hundred years ago. There was a time when a good root of ginseng, the kind that was shaped like a man, was worth more than its weight in gold. And that's not some old legend; that's historical fact."

"Where did John Bard live?"

"Nobody knows, Russell. According to Grandma, he had a cabin way up in the mountains, maybe several cabins. Some folks claim that they've met him in the forest, or at least have seen him, but you know how people are. Some just want to get some notoriety, no matter how wild the story."

"I've heard some of those accounts, Bill. Some of them are pretty recent. I know of at least one solid citizen who believes that he recently met and talked with somebody that matched the description. This supposedly happened –"

"Who told you that? Robert Kaiser?" Bill interrupted.

Russell hadn't ever heard or seen Robert's name before in connection with John Bard. He wondered why Bill mentioned him.

"Uh, why no," Russell answered slowly. "I'd have to check my notes, Bill. I don't remember exactly who it was now. It might have been Robert who told me about somebody else sighting John Bard."

Bill looked at Russell with a blank expression for a second.

"But that's not important now, Bill." Russell wanted to get the discussion back on track before he scared Bill away.

"So, getting back to what your grandmother told you, I think that you told me that you never actually met the man you knew as Uncle – sorry, I mean John Bard?"

Bill waited a few moments, stroking his chin with the thumb and index finger of his left hand.

"No," he said slowly. "No, I don't remember that I ever did. Perhaps when I was very little, but I don't have any memory of it at all if I did."

"Well, then," Russell nodded, "Did your grandmother ever tell you what John Bard looked like? Did he look anything like the old gent with the white beard in those old photos in your study?"

"Again, Russell, I'm sorry, but I don't remember anything specific." He paused. "But I always had this idea that he must have looked a little like Rip Van Winkle after his nap."

Russell thought of his meeting with John several days before, up at the Rocks.

"Old man? Long white beard down to his waist? That sort of thing?"

"Yeah, I guess so," Bill smiled. "Like the Disney cartoon."

"Dressed in old-fashioned clothes, like a blue Continental Army coat?"

Paxton said nothing for a second, then softly sang a snatch of a song, almost laughing the words:

His blue soldier's coat a-flashin' in the forest
Runnin' the ridges, singin' his song,
A-laughin' as he roams through the endless mountains
Askin' you kindly to come along

"What's that, Bill?"

"Oh nothing, Russell. Just a bit of a song my grandmother used to sing to me all the time. I don't remember the rest of it."

"What's it about?" Russell asked.

"Oh, I don't know. Just an old folk song from around here."

Russell asked Bill to repeat the verse as he wrote it down. He noticed that Bill seemed to have difficulty repeating all of it and changed a word or two. When he asked Bill if he knew any other parts of the song, Bill quickly said no and volunteered that he had never heard any other old local folk songs from his grandmother.

"So, all you know are those couple of lines you just sang for me?"

"That's about it, Russell. Sorry."

As Russell walked with Bill off the front porch and to Bill's car, he thanked Bill for the information about John Bard, and reassured Bill that their conversation was confidential. Bill apologized again for having misled Russell the day before.

"Look, Russell, even though we haven't known each other very long," Bill said as he got into his car, "I'd like to consider us friends, and I hope that my being less than honest about Uncle Johnny and my crazy family won't interfere with that."

"No, it's okay, Bill. I understand completely. It's forgotten."

As Russell walked back onto the porch, he turned and waved at Bill as he drove away.

He's not being completely honest with me, Russell thought as Bill's car disappeared into the woods between his house and the road. I seem to be getting too close to some of those facts that he warned me about yesterday, the ones that people want to keep secret. Something's not right.

And he knows that whole damn song perfectly well.

The Sangman's Treasure

From *Research Journal 4,* transcribed by John S. Abrams from original notes in Notebooks 6 and 7

Researcher's note: This narrative is based principally upon various interviews that I conducted in the summer and early autumn of 1972 with: the Rev. William Paxton, age 32, of Wellsboro, Pennsylvania; Mrs. Maria Santori, age 54, of Wellsboro, Pennsylvania; Paul Levesque, age 79, of Richmond Township, Pennsylvania; Miss Julie Maye Thomas, (who would not disclose her age, but is believed to be at least 80 years old), of Wellsboro, Pennsylvania; and Walter A. Wentworth, age 32, of Charleston Township, Pennsylvania. A number of other persons in the Wellsboro area also briefly mentioned (but quickly dismissed) the legendary character John Bard and the legend of the sangman's treasure (or treasures).

Because of the multiple sources for this legend, I have recorded and integrated into a single narrative only those points about which my sources were reasonably consistent. They presented slightly different versions of some parts of this account; and I have noted those variations. For example, Mr. Wentworth, who claims to descend from a long line of sangmen, said that the sangman legend was based on one of his ancestors whom he says made his living harvesting wild ginseng in the mountains of northern Pennsylvania in the nineteenth century. Mr. Levesque disputes this, saying that the story is only another variant of the myth of a mysterious mountain man sometimes called John Bard, who, according to a parallel legend is said to be a Druid who fled Wales to escape English persecution and is, according to the varying accounts, between seven hundred and nine hundred years old.

The Sangman's Treasure
as told by various citizens of Tioga County, Pennsylvania

During the first half of the nineteenth century, there wasn't a big trade in ginseng in the mountains of northern Pennsylvania. It gets too cold for the big-time production of sang. It grows more abundantly down south, in Fulton and Bedford Counties and into western Maryland, Virginia, and North Carolina. Spring comes too late up here for the sang roots to grow really big, and there aren't as many good spots for it to grow.

When the big foreign market for sang developed in the 1840s and continued through to the 1880s, a man could make some extra money harvesting sang, if he knew where to look. There wasn't a lot of sang that grew in this area, but there were pockets of it, especially on the south-facing sides of the mountains, that was very high quality.

There was one old ridge runner named John, who knew where the highest quality sang grew and got rich off from it. Nobody remembers John's last name, but everyone just called him Old John. Some people say that his name was John Bard, but others say that this confuses a real man with the myth of an old mountain man who supposedly is immortal.

Everyone agrees that Old John is a good name for him, because everyone agrees that, whether a myth or a real person, he is very old. Some say that he was the last surviving soldier to have fought in the Revolutionary War – was with General Washington himself at Valley Forge – and wore a fancy blue and white cockade that Washington had given him for bravery. Still others say that Old John was a Tory spy, who escaped being hanged by Washington and fled inland to the mountains of north-central Pennsylvania. Most likely these stories are just old tall tales, but the truth was at least this: Whenever he lived and died, Old John was the oldest man in the Endless Mountains, and he knew them better than anyone.

Old John lived by himself up in the mountains. He'd been up there for a long time even by 1880. Nobody knew for sure where he lived. Some say he had a cabin that was so far up in the woods that you had to walk to it and couldn't even take a mule. Others said that he had several camps to the north and east of Wellsboro and just moved from one camp to the other. Others say that his camps were to the south and west. There was even one old story that Old John had built a lodge in the trunk of a living tree and hid the door so well that you could walk right past him and not know he was there. In fact, several old trees have been found in the hills in the northeastern part of Tioga County that have hollow trunks large enough that a person could find temporary shelter, at least, inside.

Old John was a wealthy man by all accounts. He had a secret stand of sang somewhere in the mountains. Some say that it was overlooking the Tioga River, somewhere between Mansfield and the village of Tioga. Others say that it was in a forested area further east, near the ruins of the old settlement on Spanish Hill. Still other folks said that he had several sang patches deep in the mountains and moved from one of them to the other. Nobody knew exactly where Old John's sang grew, and nobody knows to this day.

In the late 1800s and early 1900s, people would see John from time to time during the year, walking into Tioga or sometimes Wellsboro with a couple of sacks of sang. He'd get on the Erie Railroad and take it to New York City, where he'd sell his dried crop to some Chinese merchant for its weight in gold. It is said that he also sometimes sold it in Scranton or even as far away as Philadelphia.

Old John would then come back about a week or so later with a bag of gold coins, some of which he'd spend at the old Emporium store in Wellsboro (which is now Dunham's Department Store) for clothes and supplies, and then he'd head back up into the mountains.

Some of the other sangmen from time to time would try to follow Old John when he left town, hoping that he'd lead them to his stand of sang. They said they didn't want to steal it, just to admire it. But John would lose them not more than two miles outside town. A couple of those old sangmen went up into the mountains looking for John and never came back. In the 1920s, one old sangman, Cletus Pfalz (sometimes known as Clete Falls), went up there and tramped around for almost three months looking for Old John and his treasure, as it was known by that time. Some hunters found Cletus in the fall, sitting up in a tree and gibbering like a monkey. They brought him back to town, but he was never "right in the head" again and died at the old County Asylum in 1923. Even on his deathbed, Cletus claimed that he had found Old John's patch of sang, and that it was guarded by fiery panthers and ghosts in white robes.

Nobody knows when Old John passed away. He just stopped coming into town one spring, sometime around 1910; but people kept reporting sightings of him now and then up in the mountains, or sometimes fishing from the bank of one of the rivers or streams. As late as the Second World War, a group of deer hunters claimed they saw on old man in a Revolutionary War hat tramping silently through the woods, carrying a gunny sack and an old rifle. So, maybe he's still up there with his gold guarding his secret stand of sang.

People have mounted big expeditions to find any traces of one of Old John's camps. They tramped all over the mountains, claimed to have covered every inch, and never found a thing. So, perhaps that rich stand of sang is still up there. It was considered to be common knowledge in the 1880s, even though apparently nobody had actually seen it. Assuming that it ever existed, and unless it has been disturbed by anyone, it would still be there today.

So is Old John's gold. There are no reports of exactly how much money Old John would bring back from one of his trips to sell his crop, but descriptions of "one or sometimes two bags" of gold coins suggest that it could have been as much as between one and two thousand dollars, worth probably thirty times that amount in today's money. Old John was never known to have spent more than five to ten dollars upon his return to Wellsboro, before he would retreat back up into the mountains.

So, there probably really is a treasure – maybe two of them – somewhere up in the mountains of Tioga County: Old John's gold and his secret stand of ginseng. But nobody will ever find them. Old John hid his treasures too well, and the mountains guard his secrets to this very day.

The Old Holiday House

From *Research Journal 2*, transcribed by John S. Abrams from original notes in Notebooks 3, 7, 8, and 9

Researcher's note: This story, or some variation of it, was mentioned over the course of this project by too many people to mention. Whenever the interviews turned to ghosts, the legend of the "haunted" Holiday House was almost always mentioned. The most consistently corroborated and detailed source was the Rev. William Paxton, pastor of the Mountain View Chapel, who said that he had heard the account from his grandmother, Belle Paxton, who claimed to have heard the mysterious voice in the Holiday mansion herself. Thomas "Tommy" Girty also contributed details about the history of "General" Darius D. Holiday. Where discrepancies exist, I have resolved them in favor of the version that is most consistent with a classic ghost story.

The Old Holiday House
as told by Tommy Girty and Rev. William Paxton

There is a haunted house in Wellsboro, the old Holiday Mansion. The whole house isn't haunted, just a closet in one of the bedrooms.

The Holiday house was built in the 1880s by one of the timber barons, General Darius D. Holiday. They called him "General," but some folks say that he was just a foot soldier in the Civil War, and that the "General" was just something he added to help himself in his business. Lots of people did that after the Civil War.

General Holiday had a questionable past. He came from a dirt-poor family that worked a farm just on the other side of the New York state line. He enlisted in Company H of the 35th Pennsylvania Regiment – the "Tioga Invincibles" — in 1861 as a private. He fought at Antietam, Fredericksburg, Gettysburg, and in the Wilderness campaign. A letter that he wrote on the battlefield at Fredericksburg in December 1862 is still in the County Historical Society Museum. By 1863 he supposedly had been promoted to captain, and he came home in October 1864, after having been mustered out with his regiment in Harrisburg. He returned with a chest full of medals and told folks he had received a temporary promotion to one-star general at Gettysburg. Some people say that his Civil War stories were all fabricated, and that although he served honorably and was wounded at Fredericksburg, he never advanced beyond corporal.

In any event, Darius D. Holiday set himself up in a timber business with his uncle, Abraham Carson. They formed the Carson and Holiday Timber Company sometime around 1868. There were rumors at the time that Carson put up all the money and took his nephew in as a partner in response to a deathbed plea from his sister, Holiday's mother, to "look after my boy." The truth is that Holiday put up two thousand dollars in gold coin. Nobody knows where he got that kind of money, but even back in 1868, people had learned not to ask Darius D. Holiday too many questions.

The Carson and Holiday Timber Company was a small operation at first, just Abraham Carson and the General and a clerk working out of an office above the old Emporium Department Store on Main Street. The business grew quickly though. In 1876, Carson and Holiday built the Centennial Building, which at that time was the tallest building in town – five stories! The timber company occupied the first floor, and they rented out the other four. Rumor had it that by 1876, the Carson and Holiday Timber Company either owned outright, or had timber rights to, ten percent of the land in north central Pennsylvania, and several hundred thousand acres in New York State.

Shortly after they built the Centennial Building and moved into it, Abraham Carson's health began to fail. General Holiday bought out Carson's interest in the company, and Carson died shortly afterward. The General kept the name of the company the same, though: Carson and Holiday. At the time there were rumors that the General somehow caused his uncle to get sick, so he could force him out of the company and take over, but jealous people will always say vicious things.

Now, before long the General was rolling in money. They say it was Cornelius Vanderbilt who would light his cigars with hundred-dollar bills, but the General did it long before. In fact, there is still a charred end of a hundred-dollar bill on display at the County Historical Society, with a brass plate that says that it was used by General Darius D. Holiday to light a cigar at the annual Formal Dinner of the Grand Army of the Republic in 1879. Commodore Vanderbilt was still using matches back then.

One of the strange things about the Carson and Holiday Timber Company was that although the company made lots of money, and General Holiday paid his employees well, they never actually cut that much timber. The General would just buy timber rights, usually from some poor farmer who was about to be foreclosed by the bank, and then sell them a few years later for a lot more. When Carson and Holiday Timber did send men up into the forest, they would usually clear just a small stand of trees, sometimes even less than an acre. All the same, the money kept rolling in. Nobody knew where it came from.

On Christmas Day 1881, the General married Catherine Palmer, the daughter of a lawyer and state senator from Clinton County, Aaron Palmer. At that time, the General lived in the Penn Wells Hotel, in a big suite of rooms on the top floor. Catherine moved in there at first, but the General decided to build them the finest house in all Pennsylvania, maybe in all the United States.

It took two years to build the General's house. He spent a fortune on it. It was custom-designed, and he used only the finest materials. For example, instead of using pine for the framing, the General insisted on oak. The gas light fixtures all came from Germany, except for the chandeliers, which were made of the finest Austrian crystal. The wallpaper was imported from France. It was, and probably still is, the best-built house in this part of the state.

The old folks around Wellsboro still talk about the housewarming party the General and Mrs. Holiday gave on a summer evening in 1883. These folks weren't born yet, of course, but they heard their parents and grandparents talk about it. They say that the General spent tens of thousands of dollars. He brought in two orchestras from Philadelphia. One played in the large dining room, which had been turned into a ballroom for that night. The other played outside on the back lawn, while guests strolled in the

General's gardens. He hired the entire kitchen staff from the Penn Wells Hotel – chef, waiters, and all.

The party lasted all night and ended with a big breakfast early the next morning. As the guests left, the General and Mrs. Holiday personally said goodbye to each person. The General gave each of the men a gold-plated pocket watch engraved with the General and Mrs. Holiday's names and the date. Mrs. Holiday gave each of the women a rose that had been dipped in pure gold. You'll still see some of those watches around town, in antique stores and such. Although they were gold-plated, the works were cheap, and most of them quit running after a year or so, but they were prized by the guests and their families. And you will still find some of those golden roses tucked away in the bureau drawers of the grandchildren and great grandchildren of the guests at the Holidays' housewarming.

The first few years in the house were happy ones for the Holidays. Their only sorrow was the lack of children. Still, they entertained lavishly, and the General's timber business appeared to prosper. People also still talk about the big New Year's open house that they would have every year, with the workers from the timber company being the honored guests.

Just around the turn of the century – the most commonly mentioned date is 1899 – things began to change. The parties stopped, and the Holiday house was always closed up tight as a drum, even in summer. Folks would know that the Holidays were at home, because at night they could see lights on inside. Also, people would still see the General leave his house for his office at seven o'clock sharp every morning, just as he always did – not every day, but often enough so that folks would know that the General was still among the living.

Even so, the General would sometimes disappear for days on end, sometimes without even canceling his appointments. One of the clerks from the timber company would go to his house to see where the General was and whether he would be coming into the office that day. They couldn't telephone because the Holidays refused to have a telephone in the house. The clerk would knock and knock, but nobody would answer the door, even though he could hear people moving around inside.

Well, to get to the haunted house story, in 1905, General Holiday's body was found in the closet of one of the guest bedrooms. He had apparently shot himself in the head. A Colt 1860 Army Revolver was by his side, still clutched tightly in his right hand. He left a strange note. It simply said, "I cannot go through what I must face. I know too much. This way is better. Forgive me."

People puzzled over that note for years. There were all sorts of wild stories, but not a bit of evidence, that the General was in some sort of trouble. He had no reason to kill himself. Sure, he had been acting strangely in those final years, but he was still sane enough to run his business. Business was good, as was his marriage. Like any captain of business, General Holiday had enemies, but none who would want to kill him or drive him to take his own life.

When the General died, everyone expected a big funeral, but Catherine insisted on no visitation or viewing and a private burial, which was unheard of in those days. So General Darius D. Holiday was quietly laid to rest one Sunday evening in the old churchyard at First Presbyterian, and that was that.

Catherine Holiday lived for another forty years. She stayed in the house her husband had built for her. It was like time stopped for Catherine in 1905. When she died, the old Holiday place still did not have electricity or a telephone. She still used gas lights, probably the last person in the state to do so, and still had blocks of ice for her huge old oak icebox delivered to her kitchen door three times a week.

People would see Catherine about three or four times a year, doing some shopping, but she would never say much. When she would go out into town, she would dress up, but her fashions were always about twenty years behind the times. If you made an effort to go up to her on the street and start a conversation, she would be polite, but would quickly make her excuses and leave.

The only event in Catherine Holiday's life seemed to be her going to church at First Presbyterian once a year, on the Sunday before the anniversary of her husband's death. She would show up, as regular as clockwork, just as the organ prelude began. The choir would always sing an anthem "contributed in the memory of

General Darius D. Holiday." She would sit by herself in the next to last row and leave quickly at the end of the service. She did this every year, the last time being just four days before she died.

Catherine Palmer Holiday passed away on April 12, 1945 – the same day as President Roosevelt – just four days shy of her eighty-third birthday. Her cleaning lady found her in the guest bedroom where the General had died forty years before. She was sitting on the floor, her back leaning on the door to the closet where the General had shot himself. The cleaning lady said that Mrs. Holiday had a half-smile on her face, and her eyes were closed, as if she was dreaming a beautiful dream. She was buried next to her husband in the First Presbyterian cemetery in Wellsboro.

Catherine's only survivors were two younger sisters who lived together on a small farm outside Lock Haven, Pennsylvania. Catherine's will left several bequests to local charities, which exhausted what little remained of her savings.

The Holiday place stood empty and closed for almost seven years after Catherine died. Nobody wanted to take on the expense that would be involved to put in electricity and make it modern. Catherine's sisters directed the law firm that handled the estate to sell the house and its contents at auction. The furniture, all of it antique, sold quickly, but nobody would even make a bid for the house.

Finally, in 1952, the Sheriff auctioned off the Holiday place for back taxes. A young doctor and his wife bought it and must have spent a fortune putting in new plumbing and electricity. Now, there had always been rumors that General Holiday had stashed a treasure somewhere in the walls of the house when he built it back in 1883. The story must have been partly true because, when the doctor and his wife had the walls opened to put in the new pipes and wires, they found an old wooden fishing tackle box holding twenty stock certificates from several long-defunct mining and timber companies, five twenty-dollar gold coins, and a handful of silver dollars. That was the sum and substance of the Holiday Treasure.

The noises in the guest bedroom closet where General Holiday had died began shortly after the doctor and his wife discovered the so-called treasure. At first, the young couple thought that it was just the noises that any old house makes; but the noises kept getting louder. Also, they always occurred at 7:00 p.m., no matter what the season, which was the hour that General Holiday is believed to have killed himself. Usually the noises sounded like someone groaning, but the doctor swore that once he distinctly heard a man's voice saying, "Catherine." When that happened, the couple moved out, and the place stood empty for about another two years until another family moved in.

The strange thing about the Holiday Place is that people nowadays tend to move in and stay put for five years or longer, even though everybody knows the place is haunted. Everyone who's lived in the house tells the same story. There's no moaning, chain-rattling, footsteps, or anything like that. Instead, every evening, just at seven o'clock, you can hear a soft tapping from inside the guest room closet. When you approach, if you are very quiet and get there in time, you will always hear the same thing: a man's voice, very gentle but also tired sounding. He says only one thing, again and again:

"Catherine, I love you."

No Way Back

Kenny Kelso could tell that Brendan was unhappy with him. The Lesson had not gone well. Kenny kept losing his place as he tried to recite the Knowledge that he had to commit to memory. Sometimes he could pick it up and continue, after a quiet prompt from Brendan. Most of the time, however, he had to go back to the beginning of the passage and try again from the start.

It would be dark soon. The temperature was beginning to drop as dusk filled the valleys. Through the trees, Kenny could see the western sky, beyond the next mountain, shifting to purple. Kenny was not sure that he could find his way down off the mountain to the road where he had parked. Brendan would simply disappear into the forest, as he always did, and return home by some other way. But Brendan would not leave until Kenny had mastered the Lesson, until he could repeat that day's part of the Knowledge perfectly.

"Try it again, Spook," Brendan said softly.

Kenny closed his eyes. Let the Knowledge take over, Brendan had advised during their first Lesson. It will not come if you try to force it.

"Blessed be the Oak Moon. Blessed be the Moon of Strength in its full flowering of glory. As its light shines on me, may its blessings and energy –"

"Energy and blessings."

"Energy and blessings, blessings and energy, what's the difference?"

"You will come to understand that it's a big difference," Brendan said slowly. "The blessings that we receive flow from the universal energy transmitted by the moon, our closest neighbor in the cosmos."

"Energy and blessings fill me in this sacred space tonight." Kenny stopped, listening inwardly for the next words. They didn't come.

"I'm sorry, Brendan. It's just too hard. Isn't there a book that has this in it and that I can study? I never could memorize stuff."

"No, Spook, you know why the Knowledge can never be committed to writing."

"Yeah, but—"

"Spook, the Drawing Down of the Moon is one of the most basic exercises. Even a novice must learn it. You have been doing so well, but your mind isn't here today."

"This stuff is so hard, Brendan. I'm doing my best to learn all this stuff, but I don't understand it."

"Understanding will come. Trust me on this, Spook. More importantly, trust yourself. Have some faith in yourself. It will come to you in time."

Kenny shook his head. "Not for me, it won't. I mean, take the Drawing Down of the Moon. We can't really bring the moon down to earth. I know it's a symbol for something else. But all this symbolism just doesn't make sense to me. I know it does to you and the others, but I'm just not at your level, and never will be."

Brendan reached out and lightly put his hand on Kenny's shoulder.

"You know that it's a symbol," Brendan said, smiling. "That shows that you are already beginning to understand. This is a spiritual exercise that allows us to center ourselves and to bring the powers of nature, of the universe, into our lives."

"Yeah, but I never did well in school," Kenny replied, feeling tears coming into his eyes. He thought his voice must be trembling and he swallowed to control it. "You guys must have known that, even that first night last fall. I'm just not cut out for this. Maybe we should just let it go. I mean, you go your way and I go mine."

That was the last thing Kenny wanted. Since that first night with Willy and Claw, the night he met Laurel, Kenny had sometimes felt a strange power inside him. He knew that he could learn the Knowledge. He had already mastered passages twice as long. For the first time in his life, he belonged to something important.

Brendan showed no reaction.

"I'm sorry, Brendan. I don't mean that."

"That's okay, Spook," Brendan replied. "I know that it was just the frustration talking.

"But you're distracted, Spook. That's why you're having problems. Maybe we should pick this up some other time. There's no hurry." Brendan stood up. "It will be dark before long. I need to go soon."

Kenny stood and brushed off his jeans. "Yeah, I guess we should be heading down the mountain."

"Not you, Spook. You need to stay here just a bit longer. Listen for the Knowledge in the gathering night. Listen with your ears, don't worry about listening with your mind or your heart or any of that New Age nonsense. Get basic. Listen with your ears. You will actually hear the Knowledge and the power in the twilight.

"You know, astronomers have proven something that we have known for centuries, that the sun emits sound that actually can be detected. Listen for it at sunset. And the stars, too, they emit sounds, Spook, night sounds that have travelled for hundreds of millions of years to arrive at this place this night. Listen for them."

Kenny didn't know what to say. He was afraid he looked stupid, standing there with his mouth open in amazement.

"So maybe this is one of those times that you could do better by yourself. The universe is a far better teacher than I could ever be. And maybe I'm making you nervous for some reason.

"So just stay here a little longer by yourself. Think about what it is that is keeping the Knowledge from you. And listen with your ears. Maybe they can hear what something in your mind is blocking."

"I already know what it is, Brendan. It's my girl."

"I thought as much. You want to talk about it?"

"No, there's nothing you can do. I have to work it out. She's just bugging me about stuff."

"You mean, Cathy?" Brendan asked quietly. "I hate to say this, Spook, but I was happy when I heard that she had dumped you. I know that she was being a real pain in the ass. Why'd you guys ever get back together?"

Kenny wondered how Brendan knew all about him and Cathy but didn't ask. He knew that Brendan would just say what he always said: "We always watch out for our own, Spook."

"Yeah," Kenny replied. "It was after that night that Willy and Claw took me up onto the mountain and did their sacrifice, or whatever it was, I was scared shitless and decided to get away for a while."

"Yes," Brendan interrupted. "And remember it was Claw who picked you up walking along 287 almost all the way to Lawrenceville and drove you back home to get your stuff and then took you to the bus station."

"Yeah, it was Claw." Kenny acknowledged. "He even gave me some money – not loaned it but gave it to me. You know, he looks scary, but he's a really nice guy."

Kenny was surprised when Brendan didn't respond to his comment about Claw, so he continued.

"Well, I ended up in Allentown with just enough money to rent a room at the YMCA for a couple weeks, so I did day labor on a couple of jobs. I did a lot of thinking about things and decided that I was being stupid, running away like that. So, I took what money I had been able to scrape together and took the bus back home.

"When I got back into town, I went to my landlord to see if I could get back my apartment. I'd skipped out on the rent at the end of the month. He looked at me like I was crazy and said that the apartment was still mine and that someone had paid the rent while I was gone. I just said, 'Oh yeah, I'd forgotten.' But I just assumed that maybe Cathy had covered it."

"Why would she have done that? She had just broken up with you, Spook."

"Oh yeah, that's right. So, maybe it was you guys that paid my rent?"

"Let's just say that we look out for our friends," Brendan replied with a smile. "I can't tell you anything more."

"Well," Kenny continued, "there were a couple of letters from Cathy. She said that she loved me and wanted to be with me, but it would never work out as long as I was involved with a cult, as she called it. So, I called her, and we had a couple of dates and sort of straightened things out between us."

"So, what are you going to do?" Brendan asked. His eyes seemed to narrow. He looked serious, almost grim.

"Well, Cathy and I are together again. I promised her that I would have nothing to do with any cults, that she was more important to me than anything else."

"But here you are," Brendan said. "What's that all about?"

"Hey," Kenny shrugged, "I lied to her. I didn't want to, but if I have to keep the Knowledge secret, she will never find out."

Brendan turned away from Kenny and stood silently for a few moments, as if he were following a movement in the forest. He turned back and stepped forward toward Kenny, his body outlined black against the deep purple light filtering through the trees. Even though he was only inches away, Kenny could not make out the details of his face.

"Think about the risks, Spook. Are you trying to tell me that Cathy hasn't asked you about us since the two of you got back together?"

"Well, she's still bugging me about the Children, kind of indirectly. Like when she calls and I'm not home, she grills me about where I was and what I was doing. When she comes over to my place, she's always looking for clues of some sort. I really got her good one day, though. She came over and I had a big old Bible sitting on the coffee table. That shut her up. She seemed happy to see it but didn't know what to say."

Brendan chuckled, "Well done, Spook. But what do you say when you talk in your sleep?" Brendan's voice was suddenly flat. Kenny was sure that he was walking into a trap.

"How do you know that I talk in my sleep?"

"Relax, Spook, we all do at one time or another," Brendan responded. "I just want to understand if there's any risk. Besides, if you'd ever say anything in your sleep, you could always explain it away as some sort of crazy dream."

Kenny was not entirely reassured by Brendan's explanation, but he continued cautiously. I have to be careful, he thought, not to say anything that could get him or Cathy into trouble. If I lie, Brendan would know it or find out.

"Well," Kenny replied, "there was one time when she came over and spent the night with me, she said that I talked in my sleep. That scared me a little, because it was the only time it ever happened, and what if I had said anything about the Children or started reciting the Knowledge in my sleep? But I asked her what I had said, and she said she couldn't understand any of it, that it was just a lot of mumbling."

"You're sure about that?"

"Sure, Brendan, I mean, I'm pretty sure. Cathy wouldn't lie about it. She never lies."

Kenny knew that Brendan was staring at him. With the fading sunlight to his back, Brendan's face was just a gray silhouette. Kenny squinted, trying to see any expression in Brendan's face. All he saw was dark gray against deepening purple.

"Honest, Brendan. We can trust Cathy. She can be a pain in the ass, but we can trust her."

"But can I trust you?"

"What do you mean? Sure, you can trust me, Brendan. You know that."

Brendan's voice seemed to rumble, sending out vibrations like those super-woofer bass speakers Kenny had always wanted in his car.

"You just don't get it, do you, Spook?"

"Get what?"

"The need to keep our secrets from the rest of the world. You just don't understand. You never will."

"But I do. Honest, Brendan, we don't have to worry about Cathy. I'm going to dump her anyway, for good this time. Like you said, she's getting to be a pain in the ass. Always asking me where –"

Brendan took a step even closer. Kenny wanted to step back, but maybe this was a test. It was better to stand his ground.

"The problem isn't Cathy. It's you, Spook. It's not just a matter of not answering questions from the outside. You also have to keep questions from being asked at all."

"What's the big deal if my girlfriend knows I'm in the Children of Bel?" For a moment Kenny worried that his voice was too defiant. "I mean, just so long as I don't tell her anything about it. My uncles were in the Masons. Everybody knew it. They even had Mason bumper stickers, but they never told anyone any of their Mason secrets. So, what's the big deal with us?"

Brendan turned away. As he turned, the deepening sunlight caught his eyes. They seemed to flash red, like one of those laser pointers Kenny had always wanted. Brendan again had his back turned to Kenny now, facing the sunset. Kenny couldn't tell if his eyes were open or closed, but he thought that Brendan's lips were moving silently. Was Brendan somehow drawing power from the setting sun? As he did, he appeared to Kenny to be growing larger, not all at once, but gradually.

Kenny looked around the clearing for the path down the mountain. He was sure he was faster than Brendan. If he got a head start, he could get away easily. But if he got lost in the forest, Brendan would surely find him. Just as Kenny spotted the path, the one he thought he had come up with Brendan, Brendan turned back to him. Kenny flinched, expecting Brendan to move in on him. Instead, Brendan just stood where he was for a moment and then sat down, his back against the trunk of a dead tree, almost invisible against its outline.

"Spook, just remember this. This is what you'd call a no-shitter. You've already had your second chance. You're now on your third. I don't care what Willy and Laurel see in you. There'll not be a fourth."

Kenny started to speak, but he could just barely see Brendan raise his hand, palm outward.

"That morning that you woke up in the woods. Normally that would have been the end of it. You would never have heard from the Children of Bel ever again, unless, of course, you ever violated any of the trust we had already placed in you. Then we would have been forced to take action to protect ourselves from you."

"Brendan, I would never –"

"Betray us? That's what every failed candidate says. But you might. You might see one of us on the street someday. You probably know my other identity, for example. Lots of people do. And for whatever reason, maybe just to show off a little, you might break your promise to us."

"Never."

"Of course, you probably wouldn't ever intend to reveal everything, or even anything important. But you'd still be pissed off that we rejected you. So, you'd be walking down the street, maybe with your new girlfriend. You'd see me, and you'd think back to how Cathy was always asking you questions about us."

"No, Brendan, I swear."

"So, here's your chance to sort of make up for all the secrecy with Cathy, and maybe to show your new girlfriend what a smart guy you are. You wouldn't mean to break your word to us. You wouldn't actually give away any really important information, but you wouldn't be able to help yourself."

"Honest to God, Brendan."

"So, you'd just say something you thought was innocent. You might say, 'Oh, I know that so-and-so over there has a secret life.' Or maybe, 'Someone should look into where so-and-so goes on nights of the full moon.'"

"No, I swear, not even that."

"But don't you see, Spook? That's all it takes: just one little crack in security, just one little leak. And before long, everything has broken open, just like a small leak can cause an entire dam to burst."

"I understand, Brendan. Honest, I do. And even if you decide to throw me out, because I can't learn my Lessons, or even because you don't trust me, I'd never break my word. Never."

"But getting back to the morning you woke up in the woods, Spook. I had decided to give up on you. But the one you know as Willy thought you still had promise. So, do you really think it was some sort of coincidence that Claw picked you up along the road? He decided to see which direction you were headed and let you hoof it for a while, to give you time to get over the panic and try to think about things rationally. But giving you the bus fare was his own idea, and yes, Claw really is a very good person.

"But Willy has the insight, Spook, certainly more than I ever will. He knows people and knows how to get inside their souls. I have trusted my life to his judgment hundreds of times. So, when I said that I wanted things ended, once and for all, that night on the mountain, Willy said no. 'Spook has gifts that must be brought out,' he said. 'For all of his young life, and for all his lives before this one, Spook has been a Child of Bel.' So, once again, I trusted Willy. I hope that he wasn't wrong about you."

"You guys – the Children – all of you, you have given me something that I've been looking for all my life." Kenny was ashamed. His voice was shaking. He felt the tears return to his eyes.

It was almost dark now. The last traces of deep purple were almost gone. The first stars were out, sparkling behind the dark shape from which Brendan's voice rumbled.

"Even so, Spook. I still had doubts. I even consulted John Bard about it."

"You actually talked about me to John Bard?"

"No, actually John Bard spoke to me about you. Listen well, Spook, like I did. Your life and all your lives to come depend on it."

"John Bard knows about me?"

"John Bard agreed with Willy and told me that I must give you another chance. He said that you have the Inner Knowledge that very few ever possess. He knew you in your earlier lives, Spook. He has known you for all his nine hundred years and in his lives even before then.

"You and John Bard studied the heavens together in Babylon. You built the Pyramids together. The great mountain cities of the Incas were designed by the two of you, and together you taught our ancestors how to build Stonehenge. But somewhere along the way, Spook, you drifted away, were lost. Now you have been found again."

"Wow. This is really –" Kenny could not find the right word. One corner of his mind told him that this was a load of crap, but he wanted it to be true. It could be true.

"So, I decided to trust Willy's insight and to follow John Bard's advice. But you should know one thing, Spook."

"I'll do my best to live up to your –"

"John Bard also gave me this prophecy. Heed it, for I know it is true."

"What did he say, Brendan?"

"John Bard said that if Spook can draw forth the Inner Knowledge, he will surely live forever as one of the greatest of the Children. But John Bard also gave me this warning, which I know is also true, and which you must always remember, Spook."

Brendan stood up and moved away from the tree. He had a small crescent-shaped blade in his hand. The light from the rising moon, just coming over the ridge behind Kenny, faintly glowed on it. Kenny could not take his eyes off it. He remembered when he had seen it before.

Brendan picked up a dead branch about two inches think. He cut through it with a single swipe of the blade.

"Hear this prophecy, too, Spook." Brendan stepped forward, still holding the blade in his right hand, gesturing with it as he spoke, as if to emphasize every word.

"John Bard said that you have the promise of greatness inside you. You also possess the forces of everlasting night. If I cannot draw out the Inner Knowledge from you, then the evil in you will bring about my eternal death as well as yours."

"Jesus. Brendan, I'd never –"

"I can't take that chance, Spook. Not again. I will do John Bard's bidding this time. But I can't risk our security, no matter how much I love John Bard. So, you see, Spook, we cannot allow any more of your little mistakes."

Kenny wanted to run. He wondered if he could get out of the clearing and into the woods before Brendan could react. He wondered if Brendan could throw the blade. How accurate was it? How far would it go? He took a deep breath and tried to calm down.

"Brendan," he whispered.

"Speak up."

"Brendan, I understand. I understand completely. I owe you so much. You showed me that I don't have to be some stupid loser, that I can learn, that I can be respected. I owe you."

"Get to the point, Spook. It's getting late," Brendan said, but there was no impatience in his voice.

"What I mean is maybe John Bard and Willy are wrong," Kenny said. "Maybe it would be better for everyone if I should give it up, give up the Children of Bel. I mean, let's just walk away from here, just walk away. You go one path, I go another. I owe you too much for you to always have to worry about me screwing up again."

Brendan's shape was perfectly still.

"I mean, Brendan, maybe I should just get out of this. You won't have to worry, not ever. You don't have to give me another chance."

"You're learning, Spook." Kenny could just barely make out Brendan's voice above the early evening breeze whispering through the half-empty branches. "You have learned to put your brothers and sisters above yourself. The Spook I first met, the Spook that Willy saw in that bar just a few months ago, that person would never have said what you just said."

"Thank you."

"But it's too late, Spook. When I said we couldn't take another chance, I meant it. We cannot let you go. We have been looking for you for hundreds of years. We simply cannot let you go now."

Starlight twinkled off the blade as Brendan shifted it from one hand to another.

"I cannot let you go."

Kenny saw Brendan's black shape moving from one tree to another. The blade sparkled. Kenny strained to spot where Brendan was now. His voice seemed to come from Kenny's left, almost from behind him.

"I must go now, Spook. Think about what I said. There is no way back. You'll walk down the mountain to your car and go home to your Cathy. And she'll bug you about where you were, and you'll make up some story that she probably won't believe because she is a lot smarter than you are. But just remember, Spook, there's no way back, no way back."

Kenny tensed. He expected to feel the blade any second. It would be so sharp, he wouldn't notice it at first. He knew Brendan was a kind man. He would make it quick. Kenny closed his eyes. He wouldn't feel any pain, just surprise as everything dimmed.

The woods were silent now. For a moment Kenny wondered if he was already, in fact, dead. Had it been that easy? He opened his eyes and looked around. There was no sign of Brendan.

I'm in, Kenny thought. One way or the other, I'm in. He looked around the clearing one final time, found a path, and started his walk down the mountain.

A Walk Around Town

At first, Kenny didn't see the other car when he arrived back at the road. It was dark. He jumped when he heard Cathy's voice in the darkness.

"So, there you are."

She was almost invisible, dressed in dark colors and standing on the far side of her car, which was parked far off the road, about fifty feet from where Kenny emerged from the forest. As she walked towards him, Kenny could tell that she was angry from the flat, tightly controlled tone of her voice and the hard, fast crunch of her footsteps after she reached the gravel shoulder of the road.

She stopped only a foot away from him. Kenny took a couple steps back, almost expecting her to slap him.

"Kenny, we have to talk about this. I can't take this any longer, your running off with some cult and me not knowing where you are or when you'll be back."

"How did you know I was here?"

"Pretty hard not to, Kenny. You left the directions on the kitchen counter, right by the phone, you stupid shit."

Kenny felt like he was a tire that had just run over a nail. *Stupid shit* is right, he thought. When Brendan called him to set up the Lesson, he had scribbled down the directions. Brendan had told him not to write them, but Kenny was afraid that there was no way he could remember the references to paths, trees, and other landmarks on the mountain.

Kenny had jotted the main points down on the cover of an old *Popular Science* magazine. He then copied them onto a tiny piece of a page torn from the magazine and planned to eat the scrap of paper when he arrived at the site of the Lesson. Hurrying to make the appointment with Brendan, Kenny had forgotten to throw away the magazine with the original notes. That is what Cathy must have found.

"Please, Cathy. You shouldn't have come. I can get in a lot of trouble. I probably am already. They're probably watching you and me right now."

Kenny hoped this wasn't true, but it might be.

"Who are *they*, Kenny? I want some answers and I want them now. First you lied to me about your cult, and then you decided to say nothing about it, which was worse. I'm tired of this, Kenny. I can't take it anymore."

"You know I can't tell you that."

"Fine." Cathy turned and started walking back to her car. "I wouldn't want you to get into trouble. Goodbye."

Kenny ran and grabbed Cathy by the elbow, turning her around to face him.

"Let go of me!" she said quietly, pulling her arm free.

"No, Cathy, we have to talk this out. I want you to understand. None of this is about you. Hell, they would probably welcome you, too. They're good kind people."

"Good kind people who go running around in the woods doing human sacrifices and worshipping Satan and who knows what else? And making other good kind people keep secrets from their loved ones? Those kinds of good kind people? No, thank you, Kenny. Not for me."

"Come on, Cathy, you know none of that's true."

"That's the problem, Kenny. I don't know what's true and what's not anymore. Not about your lodge, as you call it. Not about us."

"I love you, Cathy. Isn't that true for you?"

"I don't know, Kenny. I just don't know anymore."

Headlights from a car approaching from behind Kenny lit up Cathy's face for a second. Kenny could see tears on her cheeks before her face went back into the darkness. The car slowed as it approached them. Kenny and Cathy both waved at the car, and it sped up and continued up the road. They continued to Cathy's car.

"Kenny. I don't know who these people are in this cult with you, and I don't want to know. But I do know this: Whoever they are, they are probably involved in something that will get you in a lot of trouble, a lot more than you'll ever get into if someone saw me come here. I know for sure that they're Satanists – my pastor agrees with me – and they're probably criminals, involved in drugs and kidnapping and murder and who knows what else. You know they are, or you wouldn't be so secretive about everything."

"No, Cathy. They're just good, honest people like you and me. They have an ancient philosophy, I guess you'd call it, about people coming together and being one together with nature. That's all I can tell you, and maybe I shouldn't have even told you that. Like I told you before, it's like the Masons, with their secret stuff. If you want to know more, I can see whether they would accept you into the group. But they're good people. For the first time in my life I feel like I am worth something, not some stupid loser.

"That, and thanks to your love for me," he quickly added. He tried to look for a reaction on Cathy's face, but it remained in the dark, unreadable.

"No, I give up, Kenny. I just give up." Cathy dropped her hands to her side, palms outward gesturing toward Kenny. She sighed and looked toward the wooded hillside at her right. "Oh, I don't know. Maybe you really do believe all the lies they're handing you."

Cathy turned to face Kenny again. She took two steps forward, her face only inches from him. At first Kenny thought she was going to kiss him.

"But I don't have to believe yours," Cathy hissed. "And I don't have to believe your lies of silence."

She moved back three steps. "You're going to end up either dead or in prison. I just can't handle that. I can't live my life wondering where you are or whether you're in trouble somehow. Not if you won't share with me."

Cathy opened the door to her car and flung her purse across the front seat to the passenger's side. She stood behind the open door, staring back at Kenny. He could hear her tapping her toe rapidly on the gravel.

Kenny half-heartedly reached for Cathy as she slid behind the steering wheel.

"Goodbye, Kenny. I don't want to see you again, or hear from you again, or have anything to do with you. I already cleared my things from your apartment. If you ever try to contact me again, or stalk me, or anything like that, I'll report you and your gang of Satanist weirdos to the police."

She slammed the door shut. The echo cracked around the valley, like sharpshooters firing at Kenny from all sides.

Cathy revved the engine and did a sharp U-turn onto the road, almost hitting Kenny. She was headed back to town. One taillight was burned out. The other disappeared around the first curve. Kenny stood listening to Cathy's car until he could no longer hear it.

He continued to listen for any last echo of Cathy. He thought he heard a voice. It sounded a little like Brendan but was the voice of a much older man. The voice spoke slowly, as if it was choosing the words carefully.

"Your carelessness almost betrayed us tonight, Spook," he thought the voice said. "But you handled yourself well. Learn from this."

Kenny looked around for any sign of the presence of someone else. All that he could see or sense was the silent forest and silver patches on the road, where the moonlight broke through brief openings in the clouds.

"She is truthful when she says that you will not see her again, and you are well rid of her," the voice continued. "No harm will come to you because of her delusions."

Kenny stood as silently as he could, waiting for the owner of the voice to come out of the forest. After what seemed like an hour, but probably was only five minutes, Kenny took one last look along the road and into the forest and walked back to his car, parked almost at the bend where he saw Cathy's taillight disappear.

When Kenny arrived home, all traces of Cathy were gone, almost as if she had never been there, not even as a guest. It was after three o'clock in the morning by the time Kenny went to bed. He pulled one of the pillows close to him, hugging it. He had hoped to be able to detect a trace of Cathy's perfume, but there was none. Kenny tried to sleep but kept waking up. He gave up at seven, got up, showered, and made his breakfast. He spent the morning trying to read a book that Brendan had recommended about ancient Babylonian religion. He had hidden the book behind the refrigerator, where he was sure Cathy would not find it. It was slow reading. Kenny could understand the words on a literal level but could not understand what relevance they had for him or for the Children of Bel.

The telephone call came at ten.

"Meet me at Shannon's in an hour. I want to help," was all Claw said before hanging up.

Kenny had half expected a telephone call all morning. Even if no one had seen Cathy and him together last night, he was sure Brendan had somehow found out and was displeased. In a way he was relieved when the phone rang. For a moment he hoped it was Cathy, calling to ask his forgiveness and promising to be more understanding. But he knew better. He remembered the voice in the forest – or was it only in his head – from the night before. Nonetheless, Kenny was sure that she would come back to him in her own time. And if she didn't, there were others. There was Laurel.

The only surprise was that it was Claw who had telephoned him. Usually it was Willy or Brendan who called, never announcing himself, just delivering the message. Meet me here at such and such a time. Be there and wait for instructions. When Claw called, it took Kenny a moment to recognize his voice. And why had he said that he wanted to help? Maybe it was to ensure just that Kenny showed up.

Kenny had been in Shannon's for only a minute, and was still waiting for his beer, when Claw came in and sat beside him.

"We got to go someplace else, Spook."

"Well, okay. But do you want a beer first?"

"We got to go now. I don't want to be here long enough for people to notice me." Claw's hand wrapped around Kenny's wrist. Claw could crush it if he wanted to.

"Okay. Let's go."

"You got wheels, Spook?"

"No, I walked over."

Claw glanced around. Kenny couldn't tell who or what he was looking at.

"Well, okay. I'll go out right now and wait in the alley out back. You wait five minutes, have your beer, and come out and meet me there."

Kenny expected another ride up into the mountains and a "counseling session" with Willy. This is it, he thought, as he watched in the mirror as Claw quietly left the bar. This is it. He must have just imagined the voice in the forest, telling him that he had done well.

Willy was probably waiting, too. He knew that Willy would not physically hurt him. No, when Willy was finished with him, Kenny would not have a single mark on his body, no signs at all. But Kenny knew that he would wish he were dead. Willy was that good.

Kenny had no choice. There was nowhere else to go, no place to run. After four minutes had passed, he chugged his draft, turned around, and marched out the door and went behind the building and into the alley.

Only Claw was there. He smiled as Kenny approached him.

"Let's just take a walk around town," he said, lightly putting his hand on Kenny's shoulder.

They walked two blocks and then turned off the sidewalk to follow a path that ran along a narrow creek behind old flat-roofed buildings with stores on the first floor and one or two floors of offices and apartments upstairs.

"I never knew this stream was back here," Kenny remarked.

"Most people never notice it," Claw said. "It runs almost the whole length of the town."

"So why are we back here?" Kenny tried to sound casual.

"Well, it's kind of nice back here, and besides," Claw responded, "it's better if no one overhears what I have to tell you. So, don't worry, okay?"

Claw was careful to stay exactly at Kenny's side, never a step ahead or behind him. Kenny wondered why the sounds from the main street, only a half block away, didn't get back this far. Claw said nothing as they walked together, sometimes maneuvering around old tires, beer bottles, and plastic bags.

Claw stopped behind a little Italian restaurant. Kenny could smell the food cooking, indistinct aromas that he couldn't identify but that made him hungry. The faint clink of dishes and flatware tumbled out through the kitchen door.

"You said you wanted to help me," Kenny said, hoping somehow that he could control the conversation.

"No, Spook. I said I wanted to help."

"What's the difference?"

"What you just said was the difference, man. It's all about you, isn't it?"

"Well, I just thought you meant –"

"You? That I wanted to help you? What if you're wrong?"

Claw stopped and turned to face Kenny. "You don't fucking get it, do you?"

"Get what?"

Claw's punch to Kenny's stomach came from nowhere. He doubled over, wanting to vomit.

"Sheesh," Kenny gasped. "What the fuck was that for, man?"

He felt Claw's hand on the back of his jacket. He tensed, expecting Claw to snap his head back. Instead, Claw just kept his palm on Kenny's back, patting gently.

"That's to get you to quit thinking only about yourself, Spook." Claw's hand gently moved up to the back of Kenny's neck. Kenny felt himself being straightened up. He wanted to remain doubled over, but Claw wouldn't let him.

Kenny started to say something, but Claw stopped him.

"You know what I'm talking about, so don't play dumb."

"Cathy?"

"Yeah, Spook. Cathy."

"Listen, she dumped me last night. She's history."

"That's right, Spook. She's history. And you better make sure of that. Or Willy and I will do it for you."

"Come on, Claw. Give me a break. She doesn't know anything. She's just worried about me. And she's got all these Bible-thumping beliefs. That's all."

"We can't take any more chances with her, Spook."

"Please, Claw. Leave her alone."

"Can't, Spook. Willy and I have a date with her later tonight. A surprise date, Spook. But maybe you'd want to come along, make it a foursome."

"Me? Are you fucking out of your mind?"

Claw's hand tightened around Kenny's neck.

"Don't ever say that again, Spook. I could pop your head off, just like squeezing a zit, man. Don't ever say that."

Kenny swallowed hard. Pain shot out from his Adam's apple and around his neck like a collar.

"Sorry, man," he croaked. "I didn't mean nothing by it."

Come on, Spook," Claw said, his voice suddenly taking a friendly tone. "We've been hanging around here too long. We need to keep moving."

They resumed their walk down along the creek.

"I asked if you wanted to come along," Claw said, "so you'll see that we won't actually hurt your precious little Cathy. Might be a good thing for you to see. But she's a pain in the ass, man. The only way we can keep you is to get her out of your life for good."

"Couldn't she join us? I know she'd keep our –"

Claw cut him off. "Are you shitting me, Spook? That stupid bimbo? No, we need to have you, Spook. She could never be one of us."

"But why not, Claw? She could –"

"Sorry, man. Like Willy would say, that's above my pay grade. I just do what I'm told, and so should you."

"Do I have to go with you guys?"

Claw stopped and turned to face Kenny. Kenny jumped when Claw placed his hand on Kenny's shoulder.

"No, man. It's okay. Be cool," Claw said, patting his shoulder.

"No," he continued. "You don't have to go along. We just thought you'd want to see for yourself that we didn't hurt her, so you don't spend the rest of your life worrying about her. But you got to get her out of your life, before she blows everything. And you can't do it by yourself."

"Sure, I can," Kenny said. "I just told Brendan that I –"

"You didn't tell Brendan shit, Spook. Fact is, you can't control her, and you're too fucking stupid to keep security when she's around. So, we got to take care of her for you."

"When?"

"We're going to do it tonight. But I told Willy that I thought I could talk to you and maybe you could break it off clean with her. Tell her you never want to see her, or that you've found somebody else, or you've decided that you're queer – anything that might chase her away for good. But Willy said that would be a bad idea, that it wouldn't work and would only make her more suspicious. And we can't be sure of what you would tell her. You might even accidentally tip her off."

"No, man, I swear," Kenny protested. "I would never –"

"Sorry, Spook, but we just can't take that chance." Claw's voice seemed almost sad. "And then when we do – well, you know – what we got to do with her tonight, she'll put two and two together and know that you're the cause of it. She'll hate you for sure and want nothing more to do with you ever again."

"But she's already dumped me. She told me so last night. You guys don't need to –"

"Yeah, that's what you said," Claw interrupted. "She dumped you, you didn't dump her. But she's done that before, Spook. The two of you will just keep coming back together, like two pieces of toilet paper floating in the same toilet. She'll be back. I know the type, and we can't have that."

"Honest, Claw, I didn't tell her anything, not anything important."

"We know that, Spook, but we just can't risk it anymore. As you learn more, she becomes more of a risk to us and to you. Besides, if you're there when we – when we do what we got to do – and she sees you, that would definitely finish it between you. Hell, Willy might even let you have a turn with her."

They had come to the end of the block and looked up and down the intersecting cross street. Kenny saw the police cruiser two blocks up the street, heading in their direction. Claw glanced in the same direction, then stepped back into the shadows at the entrance to the path.

"But what if she tells the cops, Claw. Aren't you guys risking a lot just to teach her a lesson?" Kenny asked.

"Come on, man," Claw smiled. "You know how Willy works. We don't leave any clues. Yeah, she'll probably call the cops, but there's nothing really that she'll be able to tell them. Don't worry, we'll all be in the clear – you, too, no matter whether you come with us or not. It'll be cool.

"Listen, Spook. I can't waste a lot more time on this" Claw said, looking back toward the street. "So, here's the message to you. We're going to have to pay this visit to Cathy, just to scare her off. And I wanted you to know about it and that it's for your own good. It's nothing personal, and I promise that we're not actually going to hurt her, just scare her shitless. I'm telling you this so that you'll know what's going on, and because we don't want you going off and trying to be a big hero or to get revenge after it's over."

Kenny and Claw turned and walked slowly back along the path, past the Italian restaurant. They stopped outside the back door, which was open. Kenny could see shapes moving around on the other side of the screen door. A man was singing, in Italian Kenny assumed.

"Smells great, doesn't it, Spook? I'd treat you to lunch, but we really shouldn't be seen together."

"Maybe some other time, Claw," Kenny responded. "Just one question though, and maybe you can help me and maybe you can't. Why all the secrecy? What do we do that is so terrible that we have to hide it? Why do we have to scare somebody shitless if they let something slip?"

"You'd have to ask Brendan or Willy that, Spook. I just do what I'm told."

Claw faked another punch to Kenny's stomach.

"Gotcha," he said, grinning. Kenny forced a smile and a few chuckles.

"But all kidding aside, Spook. Remember what I said. Your lady is bad news, for you, for me, for all of us. And like I said, it's nothing personal against you, Spook. I hope you know that I like you, and I want you to succeed. We all do. So, I promise you she won't be hurt, but we've got to do what we've got to do.

"And I know that I don't need to remind you of this," Claw continued, his voice suddenly dropping into a deep serious tone, "but I'm going to, just so there's no misunderstanding, Spook. If you try to warn her or communicate with her in any way, we'll know about it, and, well, I won't be able to control what might happen to her tonight."

"No, Claw, I swear that I –" Kenny started to reply, raising his right hand as if taking an oath.

"And then we'll come for you," Claw finished.

Claw disappeared through the back door into the Italian restaurant. Kenny heard him say something in Italian, he supposed, as he went inside. Kenny started to follow him, but instead turned and walked home. He would stop at a store on the way and buy some frozen lasagna for his lunch. He hummed the few bars of the Italian song that he had heard coming from the back door of the restaurant.

A Report of Rape

Bill Paxton groped his way in the dark from his bedroom to the ringing telephone in his study. It stopped ringing when Bill was only three feet from his desk, but it resumed ringing a few seconds later. The clock on Bill's desk said 4:10. When Bill said hello, Ray Davis identified himself and got to the point.

"Reverend Paxton, can you come to Soldiers and Sailors Memorial Hospital? There's been an incident involving one of your parishioners, a Miss Cathy Wallace."

Upon hearing Cathy's name, Bill was suddenly completely awake.

"Cathy? What is it about?"

"I'd rather not discuss it on the phone, sir. I know it's still the middle of the night, but could you please come in as soon as you can?"

"Well, sure. I'll be there in twenty minutes. But can't you tell me anything?"

"I'd really rather not, sir. If that's all right with you. We don't have all the facts yet."

"Has there been a death? It would really help me to know what I'll need to do when I get there."

"No, nobody's dead. I'm sorry, I should have made that clear. It's just that Miss Wallace says that you're her pastor, and she is asking to see you. And I need your help, too. I'd really appreciate it if you can just get here first. Then I'll brief you on what we know, before you go in to see her. Go to the emergency room and ask for me."

Ray Davis was sitting in a corner of the waiting area, farthest from the entrance, writing in a notebook when Bill arrived. He stood, shook hands, and sat down without saying a word.

"Be with you in a second. Didn't expect you here quite so soon."

One of the hospital staff brought two mugs of coffee to them. Bill looked around for another policeman, and then realized the second mug was for him.

"I figured you could use a jolt of coffee," Davis smiled.

"What's happened to Cathy?"

Davis finished writing and closed the notebook. He clipped his pen to the buttoned flap on his shirt pocket.

"We're still waiting for some preliminary blood tests," he said, "but the doc says that, as far as they can tell, she's okay physically."

Bill felt an almost seismic wave of relief but tried to control any outward signs.

"So why is she here? How can I help?"

Chief Davis picked up his coffee and stood up.

"Let's take our coffee and go somewhere else," he suggested.

Davis led Bill out of the waiting area, down a bright clean hallway. Without knocking he opened a door and invited Bill into a small examining room. There was only one chair.

"All the offices are locked up at this hour," Davis said, sitting on the examining table. "You take the chair."

"Here's the situation, Reverend," he continued. "I'll come to the point. Miss Wallace was brought here about two hours ago, claiming that she had been gang-raped tonight."

"My God."

"Well, it's more complicated than that. The doctor says that there are no signs of sexual trauma. There are a few bruises on her forearms and some light abrasions and residue – we think that it was from a heavy tape like duct tape – on her wrists. But there were no cuts or signs of serious physical trauma anywhere on her body. Her clothes were wrinkled, but not torn or damaged.

"There are some tests that we're running: internal fluids, hair, and fibers, and the like; and the State Police have already been here and have done a rape kit. We probably won't get the results on the rape kit for about ten days since, thank God, nobody was killed. I hope to get the preliminary toxicology reports later today or tomorrow, but there are no outward signs of alcohol or drugs.

"But the difficult part, Reverend, is the absence of any medical signs to corroborate her story. Even if she had chosen not to resist physically, there should have been some signs of multiple instances of intercourse, at least how she described it."

"Poor Cathy. You mean they even examined her –"

"Yes. It's standard procedure to determine the extent of any internal injuries. That's the most important thing. I don't need to go into detail, but cases of multiple forced intercourse are frequently accompanied by serious internal trauma, sometimes by foreign objects and often life-threatening."

Bill sipped his coffee. "Sweet Jesus," was all he could say. He took another sip and coughed.

"I'm sorry, Reverend," Davis said. "I don't mean to upset you, but you need to know how serious this might be.

"The examination is also required by state law. If we're going to make a rape case, we have to have all the physical evidence we can. Without it, there's no point taking it to court. These days, without corroborating physical evidence or an eyewitness, the DA in this county won't touch it."

"I see," Bill replied. "And by the way, please stop calling me Reverend. My name's Bill."

"Okay, Bill. But we're a long way from any of that, and I have some more immediate concerns," Davis continued. "Well, like I said, the State Police left about ten minutes ago, and asked me and Ms. Schwartz – she's from County Social Services – to try to take a detailed statement from Miss Wallace. Officer Passarelli is still here. She's on the phone trying to expedite the lab tests – not easy to do at this hour."

"Just curious," Bill interjected, "but what's the urgency with the lab tests? Is Cathy in any kind of medical danger?"

"No, nothing like that," Davis replied. "I just want to rule out the possibility that she might have been drugged."

"But to get back to why I asked you to come in," he continued, "I asked Miss Wallace if she was up to giving us some details. That's when she asked me to contact you. She said she wanted to talk to you before she said anything else to us."

"Did she say why?"

"No, just that she needed to talk to you. That's not too surprising. We see it a lot. A person makes a false report and, when we get serious about it, they realize they have to retract it. Or, she might start wondering whether she had done anything to provoke the assault or make the guy mistakenly think that she consented. Sometimes there are underlying personal issues that the victim needs to resolve, the things that precipitated a false report or an exaggerated one."

"So, you have already concluded that Cathy isn't being truthful?"

Chief Davis looked at the notes on his clipboard for a moment before answering.

"No, I haven't concluded anything yet," he replied slowly. "And I apologize if I gave you any false impressions. All I know is that I have one very upset young woman who has reported that she has been the victim of a very vicious crime. That's the only fact that I have at this point. What I believe isn't important right now."

"But you, personally, don't believe she was raped," Bill pressed. "It would really help me to know what your gut feeling is, as an experienced police officer, before I talked with her. What's your hunch?"

"I'm sorry," Davis replied. "I save the hunches, as you call them, for the detective novels. I have to work only with the evidence. Hunches don't convict rapists."

Bill was about to respond when Davis held up his hand, as if to signal him to stop.

"But I'm not going to sit here and fence with you about this. So, I'll cut this short. No sir, I don't, not yet. I might change my mind about this later, but right now I do not have enough evidence to believe her story, not yet."

"Fair enough," Bill replied. "But you said that something happened to her. Any ideas?"

"Let me tell you what we know." Davis opened his notebook and flipped through three pages. "It isn't much."

"About two hours ago," Davis glanced at his watch. "No, make it more like four hours ago. I didn't realize it was so late. At 12:55 a.m. we received a 911 patch call from a trucker out on Route 6, about two miles east of town. He found a female Caucasian, in her late twenties, he thought, walking on the road. In fact, he said he almost ran her down.

"He figured she must be in some kind of trouble, so he stopped and asked her if she needed help. She said that she had been raped and needed to get to a police station. He asked her if she needed medical attention, but all she said was 'Please take me to the police. I don't want to talk about it right now.' She refused to give him her name or any other information. He said she appeared to be calm but was insistent that she needed to talk to the police.

"So, he called in on Channel 9 on his CB radio, and since he was just a few miles outside Wellsboro and headed our way, the call was forwarded to us. When our night sergeant heard it was a rape complaint, he told him to bring her straight here, to the hospital and we'd meet them here. Since the alleged crime appears to have taken place outside our jurisdiction, we notified the State Police. And since it was an alleged sexual assault, we also notified County Social Services. All standard procedure.

"I was already here when the trucker and Miss Wallace arrived. Officer Passarelli from our department and Ms. Schwartz from County Social Services arrived about the same time. I took a brief statement from the truck driver, and Officer Passarelli accompanied Miss Wallace into an examination room.

"A nurse practitioner checked her vital signs. The State unit arrived a few minutes after that, and they witnessed the doctor's examination of her and took the specimens. Ms. Schwartz and Officer Passarelli have been with her since.

"All Miss Wallace has told us – Officer Passarelli actually – was that she was abducted by two men outside her home here in Wellsboro and taken up into the mountains, where they repeatedly raped her. They then left her alongside Route 6 and drove away headed east. So, she started walking home, back to Wellsboro."

"Did she give a description of the men?" Bill asked.

"Nothing useful, basically just a big guy and a smaller guy. She said it happened so fast she didn't get a good look at them when they abducted her. She said that they grabbed her outside her house, threw a bag over her head, and stuffed her into the trunk of a car.

When they got to where it happened, they took the bag off her head and led her up into a wooded area."

"They led her? Voluntarily?" Bill asked.

"Officer Passarelli said she asked about that, and Miss Wallace said that, after the ride in the trunk of the car, she felt that she didn't have any choice. Her wrists were tied behind her back, and she was afraid that if she tried to escape, they would hurt her worse. 'So, I just went with them,' was what she told Officer Passarelli.

"She said that when they were raping her and when they finally let her go, they kept shining a bright flashlight in her eyes. All she could see were outlines of a big guy and a smaller guy. She started to tell Officer Passarelli that she thinks that there was a third man because she thought she heard a third voice, but she can't be sure. When it was all over, they put her back into the trunk of the car, drove for what she believes was about five minutes, and left her on Route 6. She says that when they lifted her out of the trunk, they cut her wrists free but left the bag on her head. They told her to leave the bag on her head until she heard them drive away."

"That's all that she remembered?" Bill asked.

"No, that's all that she would tell us." Chief Davis opened his notebook, glanced at it, and snapped it shut. "When Officer Passarelli asked for details about the men, or the car, or specifically what happened to her, she simply clammed up. When Officer Passarelli asked her why she didn't want to say anything else, Miss Wallace said that it was too horrible and that she didn't want to talk about it anymore until she had a chance to talk to you. So, Officer Passarelli backed off, and I called you."

"So, how's Cathy holding up?" Bill asked.

"Physically, she appears to be fine. I looked in on her a little while ago to tell her that you were on your way. But, emotionally, I don't know. She's very quiet, almost non-communicative. She showed almost no emotion at all when she told us she had been raped. The staff here say that likewise she showed no emotion during the exam, which can be very upsetting for many rape victims."

"Isn't that surprising," Bill said, "given what she described – kidnapped, stuffed into the trunk of a car, carried off into the woods and gang-raped? It sounds terrifying to me."

"Actually, that kind of a reaction is not uncommon," Chief Davis said.

"But, Chief, you still don't believe she was raped?"

"Reverend Paxton, I've told you the pertinent facts." Bill could sense growing annoyance and impatience in Chief Davis' voice. "Let's not waste any more time. Miss Wallace wants to see you – needs to see you – and I'm not going to ask her for a further statement until she's ready. But every minute that I'm delayed in getting more information makes it harder for us to do our job."

"Understood," Bill replied. "But you must understand that I can't advise her one way or the other about whether she should tell you anything else, and that I can't share anything with you unless she consents?"

"Priest-penitent privilege," Chief Davis smiled. "I do know my job, Reverend."

Davis led Bill further up the corridor to another examining room. He knocked lightly. A tiny woman with the brightest red hair Bill had ever seen stepped out into the hallway. Davis introduced her simply as Ms. Schwartz from County Social Services. She nodded, but did not speak, smile, or offer her hand.

"Anything new?" Davis asked.

"No, she's not in the mood to be a brilliant conversationalist right now. I've done all the talking. All she said was that she just wants to sit quietly until her minister arrives. I think that she might have been praying."

"How is she doing, emotionally I mean?" Bill asked.

Ms. Schwartz stared into Bill's eyes for a moment before answering. She seemed a little annoyed by the question. Bill expected her to say something like, "How do you think she's doing emotionally after a gang rape, you moron?"

Instead, she said very quietly, each word spoken like a stapler being operated by an angry person, "Cathy is very calm and composed right now. Not weepy or hysterical, if that's what you're expecting."

"Please, Ms. Schwartz, I'm only here to help. Anything you can share with me will help me do my job."

"And what is your job, Mr. Paxton?"

"I thought you knew. I'm Cathy's pastor. I understood that she asked for me to come. So, I came here. I only need to know that she needs me. I don't need to know why."

"I know that, but what are you trying to do here, Pastor?" Ms. Schwarz took two steps toward Bill. Her hands were at her side, loosely forming fists. Bill automatically took a step back.

Ray stepped partly between the two of them. "Come on, Donna," he said quietly. "Lighten up. It's early in the morning, and none of us have had a good night."

Donna Schwartz pulled Chief Davis two or three steps back from where the three of them had been standing. "We need to talk," she said to Davis.

"Excuse us a second," Davis said over his shoulder. Bill could hear the two of them whispering but couldn't make out any of the conversation. Donna's words came out like shots of steam from a leaky radiator. Her left arm appeared from time to time, waving in the direction of where Bill was standing. Davis reached out, placed his right hand on her left shoulder, took one step toward her, and spoke quietly. She nodded, she stepped around Davis, held out her hand, and smiled at Bill.

"I have to go. It really was nice meeting you, Reverend Paxton. I'm sorry if you and I might have gotten off on the wrong foot just now. Like Chief Davis said, it's been a long night for all of us, and I know that I'm probably not at my best. So, thank you for your help."

Before Bill could reply, Donna Schwartz started to walk away.

"I'll be out front when you need me," she said to Davis, not looking back.

"I was hoping she would stay when I talked with Cathy, at least at the beginning," Bill remarked. "I don't know whether I should be in there with her alone."

Davis said nothing but knocked lightly and opened the door.

Cathy was sitting in a cheap armchair, an unopened Gideons Bible on her lap. Cathy looked a little tired, which was normal for someone who must have been up all night. She smiled when she saw Bill.

"Pastor. Thank you for coming. I'm sorry to have dragged you out in the middle of the night."

Bill sat down on the straight-back wooden desk chair, which had obviously been brought from somewhere else in the hospital. It was uncomfortable, so he turned it around so he could straddle the seat and lean on the back. He hoped it would put Cathy at ease.

"No problem. That's what I'm here for, to help you whenever and wherever. I'm thankful that you thought I could help you."

Cathy smiled. "I'm not sure anyone can help me now."

"Chief Davis said you wanted to talk with me before you answered any more questions."

"Pastor, I don't know what to do."

"Do what's right, Cathy. Do what is the truth."

"But if I tell them the truth, Kenny might get hurt."

"Kenny?" Bill asked. "He's your ex-boyfriend, isn't he? Was he involved in this somehow?"

"No. I mean I can't believe that he could be," Cathy said. "Not of his own free will. But they said that they will kill him if I ever told anybody. I don't even know how they knew who he is. They even told me how they would do it. It was horrible."

She buried her face in her hands. The Bible slid off her lap and onto the floor, bouncing quietly then flipping to land on its side with a smack.

Bill gave her a moment, as he picked up the Bible, then quietly asked, "Why don't you tell me what happened? Then I'll help you decide whether you should talk again to the police."

Cathy looked up. There was a strange look in her eyes.

"You trust me, don't you?" Bill continued. "Because if you don't trust me one hundred percent, Cathy, it's okay. I'll just butt out and leave you alone, if that's what you want."

"Oh, Pastor, I do trust you. I truly do."

"Cathy, didn't I tell you a long time ago that you should break up with –I'm sorry."

"Kenny. Kenny Kelso."

"That's right. Kenny. You even mentioned his name less than a minute ago. Forgive me. It had just slipped my mind. I guess I'm not at my best this early in the morning."

"You and me both." Cathy smiled.

"So, we'll fumble our way through this together, okay?"

"Okay." Cathy's voice was little more than a whispered trembling squeak.

"Would you like Ms. Schwartz, or Officer Passarelli, or one of the ladies from the hospital to be in here with us?"

"Do I have to?"

"No, everything you tell me is confidential by law. There's no way they can ever make me reveal anything you tell me, unless, of course, you say I can."

"I'd rather not have Ms. Schwartz in here. She doesn't believe me, you know."

"Did she say that?"

"No, it was just the look on her face. I could tell. Chief Davis doesn't believe me either."

"Did he say that, or was that just the look on his face?"

"Just his look. Just all their looks." A single tear rolled down Cathy's left cheek. She quickly brushed it away. "I can tell."

"Well, I believe you, Cathy."

"But I haven't even told you what happened."

"That's okay. Whatever it is, I'll believe you. You said you trust me. Well, I trust you, too. So why not start at the beginning and tell me anything you want to."

Cathy was silent for a moment. She looked down.

"Or you don't have to tell me anything. That's okay, too. I respect your privacy. And if you don't want to tell the police anything else right now or ever again, that's okay too. I'll take you home, and maybe we can even stop for breakfast on the way, if you feel like it. It's entirely up to you."

Cathy reached over where Bill had set the Bible. She picked it up and placed it on her lap, then folded her hands on top of it. She shrugged her shoulders slightly and exhaled slowly.

"No, I'll tell you, Pastor," she said. "Maybe then you can tell me what to do."

Forgiveness

Bill waited for Cathy to speak next.

"I know this sounds crazy, Pastor, but I think that Kenny is somehow responsible for my being – for what happened to me."

"How? I don't know Kenny, but from everything you've told me, I can't imagine that he would ever hurt you."

"Well, I told him I was through with him," Cathy said. "Last night, or I guess now it was two nights ago now."

As Cathy told about following Kenny out into the mountains and waiting for him to return, anger and frustration seemed to replace the flat, outward calm that Bill had first observed. She trembled as she told about her confrontation with Kenny, when she waited for him near his car as he walked out of the forest.

"So, once again, it's all about that secret cult he's mixed up with, isn't it, Cathy?" Bill said when she had finished.

"I know, Pastor. You told me that a Christian shouldn't have anything to do with secret societies. I told him that. I begged him to quit. Like I think I told you before, he said it was just another lodge, like the Masons or the Elks. But none of them ever go off for two or three days at a time and never tell their wives or girlfriends."

"Cults lead only to darkness, Cathy, never to light. Oh, the ordinary member means well. Some of those groups actually do lots of good works. But Satan lies in wait for them, Cathy, to seize their souls. Their secrecy cuts them off from the fellowship of other believers. Eventually it cuts them off from the love of God."

"To be honest with you, Pastor, I didn't believe all that stuff you told me about Satan. Not at first. Then I started –," Cathy blushed and smiled. "Then I started hearing the things he'd talk about in his sleep."

"What kind of things?"

"Horrible-sounding things, Pastor. Foreign words, some of them. But Kenny doesn't know any foreign languages. He would even sing strange songs in his sleep."

"Do you remember any of the words? This could be important."

Cathy looked up toward the ceiling. Bill saw the twinkle of a tear forming in the corner of her eye.

"No," she said, looking down again. "No, I'm sorry. I can't remember any. They were words I had never heard before."

"Remember that list you showed me a while ago, the one that you found in Kenny's bedroom? Were any of the words that Kenny said in his sleep, were any of them on that list?" Bill asked.

"Maybe. But I really don't remember. Is that important?"

"No, not really." Bill said.

"But there's more. He's going off to these secret meetings. He won't tell me where or who with. He says that terrible things could happen to him if he ever told. Pastor, I think he's gotten mixed up with a bunch of criminals."

Bill smiled, trying to be reassuring. "I don't think so, Cathy," he said. "I don't think there is any organized crime around Wellsboro.

"But what we all are concerned most about – Chief Davis, Officer Passarelli, even Ms. Schwartz – is you, Cathy. Right now, I don't really care about Kenny and his stupid cults. You are what means the most to me in all the world, right now.

"So, we need to talk about what happened to you last night. Are you up to telling me about it?"

Cathy nodded.

"Yes," she said, placing the Bible on the small desk beside her chair.

"Kenny called me around nine o'clock yesterday morning," she began. "I was on my way out the door to go to work. He said he was sorry about our argument the night before and wanted to see me. He wanted to talk about it, he said. I told him he could come meet me for coffee at the diner, if he wanted, that afternoon after work."

"So, you guys met?"

"No, he called about five o'clock and said that his car had broken down up in Middlebury and he was still at the shop getting it fixed."

"What was he doing up in Middlebury?"

"I don't know," Cathy shrugged, "Maybe he had a job up there yesterday.

"Well, I told him that I definitely wanted to see him and sort of have things out with him, once and for all. I told him I'd still like to see him, provided it wasn't too late, and he should just call me when he was on his way to the diner and I'd meet him there.

"Well, Kenny called again about eight o'clock and said that they couldn't fix his car because they needed to order a part. He said that someone was giving him a ride back into town and that he'd meet me in about a half hour at his place. By that time, I was feeling a little guilty about having spied on him and everything. I didn't want him in my house, so I said I would go over to his place, but I wouldn't come in. We could meet out in front of the building he lives in and talk there.

"So, he said okay. Come over whenever I wanted. He would be there the rest of the evening. I said I would honk twice when I arrived, and he was supposed to come outside."

"So, you went over?" Bill asked.

"No, that's when they grabbed me. I mean I started to go. I went out to the street and was getting into my car. It had just gotten dark, maybe a little before nine o'clock, I think. As I was closing the door and starting the engine, a guy came walking up beside me and asked me directions. Just then the second man –he had been hiding in the back seat – rose up and grabbed me."

"Grabbed you?"

"Yes. He put one hand over my mouth and nose and put his other arm around my neck. He didn't squeeze my neck or anything, but I could feel how strong he was. I was so scared that I couldn't scream. I couldn't breathe. I almost blacked out."

Cathy paused, breathing heavily. Bill wondered whether she was reliving what she had felt.

"You don't have to go on with this, if you don't want to," Bill said quietly.

"No, I don't want to," Cathy said, "but I have to."

"So, there was a big guy – the guy in the back seat – and a smaller man, the man outside. The small guy said something like, 'Don't worry, Cathy. We're friends of a friend of yours. We won't hurt you.

We just need to talk to you about something really important about him."

"Those were his exact words?" Bill wished that he had a piece of paper and a pen or pencil. He looked around the examination room but didn't find anything that he could use. He concluded that it would probably be better if there weren't any notes of this conversation.

"Well, something like that," Cathy said. "They made me get out of my car, then the big guy grabbed my arms and tied them behind my back, and the little guy – at least I think it was the little guy – put some kind of a cloth bag over my head. I started to scream when he did that, but the big guy wrapped his arm around the front of my neck and told me to be quiet or he'd break my neck. I managed to pull free for a couple of seconds but tripped, over a curb I think, and fell in the grass. They picked me up, took me by each arm, and guided me away. They squeezed so hard, I thought that they were going to break my arms.

"I remember one of them – I think it was the smaller guy – saying something like, 'Please don't try that again, Cathy. We don't want you to get hurt.'"

"Wait a second, Cathy," Bill interrupted. "He called you by name?"

"Yes, but I don't think that I had ever seen either one of them before. I couldn't really tell; it was really dark in that part of the block. One of the streetlights wasn't working."

"And this was all happening out on the street?" Bill asked. "Isn't it possible that someone might have seen you?"

"I don't think so, Pastor. Remember that we live on a quiet part of West Avenue. When I went outside there was nobody else that I could see in the entire block."

"I'm sorry, I was just curious," Bill said. "Please, go ahead. No more interruptions, I promise."

"Well, when we got to the car, the big guy picked me up and put me into the trunk of their car. I whispered, 'What have I done? You've got the wrong person." But the small man just kept telling me not to worry, that they weren't going to hurt me. And they locked me in the trunk. I kicked as hard as I could, but my sneakers didn't make much noise, and I guess nobody would have heard me."

Cathy bent over and sobbed quietly. Bill imagined how terrifying it must have been. He wanted to reach out and touch her, but the back of the chair he was sitting on was in the way. He scooted the chair a quarter turn to the left; its legs screeched on the floor. Cathy didn't seem to notice the noise. Bill placed his hand on top of hers.

"It's okay, Cathy. It's okay. You don't have to tell me anything that you don't want to. Why don't we forget about it for now? You can tell me some other time, after you've gotten a good meal and some sleep."

"No." Cathy sat up. Bill could see that the anger was back in her eyes. "No, I want to talk about it now. I want to tell you about it first, all of it, before I have to tell the others. Then maybe you can convince them that I'm telling the truth."

There was a tap at the door. Ray Davis stuck his head in. "Sorry to interrupt, but I have some coffee here, if either of you would like some." Davis entered carrying a tray with a small plastic carafe, two plastic mugs, and envelopes of creamer, sugar, and sweetener. "Sorry to interrupt. Just shout if you need anything. I'm sitting in a room just down the hall. I've got the door open, so you can just step out into the hall if you need anything. I'll hear you."

Cathy had regained control during the interruption. She declined the coffee. Bill poured a cup for himself. In the meantime, Cathy had picked up the Bible again and was holding it in her lap, her left hand clamped down on it. Before sitting down, Bill turned the wooden chair completely around, so that he could face Cathy. He sat down and scooted closer, until Cathy's knees and his were almost touching. Cathy didn't seem to notice.

"So, we drove for what seemed like forever," she said. Her eyes were locked on the Bible in her lap. The tip of her finger traced the gold embossed cross on the cover, back and forth, side to side.

"Then we stopped. The big man came around and opened the trunk. He told me to lie still and he'd lift me out of the trunk. When he set me on the ground, he asked me if I was okay.

'We're sorry we had to scare you like that, but it really was necessary,' he said. There was a kindness in his voice."

"You mentioned a big man and small man," Bill asked. "After you got there and they took you out of the trunk, did you have a chance to get a good look at them then?

"No," Cathy said. "They somehow always kept in the shadows or sometimes would shine flashlights in my face. Really all I saw were shapes, even when they were –" Cathy's voice trailed off and she closed her eyes tightly.

"Take your time, Cathy."

Cathy opened her eyes and sighed.

"But you heard their voices. Could you identify them again?"

"Maybe, but there was nothing special about them."

"So, what happened then?" Bill asked, taking another sip of coffee.

"The small man came around, took the bag off my head. He shined the flashlight in my face and held up a plastic cup to my lips. 'You must be thirsty,' he said. 'I'm sorry we locked you up, but we had to.'"

"So, he apologized, too." Bill said.

"Yeah," Cathy replied with a half laugh. "For rapists, they were really quite polite gentlemen.

"I said I didn't want anything to drink," she continued, but the big man said, 'You'd better drink it. It's going to be a long night.'

"But I said that I didn't want anything. I just wanted to know what they wanted and to get back home. But the small man said, 'You'd best drink that. If you don't, we can't be responsible.'"

"What did you think he meant by that?" Bill asked.

"I didn't have time to think. I told them that I wasn't going to drink, and that they were already responsible. Finally, the big man just grabbed me by the throat, opened my mouth, poured it down, and held my nose and mouth shut.

"'You got two choices, lady,' he said. 'Drink it or drown in it. It's just water.'"

"Was it?"

"Water? I don't know. I don't know. It had a little bit of a metal taste to it, like mineral water from a spring. But I don't know why they made a big deal of my drinking it, if that's all it was. I really was too scared to do anything else but swallow it."

"Where were you when this happened?"

"We were somewhere out in the country, alongside a road. I don't know which one. As soon as I drank the stuff, they put the bag back on my head, but left it loose around my neck, so that I could see my feet and wouldn't stumble. They kept my hands tied behind my back. They took me and led me up a path. We came to a clearing of some kind. I kept asking them what they wanted. They would say stuff to me, but their voices seemed to get farther and farther away, but they still were there alongside me. Finally, I heard a voice – I think it was the small man – tell me that they needed to show me what happened to people who ask too many questions about things that are none of their business."

"He said that?" Bill asked. "Those were his exact words?"

"I don't know for sure, Pastor. Something like that. I more felt the words inside my head than actually heard them. I think that there might have been something in that water that they made me drink."

"Go on," Bill said. "What happened next?"

"I asked them what they meant, and one of them – I think it was the big guy – told me to lie down. He pulled off my jeans and panties. I realized what was going to happen, and that the only way I was going to get out of it alive was to do what I was told."

"You don't have to tell me anything else, Cathy. I believe you."

"The big guy told me not to struggle," Cathy continued, speaking rapidly, enunciating each syllable. "'Don't struggle,' he said. 'It will just make it worse for you.'

"I couldn't have struggled if I wanted to. They kept my hands tied behind my back. They pulled my legs apart and tied long strips of cotton, like from an old bedsheet, around my ankles. I think that

that they had the ropes tied to trees or something, but I couldn't move my legs. Then they took turns raping me. First the big man and then the small one. Again and again in the dark. I don't know how many times, maybe three times each, maybe five. I lost count. Back and forth, it seemed like forever. They never said anything to me or to each other. Just back and forth, one then another."

"You poor child." Bill said. He took a deep breath.

"I think that eventually I just blacked out," she continued. "I just couldn't take it anymore. The pain was getting worse each time one of them – well, you know. But I knew that they were going to – I'm sorry, Pastor, I don't know how else to say it – I knew that they were going to fuck me to death. So, I closed my eyes and prayed to Jesus to forgive me for whatever sins had led me to this end, and to receive my soul unto himself."

"The Lord heard your prayer, Cathy."

"I knew the end was almost near. Suddenly I felt no pain, no fear, just calm. So, just before I was ready to commend my soul to the Lord, I opened my eyes one last time, to take one last look at the two men, to try at least to see something of their faces, so I could leave this life praying for their forgiveness. I knew then that the next time I opened my eyes, I would see the loving face of Jesus welcoming me."

Bill felt the tears welling up in his eyes. He tried to control the tremble in his voice. "What a beautiful act. Oh, Cathy, I am so sorry."

Tears started to flow down Cathy's cheeks.

"I saw the small man. I couldn't make out any of the details of his face. It was all blurry, but I think he was an older guy. He was – was doing it to me right then. I could see the big man standing behind him, waiting for another turn, I guess. And then, just before I blacked out again, I heard a noise and turned my head in the direction of the sound. I saw a third man looking out from the edge of the clearing. The light from the flashlights caught his face for a moment before he stepped back out of the light.

Cathy hunched over; the shaking sobs were more violent. Bill had to ask her gently to repeat what she was saying. After his third request, Cathy looked up. Bill had only seen such pain in a woman's face once in his whole life. It was a Christmas morning long ago. A young mother in his church had awoken to her baby's first Christmas, only to find that the child had died sometime in the night. Now, as he looked at Cathy, Bill could smell the freshly cut Christmas tree in the living room, surrounded by presents that would never be unwrapped. He felt sick.

"It was Kenny," she sobbed. "It was Kenny."

Bill waited a few seconds, watching Cathy sobbing, just like that young mother had wept, in a way that Bill knew that he would never forget.

"Cathy, I am so sorry," he said. "Listen, let me get Ms. Schwartz in here to talk with you. You would probably feel a lot more comfortable talking about this to another woman."

"No, I need to talk to you about it, Pastor. You're the only person I can trust."

"Okay. If that's what you need. I'm here for you." He stood up, poured Cathy a half-cup of coffee, and handed it to her.

Cathy took a sip. She grimaced when she tasted it. Bill grabbed a paper towel, expecting that her shaking hand would spill it all over herself. She steadied her hand and quietly, almost thoughtfully, set the cup down.

"Do you want to tell me what happened next?" Bill asked. "Did Kenny do anything to you?"

"No. At least I don't think so. After I saw him there, I closed my eyes and waited for Jesus to take me. The next thing I remember, I was back at their car, fully dressed. The motor was running. The bag was back on my head. One of them raised it slightly and put a plastic cup to my lips. I was too scared not to drink it."

"Did they force you to drink it?"

"No, it really seemed like it was an offer. I could drink it or not. It was just water, they said. I was really thirsty, so I figured I might as well.

"The big man seemed to have a kind voice then. He made me turn around to the right and put his arm around my shoulder. 'Your home's that way. If you start walking, someone will pick you up.

Nobody's going to let a pretty girl like you walk all alone at night out here in the country.'

"It was then that the smaller man came up close to me on the other side from the big guy. I could feel his lips through the bag lightly against my ear. He told me to remember that Kenny would get hurt really bad if I ever told anyone about this."

"He used Kenny's name?" Bill asked.

"No," Cathy said. "I think what he said was 'your boyfriend,' but I'm sure he meant Kenny. Then he said, 'And we only showed you half of what happens to people who mess around with things that don't concern them.'

"One of them cut my wrists free. They told me to keep the bag on my head until I heard them drive away. They said that they'd be watching me as they drove away. The little guy said, 'And if we see you turn around and look back even once, we'll take that to mean that you want more, and we'll be very happy to come back and make your dreams come true.' I'll never forget those words – they were so weird – *make my dreams come true*. So, I just stood there with the bag over my head and waited until I heard them drive away.

"So, they drove off," Cathy shrugged. "I took off the bag and started walking, not looking back, and after a while that trucker picked me up and brought me here."

"Oh, Cathy, I'm so sorry all this happened to you."

"It's not your fault, Pastor. You gave me the strength to get through it, you and the Lord."

Bill Paxton closed his eyes and bowed his head. He tried to clear the emotional clutter from his mind and focus on what he had just been told.

"Pastor?" Cathy whispered.

"Pastor?" Her hand touched his forearm. "I'm sorry to interrupt your prayers, but what should I do?"

"What does your heart tell you to do, Cathy?"

"But you said that you would tell me whether I should give my statement to the police."

"No, I said that I would help you decide what you should do. So, let me ask you some questions to help you decide."

"Okay, I understand," Cathy replied quietly.

Bill took her hand firmly in his.

"Okay," he said, "Try to think back to that moment just before you blacked out, just as you readied yourself to meet the Lord. What were your last thoughts, the ones that you intended to be your last thoughts in this life and your first thoughts in the next one?"

Cathy's voice was calm. She did not hesitate. "Forgiveness."

"Now, think about this," Bill continued, loosening his grip on her hand slightly. "If you have forgiven those men – including Kenny – for the terrible things they did to you, and you have asked our Lord to forgive them, what more can earthly powers do?"

Cathy frowned. "I don't think I understand," she said slowly. "Shouldn't I tell the police the truth?"

"You should always tell the truth, Cathy. But didn't our Savior tell us to render unto Caesar the things that are Caesar's, and unto the Lord the things that are the Lord's?"

"Well, yes."

"Maybe – just maybe – as you were lying there up in those woods, and preparing for what you were sure would be the end of your life in this world, maybe your prayer of forgiveness took all this out of the hands of Caesar and placed it into the hands of the Almighty."

"But they can't be allowed to go scot free," Cathy replied. "That isn't right."

"Vengeance is mine, sayeth the Lord. I will repay," Bill quoted.

Cathy ran her fingertip along the golden cross impressed into the cover of the Bible. Her warm pink nail polish looked fresh.

"So, I shouldn't tell the police anything else?"

"That's between you and the Lord, Cathy," Bill said. "Your beautiful prayer of forgiveness, the last prayer that you believed that you would ever make in this life, was an act of true sainthood. Hearing that, I know that for every day that I have remaining in this life, I will pray to God to make me more like you.

"Think about this," he said. "Ask yourself this final question. It's not one to ask God or to ask me. It's only for you to answer.

"When you entrusted your anger, and frustration, and pain, and outrage to God through your Christ-like prayer of forgiveness, you took all of it out of the hands of earthly authorities and placed your trust in the Lord. Do you now want to take it back from God's hands?"

Cathy looked confused.

"All I am saying," Bill concluded, "is do what you think is right."

Bill and Cathy joined hands as Bill prayed for comfort and wisdom from this terrible trial that the Lord had visited upon Cathy and for forgiveness for her attackers. They said the Lord's Prayer together.

Bill got up to leave, promising to call Cathy later that day. Cathy stood and hugged Bill.

"Thank you for showing me the way."

Bill bent over and kissed Cathy on the forehead. She smiled at him as he backed out the door, into the hallway.

Once outside, Bill turned sharply to the left and walked briskly, almost marching, down the polished hallway. Ray Davis must have heard him coming. He suddenly stepped out into the hall. Bill jumped back a step when he did.

"Sorry, Reverend," Davis grinned. "Didn't mean to startle you like that. How is she?"

"I think she's ready to make a statement now, as best she can remember."

Davis nodded, smiling softly. "I'm glad. That will be best. I'll get Officer Passarelli."

Bill explained that he had to leave on other church business. As he walked into the waiting room, he could hear, over the happy banter from the *Today* show on the television, mounted high on the wall, Ray Davis quietly tapping on the door to the examining room where Cathy was waiting. He could hear Officer Passarelli whisper, "Cathy? It's Gina and Chief Davis."

The automatic doors hissed open and Bill stepped out into the crisp morning air. Bill knew that Cathy would have nothing to say, nothing to remember, nothing to tell, no accusations to make. He knew that part of it would be her sense of Christian forgiveness.

Manipulation was such a slimy word. He knew that he had persuaded and counseled, but never manipulated. He could see Cathy sitting in that tiny room, smiling faintly as she stared at the floor, just to the right of her feet. Part of it would be Christian forgiveness, but part of it would also be that Cathy would never again be sure about how much of it had been real.

Robert and the Panther

"Why, Mr. Poe, it's been almost a month since you've come in," Janice Kaiser's voice almost sang as Russell Poe entered the grocery store. "You haven't started shopping at that other place, have you?"

Russell couldn't tell whether she was joking or half-serious. "No, I've just been eating off that big order I bought from you the last time I was in."

"Oh, that's right. I thought it might have had something to do with your books. Wanda Abrams mentioned to me that you were doing a lot of work on your books, the last time she came in. How's it going?"

Russell started to discuss his field work for the Braddock book. Janice listened politely, but impatiently. Finally, she waved her hand and interrupted. "No, not the history book. I meant the one about all the local ghost stories. How's the spook hunting coming along?" Her brief laugh sounded like crystal stemware clinking together.

"Oh, you mean Jack Abrams' book? I'm sorry. I didn't know the word was out that I was working on it."

"Now Mr. Poe," Janice smiled. "You know that you can't keep a secret from Robert and me."

"Well, I'm not really writing a book. I'm just organizing Jack Abrams' old notes, finishing up the book that Jack always intended to write."

"Poor Wanda," Janice said. "She's never really gotten over losing Jack, and in such a horrible way."

"Yes." Russell started to push his cart up the aisle. "Well, I need to stock up."

"You know, Mr. Poe," Janice continued, following him. "I just have never believed that wild animal story. The police just made that up because they never caught the people who did it."

"Well, I believe it," Robert Kaiser emerged from the tiny office behind the checkout counter. Janice rolled her eyes.

"There have been wolf attacks and panther attacks around here for hundreds of years," Robert said.

"Oh, Robert," Janice said, almost singing the two words. "Everyone knows there aren't any wolves or panthers around these parts anymore."

"That's what everyone would like to think," Robert said. "Now, I'm not saying for sure that's what killed Jack, but there are a lot of strange things that go on up there in the mountains."

Russell asked, "But have there actually been any confirmed sightings, Robert?"

"Sure, dozens of folks have seen them," Robert said, as if he were discussing yesterday's weather. "I did too once, when I was younger. Problem is that the authorities are always coming up with some other explanation. And when you go back to the scene to check things out, there are never any signs. They've all been cleaned up."

"Wait a minute, Robert," Russell interrupted. "You actually saw a panther?"

"Saw a panther? Why, Russell, I didn't just see one. I saw one try to attack my cousin Margaret and her baby. And you won't find that in any of Jack's notebooks, because it is the truth, not just some old legend."

Russell glanced at Janice. She faintly shook her head and looked away.

"Wow. I'd really like to hear about it sometime," Russell said.

"Sometime? Why not right now?"

"Well, I have my shopping to do."

"Nonsense. You have a list?"

"Well, sure."

"Well, then, give the list to Janice and she'll fetch the stuff for you."

Janice looked at her husband, her hands on her hips and her mouth slightly open. She was smiling slightly, but Russell could see read the annoyance on her face. Russell was afraid that he was about to be a witness to a fight.

"Well, I'm sure you both have better things to do right now," Russell said.

"I don't," Robert chuckled. "Come on back."

Russell looked at Janice. "Are you sure it's okay?"

Janice laughed and waved her hand in the direction of the office. "Oh, don't worry, Mr. Poe. You just go ahead with Robert. It's fine."

The first thing Russell noticed in the tiny office was an old calendar with a picture of a car captioned as a Hudson Terraplane. The month displayed was May 1934.

"Are you interested in old cars, Mr. Kaiser?" Russell asked as Robert cleared a stack of mail off a chair.

"Old cars?" Robert seemed puzzled. "Oh, the calendar. No, actually I collect old calendars. The new ones – the ones that cost you ten bucks in bookstores – aren't nearly as nice as some of the old ones. And you don't have to keep buying new ones."

"How so?"

"Look at that one: 1934, same as this year, once you get past February, because '34 wasn't a leap year."

Russell sat down. Robert opened the deep drawer at the bottom right of the old steel desk and pulled out two cups and a jar.

"Care for some Postum? It's all I have. Can't stand coffee."

"No thanks."

Robert extracted a bottle of mineral water from the drawer and an immersion heating coil. He shook an unmeasured quantity of Postum granules into the cup, splashed in the water, and stuck in the coil. He devoted all his attention to making his drink. He turned back to Russell only after he had taken the first sip.

"Ah. Hits the spot. Sure I can't make you one? Started drinking this stuff back when I got home from the war. Even the smell of real coffee – you know, even thinking about it – takes me back to the Pacific and too many bad memories out there, too many last cups of coffee with buddies that I lost hours, sometimes minutes, later." Robert turned away from Russell for a moment. Russell could see him take off his glasses and rub his hand across his face. When he turned back, he seemed to be forcing a smile.

"But this really does taste better, so I never went back," he said. "Sure you don't want to try it?"

"No thanks. Now, about your experience. I'm really interested in it. And no, I don't think I saw any reference to it in any of Jack's notes."

"Well, Russell, I need to give you a little background first. This all happened when I was fifteen, about a year before my grandfather passed. So that would have been—" Robert did the math on his fingers. "I guess that would make it the summer of 1929.

"So, like I said, I was fifteen at the time, and as it was summer, my grandfather would hire me to do odd jobs around his place. Usually during the week, if he had a lot of work for me, I'd just stay at his place for several days. So that's how I came to get involved in all this."

About two years previously, Robert's first cousin, Margaret, had come to live with Robert's grandparents. Margaret was four years older than Robert. Nobody would discuss why Margaret suddenly moved in, but Robert always suspected that she must have gotten herself into some sort of trouble down in Scranton, where her parents lived.

"About a year or so after Margaret moved in, she started seeing an old boyfriend from Scranton, who would drive up to visit her several times a week," Robert continued. "My grandmother would complain that sometimes the two of them would be gone all night. Once they were gone three days, and when they returned – and I think that it was sometime around the Fourth of July in 1929 – they told the family that they had driven down to Maryland and gotten married. There was no waiting period for a marriage license in Maryland, so lots of crazy kids would go there when they eloped.

"Doug, as it turned out, didn't have a job. So, my grandfather was able to help Doug get work at a sawmill that was run by one of his former partners from back when he was in the logging business. Doug and Margaret moved out of the house and into a trailer, which Granddad had bought for the couple and had hauled into a nice little grove of trees about a hundred yards or so behind the house.

It gave them their privacy but was close enough, you know, so that Granddad and Grandma could sort of watch out for them."

Robert described how the marriage appeared to be a happy one at first. The only dark clouds were Doug staying out all night. Not often, but a couple of times every month, Doug would take his shotgun and tell Margaret he was going hunting. She would watch him hike away down the road toward town, and he would always return just at dawn.

"We all thought that Doug was running around on Margaret, but we could never get the goods on him, you know. Grandma even had me hide one night at the bend in the road, where she was sure that Doug's lady friend would be waiting to pick him up in her big fancy car, but all I ever saw was him continuing down the road, toting his shotgun, until he was out of sight," Robert said. "And when he came back in the morning, he'd usually have some fresh game. I never heard of anyone going hunting at night, but Doug was a strange guy. So, after a while, we just took strange things as being normal for him.

"Well, that fall Doug and Margaret announced that they were expecting. Still, Doug continued his hunting trips, about twice a month just as before, even in the dead of winter. Then, one night in February, Doug didn't return. A search party was formed, and Doug's body was found on a path up in the woods, about eight miles from home. The police said that Doug must have been coming down the path off the mountain when he must have tripped, and the gun accidently went off.

"Now here's where the panther comes in," Robert continued. Russell suddenly realized that he should be taking notes, but he hadn't wanted to be distracted.

"You don't mind if I take notes, do you?" Russell asked. "I don't want to miss anything."

Robert looked puzzled by the question, and looked as if he wanted to respond, but instead continued with the story.

"Well, after the funeral," he continued, "Margaret stayed on in that trailer. It wasn't much – didn't even have electricity or running water – and she could have moved back into the house. Being pregnant and all, she would have been more comfortable, that's for sure. But the trailer had been her and Doug's home, and that's where she wanted to stay.

"This all started about a month or so after Doug's death, in March or maybe early April, I guess, in 1930. Margaret was seven or eight months pregnant at the time. I was staying over at my grandparents' house that week, and their two dogs, Moonbeam and Scalawag, started whining and barking. Something was outside, and they wanted at it. The next morning Margaret came over to the house while Granddad and I were having breakfast. That was unusual, because she usually never seemed to stir out of her trailer much before nine or ten o'clock. In fact, being pregnant at the time, she didn't stir much at all, but she did her best. But that morning, she came into the kitchen just before seven. She looked awful and said that she had been up all night.

"'Grandpa, Robbie,' she said to the two of us, 'Don't tell Grandma, but something was walking around on top of the trailer last night. Back and forth it went all night.'

"'Must have been a coon,' I said. But Margaret said that it sounded too heavy for a raccoon. Granddad looked around the trailer but couldn't find any tracks or any other signs of a big animal. So, Granddad and I went about our work and we didn't think much more about it. The next night, and the one after that, the same thing happened. The dogs set up a ruckus for a little while, and Margaret reported hearing the same noises. Then everything stopped."

"Did the dogs chase whatever it was?" Russell asked.

"No, my grandfather kept them inside at night, not knowing what it was that was prowling around outside. Where Granddad lived it was sometimes dangerous to allow dogs out after dark. Dogs can get into trouble too easily. He had lost one poor dumb dog that decided one night to mess around with a bear. After that, he might let them out for a minute or two to do their business, right before he turned in for the night, but he always brought them back in.

"Well, about a month later, whatever it was had come back. Margaret told Granddad that she also heard a low rumbling noise, like a big diesel truck engine idling. She could feel it through the walls and floor of the trailer. Granddad looked around the area and, once again, didn't find anything unusual. So, once again, nobody really thought anything about it. Even Margaret thought that it might just be her being nervous about her pregnancy and imagining things. And even a small raccoon can make a hell of a lot of racket running around on the roof of one of those old trailers. And once again, after two or three nights the noises stopped.

"This happened once more, just after Margaret gave birth to her little girl at the end of May – Carolyn, or Carrie as we always called her."

Robert sipped his Postum. "Sure I can't make you one?"

"No thanks," Russell said. He hoped he didn't sound impatient.

Robert set his empty cup down on the floor beside him.

"Well, to get back to the story, Carrie was about a month old, so I guess this would make it around the end of June 1930," he continued. "I was staying again out at my grandparents' place all week, helping with some painting and odd jobs. One morning, just at dawn, Margaret brought Carrie into the house and woke everyone up. She said that the animal had returned and that it had tried to get into the trailer the previous night.

"'It was like it was trying to tear the roof off,' she told us. She said that it started walking around up there just about midnight. It woke Carrie up and she started crying. As soon as Carrie started crying, the thing up on the roof started growling and scratching at the roof, like it was trying to get in. She said that she finally got Carrie quieted down around 1:00 a.m., but the thing stayed up on the roof all night, walking back and forth, with the low rumbling noise. And every once in a while, it would scratch at the roof, like it still wanted to get in."

Russell jumped in his chair at the sound of Janice pushing the shopping carts into each other to form a row. Robert noticed and smiled.

"Got you up a tree, don't I?" Robert smiled.

"Yeah. So, what did you guys do?" Russell asked.

"By this time, Granddad and I were convinced that something was coming around the trailer. We both were sure it was a raccoon. They can get pretty big and can sound even bigger if they get on top of a metal trailer, what with all the vibrations being transmitted through the thin metal walls, just turning it into one big drum.

"Granddad reckoned that whatever it was, it would probably be back the next night, like it had the two times before. So, he asked me to stay over one more night and help him try to catch whatever it was. The first thing we did was to climb up on top of the trailer and have a look. Something had been up there all right. We could see long scratch marks in the roof. That's when I gave up on my raccoon theory. We found one set of four claw marks that were a good five inches across, from side-to-side, I mean. They were too small for a bear and too big for a wolf. There was only one thing that would have made marks that size: a panther.

"Granddad called the Fish and Game office right away. They asked us to take pictures and they would send someone out in a few days. We didn't have a camera, and we knew we couldn't wait. Since whatever it was would come for two or three nights in a row and then go off somewhere, Granddad had a hunch that it might be back that night, especially if it had smelled a baby, he said.

"So that second night Granddad loaded two shotguns and parked his truck by some trees about thirty yards away. We had a clear view of the trailer, but hoped that we wouldn't be that noticeable, sitting in a dark truck and not out in the open.

"The plan was that, if Margaret started hearing the noises, she would light a candle in the window of the trailer. Granddad would get out and move in on foot. I was to stay in the truck and, if Granddad got into trouble, I would start it up, turn on the headlights, and drive toward the trailer to rescue him and scare away whatever it was.

"Like clockwork, just before midnight the dogs started howling in back of Granddad's house. I must have been dozing, because Granddad shook me.

"'Mount up,'" he whispered. He silently slipped out of the truck and crouched behind it.

"A minute or two later, Margaret lit the candle in the window. There, on the top of Margaret's trailer, I could see something big pacing around in tight circles. I caught only a fleeting glimpse of it, because it was so black against the backdrop of the trees and hillside behind the trailer.

"I panicked, I guess, and switched on the headlights. It was a coal black panther, at least four feet tall at the shoulder."

"You mean a cougar?" Russell asked.

"Not this one, no sir," Robert replied. "This was a panther, not a cougar. No doubt about it. It was much bigger than any cougar from around here.

"When the lights came on," Robert continued, "it looked our way. Granddad was already a third of the way to the trailer. I thought he was a goner for sure. The cat could have gotten to him in a second or two. He couldn't shoot at it, not even over its head, because at that range the buckshot pattern would have been too wide and could have hit the trailer. I could see him tense up.

"'Start the motor,' he said in a loud whisper, 'but stay put.' It was obvious to me what he was planning. He was going to wait until the panther came after him and would try to get off a clean shot once it was away from the trailer.

"So, I started the engine. The panther hadn't moved. My foot was on the clutch ready to move forward so he could jump into the truck before the cat got to him. I waited for even the slightest sign from him, but he stood frozen in his tracks.

"The panther looked at my grandfather and let out a howl that I'll never forget. It was like it was trying to communicate with him somehow. It then started clawing at the roof of the trailer. Margaret was right. It was trying to rip the roof off. It wanted inside.

"My grandfather must have sensed this too. When the panther started tearing at the roof, Granddad started moving forward, like a soldier advancing steadily across no-man's land. I put the truck in gear and started forward, moving slowly, but fast enough to gradually close the gap between me and Granddad.

"I was about ten yards away when the panther then let out another roar and ripped a section of the roof clear off the trailer. The panther peeled it back like the lid of a sardine can. I could see him sticking his head down into the opening. I could only guess at the terror Margaret must have been feeling at that moment."

Russell had been staring intently at Robert, looking for any sign that this was just a tall tale, but Robert's face had changed. There was a youthfulness in his face now, and the intensity of a young man facing overwhelming danger for the first time. Russell heard a faint sound to his left. Janice was standing in the doorway, watching her husband intently.

Robert hunched forward in his chair. "Afraid to shoot so close to the trailer, my grandfather let out a ferocious scream and charged just like he was back in France in 1918. At the same time, I blasted the truck horn, revved the engine and roared forward, hoping that I looked like a tank, hanging my shotgun out the window so my grandfather could grab it if he needed to get off another shot. The panther jumped off the roof, but rather than running off, he turned and faced us head-on, silently. Granddad fired both barrels, knocking the cat off its feet. The panther then got up. I knew Granddad had hit it. I could see a moist-looking, glistening patch on its side, reflecting the lights, as it turned and retreated into the woods behind the trailer. We knew it couldn't go very far."

Russell was almost breathless. "Were Margaret and Carrie okay?" was all that he could think to say.

"I stayed outside with the other shotgun, in case the panther came back. Granddad went into the trailer. Margaret was scared out of her wits – hell, we all were – and Carrie was crying like a banshee, but both of them were unharmed. The next morning, we tried to track the panther up into the woods, but we never found any trace of it, not even blood where it was standing when Granddad shot it."

"What did the Fish and Game people say?"

"They just poked a lot of holes into our story. Same old company line: Panthers have been extinct in Pennsylvania since the early 1800s, and black ones never lived here."

"But, Jesus, there was something there, Robert. How on earth did they explain away the claw marks and the ripped open roof?"

"They said that my grandfather and I were mistaken, and that what we actually saw was a bear. But that was no bear. It was a cat, and a big one."

"So, do you think that's what got Jack Abrams, a panther?"

"Well, I know that most people think it was a pack of wolves, but even if there are still wolves in these mountains, they wouldn't attack a man. Wolves are afraid of man, unless things get too extreme for them, especially if they live in close proximity like they would around here. No, if it was anything, it was a panther. Anything that would try to rip a house trailer apart wouldn't think twice about attacking a man. Not a second thought."

Janice announced that Russell's groceries were ready, if he wanted to check them before she rang up the order.

"Well, I got to get going, Robert. Thanks for sharing that with me."

"Well, you can quote me. Every word is the truth. I hope it helps with your book – with Jack's book, I mean."

As Russell walked out of the office, Robert spoke up. "Just one other thing."

"Yes?"

"If it was a wild animal that got Jack Abrams, I sure hope it was a panther."

"I know. I'd hate to think that there was someone around here capable of doing that to another person."

"That's true, Russell, but it's not what I meant. If it was a panther, it was over quick."

Red Eyes

From *Research Journal 5,* transcribed by John S. Abrams from original notes in Notebook 38

Researcher's note: This account is based on my last interview of Paul Levesque, age 82, on December 17, 1977, two days before his death at the Veterans Administration Hospital in Wilkes-Barre, Pennsylvania.

The weather was sunny and warm for December, so Paul and I toured around the grounds outside Paul's residence. Paul was in a wheelchair, which was the first time I had ever seen him consent to use one. He was in worse physical condition than during my previous visits, but he also was more lucid than he had been recently. Occasionally he would meet another patient, greet the person, and call him or her by name. Paul's mind seemed focused for the entire two hours I was with him. He did not go off on tangents or forget what he had just told me. Whenever I asked him a question as he told his story, Paul responded promptly and clearly. When I read my notes back to him, he did not interrupt with extraneous comments as he frequently had done in the past. This time he listened very closely.

I was concerned about Paul's emotional state during our meeting, as well as his badly deteriorated health. Sometimes, he sat quietly, biting his lip or trembling, fighting to hold onto his composure. I wonder now what parts he may have deliberately repressed. On the other hand, Paul sat calmly and attentively as I read my notes back to him for verification. When I was finished, he simply looked at me and said, "That's it, Jack. You've got it all right. Every last word."

He then said that this had to be our last meeting, that he had received threats from someone he apparently knew, but refused to identify, warning him not to participate further in my research. As we parted, Paul said "Jack, I guess this is goodbye. You've been a good friend all these years." He then got up from his wheelchair, shook my hand, and walked unassisted back into the hospital. His last words as he walked away from me were "Please. Don't follow me. I'll be okay from here on."

The next day I received a telephone call from him inviting me to return the following day, but when I arrived for our appointment, I learned that he had died during the night of natural causes.

Red Eyes

as told by Paul Levesque

This is a true account of an incident that happened to me shortly after I returned from the Great War.

As a child growing up in northern Pennsylvania, I had heard stories about how the ghosts of people would take animal forms and haunt the forests at night. These were the ghosts of Indians who swore a blood oath to protect the forests forever against all evil. When they died, they were fated to return to haunt the forests, but only in animal form for their own kin had long since been driven out of the forests by the white man.

Some areas were supposedly more haunted than others. There are a lot of places in the forest that were sacred to the Indians. Some of them can still be found, marked by stone circles. Some of the stone circles, like the White Indian Rocks on the Paxton property near where I used to live, can still be seen. Others are marked only by small stones. You could walk through one and never notice. Still others have had the stones kicked away or buried over the centuries, but they retain their magic. Even those are guarded by an Indian spirit.

One Saturday in the late fall of 1919, I was out hunting. I say hunting, but to be honest, it was one of those days when I didn't really care if I shot any game or not. I was simply enjoying the crisp, sunny day. It was a perfect day to be up in the mountains. Most of the leaves had fallen, so I could see hundreds of yards into forest that would have been overgrown and impenetrable only a month before. However, there were still enough leaves left on the trees to keep things shady. I don't think there was ever a day as perfect for walking through the forest as that one.

I was having such a good time that I lost track of time and how far I had gone. When I came to the top of a ridge, I would look across to the next one, several miles away and say to myself, "Well, maybe just one more." It was only when I began to feel some hunger pangs, and started thinking about supper, that I realized that I had come too far to get home before dark.

I wasn't worried about getting back home after dark. I knew the forest pretty well and had kept to the trails on my outbound hike that day. So, after sitting and resting for a few minutes, I jumped up and started home.

Being November, it started to get dark down in the valleys around four-thirty, and by five-thirty it was full night. I had never seen the forest so beautiful, though. The moon rose shortly after dark and turned the forest into a wonderful pattern of grays and silvers. The temperature was beginning to drop fast, but I was so happy to be experiencing all the beauty of the woods at night that I walked along briskly and kept warm.

After a while, though, I thought I heard something travelling through the woods to my left, about thirty yards away, I reckoned. I assumed it was an animal, because a person would have stuck to the trail at night, even as bright as it was. The animal seemed to keep up with me and moved parallel to me, always keeping about the same distance away. I was starting to get a little worried, because I didn't like the idea of an animal stalking me in the forest at night. But I was more curious than worried. I wondered what kind of animal would play at stalking a man like that. So, I stopped and looked into the forest. I heard some faint rustlings as the animal stopped. Then I saw its eyes.

Two glowing red eyes looked at me from about thirty yards away. I had never seen red eyes on an animal before, and never since. I was a little frightened but more curious, so I kept staring, trying to see the animal's outline against the deepening darkness of the forest. I couldn't make out its shape. Instead, a whole large section of the woods behind the eyes was deep in darkness. Only those two red eyes dimly glowed out of the forest.

As I watched, I noticed that the eyes were too far apart, and a little too large, to be a single animal thirty yards away. I thought for a moment that I might be looking at two animals, with the moonlight bouncing off each animal's eyes so that I saw the reflection in only one eye of each one. Maybe each of their individual sets of eyes must have appeared to be a single eye from this distance. I relaxed a little, and was about to get on my way again, when I saw the two "sets" of eyes move in perfect unison. Then they blinked at the same time.

I stood there wondering what to do next. My first instinct was to get out of there as fast as I could, but that might invite attack. Also, even though I could tell I was getting a little more scared, I was so curious and fascinated by what I saw that I couldn't leave, not just yet.

I thought for a moment that the animal must be closer than I had originally thought, perhaps only ten yards away instead of thirty. The eyes blinked again, several times, but did not seem to come closer. I also realized that I could see at least ten or twelve trees clearly outlined in the moonlight between me and the animal. No, I thought, it had to be at least thirty yards away, maybe more.

I let out a sigh of relief. The animal must have heard it, because it suddenly moved to its left, in the direction I was headed, but still keeping its distance. It was only then that I realized how big that animal back in the woods must be. Those eyes must have been four feet apart, and each one must have been the size of a man's hand, for them to look as they did from thirty yards away. It was only then that I realized that I had wet my pants, I was so scared. And at the same time, I found myself frozen to the spot, unable to stop watching.

The eyes started to come closer, maybe one-third of the distance, and stopped. My rifle fell from my right hand. It was only when I heard it thump on the ground that I remembered I had it. I didn't even bother to pick it up, though. The animal moved a little closer. I squinted into the forest, again to try to pick out its shape. All I saw was an indistinct gray area behind the eyes, slightly larger than it was a moment before. I heard a distant, soft rustling of leaves against the absolutely silent night. The eyes blinked again, and then opened, slightly larger and slightly closer, glowing steadily.

I was scared, but I realized that I wasn't afraid of being killed or hurt. It was more a fear of being confronted by something completely unknown, something that I had never experienced, never heard about, and could not begin to understand.

It was waiting for me. It seemed to want me to follow it deeper into the forest. It would not harm me if I did as it wished. There are no words to describe how these feelings got into my mind. They weren't thoughts, at least not ones that were expressed in language. I didn't hear voices. Instead, there were feelings and presences that came to the surface in my mind. These feelings had to have come from outside me, because I was scared silly, but they seemed to rise up from inside my own mind. They were just there. The being with the softly glowing red eyes was somehow communicating with me. It was no longer a wild animal, not even a creature, in my mind. It was a being, not a human, to be sure, but a thinking being. I remember even giving it a name at the time: Red Eyes.

I left the trail and took three or four small steps in the direction of Red Eyes. I walked as quietly as I could, not wanting a broken stick underfoot or any other noise to startle it. I walked with my arms out from my side at an angle, the palms of my hands turned toward the being. I stopped and watched.

The eyes closed and I heard movement in front of me. I braced, momentarily fearing attack. The faint noise was clearly moving away from me, however. When the eyes turned back in my direction, they were five or ten yards further away, staring at me, waiting for me to follow.

Red Eyes and I continued that way for some time. I would take four or five steps and stop. Red Eyes would move ahead, stop, and wait. After a while I got bolder, covering ten or fifteen yards before stopping, but Red Eyes would never let me get closer than about thirty yards. I knew that I was headed in almost a ninety-degree angle away from the direction of my house, getting farther from home with each step. But I knew I had to follow.

At one point I decided to test Red Eyes. I stopped and would not move forward. The glowing red eyes turned to me and stared without blinking. It seemed like hours but could have been only seconds. The feelings and thoughts in my head, the communications I thought were coming from Red Eyes, had stopped. There was complete silence. I could hear my heart beat calmly, at rest even though I had just walked many miles. The glowing red eyes just stared, steadily, silently. I felt like I had regained control over my own wild imagination.

I started to relax. We continued this way for several hours, it seemed. I realized that I was just as much in control of the situation as Red Eyes was. Just as I had that thought, though, the eyes started moving toward me. The blackness was growing, eating up more and more of the lighter gray background of half-bare trees. I started to back away but couldn't move. The eyes grew larger and more intense, a faint but deep ruby red that seemed to pulse slightly. I peered desperately into the near distances, frantically trying to see clearly and understand what it was that was silently approaching me in the night.

Many times in the war, I had prepared for combat knowing that today was the day I probably would die. Standing in the trenches at dawn, I had even prepared myself for death the moment I went over the top, or so I thought. But as Red Eyes drew closer, what I thought was surely going to be my last thought on earth was this: All those times before, I had prepared myself only for dying, but never for death itself. And I realized I was facing pure death, not just the experience of dying, but pure eternal death itself, coming at me out of the forest.

I felt like my body was being pressed in from all directions. The eyes stopped their approach. I could no longer even try to estimate how close or how far they were, how large the being was, what it truly looked like. I tried to close my eyes but couldn't. I could only stare into those faintly glowing red eyes. I tried to say a prayer but couldn't. All I could think about were those glowing red eyes and what they possibly meant.

And then, just before I blacked out, I heard the voice of the being deep inside my skull. No, it was more than hearing. I felt it throbbing. This time, though, in plain English it said these words that I want to forget but never will:

"I am real."

When I woke up, it was well into the morning. I looked around. I was lying unharmed in the center of the stone circle known as the

Indian Rocks, in the forest above the Paxton place. I picked up my rifle, brushed off my clothes, and hiked home.

The Toxicology Report

Ray Davis stood up and walked around to the front of his desk as soon as Bill Paxton appeared at his office door.

"Reverend, you said that you had to tell me something about Cathy Wallace's case," Ray said, "Please, sit down." He gestured to a chair and then wheeled his desk chair around to sit beside Paxton on the same side of the desk. "You sounded very serious when you called. How can I help you – or Miss Wallace?"

"Please, Chief, like I said before, please call me Bill."

"Sorry, Bill, I forgot. Because this is official business, *Reverend* just seems more natural. It's a habit I guess I might have to break. Please call me Ray. Now, what did you want to tell me about Miss Wallace?"

Bill turned in his chair to face Chief Davis. "Ray, I'm really worried about Cathy. Since the night of – of the incident, she has shut herself up at home and refuses to go out. I understand that she's lost her job at the newspaper.

"Her grandmother called me and asked me to come to see her. I was horrified when Cathy walked into the living room, where her grandmother and I were waiting for her. She has lost of lot of weight, looked positively anorexic. She wouldn't say anything at first, and just stared at her grandmother until the old lady left the room.

"Has she seen a doctor," Ray asked, "or a mental health professional? I know that we gave her a referral to a psychologist up in Corning and offered to make an appointment for her. I even offered to drive her to the appointment, but she declined."

"I asked her about whether she had seen a doctor, Chief, but she said that nobody could help her," Bill replied. He paused for a second.

"She also told me – and this is what really concerns me and why I asked to speak with you – she told me that your department had dropped the case. I knew that she must be mistaken, so I thought that maybe you could clear things up for me."

Chief Davis stood up and reached for the telephone. "Sergeant, is Officer Passarelli on duty this morning? I see. Could you please call her into the station ASAP? I think that she should be involved in the conversation that I'm having about the Wallace case. And could you have someone bring me the file?"

After Ray resumed his seat, he said, "I want Officer Passarelli in here because she was with me the times that we tried – actually Officer Passarelli tried – to interview Miss Wallace to get more details."

An older man, wearing a shoulder patch that said "Wellsboro PD Auxiliary" knocked once and then, without waiting, brought in a thin folder and handed it to Chief Davis.

"Why, Donald!" Bill exclaimed, "I didn't know you worked here."

"You two know each other?" Ray asked.

"Sure, Chief Davis," Donald said, shaking Bill's hand. "Bill here is the pastor at my church."

"Mr. Finch is one of our auxiliary volunteers. He's been part of our force forever – used to direct traffic downtown before they put in the new stop light at Central and Main," Ray said, smiling for the first time during the meeting.

"Well, not exactly forever, Chief, "Donald laughed, "Seventeen years, that's all. It's a way I can give back to my community, nothing special."

"Well, I think it's special," Bill said, shaking Donald's hand again. "Thank you, Donald. And it's good to know that you're there every Sunday keeping an eye on the collection basket."

"Thanks, Mr. Finch," Ray said. Donald smiled at Bill, nodded at Chief Davis, and left, silently closing the door behind him.

Ray extracted a paper from the file, looked at it, but did not put it into Bill's outstretched hand. Bill quickly withdrew his hand.

"Before we go any further, Reverend, I need to remind you that this conversation is strictly confidential. I'm sharing this information with you only because you are Miss Wallace's pastor and are trying to help her. Normally I would need her written consent, so I want you to know that I feel a little uncomfortable about how much I can tell you. But I know that you're helping her in your pastoral capacity and that she would not object. So, do we understand each other, sir?"

Bill was a little annoyed by the dramatic, formal tone in the Chief's voice, but he looked him in the eye.

"You have my solemn word, Chief Davis," Bill intoned. "I promise that I will never disclose any of this and would use it only to help me in my pastoral duties to Cathy. If you want me to sign something –"

"No, Bill, that won't be necessary. I trust you.

"But as I said," Ray continued, "I do want Officer Passarelli here when we talk about the two interviews we had with Miss Wallace after you and I met with each other at the hospital that morning. She's pretty good at reading between the lines of what people say.

"But here's one of the big mysteries of this case," Ray said, tapping on the paper with his index finger, "and also one of the big problems."

"What kind of problem?" Bill asked.

"It's the toxicology report," Ray said flatly.

"You think that Cathy was on high on drugs and imagined all of it?" Bill said, hoping that he communicated a genuine sense of disbelief and outrage.

"No, nothing like that, Reverend," Ray said. "It's standard procedure to do a forensic toxicology panel in a case like this. Miss Wallace had told us that they made her drink something right before they assaulted her."

"So, they drugged her?"

"Well, we can't be sure that's what happened, so let's not get ahead of the evidence," Ray said. "The first run of tests showed traces of a couple of unknown substances, so they sent the samples down to Harrisburg to run some more tests to try to pin them down. It took a couple of weeks to get the results. Her blood tested positive for Salvinorin A, which is classified as a dissociative hallucinogen. There was also a trace of another substance, too small to confirm, that the lab thinks – and they would never be able to testify to this – was myristicin, which can produce hallucinations."

"Whoa, Chief," Bill held up his hand. "Now you're getting ahead of me. I'm just a poor old country preacher."

Ray gave Bill a look that Bill took for sarcastic disbelief. He could almost hear Ray thinking, *Yeah, right. Poor old country preacher, my ass.*

"I mean," Bill said quickly, "I know a little about hallucinogens, unfortunately, but I've never heard of this."

"Let me explain," Ray said, "as best as a poor old country cop can." He paused and smiled. Bill smiled back.

"The Salvinorin A – the substance that the lab could positively identify – is a hallucinogenic substance in the category known as dissociatives. They produce a sense of detachment from the surrounding environment, like you're in a dream. They can also produce what is known as depersonalization, which is feeling detached from your body. It feels unreal. It's like you're observing your actions from outside, but not able to take control."

"That sounds pretty frightening," Bill said. "So, it's not like LSD?"

"No, that's a different category of hallucinogens, called deliriants – like the word delirious," Ray replied.

"I'm sure you've even been under the influence of a dissociative," Ray smiled. "Nitrous oxide – the gas the dentists use – is a dissociative hallucinogen. It doesn't really kill the pain, but you just don't notice it."

"So, where do you think these guys got this stuff?"

"Well," Ray continued, "I had to go back to my textbook from a forensic pharmacology course I once took, because we don't see this very often around here. The specific substance that was in Miss Wallace's system is produced naturally in the *Salvia divinorum* plant. You just make a tea from it, and you can mix it in water at any concentration you want."

"Where would they get this plant? It's illegal, isn't it?" Bill asked.

"Nope," Ray said. "It's not a Federal controlled substance. The plant is legal in Pennsylvania, New York, and New Jersey, and a number of other states. The common name for it around here is seer's sage."

"So, it grows around here?" Bill didn't want to give Ray any hint that he already knew all about seer's sage.

"Well, it's not native," Ray said. "It's native to Mexico, where it grows in the mountains. Some of the Indian tribes there still use it in religious rituals. But it could be cultivated here. I understand the stuff looks like just another forest weed, nothing distinctive like the five leaves of a marijuana plant."

"And the other stuff, the stuff they couldn't confirm for sure?" Bill asked.

"The myristicin? Oh, that's just another everyday household hallucinogen," Ray said. "It's commonly found in nutmeg, the same stuff that you probably have in your spice rack. In sufficient concentrations it can cause hallucinations."

"And you think that Cathy was high on these drugs?" Bill asked.

"Well, Bill, based on the lab results, I know that she had a dissociative in her system several hours after the incident. I wouldn't use the word *high* exactly, and I wouldn't want to estimate to what extent she was under the influence of it at the time. I can't say. Like nitrous oxide, it can wear off pretty fast. So, she could have been completely out of it, so to speak, from a big cocktail of Salvinorin A and myristicin at the time of the incident, and then, just an hour or so later, sufficiently back in touch with reality to flag down that truck driver.

"And the presence of at least one hallucinogen, possibly two, could explain the problems we would have with her testimony, at least based on the two interviews that we've done. And that's even putting aside the problems with the equivocal physical evidence.

"And that's why I want Officer Passarelli to be here, so you can get both of our impressions."

As if on cue, the door opened, and Gina Passarelli came in, wheeling a chair from the outer office. After introductions and a handshake, Ray explained that he was meeting with Bill Paxton about the Cathy Wallace case and that all communications were to be strictly confidential. Officer Passarelli nodded but said nothing in reply.

"Now, to get to the status of the investigation itself and Miss Wallace's concerns that nobody is helping her," Ray said. He paused, as if searching for the best way to explain things.

"Let's go at it this way," he said. "Officer Passarelli and I conducted – or I should say, attempted to conduct – two interviews with Miss Wallace after you left the hospital that morning. To be honest with you, she didn't give us anything that we could work with."

"That's sums it up," Gina said. "I spent a few minutes with Ms. Wallace after you had met with her, Reverend, and she said that she was unable to give me any more details about the two alleged assailants. The only thing that she added was that at one time she had thought that she had seen a third man there, but now was sure that she had been mistaken, that it was only a bush or a small tree. I asked her if she had any objection to Chief Davis being in the room, because we couldn't conduct a proper interview in a serious case like hers unless there were two of us present. She said that she agreed that he could be present."

"That's when I entered the room," Ray said. "We asked her to tell us every little detail, no matter how small or unimportant it might seem, but she wasn't able to tell us anything more than when she first arrived at the hospital."

"And we couldn't start pressing her about details," Gina said, "because for someone who has just gone through what she described, that could cause her to tell us about details that she assumed were true or believes probably to have been true, but that she didn't actually remember. Victims that have gone through what she said she experienced can be very susceptible to suggestion. We really have to be careful when someone says they don't remember."

"I've known about some pretty serious cases that were lost because the investigators pushed too hard on details that the victim honestly couldn't remember," Ray agreed. "We have to turn all the statements over to the defense, and if there's any hint that we were coaching a victim or leading her to make up facts that she didn't remember, the case is over. The DA won't even take it into court, and she probably shouldn't."

"So, the bottom line of the first of these two interviews was?" Bill asked, already confident that he knew the answer.

"The bottom line was that there was no bottom," Ray replied, "nothing solid that we could develop, not even if the two suspects strolled into the station and confessed to the desk sergeant.

"So, we let it go for the time being, and just asked Miss Wallace to try to remember whatever she could, and we would come back in a few days in case anything else came to mind."

"I think that we both had a hunch that Ms. Wallace knew more than she was willing to tell us just then," Gina said, "and maybe she wasn't telling us because she just wasn't sure what happened. The light abrasions on her wrists and the small bruises could have been consistent with her report that she was bound and forcibly put into the trunk of a car. But that was about it, as far as corroborating physical evidence goes."

"And she said that she was raped on the ground, but there were none of the external signs that you would expect to see, even if it were consensual and all romantic – no minor scrapes or bruises at all where you would expect to find them. There were traces of soil on her jeans and jacket, but those could have come from anywhere at any time." Ray added.

"And, of course, the medical exam was completely negative," Gina added.

Ray picked up the toxicology report but did not hand it to Bill.

"So, when we got this," he said, "a lot of things seemed to fall into place."

"And not the way we wanted them to," Gina finished the thought. "Ms. Wallace had told us that they had made her drink something before they raped her, and then gave her something afterward. When we saw that she had those drugs in her system, that explained why she couldn't tell us much."

"So, we went out to her home on Wednesday, two days ago," Ray continued.

"That was the visit that caused her to ask me to come in and see you," Bill said.

"Well, we had received the lab reports of a couple of days before and had reviewed the case file with the DA," Ray continued. "We needed to update Miss Wallace on the status of the case, and we were going to tell her that the lab reports tended to corroborate her account of having been forcibly drugged. I also wanted to reassure her that we weren't going to press her for details that she couldn't be expected to remember."

"She looked awful," Officer Passarelli remarked, "like she hadn't had a decent night's sleep since we took her home that Friday morning. I asked her if she wanted us to come back later, and she said no, that she wanted to speak with us."

Ray continued, "I started by beginning to say that we were hard at work looking for the two suspects and that the lab reports indicate that someone had drugged her, much like she said.

"She interrupted me and said that she had been doing a lot of thinking and praying about what happened to her. She said that, looking back on it, she can't say for sure how she ended up walking along the highway that night or what had happened. She still believed that two men had abducted and repeatedly raped her, but after thinking and praying about it –"

"She used that phrase – thinking and praying – a lot," Gina said, looking directly at Bill Paxton.

"Yeah, she did," Ray continued. "But we sometimes see victims who have been through a horrible trauma, like a gang rape, sometimes fall back into repeated phrases like that. It helps them.

"But she said that she could not swear to God that any of it ever happened. She believed it happened, but she said that she could never put her hand on a Bible in court and swear to Almighty God that it did."

"Wow," Bill said, "What did you do then?"

"Well, we told Miss Wallace that we appreciated the help that she was able to give us. I had to tell her – maybe I misread her ability to handle it and shouldn't have said this – but I felt that I had to be honest with her and tell her that we didn't have much evidence to work with, and that, unless something else turned up, I couldn't say for sure when we would catch the men who did that to her, if ever."

"She told me that you said that there was nothing else you could do, and that you were dropping the case," Bill interrupted. "Giving up."

"That's not really accurate. But I realize that I really shouldn't have said that last bit," Ray replied, nodding his head. "To be fair, Officer Passarelli, you told me the same thing after we left, as we were driving back to the station, that you hoped that she didn't misunderstand. I said that maybe you were right. I think now that you definitely were.

"But she seemed to me to be calm and alert, and I thought that I owed her at least some information. So, what I told her was what I just told you. I stressed that we were not going to give up, as you put it, trying to find the men who did that to her. If we could find them or any evidence that could lead us to one or both of them, they would be brought to justice. I remember emphasizing that she should never give up faith in that."

"That's right, Chief," Officer Passarelli said. "I remember that the last thing that you said to Ms. Wallace was 'We never close an unsolved rape case. Never.'"

Chief Davis and Officer Passarelli assured Bill that they would continue to look for any clue, any lead, anything at all that could help them find the men whom Cathy accused.

"I appreciate your time, and your honesty with me," Bill said as he shook hands with Chief Davis and Officer Passarelli at the door to the Chief's office. "And you can be assured that I swear to keep this meeting absolutely confidential."

"Well, I really appreciate the help you've given us," Ray said, "and to me individually, in this case. We'll do everything we can, but I think that you now understand the difficult posture of the case. Without a victim who can take the stand and testify, the DA won't take the case, probably not even – and I wasn't joking about this – if the two guys came in and confessed."

"I know," Bill said. He shook Ray's hand again and left the police station.

Driving back to the church, he thought about how he could best help Cathy now. Even if she couldn't remember all of it, she had been through a lot this year. Somehow, Bill could not escape a vague feeling of guilt, that he had let her down.

When Cathy was ready to move on with her life, maybe six months from now, the Mountain View Chapel could help her and her grandmother relocate up in the mountains south of Wellsboro, where a couple from the church operated a small assisted living community. Cathy wouldn't want to leave her grandmother, so she could live and work there as a resident assistant, making good money with free room and board.

On a clear warm autumn evening, Cathy and her grandmother, if the Lord had not already called her home, could sit on the porch and watch the sun set over the Grand Canyon of Pennsylvania, disappearing into the rapidly fading brilliant colors of the mountains beyond.

Some Old Battlefield Out Near Pittsburgh

As Wanda waited for Russell to arrive at her house, she could not escape a feeling that she really did not want to do this.

Wanda had seen Russell only six times during June and early July, all of them just short unannounced visits for coffee at one house or the other. Russell had seemed almost completely absorbed with finishing his book on the French and Indian War. One time when Wanda dropped in on Russell, she found his kitchen table piled with file folders, note cards, and legal pads. "I ran out of room upstairs," Russell explained before she could ask the question. Several times he mentioned that he wanted to complete the research before the weather turned bad in the fall, and to have it written by the end of the year – "my Christmas present to myself," he said. He also said that once he finished the research on what he called "the Braddock book," he could focus all of his attention on what he always called "Jack's book."

Russell had called her last night. He said that he was going to do what he described as "a final piece of field work" and that he would really like her to come along. He explained that he would be going out to Pittsburgh early Saturday morning and would pick her up around 10:00 a.m.

Even before accepting the offer, Wanda had said, "Can I fix anything to bring along?"

"No," Russell had replied. "I'll bring a Thermos of my famous coffee and some pastries. We can stop for lunch on the way."

Thinking back on it, Wanda now could not really believe that she had asked, "Well, will we be spending the night anywhere?"

Russell had not surprised her at all by the surprised tone in his voice. "Why, no. We'll be back late tomorrow night. Why do you ask?"

She was relieved by the cluelessness of his question and decided not to answer it.

Had Russell sensed some uncertainty, perhaps some crossed signals, about the trip? He quickly added, "Wanda, it's just that I have been going on and on, yammering endlessly to you for almost a year now, about my Braddock book and the field trips and everything. You always seemed interested, and I really feel bad that I have never asked you to come along. So, I hope I can sort of make amends by asking you to come with me to where it all ended, the most important place in the story."

Wanda felt that she could not refuse.

So now Wanda waited on her front porch. Saturday had just dawned clear and warm. It would be a good day for a drive across some of the most beautiful country in the eastern United States, she told herself. But the more she thought about it, the more she really didn't want to go with Russell out to Pittsburgh or wherever. She was almost angry with herself because she really didn't know why. She could rule out any ulterior romantic motive. She probably felt closer to Russell as a friend than he did to her. Maybe she was afraid that Russell would use the long drive out to Pittsburgh to talk about what he had found out about Jack's death. She wasn't ready for that. She wanted to be at home when that happened, in the home she had shared with Jack. Whatever she expected would happen on the trip, the thought of being cooped up in a car with Russell Poe for a whole day scared her a little.

"Come on, Wanda," she said aloud to herself as Russell's car came up her driveway, "you can do this." Russell is a what-you-see-is-what-you-get kind of guy, she thought. If this is a trip to some old battlefield out near Pittsburgh, that's all that it is.

After the initial pleasantries, Wanda was determined that she did not want to allow Russell to use the occasion to talk about what he had learned about Jack's death. So, before Russell could raise the subject, if he was going to do so at all, she took control of the conversation, and Russell appeared to be willing to go along.

"You know, Russell," she began, "I really don't know that much about you, other than you're a Philadelphia lawyer who became my neighbor." She started to say "good friend" but was afraid to push it that far.

That comment triggered something in Russell. Wanda had expected a response something like "nothing much to tell" or "there's nothing special about me." Instead, Russell told her about how he was born in 1936 in Ligonier, Pennsylvania, at the western edge of the Allegheny Mountains. His father, Randolph, taught English in high school, first in Ligonier and then later in Johnstown, Pennsylvania. His mother, Jeanne, worked in the home. Russell once mentioned having an older sister, Christine, who died of polio when Russell was still a baby.

Russell's parents were drowned in a canoeing accident in the Conemaugh River when he was five.

"Oh, my god," Wanda exclaimed quietly.

Russell continued without acknowledging her interjection. He said that he was there, watching with a family friend from the shore, and must have seen it happen, but he has no actual memory of their deaths or their funeral.

"One day my parents were there, and the next day they were gone" he said. "They never came back, and I really don't have any independent memory of what they looked like, other than a few old photos. Even now, whenever I look at them, they look like complete strangers."

He then went to live with his mother's older sister, Rachel Robinson, in Waynesburg, a small town in southwestern Pennsylvania, where he went to school and then to college, graduating with a degree in history. At that time, Rachel's husband was in the Army Air Corps and died during a bombing mission over Germany in September 1943. They had no children.

"I don't remember much about my uncle Bob's death," Russell said, "just my Aunt Rachel receiving the telegram from the War Department and her putting up the little gold star flag in her front window. I just blotted out everything else about it. They never recovered his body, of course, but they did put up a marker for him at the Eighth Air Force Cemetery in Cambridge, England. One of the great regrets in my life, Wanda, was that by the time I was earning enough money to take Aunt Rachel to England to visit his memorial, she was too frail to travel."

Russell described how he would drive out to Waynesburg from Philadelphia to visit her two or three times each year, spending a long weekend or three or four days of vacation time, and how he sent her money each month, until she passed away four years ago.

"I must be boring you with this," Russell commented at one point.

"No, this is your life story, Russell," Wanda said, "It's important to me. I want to know." Wanda instantly regretted the "important to me" statement, but Russell had not appeared to take any notice of it.

Russell mentioned only two other family members: a grandmother, Clara McCarthy, and a great-grandmother, Augusta Carson, both on his mother's side. He said that he never knew his grandmother, who lived in Ligonier and died when Russell was four. He had only sketchy memories of his great-grandmother, who, like his Aunt Rachel, lived in Waynesburg. Augusta Carson died when Russell was nine. All that he remembered clearly about Augusta was that she was a big, jolly lady with white hair, who lived in a little cottage on the outskirts of town and made the best peanut butter cookies.

Russell described how he earned his law degree at the University of Pittsburgh, while working part-time at the Carnegie Library across the street from the campus. When his student draft deferments ran out when he graduated from law school, the Army tried to draft him, but he was medically disqualified.

"Flat feet?" Wanda asked.

"Just kidding," she quickly added. "That's personal; you don't have to tell me."

"No, I don't mind. Actually, they said it was a heart murmur," Russell replied. "The Army doctor who examined me said that it was serious, that I might have a bad heart valve, and that I should see a cardiologist right away. The strange thing is that the cardiologist I consulted, as well as every doctor since then, couldn't detect it, and all my cardiovascular tests have always checked out fine. The only explanation I have is that, as a couple of my doctors have said, the Army doctor heard something unusual and was just being cautious."

Russell told Wanda about how, about six months later, he found a job as an entry-level associate in a law firm in Philadelphia, worked his way up to become a partner, and spent his entire legal career, more than twenty-two years, as a general business lawyer.

After about an hour on the road, Wanda said, "This is interesting, Russell, and I'd love to hear more, but I didn't have a very good night and I need to catch up on my sleep. Do you mind?"

Russell said, "Of course not." Wanda quickly fell asleep.

The slowing motion of the car woke Wanda when they stopped for a late breakfast at a diner outside Bellefonte.

"I hope this is okay," Russell commented. "I like to eat at the traditional Pennsylvania diners, not those fast food places."

After they perused the massive menu and ordered, Wanda asked, "So, what do we want to achieve today, Russell?" She was a little surprised, but also pleased, that she had said "we."

Russell started to conduct a briefing, not a real conversation, about the research for his book. Wanda already knew a little about his long weekends poking around overgrown pastures in western Maryland or Pennsylvania.

"You can't understand eighteenth-century history on the Pennsylvania frontier," Russell said, "unless you have actually stood where it happened. That's the problem with most of the histories of the French and Indian War, of most wars for that matter. They are written by armchair types who never –"

"Got up off their fat academic butts to waddle out and see where it all happened," Wanda finished.

Russell reached across the table and grabbed her hand. "Exactly!" he exclaimed, releasing it quickly.

As she ate her buckwheat pancakes and turkey sausage, Wanda enjoyed listening to Russell's lecture. He spoke with such passion, but also seemed to make a lot of sense.

"When you go on a site, you have to visualize what it looked like more than two hundred years ago. What trees and rocks were there back then, and who had hidden behind them?"

Russell explained how he could deduce and visualize from whatever evidence was available to him: the writings of people who were part of the marches and battles; and the clues that a brambly overgrown mound of dirt or three large rocks in a row still offered after two centuries.

At one point, Wanda said, "I think I understand."

Russell replied emphatically, setting his coffee cup down hard on the table. Drops splashed out.

"Eureka! That's it, Wanda! That's the word that I have been looking for: *understanding*." He went on to describe how nobody – not even the most learned historian – could ever fully understand a historic event without experiencing first-hand the place where it happened.

"Wanda," he continued, "I don't know how many times I have stood in a field or orchard or in a ravine, and I have thought to myself, 'Now I really understand.' But I didn't use the word *understand*. But that's what I felt, for the first time: a complete understanding of what really happened, who was involved, and what each person, from the generals down to the privates on both sides, as well as the Indians, must have experienced and felt."

Russell explained that this was the day that he hoped to finish his field work on his book about General Braddock with one final visit to the site of the ambush in 1755.

"I've been there three times already, but I need to make one last visit, just to make sure I understand everything correctly.

"The standard histories are badly confused. Years ago, the state set up one of those blue historical markers, just outside Pittsburgh, and it's at least a half-mile northwest of where the worst fighting actually happened. But I think that I have figured out the true site. So, today we're going to go there for one final confirmation, to stand on the exact spot where so many men died."

Wanda felt a shiver quickly move up her back and across her shoulders.

"I want to stand exactly where they fell, and that's where I'm going to wrap it all up," Russell concluded.

Wanda and Russell arrived in the borough of North Braddock, Pennsylvania, in the middle of the afternoon. After stopping for a quick sandwich at a neighborhood bar, they drove very slowly around the streets of what used to be a neighborhood on a hill above a partly closed steel mill and a small railroad yard.

Every two or three blocks, Russell would stop, and flip through one of his notebooks or look at one of the hand-drawn maps that he had in the back seat of the car. Sometimes he and Wanda got out of the car, checked their position with a compass, and paced off a distance, taking and counting precise strides past saloons, vacant lots, old houses, and shuttered storefronts. Several times he and Wanda used a long cloth tape measure to check his paced estimates. In a few of the vacant lots, Russell probed the soil with a long metal rod.

The neighborhood was like a ghost town, except for the people who would occasionally come out onto their front porches and silently stare at Wanda and Russell until they had gone a safe distance away.

"I've been here several times before," Russell explained. "Maybe they remember me. We have to be very discrete about taking pictures or writing notes. I had one guy fire a shotgun at me the last time I was here. But I need to check my calculations one final time. I have to be precise. I can't make the same mistakes that everyone else has made."

Even after discussing his techniques with him, Wanda still did not completely understand how he could find his way through a forest landscape that now existed only in his mind and had been replaced by brick and concrete more than a century ago, and more recently by vacant lots, junk, and weeds, bordered by old cobblestone streets – "technically they're called Belgian blocks," Russell had said – and dirt alleys. They spent five hours doing this, pausing only to finish off the last of the pastries that Russell had brought with him.

It was now eight o'clock. Russell and Wanda stood in one of those vacant lots, with a view looking west across the Monongahela River. The reddening evening sky outlined the hills across the river, as the first lights began to emerge from the superstructures of the roller coasters at an old amusement park. A cool evening breeze carried the sounds from across the river, the water reflecting the distant shrieks of delighted children.

"This is it. This is the place. This is where it happened. This is where almost nine hundred men died," Russell whispered. "This is where the bones were found. Some of them are still there, right beneath our feet.

"It was a disaster. The British crossed the river just below where that amusement park is now. They were only eight miles from their objective, Fort Duquesne. The French and the Indians attacked in the early afternoon and almost completely surrounded them. Instead of going into the woods in squads and fighting man-to-man, and probably disrupting the attack, the British stayed in the clearing and went into standard European formations. While the British kept firing blindly into the woods, the French and Indians were able to stay covered, tighten the circle, and pick off the British soldiers almost at leisure. Still, the British managed to fight off the attack for about three hours. When Braddock himself was wounded, they panicked and tried to run, but were overwhelmed as they fled. Of the fourteen hundred soldiers who came up this hill that morning, fewer than five hundred escaped. Only about a dozen were taken prisoner, and it would have been better for them had they died in battle."

Russell paused, looking down at the cigarette butts and two crushed beer cans on the ground.

"The British didn't always believe in taking out their dead, you know. The ground around here was almost carpeted in bodies. When the British finally tried to escape and started running down the hill toward the river, most of the wounded were left behind," he continued. "There were just too many dead and dying. And most of them didn't die instantly but lingered for several hours – almost a full day in some cases. If they were lucky, the last thing that some of them might have seen was a glimpse of one last beautiful sunset behind those hills beyond the river."

Wanda had to summon up all the will power that she had to control her own emotions. She could not understand why she felt a dull deep grief for those soldiers, one that was perhaps even worse than what she still felt every day for Jack.

"George Washington was the hero in this disaster," Russell continued, placing his hand lightly and briefly on her shoulder. "He took four bullet holes in his coat and had two horses shot out from under him, but he was the only officer who wasn't hit. He managed to restore some order and organize a retreat of those who could get out. He hauled Braddock away, a dying man. Braddock died four days later, up above Uniontown. Washington buried him in the middle of the trail and ran the wagons back and forth over him, so the Indians wouldn't find his grave and take his body as a trophy.

"But not the rest of those guys. Washington had to leave them, dead and dying, some of the bodies thrown into heaps in the woods in a panicked attempt to hide them. He had no choice, but that decision tormented him the rest of his life. Even when he was President, there are stories that he would wake up at night, weeping uncontrollably for the comrades he had to leave behind almost forty years before. They say that on the anniversary of his death, Washington's ghost comes back here on foot, dressed in a colonial Virginia uniform, looking for the men he left behind."

Russell's face was expressionless, glowing in the red rays of evening. His voice was a husky whisper. He faced uphill and seemed to be watching something far off in the distance.

"You know, when Anthony Wayne came through here on his way to fight the Indians in the Northwest Territory in 1794, some of the bones were still here, overgrown by the dense brush just off the trail. Some were still in piles, right where we are standing now. Some were scattered. Some even had bits of cloth still on them. If we'd dig down just a few inches right now, more than two hundred years later, we could still find some of them.

"Those poor bastards. For all those years, people would pass by where that street is today." Russell turned and pointed down the hill. "Not more than a few yards away, not even knowing that the dead were still up here, or if they did, not bothering even to look in their direction and say a quick prayer for them, much less try to give them a decent burial."

Russell and Wanda stood silently in the deep twilight. The lights at the amusement park across the river were brighter now, and the sounds of children drifted more quietly, more intermittently across the already dark Monongahela. Without realizing that they had moved toward each other, close enough to embrace had they wanted to, Wanda and Russell stood together in that wilderness among scattered bones which were still glowing faintly pink and purple as the night sky crept up behind them and the last traces of day disappeared. Russell's lips were set tightly in a frown, and he said nothing. Weeping quietly, Wanda took his hand and held it gently as she stood beside him, looking with him toward the last traces of sunset.

Coffee and Pie at Roxy's

Russell had two messages on his answering machine when he woke up at 10:30 a.m. At first, he wondered why he hadn't heard the telephone ring, but quickly remembered that he and Wanda hadn't returned until after midnight last night, and then he stayed up for another two hours organizing his notes.

The first message was from Wanda, thanking him again for what she called "a great adventure" and promising to call him again later in the day.

The second message was from Susan Kline.

"Hi, Russell, it's Susan Kline from the *Bulletin.* Happy Bastille Day! Seriously, I just wanted to check in with you about anything new in the Abrams case. I've decided to do a piece on it – lingering mystery, unsolved grisly death, strange local legends, that sort of stuff. And I was wondering whether we could get together later today to compare notes. I'm sorry for the short notice, but this is a free-lance piece and I'm working against a deadline next week. Call me."

Russell returned Susan's call immediately and they agreed to meet at Roxy's, which he always considered one of the last true "Main Street" restaurants in America: small, family-owned, with ancient wooden floors, plain decor, faded pictures on the walls, and basic, low-priced mediocre food. The faded gold paint on the sign announced that Roxy's had been "on this spot since 1908." The Rotary and the Kiwanis had both met in Roxy's back room for years.

Russell arrived five minutes early at Roxy's and selected a booth near the door. Susan arrived exactly on time. She was dressed as if she was going to a job interview: dark blue suit, and a white silk blouse with a big bow. Her bracelet and earrings were plain, but also looked expensive. She looked as if she should be eating lunch in a restaurant in Manhattan rather than a glorified lunch counter in Wellsboro.

"This can't all be for me," Russell told himself. "She wouldn't have suggested this place if it were."

"I hope I didn't take you away from anything important," Russell remarked as Susan settled into the booth.

"Well, yes and no. It's a busy day, and I have another appointment later, but nothing special. Nothing more important than this."

Susan paused, smiled, and cocked her head slightly. She seemed to be looking past Russell's shoulder, out the front window. A waitress appeared alongside her and took their orders for coffee.

"We might have something to eat in a couple of minutes," Susan said, "but just the coffee for now." She waited until the waitress had left before continuing.

"Like I said, Russell, I've been thinking about our meeting at the office back a while ago, and the more that I looked through the file and thought about our discussion, the more convinced I became that there's a story that hasn't been told. What with the Paxton boys – and I mean both of them, that preacher and our publisher – trying to warn us off the story, that made me only more interested.

"So, I got an old boyfriend at the Pennsylvania Desk at the *Inquirer* down in Philly interested – in the story, not me, Russell – and the *Inquirer* agreed to publish something on it, if, of course, it was any damn good."

"Congratulations," Russell said.

"Yeah, well," Susan made a face and shrugged. "We'll see. There's not much money in it, but it might get picked up by a wire service – either in the human-interest category or more likely the weird-shit category – and might get me a little better known. There's not much money working for a semi-weekly in Wellsboro, Pennsylvania, even if I am supposedly full time." She made quotation marks with her fingers.

"But enough about me," she continued, apparently without taking a breath. "How is your project coming?"

"Oh, great," Russell replied. "In fact, I finished my field work yesterday out near Pittsburgh, at the site of the ambush."

From the puzzled look on Susan's face, Russell immediately sensed that she had no idea what he was talking about.

"The book on General Braddock," he added.

Susan sighed and smiled. "You almost scared me to death, Russell. I thought for a second there that you were talking about the Jack Abrams book. And I'm sitting here thinking, 'Oh, shit. There's a Pittsburgh angle to the story? What am I going to tell the guys at the *Inquirer*?'"

The waitress returned with their coffees to find them both laughing. She smiled but didn't say anything and left, saying, "I'll be back in a couple of minutes to check up on you two."

"Oh my god," Susan whispered. "She thinks we're a 'you two'." They laughed again.

Russell said, "I'm sorry, I've been thinking so much about the book about the French and Indian War lately. As I said, I was out at the site of the battle just yesterday and invited Wanda along. It was a pretty moving experience for her when she learned what had happened there, in what looks today like a run-down neighborhood in a dying mill town. I don't think she had ever done anything like that. I guess it was kind of emotional for me, too – it would be for anybody – and really intellectually satisfying for me, as well, because it brought the research phase of my book to a close."

"Wanda? Wanda Abrams, as in Jack's widow? She was with you?"

"Sure," Russell replied. "You know, she's my neighbor and a friend, and because this was the last piece of field work and it was a nice day, I thought it would be nice to invite her to come along." Russell felt a little annoyed that he felt that he had to explain himself.

"And the two of you are friends?" Susan pressed. "As in 'you two'?" She smiled.

"To answer your impertinent questions precisely, yes and no, in that order." Russell replied, hoping that his teasing tone covered his annoyance. "What of it?"

"Nothing," Susan replied. "Nothing at all. Just curious, that's all."

"Well, to get back to your piece for the *Inquirer,* Susan," Russell said, wanting to change the subject.

"No," Susan said. "This is much more interesting – not you and Mrs. Abrams, I mean, but your field research. Please, tell me more about it. We journalists are something like historians ourselves. I think that I could really benefit from learning more about what you were doing out there in Pittsburgh yesterday."

"Well," Russell responded, still feeling a little awkward. "As I said, I'm finishing a new book about General Braddock's campaign in the French and Indian War. He led a force of British regulars and Virginia militia on a march from Cumberland, Maryland, to capture Fort Duquesne, which was an important French fort where Pittsburgh is today. It ended in disaster just a few miles from their goal. Had they succeeded, it might have hastened the end of the war, at least in North America.

"So, I'm tracing the march literally foot by foot, as best as I can over a trail that's more than two hundred years old. A lot of the landmarks are still there, especially up in the mountains. So, it's not too hard to find most of the camp sites and, of course, the battlefield."

"Sounds interesting, but why do you have to go there? Especially tracing their route step by step? Hasn't that already been done?"

Russell nodded and half closed his eyes. "It's hard to explain, Susan. Maybe there's nothing to it. I know I'm not a serious historian, or anything like it. I don't have the academic credentials. I do this just as what I guess you could call a very serious hobby."

"Very serious hobby," Susan said. "I like that. But I'm sure your work is just as good. Sometimes the dedicated amateur is better than the complacent professional."

"Thanks," Russell smiled. They paused as the waitress returned.

"I'm a sucker for their blueberry pie," Susan said, ordering a slice, "even though I know the berries aren't in season yet." Russell ordered one, too.

"So," Susan continued once the waitress had left, "you were telling me why you go to all these sites."

"I just have to, Susan. It's hard to explain. But you can't separate the story from the place. When I visit these places, any historic site for that matter, I get a real sense of what happened there."

"Like clairvoyance? No, that's seeing the future. I guess you'd call it retro-clairvoyance – like seeing the past?" Russell could tell from Susan's questioning expression that she wasn't trying to be witty.

"No, nothing that vivid. But some places are special because of what happened there. They can speak to us if we listen the right way. Little things can trigger it."

"I suppose so. I never thought of it that way," Susan said.

"Well, anyhow, I just feel that I can understand events better, and write about them more accurately, if I have actually been where they happened."

Russell quickly changed the topic away from himself, asking Susan about the types of articles she writes, which were her favorites, and the other writing projects she was working on. But he really didn't pay close attention.

He glanced up and saw the old framed print of a great Baldwin steam locomotive pulling a train through the Horseshoe Curve. Through some convoluted mental linkage he couldn't trace, Susan's questions about his field work and the picture of the locomotive had taken him back to a cold dark railway station in Scotland, many years ago.

He had been in Aberdeen, helping his client close a lease on a North Sea oil platform. The professional chemistry between Russell and the other party's solicitor had resulted in the deal closing much faster than either side had expected, and at substantial savings to his client. Buoyed by the unexpected promise of a handsome "success fee" from his client and the prospects of a few unplanned free days before his return flight from London, Russell decided to see some of Scotland. Arriving by train in Glasgow, he realized at once that the platform was familiar. He knew that he had never been there before – never even been to Glasgow before – or on any railroad platform or in any train station like it. But he knew it intimately.

It wasn't déja-vu exactly. He remembered a sermon preached a long time ago, when he attended church with his aunt. The minister told of how, in 1865, David Livingstone boarded the train that would take him from Glasgow to his final mission and eventual death in Africa. As the train slowly pulled out, the many friends who had come to send him off quietly began to sing, the coarse smoke from the engine adding to their tears:

Jesus shall reign where'er the sun
Does his successive journeys run.

It was the same hymn that, as a boy, Livingstone had heard others sing to a missionary who was departing that station for Africa. Perhaps it had called him to Africa as well. But now they were singing it for him. Others that were there joined in, perhaps not knowing the occasion but understanding that something significant was happening and they had become part of it, just as Russell had become a part of it.

His kingdom stretch from shore to shore,
Till moons shall wax and wane no more.

More than a century later, standing in the reddish gray afternoon light, filtered through skylights made translucent from grime, Russell could hear the song still echoing, as if the atoms in the ironwork supporting the roof still resonated to the long-dead voices.

Somewhere a spoon clattered on the floor and retrieved Russell from Scotland. He must have been humming the hymn softly. Susan looked at him and asked if he had said something. She had an expression that seemed to be half puzzlement and half concern.

"No, I'm sorry. Just enjoying the meal. And the company."

Susan's expression seemed to say, *yeah, right*. But she only said, "Oh." She unzipped her purse and pulled a leather covered notebook from it, without looking.

"So," she said briskly, but cheerfully, "the subject once again is wolves and cougars and bears, oh my!"

Russell said, "Well, at your suggestion I met with Clay Collins, and he more or less confirmed that if Jack Abrams was killed by anything, it was a cougar, not a pack of wolves."

"A cougar?" Susan said, "Well, there was some talk about that at the time, like your uncle's letter to the editor. I talked to a couple of other people that were on the *Bulletin* staff at the time, and they say that after Chief Davis misstated the Coroner's finding about how Abrams had been killed by a wolf or a pack of wolves, there wasn't much more talk about cougars or mountain lions or anything else, at least not from what I have been able to find out.

"Chief Davis really messed up," Susan continued. "To be fair, the word was spreading that there was a pack of man-eating wolves on the loose, and he and the guy from the Fish and Wildlife Commission wanted to stop the panic. The problem was that by the time the Commission rep, Del Greco, got involved in it, everybody thought that it was just a big cover-up, and nobody would believe him."

"Well, in fairness to the Chief," Russell said, "I don't think he ever said it was a wolf pack or anything like that. My understanding is that he was just quoting the coroner's report and people conveniently forgot about the 'consistent with' language. At least that's what your paper reported."

"Fair point, Russell," Susan replied, "but it would have made more sense, in terms of stopping all the conspiracy theories and claims of coverup, to talk about the real level of risk even if the wolf attack story was true, rather than try to deny it at that point.

"You wouldn't believe it, Russell. From what I've heard, people were walking around town carrying shotguns and pistols. It was like Dodge City. Pets were being mistaken for wolves and were getting shot at."

"That's what Chief Davis told me."

"Well, the good news – if there is any good news to come out of all this, Russell – was that there are no reports that any pets actually got hit. But it was just a matter of time before someone – worse yet, a kid – would have gotten killed."

"Well," Russell said, "I suppose that sometimes the best way to feed a rumor is to have somebody from the government deny it."

Susan sipped at her coffee. She frowned at the lipstick mark she left and quickly wiped it with her napkin.

"I guess the authorities thought that once people knew the facts, they would be less likely to let their imaginations run away with them," she said.

"Still, some people thought it was a bonehead move by Davis, because apparently he never had any human suspects. So, blame it on the Big Bad Wolf," she continued, raising her hand and fingers like claws.

"But he didn't blame it on the Big Bad Wolf. That's the problem I'm having with the way you're describing this," Russell said.

"Well, as soon as anyone said *wolf,* about a third of the folks around here probably believed it. That's all that I'm trying to say," Susan replied.

She batted Russell's forearm with her napkin. "So, lighten up, Russell. Sounds like you're running for President of the Ray Davis Fan Club." Her smile signaled Russell that it was time to move on.

"So, what happened after the press conference?" Russell asked.

Susan took another sip of coffee and swallowed quickly. "Umm. That's when it really got nutty. Again, I wasn't here, but this is what some of my colleagues at the paper have told me. A bunch of so-called concerned citizens organized a search party for the wolves. Dozens of people – one of my sources said more than forty and half of them drunk – participated. It was like the peasants storming Frankenstein's castle with torches and pitchforks. People tramped through the woods for three or four days.

"Poor old Ray Davis, he tried to put a little order into it. I guess he figured it was better to try to control the search to keep it safe. It would have been comical if it hadn't been so dangerous – a bunch of scared, intoxicated people running around with guns, ready to shoot at anything that moved."

"No luck, I take it?"

"No. Even if there had been a pack of a hundred wolves, they would have cleared out the moment Ray's Army – that's what they called it around here – started galumphing their way through the woods. The wolves could have heard them five miles away. The poor critters would have probably thought that an elephant stampede was headed their way."

The waitress appeared with the pie, and they each asked for more coffee.

"Okay," Russell said once the waitress left. "So, let's rule out the wild animal theories for a minute. Let's assume that it was somebody who was really sadistic or who needed to make it look like an animal attack. Who – not what – who killed Jack Abrams?"

"Someone who thought they needed to," Susan replied.

Susan started to say something else, but the waitress returned with the coffee pot and refilled their cups. Russell thought that Susan's smile as she thanked the waitress conveyed a message that she felt that the waitress had just done her an unexpected, wonderful favor. She held her smile until the waitress moved away.

She's either a really nice person under that tough exterior, Russell thought, or a real pro at public relations.

"Maybe we should be talking about this someplace else," Russell said quietly.

"Well, if you like," Susan replied. "But there are two problems with doing that."

For a second Russell was afraid that Susan had misunderstood his suggestion.

"The biggest problem," she continued, "is that I have to be back at the office in about a half hour. The second problem is that I can't really help you with any murder theory about Jack Abrams."

"But you just said –"

"What I just said is that I don't buy the wolf attack theory. Neither do you. Like I said, the cops didn't have a single clue, the citizenry was beginning to panic, and they pinned it on a bunch of imaginary wolves. It was stupid. It didn't make sense. But they did it."

"So, who needed to kill Jack Abrams?"

"I don't know, Russell." Susan sounded like a teacher lecturing a small child. "But I do know that most people don't kill other people unless they think that they really need to. Beyond that, I'm sorry, but I don't have any more information or clues or hunches to give you about that."

"But I thought you said that you wanted to compare notes," Russell said.

"Well, yes, I did, but what I really wanted to hear was whether you had found any clues in Jack's notes and papers." Susan sounded defensive.

"Russell, I need your help," she continued. "I've pretty much exhausted the sources I have – just a few people who worked at the paper at the time, basically. Reverend Paxton and Chief Davis were both very nice, but they stonewalled, claimed they didn't know anything. Davis said he couldn't discuss an open investigation, except what was already public record, and Paxton sat there for a half hour saying 'I don't know' in response to each of my questions. He even denied asking the paper not to contact Mrs. Abrams.

"Is there anything that you have learned, Russell? Maybe we could join forces here."

"No," Russell replied, "I haven't turned up anything that anyone could consider a clue – not unless you're willing to believe that the White Indians or the Sangman's ghost or evil spirits of the forest did it. I'm still organizing the notebooks and the journal entries Jack compiled, but, no, there's nothing concrete in any of it."

"This is really frustrating," Susan said. "Here we are, trying to figure out the death five years ago of some poor guy that neither of us knew."

"Six years," Russell said quietly.

"Yeah, right," Susan said, "more than six years now."

"Well, let me ask you this, Susan, since you've apparently done some asking around recently. What kind of a reputation did Jack have, according to your sources?"

"What do you mean?"

"Well, Susan, for example, did he have any enemies?"

"Just all the other insurance salesmen in town," Susan laughed. "Really, Russell, you're beginning to sound like a detective in a bad movie. Did he have any enemies? Sheesh!"

"I'm sorry, Susan. I'm not very good at –" Russell started to reply.

"Oh, come on, Russell. Lighten up. And to answer your well-intentioned question precisely, no, I don't think so. I haven't heard of anything like that.

"Oh," Susan added "and my sources say that everyone in town seemed to know about his interest in local folklore, of course.

"Most people didn't know all the details, but everyone seemed to know that he was collecting oral history about the legends of the Wellsboro area. I sure wish that I could have known him. He could have provided some good local color for some of my pieces."

"That's too bad," Russell said. "I wish I had known him, too. I guess, in a way, I do know him from his notes and journals, and from a few things that Wanda has told me about him."

"Yeah, well, that's the way it is sometimes." Susan shrugged. "But to get back to your question: Yes, people were generally aware that he was compiling some sort of collection of area folklore. But, no, as far as I can tell, he didn't have any enemies based on that. As I understand it, all those legends were about things that happened hundreds of years ago, if at all. But maybe, just maybe, he was getting too close to a secret that someone still needed to protect.

"So, that's why I need your help, Russell. Have you come across anything in Jack's notes that could possibly give someone a motive to make him stop his research, to silence him?"

"No, Susan, I haven't. I can't really help you there. I mean, I've read through all his papers several times, but there's nothing that stands out. I'm sorry. If something comes up, I'll let you know."

"That's fair," Susan said, putting her notebook back in her purse and picking up the check. "This one's compliments of the *Bulletin*."

Susan glanced at her watch. "I have to get back to the office, Russell; I'm going to be late," she said as she stood.

Out on the street, Susan offered her hand to say goodbye. Taking it, Russell held it for a moment.

"Before you go, Susan, I think we need a few ground rules," Russell said. Susan looked surprised.

"What kind of rules, Russell?"

"There are two things that are important to me. First of all, I prefer that you do not try to talk to Wanda Abrams – don't approach her or contact her – without clearing it with me first. I am making this request as her attorney in the matter of her husband's death."

Russell knew that he was stretching the truth a little, but that Wanda would not object to that characterization.

"Agreed," Susan said. "The last thing I want is to make things worse for her. I really am trying to help her. Please believe that, Russell. But, of course, I'll respect your wishes about this. I have ethics, too.

"What else?"

"Good, thanks for your understanding, Susan. I really appreciate it," Russell replied.

"Now, for the second point, you and I need to promise each other that if either of us develop any credible evidence about who or what – and *what* still isn't entirely ruled out – killed Jack Abrams, we will go together to the police with it, with emphasis on the word *together*."

"Well, I don't know if I can agree to that, Russell. I don't know that I trust Chief Davis."

"Look," Russell replied, "I don't have much confidence in Ray Davis, either, but that's different from not trusting him. I think that he's basically an honest guy trying to do his best. I think we can trust him."

"Okay," Susan said, "agreed. Maybe I was being unfair. Now I have one request for you."

"Which is?"

"Which is that at some time, when you're through with them for the time being, that you let me see Jack Abrams' papers, or copies if you have to maintain custody of the originals. I don't disbelieve you when you say there are no clues there, but I need to see for myself. It's a journalist thing. Okay?" Susan smiled.

"Well," Russell replied, "I don't think that I am able to show you any of Jack's papers without Wanda's consent. She and I have never discussed letting someone else see them. I would have to ask her first."

"Fair enough. I understand," Susan said. They shook hands again, Russell thanked Susan for the coffee and pie, and Russell watched Susan walk quickly away. She was headed the wrong way to be going to the *Bulletin* offices, not looking back. Russell turned and walked to where he had parked his car. As was his habit, he put a dime in the parking meter for the next person. He looked back; Susan had disappeared. For uncomfortable reasons he couldn't quite articulate, Russell realized that he and Wanda should never let Susan see Jack's notes and journals.

Spanish Hill

From *Research Journal 4*, compiled by John S. Abrams from his original notes in Notebooks 4, 7, 8, 14, 22, 23, and 30

Researcher's note: In my interviews of older residents of the area, I have heard multiple tales about a band of white people who lived in the forest as Indians, usually described as the White Indians. There are various stories about the origins of the White Indians, if they in fact ever existed. Some of these stories are linked to a steep-sided hill, of glacial origin, rising approximately 230 feet above the surrounding countryside in South Waverly, Bradford County, Pennsylvania, just to the east of U.S. Route 220 and straddling the Pennsylvania-New York state line. This site is commonly called Spanish Hill and is also believed by some archeologists and historians to be the site of a village or fortification of the Carantouan nation, a Native American group first mentioned by the French explorer Samuel de Champlain in approximately 1615. The Carantouans are believed to have been a nation known today as the Susquehannocks, after whom the Susquehanna River was named.

The name Spanish Hill arose from the discovery there of Spanish artifacts, including several gold coins and a small gold crucifix, in the nineteenth century. Some people believe that Spanish explorers had penetrated the northern reaches of the tributaries of the Susquehanna River, including the Tioga and Chemung Rivers, in the mid-1500s, searching for gold, and that Spanish Hill is one of several treasure troves that they used to secure the gold that they could not take back with them downriver to galleons waiting offshore at the mouth of Chesapeake Bay. The more likely source of the Spanish artifacts is that they were introduced into the region in the mid-1500s by French explorers and traders coming south from the Saint Lawrence valley. It is therefore believed that Spanish Hill was one of the first places in Pennsylvania to have been visited by Europeans, as early as the late 1500s.

Aside from a few nonsensical tales of ancient giants from the lost civilization from Atlantis, Spanish Hill has few credible links to local folklore. The only detailed account that appears to be at least partially corroborated by more than one person and some external evidence was provided by Wilson Profit, age 47, who currently lives in Athens, Pennsylvania.

Wilson Profit claims to be a direct descendent of Jonas Profit, an English sailor who arrived in Jamestown in 1607. Wilson documented his ancestry by showing entries in a family Bible, which bears a printing date of 1837. Although most of the earliest ancestry was entered no earlier than the 1840s, if accurate, they would appear to support Wilson's claim to be a direct descendent of one of the first Jamestown settlers, and who was also one of the first English people to settle permanently in Pennsylvania.

Jonas Profit was listed as a "sailer" in Captain John Smith's two expeditions in 1608 to explore Chesapeake Bay and its tributaries. On the second expedition, in July 1608, they discovered the mouth of the Susquehanna River and followed it upstream into what is today southern Pennsylvania, until they were stopped by rapids.

The following year, Profit decided to leave Jamestown to seek his fortune trading with the Native American people in the upper Chesapeake Bay and Susquehanna valley. Traveling alone and relying on the hospitality of Indian settlements that he had visited the previous year, Profit followed the Susquehanna north, eventually arriving at a small Indian settlement at Tioga Point, near where the town of Athens, Pennsylvania, stands today. Learning of another settlement farther north where, according to his hosts at Tioga Point, a small group of white people lived, he ventured up the Chemung River and, on the second day, arrived at an unnamed settlement of about twenty people living atop what today is called Spanish Hill.

Jonas Profit settled near Spanish Hill and worked as a boat builder and repairman and had a small subsistence farm. Wilson Profit showed me, but would not allow me to copy, three almost completely faded pages that he claimed were a transcription, made by his great-great-grandfather from parts of Jonas Profit's diary. According to Profit family tradition, the diary was shown to a Captain James S. Clark, who explored Spanish Hill in the 1870s, and Captain Clark said it appeared to be authentic from the early seventeenth century. Wilson Profit says that the original diary was given to the Tioga Point Museum shortly after it opened in 1895, but inquiries at the Museum revealed that, if such a diary ever was given to the Museum, there is no current record of it, and it must have been lost.

The European Origins of Spanish Hill
as told by Wilson Profit

The first colony of English people in America wasn't at Jamestown. In August 1585, Sir Walter Raleigh sent a group of men to look for a site for an English colony in what is today the Outer Banks region of North Carolina, an area that had been explored and briefly visited the year before. That group camped there for about a year. Most of them returned to England, but a detachment of fifteen men stayed behind. When a supply ship arrived in 1586, shortly after the main group had returned to England, the detachment had disappeared, and were believed to have been killed or captured by the local Indians, who were known as the Secotans and the Croatans.

In 1587 a second group of about 115 people arrived and built a small settlement on Roanoke Island. The first English child born in America, Virginia Dare, was born there in August 1587, shortly after they arrived. But when a supply ship arrived at Roanoke three years later, all the people had disappeared. They left behind the word CROATOAN carved in the wood of the stockade wall, which might have referred to an island toward the southern end of the Outer Banks, or possibly to the Croatan tribe. The authorities concluded that the colonists simply had moved or been taken somewhere else, but no reliable traces of them were found, only shadowy legends. What most folks don't know is the true story of what happened to twelve people from the lost colony.

As soon as they arrived in America in 1587, the English colonists realized that they had to get along with the Indians in order to survive. But there already was bad blood as a result of bloody conflicts with the previous expedition to the area two years before. There were food shortages and misunderstandings between the English and the Indians, and relations, which had always been delicate, quickly deteriorated. Less than a year later, the Indians attacked Roanoke, but were repulsed. Tensions would remain high, however.

Some people think that the Roanoke colony were all killed or disappeared without a trace. That isn't exactly what happened. The colonists realized that the Indians were going to continue to attack and would probably eventually overrun the colony. They debated what to do. They knew that Roanoke couldn't be defended against even only a few hundred Indians. Some of the colonists said they should go back to England. Others said that they should tough it out until the next ships, with more people and supplies, arrived from England. Still others said they should look for a place where the natives were friendlier and would let them live in peace.

Ananais Dare was the son-in-law of the colony's governor, John White, who had returned to England to bring more supplies. Ananais had heard from one of the Native American go-betweens, Manteo, about a tribe of Indians, the Potowmacks, who lived to the north along a great river in what is now Virginia. Today we know that river as the Potomac. Ananais believed that the Potowmacks were peaceful and would welcome the colonists. Over the course of the summer of 1588, as the situation in Roanoke continued to get worse, Ananais quietly persuaded his wife, two other families, and several of the single men of the colony that they should leave Roanoke soon or face certain death.

In the late spring of 1588, a group consisting of the three families and four single men – twelve people in all – secretly set out one moonless night in three small boats from Roanoke to find a new place for a settlement along one of the many rivers and bays that went deep inland.

Ananais Dare was accompanied by his wife Eleanor and their eight-month old infant, Virginia Dare. The other two families were: Elizabeth and Ambrose Viccars and their son, Ambrose, Jr., who was ten at the time; and Alis and John Chapman. The four single men were William John Berde, Anthony Cage, Peter Little, and Thomas Scot. All of these people are supposed to have died or vanished at or near Roanoke by 1590, but that is not what really happened.

When the Secotans saw the group of twelve colonists early the next morning making their way in three heavily loaded boats across Abermarle Sound toward the ocean, they did not interfere nor alert the English colony back on Roanoke Island. The fact that there were two children on board assured them that the colonists did not pose any threat. The Indians also knew that the Europeans liked to explore. They had seen expeditions leave Roanoke and come back several weeks later. They had heard of other white men who spoke other tongues exploring along the coasts near their lands. So, they didn't think much of it and decided not to do anything about it. This gave the twelve colonists the time they needed to get out of the area.

One of the four single men in the group was an older man, William John Berde, who was a Welsh sailor who had served as an assistant navigator for the voyage from England. So, he became the unofficial navigator and guide for the group. The others in the little fleet called him "Admiral Johnny." Even with Admiral Johnny's expertise, it took the colonists almost a month to find their way north to the lands of the Potowmacks.

When they arrived there, they found that the Indians weren't as friendly as they had expected. The Potowmacks let them camp along the river, today known as the Potomac, just outside one of their villages, and they supplied the colonists with fresh food. However, they would not let the group build a permanent settlement unless the colonists handed over almost all their modest supply of tools, clothing, and supplies. When the summer was over, and the colonists refused to pay, the Potowmacks told them they had to leave, or they would be enslaved.

The twelve colonists argued about what to do. They knew that they couldn't return to Roanoke to face punishment and likely death for theft and desertion. Two of the families – the Viccars and the Chapmans – and one of the single men argued that the best thing to do would be to accept the Potowmacks' terms and stay there as part of the Potowmack community.

The others wanted to push onward. From the Potowmacks they had learned of great Indian nations to the north. The Potowmacks traded with two of them, the Lenni Lenape and the Susquehannocks. The Dare family, Berde, and two of the other single men voted to push further inland. The colonists divided their small store of supplies in half and agreed that the six who were leaving could take two of the three boats.

Early on a Sunday morning at the end of September the twelve colonists had a worship service on the riverbank, thanking God for having survived so many trials and dangers and praying for protection for those who were staying, as well as for those who were going on. As they sang a last hymn together, the Dare family climbed into one of the boats, and Admiral Johnny and the two other single men pushed the boats into the river, climbed in, and began to drift downriver. As they began to raise the small sails in each boat, about ten yards offshore, the single man who had voted to stay with the Potowmacks, Anthony Cage, changed his mind and went splashing into the river to catch up with the two boats. To this day, nobody knows what happened to the two families who remained behind, the Viccars and the Chapmans. The last traces of them were their distant voices still singing hymns at the shore, carried over the water to the boats as they sailed out of sight.

So, Admiral Johnny piloted his two-boat fleet down the river. Go back downriver, the Potowmacks said, and then turn north. Find the great inland sea, which they called Chesapeake, and follow it until you come to a great broad river with many islands. That river will take you to lands of the Susquehannocks, which had fertile land, timber, and abundant game. The Susquehannocks were a great trading nation, the Potowmacks said, who did not barter ordinary trade goods but, instead, traded in gold that they plucked in small nuggets directly from the great river and along its banks.

Captain John Smith claimed that he discovered Chesapeake Bay and the Susquehanna River, but it was William John Berde and his companions who were the first English people to set eyes on it, almost twenty years before John Smith's explorations from Jamestown.

All through October and part of November 1588 they pushed north. They spent the winter on an island in the mouth of the Susquehanna and were given food and furs by the Susquehannocks. They thought about staying there and building their permanent settlement. The bay was full of crabs and fish, and the forests teamed with game. The land was rich and would produce abundant crops. But the Susquehannocks themselves were a poor people, and Berde and Dare still dreamed of settling in the fertile lands that had been described to them, and fishing gold nuggets from the river.

William John Berde seemed to have a natural knack for languages, and he had learned enough of the native languages of the region to communicate in very simple terms with the Susquehannocks. Using a mixture of dialects, crude maps, and a lot of hand gestures, the Susquehannocks told Berde about their "rich brothers" who lived far to the north, "a half moon's journey" up the great river. Continue north along the great river, past many islands, forks, and bends, the Susquehannocks said. They told Berde that, whenever they came to a fork in the river, they should always follow the one with more islands, which were stepping-stones to the great lands to the north. "Always follow the trail of the islands," they said. Eventually the colonists would come to a great trading village on a narrow neck of land between two rivers, which was visited by many tribes and nations.

Early in the spring of 1589, the seven refugees from Roanoke left their island camp and started north along the great river, which would later be named for the Susquehannocks. Berde designed and supervised the building of two shallow, flat-bottomed rafts to pole their way upstream against the slow, easy current. The river became so shallow that they frequently had to jump in the river, which sometimes was only waist deep, and tow their boats upriver to deeper water or around small rapids. Although they often saw what appeared to be potentially fertile farmlands, the prospects of the gold called them further upriver.

The colonists never found the gold that they had heard so much about from the Potowmacks. The great trading village, near what today is Athens, Pennsylvania, was just a small, sad collection of two longhouses and fewer than a dozen huts. There were no riches.

As autumn approached in 1589, the seven colonists withdrew to the top of a high bluff just north of the Indian village, overlooking one of the two rivers that joined at Tioga Point. They built a crude small stockade and three huts: one for the Dare family, one for the four single men, and one for food stores and tools. Although they had not found any of the promised wealth, the Indians in the village just downriver were peaceful and helpful, if not entirely welcoming. The colonists decided to stay, and by the time that Wilson Profit's ancestor, Jonas Profit, arrived from Jamestown approximately twenty years later, the little colony had grown to become a village of at least twenty-five people living in the small compound atop Spanish Hill or between the river and the top of the hill.

The manuscript excerpts from the Profit diary state that Jonas Profit met Virginia Dare at Spanish Hill when he settled at the foot of the hill in 1609. She had married William John Berde in 1604, when she was seventeen. There is no record that the Berdes had any children. Profit would sometimes go hunting with William John Berde, whom he called "Johnny." Berde was an expert pathfinder who could find his way through the forest at night guided only by the stars. The manuscript's only other mention of the Roanoke settlement on Spanish Hill records that Jonas helped Johnny and Virginia to bury Ananias Dare alongside his wife, who had died several years before, somewhere on Spanish Hill at a place he swore never to disclose. This probably was sometime shortly before Profit's death, because the manuscript says that Jonas Profit believed himself to be near the end of his life at that time and, in return for his promise of secrecy, the Berdes promised in return to bury him at the same peaceful place. After that the Profit account of the final remnants of the lost colony of Roanoke falls silent. No traces of the graves on Spanish Hill have ever been found.

This place is known today as Spanish Hill, because, hundreds of years later, farmers found some of the Spanish coins that Eleanor Dare brought with her, sewn into her clothing to avoid detection by any hostile Indians along the way. The farmers believed that the Spanish had built a fort there sometime around 1600, hence the name Spanish Hill. Later scholars theorized that the Spanish artifacts had been left there by French traders, who had come down from the St. Lawrence River and followed the headwaters of the Susquehanna River south into what is today Pennsylvania. But they actually were artifacts of the refugees from the lost colony of Roanoke, who settled Spanish Hill in 1589.

By the time the next European settlers arrived in the area, almost a hundred years later, the timber fort and the houses built by the Roanoke refugees had completely rotted away. The inhabitants of Spanish Hill had abandoned the site and disappeared with even less of a trace than their ancestors at Roanoke. By that time, the village at the fork of the rivers, which had welcomed the seven Roanoke colonists in 1589, had grown into the Tioga Point settlement and had become a major trading point between the Susquehannocks and the other nations to the south and the nations of the Iroquois Confederacy to the north. According to Wilson Profit, his ancestors also moved away from Spanish Hill sometime in the mid-seventeenth century into Tioga Point, where they operated a trading post for many years.

Wilson Profit and several other contributors, who insisted on remaining anonymous, relate that the Indians who still lived in northern Pennsylvania and southern New York in the nineteenth century told tales of a tribe of white people who lived Indian style in the forest. They were said to be the descendants of a small group of white people, known as the People with Two Chiefs, who came to the region from the great waters to the south. They lived there and prospered for a little while, then departed suddenly. But one of their chiefs became a manitou and still protects Spanish Hill and the endless mountains as far as the setting sun.

Pear Strudel

"Russell, Russell. Over here!"

Russell looked up and down Main Street as he left the Post Office on a Saturday morning.

"Over here!" two female voices called. He looked again to the right. The sun momentarily blinded him, until he made a visor with his right hand and saw Connie Graybill and Susan Kline across the street about twenty yards away. They waved and motioned him over.

"Well, this is a surprise," Russell said when he walked up to them. Susan came forward and gave Russell a quick hug. Connie stood back and nodded.

"Well, obviously you know Susan," Connie said.

"Sure," Russell said, "we met at one of your parties a couple of months ago."

"I also interviewed Russell for a piece that I was writing," Susan added. Russell tried to remain expressionless at Susan's half-truth. "He told me about some of the research that he's doing about the local folklore."

"We were just on our way to the Diner for some coffee and maybe some of their strudel," she continued. "You know, they make it fresh every Saturday morning. I hope there's some left."

"Won't you join us?" Connie asked.

The Wellsboro Diner was an old-fashioned green dining car replica firmly planted on one of the busiest corners of town. Finding the last free booth, they sat down, Connie and Susan on one side, and Russell across from them.

"This place hasn't changed very much since it opened in the 1930s," Susan said, beginning a summary of the place, its history, some of its famous points, such as the strudel. "People come from as far away as Scranton and Corning." Her guided tour was interrupted by the waitress, who took their orders for coffee and assured them that there still were at least three servings of the strudel, which that day was pear.

"Pear strudel?" the three of them said simultaneously.

"Trust me, folks," the waitress said, "you'll love it. We make it with pears that we get locally."

They cautiously began with small talk, about old-fashioned diners, events in town about which Russell knew nothing, and recent movies which Russell had not seen and had no plans to see. Connie remained unusually quiet. Of course, it was hard sometimes to compete for airtime – even air itself – when Susan was part of the conversation.

"Connie," Russell said during a momentary break as Susan was taking a bit of strudel, "how are things going at the university?"

"Okay, I guess," Connie replied. She turned her head to the right and looked out the window. She nodded her head, as if she was greeting someone she knew outside on the sidewalk.

"Yes, it's going well," she continued, turning to look directly at Russell. "The 100-level classes get to be a little dreary at times, covering the same material year after year. I guess the students are what keep me at it. Most of them leave my introductory course never even able to spell anthropology, much less being able to explain what it is. But every term there are always two or three students who really make it all worthwhile. They're taking the course because they're really interested, and not just to satisfy an elective requirement. They're the ones that I see again in the 200 and 300 level courses. I just finished an Anthropology of Religion class that was like that. I had only six students, but every one of them was committed one hundred percent."

"Anthropology of Religion," Susan interrupted. "What's that?"

"Oh, we examine the role of rituals, shamanism, sorcery, and even primitive concepts of sin and salvation, and then try to compare and contrast them in the traditional and modern contexts," Connie continued.

"I'm also trying to finish up a comparative paper on religious death rituals in preliterate cultures in northern Europe and North America," she added.

"Like the Vikings?" Susan asked.

Russell started to say something but decided not to.

"No, Susan, not really the Vikings." Russell thought he detected a note of condescension in Connie's voice. Maybe she didn't intend it. Susan did not seem to notice.

"No, actually," Connie continued, "I'm looking at the similarities among religious practices of four distinct cultures in the period before 1000 C.E. in northwestern Europe and before about 1500, give or take a few decades, in North America: the Celts and the Frisians in Europe, the Native American forest cultures in the northeastern part of North America, and the Innuits in the far north. What explains the common themes? As humankind expanded across the globe, how did this information travel with us, and what factors could account for variations? Or is this, as Joseph Campbell seems to suggest, part of a common human awareness of the universe, perhaps even the divine, something that makes all of us human?"

Connie paused. There was silence. Russell and Susan simultaneously took a sip of coffee. Russell broke the silence.

"That's really impressive, Connie. I mean it. You described this as a paper, but it sounds more like a book to me. I want to read it when it comes out."

"Well, Russell, it has been my life's work, I guess. Hey, I'm sorry if I got a little carried away there. You're right. It might end up a full-blown book."

Susan reached across the table and touched Russell's arm, just as he was setting down his coffee cup. "You're doing something similar, aren't you, Russell. How is that coming along?"

"That's right," Connie said. "Here I am going on about my work, and you're doing two projects right now, aren't you Russell?"

"Well, I have finally dived into writing the Braddock book, now that the research is mostly finished," Russell said. "I guess you might say that I spent a lot of time going over old ground, figuratively and literally, but I have found some new perspectives, I think."

"Do you have a publisher lined up?" Connie asked.

"Not yet, Connie, but there has been some interest at Penn State and Pitt."

"But you're also working on organizing all that material that Jack Abrams compiled, aren't you?" Susan asked.

"Yes," Connie added, "that has to be a challenge. I think I recall your telling me that he had compiled something like forty notebooks of material."

"Thirty-nine, actually."

"Right," Connie replied. "But Jack wasn't very systematic in his research, was he?"

"Well, he tried to be," Russell said. "His method was basically to listen to people recount the legends – stories that they had heard all their lives – and ask a few questions, then try to draw links among all the bits and pieces he had collected. The raw material is there, but he never really had a chance to pull it all together. He tried to organize a lot of the notes into narratives in several journal books, but I think that even that was more of an interim organizational step than the finished product, more like a first draft of some of the chapters. I hope to finish the work and publish it in Jack's name."

"Well," Connie said, "as I think I told you before, the impossible challenge with the folkloric research like you're doing, Russell, is that there is little if any factual basis that can ever be found. Myths are always much more interesting than facts. That's why myths endure and take on special meanings of their own. That's what makes them different from tall tales and ghost stories. Some of them even evolve into the complex belief systems of religion. Your work is a lot harder than mine in that regard, Russell. I'm not trying to trace myths and legends back to whatever factual origins they might have. I don't need to; I just take them as they are."

"But you have another project, Russell, don't you?" Susan said. "What have you found out about the death of Jack Abrams?"

Connie seemed to startle at the mention of Jack Abrams' death. Russell thought he detected a quick, sharp intake of breath from her. Her eyebrows shot up above the rims of her glasses. Then she quickly returned to an expression of detached academic interest.

"Well, Susan," Russell said slowly, "that's not really a book project. It's just a little inquiry I'm doing to try to resolve some of the unanswered questions. It is just a natural offshoot of my work with Jack's research. I don't have any hard conclusions yet, but I don't buy the wolf-attack theory."

"What do you think happened?" Connie asked. "I mean, is it possible that it wasn't an accident?"

"Well, all I can say, Connie, is that I can't rule out human involvement. And before we all start jumping to conclusions" Russell glanced at Susan, "let's keep in mind that this is not the same thing as saying that I think that Jack was murdered. All I can say is that at this point, I can't rule it out, not entirely."

"Russell, I believe you talked to Chief Ray Davis about the case?" Susan prompted.

Russell was beginning to feel like he was being cross-examined. Perhaps he had said too much. He thought about how to escape this conversation, which was beginning to push beyond intellectually comfortable limits.

"Yes, Susan. And you also were a big help to me in digging up some of the files at the *Bulletin*. I obtained permission to look at the police files, and Chief Davis and I had several discussions about the case, which, by the way, is still an open investigation."

"Why are you getting involved in all this?" Connie asked in a matter-of-fact inflection.

"Let's just say that I'm doing a favor for a friend."

"Wanda Abrams," Connie stated.

"Of course, Wanda. She has asked me to help her bring things to closure."

"I can understand that," Susan said quietly. "God, how that lady must suffer even now, years after it happened. I know if that happened to someone I love, I would never be able to get that horrible image of it out of my mind, not until the day I died."

The waitress brought the check, which Russell grabbed, overruling what looked like half-hearted protests from Connie and Susan. They sat silently for a few moments, nobody looking at each other.

"You pay at the cash register," Connie finally said, reaching into her purse and leaving a three-dollar tip on the table.

As they walked out onto the sidewalk, Russell said, "Well, this was a lot of fun. What a pleasant surprise!"

Susan quickly said goodbye to Russell and Connie and crossed the street, ignoring the *Don't Walk* signal. She turned, smiled, waved, and then quickly walked away.

"Well, it's always a pleasure," Connie said preparing to leave Russell. "By the way, Dick and I will be having a few people over on Sunday afternoon – not tomorrow, but next Sunday – and we'd love to have you."

"Well, if I'm around – which I almost always am these days – I'd be delighted," Russell said. "Now, I have to get up to the Red & White and pick up some groceries for the week, so I guess –"

"Well, Russell," Connie interrupted, "that's where I'm headed, too. I hope Janice and Robert can handle two customers at the same time."

"Especially us," Russell laughed.

Druids and Children in the Mountains

It was slow for an early Saturday afternoon at the Kaisers' grocery store, even more so because it was during the Labor Day weekend. Russell and Connie were their only customers. Russell was surprised when Janice Kaiser greeted Connie as one would a first-time customer: "Welcome, ma'am, I'm Janice and this is my husband Robert. Just ask one of us if there's anything that you can't find. I'm sure we have it somewhere."

Russell and Connie split up, each in pursuit of the items on his or her shopping list. Robert, as usual, lurked in the office at the back of the store, muttering over paperwork and occasionally glancing out toward the counter. When he and Russell made eye contact along the aisle with the canned vegetables, Robert waved.

Russell finished his shopping first.

"So, I see that you've been spending some time with that Kline woman from the newspaper," Janice said, keeping her eyes on the cash register as she rang up each item.

"Susan?" Russell wondered why Janice referred to her as *that Kline woman,* especially since he had come to the store with Connie, but he decided not to pursue it. "Sure, she's been helping me with some of my research."

"I thought you were working on Jack Abrams' old notebooks. That's what Wanda led me to believe. But you're also investigating Jack's death. Did I hear that right?" Janice had the faintest smile as she looked at him from the corner of her eye. Connie had just silently rolled her cart behind Russell.

"I am, and Susan is just helping me with some background research from the old newspaper files." Russell felt annoyed that he had to explain himself.

Janice hit the total button with a little flourish and took Russell's money. Robert came out of the office and the three of them started to bag Russell's groceries. Connie watched them silently, smiling.

"So," Janice continued, "You're trying to find out if any of those old stories are true? I don't think you'll find much in the *Bulletin* about some of the tall tales Jack used to collect."

"Actually," Russell said, lifting a filled brown paper bag down into the shopping cart, "you'd be surprised. For example, did you know that there's probably some truth to those old stories about the Druids up there in the mountains?"

"Druids? Oh, you must mean the White Indians."

"No," Russell said slowly. "They're not really the same, I don't think. I've heard all the legends about the White Indians, but there actually was – or maybe still is – a group of people who go up into the forest and perform some sort of Druid or old Celtic rituals.

"But, wait a minute," Russell stopped for a second. "Connie here is a professor at the state university and an expert in the religious rituals of old cultures. Maybe she can tell us something about it."

Connie said, "Druids? Here? No. Technically, the term refers to a priest, not the cult itself. But, no, Russell, I've never heard anything like that. And that White Indians legend doesn't seem to have any factual basis to it, at least none that I know about. But I don't really do the same type of work that Russell is doing, Mrs. Kaiser."

"Druids?" Janice said, her voice seemed to be half disbelief and half horror. "You mean sacrifices and the like? Like they used to do in England or Wales, or wherever it was?"

"Oh, sure," Robert said. "Sure, you know what Russell's talking about, Janice. That secret group that supposedly operates around here."

"Oh, Robert, that's just pish posh." Janice gave a tiny snort.

"No, Mr. Kaiser, please go on," Connie said. "This sounds very interesting."

Well," Russell added, "apparently there actually was some sort of a group at least about a hundred years ago or so, maybe even more recently."

"We've all heard those stories for years," Robert said. "That's probably part and parcel of that White Indian legend. They're also something far worse. But sure, we've heard about them, haven't we, Janice?" Robert winked at his wife.

"Now, Robert Elliott Kaiser, you stop that. Mr. Poe and his professor friend here are serious, and you're just trying to pull a fast one on them with another one of your tall tales." Janice smiled. "If you'll excuse me, Mr. Poe, Professor, I have to tend to some things in the storeroom." Janice quickly walked away.

It was several seconds before Robert spoke. "There really are stories, folks. Janice heard them since she was a little girl, but I don't think she believes any of them. I'm not sure I do, either, at least not all of them. But there have been stories, and about stuff that's still going on today, not long ago."

"What kind of stuff?" Connie asked.

Robert walked to the end of the counter and leaned against it, looking out the window.

"You mean about the White Indians? I told Jack all about them. It should all be in Jack's papers."

"I saw the notes from his interviews with you, yes," Russell replied.

Connie said, "But you just said that there were things going on right now, that this group – the White Indians or the Druids or whatever – that they are still active. Is that right?"

"Well, Janice and I, we hear a lot of things. It's only natural, us working in a store and Janice being such a natural talker and all."

"So, is there still a group like this out there in the forest?" Connie persisted.

"That's what some folks say, but I don't know firsthand. But over the years I've heard about them."

"What have you heard?" Connie asked.

"Nothing specific. But there's a group of people – including some of the leading citizens of this area – that meets up in the mountains to practice ancient rituals of some sort. They all use secret names and such. They supposedly call themselves the Children, with a capital C."

"Children?" Russell interrupted. "I've heard references to the White Indians, of course, and to some sort of a Druid-like group; but don't think I've ever heard them called children."

"What kind of children?" Connie asked. "I mean, like the Children of whom or what?

"I don't know, Professor," Robert started to say.

"Please, please," Connie interjected, waving her hand from side to side. "Call me Connie."

"Well, Connie, you probably wouldn't have ever heard that name," Robert said. "Most people haven't. It's supposed to be a secret. But I guess they're just a bunch of folks who like getting naked in the woods or something, probably as harmless as you or me. But some folks say there's a darker side to them."

"A darker side? How so?" Russell pulled out his notebook. Connie seemed to be looking intently at it.

"Please don't write any of this down," Robert said quietly.

"Sure. No problem."

"I mean ever, don't ever write this stuff down." Robert stared at Russell. "Not in that notebook, not anywhere else, not ever."

"Well, okay, but how can it hurt?"

"I'm not sure that it would, but I don't want this traced to me in any way."

"Okay. Fair enough." Russell put the notebook pack into his pocket. "Go on. This is all off the record, as the reporters say."

"Well, like I said, folks, I can't say for sure that any of this is true. It's just what folks say."

"What folks?" Connie asked.

"Lots of people," Robert replied, "but I don't want to give any names, for their protection and mine."

"Understood," Russell said. "So what do these people say?"

"Well, for one thing, some folks say this group is really just a drug ring that grows marijuana up in the mountains and sells it in New York and Philly. And that's what they do up there in the woods: harvest their crops like a bunch of farmers, if you will."

"That sounds pretty harmless, even if it's true," Connie said.

Robert looked stern. "We don't take much to drugs around here, Professor, no kind of drugs. It might be all right on your college campus, but –"

"Go on." Russell interrupted. "What else?"

"Well, there's the stories of white slave trade."

"White slave trade?" Russell said.

"Sure, you've heard of that, being a lawyer and all, haven't you?"

"Yeah, I know what white slave trade is, but how are the – the Children, as you called them – how are they involved? Anything specific?"

"One case, two actually," Robert replied. "About ten years ago or so, two teenage girls from here disappeared. Their names were Kimberly McFall and, I think, Tracey or Stacey – I don't know her last name – and they were best friends in high school.

"Well, during the fall of their senior year, they started staying out all night. Kimberly's mother used to shop here, in fact, and I remember she was just beside herself with worry. She said that Kim and her friend had gotten mixed up with some religious cult of some sort that met in secret up in the mountains. Well, it sure sounded to me like the Children, but nobody could prove anything, and the girls wouldn't talk about it."

Janice returned to the counter. "Robert, are you still holding up these two good people? I'm sure they have better things to do than listen to you yack all day."

"I was telling him about Jill McFall's girl."

"Kimberly? Oh, what Jill went through! Kimberly's friend ended up worse."

Russell resisted the urge to pull out his notebook. "So, this really happened?"

"Of course, it happened." Robert sounded offended.

"I'm sorry Robert. I didn't say that well," Russell said, glancing at Robert. "I mean, did you know about it too, Janice?"

"Well, as much as Jill McFall would tell me. Of course, she moved away right after Kim was found."

Robert started to move away from the counter.

"No, wait, Robert," Connie said. "You were telling us about it; please go on. Janice, jump in with anything you know, too."

"Well, as I was saying," Robert continued slowly, "Finally, the weekend before Thanksgiving, Kimberly and her friend –"

"Tracey Collins," Janet offered.

"Right, Tracey Collins," Robert continued. "I knew it was either Tracey or Stacey. Well, they told their parents that they were going to a fraternity party over at the state college."

"Mansfield State?" Connie asked. "That's where I teach. And when was this?"

"Oh, I think at least ten years ago," Janice said.

"That must have been a little before I started working there," Connie said quickly, "I don't remember ever hearing about it.

"But I'm sorry I interrupted you, Janice. Please tell us more."

"Jill told me that Kim promised she would be home no later than one," Janice continued. "She said that Kim swore she wouldn't drink."

"Well, the long and short of it," Robert said, "was that neither girl was seen or heard from for almost a year."

"What happened to them?" Russell asked.

"Kimberly just came home one day, about a year later. She said that the night she didn't come home, she and Stacey –"

"Tracey," Janet corrected.

Robert looked annoyed. "Stacey, Tracey, whatever. The McFall girl said that the night she didn't come home, she went to a religious service of this group that she had joined. She thinks it was somewhere up on a mountain a little outside of Mansfield. She wasn't allowed to leave but instead had to live with some of them deep in the forest, and they moved from one camp to another. She said that she was forced into prostitution by them as what they called her contribution to the group."

"Was this group the same one as the Children, the ones you mentioned before?" Connie asked.

"Nobody knows because nobody believed her," Janice said. "And she refused to give any details, saying that the group would kill her if she ever told any of their secrets."

"So how did she escape?" Russell asked.

"She didn't," Janice continued. "Her mother said that Kim was simply allowed to leave. Kim said that their supreme leader – like the big boss of the whole cult, not just the group that had her – their supreme leader came up to their camp one day and ordered them to let her go."

"Did she say who this supreme leader was?" Connie asked.

"No," Janice shook her head. "Although, right before they left town, Jill McFall came into the store and said that the local leader of the cult was someone who was well-known here in town, but she – Jill, not just Kim – Jill had promised the local leader that Kim would never reveal the identity of anyone in the group."

"You don't sound like you believe any of it," Russell said.

"Lands sake, no," Janice replied. "It's the wildest tale I've ever heard. The McFall girl probably just ran off to New York or somewhere to be on her own, and when she had had enough, she came home and made up this crazy story."

"I believe it, or most of it, at least," Robert said.

"Why?" Russell asked, glancing at Janet.

"I just do," Robert said firmly, almost stubbornly.

"What happened to the other girl, Tracey?" Connie asked.

"She never turned up," Janice replied. "All Kim would say is that Tracey was 'chosen'." Her fingers supplied the quotation marks.

"Chosen for what?" Russell asked. "What do you suppose she meant?"

"I don't know. That's all she would say. Tracey was chosen." Janice repeated the quotation mark gesture.

"And was any of this in the newspapers?" Connie asked.

"No," Robert replied. "At least I don't recall it being in the papers, other than just the missing persons report right after the two girls disappeared."

"And the McFall family, they moved away?" Russell asked.

"Right after Kim returned home," Janice replied. "Jill said that they needed to get away from here, from all the gossip and finger-pointing. All she'd say is that someone here in town had given them some money to help them make a new start somewhere else."

"Who was it?" Connie asked.

"I asked, but she said that she and Kim had promised not to tell, that the person didn't believe in making his good deeds public."

"What about the other girl, Tracey?" Russell asked. "Is her family still around?"

"No," Robert said. "I don't think so. As I recall, nobody knew that much about them."

"Tracey lived with her grandparents, I think," Janice said. "They were in their late seventies back then. They're both gone now."

"Moved away?" Russell asked.

"No, passed away," Robert replied, "several years ago. I remember because they used to shop here. Nice people, but they never got over Tracey's disappearance. It's a shame."

Another shopper entered the store. Janice whispered a quick "excuse me" and rushed over to greet her.

"Well, I think that we both need to get home," Russell said to Robert. "Thanks for the information."

"It was very interesting talking with you, Mr. Kaiser." Connie said, shaking his hand.

"Well, you didn't hear any of it from me."

"Agreed," Russell said. "But just one question."

"Sure."

"I've never heard of that group before – the mysterious people in the forest called the Children. Where'd you pick that up?"

Robert looked around the store before answering. "You never heard this from me, okay?"

Russell smiled, "Okay."

"You agree too, Connie. You never heard it from me?"

"Sure," Connie said. "You're being very courageous telling us this. I honor that."

Robert made a slight grimace. "I mean it. This is something that I was never supposed to know."

"Okay," Russell and Connie said together.

"The truth is, Russell, I learned all this from my father, a long time ago."

"What else did he tell you?" Connie asked.

"He didn't tell me anything, Connie. Nothing at all. I just overheard it once when he was talking to someone else. At your house, Russell, as a matter of fact."

"Your father was one of them?"

Robert moved uncomfortably close, and Connie backed away one step. His voice dropped to a husky whisper. "Please don't ask me anything more about this, Russell, Connie. Please. I could get into a lot of trouble."

"Robert," Russell whispered. "That had to have been – what? – fifty years ago. But I won't betray your confidence, neither will Connie. I won't even take notes and I'll never publish what you told me. But I'd really like to know. What can you tell me about your father? Who was he talking to?"

"You know Reverend Paxton?"

"Sure." Russell said.

"It was his grandfather."

"Your father and Paxton's grandfather were in the Children together?"

Robert's voice trembled. "Please, Russell, Connie. Please. I shouldn't have said anything. Janice is right. I shoot off my mouth without thinking first. Sometimes, I just get carried away, you know, with my own stories, even start believing some of them. So, this conversation never took place. Please don't ever speak to me about this again."

Connie's Apology

Russell was sitting at his kitchen table, reading and finishing his second Sunday morning cappuccino when the phone rang.

"Oh, I am so glad I caught you at home," the voice said. Even before she announced herself, Russell know from the breathless sounding voice that it was Connie Graybill.

"Well, I had planned to go out a little later, but I'm always glad you called."

"Well, Russell, it's Connie," she added unnecessarily, "and I've been thinking about yesterday in town –"

"Yeah, it was great to run into you and Susan like that."

"No, it wasn't that great, Russell. I acted like a snobbish, condescending academic bitch, and I feel awful about it. I need to apologize, Russell, to make amends."

"No, no, Connie, you don't."

"Yes, I do, Russell. I was condescending to Susan and belittled you in front of her."

"Honestly, Connie, I didn't take it that way, and I'm sure Susan didn't either. It was just normal conversation."

"And then I was so rude to you and Mr. Kaiser at the store."

"Rude? No, you weren't rude, Connie. You asked some good questions, but you weren't rude."

"Well, maybe I hid it, or maybe you and Mr. Kaiser didn't notice it, but in my own mind I was saying, Connie, why are you hanging around this dumpy old store listening to this crazy old man spin a bunch of nonsense. And I was a feeling a little contemptuous of you, Russell, for pretending to be so interested in what he said."

"But I was interested, Connie, and you never showed any of that. I really think that you are blowing this way out of proportion."

"No, I'm not, Russell. And I want to let you know how sorry I am. I'm really a better person than that. It was not the way to treat a friend, and I do consider you to be a dear friend."

Russell could not remember ever hearing Connie Graybill apologize for anything, so he decided that it was just better to let Connie speak her mind.

"Look, I know that I invited you over for a little get-together next Sunday," she continued, "and Dick and I still want you to come, but I would also like it very much if you and Wanda could come over this evening around seven for drinks and a little dessert. Dick would be delighted to see you, too, and this would mean so much to me. I really need to do this to show you how sorry I am for my behavior yesterday."

"Wanda? You mean Susan, don't you?"

"No, I mean Wanda. I'm going to make peace with Susan at lunch later this week."

"But I don't know if Wanda's available or not," Russell replied slowly, looking for a good way to respond. "You see, Wanda and I are neighbors and she's become a good friend, but we're not – uh – involved."

"Oh, maybe I misunderstood. But it would still be nice if Wanda could come, too, even if you guys aren't a couple. After all, we're all neighbors.

Russell was silent for a moment. Where had she heard that he and Wanda were a couple? He decided not to ask, not to make Connie feel any more foolish than she probably did already.

"Well, I agree, Connie. It would be fun for all of us to get together. If you want to invite Wanda, I can pick her up on my way."

"No, Russell," Connie replied. "Could you please invite her for me?" Her voice sounded faintly pleading.

"Tell her that you and I were talking, and I had this idea for all of us to have a little impromptu get-together tonight. If I ask her myself, she might not want to come. Dick and I really don't know Wanda that well, and, just between us, I've always had this feeling that for some reason she didn't like me very much. Maybe it's only just because we don't know each other very well, but I've always sensed that with her. But if you ask her for me, she might come. Besides, now I really feel embarrassed by my misunderstanding of your relationship.

"Jesus," Connie laughed. "Now I have two things to apologize to you for: yesterday and my stupidity right now."

"Forget it," Russell replied. "I'll be happy to give Wanda a call and see whether she can come."

Russell had rehearsed the story that Connie suggested and was surprised when Wanda said immediately that she would be happy to go. When Russell arrived to pick her up, she emerged onto her front porch dressed in a long black skirt, white blouse, a dark red jacket, and black boots, with a long silver chain around her neck. Russell felt underdressed in his khaki pants and old blue double-breasted blazer.

"You look great," Russell said.

"Well, of course," Wanda said, "I can polish up pretty nicely when I need to." Russell wondered for a moment why she hadn't returned the compliment.

On the short drive down to the Graybills' house, Russell told Wanda how Connie had extended the invitation to him for both of them, assuming that they were a couple.

"Not that I'm saying it would be a silly idea or anything," he quickly added, "but I just don't know where she got that idea."

"Relax," Wanda laughed. "We are what we are, Russell. Just enjoy it."

Connie opened the door. She was wearing a white pantsuit that almost seemed to glow in the early evening light, contrasted with the dark interior of her house.

"I am so glad both of you could come," she said. She smiled at Wanda and shook hands with her, and then took Russell's arm and led him inside, with Wanda following. Dick shouted hello from what Russell assumed to be the kitchen. Connie ushered Russell and Wanda through the living room, where all the walls were lined from floor to ceiling with bookcases. Russell tried to read some of the titles of the books, but the light was too dim for his eyes to focus as Connie swept him through into the dining room. There an assortment of breads, cakes, fruit, and cheese waited on a snow-white linen tablecloth, with black lacquered utensils and black napkins. There were unlit white taper candles everywhere, the tallest Russell had ever seen. Music by Miles Davis came softly from a hidden source somewhere in the room.

"This is gorgeous, Connie," Wanda said.

"I was going to light them all, but then I realized that it would probably get too hot in here and spoil the wine," Connie replied.

After they all filled their plates and had their drinks, Connie led them out a back door onto a large porch, which extended almost the entire width of the house. It had been painted white since the last time Russell had visited. It looked out over a small flower garden, populated mostly by six untamed rose bushes, surrounded by green and white hostas, marigolds, and pansies. Islands of violets dotted the yard behind the garden, almost like steppingstones to the woods, which began about fifty yards from the back porch.

Dick and Connie sat down in two white wicker armchairs. Wanda and Russell took the small wicker couch. Everyone was silent for a moment. Russell looked out across the garden – Paul Levesque's garden – and thought about Paul and how much he must have enjoyed this house.

"I see that you kept Paul Levesque's garden," Wanda said. "It's even more beautiful than I remember."

"Who's he?" Dick asked. "Was he someone who used to live here?"

"Paul and my late husband were friends," Wanda said. "I came over here a couple of times with Jack."

"I don't think I know anything about him," Connie said. "The realtor said that the house had been foreclosed and had stood empty for a couple of years when we bought it. The yard and garden were pretty much overgrown."

"But when we eventually got the weeds tamed, we found most of those shrubs and bushes that are out there," Dick added. "They must have been Paul's. We can't take any credit for them."

"Well, Paul spent the last couple years of his life at the VA Hospital and passed away at the end of 1977," Wanda said quietly. "I didn't know about any foreclosure, but it was empty all that time. I recall that you moved in sometime the summer after he and my – after he died."

"That's right," Dick said. "Connie had just received an offer of an associate professorship at Mansfield State, with a promise of tenure and a promotion after two years. So, we really had to hustle to get up here from Scranton and settled before the fall semester. I don't think we got unpacked for almost a year."

"So, you guys are from Scranton?" Russell asked.

"Not really," Connie said. "Dick is from Allentown and I'm originally from Morristown. We were living in Scranton out of dire necessity. Dick was teaching in Wilkes-Barre at King's College and I was lecturing part-time at the University of Scranton and commuting into New York two days a week to finish my doctorate.

"I was dumbstruck when Mansfield State contacted me out of the blue. All the Dean would tell me is that they had heard good things about me and that he had received a glowing recommendation from someone he'd 'trust with his soul' as he put it. But he refused to say who it was – 'confidential sources' he said. Well, it was one of those opportunities that, for a lot of reasons, was too good to turn down. They even offered Dick a contract as part of the deal."

"And once we came up here to hunt for a house, we both just fell in love with the area. I can't imagine living or working anywhere else." Dick added.

Connie stood up suddenly. "Listen," she said, "I just want to say this one last time."

Russell started to say something.

"No, really, Russell," Connie continued. "Let me say it one last time, then I'll drop it. I want you all to know that I owe Russell an apology for the way that I behaved yesterday, both at the Diner with Susan and then at the grocery store with Mr. and Mrs. Kaiser."

She raised her glass in a toast. "So, I hope that a pleasant evening with good friends will make amends."

Wanda looked puzzled and Dick looked a little annoyed. After glancing at Dick and Wanda, Russell stood up quickly opposite Connie. "To good friends, then" he said, raising his glass and tapping Connie's. Dick and Wanda mildly gestured with their glasses and smiled. "And that's the end of it," he finished, smiling at Connie.

Connie reached over and took Russell's hand and held it for about ten seconds. She withdrew her hand, running her palm along Russell's fingers to maintain contact longer. "Thank you, Russell," she said, sitting down.

"So, Dick, Connie, what's going on with you guys? How are things in the ivy-covered halls?" Russell said, breaking the brief silence.

Connie spoke first. "Well, as I mentioned yesterday, Russell, I'm about midway in my research to try to identify common elements in those four cultures: the Celts, Frisians, Inuit, and eastern Native Americans."

"The Frisians?" Wanda asked.

"Those were a Germanic people, the earliest indigenous inhabitants of what is today the Netherlands," Connie replied. "I'm not surprised that they're unfamiliar to you, Wanda. They're kind of obscure. The first record of them is from the year 12 B.C.E., when the Romans encountered them. The old culture is long gone, but there are still about a half million people in the Netherlands who speak Frisian. We know that a lot of them migrated to Scotland and northern England in the fifth century.

"And this week I'm starting another trimester – Introduction to Anthropology and that Anthropology of Religion course I mentioned yesterday, Russell," she concluded.

"It really sounds interesting," Russell said. Wanda turned to look at him, her face turned away from Connie. Russell thought that Wanda rolled her eyes.

"And," Dick interjected, "Connie is the top contender for chairmanship of the Anthropology Department for the next academic year."

"Yeah," Connie said. "Maybe that's why I've been such a pain in the ass recently. I guess I feel that I need to prove to my colleagues – all men, of course – in the department that I should be the next Chair. I'd be the first woman ever to hold that post at Mansfield – one of only a few in any major anthropology department in the country. So, I guess sometimes lately I have been trying to show off to people.

"Dick says that lately I don't converse, I give lectures, like just now about the fucking Frisians." Connie smiled at Russell.

"I never –" Dick protested, then said with a grin. "Well, almost never."

"So, tell me more particularly about your work with the Native Americans." Russell said. "What nations have you been studying? Have you found any common threads, with the Celts, for example? I always thought that their culture and civilization were interesting."

"The Celts? How did you get interested in them, Russell?" Connie asked.

"Well, when I was in college, one summer I read *The White Goddess* by Robert Graves. It was a hard read but fascinating. I would be just about to give up on it, but I always had to turn the next page, to see what revelations came next. Every chapter was loaded with stuff that I had never known before. I was hooked. In fact, I found an old copy of it at the township library last year and re-read it."

Connie stood up, went into the dining room, and soon returned with a fresh bottle of white wine. The red light from the early evening sky reflected in her eyeglasses. "Well, Graves got a lot of things wrong, and some of it was just wishful thinking to make a good story. But I have to agree that it's a great read." She set the bottle down on the wicker coffee table, deftly slipping a large coaster under it all in one sleek motion.

"You know, there do appear to be some links between the Celts and the Indians in the northeastern U.S. and Canada," Connie continued as she sat down. "They're probably coincidental; most of those supposed connections are. But you have to consider the early migrations. We all came from the same place in Africa. So, it's not beyond the realm of possibility that people took the same ritual elements with them to northwestern Europe where they became the Celts and the Frisians. And others took those same elements across Asia and Beringia."

"Beringia?" Wanda asked.

"The ancient land mass between Siberia and Alaska," Connie explained. "People commonly call it 'the land bridge,' but it actually was quite a large area, more than six hundred miles wide and about the size of British Columbia and Alberta combined."

"There are also some common, basic religious beliefs, even similar deities, and I'm developing a hypothesis, several actually – " Connie stopped suddenly.

"Here I go again," she said, "making it all about me and what I'm doing. Just like I did yesterday at the Diner, Russell." Connie smiled. "If it's something that I'm passionate about –"

"That's what I love about you, Con," Dick said, "your passion."

Russell felt another self-flagellating apology coming from Connie and also alarmingly foresaw the evening's conversation wandering off into academics. Wanda hadn't said much, so he tried to seize control of the discussion for a moment.

"Wanda was telling me a story the other day about her almost being shanghaied on a houseboat by a couple of amateur archeologists that had come down from New York State to see some of the Native American sites around here."

"Really?" Dick said. "Tell us more."

Wanda laughed and took a long sip of her wine.

"Well, as you guys probably remember, I'm still working as a Welcome Wagon Lady in this part of the county."

"That's how I met her," Russell said, looking at Wanda and smiling at her.

"Us, too," said Dick.

"And I love all of you," Wanda raised her glass in a toast and smiled. "So, one day about three weeks ago, as I was driving back from making some calls in and around Tioga, I decided to call on a tiny houseboat moored in the river at the Lamb's Creek Boat Ramp. It had been parked there for about two or three days, so I thought that it might be some folks on vacation.

"So, I drove up, parked my car, grabbed my basket, and went on board. Nobody was outside, so I knocked on the door and a very nice woman, maybe in her early forties, answered.

"She invited me in and offered me some coffee. I went through my pitch about all the great things to see and do around here and loaded her up with all the coupons and brochures. But I always like to get to know the people I meet on these visits, even if, like her, they are here for only a little while.

"She told me that she and her husband had borrowed the houseboat from a friend of theirs up in Elmira, where they live, and decided to take a little excursion along the Tioga and Chemung Rivers for about ten days.

"She said that local history was a hobby of theirs, particularly the Indians that used to be all over this area back before the Revolution. So, they were just putzing along the rivers for a couple of hours every day, and then they would tie up near places that they had heard were old Indian sites to look for artifacts."

"Did they find anything?" Dick asked.

"Oh, she said that they had found only bits and pieces – pottery shards, horn, bones, or scraps of what looked like very old leather – but they couldn't really say how old they were or if they even were of Native American origin.

"But she said – and I'll never forget this – that it was the looking that mattered, that had meaning, and not whether they actually found anything."

"It's the quest, not the prize, that makes the epic," Dick said.

"So, what were they doing for a couple of days near Mansfield? What were they looking for there? Did she say?" Connie asked.

"I didn't ask her. She just said that Lamb's Creek was sort of the turn-around point for them. They had heard about a site somewhere along the river just across from where the boat landing is, but they didn't find anything."

"Why, they were just below my property, if they were docked at the Lamb's Creek Boat Ramp," Russell said. "I just realized it. I wish I had known at the time. Maybe I could have given them a little tour of the Rocks, talked with them about some of the local legends."

"So, how did you get shanghaied?" Dick asked.

"Well, Mrs. Cooper – that was their name –Morrie and Mary Cooper – well, she and I were just sitting in their tiny living room and galley combination, sipping coffee and talking. I thought I felt a faint vibration and looked out the window only to see the woods passing by slowly. Morrie apparently had cast off and left the boat ramp without telling Mary or knowing I was on board."

"Oh my god," Connie said, "that's hilarious. What did you do?"

"Well, they were both really embarrassed, but, like you, Connie, I thought it was hilarious. They stopped the boat right there in the middle of the river, and Morrie brought out some very nice Scotch. We had a drink together, laughed some more, and then we turned around and they took me back to where I had parked."

"Did you get their address or phone number?" Connie asked. "They sound like interesting people. I'd like to meet them, maybe ask them a few questions about their hobby."

"I have it at home somewhere, Connie. When I find it, I'll call you," Wanda said. Russell looked at Wanda with a questioning look. Wanda kept her home almost obsessively tidy. He couldn't imagine her ever having to look for anything there.

Dick stood up, went into the dining room, and returned with the cheese plate, a freshly opened bottle of red wine, and four clean wine glasses on a tray. Russell remembered seeing eight bottles of wine on the table, including the one he had brought, and he began to wonder whether Dick and Connie planned to consume them all. He filled all four glasses precisely half-way and distributed them.

After Dick resumed his seat, Connie said, "So, Russell, how are your projects coming?"

"Well," Russell began, I'm deep into writing the Braddock book. I've finished all the field work and other research and spent almost all of August finishing the outline of the first draft and am starting to write. I guess I've been a hermit for the past month or so. But I'm confident that I will have it ready to send off to a publisher by the end of the year."

"Yeah, that's what you said yesterday. Congratulations. I know it will be special. But what I'm really a little more interested in is your research about all the local folklore. We have a lot in common there, I think."

"Well," Russell began, "first of all, it's not really my research. It's Jack Abram's work. I'm just editing it and hope to publish it in his name." Russell looked at Wanda to try to read her reaction, but she gave none. "It's a great body of work," he added. "I just hope that I can do it justice."

Wanda reached over and briefly squeezed Russell's hand. "Thank you for saying that, Russell," she said quietly.

Connie looked at Dick and then at Wanda. "I said that we have a lot in common, but only the general topic," Connie said. "What Russell is doing – I mean, what Jack did – is much more difficult than my research. I base my work on actual observations and cultural evidence – pretty obvious stuff, usually. What Russell and Jack are doing is like putting together a jigsaw puzzle with pieces that don't quite fit together. If you're not careful, it's so easy, even for skilled researchers, to try to force-fit several pieces together and get entirely the wrong picture."

"Russell, do you think Jack collected all the pieces, at least?" Wanda asked quietly.

Russell was not sure how to answer, because he didn't know.

"I think he did – at least most of the important ones," Russell began slowly. "I'm not the expert, like Connie, and will never be as knowledgeable about the subject as Jack was. I'm just an amateur, I guess, but what I'm finding is that some of the different stories seem to link together over time, like all the accounts of the different groups that lived over there on Spanish Hill and where they came from."

"How so?" Connie asked, swirling the wine in the bottom of her glass.

"Well, let's take Spanish Hill as a little case study." Russell said. "The oldest legends say that Native Americans, the Carantouans or the Susquehannocks, first settled there. That's probably historical fact. Then it was the Spanish or the French, or maybe both, who came into the area perhaps as early as the mid-1500s. Then beginning in the late 1500s, we have the legend of survivors from the lost colony of Roanoke and how they made their way up the Susquehanna into this area. They apparently were seen in the early

1600s by at least one settler from Jamestown who came up here to seek his fortune. This story, whether it's true or not, is probably the origin of the White Indians legend. And now, there are stories of other groups who have taken the place of the White Indians in the local folklore.

"So, the big question that makes all this so fascinating to me, is whether these legends are just one continuous story or a series of them, one built on top of the other like the ruins of an ancient city. Most legends are based on facts."

"That's right," Connie nodded, "in a symbolic way, at least."

Russell ignored her. "So, one legend with a factual basis is adopted by the next generation as fact," Russell continued, moving his hands one above the other as he spoke. "That generation adds their own kernels of fact to it and legendary embellishments, and so it grows year after year and generation after generation."

"Wait a minute," Wanda said. "Are you saying that some of these legends that Jack recorded might be true?"

"Well, again, I would defer to Connie and other real anthropologists."

"Oh, Russell," Connie interrupted. "I am so sorry about that."

"No need to apologize," Russell replied. "I wasn't offended then, and I am serious about it now. I know my limitations.

"But, to get back to your question, Wanda, my answer would be yes. I do think that the accounts that Jack transcribed are more than just old myths, and that there continues to be a strong factual basis for some of the stories, if one digs deep enough. That's what I am finding out."

Connie put down her glass and looked at Russell. She leaned forward, resting her chin on her left hand. Her eyes were opened wide.

"I'm pretty sure," Russell said, "that there aren't White Indians roaming around these mountains anymore, if there ever were."

Connie asked quietly. "But were there in the past?"

"If you pin me down, I would say yes, Connie, but I don't think I have the type of evidence that you and your colleagues would rightly demand. There does appear to be a group or groups who hang out together and sometimes perform old rituals in the forest.

"You know, I can identify with that. I hope that they enjoy the forest, and that it brings them peace the same way it does for me. So, maybe you could call them the legendary heirs of the White Indians, or even of the original indigenous people here, or maybe something else. It doesn't really matter. The legend lives in them. The legend might not be real, but these followers of it, believers in it, are real."

"And what about the White Indian Rocks?" Connie asked. "Is there anything to the legends about that?"

Russell looked at Wanda, whose face was expressionless. What must she be thinking? He didn't want to talk about the Rocks, because of what happened to Jack there.

"I'm sorry, Connie," Russell said quietly. "I would really rather not talk about that."

"It's okay, Russell," Wanda said, taking his hand. Connie and Dick were staring at Wanda. She glanced at each of them and then looked back at Russell. "I can handle it."

"Well, I don't know what to say about the Rocks, Connie. I know about the legends about how old they are. The formation is laid out in metric measurements, or some measurement system almost exactly like the metric system. That suggests that the formation can't be older than the early 1800s, when the metric system first came into widespread use, although not ever around here. The earliest accounts, either oral or written, come from that period. Perhaps the measurements are only coincidental with the metric system, which could mean that they are much older. The dimensions and spacing seem to have ratios that are prime numbers, which ancient people did know.

"But I do know that people sometimes come up the old Indian trail along the ridge or climb up from the river to visit the Rocks. Sometimes there are groups. I've seen where they have trampled down the grass."

"Doesn't that make you feel a little creepy," Dick asked, "knowing that strangers are going up there and doing heaven knows what on your property?"

"No, Dick. Whoever it is always respects the area, 'leaves nothing but footprints,' as the slogan says. I almost never find even a scrap of litter, only trampled paths in the grass. Sometimes they seem to indicate some type of a ritual, like people walking in single file around the perimeter. But I don't mind, provided they respect the site."

Russell was surprised when Wanda said, "I understand that you've done a little amateur archeology up there on your mountain. Have you found anything?"

"No, Wanda, not much – just some beads, bits of rusted metal, and what looked like the blade from an old hand sickle."

A cuckoo clock from somewhere inside the house chirped nine o'clock. Connie jumped up and picked up her half-empty wine glass and filled it. She grabbed a couple of slices of cheese.

"Oh, Jesus Christ," she said, "I've lost track of the time. I'm sorry. I forgot that I have to make an important phone call right now."

She looked at Russell. "It's a colleague at Trinity College in Dublin, who's collaborating with me on some of the Celtic parts of my research."

Connie hurried inside. Russell could hear a door open and close.

Russell turned to Dick, "That's got to be one dedicated colleague," Russell said. "It's got to be two in the morning in Ireland."

"Oh, that's just Connie," Dick chuckled. "She is always on the phone in the middle of the night or dashing off for sudden late afternoon conferences at Cornell or NYU or Penn State, and sometimes doesn't get back until well after midnight." Wanda and Russell exchanged glances. Russell wondered whether he and Wanda were thinking the same thing.

Dick laughed, "After all, anthropology is a lot more exciting than English."

Dick got up, went into the house, and returned moments later with another tray of cheese, crackers, and small cakes, which he set on the coffee table in front of Russell and Wanda. The three of them sat silently on the porch, sipping wine and nibbling on snacks. Connie's voice could be heard from inside the house, but it was muffled. At one point, however, Connie raised her voice, and Russell thought that he heard Connie say, "Well, I need for you to take care of it before tomorrow morning, so don't fuck it up."

While waiting for Connie to return, Russell asked Dick about what he was doing, whether he was working on anything special.

"Oh, nothing like Connie," Dick replied. "She is the star of the family. I'm just a plodding assistant professor of English, teaching English Lit 201 to kids that are barely literate."

"Really?" Wanda said. "Illiterate? How did they get admitted?"

"Well, I don't mean barely literate in the literal sense," Dick replied. "What I meant to say is that although most of my students can read, they haven't read enough to really understand even a basic literature course like mine. The first question I get every semester is 'Professor Graybill, what books are we going to have to read?' not "What ideas are we going to explore?'

"But Connie is the one who is going places," Dick continued. "I'm just happy to be part of the same university that has Connie Graybill on their faculty. And, you know, my biggest fear in life is that she is going to get snapped up by some major university that won't want to hire an old professional wrestler turned mediocre academic like me."

Russell wondered why Dick was so self-deprecating. He had never heard Dick be so hard on himself. Russell almost let out a sigh of relief when Wanda spoke up.

"English literature?" she said. "Any particular era or authors? Are you working on any research right now, Dick," she asked, "like Connie's?"

"Well, I am," he replied. "I've always had a passion for James Joyce."

"Me too," said Wanda, showing her first sincere-looking smile of the evening. "I always loved Joyce, being from an Irish family. I first read *Dubliners* when I was still in high school. He was my favorite author in the twentieth-century English literature course I took when I was an English major in college.

"Of course, our family were Ulster Protestants, really strict Calvinists, so they were sure that I was going to burn in hell for reading him. But I think that reading Molly Bloom's soliloquy was one of the things that shaped my life. God, how I wanted the transcending spiritual experience that Joyce described so beautifully."

"Have you found it?" Russell asked.

"Yes," Wanda said quietly, "with Jack."

She closed her eyes. "*And then I asked him with my eyes to ask again yes and then he asked me would I yes.* To me that was more than about sexual ecstasy, it was about saying yes and yes and yes to life."

Wanda started to say something else but stopped. She looked down. Russell saw tears in her eyes.

"So, James Joyce," Russell said quickly. "Is there any particular aspect of him that you find especially interesting?"

Dick paused, his head turned at an angle toward the left side of the porch, away from Russell and Wanda, as if trying to formulate what he was going to say.

"It might sound a little odd," he said, turning back to look at Russell and Wanda, "but I am trying to examine *Finnegans Wake* to see if it contains any coded messages. That has been a persistent obsession with some Joyce scholars. I don't believe that it does; I think that's all nonsense, but it is the persistence of that idea, and how apparently intelligent people accept it as fact, that is what is fascinating about it. I guess it's something like your White Indians."

"I loved *Finnegans Wake,*" Wanda said raising her head again and smiling, "but it's already in an unbreakable code, I think: Joyce's English." Wanda drained the remainder of the red wine in her glass and poured another half-glass.

Dick laughed. "I think you beat me to it, Wanda."

Dick, Wanda, and Russell continued talking casually about their favorite authors. Russell felt a little out of date, when he said that his favorite authors were James Fennimore Cooper and Mark Twain. Dick and Wanda shared thoughts about F. Scott Fitzgerald.

Dick said, "The great tragedy and irony of F. Scott Fitzgerald is that he wrote only one good book, but one of the greatest of the twentieth century so far, *The Great Gatsby*."

Wanda said, "Well, I haven't read anything else by him, but *Gatsby* was another one of those books that really moved me. I still identify with, but am terrified by, Nick Carraway."

"Terrified?" Dick asked. "How so?"

Wanda replied, "I'm afraid that, like him, I have become a witness to life, but not really in the game, if you know what I mean. God, I don't want to be like that."

It was just after nine-thirty when Connie returned to the porch.

"Sorry," she said. "That took longer than I thought."

The rest of the evening was devoted to inconsequential matters. It was the first hour of astronomical night, and Dick revealed another previously hidden interest of his, astronomy, as he gave Wanda and Russell a quick tour of the clear night sky visible from the porch. They all had one final glass of wine and, around ten o'clock, said good night.

On the short ride back to Wanda's house, Russell said, "I learned a lot about you tonight."

"Like what?"

"Well, your knowledge of James Joyce and all those other authors you and Dick were discussing."

"Well, I learned something, too," Wanda said, "about you."

"What's that," Russell smiled at Wanda.

"Connie's got a thing for you. It was so obvious, so brazen, even in front of her husband."

"No, she was just trying to be hospitable, and I think she really felt sorry about yesterday."

"Russell Poe, are you for real? She was trying to hook you, you big dumb fish. Just from what you told me in the car coming here, I think it's obvious that she ran into you in town on purpose, from meeting you on the street and going to the Wellsboro Diner to that nonsense about having to get some groceries at the Red & White and the two of you going together there. And then tonight, she was all over you, smiling, little touches, and all. When she hugged you at the door when we left, I thought for a moment that she wasn't going to let you go."

Russell turned into Wanda's driveway.

"Do you mean that Connie Graybill has some sort of crush on me?" he asked.

"Don't flatter yourself, Russell; Connie is already doing a pretty good job of that. No, Russell, I think she is trying to get close to you for some other reason, and I don't know what that reason is. And what about all those questions about the Rocks and Jack's research? And with me sitting there trying so hard not to relive the worst thing that ever happened in my life? And thank you, Russell, for noticing that at the time and caring whether I was okay with your talking about the Rocks.

"And I don't know how far she was going to go with her little interrogation of you had she not had to make that phone call."

Russell thought for a moment and then said, "No, Wanda, I see your point, but I really think that Connie was just trying to be friendly and show a little polite interest in Jack's work. But she really was condescending and dismissive at times, even tonight. I think that's just the way she is."

"And bitchy," Wanda added. "Don't forget bitchy."

"Yes, and bitchy," Russell admitted, "but I think that she also was just trying to apologize for all that. I know that she's not really interested in what I am doing, or that it could ever be on her level. She was just trying to be a friend who wanted to make amends, as she said."

"Well, I know I'm right, Russell. You just watch out for Connie Graybill."

Wanda leaned over, gave Russell a quick kiss on the cheek.

"Thanks for the date," she said.

Russell was going to protest that it wasn't really a date, but before he could do so, Wanda quickly got out of the car and went to her front door. Russell waited in the driveway until Wanda was inside her house and turned on the light. She stood in the open door and waved good night.

The Fire

Russell's telephone rang very early on Monday morning. Still partly in his last dream before awakening, he wondered why Connie would be calling so early, but it wasn't her.

"Mr. Poe, something terrible has happened, and Mr. & Mrs. Kaiser need to see you at their store."

"My god, what happened? Are they okay?"

"They're fine, just badly shaken up. Robert is asking for you, says he has to talk to you right away."

"Okay, but by the way, who is this?"

"Please, come as soon as you can. They're waiting for you at the store." The man's voice sounded a little familiar, but whoever it was hung up without identifying himself.

Russell went downstairs and looked for his telephone directory. While his espresso machine heated, he found Robert and Janice listed in it, but there was no answer when he called their home. He downed a double espresso, grabbed a jacket off a peg in the hallway, and drove to Wellsboro.

Arriving a half hour later, he was shocked to see fire trucks and a mixture of state and Wellsboro police cars scattered around the entrance to the Red & White market. The entire block was closed to traffic in both directions. An area of about forty feet on either side of the front door, extending halfway into the street, was blocked off with yellow crime scene tape. A small crowd had gathered just outside the perimeter, while police officers and firefighters quietly asked them to stand back. A stew of repulsive odors and smoke filled the air.

Parking his car in a parking lot on a side street two blocks away, Russell walked briskly back to the store. He saw Chief Ray Davis speaking with whom he assumed to be a fire chief, walked up quietly, and waited until Ray was finished.

"Chief Davis," he called as Ray started to walk back to the grocery store.

"Ah, Russell, good morning."

"Can you tell me what happened, Ray? I received a strange call from someone saying that I needed to come into town and see Robert and Janice."

"Well, I don't know about that, but somebody tried to burn down the Red & White early this morning. The alarm came in at 4:10 a.m."

"So, you're sure already that it was arson?" Russell knew that it usually took extensive forensic examination before the authorities would label a fire as arson.

"Yeah, no doubt in this case."

Russell looked up the street toward the store. "Are the Kaisers here? Like I said, I got this call saying that they needed to see me and that I should come here."

"I think that they're still talking with the state investigators. The State Police barracks over in Mansfield usually takes charge of arson investigations for us. We really don't have the expertise and lab capabilities in our department. Do you think this can wait, Russell?"

"I don't know, Chief. All I know is that someone said that the Kaisers needed to see me right away."

"Well, let me go check with my colleagues to see if Robert or Janice are free for the moment. Just wait here a minute." Chief Davis turned and walked to what looked like a large ambulance but was black and marked "State Police Mobile CSI Unit – Mansfield, Pennsylvania." He spoke to someone inside and then returned, lifted the yellow tape, and said that the Kaisers were in the CSI van.

"Janice, Robert, oh my god. What happened? Are you guys okay?" Russell asked as he climbed up through the back door of the van. Janice and Robert were sitting in two plastic chairs at a small table, with a cup of coffee in front of each of them. A State Police officer asked, "And you are, sir?"

"It's okay, Corporal," Robert said. "Mr. Poe is my attorney."

"Well, I'll let you have some privacy then. Mr. Poe, when you're through, I'd appreciate it if you could leave me your card, so we can contact you if necessary." He stepped down out of the van and closed the door behind him.

"What's this about someone calling you, Russell?"

"What's this about me being your attorney, Robert? You know that I've more or less retired from the law. I mean I'm happy to help out for now, but if you need legal advice about this, it would be better if I refer you to someone."

"Relax, Russell," Janice said. "I'm sure that Robert said that because that officer who was staying with us in here looked very annoyed when the Chief asked if we wanted to see you. So, Robert said sure."

"Now back to my question," Robert said. He looked stern. Russell felt more mystified about the telephone call than ever before.

"I don't know, Robert. All I know is that it was a man's voice and it sounded familiar. He said that something terrible had happened to you and that you guys needed to see me right away."

Janice and Robert looked at each other. Robert made a slight shrug and looked back at Russell. "Honestly, Russell, we don't know who called you. We didn't ask anyone to do so, but I'm glad that you came by. This gives me a chance to clear up a couple of things with you."

"So, what happened? Chief Davis said that they think it was arson. Was anyone hurt?"

"No," Janice said, "We got a call from the fire department at a little after four this morning telling us that there was a fire at the store. When we got here, the fire department already seemed to have it under control, but as you can see, the place was gutted."

"Is there any structural damage? From what I could see glancing in the window when I came here, it looks pretty bad."

"No, no structural damage as far as they can tell," Robert replied. "It's more of a big stinky mess than any real structural damage to the building, the fire chief told me. Still, it's a hell of a way to start Labor Day."

"So, they say it was arson?"

"Yeah," Robert said. "The State Police guys have been grilling us all morning about whether we had any enemies, or whether the Mafia was trying to lean on us, nonsense like that. I sometimes think those guys watch too much TV."

"So, they told you it was arson?" Russell asked.

"No doubt about it, they said. They said whoever did it wanted to be sure that it looked like arson. Either that, or they are the dumbest arsonists in the world. They broke down the front door, went in, and poured gasoline all over the place. They used burning rolled-up newspapers to light the fire. And to be sure that it looked like arson, and not some electrical fire or something, they even left four empty gas cans sitting in a neat row by the front door."

"That's really strange," Russell said.

"Not really," Janice said. "The State Police investigators told us that this sometimes happens when they want to give a warning, without actually hurting anyone."

"Yeah, but the stupid sons of bitches could have easily killed themselves. Too bad they didn't," Robert added. "Like I said before, it's one hell of a mess, especially with all the water damage sort of turning everything into soup inside, but the store wasn't destroyed."

Janice went to a coffee pot with a Pennsylvania State Police decal on it and poured Russell a cup. "Sorry, Russell. I hope you'll forgive me if I forget my manners, today." Russell took a sip. It was the worst coffee he had ever tasted.

"Well, that's a little good news, at least," Russell said. "Are you going to be able to reopen?"

"Sure," Robert said. "We have always kept our fire insurance premiums up to date, and the insurance company has already called to tell us that they'll cover all the cleanup and repairs and replacement of merchandise and fixtures. They're going to come around later today to board the place up, as soon as the police let them. We also have some business interruption insurance, but it will only cover a small part of the lost sales. Still, we could reopen in about ten days."

"On the other hand," Janice said, "Maybe this is a blessing in a way. We're probably getting a little too old to keep running the store."

Robert looked down at the floor and nodded his head slowly. "Janice has said that we should just cash out and move to Florida or California or someplace else warm."

"So, I don't know about reopening. Janice and I were talking about it a little this morning, between interviews by the investigators. So maybe it's time to move on to the next chapter. But, hell, my family has lived here since when Wellsboro was first settled. It's more than home, Russell; it's where I have deep old roots. And I don't want to be chased away by a bunch of thugs with gas cans and old newspapers."

"Well, it's really too early to make any decisions," Russell said.

"Well, I just don't know," Robert continued. "That fire was no sloppy prank by a bunch of kids. Whoever did it knew exactly what they were doing: sending me a warning to keep my damn mouth shut."

"Keep your mouth shut about what, Robert?" Russell asked.

"Jesus Christ, what do you think?" Robert raised his voice.

Janice reached over and stroked his forearm. "Calm down, Robert, you're getting a little loud," she said quietly. "Russell, maybe this isn't a good time."

"About that stuff you and I and that professor friend of yours were talking about the other day, that's what," Robert said, pulling his arm away from Janice. "Well, I got the message, loud and clear. Maybe there's one there for you, too."

"Robert, if you think that's what it was about, then you should tell the cops about it," Russell replied. "If that's the case, then we're dealing with some pretty bad people, not just a bunch of tree-hugging hippies who like to run around in the woods."

"Who'd I tell," Robert snorted. "Chief Davis? He's a nice enough guy, but he couldn't find his ass with both hands. And I'm not sure he can be trusted. I've even heard that his wife is involved with the Children somehow."

"Where'd you hear that, dear?" Janice asked. "And whose children are involved?"

"Well, I don't remember. It was some time ago. And even if I did remember, it wouldn't be very safe to say who it was, now would it?"

Janice looked puzzled. She started to say something when the State Police corporal tapped lightly twice on the door, then came in.

"Is everything okay here?" he asked. "Do you need anything?"

Turning to Janice, the corporal asked, "Mrs. Kaiser, I understand that you were – are – the business manager for the store and keep the books."

"Actually, my husband does," Janice replied.

"Well, then, Mr. Kaiser, we've retrieved some files and what look like ledgers from the little office in there, and my sergeant and I would like to ask you a few questions about them."

"Oh, dear," Janice exclaimed. "It there anything wrong with them?"

"Oh, no ma'am," the officer replied. "they're not damaged very much at all. It's just that we could use some help in seeing whether there might be something – anything – in them that might give us a clue to who did this. I'll come back in a few minutes."

He went to the front of the mobile unit and retrieved three bright yellow boxes of film, and then left, saying "I'll be inside the store taking pictures. If you need anything, just ask any of my colleagues or one of the officers from the Wellsboro police."

"So, what are the next steps?" Russell asked. "Can I help you and Janice out? Financially, I mean? I know that even if you have the greatest insurance in the world, cash flow can be a problem. I'd be happy to run up the street to the bank and tap my savings account for you."

"It's Labor Day," Robert replied. "The banks are closed today."

"Oh, right." Russell said. "But I could get a check to you later today, so you could deposit it tomorrow when the banks open again. Would a thousand dollars help tide you over until you get things straightened out? I really would like to help. You can pay me back whenever you can, or I can just take it out in trade when you reopen, whichever would work better for you."

Janice began to choke up. "That's the nicest thing, Mr. Poe – Russell. I mean, it's not like we were even friends, just your grocers and you're our customer who comes in about once a week. And other people have been so kind to us this morning.

"For example, Reverend Paxton came here this morning," she continued, "just a little while before you did, to give us almost five hundred dollars that he said was from a special fund that members of his congregation had set up. Most of the folks in his church don't have even two pennies to rub together, but he said that they all chip into the fund whatever they can, so that they can help others in need, even strangers like Robert and me. He also said that if we decided to move away and sort of start a new life, he and his congregation would be happy to help us out some more, by helping to pay our moving expenses. And he said that he has friends in Florida who would help us get settled when we arrive.

"I told Reverend Paxton that it was such a wonderful gesture, doubly so because we don't go to his church or any church at all, really. But do you know what he said?"

Russell nodded, "No. What?"

Janice smiled. "He said that God loves us for who we are and doesn't check our membership cards. And neither should we.

"Well, Robert," she continued. "we shouldn't make those nice young police officers wait for us. I can go out and see if I can help them, if you boys want to continue talking for a few minutes." She left.

"That was nice of the Reverend," said Russell.

"Yeah." Robert said without any sign of enthusiasm or even gratitude. "I still need to talk it over a little with Janice, but I think we're going to take him up on his offer."

"Wait a minute," Russell said. "I thought you just told me that you were going to stay and reopen the store, that you weren't going to let them chase you away."

"Well, I said that we could reopen, and I think that's what I'd like to do, Russell," Robert sighed. "I really do. But I'm also a practical man. People may think I'm just a crazy old coot, but I can understand a message when I hear it."

"What kind of a message?" Russell asked.

"Damn it, Russell. Haven't you heard a word that I said?" Robert stood up. He started tapping his finger on the Formica top of the table. The remaining coffee in the cups sloshed with each tap.

"What the hell do you think I'm talking about. That stuff we talked about on Saturday at the store. Jesus fucking Christ, Russell. Don't you ever pay attention?" Robert thundered. His face got red. He then paused as if to catch his breath.

"I like you Russell," Robert continued in a lower voice. "I really do. But now I am probably going to go to my grave wondering if that visit by you and your professor friend on Saturday had anything to do with our losing everything that we had worked so hard to build over the past thirty-five years. I know that you would never do anything like that on purpose. You're not that kind of man. But I'll never know for sure."

"Honest, Robert, I swear that –"

"So, thanks for your generous offer to help us, but we can't accept it. This is goodbye, Russell. Even if Janice and I do reopen the store, I don't want you as a customer."

"But even so, Robert, my offer to help you and Janice still stands."

"Don't you understand anything that I've been saying, Russell? I really appreciate the gesture, I really do. But I can't afford any more contact with you. No, it just wouldn't be safe for me or Janice, and possibly not for you as well. This fire was a warning for you, too."

Robert stood up and extended his hand. "So, it's goodbye, Mr. Poe." Russell stood and they shook hands. Robert had a sad smile. "I like you and really enjoyed knowing you, and I'll miss our little chats at the store." Before Russell could say anything else, Robert turned and exited the van, not looking back, leaving Russell alone inside. When Robert closed the door, Russell thought the air that the door had pushed inside the van smelled of burnt bacon.

Rabbit

Whitey wondered whether he should turn on the parking lights as he sat at dusk in his truck, parked about a hundred yards up a narrow dirt road that zigzagged up from Baldwin Run Road into the forest. The heavy overcast and the mist from the storm earlier that evening made it darker than normal. The sun probably had set about fifteen or twenty minutes ago, he reckoned.

Whitey reached down to pull out the knob. He really needed parking lights on. Even though he hadn't seen any other traffic, either on Baldwin Run Road or on the dirt road where he now sat, he felt unsafe. At only fifteen or twenty miles per hour, someone coming around a curve might not see him until it was too late. He wondered how many deer got hit on this road.

Parking lights – this would be one time that they were really used while parking. Whitey had always wondered how they got the name. But he hesitated. Better not attract attention. He tried to remember whether the phone call had said anything about having his lights on.

The phone had rung just as Whitey arrived home after working all afternoon at Russell Poe's place. He hadn't even taken off his jacket or had a chance to take a can of beer from the refrigerator. Sandy was already there and answered the phone.

"It's for you," she said.

"Rabbit" a man's voice said quietly when Whitey said hello. He had almost forgotten the name he had been given when he had joined the Children of Bel more than twenty years ago.

Rabbit. At first, he had objected to the name, thinking that they were insulting him. They explained that Rabbit was one of the gods of the Algonquin Indians, and that he was clever and brave. It was his true ancient name, they said. But after a few years with the Children, Whitey concluded that he had better things to do than try to learn a lot of nonsense and go to weird ceremonies in the woods at night. He told one of his spiritual guides, Zephyr, that he wanted out, and she said that it was not a problem.

They met at the Pine Tree Inn at eight o'clock in the morning, just after opening, and were the only people in the bar. "This was just not the right moment for you," Zephyr said. "Just remember the sacred promises that you have made to us, and you will always be one of us, in our hearts and in yours, in this life and in all the lives to come."

He had never forgotten those words, even though, after all these years, he still was not sure what they meant.

The last thing she said, just before leaving him alone in the bar, was "Sometime in the future, and this day may never come – we might need your help. In return for protecting you, we hope that we will be able to rely on you, even if you are no longer active in our fellowship. Until then, remember that we love you."

"Remember we love you." Whitey had carried those words with him, and at the same time had tried to run away from them, ever since.

They had kept their promises. Ever since then he had occasionally seen members of the group around town, but he never showed any sign of recognition. Neither did they. Whitey Wentworth had kept his word. Even if he hadn't heard about what happened to folks who didn't, Whitey would have never revealed anything. He felt good that he had at least that much honor.

There had been only one other contact in all those years, when Brendan had asked him to arrange a meeting between Jack Abrams and two of the Children who said that they had some folklore material about the Rocks and their history that they wanted to contribute. He had always wondered whether those two men had anything to do with Jack's death later that afternoon. He told himself that it was just a coincidence. The newspaper had reported that the police said that it was a wolf attack, not a murder. He volunteered a witness statement to the cops, and they thanked him and never indicated that he was suspected of being involved in any way. He felt badly for Mrs. Abrams, but he nonetheless feared that he could only get into trouble by starting to ask a lot of questions. It might be better not to know everything.

"Rabbit, are you there?" the voice repeated.

"Sorry, you must have got the wrong number."

"No, Rabbit." The voice sounded patient and kind, even friendly. "No, Whitey. I know it's you."

Whitey's mind raced, frantically. What had he done? He hadn't done anything. For the second or two until the voice spoke again, Whitey almost panicked. He started to hang up but stopped. It wouldn't do any good. They would always know how to find him.

"We need to talk, Rabbit. We want to meet with you in a little while."

"Hey, I ain't never said nothing," Whitey started to protest.

"We know." The voice was steady, calm, soothing. "We know, Rabbit. But we have need of you, Rabbit. We need your skills. We know you don't want to be part of us anymore, and that's okay. It really is. So please don't be scared."

"I'm not."

"Good, that's very good, Rabbit. You know you can always come back, or not, whatever you want. You'll always be one of us. But we need your help with something."

"What kind of help?"

"We can't say over the telephone, Rabbit. You know how it is."

Whitey listened carefully, repeating the directions in a whisper, hoping that he would remember them. He was relieved when he realized that he knew the place where the meeting would be.

"Be there at eight o'clock tonight, Rabbit, and come alone."

Whitey almost asked what if he didn't show up, but the caller answered his question before he could get it out.

"And Rabbit, if you're not there, or you're not alone, or you try anything, we'll just have to have our meeting some other time. And it might not be so friendly."

"Hey, I know who you are, so don't threaten me," Whitey said quietly, hoping that Sandy couldn't hear him. "You guys couldn't scare me back then, and you sure as shit ain't scaring me now. Who the hell do you think you are?" Whitey felt himself getting angry. He was gripping the phone so hard that his hand was turning red. Calm down, he tried to tell himself.

He looked across the room at Sandy. She had a worried look.

"Yes, you know who we are," the voice said calmly. "And you know what we can do. So, we understand each other, Rabbit. That's the way it should be between old friends."

The man on the other end of the phone hung up. Whitey continued to speak into the dead line, trying to have a more matter-of-fact tone for Sandy's benefit.

"Yes, that's right," he said. "I'll be there. And thank you, sir." Whitey replaced the receiver in the wall phone. He kept his hand on the receiver and stared at the wall inches from his face.

"What was all that about?" Sandy asked. Her eyebrows were wrinkled the way they always got when she was worried about something. She knows something's wrong, Whitey thought.

"Oh, nothing," he said, trying to sound casual. "I just have to go out for a few minutes, to meet a guy about a possible job," he said to Sandy as he zipped up his jacket and grabbed his ballcap. "We'll go out when I get back, or, if you want, I can meet you later someplace."

"That's really great news," Sandy replied, flashing a quick smile. She's not buying it, Whitey thought. "How long do you think you'll be gone?" she asked.

"Don't know. The guy didn't say, but it's just up Baldwin Run a little ways."

"Isn't that up in the State Game Lands west of town? Why would you be having a meeting way out there?"

"He wanted to meet me at the job site and show me some things. I think he said it was some work for the state."

"Is it someone I know?"

"I just know him as Eddie," Whitey said, making up the first name that came to mind. "He said he had just arrived in town and was putting together a crew, and someone had recommended me to be one of his foremen for some construction work. He wants to start tomorrow, so he needs to see me tonight to see whether it's the kind of job I can do." He suspected that Sandy wasn't convinced, but Sandy said that she would stay there and watch television until Whitey returned.

"Don't be too long," she said, kissing him on the cheek as he left.

It was now just a few minutes before eight o'clock and dark. Whitey had been scared just after the phone call, but now he was more curious than apprehensive. The cigarette he was smoking was calming his nerves. They're not going to hurt me or anything, he thought. He hadn't had any contact with them at all since he decided to quit. The Children just weren't for him, a lot of mumbo-jumbo and running around at night in the woods. But there also was a darker side to the Children that scared him away, something that they hinted at but never really came out and described. They accepted his decision to leave in what seemed to be a friendly way, but he also got the message. They wouldn't hassle him, so long as he kept quiet. He had heard about what happened to people who didn't. He had kept his promise, and so had they. So, why did they want to talk to him now? Maybe they were just trying to recruit back old members.

Suddenly Whitey heard footsteps to his left. He jumped a little in his seat. A big dark man had just appeared, out of the dusk. He stood by the driver's door, his hands resting on the bottom of the open window. He wore a faded, but plain, blue denim jacket over a black T-shirt. His short, black beard seemed to hide most of his face. He looked menacing until he smiled. Whitey searched his memory for the big man's name.

"Hey, Rabbit. It's me, Claw. It's been a few years, my friend," the big man said.

"Uh, yeah. Hi, Claw," Whitey replied.

A tall woman wearing a hooded sweatshirt and jeans stood behind him. She walked around the front of the truck, pausing to smile through the windshield at Whitey. Then she climbed into the passenger side beside him. She lowered her hood and shook out her long dark hair.

She reached across the passenger compartment and put her hand on Whitey's right shoulder briefly. "Hello, Rabbit. I'm Laurel. And I believe you already know my friend, Claw," she said. Claw nodded and smiled briefly.

"Rabbit and I are old friends, aren't we, Rabbit?" Claw said.

Whitey looked around quickly, looking for a parked car. Where had they come from?

"No point looking for our car, Rabbit; we came here another way," Claw laughed. "We saw *you* pull up, in fact. We just wanted to make sure everything was cool before we showed ourselves."

"Rabbit," Laurel said quietly, "John Bard sent us. He needs your help."

Holy shit, Whitey thought. John Bard? Whitey remembered him as some sort of a mystical leader, supposedly hundreds of years old. What's going on here, he wondered. What's this all about? He moved to open the door and get out. Claw's hands remained on the door. When Whitey moved the inside handle, he could feel the force the big man exerted, holding the door closed.

"No need to get out, Rabbit," Claw said. "Just stay comfortable. This will just take a second."

"What's this all about? I ain't said nothing to nobody, not all these years. Not a single goddamned word, not to a living soul, I swear to God."

Claw reached in and put his hand on Whitey's shoulder.

"It's okay, man. Don't worry," he said. "We know that, Rabbit.'

"And believe, me," Laurel added, "we appreciate it. We know we can trust you and we want you to know that you can trust us. Okay?"

"Yeah." Whitey said flatly, waiting for the *but*.

"So, what's this all about?" Whitey repeated. "What do you guys want with me?"

Laurel turned in her seat to face Whitey. "It's Russell Poe, Rabbit. You work for him," she said quietly.

"So what if I do? What about him?"

"Well, some of us are a little concerned about him, you know. We know he's been poking around at the Rocks and that you've been helping him," she said.

"Well, hey, a man's got to earn a living. But I haven't told him anything, I swear."

"Relax, Rabbit. We know that." Laurel said. "But he's also been finding things he really shouldn't see, like the underground chambers and the tunnels."

"Chambers? Tunnels?" Whitey exclaimed. "What are you talking about? I don't know anything about no underground chambers.

"He's just done some archeological research, as he calls it, just sort of measuring distances and scraping the surface, down about four inches or so, finding mostly old junk. He's never told me anything about any underground stuff."

Laurel paused and looked across the front seat at Claw, who was still leaning against the driver's door, his head partially in the window only inches from Whitey. A moment later she said, "Well, maybe he didn't. But in addition to that, Rabbit, he's been asking a lot of questions that he really shouldn't ask, about old legends and the like."

"Oh, those are just crazy old tall tales," Whitey said. "He studies that stuff and is writing a book about it. He doesn't believe any of it. Nobody does."

"That also may be true," Laurel said. "Those might be just crazy tall tales, as you call them, but he's getting close to some truths, Rabbit, really close. Things that he shouldn't know about, that nobody should."

"Honest. I know Russell Poe real good," Whitey protested. "He's just a little strange, you know, but he's a good man. He just writes books and stuff and is just curious about things, but he ain't interested in the Children."

Claw took a deep breath and held it. Whitey tensed up, wondering if he could push Laurel out of the way and escape through the passenger's door. The big man exhaled, and Whitey could smell the peppermint on his breath.

"Yeah, Rabbit, he's a good guy. We know that," Claw said, nodding his head. "But, you see, like Laurel said, we're worried that he might stumble across something that he shouldn't – you know, get himself into trouble without meaning it. A lot of good people could get hurt all the same."

"Sandy's mom, for example," Laurel said quietly.

Whitey took another drag on his cigarette. The smoke burned the roof of his mouth. His tongue felt rough and dry. He was confused. Now they were threatening Sandy's mother. His voice sounded hoarse when he answered.

"I don't want that."

"Neither do we," Laurel said.

"So, what do you want me to do?" Whitey said slowly. "I won't do anything that will get me in trouble. I still got some time to go on my probation."

Claw laughed softly.

"No, nothing like that, Rabbit," he said. "What do you think we are? I've been there myself, and we would never ask you to do anything to mess up your probation."

I know what you guys are and what you can do, Whitey wanted to say, but he didn't.

"No, calm down, Rabbit," Laurel said. "All we need you to do is to keep an eye on Russell Poe. You know, just let us know if he starts getting too close for comfort, if you know what I mean.

"No, I don't know what you mean. Too close to comfort for what?"

"Don't worry about that, Rabbit," she said, putting her hand on his arm. "We'll figure that part out. All you have to do is just keep an eye on him and tell us what he's doing. That's all."

Whitey was silent for a moment. It wasn't right to spy on Russell Poe, not after all Russell had done for him, paying him well, treating him with a little respect. No, it wasn't right.

"I mean, you owe us, Rabbit." Laurel continued quietly. "We haven't bothered you very much over all these years, and we wouldn't have bothered you now. But only you can help us. Otherwise, a lot of good people can get hurt."

Whitey took a final drag and crushed his cigarette in the ashtray.

"Shit. Okay," Whitey finally said. "Okay, what do I got to do?"

"Just what Laurel just told you, Rabbit. Just watch him," Claw said. He paused to smile. "That's all, my friend. Just keep an eye on

Poe. And let us know what he's doing, especially up there at the Rocks."

"And get him talking about his other research," Laurel added. "You know, the old legends that he's interested in, the stuff that Jack Abrams did. Ask him questions about his studies at the Rocks. Make him think that you're interested, too. Get him to share with you. And then tell us what he tells you."

"Okay," Whitey said. "Okay. But if Russell gets hurt or anything, I'll talk. I swear to God, I'll tell the cops everything I know."

"You won't ever have to do that," Laurel said. "I promise."

Claw hadn't moved. He stood there quietly, looking down at Whitey. Whitey tried to look into Claw's eyes, but his face now was hidden in the deep shadows that had arrived with the night. He could no longer see the reassuring smile on Claw's face.

"So, when do we meet again?" Whitey asked.

"We won't meet again, Rabbit," Laurel said. "Someone will call you on the telephone, just like tonight. He or she will call you Rabbit. That will be your sign. Tell that person whatever you know about what Poe's been doing. Answer all the questions they ask you as best as you can. Don't worry about it. You can trust us."

Claw reached in and grasped Whitey's left forearm. His grip was like a vise, but also gentle.

"Don't worry, Rabbit. If you do us this favor, everything will be cool. Remember, we're your friends." He patted Whitey's arm and straightened up. At the same moment, Laurel opened the passenger door. She lingered for a moment, looking at Whitey. She then reached over and touched his cheek. Whitey felt a warmth flowing from her fingers into his face. She smiled and silently got out of the truck.

Whitey watched as Laurel and Claw turned and walked away into bushes at the edge of the woods. Whitey got out of the truck and looked for any sign of them, wondering how they could be completely absorbed by the forest, as silently as they had arrived. Whitey stood by his truck. He waited for several minutes while he finished his cigarette, standing as quietly as he could, watching and listening for any sign of them moving through the forest, but there was none.

The Sangman's Map

Bill Paxton knocked at Russell's front door.

Russell had called Bill last night and said that he had been going through his uncle's books and found several that appeared to belong to Bill's family.

Bill had said, "But it's your house now and your books, but thank you all the same for calling me. It means a lot to me."

"No, Bill. It might legally be my house now, but it will always be your home, too. Please come over, if you can. I don't want to inflict any painful memories on you, but I've found a couple of things that I think that you should really have."

Bill said that he would be there at three o'clock.

"I have a couple of commitments before then at the Chapel," he explained.

Russell had a plate of sandwiches and a bowl of chips ready when Bill arrived. As before, he had a six-pack of beer chilled in the old refrigerator. After they sat down in the living room, Russell explained that he was sorting through some of the things that Simon had left in the house, mostly books and some papers.

"I really feel pain, Bill, a real physical pain, when I have to get rid of old books," Russell explained. "To tell a story on myself, there was a time about five years ago, when I got on this 'declutter your life' kick, and I decided to sort through the books I had in my place in Philadelphia. At that time, I had more than six thousand books, shelved and stacked wherever there was space. Like a mad professor. You should have seen it.

"So, one Saturday morning, I said to myself, this is the day of reckoning, I really gave myself a sermon, Bill. You'd have been proud of me. I told myself that it is not disrespectful to dispose of books, to give them to a library, for example, that could use them. I was not dishonoring the work of the authors. Still, I felt like I was picking which of my children to send off to an orphanage.

"I guess I got that from my aunt, the one who raised me. She said that it was disrespectful even to underline in a book. But, to make a long story short, Bill, after about three espressos, I summoned up the courage to go through my six thousand books. It took me two days, and I sorted out a grand total of six of them to donate to our library for their book sale."

"Well, at least you got rid of," Bill paused to do the math, "one tenth of one percent."

"Well, before you go any further, Bill, I have a confession to make." Russell chuckled. "When I went to the next book sale at the library, I bought four of them back."

"But I've been sorting through the books that Simon had left here," Russell continued. "I've got to make room for my 5,998 books that I shipped up here from Philadelphia, in addition to the thousand that were already here."

Bill laughed. "You know, Russell, one of the things that I really like about you is that, like me, you never take yourself too seriously. I just hope that the next time you're over at the Manse, you don't get the temptation to start counting my books. I'm probably even worse than you."

"I noticed, Bill," Russell said. "Unlike most preachers I know, you have more than just the Bible."

"Well, God never intended us to limit our knowledge," Bill said.

Russell invited Bill up to his study, to see whether he wanted any of the books that he was planning to discard. Bill was secretly pleased when he recognized the study as the front room that had served as his bedroom when he stayed with his grandparents.

"I see what you mean about all the books," Bill said as he browsed the bookshelves.

"I pulled out some books that I think might have belonged to your family, Bill," Russell said, pointing at a stack underneath the front window. Bill walked forward. His eyes fell on one book in particular, the gold title on the spine glowing dimly against the worn red cloth binding. He sat down – almost collapsed – on the floor and picked it up, caressing it with his hands, without opening it.

"*Indian Wars of Pennsylvania,*" Bill whispered, picking up the book from the pile. "By C. Hale Sipe. I can't believe it, after all these years."

"You know the book?" Russell asked softly.

Bill opened to the title page. There it was, written in the best Palmer cursive on the page opposite the title: "To Walter Paxton from his loving wife Belle, Christmas 1926."

Bill thought he felt a tear in the corner of his right eye. He quickly wiped it away, hoping that Russell hadn't noticed.

"I sure do, Russell." He paused and took a breath. "This book used to belong to my grandfather."

Russell glanced over Paxton's shoulder. "I read a few parts of it. It looked interesting, but pretty stiff reading for a little kid."

"Believe it or not, Russell, this was one of my favorite bedtime books when I was older. It was like Mother Goose for most kids. Whenever I stayed overnight here, my grandmother would read parts of it, usually the less bloody stuff.

"Thinking back on it, I guess Sipe had a way of making the old Pennsylvania frontier come alive. True, the book is about one Indian massacre after the other, and is terribly slanted against the Indians, but it was exciting stuff for a kid – yes, and sometimes terrifying stuff if you think about. But I don't remember it ever giving me any nightmares."

"Gee, I've done a little work in the early colonial period. I don't think I ever came across any of Sipe's work," Russell admitted.

"That's possible," Bill said. "I guess he's more or less forgotten now. As I remember, C. Hale Sipe was a lawyer in Butler, Pennsylvania, back at the turn of the century. He wrote the book as a hobby, but he must have spent years at the State Archives in Harrisburg."

"Interesting. When I looked at the index, I didn't notice anything in it about this area. Is there? Do you recall?" Russell asked.

"No, not that I recall, Russell. Most of the action in Sipe's book, if I remember correctly, took place in the southern part of the state. But I guess you'd already know that, wouldn't you?" Bill said.

"What I really meant," Russell explained, "was whether there is anything in the book about old Native American sites in this area."

"You mean like the Indian Rocks? Not that I recall. Folks back then – white people and Indians both – had more to worry about than a bunch of rocks up in the woods. No, most of the action, as I remember, was in the southern part of the colony."

"Well, no," Russell replied, "I was thinking more about some of the Native American settlements like Tioga Point."

"No, not that I remember," Bill said.

"Well, Bill, you have to take that book with you."

"No, it's yours now, Russell. It will do you more good than it would me."

"All the same, Bill, please keep it. It's part of your childhood, of who you are."

Images flashed through Paxton's mind: being tucked up on a winter night under his great grandmother's featherbed in the room where he and Russell were now standing, while his grandmother read exciting true accounts by the light of a forty-watt bulb; seeing the book displayed on the little book rack beside his bed, along with two rows of other old books, which were the only ones Bill had ever seen anywhere in the house. Bill had wondered what had happened to them. He was disappointed when after his grandparents' deaths, nobody had thought to save them for him.

"For all these years," Bill said, "I had just assumed that these books had been thrown out or given to a library or something. Do you know how they came to be here?"

"I have no idea," Russell replied. "All I can assume is that they must have been overlooked and left behind when the house was closed up after your grandparents passed away. When I moved in, they were just mixed in with all of Simon's other books."

"Well, Russell," Bill started, but he stopped. He felt embarrassed to be so choked up by an old book. He looked down and quietly, very gently, turned the faintly yellowed pages of the old book.

"Well, Russell," Bill continued as he looked for passages that he might still remember, "all I can say is thank you. You have no idea what this means to me."

"Oh," Russell interrupted. "I had almost forgotten about this." Only when he looked up from the book, Bill saw that Russell was holding a piece of paper in his hand.

"What's that?"

Russell smiled. "A mystery. A genuine, honest-to-goodness riddle. Evidently my uncle made this map of the property. I can recognize some of the things on it, but others are riddles, especially the strange symbols and numbers. I thought you might be able to decipher some of it for me."

"Let me see."

As soon as he saw it, Bill knew he had to think fast. He hoped he hadn't already involuntarily shown anything in his expression. He stared at the map, trying hard to conceal his surprised disbelief. There was more than one part to the Sangman's Map, after all.

"Hmm. Interesting." was all Bill said.

"Like I said," Russell continued, "I can identify some of the landmarks, like the Rocks, of course, and the old yew tree, and some of the old Indian trails. But, for instance, what's the Wolf Pit? I went up there and couldn't find it."

Bill was grateful for a chance to focus on something other than the symbols. Maybe Russell really didn't know what the map meant. "The Wolf Pit? I haven't thought about the Wolf Pit for decades." Bill sat down at the desk. Russell looked over his shoulder.

"The Wolf Pit was, believe it or not, just what the name implies," Bill continued. "Back in the early nineteenth century, there still were some timber wolves here in this part of Pennsylvania. Not many, but there were at least a few packs still hunting in the mountains, and not too far from town, either. I think that there were sightings of packs of them as late as the 1870s or 1880s. One of my ancestors – I don't remember which one for sure, but it had to have been either my great grandfather Samuel Paxton or his father Noah Paxton – well, one of them had shot a wolf bitch with cubs. He felt really bad about that, so he somehow grabbed all the cubs and brought them home without ever really thinking about how he was going to raise a litter of wolves. Maybe he thought he could sell them. Who knows?"

"I'll bet his wife had a fit when he brought them home," Russell said.

Paxton smiled. He could see his great grandfather, or whoever it was, coming into the kitchen with a big bag of squirming, yelping wolf cubs.

"No," Bill chuckled, "the old boy had a better sense of self-preservation than to do something as dumb as bring them home. So, he dug a big pit, about four feet deep, and lined it with stone. Every couple of days, he'd hike up into the woods to the pit and toss some meat in and lower a couple buckets of water. The cubs were old enough that they could survive on that, I suppose. They instinctively set aside a corner of the pit to do their business. Wolves are very clean animals, you know. A couple of the cubs died, but the others made it. Eventually, I guess, they figured out how to climb out of the pit and ran off into the forest.

"But the pit stayed. I remember seeing it when I was a little kid, but my grandfather decided to fill it in. He was afraid someone would fall into it and get trapped. Sometimes animals would. You could hear them howling and crying to get out. Most often their cries would just attract a predator. The cries would end suddenly."

"So, this map would be from before my uncle's time?"

Russell is sharp, Bill warned himself. I need to be more careful.

Bill examined the map closely. It looked to him like a hand-drawn copy of an older, lost document.

"Maybe not," he responded. "This might be a copy. But there might still be a few old timers who could take you to where the Wolf Pit was, even without a map."

"Could you find it now?"

"Me? Not a chance, not without the map. It was too long ago, and I was just a little kid."

"What are these other markings? Any ideas?" Russell asked.

"Not a clue. They look like dates of some sort, and some of them look like some kind of code or abbreviations. But I couldn't even try to guess what they mean. Some of them look like notations that your uncle added over time. See, the ink and the handwriting are different, and the dates – if they are dates – are after the property passed out of our family."

Bill handed the paper back to Russell and watched Russell place it in a manila envelope and put it in the top right drawer of his desk.

"Hmm," Russell said, "That's what I thought."

Bill made his excuses and left as soon as he felt he could do so without being impolite. He took *Indian Wars of Pennsylvania* and the only two other books that survived from his childhood. One of them, *Treasure Island,* he cherished for its illustrations by N.C. Wyeth. He remembered that he always thought that the pictures were better than the story.

Driving home, Bill watched the shadows of evening begin to fill up the mountain valleys. This was his favorite time of day. It made him sad in a strange way he could never articulate. Unlike most twilights, today he did not feel the great peace that this time of day usually gave him.

"It's true," he said aloud as he drove into the parking lot at the Mountain View Chapel. "Praise God, it's true." Bill pounded the steering wheel. "It's true, true, true."

Bill remembered the early spring day his grandfather told him about the Sangman's treasure and the three-part map. He had just turned eleven. Mom and Dad had to go up to Corning for something, and they didn't want to take Bill. He had hoped that his grandfather would be home that afternoon. He loved to listen to the old man's stories. Unlike his grandmother's folk tales about the Indians and ancient spirits, his grandfather's tales were of great adventures of the past, of exploration, treasure, and mysteries that remained unsolved to this day. They were a little less scary sometimes because they somehow seemed less real.

As soon as he entered, his grandfather came up the kitchen steps from the basement.

"Just in time, Billy," he said. "Need your help up the mountain."

"Up the mountain" could have been anyplace. Granddad always referred to any part of his property, other than the flat lawn in front, as "the mountain." Bill hated jobs up on the mountain. They were usually long boring chores. When Bill actually was assigned a task, it had to be done to perfection. Brush had to be cleared just so. When Granddad chopped wood, it had to be stacked, and even carried, just the right way. For some reason Granddad was never himself up on the mountain. He almost never told stories. Instead, he would become silent, as if everything Bill did was annoying him.

Bill arrived home and got out of his car, still wondering why his grandfather always had to be such a perfectionist, why nobody could meet his standards – not his grandmother, not his father, and certainly not himself. Bill looked out as the first twilight collected in the small yard behind the church and in the field beyond.

That day up on the mountain with his grandfather, the last time they were together, was different. Instead of hauling shovels and pickaxes up the path, as they usually did, Granddad just carried a thin leather pouch, more like an envelope than a bag. About a quarter mile along the old Indian trail, in the direction of the river, they stopped, and Granddad took a neatly folded piece of paper out of the pouch. The paper was thick and crackled as Granddad unfolded it. He looked around, then back at the paper, and then carefully folded it up and returned it to the pouch. They went further up the trail, past the turnoff to the Wolf Pit, and up into a part of the forest that Bill had never visited before.

Granddad removed and unfolded the paper again, looked around, and replaced it.

"Are we lost?" Bill asked.

"No, Billy," Grandad had replied, smiling and squinting into the sun behind Bill's back. "I'm never lost. I'm just checking something out."

"What's that," Bill said, pointing at the leather pouch. "A treasure map?"

"Well, Billy, you might say that's exactly what it is. Yes sir, a treasure map. We can call it the Sangman's Map. But it's for a very special kind of treasure."

Granddad and Bill sat down on a fallen tree trunk. Walter Paxton told Bill about a sangman who had made his fortune harvesting the finest ginseng in the world. It grew right in these mountains, right where they were sitting, and was literally worth more than its weight in gold.

"I knew that old boy," Granddad said, winking like he always did when he didn't want Bill to be too sure that what he said was true or just a tall tale. "He and I tramped all over these ridges together when I was a kid like you."

"Did you guys go to school together?"

"Good lord, no. He was already an old man when I knew him. But he'd take me up into the woods and teach me about the mountains and all the life that's in them, both the good and the bad."

Bill looked across the church parking lot and to the mountains beyond. Good and bad: Granddad was right about that. Sometimes nobody can tell them apart.

Then Granddad told him about the treasure, hidden somewhere in the mountains, and how, long ago, the Sangman met him one November morning up on the mountain, near the Rocks.

"My time is just about over," the Sangman had said. "My mind is going. And before I lose it completely, I need to record where the treasure is to be found."

Bill smiled. He remembered how when he was a kid, he always pictured somebody losing their mind as a little marble rolling out of an ear, bouncing once or twice, and then rolling down the road, gone forever.

"It was right about at this spot, Billy, right where we're sitting now. He gave it to me in this old leather pouch, Billy. He said that he made three maps. Each was the same, but each one had only one part of the directions to the treasure. All three were needed. The Sangman told me that he was giving me one of the maps, he was giving the second one to another person he trusted, and he was keeping the third one for himself. That way, if anyone ever found out about the treasure and stole one of our maps, he wouldn't be able to find the treasure. He'd need all three parts."

"What happened to the Sangman, Granddad? Grandma said he was Uncle Johnny."

"Oh, Billy, Uncle Johnny is just a story your Grandma made up a long time ago. I'm sure the real Sangman died long before you were born, before your father was born, even."

"Did anyone find the other two parts of the map? Does anybody know where they are?"

"No, Billy, because nobody ever found out where the Sangman lived. Folks say he had a cabin up in the forest somewhere, and a couple of other camps here and there, but nobody ever found any of them. In fact, nobody knows for sure that he's dead. But he'd have to be. He was at least a hundred years old, maybe more, when I knew him when I as a boy."

"So, this is one part and the Sangman kept one part. What about the third part, Granddad? Who has that?"

"Well, I don't know, Billy. I asked the Sangman, but he wouldn't say. All he'd say was that it would be revealed in time, or something like that. So, I let it go. You just didn't ask the Sangman a lot of questions. If he got annoyed by a bunch of fool questions or he didn't want to tell you, he'd just disappear, and you might not see him again for a year or more, and, for some folks, never again. So, I don't know. In fact, I don't know for a fact that there ever were three parts to the Sangman's Map, but I know that this is one of them."

The old man looked at the map one last time, then folded it gently and returned it to the leather pouch.

"No, Billy, if there ever was a treasure, the Sangman took that secret with him to his grave. We'll never find out. Lord knows, folks have tried. But we'll never know for sure."

Bill asked his grandfather why he was checking the map now. Granddad got very quiet, his voice almost a whisper. There was a sadness on his face that Bill had never seen before.

"Billy, all of my life – or for most of it, I guess – I kept the Sangman's secret. You're the only person I ever told about the map, and I can't even tell you the whole secret, not even now."

"Didn't you ever try to go dig up the treasure?"

"No. I had given my word, Billy. And remember, you need all three parts, not just one."

"But why are you looking at it now? And why are you telling me about it now, Granddad?"

"Billy, I don't think I have much time left."

"Granddad, no. You're healthy. You'll live to be a hundred, maybe longer, just like the Sangman."

"Maybe so, Billy, but something tells me that, just like the Sangman, my time is almost up. Like I said, I always kept the Sangman's secret. But now, I just want to try to find out whether all these marks on this map mean anything at all. I know I won't find any treasure, not now. Shoot, Billy, it might all be just some tall tale. The Sangman had lots of them. But I've always believed it, all these years, and I have to be true to that. I just wanted some sign that it was real, that's all."

With that, Walter Paxton stood up and handed Bill the leather pouch.

"This is yours now. I'm entrusting this to you, Billy."

"Why not give it to Dad?" Bill asked.

"Your father's a good man in his own way, Billy, but you'll be a better man, and I know that I can trust you."

Bill had carefully tucked the leather pouch inside his flannel shirt. His grandfather silently walked a few feet away, to a bend in the Indian trail, and stood looking into the distance, to the west. Billy followed, and he thought he could just barely see part of Granddad's house, far away at the foot of the mountain.

"Sure, I believe that there's a treasure," he said. "But Billy, there comes a time when belief is not enough, when a person just has to find out. Always remember that, son. Everybody needs faith, but there comes a time when we need to know whether what we believe could be true, whether all that believing is worthwhile."

Those were the last serious words that Bill remembered from his grandfather. Still in the parking lot, enjoying the cool early evening air, Bill looked to the west, to the fading glow of the day that was ending. As he often did, he wanted to watch the stars emerge one by one. He sometimes did his best thinking watching the stars come out. It was almost like praying.

How did Simon Poe come to have part of the Sangman's Map? It could only have been left undiscovered there when the house was cleaned out after Grandma died. But how did Granddad get the second part of the map? And why hadn't Granddad given the second part to him that day, at the same time, or at least told him about the second part? And where was the third part? Maybe Russell's part of the map contained clues to find the third and final part.

Bill felt a great sadness settling on him, pushing away the happiness he had felt all afternoon, having been reunited with the books and discovering the second part of the map. He liked Russell but knew that Russell was dangerous.

The fact that Russell Poe had a piece of the map was only the latest threat. Even if Russell didn't know its significance now, he would certainly figure it out eventually. He had to be – Bill groped again for the right word – neutralized.

"Dear Lord," he prayed, "Why have I gotten myself into this? Please, please show me a way out of what I know that I must do about Russell. He's a decent man and doesn't deserve this, but Thy will be done."

Bill looked at the last traces of sunlight and wept as he sang an old hymn. He had first heard it from a wonderful old lady, Jane Mackenzie, who literally sang it on her deathbed only a few hours before she went to meet Jesus after 106 years in this life. Jane's smile was brilliant, like that of a young woman on her wedding day, and her strong voice rang out:

My latest sun is sinking fast,
My race is nearly run,
My strongest trials now are passed,
My triumph is begun.
Oh, come, angel band,
Come and around me, stand,
Oh, bear me away on your snow-white wings
To my immortal home,
Oh, bear me away on your snow-white wings
To my immortal home.

"Please, Lord," Bill sobbed to the emerging stars. "I am so unhappy. I will do what I must do. I will do Thy will. But when will my triumph begin?"

A Little Burglary

The sun would soon be rising behind the thick clouds and mist. Brendan wondered why September days often begin like this: obscured, mysterious, even a little frightening, only to turn out to be so beautiful by midday. He could hear Willy and Claw trying to approach as quietly as they could through the underbrush between the clearing and the old Indian path. Claw could move as silently as the clouds across the night sky. He had amazing grace for such a big man. Brendan chuckled at the pun but remembered just what it was that he feared about Claw: the big man's ability to approach, strike silently and quickly, and then vanish.

It was Willy who was giving them away. Willy could move through the forest more quietly than almost any other man, except Claw of course. But this morning Brendan could hear the soft whisper of leaves being bent underfoot. Each man said nothing as they approached, but Brendan could hear Willy breathing. He wasn't out of breath, but he was exerting himself. Claw, who must have weighed at least three hundred pounds, breathed like a man at rest.

As usual, it was Willy who led Claw out into the clearing. Brendan stood in front of a tree, just opposite to the direction of their sounds, so that he would present no silhouette as they approached, and his gray jacket and pants would blend into the pre-dawn light. Willy and Claw showed no surprise when he appeared to materialize from the shadows.

"Morning, Brendan," Willy said, smiling.

"Hey, Brendan," Claw said. "What's so important to bring us out here in the middle of the night?"

"Middle of the night?" Willy responded. "It's six o'clock, the day is one-quarter gone. Besides, this can be the best part of the day, man. You should try it more often."

"Well," Claw began, "maybe for you but –"

"Whom can I trust?" Brendan interrupted quietly.

"What?" As usual, Willy was going to do the talking.

"You heard me, Willy. Whom can I trust? Which of the Watchmen can be trusted with the fate of the Children?"

Willy stared at Brendan. The smile had vanished. Claw moved closely behind him.

"Why, me, of course, Brendan. You can trust me. And Claw, too. You know we've risked our lives for you."

"But who else, Willy? Who else do I have but you and Claw?"

Willy's eyes did not wander from Brendan's for even a blink. "Does it matter, Brendan? Does it really matter if you still have us?"

Willy stepped closer. He put his left hand on Brendan's right shoulder and kissed his left cheek. Brendan could not detect any alcohol on Willy's breath.

"You know we would die for you," Claw added softly. "If I died for you a thousand times, I could never pay back all that you and Willy did for me. You were there when I had nobody else." Claw's voice was trembling as he ended the sentence.

"And me, Brendan," Willy said. "You took a drunken old Marine and showed me that I could be part of something good again. You know that."

Brendan was satisfied. A large part of Willy and Claw was an act, but they really were grateful. Their relationship with him operated as it should, in a borderland between respect and fear. Brendan relaxed.

"Okay," he continued. "You guys know I trust you. I've trusted you with my life on many occasions. But tough times are coming, and our future is going to depend on people like you, people with strong souls and strong minds that I can trust."

Willy and Claw glanced at each other. Brendan could see the question on Willy's face. *What the fuck is this guy talking about?*

"I need to trust you now. From this point on, you are never to reveal anything that I am going to tell you. I don't even want you to talk about it between yourselves. Agreed?"

Willy said, "Agreed, Brendan."

"Yeah," Claw said, "agreed."

Brendan looked at Willy, watching for any expression visible in the dim light. "I have found the second part of the Sangman's map,"

Brendan said. 'I don't have it in my possession, actually, but I know where it is. And I need you two to obtain it for me."

"Shit, man," Willy said. "You brought us all the way up here to the middle of East-fucking-Geek, just to tell us you want us to do a little burglary for you? So, where's all this fucking danger and trusting us with your life come in?"

Brendan decided to ignore him.

"Russell Poe has the second part of the map," he continued.

"You mean the guy that lives up near the Rocks, the guy that we've got Rabbit watching?" Claw said. "Piece of cake."

"Not a piece of cake, Claw," Brendan said. "Russell Poe is a dangerous man." Jack Abrams was dangerous too, Brendan thought. We hadn't realized it until it was almost too late.

"How's he dangerous?" Claw asked.

"He just is, Claw. You have to trust me on this. Poe is closing in on us. He doesn't realize how close he is, not yet. But he's close. Just like Jack was getting too close."

"Come on, Brendan." Willy sounded annoyed. "Come on. Quit treating us like a couple of children. If we're going to go around committing felonies, we at least have the right to know what for."

"For the final time, Willy, you have to trust me on this. Let's just say that Poe is getting too close to too many truths: the Children, you, me, the treasure, all of it."

Claw had been looking up through the tree branches. Now his head snapped down suddenly.

"Treasure? That map you want us to get from Poe, it's a treasure map? What kind of treasure?" Claw's voice sounded excited, which was rare for the big easy-going man.

"You ever hear of the Sangman, Claw?"

"No."

"Remember he's not from around here, Brendan. Claw grew up in West Philly."

"Okay. Willy, you can tell him about the Sangman, but just what he needs to know."

"Don't you trust me, Brendan?" Claw's voice betrayed a little hurt.

"Sure, I trust you. You know that, Claw," Brendan tried to sound sincere. "This is just a matter of information security, nothing personal against you."

"For now, just find the map," Brendan continued. "It's somewhere in Russell Poe's house, for sure. People have seen it. My guess would be in his study on the second floor."

"Fuck, man," Claw grunted. "If it's a treasure map, the man's probably got it locked up in a safe or something. It ain't going to be easy. Neither of us are safe crackers. You want us to take the whole safe?"

"Slow down, Claw." Willy said, "Let Brendan explain it to us."

"That's a good question, Claw," Brendan said, "but don't worry about it. "I don't think it will be locked up, at least not in a safe. I don't think Mr. Poe has any idea of what it is. He's told people as much."

"What people?" Willy asked. "Who else knows about this?"

"Let's just say that I have some reliable information."

"From Rabbit?" Claw asked.

"No, from someone else who has seen it," Brendan replied. "But that's not important. What's important now is that we need to find out what's on that map. It's important to all the Children, a part of our heritage and a part of our future."

"But if we take the treasure map, won't he notice it's missing, even if he doesn't know what it means?" Claw asked.

"That's right, Claw. Poe's a smart man. So, this brings us to the second part of this job. Once you find it, take some pictures of it. Use a Polaroid, so you'll be sure you have some good clear photos of it and so there are no negatives that could get traced back to us somehow. Then put the map back exactly where you found it."

"Oh, I see," Claw nodded. "He'll never know we were there."

Claw was smiling. Brendan clapped him on the shoulder. "You got it, my friend," he replied. "Russell Poe's smart, like I said, and pretty observant. Our source says that he's got papers and books all over that room, piled everywhere, but he'd know if anything was disturbed. So, if you guys do your job right, he'll never know."

"Where do you want us to deliver the goods?" Willy asked.

"I'll contact you. Once you have the pictures, leave me the sign that you want to meet."

"Okay."

Brendan turned and started to walk away. He would go up over the ridge, follow the Indian trail, and hike the four miles home. It would be a beautiful morning for it, once the sky cleared and the fog lifted. Before he stepped through the blackberry thicket that hid the path to the ridge, he turned.

"And guys," he said, "Don't fuck this up."

Planning

Willy and Claw watched Brendan disappear into the woods, then they hiked down the steep slope of the mountain to the road, where they had left Claw's old car.

Willy knew it would be easy to get into Poe's house. Rabbit might be able to tell them when Poe was going to be away, but Willy didn't want to contact Rabbit, not yet. Rabbit was still an unknown factor. He had promised to keep an eye on Poe, but he was sure to get suspicious if Willy asked about Poe's movements. Brendan had said they would have to find the map without disturbing anything. This probably also meant not disturbing Rabbit with questions.

This was so like Brendan, Willy thought. The assignments that looked easy always turned out to be the most complicated.

Claw switched off the radio. Willy hadn't even noticed it had been on.

"So, what's the plan, Willy? And what's this shit about a sangman and treasure?" Claw asked. "And what the fuck's a sangman?"

"Shit, man, that's just an old fairy tale around here," Willy said. "Back about a hundred years ago or so, John Bard supposedly made a living as a sangman."

"Yeah, a sangman? What's that?"

"You've heard of them, Claw. It's a guy who goes out into the forest and gathers and sells ginseng."

"Oh, yeah, the herbal stuff."

"Yeah. Back in old times, it was supposed to be worth its weight in gold. The Chinese used it as some kind of a sex aid, like Spanish Fly. And they thought it would bring back their youth."

"Sounds like good stuff. Maybe I should go looking for it." Claw chuckled. "And John Bard was one of these sangmen?"

"That's the legend."

"I mean, *the* John Bard, *our* John Bard? Come on, man. He'd have to be over a hundred years old."

"That's what they say. He supposedly put away a pile of gold from the sang trade and has it hidden some place up in the mountains. They say it's hidden so deep in the woods that no man can remember how to get there. So, John Bard wrote out the directions in code and divided them up into three parts."

"Why three parts, Willy?"

Willy reached into the back seat, pulled two cans of beer from the Styrofoam cooler and tossed one into Claw's lap. Claw jumped slightly in his seat.

Willy took a deep drink and wiped the foam from his lips.

"Well, they say that the directions to where the gold is hidden were so complicated that no single man could memorize them all. So, John Bard wrote them down in the form of three maps, with one third of the directions on each one. He gave two of the maps to friends and kept the third one for himself. That way no one could grab the treasure all for himself."

"Yeah, but what if John Bard wanted to get at the treasure himself, you know, maybe to spend some of it?"

"I guess John Bard knows where it is, even without the other two pieces of the map."

"So why give the other two pieces away to anybody? It just don't make sense, Willy."

Willy took another sip.

"I don't know, Claw. I just don't know. There's a lot about John Bard that doesn't make sense."

"So, who did John Bard give the other two pieces to?"

"I don't know that either, Claw. I guess he might have given one of them to one of Brendan's ancestors, since he has one of the parts."

"You mean the Paxtons?"

Willy swung his right arm around and grabbed Claw by the throat. Claw slammed on the brakes.

"Hey man, what the fuck you doing? You want us to get killed?"

Willy didn't let go. His lips were less than an inch from Claw's right ear.

"Don't you ever use that name again."

"Hey, man, it's just you and me."

"I don't care, Claw. We don't betray each other, even if we know everything about our brothers or sisters. We do not betray, not even to each other."

"Come on, man."

"I mean it, Claw. I love you like a brother, but if you ever betray again, I'll rip your fucking head off. I mean it, and I know how to do it. Literally."

Willy released his grip. Claw sat silently. Claw was trying to compose himself, but Willy could see the gentle trembling up and down his body. Willy gave Claw another moment, then said softly, "Come on, man, let's get going."

They drove in silence the rest of the way to the bar where Willy had left his motorcycle. After Claw pulled the car alongside Willy's bike, he waited for Willy to get out. Willy sat looking straight ahead, waiting for Claw to say something.

"Willy," Claw was almost whispering.

"Willy," he repeated. "I'm sorry, man, about what I said back there, about Brendan."

"Maybe I just overreacted, Claw. But you really got to watch what you say."

"Yeah, I know. I just had one other question, about John Bard. Do you really believe all that shit that he's like more than a hundred years old, and the treasure and all that?"

"Sure. That's the story Brendan told me. I got no reason not to believe it."

"But Bard would have to be like the oldest guy in the world, man."

"They say he's over nine hundred years old, Claw. You know that."

"Well, yeah, I heard that, but that's just a legend, man." Claw said, "But maybe it's just symbolic, you know, like Jesus walking on water and stuff. Nobody really believes it's actually true."

"Brendan believes it, and that's good enough for me," Willy replied. "It should be good enough for you, too."

Claw lightly pounded his fist on the steering wheel, shaking his head. "No, Willy. No fucking way, man. It just does not make sense."

"It doesn't have to, Claw."

"And the treasure. You mean there's really a treasure out there in the woods?" Claw sounded hopeful.

"I'm not going to bullshit you, Claw. I just don't know. But I have to take Brendan's word for it. He's never lied to me."

"And the map? You really believe we're going to find a fucking treasure map in Poe's house? And he doesn't even know he's got it?"

"That's what Brendan says."

"The one part of the story I still don't get, Willy, is why John Bard divided the map into three parts. He gave one of them to Brendan's ancestor, kept one for himself, and gave the third one to some unknown guy?"

Willy shook his head and reached into his pocket for a cigarette. "Yeah," he said after lighting it, "and I guess somehow the third part came into Russell Poe's possession somehow. John Bard must have figured that if he kept one part of the map for himself, and he was the only one who knew who had the third part of the map, that way he'd keep control."

Claw reached behind Willy and took another can of beer from the cooler. He opened it and must have downed half of it in a single gulp.

"Wow," Claw said. "This is fucking unreal, man. Nine-hundred-year-old guys. Treasure."

"Believe me, Claw. It's real. I can't prove it to you, but I know it's real."

"And now, if Brendan can get hold of Poe's part of the map, that will give him the upper hand with John Bard," Claw said.

Willy was silent for a moment. Claw might be right. That was the amazing thing about Claw. He came across as a big dumb guy, but wheels in his head were always turning.

"No, man," Willy said, "Brendan would never go against John Bard. There must be some other reason why he wants to bring the two pieces of the map together." Willy knew he didn't sound convincing.

Willy got out of the car and closed the door quietly. He stuck his head back through the open window. Claw was looking at him strangely. Willy couldn't interpret Claw's expression, but he felt that Claw's mind was working hard.

"Don't worry about it, Claw. I'll figure out when we need to go out to Poe's house. Just be cool, and don't forget what we talked about earlier. If this Poe guy is as dangerous as Brendan says he is, we got to maintain security."

Claw started the engine. He shook his head, looking straight ahead. "This is fucking nuts, Willy. What have you gotten us into?"

"We're Watchmen, Claw. You know that. We do what Brendan tells us. You of all people owe Brendan your life. If it wasn't for him, you'd be in prison, man. Maybe even dead. Me too, probably."

"And you really believe this stuff, Willy?" Claw wasn't going to let go. "I need to hear you say it again, Willy. You really believe all this shit?"

"It doesn't matter what I believe, Claw. All that matters now is that we do what we're told."

Claw pounded the steering wheel again, shook his head, and drove away. For the first time since he met Claw, Willy felt afraid of him.

Tension Like a Silent Thick Fog

Sandy was determined to stay up all night if she had to. Sitting at the tiny Formica-topped kitchen table in her eat-in dining area of her trailer, Sandy started to take another sip of lukewarm coffee. She set the cup down, tossed her just-lit cigarette into it, and pushed it across the table. Musty coffee-smelling steam hissed up for a moment.

"You silly, naive, stupid little girl," she muttered. "Look at the mess you've gotten into, and there's no way out."

She had been almost relieved when Whitey called yesterday afternoon to cancel their date that evening.

"I'm really sorry," he said. "I picked up a little bit of work just on the other side of Towanda – not much, just a one-day job doing some landscaping and the like – but the contractor is up against a deadline or he'll lose a lot of money. So, the pay will be good, and he'll pay in cash as soon as the job's done."

Whitey claimed that he had to start work at six the next morning, so he was going over to Towanda tonight. "The boss said he'll even put me up in a motel near the site and pick me up in the morning, just to make sure I'm all rested and ready to work."

"He must be a really good guy," Sandy said. She had never heard of such an arrangement.

"Yeah, well," White said slowly, "I guess he's really in a tight spot with the project, and he said that he heard that I work fast and don't make a lot of mistakes."

Whitey said he'd stop by to see Sandy on his way home after he finished the job. He called shortly before six that evening to say that he might not be back until very late, because the job ran a little longer than he expected. They might have to work almost all night to complete the work.

"Don't worry," Sandy had told him. "I'll wait up for you." Whitey did not respond.

She really didn't want to wait up for him, and she had never felt so confused or alone in her life. Things with Whitey had been wonderful until about six weeks ago, when he started acting strangely. When she would ask him if anything was wrong, Whitey would say no, and then try to change the subject. She had planned to confront him tonight with her concerns and even a few suspicions, if he showed up. But now, sitting at her kitchen table trying to concentrate on an old issue of *People* magazine that she had taken from a doctor's office, she was trying to convince herself that she really didn't care. After all, she reasoned, she and Whitey were just a temporary thing. Eventually he'd go his own way, and she would go hers.

There had been some good things in Whitey's life recently. He appeared to have cut back on his drinking. At least there had been no more of those embarrassing calls from her father, "Just to let you know in case you're worried, dear. Whitey is going to be spending the night with us in town." That had become his cute phrase for "Whitey's drunk and sleeping it off in a cell at our station." She could almost see Ray Davis smirking as he said it. Or maybe it was unfair to think that. Sandy knew that in most places, a guy like Whitey would have been sent to the county jail for a month on some trumped-up charges like public drunkenness or disturbing the peace.

Whitey also seemed to have a steadier stream of work, good-paying work and not just day labor or odd jobs around town. He even gave Sandy a hundred dollars to buy a small microwave oven for her trailer. He was secretive about what he did to earn money, but that was just his way. "Don't worry about nothing," he would tell Sandy, "and everything will be okay."

Their relationship wasn't going anywhere permanent, but she was beginning to see a gentler, caring side to Whitey that she hadn't really noticed before and which she was starting to like. Earlier that summer Whitey had hinted that he'd like Sandy to move in with him, but she changed the subject and Whitey had not mentioned it since. She didn't want to give up her independence, not now and maybe never. But she also realized that she was beginning to care about Whitey, but not as some sort of soul mate. There was no such thing, she told herself, not in real life, at least not in her life.

"But, Sandy, for the first time in a long time, you're kind of happy," she said aloud, as she looked into the coffee cup and ran her finger around its rim. "It's not going to last, so why can't you enjoy it while you have it?"

The two dogs that lived in the next trailer started barking and whining. It was obviously supper time. A few minutes before, she thought that she had heard her neighbor drive by on the gravel road that ran through the trailer park. She smiled, thinking about how Edie always came home from her job at the coffee shop to feed them, right at seven o'clock.

Sandy walked over to the kitchen sink and watched Edie taking her two dogs out for their evening walk. She always took them into the trees, about twenty yards behind the trailers, so that they wouldn't crap all over the place. They tried very hard to be good dogs, but they were still dogs.

Maybe that explained Whitey, she thought as she returned to the table with a fresh pack of cigarettes. He tries to be good, but he's still Whitey. She lit a cigarette, took one puff, and tossed it into the sink, amazed by her own accuracy. It tasted awful. She had tried to quit smoking and had somehow conditioned herself into being revolted by the smell and taste of cigarette smoke.

The problems seemed to begin on a Saturday early last month, coming back from a picnic she and Whitey had at the "beach," which is what local people called the stony, narrow shore of Tioga Reservoir. When Whitey came into her trailer and set down the plastic cooler, he reached into his jacket and started to light a cigarette. Sandy asked him not to smoke inside, because she was trying to quit. He suddenly lost his temper and screamed about her being a bossy bitch and stormed around the close confines of the trailer yelling and waving his arms about. It had been almost like a dance, with Whitey moving around and Sandy backing up, staying just out of his reach. She was frightened. Whitey wasn't someone to lose his temper like that, certainly not over something like not smoking inside. She didn't believe that Whitey would hit her, but she was relieved when he finally stomped – literally stomped – out, slamming the door and then pushing against the side of the trailer as if he were trying to rock it. But he returned two nights later, after obviously having eaten a whole package of breath mints. His breath actually smelled worse, but Sandy didn't say anything. He stayed the night, but whenever Sandy thought about it, she had to laugh at the strong smell of peppermint on his breath, which lasted all night. Although Sandy soon realized that she was unable to follow her own rule against smoking inside, Whitey never smoked a cigarette in her presence again.

That's like everything else in your life, Sandy thought; you always break down under pressure. Whenever she felt under pressure, Sandy lit a cigarette, most of the time without thinking about it. Now, almost six weeks after declaring that she had quit smoking forever, she was still going through a pack of cigarettes – each one lit and then almost immediately discarded – every day.

An unspoken tension, almost like a silent thick fog, had come between them. The next incident, about two weeks ago, was when she found four rifles in the back of a closet at Whitey's apartment, partially hidden by some boxes of old clothes. Two of them looked like military weapons. They hadn't been there before. Sandy didn't think that it was unusual for Whitey to own a gun – most of the men she knew owned at least one – but for there to suddenly be four when there previously hadn't been any shocked her deeply for reasons she couldn't clearly explain to herself.

She asked Whitey about them, trying to be casual. It was difficult for her even to think about firearms, after having experienced second-hand, through the stories her father brought home from the police station, all the senseless damage and everlasting pain they could cause. She hated the culture in northern Pennsylvania that equated owning a gun with manhood. One evening several days after that, as they were watching television at Whitey's, she summoned up the courage to ask him. He looked a little surprised, then a little annoyed, and then said that he was just keeping them for a friend.

"Oh, who?" she asked.

"Nobody you'd know," Whitey replied, "just a friend who doesn't want to keep them at his house because his young niece and nephew are staying with him right now."

There also were all the strange phone calls that started coming into Whitey's apartment. The calls always were in the early evening. Sometimes, when Sandy was at Whitey's, she'd answer the phone for Whitey if he wasn't there or couldn't come to the phone. The first caller, who called while Sandy was waiting for Whitey to return home from work, was a man – Sandy guessed he was young – who asked for "Rabbit." When Sandy said there was nobody there by that name, the caller seemed to get flustered. He stuttered and stumbled over his words as he said that he must have dialed the wrong number and apologized. A few other times, other people called and, as soon as Sandy answered the phone, they would simply say "sorry" and hang up.

She had never remembered Whitey getting so many telephone calls before. In fact, when she had first started spending time at Whitey's apartment, she assumed that he didn't even have a telephone. One evening, shortly after the smoking argument, Whitey answered the phone, put his hand over the mouthpiece, and mumbled something into the phone.

When he returned to the couch, Sandy asked who called.

"Oh, nobody," Whitey answered, "just a guy calling about a job for me."

"Well, you're certainly a popular guy all of sudden," she commented, smiling at him, trying to communicate that she was proud of him, not suspicious.

She remembered that Whitey had that funny, puzzled look on his face when she said that, the one he often had when he was trying to think of a little lie to tell her. He nodded slowly and said only, "Well, there are a lot of little projects that people want to get finished before winter, and I need the work because there's piss-all work once winter sets in." He got up, walked to the television, and changed the channel, which Sandy took as a signal for her to change the subject.

Finally, there was her strange encounter with Whitey two days ago on the road near the old Paxton Place, where Whitey sometimes did odd jobs for Russell Poe, the new owner. She had wondered what he was really like. Whitey had talked a lot about the things that they had done together, fixing up his house, working up on the mountain behind his house, and sometimes just hanging out at the Indian Rocks telling stories to each other. In school she had seen a picture of Edgar Allen Poe and imagined that Russell looked like him. But she had never met the man, and when she suggested that sometime she could go along with Whitey and help him do chores for Poe, he refused her offer, saying that it wouldn't be proper since he was Whitey's employer and it would look like Whitey was taking advantage of him.

Sandy had been taking the fire tower road as a short-cut over the mountain and saw Whitey's truck parked about two hundred feet on the other side of a bend in the road, just above the entrance to Poe's place. She pulled up behind him, honked her horn, and waved at him. She could see him sit up in the driver's seat. Their eyes met in his rear-view mirror. Then he quickly started the engine and drove off down the road, so fast that he almost missed the sharp turn to the right. When she asked him about it that evening, Whitey said that she must have been mistaken, and that he was in Wellsboro all afternoon.

She walked over to the kitchen sink and tossed the coffee-tobacco sludge from her cup into the sink, then heated some more water for instant coffee. Something is wrong, she told herself, lighting another cigarette. She had almost convinced herself that Whitey was seeing somebody else. That would explain his going out in the evenings and being vague about the details when he came back. But if he were seeing another woman, why would Whitey always call or stop by the trailer later, sometimes around midnight? And there had never been a trace of perfume or alcohol on him, not even breath mints. Or, maybe was it just him having a guilty conscience and cleaning himself up before he arrived?

She stared into the tiny mirror on the side of one of the kitchen cabinets. She studied the face that she saw, which no longer really looked like her. She wanted to say something out loud to the strange woman in the mirror but couldn't find any words.

It had been the same way, at first, when she went to her parents' house at lunchtime earlier that day. She had to talk to somebody. Her father was clueless when it came to things that really mattered to her, but she had learned over the years that just trying to explain things to Ray, trying to get him to understand how she felt, helped her.

Ray Davis always took Friday afternoon off, walking the five blocks from the police station for lunch at one o'clock and then spending the afternoon reading or working on little projects around the house. Usually he would need to go back on duty Friday night and sometimes work all night. Sandy had planned her arrival so that Ray would already be there, and she wouldn't have to be alone with her mother. However, when she arrived at the front door, it was locked. She could hear the television inside, tuned to one of the soap operas that her mother loved. She thought about turning around and quietly leaving, perhaps coming back later when her father was sure to be home, but how would it look if he came up the front walk just as she was leaving? So, Sandy leaned on the doorbell button, to be sure that June heard the bell over the television. It took almost a minute for June to come slowly to the door and pull away the lace curtain on the tall narrow window on the left side of it, just enough so that she could see clearly outside. Sandy then heard locks being unlocked, clicking back and forth several times as June opened the door.

"Hi, Mama," Sandy said, giving June a light hug and a kiss on the cheek. "How are you? Is Daddy home yet?"

He wasn't. June led Sandy into the living room, turned off the television, sat on the sofa, and motioned for Sandy to sit beside her.

"Your father will be home presently," June said. "He was detained by something important at his office, but called me to say not to worry, just like he always does. This will give us a time to talk, Sandra. You know, we almost never have a chance to talk like we used to."

Sandy nodded. The problem was that June was no longer in touch with reality long enough to carry on a conversation. Instead, she would either become stone silent or would ramble off into disconnected bits of stories about her life long ago.

"You know, Sandra," June said, lightly slapping her hand on Sandy's leg. Sandy jumped slightly in surprise. "You know, I was just thinking this morning about your friend Whitey Wentworth. I hadn't thought about him for years.

"I do hope that you're not involved with him," she continued, "romantically, I mean." She smiled at Sandy and raised her eyebrows slightly, suggestively Sandy thought. "I mean, Sandra, I have been picking up little bits of information here and there. Oh, I'm not just a poor old shut-in like some people think I am. I hear things. I have my sources."

"No, Mama, we're just friends, that's all." Sandy could feel a warm anger slowly build up inside her. Why not just tell June that she and Whitey are lovers, that they were going at it in bed all day and all night? Maybe that would somehow shock June back to reality a little, like the electric shock therapy she said that she had been given at the hospital. June had this crazy obsession about Whitey Wentworth.

"That's just as well, honey." June said. "I mean it's okay to have Whitey as a friend because he can be so charming." June smiled and looked off to her right, in the direction of the front door.

"I'll tell you a secret, but only if you promise never to breath a word of this to your father or anyone else, but especially not to your father."

"I promise, Mama."

"Well, you know a long time ago – maybe I already told you this, but I don't remember so I'll tell you again – Whitey Wentworth and I went to high school together, and he was sort of sweet on me, even though he was younger than me." Sandy smiled. She had heard that story before and she knew that wasn't true, because she had always been told that her mother had grown up in Ithaca, where she met her father when he was an undergraduate and she worked in the university library.

"And then he went away, and I didn't see him for many years, until he showed up one night at a little group that I belonged to."

"What group was that, Mama? Was it around here?" Sandy began to feel happy that her mother was at least able to piece together a story in more or less a straight line, even if it was a complete fairy tale.

June smiled, looking like someone remembering happy times long ago. "It just was that lovely little group I think I told you about before. I forget now the little name we had for ourselves, but we'd go out on lovely picnics and sometimes even campouts up in the mountains, and sometimes stay out under the stars all night."

"Sounds lovely, Mama. And Whitey was in that group?"

"Oh dear, I must have gotten all confused," June said suddenly. "No, Whitey wasn't my sweetheart then. It was a man named John. It's funny, Sandra, but I can't for the life of me remember his last name. But he was the leader of our group. He even called me his queen – that's the word he used, *queen* – although we never were together like husband and wife, except that one time.

"Or maybe we were together more than that one time." June, continued. "And late at night I sometimes think about the child I had with Whitey."

"What!" Sandy almost shouted. "Mama, please, you're just imagining things again." June seemed to ignore her interruption.

"John and Whitey and I spent the night up on a mountain just near here," she continued, her face turned to the window. Her hands were together under her chin, as if in prayer. "It was a beautiful night, with lots of stars shining through the branches of the trees and shooting stars and all. And the three of us made love. John and Whitey took turns with me, again and again and again. Or at least I think they both did. Yes, I know they both did, because I could sort of leave my body and float over us and watch them make love to me, one then the other, and I could still feel all the pleasure again and again and again, all night long. We fell asleep, all three of us together, and when I woke up in the morning, John had left, and Whitey took me home."

"Where was Daddy when all this was going on?" Sandy asked.

"Oh, your father never really noticed my comings and goings. He spent most of his time at the station. He was just a patrolman back then. That night up on the mountain, he was down in Harrisburg for the weekend at some special police training of some sort. He never knew. Oh, he's a very smart man, your father. If he had really cared about it, he could have found out easily enough, even though our little group liked to keep things secret."

June paused. She wiped a tear from her eye and looked out the window again. She reached over and took Sandy's hands in hers. She was smiling, one of the special radiant smiles that Sandy used to see on her mother's face many years ago.

"And nine months later – you were seven at the time – I gave birth to our child."

Sandy felt sick with disgust that her mother could sit here in the home she had shared with her father for so many years and enjoy such a fantasy, but she had to hear more.

"So, who was the father? John or Whitey?" she could not help but asking. "Do you know?"

"Why, Sandra, it was Whitey Wentworth, of course. No question about it. I just know it."

"Then what about this John person?" Sandy asked. She wanted so much for her father to come home and rescue her from this craziness, but she also wanted to keep June talking, talking about anything, even sickening nonsense like this. As long as June was talking, her mind was working. Just tell yourself, Sandy thought, that you are listening to all this as a kindness to the person your mother used to be.

"Well, John took the baby, saying that I was his queen and the child was his and that it was holy in some strange way and had to be taken away, where it would not be harmed by the world. But I knew that the father was really Whitey."

"It?" Sandy asked. "You called the child *it*. Was it a boy or a girl? Do you remember."

"No," June said. "I never got to see my baby. When the time came, John came here and took me back up into the mountains. I gave birth in a clearing in the mountains, one beautiful autumn afternoon – a day a lot like today. There were two women there who were like midwives. When I delivered, John took the baby away. The two women gave me some medicine and I fell asleep while they sang old songs to me and stroked my hair. Sometime later, when I woke up, Whitey was there, and he brought me back home."

"And did you ever see John again?" Sandy asked. "Or Whitey?"

"Whitey?" June looked puzzled. She started to speak rapidly, her voice almost dreamlike. "Why I haven't been with Whitey since then. Or, maybe, yes, maybe there was that one time when we went alone back up to the Indian Rocks and he and I made love all night. Oh, Whitey was such a wonderful lover." June sighed.

At that point Sandy wanted to leave, to walk out, slam the front door, and never see her mother again. Her mother didn't mean to be cruel, but every word of her fairy tale about Whitey was making her angrier, word by word. She didn't know whether she was angry with her mother or herself. Sandy could give her mother the benefit of the doubt, but she couldn't take any more of it, and she started to get up.

"Mama, I don't have to sit here and listen to this crazy talk," Sandy said quietly, trying to control her voice.

June seemed to ignore her.

"Or maybe it was John all along somehow taking the shape of Whitey. He could do that, you know. He told me he was a special kind of spirit. This was years later, right after I came home from the hospital that time. No, it was before the hospital, before. I think that your father found out about us and had me put in the hospital for that little while."

"Mama, you just said that Daddy didn't know about this. Please slow down," Sandy said. "You're confusing me. You're confusing yourself. Just stop it. Stop it!"

June was starting to get visibly agitated. Her hands were moving back in forth like tiny windshield wipers. Her head was nodding side to side.

"Oh, I don't know, Sandra. I just don't know. I have all these pictures in my mind, all these memories, and it's like when you change TV channels real fast and see just a tiny bit of this show and a tiny bit of another one. Oh, it's all jumbled up, Sandra. Everything is all jumbled up."

Sandy sensed a quiet presence behind her at the entrance to the living room. It was her father. She didn't know how long Ray had been standing there, silently listening.

A Kitchen Table Investigation

"Hi, Daddy," Sandy said, turning around to face Ray. "I didn't hear you come in."

"Sandy, this is a surprise," Ray smiled. "Hello, June. How are things going today?"

"Oh, this has been a good day," June said. She touched the back of Sandy's shoulder. "Sandra came to visit."

"So, I see," Ray said. "What brings you here, Sandy? You usually call first."

"Well, I have things to do," June said, turning around and walking toward the stairs that led up to the bedrooms. "Lots of things to do. So little time. So many things. So many things." She was almost singing the last words as she went up.

Ray shook his head sadly. "That's fine, June. You just rest now. We'll get everything done, just like we do every Friday afternoon."

June's voice tumbled down the stairs from the landing. "I didn't get a chance to fix your lunch, Raymond, what with talking with Sandra and all, and you saying that you'd be late. I didn't know what to do. I had so many things to do." Her voice faded.

"Don't worry about it, dear," Ray called up the stairs.

Ray bowed his head for a minute, his eyes closed. He sighed, opened his eyes, and looked at Sandy.

"I'm sorry I didn't call first," Sandy said. "I just wanted to talk to you about something, and I knew you'd be home about now. You always are on Friday afternoon. I hope I'm not intruding or anything."

Sandy disliked the sharp tone she heard in her voice. Ray looked hurt for a moment.

"I'm sorry, Daddy," she said softly. "That didn't come out right."

"You seem upset about something, Sandy," Ray said. "I hope your mother didn't upset you. I heard some of it when I came in."

"No, I don't want to think about it anymore," Sandy replied quickly, at the same time realizing that she had to talk about it more. That's why she was there.

"I mean, you know how she gets like that. All those stories she likes to tell. She doesn't mean anything by it, Sandy."

"But she has this thing about Whitey Wentworth," Sandy said. "It's like some kind of an obsession or something. And she says terrible, crazy things about him."

"Yeah, I know, Sandy. And all those stories about the White Indians or whatever they are. You know none of that's real. That's just her mental illness. She just makes up stories about the last person she hears about or thinks about. You came here and for some reason your relationship with Whitey set her off, got her going like she did. There's nothing real there, not anymore."

"Isn't there, Daddy?" Sandy said. "Nothing at all? She makes it sound like she and Whitey were having a good old time behind your back." Sandy smiled, turned her head slightly, and looked at Ray from the corner of her eye and winked. She hoped he realized that she was joking. Ray showed no reaction. "Sounds like I even have a half-brother or half-sister I didn't know about."

"Well, I'm sorry, Sandy. You know your mother loves you and is just trying to look out for you as best she can, given how she is. And I also want you to know that there's not a bit of truth to all those crazy stories. I would know if there were."

"I know," Sandy said. "I also know that it's got to be hard on you."

"No, Sandy, surprisingly it's not," Ray said. Sandy thought she detected a little tremble in his voice. "I made vows with your mother many years ago, and I renew them every day to myself. I'm going to be there for her, helping as best I can, showing as best I can that I love her no matter what, and –"

His voice trailed off. Sandy couldn't hear the rest of what he said. He sat down on the sofa, where June had been sitting earlier.

"Come on, Sandy," he said, patting the couch with his palm. "I'm really glad to see you. Like I said earlier, what brings you here?"

"Whitey."

"You mean the stuff your mother was telling you about him? Please, Sandy, let that go. That's just a poor woman's – I don't know

– fantasy? Delusion? You know she probably should be institutionalized, what with her schizophrenia and all, but I couldn't allow that to happen, not permanently. She's such a gentle soul and –"

"No, Daddy, what I have to tell you about, ask you about, is all real. At least, I'm pretty sure it is." She sat down in her father's chair across the coffee table from Ray.

"Gosh," Ray said. "You sound like it's serious. What's wrong, Sandy? What can I do to help?"

"I really don't know where to start," Sandy said.

"The beginning is usually the best place," Ray said quietly.

"That's the problem," Sandy said. "I don't know where it begins, and I don't know where it's going to end."

"Can I get you something to drink? Maybe some coffee?" Ray said, starting to get up. "It will only take a minute to make some. I can even give you something a little stronger, if you like."

"No," Sandy said. "No, I'm fine. Just quit fussing. I know you're just trying to be helpful and all, but just please listen and let me try to get it all out."

"Okay," Ray sat back in the couch. He crossed his arms and then suddenly unfolded them, putting his hands on his thighs. "Okay."

"Daddy, I need your advice. Now please don't make any of your little digs about how this is a first or I never ever showed that I even gave a damn about what you thought about things. That was all different. And don't think that I don't appreciate what you've tried to do for me. And I don't doubt that you always loved me and meant well."

"Sandy, I wasn't going to say anything. Please, go on."

"Well," Sandy took a deep breath. "I think that Whitey's gotten into some kind of trouble with some bad guys."

"Bad guys? What kind of bad guys? What makes you think that?" Ray said. "Go on, why do you think Whitey's in trouble?"

Sandy could hear the faint dialogue from a soap opera on the television in her parents' bedroom. She couldn't make out what the man and woman were saying.

Ray turned and looked toward the stairs. "Listen," he said, "why don't I just go up and ask your mother to turn that down or close the door."

"No, that's okay."

Sandy described the recent experiences with Whitey: the strange telephone calls, his sudden disappearances, the sudden money, and the episode when she found him parked on the road near the old Paxton place, obviously watching something, and then how he had denied it.

Ray nodded several times but didn't say anything.

"So, what do you need to know?" he finally said.

"I don't know," Sandy said. "But doesn't that all sound strange to you? Aren't there any clues there of something illegal going on, or maybe planned, something that maybe the department has heard about. I know Whitey's got sort of a shady reputation around town, but I'm worried that he's going to get sucked into something without knowing it."

"Well, Sandy," Ray said. "First of all, I've known Whitey Wentworth longer than you have – maybe not as well, but longer. Yeah, he's got a reputation as the town drunk and likes to play the village idiot sometimes, but he's nobody's fool. He's a smart guy. I can't go into any details, but he's helped us a couple of times with some information. So, I wouldn't worry about Whitey getting sucked into anything, at least not anything really serious.

"There's nothing unusual about anything he told you, not on the face of it. Take his overnight absences, for example. I'm not the county building inspector, but it's fall, and I know there's a lot of pressure to finish up some projects before the weather gets bad. We get complaints down at the station about the noise from work on Sunday mornings."

"But all the way over in Towanda?"

"Yeah, there too, I'm sure. Like you, I never knew Whitey had such a reputation for being a skilled craftsman that people would be calling him up to go out of town on a job and putting him up in a motel, but it's possible, I suppose."

"But can't you do something, Daddy, like keep an eye out for him or check some things out?"

"Honey, I can't open an investigation if there's no evidence of a crime, and I haven't heard anything that would make me the least bit suspicious of him or that these bad guys that you're worried about even exist. I'm not a private detective. Sure, he's done some strange things – well, maybe not strange, but not like him – recently, and it's okay to be concerned. But, in my experience, most of these things have a completely innocent explanation."

"So, you're not going to do anything?" Sandy said, as she reached for her purse. "Then I'm sorry if –"

"No, I never said I wasn't going to do anything. Let's go sit at the kitchen table so I can ask you a few questions and make some notes." Ray stood up and walked into the kitchen. He sat at the table, took off his jacket, and produced a notebook. Sandy looked at him, not sure what to expect. He gestured for her to sit down across the table from him.

"Now, Sandy," he said, sounding like a teacher trying to explain something to a slow student. "You have to understand that I just can't go around investigating things based only on hunches, even if those suspicions seem reasonable. I've got to follow some procedures, or they'll have my head."

"Who'll have your head?"

"Well, the DA for one. She keeps close tabs on investigations in the county and gets a little nasty when they don't produce anything. And she tells the Borough Council and then they get all over me about wasting taxpayers' money on a lot of dead-end cases. And remember, dear, that I've got only five full-time sworn officers, and we're the largest police force in the county, and two of those guys moonlight in a couple of the outlying townships. And on top of that, we're always being asked to back up the police in the townships and smaller boroughs. Some of them don't even have a single full-time officer."

I really don't need this lecture, Sandy thought, but she just nodded and said, "I understand. I'm not sure if there's any real evidence or anything there, but maybe it might fit into something else. I don't know. I just don't want to see Whitey get into trouble or into some kind of danger, that's all."

"Well, let's see what there is, Sandy." He opened his notebook.

"There are a couple of things that you mentioned that I'd like to ask you a few questions about, if you know the answers," he said.

"Well, sure." Sandy was a little surprised at his business-like tone, almost like the cops on television. She had assumed that he hadn't really been paying attention and was only trying to be polite just to soothe her fears. But he seemed to switch instantly from his father mode into his police mode. Maybe this is serious, she thought.

"I'm interested in the phone calls," he continued. "You might not know this, but it's a felony in Pennsylvania to repeatedly make threatening or harassing telephone calls, especially anonymous ones. Now, you said that these calls were made to Whitey's apartment."

"That's right."

"And you were there, and you answered some of them?"

"Yes."

"Where was Whitey? Why didn't he answer them?"

"Well, on two of the days, I had gotten there early, and he wasn't home from his job yet. And the other time he was in the john. And then there were a few calls that he answered and mostly listened and then hung up. He said they were telephone sales calls, you know, like for magazines and such."

Ray continued to ask her about specific dates and times. Where had Whitey been working those days? Did he say anything about the calls? Sandy hadn't expected to be – the only word that came to her mind was *interrogated* – by her father. She didn't remember the answers to a lot of the questions.

"I think it was –" she began to say in response to one of them. Ray slapped his hand on his open notebook. She jumped a little.

"No. No guesses. None of this *I think it was,*" he said. "I need facts, not guesses. If you don't remember, just say so. That's fine. The fact that you don't remember something is important information, just as much as a detailed description of a criminal."

"Okay, I'm sorry Chief." Sandy said, smiling. Ray did not seem to notice.

"Did he ever mention any similar calls that he received anyplace else?"

"Well, where would he get –" Sandy started to ask.

"Your place, for example."

"No, not that I know about. Whitey has never been to my place when I wasn't there, and I surely didn't get any weird calls like that."

"Okay," Ray said. "Now let's go back to that first call, when the caller asked for 'Rabbit'."

"That's right." Sandy felt more relaxed.

"Did you ever hear anyone call Whitey *Rabbit*? Or maybe Whitey had a friend whose nickname was Rabbit?"

"No, never."

"When these people called, did they use any other animal names?"

"No."

"Or any other names at all?"

"Well," Sandy paused for a moment, trying to remember as accurately as she could. "I think one time they asked for Whitey by name. But all the other times, when I answered the phone, they'd just hang up without saying anything." Sandy said. "Is there anything about the names that means anything? Are they gang names or something?"

"No, Sandy, I'm just a little curious, that's all. And one last thing, I believe that you said that it seemed to be different people who called. Can you tell me anything about the voices?"

"Well, the first call, the guy who asked for 'Rabbit,' he sounded like a young guy, with a little bit of a high voice."

"Could it have been a woman?' Ray asked. "I know I'm asking you to speculate a little, but it will help understand better what the caller sounded like."

"No, I don't think so. I'm pretty sure it was a guy."

"And the others – the ones who called and asked for Whitey – were those men's voices?"

"Yes, definitely."

"Were there any accents, like a foreign accent or Southern or somebody from New York City?"

"No, nothing like that. They all sounded just like people from around here."

"And you said there were some calls when they hung up as soon as you answered?"

"Yes, there were at least five, maybe six, like that."

"In any of those calls, both the ones where somebody said something and the ones when they just hung up, did you hear any background noises of any kind?"

"No, I'm sorry."

"No, that's okay, Sandy. I just want to get as many facts as I can, just in case there's something going on that I should know about. I'm not saying that there is. I don't want you to get worried because of the questions that I'm asking. I just want to find out whatever I can.

"Two last questions about the phone calls, Sandy. You've already told me as best as you can remember, what the callers said to you."

"Well, it wasn't much."

"I know. But did they say anything that you felt was threatening or menacing?"

"No, they were all very polite."

"And when you asked Whitey about the calls he had taken, he told you they were just sales calls, like telemarketing?"

"That's right."

"And when you asked Whitey about the calls, did he give any indication to you that he was frightened or felt threatened by them or even annoyed?"

"No, but I had a sense that he wasn't telling me the truth about the calls. But no, he didn't act scared or even bothered by them."

Ray gestured to his left to the refrigerator. "Can I fix you something to eat, or get you something to drink? Do you need to take a little break?" Sandy felt a little annoyed that he said "need to take" instead of "want to take."

No, she thought, he's humoring me. He's making fun of me. So, you want to play cops and robbers, little girl? Here's how we do it in the grownup world. She wanted to leave.

Instead, Sandy said, "No, I'm fine, Daddy. I know you're just trying to help."

"Well, this won't take much longer," Ray said, smiling for the first time since they had moved to the kitchen.

"Well, what about him spying on Mr. Pope?" Sandy had almost forgotten about it.

"It's Poe," Ray said. "And thanks for reminding me about it."

"Yes, of course, Mr. Poe," Sandy continued. "I guess I'm a little nervous about all this. But what do you know about Mr. Poe?"

"Oh, so now it's your turn to ask the questions," Ray said, smiling. Sandy smiled back. "I'm being schooled by a master, Daddy." She hoped that Ray caught the slight note of sarcasm in her voice.

"Well, I know Mr. Poe," Ray said quietly, apparently ignoring her last remark. "He's a lawyer and writer who moved here from Philly about a year and a half ago. He's consulted me on a legal matter he was handling. He appears to be a quiet, honest person who sort of keeps to himself."

"But Whitey was spying on him."

"Come on, Sandy," Ray said. "We don't know that. In fact, you can't even be sure it was Whitey you saw parked on the fire tower road. For example, how close –"

"Oh, no," Sandy interrupted. "I know it was him." Why didn't her father believe her? She began to feel frustrated, maybe a little angry. When will he stop being a cop and start being a father? He'd believe anyone else who reported that, why not her?

"Okay," Ray said. "okay. Let's talk about Whitey and Russell Poe. I know, for example, that Whitey sometimes does odd jobs for Mr. Poe."

"That's right," Sandy said. 'He sometimes mentions Mr. Poe – Russell as he usually calls him."

"What does he tell you about his relationship with Russell Poe?" Ray was flipping through his notebook. Sandy could see that almost all the pages were filled with her father's tiny neat writing.

"Most of it is just ordinary handyman work, he says, nothing to talk about. But sometimes he talks about the work he and Russell – Mr. Poe – do together at the Indian Rocks. He says they're on Mr. Poe's land and that the two of them have been clearing the area out and doing some measurements or excavations or such like there. He says that Russell calls him his research assistant and pays him a little extra for it."

"Excavations? You mean digging?" Ray asked. He sounded surprised.

"Well, I don't know what kind of excavations," Sandy said. "It didn't sound that interesting to me. Whitey said it mostly involved making a lot of measurements and sifting dirt for old Indian things."

"Let's go back for a minute to the time you believe you saw him parked near Mr. Poe's house, up on the fire tower road. Do you know of any reason why he would be spying on Russell Poe?"

"Spying? I never said he was spying."

"Well, yes, you just did, but that's okay. Let's just treat it like a 'what if' type of question – we call them hypotheticals – to help me understand his relationship with Mr. Poe and what you believe that you saw."

"Well, no, Daddy. I mean Whitey doesn't talk a lot about Russell – Mr. Poe – but he's always said nice things about him. He told me about some of the old Indian tales that Mr. Poe told him. Apparently, Mr. Poe collects those stories. Whitey says that Mr. Poe is writing some sort of a book, that a former neighbor of his started but died before he could finish it."

"What type of stories, Sandy?" Ray started flipping through his notebook.

"Well, he never told me a lot of them. They sounded pretty boring to me. I do remember him one time coming home from working at Russell's place and, after a couple of beers, he told me that he thinks that Russell might have come across some old information about a treasure that his grandfather – Whitey's grandfather – always claimed that he had hidden up in the mountains somewhere."

"That doesn't sound boring to me, Sandy. Tell me more."

"No, that's all he said. A little later that night he told me not to take the treasure story seriously, that he didn't believe any of it because his grandfather was just a crazy old sangman who eventually went nuts from alcoholism."

"Did Whitey ever tell you why he and Mr. Poe were doing that work at the Indian Rocks?"

"No, is that important?"

"No, not really. I was just a little curious, but it makes sense, what with the Rocks being on his property."

Ray reached into his jacket pocket and took out a red pen. Sandy could see him underlining things in his notes and drawing a couple of arrows. Ray looked up and apparently noticed, because he shifted his left hand so that she could not see.

He closed the notebook and looked up, staring at Sandy for a few seconds, as if he was wondering whether he should say something.

"Sandy," he said quietly. "I know that you don't want to talk about the next thing that I want to discuss with you, but there are some things I need to know."

"Father," Sandy said, "I do not want to discuss my personal relationship with Whitey Wentworth. I know that you and Mama don't approve, that you both think that he's too old for me, has a bad reputation, and will only cause me trouble."

"No," Ray said. "No, that's all your business, Sandy. You're an adult woman with a life of your own that you need to live. No, what I want to know is whether Whitey has ever mentioned anything about – well, about a group like the one that your mother is always talking about?"

"I thought that you said that the White Indians, or whatever they're called, aren't real, that they're just something she made up."

"Not entirely, Sandy. Now please listen very carefully, because I don't want you to make more of what I'm going to tell you than what are the basic facts. You're right that most of those stories are just old legends and tall tales. But some of them sometimes are based on one or two facts that have gotten all twisted around."

"You mean all that stuff that Mama has been saying, about White Indians, and Whitey and her – some of that's true?"

"No," Ray said quietly. "That business about her and Whitey and that other guy, John Bard, having been lovers – all that is part of her delusions. Over the years, especially since your mother has been ill, there hasn't been a day go by but what she hasn't talked about the White Indians, or sometimes the Children, as she calls them. Sometimes she has –" Ray took a breath.

"Sometimes she has even told me in graphic detail how Whitey was a better lover than me. The woman has quite an imagination, and I love her for it even when it hurts. But almost none of that is true. It couldn't possibly have happened."

"So, why are you telling me this, Daddy? I know that Mama's sick. I remember the old days when she was a different person. I miss that person so much." Sandy felt the tears welling up. She quickly ran an index finger along each lower eyelid.

"We all do," Ray said. "But what I want to ask you about is whether Whitey has ever mentioned any groups like that – not that he belongs to any of them, but even if he has ever heard of them. I ask, because he seems to know so much of what is, well, hidden around here."

"No, not that I recall. Why?"

"Well, Sandy, I've got to trust you now. You came to me, and so I owe you this. There apparently is a secret society of sort, some type of cult, that operates around here –possibly more than one. You know those stories that your mother sometimes tells about ceremonies and sex rituals and gang rapes and the like up in the mountains at night?"

"You mean that –" Sandy started to say.

"Well, these probably are just coincidences, Sandy, but over the past few years, we have had occasional incidents up near the Indian Rocks. You might remember the man who ran the insurance office who was found dead up on the mountain, and a couple other people have been found in the forests badly injured or, in one case last winter, left out to die in the cold. Then, a couple months ago we had a serial rape complaint from a young woman who claims that she was drugged and taken up onto a mountain. From where she was picked up afterward by a passerby on the road, I believe that it was somewhere at or near the Indian Rocks. She described being raped multiple times by two or three men in a sort of ceremony a lot like what your mother was telling you about when I came in."

"What happened? Did you catch the guys that did it?"

"This is the tough part, Sandy," Ray said quietly. "There was no corroborating physical evidence from the exam they did on her at the hospital, and the toxicology report said that she might have ingested a sufficient quantity of drugs to have hallucinated the whole thing. After reporting it to us and making a statement, the victim changed her mind and said she no longer wanted to cooperate, and she left town. I'm still carrying it as an open case, but it's at a dead end. Even if she changed her mind, there's nothing the DA can take into court.

"All these cases went nowhere – no corroborating witnesses, ambiguous physical evidence, nothing – even the death case. You might remember it: the man who they say was attacked and killed by wolves about six years ago."

"Oh, yeah. I remember. But you don't think that Whitey –" For the first time ever, Sandy felt afraid of Whitey.

"No," Ray said, reaching across the table to touch her arm. Sandy took his hand. "No, I don't think that Whitey was involved in that incident. He gave us a statement because he happened to be with the victim a few hours before he was killed.

"But it is possible – just possible – based on what you told me that there might be some connection between him and such a group. I've known Whitey for a long time, like I said, and I know that he's not a violent man, even when drunk. But he might be involved somehow with this group, or maybe at some other time in the past might have been involved with them.

"You have nothing to worry about from him. But I'm glad you shared this with me, Sandy. I know that you're genuinely concerned, and it took some courage on your part to tell me this."

"What's the next step?" Sandy asked.

"Well, like I said, I don't have anything new upon which I can justify opening a formal investigation. But the next step in the process would be for you to make a formal statement, over at the station, just like any other citizen. You and I could even walk over together right now and take care of it, if you're free, or you could come in any time that's convenient for you. Then we will file it and cross-reference it to anything we hear involving gangs or group criminal activity. That's about all we can do at this point. There's nothing to go on right now, but your statement could help us build a foundation in the future."

"But I don't want to make any statement accusing Whitey of anything."

"Based on what you told me, Sandy, there's nothing to accuse him of – just some observations of uncharacteristic behavior, that's all. You don't need to do anything right away, if you want to think about it. I'll keep my notes to myself, and nobody will find out what you told me, at least not from me. But without a formal statement from you, there's nothing else that we can do."

Sandy tried to conceal her growing anger. "I'll think it over. Like you said, there's probably nothing there. But thanks for listening."

As Sandy was walking toward the front door, June came down the stairs. She stopped at the bottom and waved.

"It was so nice to see you today, Sandra. Do come again. And be sure to wish your boyfriend a Happy Samhain."

Ray and Sandy looked at each other. Samhain? Or had June said *Sam Haynes,* maybe some imaginary character that her mother knew or thought that Whitey knew? Neither Ray nor Sandy said anything in response.

For the first time in years, Ray and Sandy hugged tentatively. Sandy hoped that he didn't notice her pulling away. Then Sandy waved goodbye at her mother.

"Bye Mama. Stay well."

It was now past nine p.m. The kitchenette was completely dark, except for the light from a streetlight coming through her living room window, filtered by the venetian blinds and the still-open curtains that cast faint moving shadows on the wall. Thinking back on the day, Sandy still wasn't sure that her father had been any help. At least he had listened carefully and pretended to take her seriously before patting her on the head and sending her home. She was more confused and worried than ever. It's all made up, he told her, by her crazy mother, except for maybe a little bit. And there might be gang rapists running around loose in the mountains.

"Screw Whitey," she said, picking up her purse and car keys. "That stupid bastard's running around with some woman he's picked up at a roadhouse somewhere. He's probably going to show up at three in the morning, wanting me because he struck out at closing time." She realized she didn't use the word *cheating,* because she didn't own him any more than she was committed to him. She also realized that she had been talking out loud to herself more than she used to do.

Sandy saw the lights on in Edie's trailer. She walked over to see if Edie would like to go to the Valley Inn for a couple of drinks and talk about what shits men were – boyfriends, bosses, fathers, whatever. She made sure that both of the locks on her door were locked. Whitey had a key only to one of them.

Jack's Death

Wanda looked out the window, waiting for Russell to arrive. She thought for a moment that there was a problem with her eyes. The vivid colors of mid-October all seemed to her to have turned gray. She closed her eyes tightly and reopened them, hoping for the color to return. Ever since Russell telephoned earlier that afternoon, Wanda had dreaded this moment that she knew was almost upon her. She had dreaded it for endless, countless hours and days and years ever since Jack was killed. She drank a glass of wine while she looked out the window in disbelief at the dreary, death-like afternoon, as she mentally replayed the phone conversation from several hours before.

"Wanda," Russell had said, his voice husky but very calm, "I'm ready to tell you what I think happened to Jack."

She hadn't known what to say or even what to feel.

"Wanda, are you there?"

"Yes, Russell, I'm here."

"I think I know how Jack died. Can I come over this evening?"

"Can you come over now? Can you at least tell me a little bit over the phone, so I can prepare myself?"

"No, I can't. We need to be face to face when I tell you what I've learned. And I still have one or two last details to double check this afternoon. I'm at Chief Davis's office right now. But I'm sure that I know what happened."

"Chief Davis?" Wanda gasped. "Why are you seeing him? Was it –" She couldn't finish the sentence.

"Wanda, let's not jump to conclusions until I have the chance to get it all organized and we can go through it step by step. I'm sorry. Maybe I shouldn't have mentioned Chief Davis. I didn't mean to upset you. There are just a couple of details I want to be sure that I understand, that's all."

Wanda was standing at the door waiting for Russell when he drove up. In fact, she had been standing in the front of the house, looking out the window for much of the time since Russell called.

She silently held the door open. Their usual greeting, a prolonged handshake or, more recently, a quick, partial hug, was omitted. Russell walked straight into her living room. He took off his woolen tweed sports jacket and draped it over the back of Wanda's couch, where he sat down. He gestured for Wanda to sit next to him on his right. Instead, she moved one of the living room chairs around to the opposite side of the coffee table, sat down, and tried to look into his eyes while he gathered his thoughts. He doesn't know how to begin, she thought. She had never seen his eyes so sad.

"Wanda, let me start by saying that I can't prove anything that I'm going to tell you, at least not in a court of law. All I have are little scraps of circumstantial evidence here, a possible inference or two there. But, as Sherlock Holmes used to say, when you have eliminated all the possible explanations except one, what remains must be the correct theory, no matter how implausible."

Wanda smiled. Had Russell learned how much Jack had loved the Sherlock Holmes stories? She didn't remember ever mentioning them.

"Let me say something first, Russell." Wanda reached across the coffee table and took Russell's hand. She held it lightly with both of her hands. Russell's face was serious, his eyes constantly looking at her. "No matter what you have to tell me, I want it to be the whole truth. Don't hold anything back for fear of hurting me. I've had so much hurt in my life, so much pain every day for all these years, that a little more won't make any difference."

Russell continued to look silently into her eyes.

"I also want you to know, Russell, that whatever you tell me, I don't plan to take it any further. It would only open old horrible wounds deep inside me, and it wouldn't help Jack. So, we can be honest with each other."

Russell swallowed, took a breath and began. Wanda had decided that, while he talked, she would say nothing. She would only look into his eyes, hoping that somehow she might see some little part of Jack as Russell talked about him.

Stop it, she thought. Stop it! You can't get all emotional now. You have to listen with every bit of your attention. You will never want to hear this again, so pay attention now.

"Wanda, both theories are true."

"What? Both theories? What are you talking about, Russell?" Wanda could not restrain herself. Then she immediately felt foolish, like some quarrelsome old lady. "I'm sorry," she said quietly.

"I'm sorry, Wanda," Russell said, sounding frustrated. "I'm not making a good start of this. I mean, the theory that Jack was attacked and killed by a wild animal or a pack of them is probably what happened. At the same time, I am also convinced that it was foul play.

"Let me get the painful part of it out of the way first. And if you don't want to talk about it, or want to take a break, or not go into any details about anything, just stop me, okay?"

"Okay."

Russell paused and looked down. "There's no good way to lay this all out, so I'll just start. You never had to identify Jack's body, did you? You told me that you never saw him after he was found."

Wanda nodded. She felt the tears build up in her eyes. She suddenly found herself struggling so hard to keep her voice under control. She looked away, at a vase of fall flowers on a table by Jack's old chair.

"No, that's not entirely true, Russell." She turned back to look at him. "I don't know why I lied to you about this. Maybe I was too frightened by the pain that I knew that thinking about it would bring, that I would be back in those horrible final moments at the funeral home and would never ever be able to escape them."

Wanda hunched over, her face in her hands. She stayed like that for what seemed to her to be hours, trying to summon up the courage to continue or the hardness to block it all out of her mind.

"Wanda?" Russell said quietly. "You know, we don't have to go into details, if you can't."

"No, Russell," she said, straightening and pushing her hair back. "No, I need to tell you the whole truth. I didn't see Jack right away. They said that they didn't need me for the identification."

"That's right. It was my Uncle Simon who found Jack, called the police, and preliminarily identified him. They used his driver's license for confirmation," Russell said quietly.

Wanda continued, "But I didn't have to identify him, that's the point I was trying to make. I asked Chief Davis if I could see Jack, but he said that Jack's remains weren't in a condition for me to see right then. He used the word *remains,* Russell. At first, I thought he was just using police talk, but there was an earnestness in his voice, almost like a pleading, that told me that he was trying to communicate something really horrible, without having to use the actual words.

"After the autopsy, the undertaker strongly recommended a closed casket. I had accepted that and decided to remember Jack as I saw him every morning of our life together, just as he was waking up. He always had a big smile on his face when he woke up and first saw me.

"But something came over me, Russell. I just couldn't let it end like this. I couldn't turn our life together, all those special mornings, all that we shared, I couldn't just turn it into some fairy-tale ending. I needed to know the whole truth, not just all the good memories. I owed it to Jack. I could carry the good memories forward, and I knew that I had to carry the bad ones, too, no matter how horrible. Somehow, I knew that I would never ever have another peaceful day in my life if I didn't know the truth. I had to see him one final time."

"I understand," Russell said quietly. "Jack would understand, too."

"Thank you for saying that, Russell," Wanda said. "But I feel so bad about having lied to you."

"No, that's perfectly understandable, Wanda."

She took a deep breath and looked to her right, across the room to the window that opened onto one of the apple orchards.

"So, it was after the service. I asked the funeral director if I could just have a minute or two alone with Jack before we went to the crematorium. Jack had always said that he wanted his ashes scattered in the oldest part of our orchard, but that I had to be careful not to let the Department of Agriculture know about it."

Wanda smiled as she wiped a single tear from her eye.

"Well, the funeral director told me to take whatever time I needed. I sat there for a few minutes. I tried to cry, but there were no tears left. So, I just sat quietly and talked to Jack about all the good times we had together.

"After about five minutes, the funeral director tapped very lightly on the door and came in. He asked if there was anything I needed and if I was ready for them to go on with the arrangements, as he called them. I asked if I could just see Jack, just for one minute, even thirty seconds, to say goodbye.

"He said he understood that it was important to me and that I could, but it would take a while for them to prepare Jack so that I could see him in a way that I would want to remember him. I remember them wheeling Jack's casket out of the parlor into a small room and closing the sliding doors. The funeral director escorted me into another small parlor. There was music softly playing.

"About twenty minutes later the funeral director said I could go back in and he walked me back into the room where Jack had been. They had moved Jack's body into a different casket, one of those with a lid in two halves, and the upper half of the casket lid was raised. Jack's body was completely covered up to his chin and another blanket was drawn up around the sides and top of his head. He looked like he was wearing a white, silky babushka. His face looked waxy. I could see where they tried to cover up the gashes across his face with putty or something, and he had makeup on his cheeks and lips. At first, I wanted desperately to think that there had been some mistake, that this wasn't really Jack, that they had found some other poor soul up there in the forest. But I knew there had been no mistake, that this was real.

"And then, after I got over the shock of seeing my poor darling in his casket and knowing that I would never see him again, I remember thinking that he didn't look so horrible like I had feared. He actually looked beautiful in a way – maybe not to anybody else in this world, but to me he looked beautiful.

"The undertaker asked me not to touch him, so I didn't. I stayed with him for a few moments, and then said goodbye."

Russell quickly wiped his eyes with his index fingers. He then held a hand over his eyes for a moment and sighed, slowly shaking his head.

"I'm sorry, Wanda," he said, clearing his throat. "I really didn't intend for you to have to go through all that pain again. The only reason I asked is that I studied the report of Jack's autopsy and spoke to an expert. Did Chief Davis or anyone ever tell you about the Coroner's report?"

"Only that the Coroner decided that Jack probably died as a result of an attack by a wild animal, possibly a wolf or even a pack of wolves."

"That's basically what the report said, but it's only partly correct, Wanda. Let me explain some things about – about some of the wounds on Jack's body, the ones you couldn't see. I don't want to go into a lot of detail, but it's important to understanding how he died. But please stop me if you don't want to hear any more."

Wanda knew that Jack's beautiful body had been mutilated. She wasn't a fool. She knew why the undertaker only let her see his face.

"Jack died as a result of several massive wounds. One was to the back and sides of his neck." Russell pointed at himself. "It was a very deep wound that severed one of the arteries and several smaller blood vessels in the neck. There were also what appeared to be bite marks in the back of Jack's scalp and long slicing cuts on his upper back and shoulders."

"What was the other massive wound?"

"The Coroner believes that the deep wound in the neck was the fatal one, and that Jack probably lost consciousness almost instantly from shock and died within a minute, maybe less."

"Yes, but what was the other wound?"

Wanda could see Russell take a long deep breath. He looked like he was trying to compose himself. Wanda braced herself. She remembered that Russell said that she could stop him whenever it became too much. But she had to listen. She knew that Russell was glossing over the worst of it. But she had to listen. She had promised it to Jack so many times since he left her.

"There was also a large gaping wound in the abdomen, with massive damage to Jack's internal organs, and several of them were missing."

"My poor darling."

"I know it can't really lessen the pain, Wanda, but, believe me, there can be no doubt that Jack passed away very quickly. He almost certainly went into shock and lost consciousness in a matter of seconds. After that he didn't feel anything. As massive as the blood loss was, he passed away in a minute or two at most. The wounds to the abdomen were almost certainly post-mortem."

"That's what Chief Davis said to me, too, that he probably didn't feel very much, probably felt more surprised than scared," Wanda said quietly. "But there was more, wasn't there? What else happened to him?"

"Wanda, I really don't want to go into a lot of detail with this. What specific questions do you have?"

"Well, I had heard rumors that his arm or leg was – was torn off."

"Who told you that?" Russell asked, but he didn't wait for a reply.

"Well, yes, his left arm was –" Russell paused for a second, then continued, "completely detached at the shoulder, and his right arm was partially detached. His right leg was almost completely severed at the knee. Large chunks of muscle tissue had been, uh, removed. But all these terrible wounds almost certainly happened port-mortem, after he was gone."

"And a wolf did all this?"

"No. I'm sure that it was not a wolf."

"Then what, or who, could do such a thing?"

Russell spoke quietly and slowly. "The reason I described these details to you was that these are all the classic signs of an attack by a cougar. People around here also call them panthers."

"I know what a cougar is, Russell," Wanda snapped.

"I'm sorry, Wanda," Russell said. "I didn't mean to be condescending. I only recently learned myself that they're all the same species."

"Forgive me," Wanda replied. "I know you didn't mean to be condescending, only precise. Just like a lawyer." Wanda tried to smile.

"This is hard for me," she said, "so please don't pay too much attention to my reactions. Please go on."

Russell paused for a second, as if he were collecting his thoughts. Then he continued, "There's no way a wolf, or even a pack of wolves, could have caused those injuries. It's a blessing in a way, Wanda, because cougars kill almost instantaneously. That would have been the wounds to the neck and scalp. They attack from behind. A wolf will – well, let's not talk about that, because wolves weren't involved."

"And you're sure of this?"

"Yes, I even consulted with an expert on cougars."

Wanda began to feel anger seeping like a bloodstain through the fabric of her grief.

"That can't be, Russell. There aren't any cougars around here. They all live out west, in the Rockies."

"Actually, Wanda, at one time the cougar ranged all over North America. There were two confirmed kills just west of here just a little over a hundred years ago. And there have been reported but unconfirmed sightings ever since. That's not surprising, because they are reclusive, which is why they're so seldom seen.

"Jack's notes are full of accounts about them, big ones too. There has to be a factual basis for all those legends. There are people alive today that say that they have seen them in this area. There's even a guy who runs a non-profit center near here for the study of them."

"Oh, that would be Clay Collins," Wanda said quietly.

"That's right. I met him at one of Connie and Dick Graybill's get-togethers."

"But you said that you couldn't prove any of this," Wanda continued. "Aren't Jack's wounds proof enough?"

"No," Russell said, "and this is where the mystery begins to come in. From what I have learned, the police who responded to the scene probably destroyed any other clues that might have been at the scene where Jack was found and could have confirmed a cougar attack. They leave some tell-tale markings in the area of a kill. If there were any, the cops trampled them down. They obviously didn't know what they were dealing with, or they would have been more careful."

"But aren't the wounds enough?" Wanda persisted.

"No, Wanda. Horrible as it sounds, those same wounds, especially the post-mortem ones, could have been made by a man."

Wanda felt like she was going to throw up. She almost got up to retreat to the bathroom. Control yourself, she commanded. You wanted to know these things. You needed to know these things. You can never get on with the rest of your life until you hear them. You can't run away back into happier times. You owe it to Jack. You owe it to yourself.

"But surely, Russell, there's nobody so sick that they would deliberately –"

"No, I don't think so either. Neither does Chief Davis. We talked about that possibility. That's why it has to have been an animal, and I'm sure it was a large, very powerful cougar."

Russell sat there, obviously watching for Wanda's reaction. She was not prepared to give him one. Not yet.

"But you said that it was also foul play," she said quietly. "How can it be both?"

Russell hesitated again. It seemed like he was still debating how much he should tell her. Wanda noticed a lack of confidence in his voice when he resumed.

"Wanda, the only likely explanation is that a cougar killed Jack. But I'm also pretty sure that Jack was set up somehow, that someone arranged it. The cat was just the murder weapon. For one thing, cougars only hunt at dawn and dusk, and Jack was attacked in the afternoon. A cougar out on its own wouldn't have attacked a man, not in the middle of the day, not on its own."

"But who? Who killed my husband?" Wanda wished that Russell would just get on with it.

"I have to be careful what I tell you, because I don't have much evidence. But I think that Jack's research, especially toward the end of his life, uncovered some secrets that weren't just legends, but were true."

"I know that's what Jack was beginning to think, right toward the end," Wanda said quietly. She thought about how Jack had changed so much in those last months of his life.

"And, for reasons that I don't know yet, some people didn't want them to be uncovered for what they were: facts, not legend," Russell continued. "I think that Jack was getting too close to what those facts were and maybe even who those people were.

"True, some of the stories that Jack recorded are just tall tales that people around here have been passing down for generations, maybe hundreds of years. But Jack also found out some of those legends have at least some factual basis. I checked out some of Jack's notes about the Indian Rocks, for example, and they have quite a history backing them up."

"Who'd you talk to," Wanda demanded. "Not Bill Paxton? I told you before that I always felt that he had something to do with Jack's death."

"No, calm down, Wanda." His voice was stern but also sounded a little defensive. "As you know, Bill's family owned my place for more than a hundred and thirty years. He spent a lot of time there as a kid, almost like a second home. I just asked him some background questions about some of the references in Jack's notes. He was very helpful, but – and I want to make this clear, Wanda – Bill quickly pointed out that most of those old tales were pure fiction, nothing more."

"I'm sorry, Russell, I didn't mean to lash out at you like that," Wanda said. "But something about Bill Paxton and all those people at his church have always given me the creeps."

"Yeah, I understand. Me too." Russell said quietly. "But, to get back to what we were discussing, there is one legend that I am convinced is true or mostly true. Jack found that out right before he died. It's in Notebook 39, the last one."

Wanda suddenly got up and went to the kitchen.

"I'm making some tea," she called out. "Do you want some, Russell?"

"No, thanks."

Wanda returned in a minute with her tea. Russell was still on the couch, looking out the same window that Wanda had looked through, the one that opened onto the orchard.

"Russell," Wanda said as she sat down next to him. "You're a good friend, a very dear friend. I can accept that Jack was killed by a cougar, especially since it was quick and, from what you tell me, probably painless. I don't understand it, and I probably never will.

"But you don't have to conjure up some wild theory about it being a murder just to make me feel better about it. I mean, I had my suspicions about what happened to Jack. That's why I asked you to help me. Maybe there's nothing that you can tell me that will ever wipe out those suspicions entirely, at least not in my heart. But I can accept the facts as you found them. I don't need to believe in a legend to help me understand what happened."

Russell looked at Wanda. He said very slowly, deliberately, "But I need to tell you everything, Wanda, at least everything that makes sense. You can't have one without the other."

"Okay," was all Wanda said, as she sipped her tea while keeping her eyes focused on Russell's left hand as he twisted and reached awkwardly behind him into an inner pocket of his jacket.

Russell Presents His Case

Russell pulled Notebook 39 from his jacket pocket.

"Wanda, here it is. As I said, I probably couldn't prove any of this, not in a court of law at least, not beyond reasonable doubt. But I'm sure this is what happened.

"Let's start with the old stories about a band of so-called White Indians who used to live in the mountains around here. Some people claim they still do."

"Sure, Russell, lots of people have heard those stories." Wanda's annoyance showed in her voice. I don't need a lecture, she thought.

"Yeah, right," Russell said. "Sorry, of course you know about them. Well, in Jack's notebooks, there are repeated references to a sort of Paul Bunyan type of character. Sometimes he's known as John Oakman, sometimes as the Sangman, but most frequently he's known as John Bard. I'm convinced that all three references are to the same person."

"I've heard all about John Bard," Wanda smiled. "Remember that time that you dreamed that you had met him up at the Rocks and talked with him, and we talked about the legend a little."

"Yeah, that's right," Russell said, smiling and shaking his head. "I almost completely forgot talking to you about it. But my meeting him up at the Rocks seemed so real at the time."

"Maybe to you it was," Wanda smiled. "Dreams on a warm afternoon can be like that. And as for the Sangman, Whitey Wentworth's full of old stories about how they used to hunt for wild ginseng in the mountains around here, a hundred years ago or so, and how it was worth its weight in gold. I remember one day when he was cleaning out some brush at the back of one of the orchards, he told one of my regular guys that he had spotted some wild ginseng at the edge of the forest, but that it was poor-quality stuff. I saw them talking for about ten minutes, so I walked over to see if they needed anything. Whitey started telling me about how when he was young, he and his father and grandfather would all go hunting sang together. I wish Jack had been there with one of his notebooks.

"And, yes, Jack would share some of those old stories with me, and sometimes I would help him transcribe them from his notes into the journal books, but I never really paid that much attention to those stories. I'm still a city girl, I guess, and I don't have much time for old country legends. But Jack loves – loved – them and had a real passion for collecting them and preserving them before they were forgotten. That intellectual passion of his is one of the things I will always love about him."

"Well, I guess Whitey could have filled half of Jack's notebooks all by himself," Russell smiled. "But getting back to John Bard – let's call him that – he has supposedly lived in these mountains for hundreds of years. And, as you know, there are references in Jack's notes to John Bard being nine hundred years old. There are a couple of stories, too, about how John Bard was one of the last practicing Druid priests in Wales. During the subjugation of Wales by the English, back in the 1300s, the last few remaining Druids were persecuted by the Catholic English. John Bard, and several other Druid priests and scholars supposedly escaped to Ireland and eventually to North America. This would've been at least a hundred years before Columbus."

"I've heard of the legends about the Irish monks, but weren't they much earlier, before the Vikings?" Wanda asked.

"They were. The Irish had probably been making the journey to North America for over five hundred years by the time John Bard came over. And, like I said, some people say that he's still alive."

"Well, that part's just crazy."

Wanda felt the impatience returning. There was no need for this. She had already told Russell that she was prepared to accept his opinion about Jack's death. Over the years, she had gradually come to terms with the possibility that she might never know all the truth and would just have to live with the ambiguities and unanswerable questions. She didn't need to hear a bunch of folk legends.

"Wanda, I know none of this really makes any sense," Russell continued. "I didn't believe it at first, either. But please hear me out.

Whether John Bard is real or not isn't what really matters. What matters is that there are some very dangerous people out there who believe it and are willing to kill to preserve their secrets."

"No, what matters to me right now, Russell Poe – right this instant, before you go any further with this – is whether you believe, as best you can, that what you are about to tell me is true." Wanda was surprised by, and didn't like, the soft hints of anger she began to hear in her own voice.

"You deserve the truth, Wanda, even if you don't like the answer or the possibility that there is no clear answer. So, this is the best answer I can give you: even though I don't have all the proof: Yes, what I am about to tell you is what I believe happened to Jack."

"That's just not good enough," Wanda said, standing up. "Russell, you'll always be a dear friend to me, but I just can't take any more of this. Every day for the past six and a half years, I have woken up wondering what I could have done so that it would be Jack who would be still sitting here with me. Will what you want to tell me – this truth – answer that question?"

Wanda resisted when Russell reached for her hand to ask her to sit back down onto the couch.

"I don't know, Wanda. Maybe we've talked about this enough for today. Maybe we should just leave it where it is, and I can come back."

"Jesus, Russell, I'm sorry. I didn't mean it." Wanda closed her eyes for a moment to try to regain at least an external calm. "This is very upsetting to me," she continued with her eyes closed, "I am trying very hard to – to handle all this, but please go ahead with it."

She really didn't want to hear any more, but Russell had spent a lot of time trying to learn what really happened to Jack. She owed it to Russell to hear it all. She owed it to Jack to not give up trying to find out what happened. She moved to Jack's old chair, which was ten feet to the right of Russell, so that she could look out the window at the orchard while she listened.

"Okay, I'm ready," she said.

"Wanda," Russell continued, "I'm convinced that there is a secret cult operating in this area. It's very old and it is probably the basis for the legends about the White Indians. The cult probably has been around for a long time, maybe a hundred years or more.

"The Rocks, up there on the mountain behind us, is one of their sacred meeting places. There have even been meetings or ceremonies of some sort since I moved in. When I did a little amateur archeological excavation last year, I found a few artifacts that appear to be Celtic. A few others appear to be of Native American origin. I can't say how old any of them are, but they all were found within twenty centimeters of the surface. I also discovered that there is an extensive series of underground rooms and passages just underneath the circle.

"That stone circle wasn't built by the Indians or some prehistoric people. It was built by Europeans using metric measurements."

"But how much of this did Jack know?" Wanda asked.

"Jack knew just enough to fill in some blanks, to bring some of the old tales out of the realm of legend and into the borderlands of fact. The biggest breakthroughs, and the ones that might have cost him his life, were his interviews with Paul Levesque.

"Like I think I mentioned to you before, Wanda, Notebook 39 is mostly a bunch of short notes, sentence fragments, single words, most of it not very organized or coherent like all his other notebooks.

"I know," Wanda replied. "I noticed that. It was completely unlike Jack."

"Not all of Notebook 39 was like that," Russell said, holding the notebook and opening it. "The first several pages had some clear, detailed notes."

"I remember," Wanda said, "but I couldn't bring myself to read them."

Russell said, "Is it okay if I read some of them now?"

Wanda nodded. Russell began to read:

November 17 – I had a brief interview with Paul Levesque at the VA Hospital. Paul said his health is good one day, very bad the next. He told me the story of his encounter with "Red Eyes," as he called it. He claims that there is a secret group – the name of which he refuses to disclose – that knows that he has been talking to me. This will have to be our last meeting.

Paul said that he had received a phone call last night. He recognized the voice as one of the Watchmen, as he called them, the security force for the cult. He knew who it was who called him, but says that he will never, never violate his vows to the point of revealing identities. To reveal the identity of a member of this group would be to sign his own death warrant.

He knows that the call came from a Watchman because he called him by his Old Name. Old Names are the names that members of the cult use when addressing each other. The voice said, "Hello, Torc." Torc is a Celtic name for the bear. Many of the members use Celtic names of animals for their Old Names. Paul says that in the ancient Celtic culture, the bear was a totem for the warrior spirit.

Paul reported that the caller simply said, "Hello Torc. We are just reminding you of your sacred vows, pledged in your own blood. We know you have been talking about us to an outsider. You're a foolish crazy old man, so we can make allowances up to this point. But no more. No more." (This is the substance of what Paul told me. It may not be an exact quote.)

Paul begged me not to visit him again. He said that he has participated in "corrections" that are given to people who break the oath of secrecy.

Wanda wept silently as she heard Jack's words. Russell almost sounded like Jack, the way that he read them: detached, but slowly, giving each word its proper emphasis.

"Remember the strange phone calls that Jack received just before he was killed, the ones that he said were wrong numbers?"

Wanda nodded.

Russell continued quietly. "I believe that this group calls themselves the Children of Bel. The calls to Jack probably came from the Watchmen that Paul referred to, warning him away from pursuing his research any further, just like they warned Paul less than a month before he died. Jack was getting awfully close, Wanda, to some secrets that the Children of Bel, whoever they are, didn't want revealed."

"What kind of secrets?"

"I can only speculate, Wanda. I really don't know. But Paul knew them, and, even though I'll never be able to prove it, I think that it's no coincidence that Paul died when the Watchmen found out that he was talking to Jack.

"In some groups, I guess, the fact that something is a secret is reason enough to kill to protect it. As well hidden as this cult has been over the years – how they have been able to blend like camouflage into local folklore about White Indians and so forth – I'm sure that one of the things they didn't want confirmed as fact is that they're real.

"There could be a lot of other things that they want kept secret. Maybe they know where the Sangman's treasure is. Maybe they're involved in some illegal activities, like drug running or such. Ray Davis says that he thinks that they might be involved in abducting young women and gang-raping them in the forest. I don't know. It really doesn't matter what the substance of their secrets are. What counts to them is that they remain a secret at any cost."

"Russell, do you have any idea who might belong to this group?"

"A couple of hunches, but I couldn't ever prove anything."

"Well, tell me at least."

"Should I really do that, Wanda? I mean, if I tell you that I suspect that so-and-so is in the Children of Bel, every time you see that person, you'll say to yourself, 'There goes Jack's killer.' And what if I'm wrong?"

"Russell, just a few minutes ago you told me that I had to see this through to the end. So, do you."

Wanda wondered whether Russell would just end the conversation then and there. He set Jack's notebook beside him on the couch. He looked as if he was getting ready to get up and leave.

"Okay. There's one person above all who's mixed up in this: Bill Paxton. He seems to be –"

"I knew it!" Wanda said, thumping her hands on the arms of the chair.

"Sorry for interrupting," Wanda said. "But I have always had my suspicions about him, like I told you before, but I really didn't have anything to base that on. Maybe that is just my wanting so desperately to have someone to blame, to put some – I don't know, Russell – to put some sense to all of it. Sure, there was the one incident right before Jack died, when that strange man come into the office and said that Paxton had referred him. But until now I didn't have any solid reason to think that Bill Paxton would ever do something terrible like what happened to Jack – like you say, nothing that I could prove."

"There are just too many things that point to him being involved, Wanda, maybe even being at the center of all of it." Russell said. "He and I have become acquainted from the work that I've been doing with Jack's research. From what Bill's told me about his family, it's a sure bet his grandparents were both in the cult. In fact – and this comes from a couple of sources – his great-great-grandfather even might have built the Rocks just to have a sacred circle for the ceremonies. Or maybe they're older than that. We probably will never know."

"I remember from Jack's research how the Paxton family was involved with the Indian Rocks," Wanda said, "but exactly how does Bill Paxton fit into this?"

"Well," Russell said. "Bill Paxton didn't just grow up on the old Paxton place; he also grew up on John Bard stories. In fact, I suspect that someone in his family might have even hinted to him when he was young that he actually was the grandson of John Bard – Uncle Johnny as his family called him. He might even have a couple of old photographs of him. But, when I first asked him about the John Bard legends, in just a general way, he denied having ever heard of them. In my experience, that was the knee-jerk reaction of someone who suddenly realized he had something to hide. Then, the next day, he came out to my house and admitted that he had misled me, but I'm not sure that I completely believed him even then."

"So, you're basing all this on the word of somebody who admitted that he lied to you, and whom you think lied again when he told you he lied the first time? Sounds pretty flimsy to me, Russell."

"Sounds like you would be a good defense lawyer," Russell replied, smiling. "Guilty people often act that way: get caught in a lie and then lie again to try to get out of it. Usually instead of explaining away the first lie, their stories just get more unbelievable.

"And there's more, Wanda. From what you've told me, you've never had any dealings with Reverend Paxton, have you?"

"No. Why would I have anything to do with someone like Paxton? He probably sees me as kindling for the fires of hell." Wanda smiled.

"No, Wanda, actually he can come across as a pretty tolerant guy. It might be just an act, but he seems sincere about some good things. But you've never had any contact with him, not even when Jack died?"

"No. Not a bit." Wanda made a face of what she hoped was extreme revulsion and shook her head. "Oh, I heard from one of his parishioners that he had prayed for Jack and me the Sunday after Jack died. But I never had any contact with him, not even a sympathy card, which I probably wouldn't have wanted anyways."

"Well, during the early days of the police investigation, it appears that Bill Paxton called both Chief Davis and the editor of the *Wellsboro Bulletin*. Paxton claimed that he was acting on your behalf. He said that you wanted to be left alone and didn't want to answer any more questions. He also told Kenyon –"

"Who?"

"I'm sorry, he was the owner of the paper back then. He also told Mr. Kenyon that you did not want the paper to mention Jack's research into folklore, supposedly because it would cause you too much pain."

"That's crap, Russell, and you know it."

"I do. And that's why I think Bill Paxton was somehow involved in Jack's death. And then, when Susan Kline, a reporter from the *Bulletin*, asked for access to the newspaper's files about Jack's death, Bill's cousin Greg Paxton, who lives in Wilkes-Barre and owns the paper now, tried to forbid it. But she showed me the files anyway, which is how we found out about Bill Paxton telling the paper and the police not to contact you. Susan says she recently asked Bill

Paxton about his attempt to kill the *Bulletin* inquiry and he denied everything, even though she and I have evidence to the contrary.

"So, even if Bill Paxton wasn't directly connected with Jack's death, he certainly was involved in a cover up of some sort," Russell concluded. Wanda thought that he sounded like a lawyer in the movies wrapping up his argument to the jury.

"A cover-up?" For some reason she couldn't quite explain, Wanda wasn't surprised. "You mean like the police were somehow involved? You don't really think that Chief Davis would be a party to anything like that, do you?"

"Not knowingly. Ray Davis impresses me as someone who's basically honest, but sometimes doesn't realize when he's in way over his head. He tries to be as objective as possible, but sometimes he doesn't look beneath the surface. For example, the Coroner's report said that Jack's injuries were consistent with – important words, *consistent with* – injuries caused by an attack by a wild animal, such as a wolf or a pack of wolves. Chief Davis was clear about that in the press conference about the case, but people only heard the "wolf" part. That's how the wolf attack story got started. He told me that he still has some doubts about the wolf attack theory and has never officially closed the case."

"Well, he's a troubled man, Russell." Wanda replied. "I agree with you about him being an honest cop. He has a lot of problems with his daughter, I know, and his wife, June, is basically a shut-in. That must cause a lot of stress for him."

"I didn't know that about his wife," Russell said quietly.

"Well, there's one last bit of evidence," he continued. "There are witnesses who saw Jack apparently meeting with two unidentified men out at the Pine Tree Inn a few hours before he died.

"And there was a fourth man at that meeting, whom neither Davis nor I believe was one hundred percent truthful."

"Who's that? Not Bill Paxton?" Wanda asked.

"No, Whitey Wentworth."

"Oh Lord, not him too!" Wanda exclaimed.

"Just by coincidence," Russell explained, "one of Chief Davis's officers stopped in at the Pine Tree for a couple of minutes on his way back to town and saw Whitey and Jack and two other men at the bar that afternoon. When the police interviewed Whitey, he told them that he met Jack there, claiming that Jack had some questions about some legends that Whitey had provided. Whitey said he didn't know the other two men and that they were just sitting at the bar with him and Jack at the same time."

"Well, it's true, isn't it, that Jack did interview Whitey several times." Wanda said. "I remember both Whitey and Jack telling me about it at the time. In fact, one of the interviews took place right out there on the front porch."

"Yes, but this meeting was different," Russell said solemnly. The room suddenly began to feel cold. Wanda was terrified to think about what she knew she probably would hear next.

"Shortly after Jack and Whitey met, the two other men came in. The police don't have a good description of either of them – basically just a big guy and a smaller guy – and haven't been able to locate them. The witnesses said that they seemed to know Whitey and Whitey seemed to know them. Whitey appeared to introduce Jack to them. The four of them talked for a while, sitting at the bar – but nobody knows what about – and then the two men left at the same time as Jack and Whitey."

"Did Jack go voluntarily?"

"It looked that way."

"What did Whitey say?"

"Whitey told Chief Davis that the two men may have left at the same time as Jack, but they didn't leave with him," Russell continued. "He also denied having ever seen the two men before or since, and said that he didn't talk to them, except to just say hello when they sat down at the bar next to him and Jack, and maybe to say goodbye when they left."

"There were a couple of other people in the bar at the time, along with the bartender, and none of them have a sharp memory of what happened. But the police officer who saw them, and at least one of the other customers in the bar said that Whitey, Jack, and the two men were all involved in a conversation together, although neither of them – the policeman or the other customer – could hear what they said.

"The bottom line is that Chief Davis and I both think that Whitey is lying, and that –"

Wanda interrupted. "So, you think that Whitey somehow brought Jack into a trap, and these two men took him away?"

"It's not *I think* or *somehow,* Wanda. I am sure of it. I would like to think that Whitey had no idea about what was going to happen next, but, yes, that's what happened. Whitey claimed that he stayed at the bar and left later by himself. Chief Davis says he went on a saloon crawl that afternoon and eventually was picked up that night for drunk driving outside Mansfield. It's almost impossible that Whitey had anything to do with – with what happened to Jack."

"So, the two guys or someone else led Jack up into the forest, where the panther was waiting," Wanda summarized. She felt a cold sweat breaking out.

"And there's one more thing, one last thing," Russell said quietly. He waited for Wanda to tell him he could go ahead with it.

"Yes," was all Wanda could say. She wanted to run from the room, but she knew that she had to stay and hear it.

"The cougar killed Jack, almost instantly like I said. But the post-mortem wounds, the mutilation, was not done by the cat. It was done by –"

"By those two guys or by someone else who was waiting there with the cougar." Wanda could not believe that she was hearing herself finish Russell's terrible sentence. She was shivering and, after a second or two, was shaking uncontrollably. Russell got up, picked up a crocheted Afghan that was draped over the couch, and walked to the chair to put it over her shoulders. He knelt beside her and held her gently, almost as if he were afraid that she would break like old china.

Wanda wanted to scream, to cry, at least to whimper, but her voice failed her. The tears wouldn't come. All she could do was tremble. While she was sitting in their office in town, sipping tea while she took care of some leftover paperwork, Jack was being led to his death.

Should she have been more alert to the danger signals in all those strange events just before Jack died? Should they have gone to the police? Even on that last morning, was there anything that she could have done to prevent Jack from going to that meeting and the eventual death march into the mountains? Russell had worked so hard to answer so many questions that have haunted her every day for the past six and a half years, but he will never be able to answer these most painful questions of all.

After what seemed to Wanda like a half-hour, Russell got up, moved back to the couch, and said quietly, "What do you want me to do, Wanda?"

"What can we do, Russell? You yourself say you don't have the evidence. You're a lawyer. You of all people should know if you don't have a case."

"I can present all this to Ray Davis," Russell said. "But, in all honesty, what I tell him probably won't make a difference, not without any hard evidence. But what I tell him could someday connect with evidence that would lead to the Children of Bel and Jack's killers. I'm sure that they're one and the same. Davis promised me that he'll never close the case until he has the answers, and I believe him."

"No, Russell. That's sweet of you, but you've done enough. You and I both know that Ray Davis will never be able to do anything. If you keep poking around, you'll only be risking your own life further."

"I still plan to finish Jack's book," Russell said after a moment.

"Well, I can't ask you to do that now, Russell, not with some of these legends hiding so many dangerous truths."

"I have to, Wanda. We owe it to Jack."

Wanda returned to the couch and sat beside him.

"Well then, Russell," she said, taking his hand, "please do just one more thing for me."

"What's that? Anything, Wanda. Just name it."

"Look out for yourself, Russell. Just look out for yourself. Please. I can't lose you, too."

The Blood on the Tombstone

From *Research Journal 2,* transcribed by John S. Abrams from original notes in Notebook 17

Researcher's Note: The principal source for this account is Lizanne Longwood, age 75, who was born in Newport, Rhode Island, in 1897. She moved with her parents to Wellsboro in 1900, when her father accepted a position as District Chief Freight Manager for the New York Central Railroad. Never marrying – "no one was quite right for me" – Miss Longwood taught arithmetic in the Wellsboro schools all her adult working life, until she retired in 1962. She has lived since 1911 at her family home on Cone Street, two blocks from the old train station in Wellsboro. She now shares the house with her niece, Linda Marino and Linda's husband John Marino. She was interviewed on March 12 and 19, 1972.

The basic facts of this story have been verified by newspaper accounts of the Greene murder case, courtesy of the *Wellsboro Bulletin* and records of the former Court of Oyer and Terminer of Tioga County (now the Criminal Division of the Court of Common Pleas) in the case of *Commonwealth versus James W. Glenn*. The existence and history of the tombstone has been confirmed by the Rev. William Paxton, the pastor of the Mountain View Chapel, which currently maintains the old Methodist Cemetery. Rev. Paxton had no specific knowledge of his family's charitable involvement in the case, but he stated that his grandfather, Walter Paxton, sometimes helped out people in need during the Great Depression.

The Blood on the Tombstone
as told by Lizanne Longwood

In August 1937, one of the most sensational murder trials in the country that year was held in the Tioga County Courthouse in Wellsboro. I was teaching fourth grade arithmetic at the time and was horrified to learn that the defendant was a childhood playmate and high school classmate of mine, Jimmy Glenn, who had lived on Purple Street, just down the street and around the corner from us in the north end of Wellsboro. Jimmy was two years older than me, but we associated a lot when we were growing up.

Jimmy was always a strange boy. When we were children, we liked to play together, and when we were teenagers, we would spend time together whenever my family would allow it. Sometimes, even when he was a teenager, he would run out into the street and conduct imaginary "cattle drives" with a long bullwhip. He also would go off for days on end on what he called "camping trips," but he was never seen to have any camping equipment in his possession. He was a nice enough person, with always a smile and a friendly hello to anyone he met on the street, but he always seemed to be not quite right mentally. However, he was never known to be violent or to lose his temper.

His father passed away in 1917 and his mother moved away from Purple Street and out to a small cottage in the country, just south of Whitneyville. This happened at about the same time that Jimmy enlisted into the Pennsylvania National Guard for World War I. He fought in France and came home just before Christmas in 1918. I remember that the county had the soldiers who had returned home march in the Christmas parade in downtown Wellsboro. Other than the parade, I did not see him after he returned home from the war, except on rare occasions, maybe once a year, when we would unexpectedly meet each other downtown.

At the time of the Greene murder case, Jimmy was in his early forties. Jimmy was unemployed, except for occasional day labor, which was the only kind of work that most people could find in northern Pennsylvania during the Great Depression. But everyone knew that Jimmy scratched out a living running a still that was hidden in the woods deep in the Grand Canyon of Pennsylvania, and by selling the corn liquor in mason jars for twenty-five cents a pint – "two bits for a bite," people used to say. He would haul his goods up out of the canyon and load them into an old car he had somehow managed to buy. Then he'd drive back into town and all the way out to Whitneyville, dropping off deliveries along the way. They called it "Jimmy's Milk Route" because he always made his deliveries early in the morning.

Jimmy never seemed to have any trouble with the authorities. Some people said that he paid the commander of the local state police barracks a percentage of his sales, said to be five cents per jar. I think that it was just too difficult for those big fat policemen to climb down into the canyon to hunt for Jimmy's works, and there were much bigger still operators in the area for them to chase on flat ground.

In July 1937, Jimmy was arrested and charged with the murder of Hank Greene, who was a well-liked family man, a deacon in his church, and owned a sawmill in a valley north of Wellsboro.

The only witnesses were a couple of the men from Hank's mill. Jimmy had come to the sawmill looking for work, and Hank ran him off the property. The witnesses said that Hank and Jimmy were in a heated argument, with Hank claiming that Jimmy was selling cheap corn whisky to his workers, who were coming to work drunk and were liable to hurt themselves on the job. Hank Greene was a kindly man, and he knew how hard it would be for a man who lost his job in those days. That was before unions or worker compensation benefits in the lumber industry. If you got hurt on the job, you were out of work, period.

One day shortly after the argument at the sawmill, Hank Greene just disappeared. When he didn't come home from work that night, and not the next day either, they started looking for him. Somebody tipped off the police about the argument he had with Jimmy Glenn, so they sent a search party over to his place, where he had continued to live by himself after his mother passed away in the late 1920s. The dogs found Hank's body buried in a shallow grave in the woods about 200 yards from Jimmy's back door, with a long, razor sharp sickle buried deep in poor Hank's chest. Blood was also found on a shirt in Jimmy's laundry basket, which matched Hank Greene's blood type, but also matched Jimmy's. Jimmy told the police that he had cut himself while chopping wood and showed the police a small partially healed cut on his arm.

The police found nothing else of interest except a lot of old maps of the areas around Wellsboro, which were in a dresser drawer in what used to be the bedroom used by Jimmy's mother. There were marks on them, some along roads and some far off the roads. They assumed that those were delivery points or other locations that Jimmy used in his moonshine business. Jimmy claimed he didn't know anything about them and that they must have belonged to his mother.

Jimmy continued to deny knowing anything at all about Hank Greene's death. Then, after a hardware store owner in Mansfield remembered selling a sickle identical to the murder weapon to Jimmy about a month before Hank's disappearance, Jimmy changed his story a little. When the police showed the supposed murder weapon to Jimmy, he said that it looked like his, but he couldn't be sure. He admitted that he had purchased a sickle like it from the hardware store in Mansfield to clear some brush from the back of the property, but he loaned it to a friend. Jimmy said that he had heard that the friend was a member of the White Indians and that Hank had been killed by accident by the White Indians during one of their ceremonies up in the mountains. He claimed to know nothing about the grave behind his house.

Of course, people had been telling tales about the White Indians for years, even though nobody had actually seen an Indian of any kind – white or red – around here for probably fifty years at least. Whenever a mystery couldn't be solved, folks liked to figure out a way to blame it on them. So, when asked to identify his friend, or how he knew about the ceremony at which Hank had supposedly died, or to give the names of any other witnesses or produce evidence at all that could corroborate his story, Jimmy refused. He said that he had already said too much as it was. He said that he would rather go to the electric chair than be tortured and killed like poor Hank Greene.

There wasn't much that the judge or jury could do. The evidence against Jimmy Glenn was circumstantial, but good enough to make the Commonwealth's case, and there was no evidence to support Jimmy's claims other than his own testimony, which nobody believed. The jury found him guilty of first-degree murder. My neighbor was on that jury and told me later that they didn't even bother to sit down at the table in the jury room.

When it came time to sentence him the next day, there was nobody who would come forward to speak for him, not even one good word. Before sentencing him to death, the judge reminded Jimmy that his life was at stake. The judge urged Jimmy to tell anything he knew that could support his claim of innocence. Jimmy continued to refuse to say anything more. When the judge asked Jimmy if he had anything at all to say before sentence was pronounced, Jimmy just said, "No, your honor. I know that you must now do your duty, and I do not hold it against you."

I suppose I could have come to court and said something for Jimmy, but I was at Chautauqua all that summer and didn't hear about the case until I returned at the very end of August, right before the start of the new school year, and read in the newspaper that Governor Earle had already signed his death warrant and that they had taken Jimmy away to the Death House at Rockview State Penitentiary.

Jimmy was too poor to afford a lawyer for an appeal or to request clemency, and none of the lawyers in the county would take his case for free. So, he just quietly resigned himself to his fate. About six weeks after the trial, just a few minutes before midnight, they put him to death in the electric chair at Rockview. They say he walked right into the death chamber and sat down in the chair without a second thought. Just before they pulled the leather mask over his face, the warden asked if he had anything to say.

He looked the warden straight in the eye and calmly said, "I swear to God that I am not guilty of this crime. And in a few minutes from now I will tell Him face to face the same thing that I am telling you now. But if I have to die for that poor man's death, I pray that God will send a sign after I am gone, to prove that I was an innocent man. God will make sure that the truth comes out."

Then he closed his eyes and was smiling when they lowered the mask. The witnesses told the newspapers that the first jolt of current killed him instantly.

Jimmy didn't have any family left, but an anonymous person supposedly from out in the country, near the village of Tioga, claimed his body and saw to it that he had a proper funeral and a decent burial in the old Methodist Cemetery at the edge of town. To this day, no one knows who that anonymous kind person was, but there have always been rumors that it was the Paxton family who contributed the money. They were a prominent family in Tioga County then and were known for sometimes helping out people who had nobody else.

There was no one at the funeral, though. His only mourners were the undertaker and a minister that the undertaker had convinced to come out in the rain to help lay Jimmy Glenn to rest. The undertaker, the minister, and the two grave diggers had to carry his state-issue pine coffin from the hearse to the grave.

About six months after Jimmy was executed, a long curved red stain, about two inches wide, began to appear on his tombstone. Soon it had taken the long slender shape of a sickle, with a very sharp point, the point just inches above the ground and pointing down at Jimmy's grave. In time the upper part of the stain turned dark brown, like a wooden handle. But the lower three-quarters remained bright red and moist looking. It even felt moist to the touch. As much as the cemetery caretaker tried, there was no way to remove the stain.

The person who had paid for Jimmy's burial sent a stone mason to the cemetery. He chipped off the face of the stone, re-polished the granite, and reengraved it with Jimmy's name. But about six months later, the bloody sickle reappeared as plain and as bloody as ever, and in exactly the same location. Finally, they took the stone away and put in a different stone from another quarry, but, about six months later, it also took on the same bloody stain.

Some people said that God had sent the sign that Jimmy had requested when he sat in the electric chair, but that it was a sign of guilt, not innocence. We'll never know for sure.

You can still see Jimmy Glenn's grave. It's in the oldest part of the cemetery about a hundred yards behind the Mountain View Chapel, back from the days when the little Methodist chapel was still standing there. The old chapel had been unused for years when it burned down in 1941, just before the start of the Second World War. While I was still able to get around, I would always have my niece or her husband drive me out to put flowers on Jimmy's grave on his birthday. He may have turned out bad in the end, and may be suffering eternal torment, for all I know. But I did it in honor of the sweet, kind, funny, strange boy I used to know when I was a girl long ago.

The Mountain View Chapel takes care of the cemetery now. The last couple of times I was there, I saw that they had taken away the so-called "bloody" gravestone and put a metal marker in the ground and have cleared the weeds away from it. There's no stain on it, but sometimes, when I visited his grave those last few times, I noticed a faint smell, like the fresh blood from a slaughterhouse.

The Tioga Yew

From *Research Journal 5,* transcribed by John S. Abrams from original notes in Notebooks 4, 5, 17, 22, 23, 24, 27, 30, 31, 32, 34, and 38

Researcher's Note: The principal sources of this account are Mr. Simon Poe, of Richmond Township, Tioga County, Pennsylvania, on whose property the Tioga Yew stands, and Mr. Robert Kaiser, whose family has lived in Tioga County for more than one hundred years. Additional information was compiled from interviews of too many people to mention them all. The other major contributors, in addition to Mr. Poe and Mr. Kaiser, were: the late Paul Levesque, also of Richmond Township; the Rev. William Paxton, the pastor of the Mountain View Chapel outside Wellsboro, Pennsylvania; and Mrs. Anita "Annie" Hart, the Librarian of the Tioga County Historical Society, Wellsboro, Pennsylvania. The interviews were conducted on various dates between May 1972 and January 1977, and some of the sources were interviewed multiple times. I am also grateful to the assistance of Mrs. Brenda McKnight, the Public Relations Director of the Pennsylvania Forestry Association, in Harrisburg, Pennsylvania, and materials she provided.

The Tioga Yew

as told by Robert Kaiser and Simon Poe

An ancient yew tree stands on a mountain slope on Simon Poe's property, overlooking an old Indian burial site on the west bank of the Tioga River north of the town of Mansfield. The tree is more than eighty feet high. Its main trunk reaches ten feet high and is more than fifty-six feet in circumference. It sits to the east of the Indian Rocks and is situated so that sunrise on the equinoxes is in a straight line with the tree, one of the upright stones, and the center of the rock formation.

The grave site was discovered in 1833 by William Ripley, one of the early explorers of the region. Unlike several larger burial sites nearby further down the river, this site contained only one body, that of an Indian, believed to be Susquehannock. He was buried in a sitting position with his back to the mountain. Three old long rifles were laid across his lap, probably as a warning that his spirit would forever guard the sacred lands beyond. The rifles were rusted, and it could not be determined whether they were buried with the body or sometime after. After the site was crudely excavated by Ripley, its contents, including the skeleton, were removed to the University of Pennsylvania. Its location, however, remained a local point of interest, known as the Sentinel Burial Site, well into the twentieth century.

The tree is a great source of mystery. It is an English yew (taxus bacatta), which is not native to North America. The yew that is native to northeastern North America is the Canadian yew (taxus canadensis), which is a smaller, spreading shrub. From the size of its trunk, arborists estimate that the Tioga Yew is 1,500 to 1,800 years old, perhaps even older. Unlike smaller, younger English yews that occasionally are cultivated by homeowners elsewhere in the region, the only possible explanation for the Tioga Yew, is that it was brought to North America as a seedling and planted here more than a thousand years ago. This transplantation theory is supported by the fact that even now, after more than fifteen centuries, the composition of the soil around the base of the tree is visibly different from that of the surrounding forest only a few feet away.

In Europe, and particularly in areas of Celtic influence, the English yew was revered by the old religions. One of the longest-living things on earth, it was associated with longevity and reincarnation. It also was revered by some medieval Christians. However, unlike Christians, who believed in death and resurrection, the Celtic religions believed that either of two things happened at death: reincarnation or, similar to many Native American beliefs, transfiguration, by which people who possessed certain secret knowledge and had mastered certain spiritual powers would retain their previous personalities, but as pure spiritual essence able to assume the forms of animals, plants, or even the physical likeness of their former selves. The Algonquin peoples of eastern North America called this transfigured spirit a manitou, one who, after a very long life, had rejoined the fundamental life force and had regained its powers, which are lost to people during their lives. In some old northern European legends, they sometimes were known as shapeshifters.

Some ancient European legends associate the yew tree with this transfiguration, but in different ways, such as in a sacrifice by being burned alive on the boughs of a sacred yew tree. Only a person of great age and nobility would have the privilege of being sacrificed in this way, in the promise that he or she would be transfigured and live as long as the yew tree from which the branches of the pyre were cut. These sacrifices were always voluntary, at the request of the person to be sacrificed. Some groups believed that the yew tree also had the power to absorb the body and spirit of a living person and to retain it there, becoming that person.

In Wales and northern France, doors would sometimes be cut into the trunks of the thickest yew trees, and, in Christian times, some of these were used as shrines or small chapels. This might have been associated with the ancient practice of a small number of Celtic and pre-Celtic groups to entomb their most revered holy people in the living trunk of a yew tree, thereby making the tree a living shrine, as well as the transfigured spirit of the person it held.

We cannot be sure precisely how the Native Americans in the region viewed the Tioga Yew. We do know that they sometimes brewed yew berries into a tea, which they took for medicinal purposes and yew tea remains a folk remedy for rheumatism among country people in the Appalachians. However, these yew berries came from the more abundant Canadian yew. The seeds and bark of the English yew are poisonous.

There are no first-hand indigenous sources about the meaning of the Tioga Yew or the Indian Rocks adjacent to it. By the time the first confirmed European settlers arrived in the last half of the eighteenth century, most of the Native Americans had left the region, realizing that they had been swindled out of their ancestral lands by the Penn family in the infamous Walking Purchase and the Treaty of Fort Stanwix. It is possible that a few individuals still lived in the area, but by 1780 almost all had migrated to the north and the west, to move beyond the reach of white settlers who had already demonstrated that they intended to keep pushing the Native Americans off their ancestral lands.

The earliest settlers in the region, such as the Paxtons and the Lambs, said that Native Americans passing through the area along its great network of trails, as they continued to do into at least the 1830s, would visit the Tioga Yew, which they called a "talking tree." They said that, if one stood close enough, it was possible to speak to the spirits who protected the surrounding mountains and valleys, as well as to people at other talking trees many miles away.

This is consistent with the old English and even older Celtic traditions of the ley lines, which were hidden channels of spiritual power that coursed in straight lines through the world. These were known to the ancients, but first documented only in the 1920s by the English archeologist Alfred Watkins. He charted the location of shrines, chapels, sacred groves of trees, and other holy sites in the United Kingdom, some of them dating back centuries before the introduction of Christianity. These sites were points in mathematically precise straight lines and often located at the intersection of two or more of these lines. Some of these ley lines stretch for hundreds of miles in a perfectly straight line without even an inch of deviation from the true course. Many of the ancient roads were built along them. Magnetic compasses spin wildly around at the intersection of two ley lines. The ley lines and the power that they generated at their intersections explain the ability of Native Americans to speak to other people many miles away. Even today, compasses in the immediate vicinity of the Tioga Yew all point to the tree, rather than north, as one approaches it even from one hundred feet away, and they spin counterclockwise, like the rotation of the earth, within three feet of it. Portable radios emit loud bursts of static and then go silent.

There were at least eleven such "talking trees" known to be in Pennsylvania, New York, western Maryland, and what today is West Virginia. Four similar ancient English yew trees were discovered before they were cut down, the closest of these being about twenty-nine miles southwest on a mountain top in the Susquehannock State Forest. Today, only the Tioga Yew and one other English yew high on Mt. Davis, the highest mountain in the state, in Somerset County, are known to exist in Pennsylvania. There might be more, but they have not been discovered.

There are no Native American accounts of the origins of the "talking trees," all of which they considered to be "brothers" of the Tioga Yew. As the earliest legends of the Lenni Lenape, Susquehannocks, and other eastern indigenous nations said, "We came into an empty land, but we could tell from the things that we found that the ancient ones had been here before and their spirits would return to instruct us now." Those ancient ones were undoubtedly from Europe, some of whom journeyed to North America even before the voyage of St. Brendan of Clonfort in the sixth century and then supposedly vanished, leaving only the yews as their living memorials.

The "talking tree" that used to be in the Susquehannock State Forest was, like the Tioga Yew, an English yew tree that contemporary accounts described at more than sixty feet tall, with a trunk that was twenty-five feet in circumference. It was the site of one of the greatest unsolved mysteries in the history of the region.

In late October 1921, Alexander Kaiser, who was twenty-four years old, single, and lived with his parents in Wellsboro, told his father that he was going on a three-day archery bear hunt with three of his friends up in the mountains. His parents, Conrad and Edith Kaiser, did not think that this was unusual, as it was customary to go out and tramp around in the mountains for several days with one's friends while hunting bears, usually camping out for one or two nights. Few bears were ever harmed, or even seen, but everyone in the hunting party would have a good time.

Conrad Kaiser was a great-uncle of Robert Kaiser, who contributed to this account. Conrad and Edith were not very concerned when Alex did not return when expected. His companions said that Alex had told them that he wanted to stay out in the forest for a couple of more days, "just to wander around and think about things." When Alex still had not returned for more than three weeks, his parents reported him to the police. A search was organized from the spot where his companions said that he left them, and it stretched out for many miles in each direction. Finally, as winter set in, the police concluded that Alex was either dead somewhere or had departed the area and, for whatever reason, did not want to return home.

Conrad and Edith kept up hope for many years after Alex disappeared. Sometimes there would be sightings of a young man who matched Alex's description, but these hopeful signs always produced disappointment. Conrad passed away in 1930, still convinced that his son was alive somewhere and, at the same time, anguishing over what he had done or said that made Alex not want to have any further contact with him and Edith. When Conrad died, Edith went downhill quickly, and she died in her sleep on Alex's birthday in 1931. The Kaiser family concluded that Alex was dead, at least to them.

In August 1967, a violent thunderstorm and lightning strikes started a forest fire in the Susquehannock State Park, resulting in the destruction of about six square miles of forest high up in the mountains. The next spring, the state government decided to clear the area, plant new trees around the perimeter, and build a picnic area and outbuildings in the center, and a gravel road winding up the mountain from the state highway.

In the exact center of the burned-out area there was what was left of a magnificent thousand-year-old English yew. They started to cut the tree up, using chain saws and long cross-cut saws on the branches, so that they could be burned. It was hot work and slow going, but eventually only the ten-foot high stump of the tree remained. They doused the stump with kerosene and set it afire, planning to use a bulldozer to drag the charred remains away and dump them in the forest.

They had noticed that a lightning strike had partially split the trunk into four sections that remained joined together. As soon as the tree started to burn, the four sections dropped away, like a large black flower bud opening, to reveal a human skeleton partially embedded in one of the sections. The workers acted just in time to douse the fire, pull away the smoldering sections of the trunk, and remove the skeleton. It was a difficult task, because wood had grown in among the bones and had to be cut away with pen knives. There were remnants of clothing still attached to the bones, and, by the skeleton's feet, they found a small metal container about the size of a tube that would have been used to protect an expensive cigar.

There was no cigar inside, but instead a note that simply said: "Alexander Kaiser has paid in full for his mistakes and now lives forever in the forest he loved."

When they removed the rest of the rubble, the workers found a small stone doorway that appeared to lead into an underground chamber of some type. Their flashlights did not reveal anything in the chamber, so they bulldozed dirt into it, leveled the area, and continued their work. The picnic area opened to the public in August 1968.

The Coroner was unable to confirm positively the identity of the skeleton. Alexander Kaiser's dental records had been destroyed many years ago, before dentists were required to file copies of dental charts with the state when they closed a patient's file. Nonetheless, Robert Kaiser was satisfied that it was his long-lost cousin, and he arranged to return Alex's remains to Wellsboro, where they were laid to rest next to his parents in the Kaiser family plot.

About a year after the Susquehannock Summit Picnic Area opened, visitors began to report loud screams, like someone being tortured, that seemed to come up from the ground. At first there were only one or two such reports every six to eight weeks; but they became more frequent, and eventually were almost every day. The state forest officials said that the noise was coming from hawks, but this was eventually dismissed by ornithologists who categorically disproved the hawk theory.

Responding to mounting complaints and local press stories about "the haunted picnic grove," the state forestry service investigated further in 1971 and this time confirmed that the sounds were coming from the ground. The state officials explained that the noises were the results of minor seismic shifting causing the plates of rock to vibrate and produce the sound, which then was reverberated through old abandoned coal mines far underground.

Nobody believed it. Local people stayed away, and the picnic area was too remote to attract ghost hunters and aficionados of the occult.

Researcher's footnote: At the end of the fall tourist season in November 1974, citing budget shortages and inadequate usage, the state permanently closed the Susquehannock Summit Picnic Area. There also had been protests, in the form of a petition to the Governor, signed by civic and religious leaders in the area, including Rev. William Paxton, against continuing to operate a tourist area on the site of such a horrible crime. The state removed the picnic pavilions and outhouses, tore up the parking lot, and permanently closed the access road. They announced that they were going to allow the area to revert to its natural state.

Other than the soil sampling conducted in the early 1950s by the Pennsylvania Forestry Association in the area around the Tioga Yew, Simon Poe has consistently declined requests by researchers to conduct a test boring of the Tioga Yew to confirm its age or to make any further examination of it.

In 1976, the Commonwealth of Pennsylvania erected a small historic marker at the approximate location of the Sentinel Burial Site.

Forces of Evil

"Jesus, Brendan, you scared the shit out of me. Don't ever sneak up on me like that again. You're lucky I didn't have a gun."

Brendan knew that Willy had been waiting for almost an hour for him. He had watched him drive through the break in the bushes and into the clearing about fifty yards off the road. It was almost dark.

"Where'd you park, Brendan? Did anyone see you?"

Brendan got in the back seat of Willy's old Chevrolet Impala.

"Hey, man," Willy said, trying to reach under his seat for something. "I'd be a whole lot more comfortable if you sat up here with me." Brendan watched as Willy kept his eyes fixed on Brendan's dark reflection in the rear-view mirror.

"And I'm a whole lot more comfortable sitting back here. So, shut up and have a beer."

Brendan held out a cold can inches from the right side of Willy's face. Willy's left arm hung down and slightly forward. He reached up awkwardly with his right hand. Brendan now knew that Willy's gun was just inches from his left hand, under the front seat on the left side.

"Why'd we have to meet way out here anyways?" Willy asked.

"Instead of the last time," Brendan responded, "When you and Claw came driving up to my place in broad daylight on your bikes? I wouldn't be surprised if half the county saw you two stupid clowns. I sweated it for weeks. I was sure someone would notice."

"Well, that's ancient history, man. What's your problem now?" Willy asked. "Not getting enough since your precious little Cathy had to go away?"

Brendan wasn't sure whether he was more stunned by Willy's disrespect or his vulgarity, but he had his forearm across Willy's windpipe before Willy could react.

"By the way, Willy," he said softly. "If you make a move for that pea shooter you have under the front seat, I'll snap your head off."

Willy gurgled something that sounded like agreement, and Brendan let go.

"Sorry, Brendan," Willy croaked. "I really am, man. I was out of line."

Willy took several gulps of beer, the beer can in his left hand, trying to appear to be in control, but Brendan could see his hand shaking slightly.

"What's up?" Willy said after taking a long sip.

"Get out of the car, Willy. I'm not going to sit here with that fucking gun just inches away. Let's grab the six pack and take a little walk."

Brendan could see the sweat on Willy's forehead when he opened the door and the dome light went on. Willy started to walk toward the edge of the clearing. Brendan remained by the car.

"Where are you going?"

"I thought you wanted to take a walk, Brendan."

"No, I just wanted to get out of the car. We can talk right here."

Willy returned slowly, his eyes darting to the driver's door. Brendan stepped sideways and leaned against it, standing between Willy and the car.

"Willy, it's time for the Watchmen to rise up."

"What do you mean, Brendan?"

"The forces of evil are closing in on us, Willy. We have to take action."

"Forces of evil? What the fuck are you talking about, man? What forces of evil?"

"Some are outside, some are inside, Willy," Brendan said calmly. "We need to turn back the outsiders who would steal what is ours, our faith, our heritage. We need to purge the forces that once were good and now have turned evil."

"Man, you're talking nonsense. Save that evil mumbo-jumbo for one of your sermons."

Brendan took three steps forward, grabbed Willy, and smashed his head into the side of the car, like a battering ram. Willy didn't have time to react. He lay on the ground and looked up. His face was gray, and his eyes were closed. For a moment, Brendan was afraid that he had killed him.

"I swear, Willy," Brendan said when he saw Willy's eyes open. His voice was barely a whisper. "I swear. One more smartass crack from you, and I'll kill you right here."

"Okay, okay." Willy scuttled backward several yards, trying to get out of range. He stood up slowly, his fingers probing the top of his head. He winced every time he touched it.

Brendan was surprised. Willy must be almost sixty. Brendan had hoped to knock him out and leave him in the woods. He knew that he could still rely on Claw instead or even Spook. Now Willy stood in front of Brendan, shaken but still in control of himself. Maybe he still had some value. Brendan realized that he was faster than Willy, but Willy just might be tougher.

"Okay, Willy. Let's quit screwing around with each other. We have some problems."

"I'm listening. What problems?"

"Problem number one: Russell Poe."

"Poe? The guy that owns the Rocks? Shit, he's harmless."

"No, he's not, Willy. He's smart. He's beginning to stumble onto some stuff that could really hurt us, once he figures it out."

"Like what?"

"Well, for one thing, Willy, he's nosing around about Jack Abrams and the stuff that Abrams was finding out. He's also asking questions about Abrams' death."

"Hey, we've already been through that, Brendan," Willy said. 'It was a fucking accident. We just wanted to give him a good scare, like you said. We were taking him to the Rocks, just like you told us to."

"Well, you didn't."

"Hey, how was we to know that the fucking cat would go apeshit and jump him?"

"Willy, Willy," Brendan sighed. "You're right. We've already gone through all that. And after the cougar ran off, you morons cut up Abrams to make it look like wild animals."

"Yeah, and Claw cut up a little of that old wolf-hair vest that he was wearing, and the cops bought it, and –"

Brendan interrupted. "Get real, you stupid shit. Nobody found any wolf hair around there, what with all the cops tramping around after they found the body. And if they had found it, they would have tested it and probably found out that it was some fake made in China.

"That wolf story started with an incompetent police chief who keeps his wife drugged up and a virtual prisoner in his house and a drunken undertaker who, when he occasionally crawls out of the gutter, pretends to be the County Coroner and keeps getting re-elected because there's nobody else stupid enough to want the job. Come on, get real. Had anyone with half a brain checked it out, it would have fallen apart in thirty seconds. Wolf attack, my ass. And that panther just didn't decide to attack Abrams for no reason. Why didn't it attack you or Claw? Hell, Claw would have been a better lunch than you and Abrams combined."

"Well, that is true," Willy said, chuckling. Brendan was not amused.

"No," Brendan continued, "I have never bought your story about how the cat just came out of the woods and attacked Jack Abrams for no reason. She was set on him, like a cat on a mouse. You should know that better than anyone, Willy."

"Well, I wouldn't know anything about that," Willy said quietly.

Brendan ignored him. "And now Poe's getting too damned close to uncovering the truth about all of us. He's picked up where Abrams left off, and people are talking to him."

"Nobody's going to break their vows," Willy said. "Everyone knows the consequences."

"Maybe not intentionally," Brendan said. "Maybe they don't even know what's real about what they told Abrams, and now are telling Poe, and what's just a crazy old legend. For example, I'm pretty sure that Poe knows about the Children and probably already knows about the treasure."

"From that map that you had Claw and me photograph?"

"Well, he has a part of the map," Brendan said, "But I don't think he knows what it means. When he showed it to me, he didn't let on that he had any idea. That's why I had you guys take a picture of it but not take the real thing, so he wouldn't get suspicious.

"And, of course, Rabbit's told us that Poe has been poking around at the Rocks, excavating and so forth, for over a year. So, with Jack Abrams' stories, and Poe going back and talking to some of the same people that Abrams talked to, and his excavations at the Rocks, it's just a matter of time before he puts it all together, with or without the map."

"Yeah, Brendan," Willy replied, "but Rabbit says he's harmless, basically a good guy. He says Poe knows we use the Rocks and a couple of other places on his land. Rabbit says Poe doesn't care because we don't mess up the place. Shit, Poe even noticed those nice mountain laurel that we planted last fall, although he thinks they just appeared naturally. And all that snooping he's been doing about Jack Abrams has just been to get in good with Jack's widow, the lady that owns that apple farm next to him."

Brendan tossed another can of beer to Willy and opened one for himself.

"So, what if," Willy said after he had several gulps of beer, "what if, we just scare Poe a little, just like we did to his uncle when he started nosing around the Rocks too much."

"Three reasons, Willy," Brendan said. "First, of all, I don't think we scared off Simon Poe. He was a tough guy, nothing like his nephew. Making strange stuff happen to him was not enough. Hell, he was a retired oil guy from the Persian Gulf from back in the 1940s. He wasn't the type of guy to scare easily. I admit it, I really miscalculated.

"Second, Simon Poe apparently was planning to move out west with his girlfriend anyways, but he kept the house, complete with furniture, after he left. That was another big surprise, to tell you the truth. We didn't even know anything about her. At the same time, he obviously had plans to come back, at least now and then. A scared man doesn't act like that."

"So maybe it will be easier to scare Russell Poe," Willy suggested. "He's a really smart guy, but I'm sure he'd freak out if he met – well, let's just say, some of the more exotic wildlife around here. From a safe distance, of course. It still would be enough."

"No," Brendan replied, "it's too late for that, Willy. And that's the third reason. You said it yourself, he's smart. I think he's really close to figuring it all out.

"I don't know about you, but I'm not going to prison because you turkeys killed Abrams, even if it was an accident. We've got to neutralize the threat."

"The threat? About Abrams? You mean Rabbit? Sure, he did the setup on Abrams, but he'll keep quiet." Willy said.

"Like he kept quiet when he told the cops about you guys meeting Jack at the Pine Tree Inn?" Brendan responded. "But no, I'm not really worried about Rabbit. He had no choice. The cops knew he was at the Pine Tree."

"But how'd he know that he'd been seen there?" Willy asked.

"I don't know," Brendan replied. "Rabbit's a smart guy, like a wolf. He knew he was in a tight spot and was looking out for himself while trying not to hurt us. Rabbit was trying to throw the cops off the scent. I can appreciate that. Like I said, he did the best he could.

"But that doesn't change the fact that Rabbit's still a problem. He's in too deep and he knows it. But I'm not all that worried about him, Willy. We can manage him. You and Claw already have him dancing around like a puppet. No, the real threat is Russell Poe. I know him well enough to know that we can't manage Poe like we can Rabbit."

"No more, Brendan, no more." Willy took a step back, his hands raised at his sides, the palms facing Brendan as if trying to push him away. "Claw and I are already on the hook for Abrams. Even if they ever catch us and can prove anything, it will probably be just manslaughter.

"Abrams was enough. We can explain that away as an accident, tell them that it was a practical joke that got out of hand. The worst we'd get would probably be just two to five. And they'll never be able to connect us with that stupid kid that we left to die in the snow last January."

"Yeah," Brendan interjected. "The one that fucking Russell Poe rescued. See what I mean, he's always popping up like a goddamned Whack-A-Mole."

"That may be true," Willy replied, "but I know that Claw and me are not going to risk going to the chair, not for you, not for the Children, not for nobody. Damn it, Brendan, we've been lucky so far, but enough is enough."

Brendan was quiet for a minute while he finished his can of beer. A truck drove slowly along the road, much slower than usual when it went by the opening that led to the clearing where they were standing. Brendan and Willy stood quietly, barely breathing while each picked an escape route if someone stopped. The truck did not slow down and continued on.

"Okay," Brendan said, sensing a strange rising panic in Willy. "Okay, calm down, Willy. I'm not asking you to kill anyone for Christ's sake, just help me take care of him. I'll figure out a way to neutralize Poe so that nobody gets hurt."

"So, you want us to deliver him an engraved invite to Samhain, on a fucking silver tray, maybe?"

"Don't be an idiot, Willy. You know that Poe wouldn't come voluntarily."

"Why not, Brendan? Has anyone asked?"

"I know Russell Poe. I'm probably the closest thing he has to a friend around here, except maybe Jack Abrams' widow. I'm sure he trusts me, but I know that he wouldn't want any part of Samhain."

"How do you know, Brendan? You told him about the Children?"

Willy started to move slowly toward the car. Brendan remained where he was, leaning against the car, trying to keep his body language appearing relaxed.

"No, of course not, Willy. Nothing important, just a few old bits of family history, a few old ghost stories like I told Jack Abrams, that's all," Brendan said.

"The point is," Brendan continued, "that we'll have shown him enough so that he concludes, on his own, that he needs to leave us alone. That's the only way he'll come to see the light. You know how it is. You sometimes have to tear a person down before you can build them up."

"Like Spook." Willy said, nodding.

"Yeah, like Spook, but Poe is a hundred times smarter. Never forget that, Willy."

"So, you want Claw and me to take Poe for a little ride in the country some night?" Willy asked.

"Jesus, Willy, you're beginning to sound like a gangster in a bad movie," Brendan laughed. "But whatever we do, you may have to bring him against his will."

"How am I even going to get close to him, to convince him to come with us?"

"Leave it to me and Rabbit, Willy. I'll tell you about your role after Rabbit and I get it all set up. And don't worry. I'm not going to put you or any of our brothers and sisters at risk."

Willy held his watch up, trying to read the time in the heavily filtered moonlight.

"Listen, Brendan, I gotta split. You said that the Watchmen needed to move against something internal? Is Spook causing us problems again?"

"No, I assure you that Spook is developing into a loyal, obedient Child. But we were speaking of invitations."

"Someone else?"

"I want you to deliver an invitation to John Bard to preside at Samhain this Wednesday night."

"Bard? How on earth do you expect me to find him? He's fucking dead for all I know."

Brendan looked up through the half-empty tree branches at the first stars of evening. "No, Willy, not dead," he said, "but his cycle is almost done. This Samhain, in fact, he must be reborn, at the same tree where he last emerged nine hundred years ago."

"Come on, Brendan." Willy said, mashing his cigarette into the dirt with his foot. "I mean, we all talk about John Bard and I believe in him. But, come on, this is Willy you're talking to. There's no such person as John Bard, at least not anymore. He just a spirit, a manitou, not real flesh and blood."

"He's real," Brendan said. "I swear it to you on my life, Willy. I assure you, John Bard is very much alive. He knows that you are a Watchman and he will wait for you at the old Sentinel Burial Site down by the river. He will know you and will come with you. He wants this. He has been looking forward to this Samhain, his nine hundredth in this cycle, for many years. And he has chosen you to be his guide up the mountain and into his next life."

"Okay, but how will I –" Willy started to ask.

"Just be there," Brendan interrupted. "Just be at the site two hours before midnight on Wednesday. John will know what to do from there."

Brendan turned and walked away. Rather than taking the narrow dirt path down to the road, he blended silently into the forest, following the paths home by memory and the distinct feel of each one against the soles of his shoes. When he was about a hundred yards away, he turned and looked back through a natural line of sight he had discovered years ago. He saw Willy still standing outside his car, drinking the last of the beer.

The Night Visitors

Faithful to one of the traditions of their thirty-year marriage – or was it just a comfortable habit? – Ray Davis poured the hot water into the flowered thin teapot for his breakfast with June. Soon after their wedding, Ray took over the preparation of their breakfast. He had wanted to do something every day that would be uniquely special in their life. How many breakfasts had he prepared? He started to do the math as he arranged the English china teacups on their kitchen table, but he gave up when he tried to subtract the few days that he hadn't been home at breakfast time. The toaster oven buzzed, telling him that the croissants were ready, wiping out the provisional total that he thought that he had calculated. He opened a can of mandarin oranges and put them in bowl, rinsing them first to remove the traces of the light syrup.

His grandparents' mantel clock in the living room chimed seven and, as if on cue, June came downstairs from their bedroom. Every morning she always looked so refreshed, so young, before the worry lines began to slowly come, to the surface of her face as the day continued. Today she wore a light lavender robe over her deep purple nightgown.

After all these years, Ray thought, after all the troubles, even as she had become a ghostly shadow of the woman she had once been, in the morning June still had – he groped for the word – a magnetism, an aura, a gentle glow that came from within, something that maybe only he could see when others saw only a sad fading middle-aged woman.

Sandy used to see it. Sometimes, when she was younger, right after June returned from the hospital in Syracuse, Sandy would talk with him about it, and how she missed the mother she used to have, as she described June. Those discussions ended years ago when Sandy announced that she couldn't take the sadness that she said was like a heavy, suffocating smog in the Davis home, and that she had to move out, "just to be able to breathe," she said. Ray had offered to help her find a place to live, but she declined. "Daddy, I have to do this on my own," she said.

Ray looked at the china cups, which they had bought together as a first anniversary present to themselves. Somehow – and perhaps he would never understand it – their mornings together always brought back those days, resurrected two younger versions of each of them, two people who believed in possibilities of life together and maybe even a special magic that only they could share. And then Ray would go to the station and June would stay at home, afraid to leave the house except to tend her flower garden. And somehow during the day the two of them would drift slowly apart, Ray into his world of laws and facts and rationality, of noble aspirations and human failings, and June edging slowly back into her own world, one that Ray could barely describe to himself, much less understand.

June sat down, and Ray poured her tea, a robust English breakfast tea, "steeped two minutes" he would assure June every morning with a smile. He placed the two chocolate croissants on a small plate and offered them to her. She studied them for a second and as always took the smaller one. Even when the two croissants looked identical to Ray, June would study them, almost like a surveyor. He then placed ten – not nine, not eleven – orange segments on her plate, the very faint aroma of the oranges blending with the faint traces of the chocolate drizzled on the croissants.

Just like every morning of my life, Ray thought, and yet it gives me such joy, such comfort. I could die happily today knowing that, on my last day, we had breakfast together.

June was looking at him and sending him an invisible signal that snapped him back to the reality of their kitchen on a sunny autumn morning. She sat silently, smiling at him. But June would never say a word until she had her first sip of the tea. Ray sipped his at the same time, as they watched each other. Ray would rather have coffee; June had always hated the smell of it. She never forbade it, but Ray would have his coffee at the station, and never drank the stuff after mid-afternoon. So, it never made sense to keep any in the house. And that exclusion made the tea at breakfast a sacrament.

"Raymond," June said as they set their cups back in the saucers in unison. "Raymond, I love you with all my being. Our love –"

"I know, June. I realize it every day," Ray replied.

"But today I have to tell you something that might hurt you. I know that there are things that you don't like me to talk about, that you think are just crazy talk."

"Never, I never said –" Ray started to say.

"That's okay, dear," June responded. "I've heard you talking with Sandy about what the two of you call my 'crazy talk.' You even used those words. Don't deny it. It's all right. I understand why you think that sometimes."

Before Ray could protest further, June said calmly, "Raymond, I had two visitors last night."

"Was it another of those dreams that you sometimes have, the ones that your medication sometimes causes and makes them seem so real?"

"No, darling, this was real, as real as you and I are right now."

Raymond had learned that the best thing to do was to sit silently and let June tell her stories. Don't excite her, because she would get flustered and embarrassed by it and would simply end the conversation. Let her talk all she wants, the doctors had counseled him. It's better than letting her store up all those thoughts inside her. The longer she kept them inside, the doctors said, the more real they became to her.

"Raymond," she said, her head bowed. Her right hand was arranging and rearranging the napkin in her lap. "Raymond, John Bard came to visit me last night, just after midnight. He came around to the kitchen door. He tapped his secret tap on the door, so I'd know it was him."

"You have a secret tap with him?"

"Yes, from the old days."

"Darling, I didn't hear anything," Ray said.

"You wouldn't have," June smiled. "You were so sound asleep that they could have set off an atomic bomb in our kitchen and you'd never notice."

"How did you know it was John Bard?" Ray asked, regretting almost instantly the question.

"We both know how," June said quietly. "I mean, I don't want to hurt you and bring up things from the past, but –"

"Okay," Ray said. "So, what happened?"

"Raymond," June said, looking up. Her blue eyes looked like points of light, reflecting the light coming in the kitchen window behind him. "Raymond, John Bard came to say goodbye."

Ray wanted to ask some questions, but he was afraid that June would think that he was interrogating her, that he didn't believe her, and then she would refuse to say anything else. Keep her talking, he advised himself. Ask questions only when you need to keep her talking.

Ray took a sip of tea and broke off a piece of his croissant. He moved it around his plate, soaking up some of the traces of water from the orange segments. He saw June watching him, so he set it down.

"Go on," he said. "I'm listening."

"He said that he had come to say goodbye. 'I am at the end of my time,' he said. 'My nine-hundredth Samhain is nigh, and I must pass to my next level.'"

"What is this Samhain?" Ray asked. "You mentioned that last Friday, when Sandy was here. I think it was the first time I ever heard you mention it." Ray was annoyed with himself when he remembered that he had meant to look it up but never got around to it.

June appeared to be looking far off into the distance. Her voice took a quality that Ray had never heard, almost like a Gregorian chant, but spoken. "It's a very ancient sacred day, at the first new moon after the autumn equinox, the only time of the year when the boundaries between this world and the other world can be crossed.

"The Aos Sí, the souls of those who have crossed over, return to our sacred groves and circles," June intoned. "We honor death then, just as the moon dies that night, becoming the first new moon of the dark half of the year. We dance with them to celebrate the oneness of life and death and of death and life. And when a great, ancient Druid like John Bard completes his cycle of life, we send him with great honors, with mistletoe and yew branches, across the clearing to the other side of the forest to his next level of existence, where he becomes a manitou and can take and change whatever form he wants, be it rock or tree, an animal of the forest, of people who are still on this side, or even of his former self."

June suddenly stopped speaking, the pitch of her voice as if in mid-sentence. Her eyes were closed. Ray's mind began to whirl slowly around: Aos Sí, mistletoe and yew, Druid priests and manitous, a crazy mix of Celtic and American Indian and who knows what else.

"And you are sure that this was the same John Bard that you have told me about before, and that he told you all this when he visited you last night." Ray confirmed quietly.

"Yes, he called me by my Old Name."

"Which was?"

June opened her eyes. She reached across the table and took Ray's hand. "*Is*, Raymond, is. It has been my name for all time."

"What *is* your Old Name, then, June. I want to know everything about you."

"Dearest Raymond," she said, "you are more important to me than eternal life itself, and I know that someday you and I will step across together, maybe not at exactly the same time physically, but at the same instant spiritually, and we will wander together among the farthest stars and in the forests here on earth on a million Samhains to come. But no matter how much I love you, I cannot tell you that now, not until that time comes for us. I took an oath."

"I understand," Ray murmured. "What did he look like, the man who was at our back door?"

"Well, like John Bard."

"I mean, what was he wearing, June?"

"His usual outfit for the mountains, an old hat and that old blue coat of his. Lord, it must be hundreds of years old. It looked like he had trimmed his beard a little, at least since the last time I saw him, and that was many years ago. He's gotten a lot neater since I used to know him." June smiled faintly.

"But why all these questions, Raymond? I've told you all about John Bard. Many times, many many times." She sighed.

Ray could tell that June was beginning to get annoyed. "I'm sorry," he said, "I didn't mean to interrupt. I'm just interested, that's all."

June looked around, in the direction of the back door. "Raymond, I know that all these years you have never believed what I've told you about my – my experiences – with the Children. But they were real. At least, I am positive that most of them were real, even though there still are a few things that I think are real but don't understand. And it's only because I love you so much, and because I want to be with you forever among the stars, that I am telling you these things now. I really should never have told you any of this, Raymond, none of it. I could get into a lot of trouble by telling you even the little bit that I have told.

"But, oh god, I want to walk hand in hand among the stars with you and only you forever." June buried her face in her hands for a few moments. Ray looked at her, for a moment not sure what he should say. Then he said, "And I want to be with you, too."

June straightened up, exhaled, and looked at Ray. "So," she said with a deliberate tone to her voice, "John told me he would be sacrificed at Samhain, under the blade of Brendan. John said that our son would be there. He's grown up now and is beginning to master the wisdom, but I know that he is really Rabbit's son, I mean Whitey's son. John said that someday he will become a great leader of our people. John told me his Ancient Name."

"Rabbit?" Ray asked. "Whitey is known as Rabbit? Who calls him that?"

June put her right hand to her mouth, with a look of surprise and alarm. "Oh, Raymond, please forget that I said any of that. Please, please wipe it out of your mind. I should not have given up Whitey's Old Name. Please forget it." Tears appeared at the corners of her eyes. She wiped them away quickly with her napkin.

Ray decided to ignore June's fantasy about her other child.

"Under the blade? Sacrificed?" he said instead. "You mean that John Bard is going to be killed by this person you call Brendan?"

"No, not really, only ceremonially. It is something that great holy people like John must go through so that they can live forever," June said. "It is the price that they must pay for immortality in this world. John might keep the same physical form, or he might change. His spirit will transform into whatever shape that he wants."

"So, nobody will get hurt?" Ray asked.

"No," June said, with a strange uncertainty to her voice, one that she usually had when she was fantasizing. "It's symbolic and real at the same time, like Christian communion. I mean, he won't be physically killed, no more than it's really the body and blood of Jesus. John can never be physically killed. But there will be an instantaneous death and the beginning of a new cycle of life. And because it will be the last Samhain of this cycle, they will probably burn a sacred tree, an oak or maybe even the great yew, so that his spirit may light the moonless night. I do hope it's the yew. It is so special and only he deserves it. But even so, the tree that is selected, that he selects, will not be killed but will return to life at the next spring equinox."

"And where and when is this all supposed to take place?" Ray asked.

"Only in a sacred circle or grove, like the White Indian Rocks, tonight, probably around midnight, or maybe tomorrow night, or maybe the night after that. I don't remember. I should have looked at the sky last night to see how close the moon was to becoming new. I don't think John told me, and I was too surprised to see them to ask."

"And how –" Ray started to ask.

June put her hands to the side of her head. "Please, please, please," she said, "I'm getting all confused. I know it doesn't make sense to you, Raymond, but please don't try to confuse me even more. This is the true nature of existence, of the universe, that night and day, life and death, dark and light can all exist at the same time. I don't know it all, and it was a long time ago when I did know what little I learned. Maybe I have already told you too much."

"I'm sorry," Ray said softly. "I don't mean to confuse or upset you. I understand, believe me I do. And may I ask you just one more question?"

"Sure, if I know the answer," June said quietly.

"Why are you telling me this?" Ray asked, hoping not to alarm her.

"Because John said that I am in danger."

"From whom?"

"From people who want to take over the Children, from people like Brendan and Willy. He said their names."

"Brendan and Willy? Who are they?"

"Children of Bel."

"But, in real life, I mean. Do you know the real identities of people like Brendan and Willy and this person who you say is your son?"

"Yes, I know who Brendan is. A lot of the Children do, but nobody will say; they are so afraid of him. I don't know who Willy is. But if I tell you, if I even guess out loud, they will find out and kill me. And they always find out. I don't know how, but they always do."

"And John Bard told you all this last night?"

"Yes, he did." June's voice sounded determined. "Just like I am telling it to you now."

"But how could you be in danger?" Ray asked. "You've always said that you haven't had anything to do with these people for years, that you no longer belong."

"He didn't say," June said quietly.

"And why is John Bard telling you this?" Ray asked again. "Does he want you to be there, even though he says that you are in great danger? It doesn't make sense to me, June. I don't understand."

"He never said that he wants me to be there, Raymond. He just came to say goodbye," June replied, her voice barely audible. "Oh, Raymond, it's not all logical in this world, Raymond. You wouldn't understand. Only a Child of Bel can understand."

"And John Bard was here, inside our house, last night?"

"No, Raymond, I never said he was inside. He was at the back door." June pointed at the door. "He didn't come in. He wouldn't. He waited outside and I had to go outside to him. I'm sure it was John, but sometimes I thought it was Whitey. He seemed to change back and forth."

June picked up her cup. Her hand was trembling. She grasped it with both hands and set it down.

"More tea, dear?" Ray asked.

"No, thank you."

Ray and June sat silently at the table. June looked into her cup and occasionally turned in the direction of the kitchen door. Ray continued to look at her, hoping he had a faint smile on his face, a welcoming smile, not a condescending one. After a while, Ray glanced at his watch. Neither had spoken for almost five minutes. Ray wondered what he could say or do – if there was anything at all that he could do – to restore the morning peace, the rare moments of real communication that they had always enjoyed together.

Ray knew that he would have to break the silence. He hoped he hadn't hurt June's feelings.

"And, I believe you said that there was a second visitor. Was it at the same time or later?"

"Sort of both, Raymond. I know this sounds crazy but I'm positive it was real. After John and I talked for a while "

"You talked about other things, things that you haven't mentioned yet?"

"Well, yes, but they were just about the Children and the old days, that's all. Just chit-chat between two old friends. Nothing important."

"I assume that you're not allowed to tell me what was said." Ray tried very hard to keep any kind of an accusatory or hurt tone from his voice. "If that's the case, I understand. I wouldn't want you to get into any trouble. So, who was the second visitor last night? Whitey Wentworth?"

"Yes, Whitey, and please forget that I ever said his other name, please for his sake and mine. But this is the strange part. I was standing outside on the back patio, right by the door, talking with John just as close as I'm speaking with you, and suddenly he disappeared, and Whitey was there."

"What happened to John Bard?"

"Well, I don't know," June said. "I glanced up at our bedroom window for a second, to make sure I hadn't disturbed you, and, when I looked again, John had disappeared, and Whitey was standing there in his place.

"But it could have been John Bard, too. He can do that, change form, even take on the form of another entirely different person."

"Did you see any signs of where John Bard might have gone?"

"No, it was dark last night, almost no moon at all."

"What did Whitey want?"

"He said that he came to warn me. He asked if anyone from the Children had contacted me or threatened me in any way. He said that a couple of guys – *thugs* he called them – had threatened to hurt me if he didn't cooperate with them about something.

"I asked him who these guys were, and he wouldn't say, except to say that they worked for Brendan, who's like the number two leader, next to John Bard."

"He said that they had forced him to do something really bad, to betray a friend. At first, he thought that he was just getting involved in a dispute that the Children had with his friend, who owns the land where the Rocks are."

"That would be Russell Poe."

"He didn't say who it was, but he believed that something really bad was going to happen to this friend at Samhain. He wouldn't say what it was, but he seemed really shaken up about it."

"Was there anything else that Whitey said that you can tell me?"

"Not really." June was silent for moment, her eyes closed.

"No," she said again when she opened her eyes.

"What do you think we should do about this, June, about these night visitors of yours? What did they want us to do?" If someone's going to be in danger, why doesn't Whitey report this to the police, either out there in Richmond Township or even to me?"

"I asked him that, Raymond, and he said that it would be pointless for him to tell you about it, because you wouldn't believe him. He thought that if I told you about it, you might believe me and do something."

"Did he say anything that he had in mind? Unless Mr. Poe objects to them trespassing on his land or there's other evidence that they intend actual criminal acts, I just can't send some officers up there and arrest them or chase them all away."

"Well, I don't know about what you can and can't do, Raymond. I'm just saying what he told me.

"And there was one other thing that he said," June added.

"What was that?"

"Well, two things, really. He said that it didn't matter what I did or didn't do, but he would never bother me again. He said he knows that I have been trying to escape the Children all these years and that I kept my promises to them. He wants me to have a good life with you and Sandy."

"Who said this, John or Whitey?" Ray interrupted.

"It was –" June hesitated. "I think it was John, but it also might have been Whitey. They seemed to be jumping back and forth; first one would appear and say something, then the other, right before they left – or he left.

"Oh, Raymond, I just don't know," June said, her face that of a woman trying hard to remember. "It is so confusing."

"What else did he – or they – say?"

"Right before he walked away – and I'm pretty sure it was Whitey that time – he said, something like 'I got him into this mess and I'm going to have to get him out.'

"I mean, I know that I am not crazy, Raymond. I didn't dream this or imagine it."

"It's not for me to say," Ray said, trying to sound sympathetic. "You know, it's possible, just possible, that you had one of those really vivid dreams, the ones that are brought on sometimes by your medication. Maybe you were sleepwalking, You've done that before, June. Maybe it seemed as real as you describe it. That's not for me to judge."

Ray reached over and took June's hand. He tried to look into her eyes. "Look at me, June," he said. "Look at me."

June looked up. "What is important now," Ray said, "is that I believe that *you* believe that it was real, and that makes it real to me, and that's all that matters to me. And I love you, and that will never change."

Ray wanted to draw out more of June's story, to try to let her see for herself the contradictions and impossibilities in what she believed that she had experienced. But he could tell that June had become exhausted just talking about – what was it, he wondered – her dream, her visions, her visitors, her hallucinations?

"I'd best go upstairs and rest for a while," June said, standing up, throwing her shoulders back and raising her chin. "I'll clean up later. And thank you so much for such a lovely breakfast, Raymond. I might even go into town today for a little while."

June came around the table and kissed him, then went into the living room and walked upstairs.

"That would be very nice, June," Ray said to her back. "If you do decide to come into town, call me first, and we can have lunch together, maybe at the diner." It was an invitation that June had not accepted in many years.

Ray's first telephone call when he arrived at the police station was to Whitey Wentworth. There was no answer. His next call, to Russell Poe, went to Poe's answering machine.

"Mr. Poe," Ray said, "It's Chief Ray Davis from the Wellsboro Police. Could you please give me a call when you have the chance? It's nothing urgent. I just have a couple of questions, and I thought that you might be able to help." Ray left a phone number and hung up.

Administrative matters diverted Ray's attention that morning, so it was not until early afternoon when Ray telephoned Robert Verona, the Chief of Richmond Township's two-man police department. Ray explained that he was picking up information that suggested that there might be trouble sometime that night or the next night at the Indian Rocks and that it might have something to do with the new moon.

"The new moon?" Chief Verona laughed. "Well, that's a new one. Usually all the crazies come out at the full moon."

They discussed briefly what each of them knew about reports of cults known to be operating in the county.

"That's the trouble with all this, Bob," Ray said, "Neither one of us knows how many of these reports are true and how many are based on little more than rumors and superstitions."

"Yeah, that's right," Chief Verona said. "Just a couple of weeks ago, we got a report from a motorist about a mysterious procession marching up on that slope at the bend in Lamb's Creek Road carrying torches and a body all tied up. Turns out it was three guys with flashlights hunting deer out of season and carrying a small doe that they had shot."

"Well, there is that semi-religious group – I guess you'd call it a cult – that sometimes has services up in the mountains," Ray said, "but we've never had any hard evidence or complaints of any violations. There might be more than one, but we don't have anything solid about it."

"I know that my department can't afford to send an officer up there into the forest some night to look for a bunch of hippies who probably aren't doing anything worse than smoking some weed," Chief Verona said, "not unless the landowner wants to file a trespassing complaint. And I have talked before to the man who owns those Indian Rocks up above the river, Mr. Poe, and he doesn't have any objection. He says he knows that some people use the Rocks for some kinds of ceremonies, and others like to hike up there and picnic. However, they seem to respect the place and always leave nothing but footprints, like he says.

"But I know that we're both concerned about that rape case a couple of months ago, where there were some ritualistic aspects to it. But I'm not aware of any connection to any specific group, are you, Ray?"

"No, Bob, we've got nothing new to go on over here in Wellsboro and I haven't heard anything new from the State Police. And, as you recall, the victim isn't cooperating. She made a statement and then recanted it. Even if she had stuck with it, the forensics didn't hold up. Well, at least you and I don't have to explain to our beloved DA why we haven't closed the file."

"Yeah," Chief Verona chuckled, "If we keep it open, it messes up her statistics, but if we close it without an arrest, it would make her look like she doesn't believe rape victims – neither one's the best thing for somebody who wants to run for Attorney General."

The two police chiefs agreed to stay alert and share any new information. Chief Verona said that since the supposed site was in his jurisdiction, he'd interface on their behalf with the State Police if he needed help.

Just before the call ended, Chief Verona asked, "Just so I'm sure I'm not missing anything, Chief Davis, I understand that you have developed some information that there might be ritual sacrifice – probably only a mock ceremony, not a real sacrifice – or something similar later this week, possibly even tonight, and that it is going to occur at the Indian Rocks or some similar place?"

"That's right."

"Is any of this from a reliable source?"

Ray paused a couple of seconds before replying softly, "No, Chief Verona, I'm afraid not."

The Panther Kill

As soon as Russell heard the pounding on the kitchen door, he looked at his alarm clock: 6:10 a.m. It was just beginning to get light on what promised to be a beautiful Indian Summer day. As soon as he was fully awake, he remembered that it was Wednesday. Whitey Wentworth would be coming at seven to help clear away the brush that had encroached from the woods into Poe's already small back yard. Never, in all the months that Poe had known him had Whitey ever been early, especially not this early.

Russell threw a bathrobe around his shoulders and took his time descending the stairs. His muscles were tied up in knots from cutting and stacking firewood yesterday. He felt like he didn't have full control over them. The knocking continued, and Russell could hear Whitey's voice as he approached the kitchen door.

"Mr. Poe. Russell. Wake up. It's Whitey. There's something you've got to see."

Poe made a point of yawning as he opened the door.

"Whitey, it's only a little after six. You're too early. I just got up."

Whitey had a knapsack slung over one shoulder and had rested his rifle against the side of the house, just outside the door.

"Sorry to roust you out so early, Russell, but I knew you'd want to know right away."

"Know what?"

"There's been a panther kill up on the ridge. An elk, a young one but a ten-pointer. I know you've been interested in getting some proof of all those panther legends. Well, here it is, and almost at your back door."

"An elk? I thought that they were pretty much gone from Pennsylvania."

"Well, almost Russell," Whitey said. Russell could hear the excitement in his voice. "There ain't many left."

Russell's next thought was of Clay Collins.

"Whitey, have you told anyone else about this?"

"Well, no, Russell. I figured you'd want to be the first. I mean, it's on your land, and you're interested in panthers."

"Well, I should call Clay Collins over at the Pennsylvania Cougar Research Center," Russell said as he walked back into the house, motioning for Whitey to come in. "He's been trying to get definite proof that cougars are still in the area. I should also call the Fish and Game people."

"There's no time for that, Russell. The cat could come back and finish up his meal."

Russell persisted, however.

"Sorry to wake you up so early, Clay," Russell began.

"No problem, Mr. Poe," he replied. "I've been up for a while. I'm an early riser."

When he told Clay about the discovery, he couldn't tell over the telephone whether Clay's reaction was skeptical or just sleepy.

"Who told you about this, Russell?" Clay asked.

"Whitey Wentworth. He's here now."

"And the kill is up on your property?"

"I think so, from what Whitey told me. It's up toward the top of the ridge behind my house."

"Just this side of the old Indian trail along the ridge," Whitey spoke up.

"How does Whitey know about it?" Clay said.

"Good question, Clay. I'll ask." Russell held the phone out like a microphone. Whitey's explanation was sufficiently self-incriminating to be true.

"Well, let's just say I was on my way back from a little night hunting," Whitey said. "It was about a half hour ago. I heard a lot of thrashing in the woods, like something big was struggling there. It sounded some way off, so I started in that direction. That's how I found the elk, with my light."

"You were spotlighting?" Russell asked. "And aren't you rushing the season a little?"

Whitey seemed to be surprised by Russell's knowledge of Pennsylvania hunting laws.

"Well, I wasn't hunting on your land. I'd never do that." Whitey was emphatic. "I parked out on the road because it was close to the path up to the ridge trail. I didn't think you would mind. I was over in the – well, let's just say I was well off your property. I'd never hunt on your land. I know how you feel about that, and I respect that."

"I don't want to hear any more, I think." Russell said.

"Best not, Russell," Whitey nodded. "Wouldn't want you to be an accessory."

"And that's why you don't want me to call the Fish and Game people?"

"Not just yet."

"Tell Whitey his secret is safe with me," Clay interjected. "There's another good practical reason not to call Fish and Game: They could take days to get to your place to investigate. By then the evidence could be compromised, unless you're willing to sit up there all day and all night with a shotgun to protect the scene."

Clay explained that he had to stop and get gasoline on the way, but he could be there in about a half hour or forty-five minutes. "So, don't wait for me. It's really important that you get a camera – a good one if you have it – and get up there," he said.

"I've got a pretty good 35-millimeter camera," Russell replied.

"On second thought, a good Polaroid camera would be better," Clay said. "It's harder to fake a Polaroid picture. I'll bring mine with me. But what's important now is to get back up that hill right away. Don't touch anything, but photograph everything. I mean everything as best you can within at least twenty yards of the carcass. And when you enter the area, take off your shoes and keep a sharp eye out for tracks, any tracks at all, even places where the grass or weeds look like they've been pushed down. Take a flashlight with you and use it, because there are a lot of shadows this time of day. If you see a good clear track, like in the dirt, put a ruler down beside it. If you don't have a ruler, use a pen – not a pencil – a pen."

"I have a good metal ruler and a longer tape measure, both metric, but I'm curious. Why not a pencil?" Russell asked.

Clay's voice sounded excited and a little impatient. "The problem with pencils is that they can be of any length, Russell, depending on how much they've been sharpened. With a pen you can at least determine its length from another pen of the same brand. Measurement is really important, so a metric measure like yours is always more precise than one with only inches. Centimeters can make a difference. That's how we determine how big the animal is."

"Maybe we should go in on our hands and knees so as not to disturb anything," Russell commented.

"That can actually do more damage to the site, and it's also a good way to become the cat's lunch. If he sees you on all fours, he might think you're a scavenger trying to take his kill. No, stand up as tall as you can, go slowly, and keep looking down. But only one of you should be doing this. The other person should keep looking at the forest and be ready with a rifle or shotgun. A shotgun might be better at close range.

"But whatever you guys do, remember that it's early morning and still the cat's hunting time. If that's a cougar kill, it will come back."

Russell asked, "Wouldn't be better if we just wait for you? You're the expert."

"No, Russell. It's more important that you and Whitey get up there to protect the scene. For one thing, if anyone else should come along, you'll be able to keep them from inadvertently destroying evidence. Also, try to keep scavengers, especially birds, away. Birds will go for the parts of the carcass the cat has already opened and they can destroy a lot of tell-tale signs of a cougar."

Based on Whitey's description, Russell told Clay to follow them up the trail behind his house.

'I know the one, Russell."

"Whitey says that the kill is about fifty yards below the ridge and about twenty yards to the right of the path, behind some bushes. He says that he left his ball cap on a branch to mark where you should turn. Most of the leaves are down by now, so you'll probably see us from the path."

Russell quickly returned upstairs, dressed, and collected his field bag, which already had a camera, notebook, metric tape, markers, and the rest of his archeology gear. There were two new rolls of film in the bag. He checked the camera, which had twenty exposures left.

Russell and Whitey left through the kitchen door. Whitey grabbed his rifle and knapsack and led the way. Neither man said much, saving their breath for the climb up the mountain. When they were almost to the ridge, Whitey pointed to his cap hanging on a branch and quietly said, "This is the place, Russell. We turn here."

Russell and Whitey walked side by side as Whitey described the scene they were approaching.

"See those two clumps of brush up ahead, just to the left of that oak? The elk is just behind them."

"Did you spend much time in there, when you found the elk? I'm thinking about what Clay told us about not trampling down some of the evidence he'll need to convince the state guys."

"Well, it was still kind of dark," Whitey said, "and I didn't know if there were any prints or not, if that's what you mean. I was just coming down the trail and I heard that thrashing noise off to my left. So, I took a couple steps off the trail and shined my light in the direction of the sound."

"What kind of a sound?" Russell interrupted.

"Oh, nothing special," Whitey said. "Like I said, just like a big animal thrashing around in the brush. When the elk carcass suddenly showed up in my light, I almost jumped out of my skin.

"Did you see any other animals in the area?" Russell asked.

"Nope. I looked around, because I was afraid that whatever killed the elk was still there and would go after me next. But no, I didn't see anything else, thank God. So, I high-tailed it down the trail to get you."

When they came to the two clumps of brush that Whitey had pointed out, they stopped. Whitey pointed ahead.

"See it, Russell? Dead ahead."

The body of a young elk lay at the far end of a small clearing, partly covered by leaves and dirt. Its head was twisted back almost parallel to its back. A large part of the back of the neck was missing, and there were bites taken out of the belly. Russell could see the ends of the viscera, pink, red, and brownish colored, still wet looking.

Russell felt sick. Steady, he told himself. It's no worse than a butcher shop.

"Those are the signs that Clay told me to look for, Whitey. The cougar bit into its neck and tore part of it away as it brought the elk down from behind. Then it went to work on the guts."

They removed their shoes. They moved forward slowly as Clay had instructed, Russell looking down at the ground and Whitey behind him, occasionally whispering "All clear, Russell." Russell stopped suddenly and pointed silently at the ground.

"Holy mother of Christ," Whitey said.

The paw print was at least five inches, maybe six, from front to back. Russell carefully laid his metric ruler alongside it. It measured 14 centimeters, more than 5-1/2 inches. He carefully kneeled on the ground, opened his field bag, and brought the camera to his eye.

"Clay is going to go nuts when he sees –"

Suddenly it felt like his head exploded. He fell forward, his jaw hitting the cool, dewy grass. The last thing he felt before he blacked out completely was a needle being stuck into his neck.

"Shit, man, did you kill him?" Whitey said as Claw stepped over Russell's body. "You didn't tell me you were going to kill him."

"No, he's going to be fine," Claw said as he nudged Poe with the toe of his boot. "That's the nice thing about a blackjack; it only leaves a bruise. And what with that shot that I gave him, our friend here won't even have a headache when he wakes up. He'll actually feel pretty good. So, don't worry, Rabbit. We just needed to put him out of commission for a little while until it's time to have a little conversation with him. He'll be okay."

"Okay, so my work's done, right?" Whitey asked. "I did what you guys wanted, right?"

Claw laughed. "Yeah, Rabbit. You did what we wanted. We knew we could count on you. And we know we can count on you in the future to keep quiet, right?"

Claw pulled five hundred-dollar bills from an inside jacket pocket and held them out to Whitey.

"No sir," Whitey said, stepping back and waving his hands in front of his body. "No sir. What I did was for the Children, not for money. Russell Poe is my friend. I won't betray him for money. No, you keep your money. I did it for the Children of Bel, and for the kindness you all once showed me."

"Suit yourself," Claw said, slowly stuffing the money back into his jacket. "Now you'd best clear out, Rabbit. There's nothing left here for you to see or do."

"One thing I need to tell you," Whitey said as he started to leave. "Poe invited some scientist named Clay something-or-other to meet him up here. Clay's got some interest in cougars, so Poe called him as soon as I told him about the elk. I couldn't stop him, I tried. This Clay person told Russell that he was going to get some gear and would be coming up the trail. He may be on his way up right now."

"Thanks for the warning, Rabbit, but it's okay. I sort of expected Russell would do something like that, calling somebody with the big news. But I can handle it. It's better if you clear out."

"But what if he sees Russell?" Whitey asked.

"No, don't worry, Rabbit. It'll be cool. I got it covered."

Whitey slung his rifle over his shoulder, picked up his knapsack, and quickly left. He wanted to get away from there as fast as he could. However, as he came out onto the trail to Russell's house, he thought that it might be better for him to hang around for a few minutes to see what would happen next. He went about fifty yards down the mountain and stepped behind a thicket on the opposite side of the trail. Glancing back up the mountain, he had a partially blocked view of Claw, but he was pretty sure that Claw couldn't see him in the camouflage jumpsuit that Whitey always wore for hunting.

Claw had made no effort to move Russell. Instead, he sat on the ground, his back leaning against a tree, pulled a small book from his pocket, and appeared to be reading it. He looked up from time to time and then returned to his reading. A half hour passed. Then Whitey saw a man coming up the trail. He passed within five yards of Whitey but didn't slow down, look into the thicket, or give any sign that he had seen Whitey. It was Willy.

Willy continued up the mountain, stopped briefly at Whitey's ballcap, and then turned right into the woods. Claw stood up and greeted him.

Claw had been right. There was nothing more that Whitey wanted to see. Rather than continue down the trail to Russell's house, he quickly slipped deeper into the forest, silent as a spirit.

The Box

I'm blind, Russell thought as consciousness gradually returned. He tried to touch the throbbing sore spot on the back of his head, but his arms wouldn't move. He could flex fingers and toes, but he couldn't move from side to side. His arms were lashed to his sides by a strong band – layers of duct tape, perhaps? – and would not move. He tried forcing his arms outwards to stretch the material that bound him but couldn't. He thought that perhaps repeated pressure would eventually loosen the restraints, as in some of Harry Houdini's amazing escapes. He tried to recall a book about Houdini that he had read as a boy. He had liked to try to replicate Houdini's escapes, but his attempts usually resulted in a visit by a locksmith.

Stop it, he told himself. This is not time for – he searched for the word, something like fond memories – reminiscences, he finally thought. But of what? His mind was wandering all over the place. Concentrate, he commanded himself. Put one thought together with the next one, and those two with the next, and on and on.

As his eyes became adjusted to the darkness, he could see a faint, slightly lighter – or maybe less dark – patch in front of him, extending from about a foot above his head to his shoulders, where it was blocked by his shadow. It was like a thick line made with a marker or paint brush, rough along the edges and of varying width. *Varying width,* he smiled when he realized that he could come up with that description. He could feel a firm, flat floor beneath his feet. He tried to move his feet, but, like his arms, his legs were bound tightly together at the knees and below. Short hopping up and down was the most movement he was allowed. He tried hopping once or twice, but it accomplished nothing. He fell asleep thinking that he was having a bad dream.

He awoke again. How long had he been asleep? The faint line of light in front of him was dimmer now. He tried to lean forward and from side to side. His forehead could just barely reach the surface in front of him. It felt slightly rough, like unfinished sanded wood.

"I'm in a coffin," he said aloud. "I've been buried alive." He was frightened by how his voice sounded slurred and blurred and distant, as if it was coming from outside. "I will never get out. I'll die here and nobody will ever know. Maybe I'm already dead."

"Stop it! Just stop it!" he commanded himself again. This was no time for hysteria. Think! Rule out some things. You're not dead. If you were dead, you wouldn't be conscious of your surroundings, even as strange as they appear. He held his breath for as long as he could. Gasping for breath after almost a minute, he was now convinced that he was still alive.

Russell remembered how he overcame his initial terror when he discovered the underground chambers and passages. He didn't escape by panicking. This was only one chamber. This would be easier. He took another deep breath and held it, just to confirm his conclusion that he was alive.

He then tried to take inventory of his physical condition. He started with the sore spot on his head and then noticed an aching tightness in the base of his neck. But his mind lost track of what part of his body came next. He mentally retraced his thinking: sore spot on the top of my head, probably caused by hitting something or something hitting me. Bleeding? He couldn't be sure; maybe the blood had dried. Stiff area in the back of – where was it? Neck? Shoulder? Then his mind wandered off course and he tried to start again.

He was definitely alive and was standing, not horizonal. He was tied up and enclosed in some sort of wooden box, but it wasn't a coffin. Wiggling his shoulders as much as he could, he guessed that the box was roughly round, a cylinder not much taller than he was. He tried to wiggle all the way around but could not figure out how to do that. It felt as if he were wedged into place. There was not enough room to kneel or even crouch down a little. There might be a crack in what he described now to himself as the box, which would explain the faint light before his eyes. The light seemed dimmer now. It was cold, which meant that he was outside somewhere, and not buried, at least not yet.

"Well, this is a classic tight spot," he said. He felt relieved that he could joke about it. "You're okay for now," he said aloud softly. "You don't know what happened, or why it happened, but you're okay. You know the situation. You can think your way out of this." He closed his eyes, trying to force down fear that tried to creep back in.

Calm down," he whispered. "Calm down." He repeated the phrase softly, like a mantra. "Calm down." Soon, he wasn't sure whether he was saying it or thinking it.

He thought he heard a faint hissing sound, just for a second or two. He felt his spirit wandering back in time to a beautiful October day, watching the gold from the sun setting behind him move across a freshly harvested field, the distant edge of the gold slowly, silently turning to golden brown. He began to recite his favorite passage from Thomas Hardy:

A Saturday afternoon in November was approaching the time of twilight, and the vast tract of unenclosed wild known as Egdon Heath embrowned itself moment by moment.

Is it November already, and will I ever see Egdon Heath, does it really exist somewhere, he asked himself before he drifted off, the throbbing pain in his head fading away like half-remembered golden afternoons long ago.

Russell awoke again. His first sensation was one of being completely rested, like after a long night's sleep. He wasn't afraid, but almost felt comfortable. The darkness confirmed that nothing had happened to him since he drifted off. The faint line that had become his only contact to the outside world had been replaced by a faint orange line that flickered, sometimes a dull orange and sometimes disappearing. Not much time had passed, he thought. It is sunset, and clouds are moving in front of the setting sun. He held his breath, straining to hear any sound that he could. The wind gently whooshed through the almost bare branches of the forest. He could hear it stirring up the fallen leaves. He felt relieved, almost like being home, to know that he was in the forest.

This is ridiculous, he thought. You have to take some action. Somebody brought you here. Maybe they are still around. He started to shout, but something told him that he should remain quiet. How did he get here? The last thing he could clearly remember was going to bed last night. He had a dream that he was looking at some kind of an animal carcass with someone and he passed out. But if it had been a dream, what was he doing here, locked up in a box in the woods somewhere? Or maybe he had a stroke. He was getting close to that age. But, if he had a stroke, why was he here instead of at a hospital?

"Or maybe this is the dream," he said, rubbing his forehead against the faintly rough surface in front of him, seeking any confirmation that he could find. No, he concluded, as crazy as it seems, this is real.

Who was behind this? He had lots of facts but couldn't put them together into evidence. Why would anyone want to do this to him? His thoughts seemed to point from all sides to one central point: Jack Abrams' research. Like Jack he was getting too close to some truths that some dangerous people didn't want revealed, even in the form of folk tales.

He thought again about shouting out, but if whoever was involved in this knew that he was conscious, it might make things worse. Remain quiet. Assess the situation. He thought that he heard soft voices in conversations far away. How pleasant, he thought. I hope they are having a nice evening. He heard a faint hissing sound again and fell asleep wondering if there was a snake nearby, picturing its deep black scales glittering red and gold in the faint light of evening as it slithered among the fall leaves.

Sometime later, voices, closer now, woke Russell suddenly. He snapped his head back, hitting hard against the wall behind him. The pain, amplified by waking so suddenly, bored down his spine, arms, and legs. He groaned.

The thin line of light was a brighter red now, flickering like flame. He could smell wood smoke. They are going to burn me alive in this box, he thought. He was sure now that he had nothing to lose, so he shouted, very slowly and distinctly, "Help! Get – me – out!"

"Get – me – out!" he repeated several times.

After what seemed like hours, Russell heard a distant rustling of leaves, like footsteps in the woods, coming closer. Was it a person, maybe more than one? If so, how many? Or was it an animal? No, he thought, the steps are too regular to be an animal. They were human steps, he was sure, probably more than one person, a group of persons almost in perfect step.

He never heard the steps of the person who tapped on the outside of his box. He remained quiet, afraid to give himself away.

"Mr. Poe," a voice said. "Keep quiet." He couldn't tell if it was a man's voice or a woman's. The voice sounded familiar, but he couldn't place it exactly.

"Don't you worry, now. I know all about it. We won't detain you in there very long. We will set you free very soon. Just stay quiet and all will be well."

Russell tapped three times with his forehead. There was no response. He held his breath while he listened. There was no reply, only distant voices and wood smoke. The bright red line in front of him had disappeared.

Russell heard the faint hissing sound again, like air leaking from a tire; and it lasted longer this time. He began to relax. The voices seemed very far away. The last thing he heard was a woman's voice singing. He thought the language was Gaelic.

Ordained Since the Beginning of Time

"John Bard is in this forest, on this mountain," Brendan whispered as he started up the path to the Rocks. His white robe glowed softly in the starlight. He wondered at how his sleeves seemed to glow even on this moonless night.

"John Bard will be here."

Brendan sensed a thrilling fear creeping in around the edges of his excitement. Tonight, John Bard's cycle is completed. Tonight, he will be reborn in me. When I come down this mountain just before sunrise, I will no longer be Bill Paxton, no longer be Brendan. I will have become John Bard. He will live in me, and I will live forever.

As he started up the steep trail from near the river, he saw Willy faintly silhouetted against the sky, waiting by the Guardian burial site. Willy raised his hand silently and stepped back into the bushes lining the bank. He would do as he had been directed.

Brendan received a call at home from Willy two days before. Willy didn't identify himself. He just said, "I have to see you."

Willy came on foot, taking a path through the forest and to the back door, so he wouldn't be noticed. Once Brendan had shown him into the study, Willy sat down and began to shake, slightly at first, then almost uncontrollably. Brendan was getting alarmed, but shortly Willy regained his composure.

All he said was, "He's real."

"Of course, he's real," Brendan said. "But why did you have to see me all of a sudden?"

Willy described how he was doing some field work up in the State Game Lands that morning, and an old man suddenly appeared behind him and tapped him on the shoulder.

"'I know you, Willy,' he said. "I swear, Brendan, I had never met this guy before in my life and I have no idea how he knew my Old Name. But he used it. Willy. Nobody in the world knows my Old Name except my brothers and sisters in the Children."

"What did he look like?" Brendan asked.

"Like someone out of a kid's history book: long white hair tied back in a sort of ponytail, white beard, high-top moccasins, buckskin pants, and a long blue coat, like they used to wear back at the time of the Revolution. That was John Bard, wasn't it?"

"Well, that certainly looks like him," was all that Brendan would admit.

"Did he say what he wanted?" Brendan asked.

"No, not really. All he said was 'You and I have a date on Samhain at the ancient Sentinel Burial Site, and I assure you that I will be there at the appointed hour, ready for you to guide me further. I am honored that you have been selected to be my guide.'"

"Well, that's good that it's all arranged," Brendan said. "So, what's the problem?"

"No problem, I guess," Willy said, "but he did say something strange. He said, 'I know what is to transpire at this Samhain. It has been ordained' – I think that was the word that he used – 'ordained since the beginning of time.'

"He also said that he knew what was to happen and was at peace with it, and that he did not hold me accountable for it, and that I would someday be a leader of the Children and would eventually become a great spirit. 'It was ordained,' he said again."

"So why are you telling me all this, Willy?" Brendan asked.

"I don't know," Willy said. "I know that Laurel says that I have the Ancient Knowledge and the gift of reading souls, but I don't want you to think that I'm being disloyal."

"Why would I think that, Willy?"

"Well," Willy said haltingly, "the last time we met, you know, up there on the mountain, I was kind of disrespectful to you and a real smartass. And you put me in my place, and I'm happy that you did. I deserved it and more, Brendan."

"I know that will never happen again," Brendan said.

"Well, all the same, you were talking about how there were problems with people not being loyal, and I don't want there to be any misunderstandings between us, Brendan."

Brendan assured Willy that there was never any doubt about his loyalty. After some small talk about the preparations for the

Samhain ceremony and the plans to capture Russell Poe, Willy left, walking through the old Methodist cemetery and toward the forest, where he had probably hidden his motorcycle. Ten minutes later the distant sound of a starting engine confirmed Brendan's suspicions.

Brendan did not hear anything further from Willy until that morning, when he received another phone call.

"Mr. Poe has accepted our invitation" was all that Willy said before hanging up.

Tonight, it all comes together, Brendan thought as he climbed the steep trail from the river, or at least things will begin to come together irretrievably. What had Churchill called it: not the beginning of the end, but the end of the beginning? No, Brendan thought, this would definitely be the end of the end, the point of no return.

John Bard would be there tonight to sacrifice himself for his Children of Bel. They would feast as his spirit was reborn in the fires of the sacred yew, not only as the next manifestation of John Bard's ancient spirit, as John recommits himself as a manitou protecting these forests and mountains and valleys, but as a part of John's spirit enters and becomes a new Brendan, the Son of the Son of God. For a moment, Brendan felt frightened, wondering whether he was too flawed, too ignorant, too young to assume John Bard's worldly mantle.

Tonight, Bill Paxton's worldly problems would be over, as well. Brendan hated the thought of sacrifice, but sometimes it was needed so that the Children may live. The Goddess herself taught us that through the spider, who turns her own venom inwardly, so that her spiderlings may nourish themselves on her body.

Brendan thought about Russell Poe as he approached the Tioga Yew at the eastern entrance to the Indian Rocks. It is a pity – necessary but still a pity – that it has to end this way. The two men had become friendly, if not actual friends. Russell had even been kind to him, respecting his childhood memories and returning the books to him after so many years. That is why Poe could not just be eliminated, like the others who had come too close to learning the

Ancient Knowledge that only the Children could know, as well as some things that nobody should know. No, the good in Russell Poe would be consecrated forever in this sacred grove. The gasses that Spook would inject into the hollowed tree – Brendan smiled at the near-pun – would do their work kindly. The nitrous oxide in the mixture will prevent him from noticing when the gas switches to pure nitrogen. Russell will pass out almost instantly, feeling a sense of well-being and maybe even euphoria. His heart will stop silently and painlessly, and in less than a minute Russell will become an eternal spirit of the forest, residing in the sacred yew tree.

Brendan felt a moment of sadness. It truly was a sacrifice, a personal sacrifice for him. He had genuinely liked Russell Poe. He would miss him.

The Sangman's treasure – his birthright and the birthright of all the Children – would be in his hands tonight. He now had a photograph of the second part of the map. The Children would find the third map, maybe not right away, but they would eventually. They might not even need it.

Brendan heard noise behind him. Several other Children silently made their way up the mountain, none of them carrying a flashlight or torch, each one knowing the way by heart even on this moonless night, Samhain, the night of death and eternal life in a higher plane of existence.

Brendan's thoughts returned to Russell Poe. He was sure that Russell would be reborn into a better life on a higher spiritual plane. As Brendan entered the sacred circle of stones, he quietly whispered a Celtic prayer for those about to pass from this life to the next one. He prayed for John Bard – his Uncle Johnny – who would be reborn only a few minutes from now as part of Brendan's soul. He prayed for Russell Poe.

Ten people had already arrived. Three of them wore white robes, the rest wore their everyday street clothes. Some were speaking softly, others walked alone looking up at the stars. With the five people he saw on the trail behind him, plus Willy and John Bard, they would have a good turnout. It would not be as many as in previous years, Brendan thought sadly. So many had drifted away over the years, but new ones, like Spook, had joined.

Spook had been standing by the Tioga Yew, as he had been instructed. His role tonight would be simple. When Brendan gave the signal, when he raised the sacrificial knife high, Spook would open the valve on the nitrogen cannister, allowing the contents to flow through the clear plastic tubing and into the tree. He would then light the kerosene-soaked rags, hidden by a thin layer of kindling at the base of the trunk. The kerosene would create a spectacular blaze for a few moments, but the ancient yew would survive with only superficial damage.

"What's the gas for?" Spook had asked Brendan.

"Spook, when you light that tree, it will go up in flames in less than a minute. So be careful and jump back as soon as you set the fire. The gas will kill any insects or other living creatures inside it before you light the fire. It's better that way than having them burned alive. They are innocent and have spirits, too.

"The Sacrificial Yew's destiny is to be consumed in flame, to be reborn again and again, hundreds and thousands of times for all eternity. That's why we sacrifice it only at Samhain, after its longest branches bend over to touch the ground. But any living things that may be inside the oak are innocent. We must be as loving and merciful to them as possible. That's why we shoot the gas deep inside the trunk before we set the tree ablaze."

This would be Spook's first Samhain, and sometimes the first one is troubling for new Children. Moreover, tonight is John Bard's nine-hundredth Samhain, the last in his old cycle and the first in his new one. Nobody in the Children had ever witnessed a transfiguration before. Only Laurel claimed to know all the details, which she had taught to Brendan.

"The sacrifice of John Bard is symbolic, Spook," Brendan had explained, trying to alleviate the fears that he sensed were building in Spook. "It will look real, but it is only symbolic of the sacrifice of self that each of us must make to the Goddess whose children we all are. When you have advanced in priestly knowledge, you will learn the secrets of sacrifice. Someday you will undoubtedly be called upon to perform the Samhain sacrifice yourself."

"So, no one actually gets sacrificed?"

Brendan smiled and gave him a quick, one-armed hug around the shoulder. "No Children were harmed in the making of this Samhain."

They laughed together.

Zephyr

June sat in her sewing room on the second floor, listening to her old Patsy Cline records and reading a book of Welsh folklore, when she heard Ray downstairs. It was only three o'clock; she hadn't expected Ray until five.

"Raymond, that you?" she called.

"No, your mysterious afternoon lover," he replied. June laughed.

"What are you doing home early?" June asked as he appeared in the doorway. She looked up and smiled.

"Well, knocking off early is the good news. The bad news is that Sergeant Washington called in sick. So, I need to cover the midnight-to-eight. Officer Bradley is going to put in some overtime at the station until I get back this evening."

"Can't – oh, what is her name – that nice young woman that works for you?"

"Officer Passarelli."

"Yes, that's right. That nice Italian girl. Can't she handle it?"

"No, there's no way she could get someone to watch her kids overnight on such short notice. I wouldn't even ask her. So, I'll just have a light supper and head back around nine to let Brady go home a little early. He's been there since eight this morning."

"Will you be all right, June?" Ray asked. "Do I need to run out and get you anything?"

"Oh, no," June said. "I'll be fine." She lifted the arm off the record that she was playing and gently replaced it in its album sleeve."

"If you give me a few moments to freshen up, I'll be downstairs directly and will fix us a little early supper. Is there anything special you'd like?" she said, closing the lid of the phonograph.

"No thanks," Ray replied. "I had lunch just a couple of hours ago, so I'll just make a sandwich. If it's all right with you I'll just grab a couple hours of sleep."

June promised to wake him up at eight-thirty, but she knew that even without an alarm clock, Ray would wake up promptly whenever he wanted. He had always been that way, like a human alarm clock. When she went into the bedroom at eight-thirty to wake Ray up, he was already rolling out of bed. June went down to the kitchen, wheeled the dishwasher over to the sink, and connected the hose. She always liked to do the dishes at the end of the day, just before bedtime. "A good way to close the kitchen," she would sometimes say to Ray.

June sat at the kitchen table, thinking about possibly making some sand candles that evening. She loved the random shapes that she let them take. She quit giving them as gifts years ago, when none of her friends would ever use them. "They're too beautiful," one of her friends once said. "I could never light one."

It was almost time for her to take her medication; but she wasn't ready to drift back into her "happy land," as she described it to herself. She tried to remember every detail of the visits to her last night. What exactly did she see? How can she be sure that it was John Bard and Rabbit – no, *Whitey,* she corrected herself – standing at her back door? What precisely did they say? She asked dozens of questions that Ray probably was too afraid of hurting her feelings to ask. She sipped some strong hot tea to try to stimulate her thinking and sharpen her memory, but so many things remained blurry.

She went into the living room to watch some television until Ray came downstairs. She turned on their set and watched whatever channel Ray had chosen last. She really didn't care what was on, so long as it wasn't the news or sports.

Samhain was near, she thought, but when? She went into the small room off the dining room. Ray used it sometimes as a home office, but in recent years it had become more of a storage room. She looked on the pile of relatively recent magazines. Ray would display them on the coffee table for two months and then consign them to a pile in this room, to be thrown out every six months. She then looked on the small bookcase behind the table and chair that served as a desk. There with the dictionary, some of Ray's college textbooks, and the first eight volumes of an encyclopedia that she started buying at the old A&P supermarket before it went out of business, June found what she was looking for, this year's edition of the *Hagerstown Town and Country Almanack.*

She turned to the listing for October and confirmed that the new moon would occur at 8:35 a.m. Thursday morning. That meant that Samhain would be celebrated tonight, at midnight. And tonight, of all nights, Ray would be away. It was as if it had been arranged forever. John hadn't specifically asked her to be there, but she sensed an unspoken invitation, almost a plea, to be there, even though John – or was it Whitey? – warned her that she would be in great danger. And tonight, she might see her son for the first time ever, the child taken from her minutes after birth. How would she know him? She might have to ask John Bard to point him out to her. Would she introduce herself to him as his mother? She wasn't even sure that any of it was real, but she had to find out.

The mantle clock struck eight forty-five and, about two minutes later, Ray came downstairs.

"I just wanted to stay up to say good night and see you off," June said.

"I'll try not to call you unless it's important," Ray said.

"Oh, don't worry about that, Raymond," June said. "I'm going to take my medication now and go to bed. I should have taken it earlier, but I wanted to be up to see you off, like I always do."

"Well, I won't disturb you," Ray said. "I know that once you take your sleeping pills, I wouldn't be able to wake you if they set off an atomic bomb."

June laughed. That was one of their favorite phrases.

Ray gestured at the almanac still in June's hand. "Seeing whether we're going to have a white Christmas?" He asked. June could sense that he was joking, but she decided to be serious.

"Why yes, Raymond," she said. "Actually, I was more interested in Thanksgiving and whether we'll have a traditional old-fashioned holiday. You know, 'over the river and through the woods'," she started to sing. "Maybe we could invite my brother and his family to come down from Ithaca, possibly have Sandy come over."

Ray went into the kitchen for several minutes. June could hear him preparing a lunch to take with him. He and June met at the front door, where he kissed her and, as he did every time he left for work, promised to be safe. June stood at the open door and watched him walk briskly down the street, a small paper bag in his hand, connecting the lighted dots made by the streetlamps, until she could no longer see him.

"This is it," she said to the empty kitchen. "The hour of decision, like that TV preacher says. What are you going to do, June?"

She stepped out the back door and looked at the sky, dark, cloudless, and lit by a million stars, at least. She decided not to take her medication, for the same reason she frequently skipped a dose or two when she wanted to avoid the fogginess that she knew would envelope her. Poor Raymond, she often thought. He tries so hard to pay attention. She hated the times when she would pretend to be on the pills. It seemed almost like infidelity, but sometimes she needed clarity.

June sighed and whispered, "I am so sorry, Raymond," as she flushed the two pills down the kitchen sink, allowing the water to run hot for several minutes to be sure that they dissolved and didn't clog the drain. She replaced the bottles on the bottom shelf of the cupboard above the sink. Ray always counted her pills to make sure that she didn't get confused and forget a dose or take too many, but she never did. Although he had no reason to be suspicious, June knew that he would count them tomorrow, right after she took her morning doses. Sometimes he would even take the breakfast pill from its bottle and put it on a small dish, which he set down at her place for breakfast.

June returned to the house, went upstairs, and changed into a dark sweater and jeans. She remembered that she had earned the right to wear white at the major festivals, Beltrane, the solstices and equinoxes, and Samhain. Maybe she shouldn't wear white tonight. Maybe she had forfeited that right after so many years. She found a white silk robe. It wouldn't keep her warm if it turned cold tonight, but she could keep it rolled up so it would not be noticed until she put it on just before she arrived.

June sat in the darkened house until shortly before ten o'clock. Ray would be busy at the police station now. She telephoned, and Officer Bradley answered on the first ring.

"Richard," she said, surprised that he answered. "Don't you have a home to go to?"

"Just finishing up the changing of the guard," Officer Bradley explained. "Here, I'll put the Chief on."

A few seconds later, Ray came on the line.

"June, is everything okay?" June could hear concern in his voice. She adopted her "medicated" voice.

"Oh yes, darling, it's all fine. I just wanted to say goodnight one last time, right before I turn off the light. Please be safe tonight."

"Thanks, June. I'm really happy that you called. Now get some sleep. I will try to get away a little early in the morning, so I can fix your breakfast on time."

June turned off the lights, except for the night light on the stairs and in the kitchen. She left by the kitchen door, testing the lock after she closed it. The car that was still designated as "her" car – the one that she hadn't driven in years and that Ray drove only when he took it for its routine maintenance – was in the old detached garage at the back of their house. It started on the first try.

June drove the back roads east out of Wellsboro. June had not been to Samhain, or to any of the other ceremonies, for years, since before she was hospitalized. She was amazed by how she could remember the way to the Rocks, and how easily she found the parking area at the foot of the mountain, by the river but hidden from the road by the bushes. She even remembered the hidden entrance to the parking area. Years ago, when she came to the Rocks regularly, she would drive past the entrance two or three times before she spotted it.

June parked. There were four other cars and three motorcycles there. She started up the trail to the Rocks. As she climbed, she wondered whether she should have borrowed Ray's 9 mm pistol, just in case. No, she said to herself, that's more of that crazy talk. Push it down. You are in control.

When she was almost to the Tioga Yew, she saw Brendan talking to a young man. She wondered if that was her son. She waited until Brendan turned and walked into the circle and started greeting the people there. When she passed the yew, she put on her white robe and quietly said, "Blessed be, brother" to the young man. He gave a slight bow – maybe to her white robe – and returned the greeting: "Blessed be, sister."

June took a deep breath and entered the stone circle. Some people looked at her with puzzled expressions, but then greeted her: "Blessed be, sister."

She did not see John Bard. As she stepped forward, Brendan walked up to her. She hoped that he didn't notice the slight flinch when he touched her shoulder and kissed her cheek.

"Welcome home, Zephyr," he said and then turned and walked back across the circle to the low altar that had been constructed at the base of the yew. Zephyr and the others followed him and formed into a circle.

A woman in white emerged from the forest. She greeted each person in turn. When she came to Zephyr, she simply said, "Blessed be, Zephyr. I am called Laurel. I have never met you before tonight, but I know all there is to know about your beautiful soul, and the terrible quest you have been on for so many years. Welcome home, Zephyr. We love you with a love that is as timeless and eternal as the stars above us." Then she moved on. After greeting each person, Laurel went to stand beside Brendan.

They all stood silently waiting for John Bard. Nobody said anything. They stood so still that, in the dark, it was hard to distinguish some of them from the upright stones behind them. Only those privileged to wear white glowed faintly in the starlight. After a few moments, Laurel turned and motioned for everyone to draw near. "Our circle must be small and tight tonight, so that John Bard's last vision is of all of us, together as one."

Zephyr moved forward.

Brendan started to speak in a low, loud voice that seemed to make the ground vibrate.

"On this most special Samhain, we shall witness the destruction of the universe. Tonight, a nine-hundred year cycle has come full circle, the tenth of our era. Under these stars this Samhain night, we Children of Bel are privileged to witness the rebirth of the Son of the White Goddess, as John Bard offers his body to the earth and frees his soul to be reborn, as it has been in all times past, in all of us and in the one of us chosen by the Goddess."

Where was John Bard, Zephyr wondered. Perhaps he would appear, as legend says that he has done sometimes in the past, rising out of the earth through the underground passage beneath the Rocks. Or maybe on this last night, his last Samhain, he would just quietly walk into the center from just beyond the light. Zephyr had heard the legends from Brendan and others. She believed that she knew John Bard better than anyone, but she had never seen him materialize at Samhain.

"Our leader, John Bard, is with us," Laurel said quietly.

The old man appeared to rise slowly from within the low altar in the center of the circle. Small fires ignited around the base of the altar, about two feet from it. Their light made him appear taller than Zephyr remembered. His black robe, trimmed with ivy and mistletoe, seemed to absorb all the light. He carried two boughs from the yew tree, one in each hand, crossed in front of his chest like the scepters of an Egyptian pharaoh. Even the stars seemed to dim. Without saying a word, he lay down on his back on the altar and opened his robe, exposing his chest. His hands, each still holding a bough, hung at his sides and just touched the ground.

Zephyr wanted to back away, terrified of what she knew that she was about to see, but something pushed her closer to the altar, along with the others. Brendan moved to stand behind John Bard. As he raised his arm, a long, sickle-shaped knife seemed to grow from his hand. It looked like a black shiny stone, with the lights from the small fires around the altar creating lines of red that moved back and forth. Zephyr could see that Brendan's hand was trembling. She could see sweat forming on his brow, even in the cold, clear night air.

John Bard began to chant a prayer in a high, almost falsetto, voice:

I sang the world's birth cry at
The first of all sunrises.
Now on the last of all nights,
I sing its triumphant dirge.

Zephyr recognized it at once: the ancient death prayer that only a Druid may speak once every nine hundred years. He knows what's going to happen. He isn't going to resist; he's ready. This isn't an act. Brendan is really going to sacrifice him. She started to move forward.

John Bard sat up and raised his hand in benediction. The firelight danced across his face, making him look eternally old and young at the same time. Wrinkles became canyons, but, where the light struck smooth areas of his face, his skin was like a baby's.

"For nine hundred years I have served the White Goddess, mother of us all, and you, my brothers and sisters in the great mysteries that only we have been blessed to know. When the last sacred groves in the Old World were destroyed, I was there. With my brothers and sisters, I brought the Knowledge to this New World. I carried a seedling from my home and planted it with my own hands to become this sacred tree that shelters us and gives us eternal life tonight. Since then these mountains have been my home, my sacred grove. In this sacred circle alone, I have seen the world die and be reborn more than eight hundred and ninety-nine times. Many of you have seen them with me, either in this existence or in a previous one.

"But now my cycle is over. The nine hundred years have all flowed out into the oceans of everlasting life. Wait for me. Watch for me. I shall return, joining my soul for all eternity with one of you.

"There is one among you whom Bel has chosen to pick up the flame of truth I now set down. Look to the person, who will be revealed to you in the fullness of time."

The knife hovered above Brendan's head.

Laurel stepped forward.

"No, Brendan. We don't have to do this. I know what you are thinking, but you are not going to lead the Children, not now, not ever. This has to stop, and it has to stop now. This is not what the Children of Bel are about. You and those thugs you call the Watchmen have no place here. On this nine-hundredth Samhain, we cast you out."

"Step back, Laurel," Brendan hissed.

"No," she said more loudly. Brendan grabbed her wrist and twisted her arm suddenly, making her lose her balance and fall. Brendan kicked her in the side once she was on the ground.

Everyone shrank back from the altar. Only Zephyr stepped forward. She grabbed Brendan's arm. Brendan turned and gestured with the knife, inches from her throat.

"Say one more word, bitch, and we'll have three sacrifices tonight."

"Three? Who else are you and your thugs going to murder tonight, Brendan?"

Brendan pushed Zephyr down alongside Laurel. Some of the Children of Bel began to back away from the altar. Zephyr thought she saw two of them turn and quickly walk into the forest.

"Now it becomes all clear," he shouted, "why this night of all nights that you returned to us, not as our sister but as a banshee determined to destroy us. It is all clear to me now, how you and Laurel want to deprive your brothers and sisters of my rightful leadership. It all makes sense now."

"Zephyr," John Bard sat up and said, just loud enough for Zephyr, Brendan, and Laurel to hear. "Zephyr, please let that which must be done be done. I wanted my last vision to be of you reconciled and at peace with your brothers and sisters, not at war with them. Grant me this last vision to carry with me to my new existence."

"Brendan," he said in a louder, commanding voice as he lay down again on the altar, "Do it. Now."

Brendan raised the knife again.

"Blessed be, John Bard, in all the future cycles of your life. Blessed be."

A voice shouted "No!" from somewhere outside the clearing.

At the sound of the rifle crack, Brendan flinched and grabbed his upraised right arm, just above the wrist, with his left hand. He plunged the knife downward at an angle. John Bard let out a little *umph* sound as the knife pierced his chest but appeared to slide off a rib. Blood was all over Brendan's right hand and on John Bard's chest. Zephyr could not tell how much was Brendan's blood and how much was John Bard's.

A second shot was fired. Brendan dropped down onto the altar, covering John Bard with his own body. Zephyr couldn't tell whether he had been hit, and she wondered why he didn't try to escape through one of the trap doors that she had heard were placed all over the circle. For what seemed like many minutes, nobody moved. Zephyr looked for an escape route back into the forest. She heard a voice coming from the path that led from the old Indian trail that ran along the ridge, just uphill and to the west.

"No," the voice said. "That's enough."

Zephyr took off her robe, dropped it, and ran past Brendan, John Bard, and the altar. Within seconds, she was kneeling down on the far side of the yew. Nobody seemed to have reacted to her departure. The young man she greeted when she entered the circle was still there at the back of the tree, crouching in the dark. His eyes were wide open, and his mouth was moving as if he wanted to say something but couldn't.

She wanted to keep running, down the trail to her car and all the way home without looking back, but she knew that she had to stay, if only to confirm whether or not any of this was real.

"It's okay," Zephyr said to the young man. "It's okay. Just keep low and out of sight, and we'll be fine."

Confrontation

Whitey Wentworth stepped out of the shadows and moved across the circle. He aimed the beam from his flashlight at the altar, where the light from the fires around the base absorbed it.

"Step away from that man," he said quietly. The people standing closest to the altar began moving toward him. Some of them still acted confused. Whitey shined his flashlight in their faces. He recognized some of them. He hoped nobody was armed. The odds were at least twelve to one. Suddenly, Whitey realized that he really hadn't planned what he would do from this point on.

He kept coming forward, his rifle held chest-high, slowly sweeping the crowd. He carried a loaded pistol on his hip and another rifle across his back.

"Everyone back away from me. Go to the edges of the circle." He waved his rifle where he wanted them to go "Do it." He shouted. He was amazed when they complied, everyone taking one or two steps backward, almost in unison.

"You there." He pointed the rifle at the altar. "Quite playing possum. I know I just winged you. Had I wanted to kill you, I would've done it on the first shot. Stand up. Now."

The white hooded figure draped across the altar stood slowly. The person that had been lying underneath didn't move.

"Drop that fucking hood. Now."

"Put the rifle down, my son. You've made a terrible mistake."

"Drop the hood. I want to see you."

The bloody right hand lifted slowly, then dropped. The left hand reached up and pulled down the hood.

"Hello, Brendan."

"Put the gun down, Rabbit. It's all right. You didn't understand."

Rabbit hesitated. He noticed several of the men taking slow silent steps toward him.

He fired over their heads. Most of the people dropped to the ground. A few remained standing with their hands raised.

"Everyone hit the deck," Whitey shouted. "Do it. Face down. Hands clasped behind your neck. Execution style."

Whitey moved toward the altar. Brendan remained standing, his hands at his sides. Blood had seeped onto the right side of his robe.

"You fuckers can have it one of two ways. Fuck with me and you're dead. Do what I say, and you might get out of this alive."

Whitey was now no more than twenty feet from the altar. He kept his eyes on Brendan. Brendan smiled.

"Years ago, Rabbit, we parted as friends. We know that you have kept your word all these years. We know of the service you performed, delivering a potential enemy to us so that we could show him the truth. We are friends still."

Whitey pointed the rifle at the body on the altar.

"No fucking murderer is my friend, Paxton."

"My name is Brendan."

"Let's cut that Old Name bullshit and all the other make-believe.

"John Bard isn't dead, Rabbit. You know that. You know about Samhain."

"If he ain't dead, make him get up."

"You know I can't do that."

"Where's Russell Poe?"

"He is safe."

"Where is he? Tell your people to bring him here. If he isn't standing in front of me in sixty seconds, I'll blow your fucking head off."

"Rabbit, put down the gun. Look, you haven't done any harm yet, no real harm. It's all a big misunderstanding. Russell Poe is fine. He is in no danger, at least not from us. So, put down the gun."

"I know what I've seen, and I've seen enough. I could send all you fuckers to prison for the rest of your lives."

Brendan smiled. "So that's what you want? Money? Come on, Rabbit, who would ever believe you? The town drunk comes off the mountain with some wild tale about human sacrifice up in the forest. Druids in Pennsylvania. White Indians. Stuff you made up from Jack Abrams' ghost stories."

"No, all I want is Russell Poe. The rest of you assholes can all go to hell, for all I care."

Something was wrong, Whitey thought. Paxton isn't going to deliver Poe. That could only mean that Russell was already dead. Whitey wondered whether he should just go ahead and kill Brendan. He had eight rounds left in the magazine, and three full magazines in his ammo bag, and the other two weapons were loaded. He could just start blasting away into the trees, just to get people running away, then kill Paxton, and then escape in all the confusion. Or maybe he should just kill them all. Either way, there would be no witnesses.

"Put down the gun. Come on, Rabbit."

Brendan stepped around from behind the altar. His left hand was extended. His wounded hand was tucked inside his robe.

"Both hands in view, please."

"Come on, Rabbit. My hand is bleeding pretty badly. I've got to stop the bleeding. It hurts like hell."

Brendan took another step forward. Maybe I have it all wrong, Whitey thought. A guilty man wouldn't stand his ground like that. Whitey raised the rifle and pointed it at Brendan's head. Brendan stopped.

"Come on, Rabbit. It's all a big mistake. Give me the gun, muzzle first if you like. That way if I make any false move, you can still protect yourself."

Whitey realized that Brendan was beginning to take control. He had to get out of this somehow, bring it to conclusion. Then he saw Brendan's eyes shift. Brendan's body tensed.

Suddenly everything around Whitey was moving in slow motion. He saw Brendan's arm appear from the long sleeve of his robe. He saw the knife flying slowly through the air, turning end over end, almost frame by frame in a movie. Whitey fell to his left, rolled twice, and fired at Brendan from the prone position. He heard the groan and the thump behind him.

He kept his eyes on Brendan. He must have hit him. He couldn't have missed at that range, but Brendan turned and started running away. Whitey spun around to check his rear. Claw lay on his side, his eyes open, his hand grabbing furiously at the black knife embedded in his thigh all the way to the hilt. Whitey ran back to Claw and pulled the knife out as gently as he could. In almost the same move he pulled off Claw's belt and tightened it around Claw's leg, just above the wound. Claw passed out, but Whitey knew that he would survive. He also knew that Claw would never say anything about how he got injured.

As Brendan ran past the altar the small fires that circled the altar seemed to erupt, sending spikes of flame to the top where the body lay motionless, with boughs of yew and sprigs of mistletoe on his chest. The few people still in the area seemed to be either too stunned or too frightened to move. Their inaction would give Whitey the chance he needed to leave, catch Brendan, and make him tell where Russell Poe was. He'd make Brendan talk, just before he killed him.

Whitey followed the flash of Brendan's white robe into the forest. Brendan was his. Whitey knew these forests and mountains. He had hunted in them at night since he was a boy. Brendan wouldn't get away.

Rescue

Zephyr and Spook kept as low as they could.

"By the way," Zephyr whispered, "I'm Zephyr."

"I'm Spook," the young man replied. "Blessed be, Zephyr."

"Yeah," Zephyr said, "Blessed be, Spook. Especially if we get out of this alive."

"Oh, Christ," Spook said, "I almost forgot."

He got up and crept left, going about one-quarter of the way around the trunk of the tree. He looked around the edge, toward the center of the circle. He came back with a plastic jug and started pouring kerosene on rags that were laid around the base of the tree and splashed some about four feet up the trunk.

Zephyr whispered, her voice almost a hiss, "What are you doing?"

"I know, I know," Spook said. "I've really fucked up. I was supposed to pour the kerosene and then turn on the gas. But with all that shooting and all that going on out there, damn it, I got confused and forgot."

"What? You're going to set fire to the sacred yew?" Zephyr had to restrain herself from shouting at the trembling boy that was hunched over searching the ground, reaching down with his hand to try to feel the matchbox he had dropped. Zephyr reached over, grabbed him, and pulled him back to her.

"Well, yeah," Spook said. "Brendan entrusted the lighting of the fire to me, and I fucked it up."

"Fucked it up? You idiot," she said, "not only are you destroying a thousand-year-old tree, but you'll probably start a forest fire that will kill us all." She reached down, picked up a handful of dry leaves, and shook them at Spook. Bits of leaves, almost like a cloud of dust, emerged from her fist and clung to his face.

"But Brendan said –" Spook found the matches. As he bent down to pick them up, Zephyr looked for something she could use to knock him down. He tried to light a match, but his hand was trembling so badly that he dropped it. He ignited the second match, but the wind blew it out. Zephyr reached out and brought her fist down with all her strength on his wrist. Matches flew away in all directions.

It was then that Zephyr heard a man's voice that seemed to be coming from inside the tree.

"Get me out of here!"

"Christ, somebody's in the tree," Zephyr shouted. She didn't care who heard. She put her ear up to the trunk and followed it almost halfway around the tree, listening.

"Get me out of here!"

The voice was not screaming or frightened. It sounded like someone reading the same line over and over, sometimes clearly and sometimes mumbling.

Zephyr cupped her hands against the trunk. Brendan or some of his thugs might still have been in the area, so she spoke in a loud whisper. "We'll get you out. You're safe now. Just be quiet."

Zephyr grabbed Spook by the shirt and pulled him close.

"Who's inside the tree, Spook?"

"Honest, Zephyr, I didn't know there was anyone in there. Brendan told me that I had to shoot some gas into the trunk to kill the insects, so they wouldn't suffer from the fire. And I forget to do that, too." Spook's voice was trembling. He looked as if he were going to burst into tears.

"Well, you and Brendan almost killed a man. So, pull yourself together and let's get him out."

Zephyr cautiously approached the front of the tree, the side facing the altar and the circle of rocks. It was quiet. The flames in the jars at the base of the altar were lower now. The body was gone. Only a single hooded figure, dressed in white, stood at the center of the circle looking up at the stars.

"Help us!" Zephyr called. The hooded figure walked slowly across the circle toward them. She dropped her hood as she walked and seemed almost to glide or float across the clearing. For a moment, Zephyr was convinced that she was having one of her hallucinations.

"Please, sister. Please help us," she called again.

"Blessed be," the woman said when she approached. She pulled the hood back up, keeping her face in the shadows cast by the dying flames.

"That's Laurel," Spook said.

"The Old Names are no longer important, Spook, no longer valid," Laurel said. "The cycle that ended at this Samhain is the last one, the end of our age, the end of all ages. And only we three are left. It is sad, but victorious."

Victorious? Enough of this nonsense, Zephyr thought. At least she doesn't have a gun or a knife, at least one we can see.

"Laurel, there is someone trapped inside the sacred yew. He is dying. We must save him," Zephyr said.

"Oh, that's only the transfigured spirit of John Bard speaking to us, his three last Children," Laurel said. There was a dream-like quality to her voice that alarmed Zephyr.

"Bullshit," Zephyr said. "Transfigured spirits don't need to call for help to get out of trees."

"Sisters," Spook said, "We've got to do something. Now."

"Laurel, what should we do?" Zephyr demanded. "How do we get him out of the tree?"

Laurel nodded and turned to the part of the trunk facing the altar. "Help me push," she said.

Laurel, Spook, and Zephyr pushed where Laurel pointed. A section of the trunk came loose. Together they pried it away from the trunk. A man fell out, dangling from two ropes that were connected to the inside of the trunk.

"Jesus Christ, I swear I didn't know. I really didn't know," Spook whimpered. "Brendan said –"

"If you mention Brendan one more time, you sorry little shit, I'll tie you up in the tree and close the door and leave you there to rot," Zephyr said.

The man was alive and partly conscious. Spook used a pen knife to saw through the ropes and the layers of duct tape around his arms and legs. They gently lowered the man to the ground. He tried to get up but fell down. He lifted himself up on his elbows and knees but collapsed again, his face partially buried in the leaves. Laurel and Zephyr rolled him over.

"I know him," Laurel said quietly. "It's Russell Poe."

"We have to get him to a hospital," Zephyr said.

"No," Laurel said as she looked into his eyes and felt for his pulse. "No, he'll be okay. He probably won't remember any of this. But we do have to get him home. I know where he lives. It's just over the ridge."

"But what about Brendan and Rabbit and all the others? All that shooting?" Zephyr asked.

"Don't worry," Laurel said. "Those idiots are already miles away from here."

"But the bodies?" Zephyr persisted.

"Aren't any," Laurel said. "I think that Brendan might have gotten nicked on the hand or wrist, but he ran out of here like someone half his age. Claw got stabbed, but I saw Rabbit turn his back on Brendan and run over and pull the knife out of his leg and put a tourniquet on him. That took guts once Brendan went berserk."

She swept her hand across the circle. "Claw must have crawled out or somebody must have helped him get away."

"Well," Zephyr said, "let's get out of here before anybody comes back. Thanks for helping us."

"Thanks for sort of standing up for me earlier," Laurel said, "when I confronted Brendan."

"Somebody had to."

"What are you two talking about?" Spook asked.

"It doesn't matter now, Spook. Nothing matters now except the three of us trying to get this man down the mountain," Laurel said. With Spook's help, she replaced the door to the interior of the tree. It fit so precisely that Zephyr could not even feel a crack at the joints.

They stood Russell up. With one of his arms around Zephyr's shoulder and the other around Spook's, and Laurel leading the way and acting as lookout, they slowly guided Russell across the stone circle and out the side opposite the yew. Zephyr looked back. The Indian Rocks seemed to twinkle in the starlight. The fires around the altar had burned down to the point that they cast only a faint reddish glow on the oak logs at the base.

As they started up the path the short distance to the ridge, Zephyr said, "I'm sorry, Spook. He's too heavy for me." Laurel came back to them and took Zephyr's place.

"No problem, Zephyr. I got him. The old Indian trail along the ridge is only a few more yards. We turn left, go along it a little way, and then take a path to the right. It will take us right down to his house. If he gets to be too much for us, we can probably roll him."

Zephyr laughed, wondering how Laurel still could joke after all that they had seen. Spook looked as if he didn't understand.

As they descended the mountain to the house, Russell began to become more alert and to move his legs in a more coordinated way, but descending the path in the dark moonless night was slow and challenging. At one point, Spook stumbled over a low branch, and all three of them fell. After what seemed to Zephyr to be about forty-five minutes, they could see the light in the back of Russell's house. About twenty minutes later they were in his back yard.

"Let me try the doors to see if we can get him inside," Laurel said. She left Russell, Spook, and Zephyr and tried the kitchen door without success.

"No luck," she said. "Let's take him around front."

"Can't we just break a window or something?" Spook asked. "I mean, like, it's getting cold, and we just can't leave him outside in that jacket."

"No," Laurel said, "if we break in, he'll discover it and definitely know that something is wrong."

"Well, what if we just put my jacket over him?" Spook replied.

"No," Laurel said. "If he wakes up and finds a strange jacket covering him up, he'll get suspicious. He's probably not going to remember any of this, so it's better not to leave any clues. The best thing to do is put him on that little couch on his porch. It's out of the wind. It's not that cold tonight, definitely not below freezing. He'll be okay until morning. If he gets cold and wakes up, he can get inside, even if he has to break in."

They led Russell around to the front of his house and helped him up the steps. He seemed to know where he was.

"What a beautiful night, with all the stars," he muttered as Laurel and Zephyr got him positioned on the couch in a semi-fetal position.

"That will help him retain body heat," Laurel said. "He'll be okay."

"Okay," Laurel said, "the best way out of here for me is to go out to the road. You guys will need to go some other way."

"Well, my car's parked up on the other side of the ridge," Spook said, "over by the river."

"So's mine." Zephyr said. "We'll go together. That way we can each keep a lookout if Brendan or any of his gang are still lurking up there."

Zephyr turned to say goodbye to Laurel, but she was already walking down the driveway, taking off her white robe.

As they walked back up the mountain, Zephyr wanted to ask Spook a little about his background and why he joined the Children, but she knew that she should not ask personal questions. Funny, she thought, I'm still obeying the rules. Besides, it was better if they walked as quietly as they could. Climbing the mountain, Zephyr was impressed by Spook's ability to pick his way through the dark in almost perfect silence. She also noticed that she was moving almost as quietly, quickly but not making much more noise than the faint breeze.

When they reached the parking area, several cars and a motorcycle were still parked there. She wondered which ones would never be retrieved by their owners. She and Spook embraced before she got into her car.

"Thanks for your help, Spook."

"No, Zephyr. I fucked everything up."

"We all do sometimes, Spook," Zephyr said, "We all do."

"By the way, Zephyr, just in case you were wondering, and I don't think it makes any difference now, my real name –"

Zephyr put her fingers on Spook's lips.

"No, Spook. I must never know that. Never"

She gave him a prolonged hug and said, "Goodbye, Spook. We probably will never see each other again. Blessed be."

"Blessed be, Zephyr."

She watched Spook get in his car and drive away. Zephyr started her car. The dashboard clock said 3:07 a.m. She would be home, in bed, and asleep by four. All the way home, she tried to think about anything except what she had just seen and been a part of. All the way home, she cried softly, trying not to think about it.

A Last Dance in the Forest

As soon as Brendan reached the trees, out of the light of the fire around the altar, he glanced back. He saw Rabbit kneel down beside Claw, then get up and start to run after him. Most of the Children were still on the ground, but a few were getting up, beginning to move in on Rabbit. Rabbit slowed enough to point his rifle at them as he continued to run. They hesitated. Some of them dropped back to the ground. Others raised their hands.

He wondered if it would have been better to have continued to stand his ground, to face Rabbit down, not to abandon his Children; but he knew that his survival was imperative. The Children would be okay until he returned; Brendan had taught them to take care of each other. Willy and Claw would take care of Laurel, who had tried to steal his birthright. Zephyr would never be a problem; nobody would ever believe her. All Brendan had to do was lead Rabbit away deep into the forest night.

Just before he turned back to pick his path through the woods, Brendan looked for Willy. After escorting John Bard up the mountain to the Rocks, Willy was supposed to be the security patrol just outside the clearing. Nobody could move as silently through the forest as he could. When trouble started, he had expected to see Willy come into the circle, but there was no sign of him. So, there were two key security facts: Claw was hurt and out of commission, but Willy must be in the forest already, circling around to ambush Rabbit.

Brendan had a good head start on Rabbit, thirty seconds at least. Rabbit was probably in better shape, but Brendan knew that he had gained the advantage as soon as he disappeared into the forest. He also knew Willy would take care of Rabbit. Rabbit would be a dead man soon after he entered the forest. All Brendan had to do was to escape. These were his ancestral lands. Nobody knew them better. Escape would be easy, especially from a drunk like Rabbit.

He plunged ahead into the dark, sometimes tripping over branches and roots, but always regaining his balance on the next step, like a ballet dancer. He could hear Rabbit crashing through the underbrush behind him. Rabbit would be firing soon, so Brendan started to zig and zag, sometimes doubling back three or four feet and occasionally ducking as he moved left and right around the trees.

He heard the crack of Rabbit's rifle and a whoosh by his ear. The white robe! No wonder Rabbit's shot was so close. He began to tear at the robe as he ran, but the dark green belt held it closed. As he loosened the belt, the trees seemed to reach out and grab at the robe, trying to slow him down. Finally, the forest freed him from it.

Brendan was running faster now, leaping and swerving without looking, acting on pure instinct, feeling at one with the forest at night, being part of it, something that Rabbit would never understand – none of them, only John Bard and the other manitous that protected these mountains. Brendan was listening for rocks and branches, like a bat flying through the night, not having to look for them to avoid them. He thought that he could still hear a few voices of the Children, now far away, asking each other what had happened. His hearing had never been sharper. Had John Bard's transfiguration already begun? He could feel John Bard with him, guiding him, telling him when to jump over an unseen obstacle, to zigzag left or right to avoid a shot.

Brendan danced through the forest, drawing in the cool moist night air in deep, satisfying breaths. Another shot cracked through the forest. It didn't seem to be as close as the last one. Perhaps Rabbit was shooting at his discarded robe, hanging on a tree branch and moving in the breeze.

As he ran, Brendan wondered at the sense of euphoria that was coming over him. Was it fear, or the "runner's high" that he had heard about? Or was it the strength that he was drawing from the forest as he escaped?

Strength from the forest, that had to be it. John Bard's strength had passed to him. He was running the race that John Bard had run for his own life, and for the life of the Children, so long ago in the mountains of Wales. Brendan knew now that he would escape. He had become like John Bard. He would live nine hundred years.

Brendan glanced over his shoulder for only the second time since he left the clearing. He was nearing the top of the next ridge northwest of the Rocks. He had to keep low so as not to expose himself against the night sky. All he had to do was get over the ridge and into the dense forest in the valley beyond and then head west. He would be back at the Manse before morning. If necessary, he could collect his gear and head deeper into the mountains. Rabbit would never find him. Willy would find Rabbit first.

Slowing down now to conserve strength and to be as silent as possible, Brendan walked slowly from tree to tree, looking back, listening. He heard another shot, but it was farther away. He knew Rabbit wasn't just guessing. Rabbit must be firing in Brendan's general direction, hoping that Brendan would carelessly expose himself. Brendan kept low.

One more shot was fired. It was from a different gun than the one Rabbit had been shooting. Then Brendan heard the scream that told him that Willy had taken care of Rabbit.

Brendan leaned against a tree, suddenly out of breath. Sweat stung his eyes. His chest heaved and his head pounded. In a way, Rabbit's actions will actually help. Brendan will return, no longer just Brendan but also the reincarnation of John Bard. Walter A. Wentworth, the papers will read, went on a drunken rampage, shot his way into a peaceful gathering of a religious group, killed its leader, and then disappeared, stumbling drunkenly and shooting wildly, into the woods. A scream was heard. In a few weeks, or maybe even not until next spring, some scraps of cloth and bone, and maybe part of a rotting ballcap, will be found high up on the ridge.

Brendan looked up through the trees at the Leonid meteor shower. The stars and the density of the meteors told him that it was after two o'clock. In a way, he thought, this is the end of the world. The Children of Bel have been exposed. There's no way this can be kept quiet. Even with the tightest security, the word will get out, but we can control it. The disappearance of Whitey Wentworth will just fade into legend. We won't have to worry about Russell Poe digging into it. He will become part of the legend himself. We can control it.

Perhaps this is the way it all should end. Perhaps John Bard's transfiguration will mean that the Children of Bel can come out of the sacred groves of the night forests and back into the sunlight. And Brendan Bard will lead them.

Brendan looked back to the southeast, toward the Indian Rocks, now at least two miles away. He thought he could see a faint red glow. That would be the sacred yew being consumed to be reborn for another nine hundred years. He wondered what the Indian Rocks, the yew tree, the endless mountains, would all look like nine hundred years from now. But you will be there, he said to himself. He took a last look at the meteor shower and thought about a fragment from the Book of Job:

Where wast thou when I laid the foundations of the earth? Declare if thou hast understanding.

Who hath laid the measures thereof, if thou knowest? Or who hath stretched the line upon it?

Whereupon are the foundations thereof fastened? Or who laid the corner stone thereof;

When the morning stars sang together, and all the sons of God shouted for joy?

I was there, Brendan almost shouted aloud. I have understanding. I shouted for joy as the morning stars – these very same stars that light my way tonight – sang.

A warm wind streamed up from the next valley. Still moving quickly from tree to tree, he worked his way down the mountainside. No, it would be better not to return to the Manse. Bill Paxton would have done that. Brendan Bard would not. He had two more ridges to cross. He would continue on and by morning he would be at one of John Bard's campsites, hidden deep in the mountains. He could rest there in one of the underground stone chambers for a few days before his "resurrection." Nobody would find him, just as no one had found John Bard for hundreds of years. Like John Bard, he would appear or not, to whom he chose and when he chose.

In the excitement of the escape he had almost forgotten about the third map. It had to be somewhere in or near one of John Bard's campsites– his campsites now. It might take months or years, but he would find it.

In a few days, Brendan would venture out to one of the appointed places where he used to meet John Bard. He knew that Willy would be at one of them, waiting for him. Brendan wondered how he would break the news to Willy that Spook was the Chosen One, the true son of John Bard himself. Willy had always assumed that he would be the one who would now lead the Children. But it would be Spook who eventually would bring the Children back to the sacred groves and lead them forward. Willy was a faithful follower, with great powers. Someday, when his natural life comes to its close, he would be absorbed and would live forever in a sacred yew. Willy had Sight, and he had always been the Trusted One. But he was never destined to lead. It would be a hard thing for Willy to accept at first, but through his obedience he would achieve immortality.

For a moment, Brendan felt remorse for the death of Russell Poe. He had liked Russell. Perhaps Russell could someday have become a real friend, but he was irretrievably of the Other Side. In this life, at least, he had been doomed to be estranged from the White Goddess and those who followed her. This night, with all its wonders and sorrows, was predestined before the world began. Brendan felt comfort, however, in the decision that he had made to allow Russell to become one with the Tioga Yew. Russell was at peace now, with perfect understanding, and would live there forever on that mountain that he and Brendan had both loved. Brendan prayed that in time Russell Poe could become a manitou.

Brendan's prayer was interrupted by the sound of water rushing over rocks. He was approaching the floor of the valley. He came to the bank and looked for a place to ford the stream. Looking across, he saw a shape move through the trees, probably an elk from the size of it, or possibly a bear.

He thought about Claw. Brendan always wanted to call him Art, one of the old Celtic names for the bear. The name first came to Brendan that first day when he met Claw in the visitors' room of Lewisburg Federal Penitentiary, right before he was paroled. The name had fit Claw, with his ability to draw great wisdom from the darkness of night. But Claw told him, "Shit, Brendan, Art sounds like the name of a used car dealer." He chose Claw instead, the deadliest part of a bear. So powerful and so gentle, Claw had sacrificed himself tonight.

Halfway up the second ridge, Brendan began to feel the presence of another being. Just off to the right, perhaps fifty or seventy-five yards away, someone or something was following him. Brendan moved twenty yards to his left and then glanced over. It was still there, the same distance away, no closer and no farther. Brendan could make out a vague shape, nothing more, moving like his shadow up the hill. Sometimes he thought he could make out two forms, one larger and one smaller in the distance. It was probably a bear, or maybe a bear and its cub, curious but no threat unless he moved toward the cub.

Brendan stopped and waited. The shape came ten yards closer and stopped. He stood still and waited. After a few moments, the shape moved closer. Then he saw its eyes, glowing dull red against the darkness.

He turned and ran down the hill, stumbling, tripping, almost falling. The grace that had thrilled him just an hour ago was gone. He crashed down the hillside, bouncing off trees. He tried to look back but couldn't. He heard a loud purring sound rumbling so deep that Brendan could feel it in his feet. He felt himself pushed to the ground from behind, knives digging into his shoulders. His head was caught in a vise, squeezing and pulling at the same time.

The last thing Bill Paxton heard was a scream. His last thought was to wonder whether it was coming from him or from out of the night.

The Lost Day

The morning sun and his shivering began to rouse Russell from a dreamless sleep. Then he felt someone vigorously shaking his shoulder. It was Wanda.

"Wake up, Russell. Wake up. What are you doing out here? Have you been out here all night?"

Russell tried to stretch and sit up on the couch. His body was one giant ache, not quite at the level of pain, but like every muscle had been exercised beyond its limit.

"Were you out here all night? What happened to you? There's dried blood on the back of your head."

Russell had no memory of how he ended up on his front porch or how he hit his head.

"Honestly, Wanda, I just don't know. I guess I was sitting out here last night for a while and fell asleep." His throat was dry, and he sounded hoarse.

He could see that Wanda did not believe that explanation. Neither did he. He looked at his watch. Nine o'clock. He then remembered the breakfast date he had with Wanda. He was going to go to her place for breakfast and then they were going to come back and spend the day working together on the last parts of Jack's book, as they called it.

"When you didn't show up at eight thirty like you promised, I called you, and there was no answer. So, I came over to see if anything was wrong. It looks like I was right. Let's get you inside and get cleaned up a little. I don't like the look of that bump on your head."

Russell stood up, stretched, and walked to the front door. "Ah yes," he said, "nothing like an October night on a couch on the porch to set one up for the day." He reached into his pocket for his keys. They weren't there.

"Now, I remember. I locked myself out last night and didn't want to go hunting around in the dark for the spare key I have hidden under a rock," he said, hoping that it sounded plausible.

"And it was a pleasant evening, so I just said to myself, why not just enjoy the night out here, maybe even watch the meteor shower?"

"But how did you get the bump on your head?"

"I dropped a pen under the kitchen table yesterday afternoon, when I went under to get it, I guess I stood up too soon and banged it on the edge of the table. I didn't even know that it was bleeding." Russell had no idea, but this was the best he could improvise. "I'm sure that it's nothing."

"Well, that may be," Wanda replied, "but let's get inside and get it cleaned off and see how bad it really is."

Wanda went with Russell to the rock under which he had hidden the spare key. Russell stumbled momentarily going back up the two steps onto the front porch. Once they were inside, Russell sat at the kitchen table while Wanda gently cleaned the wound with a wet paper towel and soap.

"I guess it's not so bad," she said, stepping back. "You know how head wounds are, lots of blood but usually not much damage. It probably won't even need stitches, I don't think, but we should stop at the doctor's office just to be sure."

Russell was quiet for several minutes, staring out the kitchen window at the path leading up the mountain behind his house.

"Russell?"

"Huh?"

"It that a private fantasy or can anybody come in?"

"No. I'm sorry, Wanda," he said, turning to face her. He sat down. How to explain what I can't explain, he wondered.

"Wanda, the long and short of it is that the last twenty-four hours is a complete blank." He looked at the kitchen clock. "No, last twenty-seven hours," he added.

"The last thing that I think that I remember clearly is –" Russell paused, searching for the last memory that he knew to be real. "I think that the last thing I remember is getting up yesterday morning. It was just a little after six, still dark out. I remember coming downstairs and going to the back door for some reason, but that's it."

"Why were you going to the back door at that hour," Wanda asked. "Was somebody there, or did you hear a noise out back?"

Russell was silent for a few seconds. Then he shook his head and shrugged. "No," he said, "I simply don't remember. Maybe I had dreamed something like that.

"But the next thing I remember for certain is your waking me up. Everything in between is – well, I don't know how to say it – it's like snatches of a dream that you remember the next day. For example, I have no idea how I hit my head – the kitchen table seems logical – but I have no actual memory of it. Nor do I have any idea where my house keys are, nor how I ended up sleeping on the porch. I think I remember little snippets of really weird memories that can't be real, like a couple frames in a movie, of being up in the forest and being at the Rocks and dreaming that I was being buried alive. But I honestly can't remember anything real from yesterday, other than sitting here in the kitchen early in the morning."

"Well, in that case –" Wanda started to say.

"In that case, I think that we'd better see a doc, like you suggested." Russell said. "I'm going to take a quick shower and change, then we can go."

"Who's your doctor?" Wanda asked. "I can call ahead while you're changing."

"Gee, I haven't hooked up with anyone local yet."

"Russell Poe! You've only lived here almost two years!" Wanda said. "Well, I can call mine and see if he can fit you in. You go get cleaned up and put on some clean clothes. But be careful of that place on your head. You don't want it to start bleeding again.

"Do you want me to come upstairs with you while you change clothes, just in case you pass out?" Wanda asked. "I can wait outside your bedroom, if you like. But those stairs can be tricky and you're not very stable right now."

"No, I'll be fine."

Russell heard the phone ring while he was changing. He thought that a cup of coffee might help stimulate his memory. He wondered whether he was suffering a short-term amnesia from the blow to his head.

When he came back downstairs ten minutes later, Wanda was just hanging up the telephone. She had already made some coffee and poured each of them a cup.

"First of all," she said, "I spoke with Dr. Benet. He's my GP and a pretty good guy. He said he would be happy to see you, but when I described the loss of short-term memory, he said that it would be better if we run into the hospital to get you checked out to rule out a concussion or possibly even a stroke. He told me whom you should ask to see when we get there. His office is going to call ahead so they will be expecting you whenever we can get there. Doc Benet doesn't think it's anything really serious, that these things happen with hard blows to the head sometimes, but he says that we need to rule out some of those more serious things. It's not an emergency, he said, but you really should be seen today."

"Okay, so I guess we can go whenever. Was that him calling back just now?" Russell asked.

"No, it was Chief Verona. He said that they had gotten a report about what he called some strange activity up on your mountain last night, and he'd like to come and check it out. He asked if it would be possible to come right away so that if it turns out that there is a crime scene, it won't be disturbed by the weather or animals or such. He said that you'd understand that."

"Well, I won't be the best witness for him."

"He said that they just want to go up there and have a look, and that they need for you to be here when they do, since they won't have a search warrant."

"Well, that's correct. Did you tell him to come on over?"

"Yes. He said that he'd be here in about thirty minutes, if that's all right. Chief Ray Davis from Wellsboro might come also, since some of the information came from Davis and he's asked the Wellsboro police to assist. I told Chief Verona that you had a doctor's appointment in Wellsboro, and he said that he really needed to speak with you this morning, and that he would be here as soon as possible. I told him that your appointment wasn't until early this afternoon, so that it would be okay."

"We have an appointment?" Russell asked.

"No, not really," Wanda said. "I didn't want to tell them that we were taking you to the hospital. It's none of their damn business."

About twenty minutes later, Russell heard a car in the driveway. He saw a Richmond Township police car drive to about ten feet from the house and park, followed less than five minutes later by one from Wellsboro. Chief Verona and Chief Davis got out of their cars at the same time, shook hands, spoke for a few moments, and then walked together up onto Russell's front porch.

"Well, I'm glad my nosy neighbor, Wanda, is here," Russell said when he opened the door, "what with two cop cars from two different jurisdictions in my driveway. Otherwise, what would she think?"

Wanda poked Russell in the ribs. "Be serious, Russell."

Chief Verona and Chief Davis laughed, and shook hands with Russell and Wanda. The two officers came in and sat side by side on the couch in Russell's living room.

"Can I offer you guys some coffee" Russell offered. Ray Davis accepted and Chief Verona declined. Wanda offered to get it.

Chief Verona explained that early that morning, at 1:35 a.m., his night duty officer received a call from two men who were night fishing in the Tioga River, just south of the Lambs Creek Boat Ramp and across the river from the east side of Russell's property. They heard what sounded to them to be multiple rifle shots coming from the mountain across the river from them. When they looked in the direction of the sound, they saw what they described as one or more fires on the mountain. They looked like campfires. They also thought that they heard voices, but they couldn't be sure that the voices came from the same area.

"You know how sounds reverberate in these valleys," Chief Verona said, "so nobody can ever be one hundred percent sure."

"The other piece that we have is that Chief Davis received information from a confidential source that there was going to be some sort of a religious gathering last night in the mountains, possibly at the Indian Rocks on your property."

"That's right," Ray said. "I left a message on your answering machine late yesterday afternoon. I just wanted to ask you a couple questions about what I'd heard. Did you get the message?"

"Uh, no," Russell replied. "I've been having some problems with my answering machine lately."

"Yeah," Chief Verona said, "they're not really that reliable, are they?

"But, as Chief Davis and I were saying, and as you already know, there have been some other unusual events up there, including that kid that you found up there last winter, Mr. Poe, and also that unsolved death a number of years ago."

Ray looked at Wanda, with a sudden pained expression. "Oh my god, we're sorry, Mrs. Abrams."

"That's all right," Wanda said. "It happened."

"Well, I'm truly sorry, Mrs. Abrams. I really didn't need to remind you of it. Please accept my –"

"Go on, Chief Verona." Wanda replied, "You were saying?"

"Well, we would like your permission, Mr. Poe, to go up there and have a look around a little – just to see if there's any evidence of anything that we should be concerned about," Chief Verona said.

"It's only fair to tell you," Chief Verona continued, "that we have no probable cause to believe that any crimes have been committed up there – having a midnight church service out in the woods is not a crime around here, as far as I know – so if you don't want us poking around up there, that's not a problem at all. But we thought that you would be interested. You can come up with us, if you like."

Russell said that he wasn't feeling well and had an appointment to see a doctor later that day, and that, even if he were feeling okay, he didn't need to be there. They were welcome to look around wherever they wanted. He suggested that they leave their cars in his driveway and take the trail from his back yard.

"It's faster and an easier climb," he said. "But if you need any help or have any questions, let me know. We won't be leaving until about twelve thirty or one."

Russell guided the police officers to his back yard, pointed out the trail, and gave directions. Then he told them about the other trail leading to the Rocks, which went down the eastern slope almost to the river and then south to Lambs Creek Road.

When he returned inside, Russell suggested that Wanda could go back home until it was time for him to go to the hospital, but she said that she wanted to stay with him.

"Head wounds can be unpredictable, and you shouldn't be alone until we get everything checked out," she said. "I'm worried about you, Russell. Something really strange happened to you yesterday, and I'm just not going to relax any until we get some answers, both about your medical condition and whatever the cops find up on the mountain. I think there might be some connection there."

Her tone persuaded Russell to give in. They went upstairs to Russell's study to work on Jack's book together. Russell had several final questions about some of the details in Jack's notes, references that he did not understand but which Wanda might know. He was a little worried that he was having trouble connecting some of his thoughts, even constructing coherent questions. Wanda didn't seem to notice. She simply asked for clarification and answered his questions point by point.

It was almost noon when Chief Verona knocked at the front door. Chief Davis, he explained, had to return to Wellsboro. When the Chief, Wanda, and Russell were all comfortable again in the living room, sipping coffee, Russell asked what, if anything, he had found.

"Nothing of any importance," he said, "except these." He handed a set of keys to Russell.

"They're mine. I've been looking all over for them. Where did you find them?" Russell asked, not knowing what answer to expect.

"About ten yards up the trail. They must have fallen out of your pocket recently. There's no rust on them and they're still clean."

"Why yes, I must have dropped them yesterday." Russell replied. "I didn't notice that they were missing until this morning. Thanks." At least that was the truth, he thought.

"But you said that you found nothing of importance?" Russell asked.

"Well, we didn't do a full crime scene investigation," Chief Verona explained. "It was just me, Chief Davis, and one of the auxiliary officers from my department, who didn't have his radio on so we could tell him about the shortcut through your back yard. The poor guy hiked up the back way lugging our crime scene bag. Basically, what we found were signs that a group of people had been there within the past twenty-four to forty-eight hours. There might have been ten or twenty; we really couldn't tell for sure. The grass and low brush were trampled down in places.

"The first thing we looked for was evidence of gunfire, but we didn't find any shell casings. If someone did fire a firearm, they or someone else scooped up the brass and took it with them.

"We also found a piece of 3/8 inch plastic tubing, about five feet long. There was an empty two-gallon plastic gas can, which had held kerosene. We think that there were some traces of kerosene spilled in places on the ground, but we'd have to send the State Police lab guys up there to confirm it. We found some small wooden matches, most of them unlit. We also noticed some singed spots on the ground where we believe there might have been lanterns or small fires. These surrounded an odd little pile of oak logs and yew branches at the eastern end of the circle, near that magnificent yew tree you have.

"By the way, Mr. Poe, those English yews, I think they're called, they are very rare around here, and that one has to be at least five hundred years old. You're lucky to have one. Does the Pennsylvania Forestry Association know about it?"

"I don't know," Russell said.

"Well, it's a beauty," Chief Verona smiled. "I was concerned when I saw that those morons who were up there, whoever they were, were sloshing kerosene around and trying to build a bonfire so close to the tree. We were lucky that we didn't have a forest fire up there last night, as dry as everything has been the last few days and with all those dry leaves on the ground.

"Do you know who those people were?" the Chief asked.

"No, I don't."

"Aren't you a little concerned about who goes onto your property?"

"Well, I am now, Chief," Russell said. "But my rule has always been that I don't mind people going up there along the trails, taking a break at the Indian Rocks, enjoying the forest, provided that they leave things the way they found them. I know that there is a group, maybe more than one, that sometimes meets up at the Rocks. I've seen the same signs that you saw up there this morning: trampled down grass, usually in paths around the circle, sometimes a broken twig or two. But there's never been any damage, and never any of the junk that you found strewn all about. And I've never seen any signs of a fire of any type."

"Well then, that suggests to me that whoever they were, they left in a hurry, not tidying up like you say they always do." It sounded more like a question from Chief Verona than a conclusion.

"I don't know," Russell said. "Like I said, I've never seen any signs of any of the stuff that you found."

"You know, sir," Chief Verona said, "you are entitled to post your land, and we will prosecute anyone caught trespassing. If, as you say, you have no objection to people enjoying your mountain and forest, this would be a good way to control access. They'd have to ask your permission before going up there. Otherwise, they'd be committing an offense."

"Well, my uncle, when he owned the land, did post it for no hunting," Russell explained. "Some of those signs are still up, but pretty faded, So, I put up a few no-hunting signs myself last summer, when I first moved here. But I concluded that it would be more trouble than it was worth to try to post a piece of land so large."

Wanda gave Russell a look that seemed to say, "You're wandering."

Chief Verona took out a small spiral-bound notepad. The end of the wire binding caught momentarily on the flap on his shirt pocket. "Well, that's your call, sir. I just need now to ask you a few questions about anything unusual that you might have observed last night. I know you have an appointment this afternoon, so I won't take long."

Russell could hear distant alarm bells in his mind. He had no memories of last night or most of yesterday. But something had happened up at the Rocks. How could he answer even the most innocuous questions without lying or looking evasive?

"Sure," he replied. "I want to help any way that I can. I mean, I appreciate you and Chief Davis and your other officer all coming out here this morning to check this out."

"Well, I don't need to ask you a lot of biographical questions, like where you live, *et cetera*. If I need any of that information, I can ask you for it later. I don't need a statement from you or anything like that. I know that you're a lawyer, so –"

"So, Chief, that makes me all the more anxious to help you however I can."

"Well, basically, where were you yesterday?"

"I was here at home all day, except for a time sometime in the late morning when I like to take a little hike up the mountain. It's great exercise, and I try to do it at least three or four times per week."

"And when was that?"

"I was up early, so it would probably have been around eight o'clock, maybe a little earlier. I didn't really notice when I left."

"For how long were you away?"

"Not more than five minutes, maybe seven. I started up the trail and had gone maybe ten or twenty yards when I thought I heard my phone ringing and ran back down. That must be when I dropped my keys."

"Were you expecting a call? Is that why you returned to the house?"

"No, not really, "Russell said. "But sometimes I get calls from my old law firm, usually early in the morning. For some reason, I thought it might have been from them."

"Any particular reason why you would be expecting a call from them yesterday morning, specifically?"

"No, Chief. I just had a hunch, but I was mistaken. By the time I got back to the house, the call had disconnected, of course. There was no message on my answering machine, but it's been malfunctioning lately."

"Yeah, that happens to all of us sometime," Chief Verona said. "So, did you return to the trail?"

"No, I decided to stay at home and work on my books."

"Rather than go back on your hike?"

"Yeah, the telephone call had sort of broken my mood."

"So, you worked on your books then. These were financial records?"

"No, two books that I am doing: one on the French and Indian War and one that I am editing about old folk legends of this part of the state."

"Sounds interesting. I'm a history buff myself. Let me know when you publish them. And did you have any occasion to leave the house later, like to go out to the road and get your mail?"

"Well, yes, I must have. The mail usually comes around three o'clock. It takes only five or six minutes.

"You say that you must have. Does that mean that you don't have a specific memory of doing so?"

"No, not really. It's kind of an automatic chore, like doing the dishes. But I'm sure I did."

"Any other times after that when you were outside the house?"

"No, not that I recall."

"And when did you turn in for the evening?"

"It was probably around ten-thirty or eleven. I don't really remember the exact time."

"And at any time during the night, did you hear any unusual noises, like gunfire, or any people talking, or anything unusual like that from up on the mountain behind your house?"

"No, sir." Russell felt relieved that at last he could answer truthfully. "No, I didn't hear anything at all unusual. I couldn't go to sleep right away, so, after about a half-hour, I decided to go out on the front porch. Sometimes the crisp autumn air is relaxing, and it wasn't very cold last night, so I thought that I would sit outside on the front porch for a while. It was probably eleven or eleven-thirty. I guess I fell asleep on the couch and didn't wake up until almost nine this morning. Had there been gunshots anywhere close, they would have woken me up, I'm sure."

"Now please don't take these next two questions wrong, Mr. Poe, but I need to ask them because they go to your opportunity to observe."

Russell smiled, "No, I understand. I fell asleep outside on my porch and slept until nine o'clock the next morning. What, if any, alcoholic beverages had I had to drink? None the entire day or evening. What, if any medications, do I take? Again, none. Don't worry, Chief. Those are fair questions."

Chief Verona turned to Wanda. "Now, Mrs. Abrams, I understand that you live at the next place, just down the road.

"That's right."

"And you are Mr. Poe's closest neighbor?"

"Right again."

"Did you have any occasion to visit Mr. Poe yesterday?"

"No, I spent the day at my place wrapping up the paperwork from this year's harvest. I grow apples."

"I know, and they are wonderful."

"Thank you, Chief. I was home all day and evening. I don't think that I would have been able to hear any gunshots from the Rocks, depending on which way the wind was blowing. I think I might be too far away. I really don't know. But I didn't hear or see anything unusual last night."

"And I can corroborate Russell's story about sleeping out on the porch all night. He was just waking up when I came by around nine this morning. We had an appointment for breakfast and for me to help him work on one of his books."

Chief Verona thanked them for the information and Russell for allowing them to look around on his property. He gave them each his card, smiled, shook hands, and left.

Wanda went home, changed clothes, and returned thirty minutes later to drive Russell to his appointment. "There's no way in hell that I'm letting you loose on the roads of our fair county with a possible concussion or brain damage or who knows what," she insisted.

"Any brain damage is, I am sure, a pre-existing condition," Russell laughed.

They arrived at the hospital just before two thirty. After dressing the wound, x-rays, and blood tests, Dr. Patel, an emergency room resident whom Dr. Benet had described as a "great skull guy," discussed the results with Russell. Russell asked Wanda to be in the consultation with him, "in case I don't remember something," he said.

"Mr. Poe, the short-term memory loss you're experiencing is consistent with a sharp blow to the head, such as the one that you sustained. The wound was superficial, but, as you know, they can produce spectacular bleeding. The good news is that there are no signs of fracture. At most you might have suffered a mild concussion, which might explain the slight loss of balance that you experienced earlier this morning, but which is better this afternoon. There are no signs of a stroke, which was my biggest concern, but which would be unlikely for someone of your age with your good blood pressure and low cholesterol levels. Drugs – even over-the-counter antihistamines for some people – can also cause short-term memory loss, but you say that you haven't needed to take any for years, so we can rule that out.

"A solid blow to the head, such as you sustained, even if it doesn't produce a significant cut, can affect people differently. Likewise, the extent of memory loss, if it occurs at all, can vary widely. You say that yesterday is almost a complete blank, except for what you describe as fleeting, but – your word – bizarre memories like the one about being buried alive, or the one where you're looking at a dead animal, the one where you're walking down a hill with three other people. Completely false memories, even though they are vivid and seem real, also are very common."

"But Doctor, as I told you, I don't even remember being hit on the head or bumping my head on something, or any trauma like that."

"That's not unusual Mr. Poe. I have seen cases where the patient not only loses all memory of the injury, but even memories from before the injury – sometimes as few as hours before and sometimes even for weeks or months before.

"It is possible that, in time, your memory of yesterday will return. When it does, and if it does, it might be just in bits and pieces, like a few pages in a larger book. You might eventually be able to reconstruct much of what happened from external stimuli, like a newspaper, or documents, or other people or places with which you interacted. You'll never be sure, because these reconstructions sometimes are what we assume must have happened, but not what really happened.

"Or the lost memory might never return. Just as you are not normally able to remember every single day of your life, yesterday might be a lost day forever."

Russell was instructed to contact Dr. Patel if his memory loss expanded to block out a greater period of time, or if it recurred without another blow to the head.

Russell was quiet on the ride home, still not wanting to accept the logical medical explanation that he knew that he had to accept. He felt frustrated just one degree below angry, that, in a very real sense, he was losing his mind – at least the part where yesterday was stored. He felt trapped by being detached from his own reality, constrained by the futility of reaching out in the dark to probe his memory. He closed his eyes and could see only thin reddish blurry shadows dancing on a wall where there should have been inscribed his yesterday.

Changing Seasons

On a sunny Friday morning two days after the Lost Day, as Russell called it, he and Wanda climbed the trail to the Rocks. He didn't know whether it was his memory of the Lost Day beginning to come back to the surface or just suggestions from Chief Verona's description about what he found at the scene. The scene – Russell kept thinking of the area around the Rocks as *the scene,* but the scene of what?

As they hiked up the trail, Russell realized that, as far as he knew, this was Wanda's first visit to the Rocks. This might not be a good idea. About halfway up the mountain, Russell stopped.

"I just wanted to show you the view. When you're focused on getting up to the top, sometimes you forget to turn around and enjoy it," he said.

"It's very nice," Wanda said, "but I'm really anxious to see these famous Indian Rocks."

"Well, about that, Wanda," Russell said. "I don't know how to say this, but are you sure that you want to go there? I don't mean just go there to the location, but also go there to the horrible memories even the mention of them must bring. It's all right if you're not ready, or even if you'll never be ready."

"Can we sit down for a moment, Russell?" Wanda asked.

Russell found a grassy spot along the path. They sat beside each other and looked down the mountain. They could see the roof of Russell's house and the forest on the other side of the road, stretching to the horizon. Russell pointed to the left.

"If you look over there, you can see your house and even a few of the apple trees," he said.

Wanda said, "Russell, I know why you stopped. I know what happened at the top of the ridge six and a half years ago.

"One of the things that I really love about you, Russell, is that you have always been so thoughtful towards me and so respectful of Jack's memory."

"Well, it's nothing –" Russell started to say.

"But, Russell, I'm not a fragile china doll. I knew that this day would come, when I would need to – no, *want to* – come here. It's something that I need to do if I am ever going to be able to live with the grief that I still feel every day of my life, if I am ever really going to be able to get back out into the world. And I don't mean the superficial Welcome Lady stuff, but really out in the world and part of it again, perhaps even being able to form and enjoy new relationships.

"Jack wants me to take this hike with you, Russell. He wants me to see where it happened. I know that he really appreciates my courage – and, yes, even my sacrifice – in going to the Rocks. Jack always told me that the best way to face fears of the unknown is to look at them, to stare them down, and not to turn away. And Russell, you have helped me to remember that.

"So, I'm ready, Russell. This is something I want to do – for Jack, for me, and maybe even for you, too." Wanda jumped up and looked down at Russell, who was still seated.

"So, let's go," she said, as she turned and resumed the climb to the ridge.

When they arrived at the Indian Rocks, Wanda remained outside the circle. Russell looked back at her, fearing that she was emotionally unable to enter.

"Don't worry, Russell, she said. "This is the first time I've ever seen them. It might be the last. So, I just want to take everything in."

A few moments later she joined Russell in the center of the circle. The area was as Chief Verona had described. Even two days later, Russell was able to point out to Wanda where the people had been, where they entered, and where they must have been standing. He walked around the base of the yew tree and found four more unburned matches. He noticed the round discolored spots, each about eight inches wide, which circled the pile of logs neatly stacked in a rectangle in front of the tree. The still fresh yew branches were laid in a herringbone pattern on top of the logs. Most of them were still in place.

Russell pointed out the grid where he and Whitey had begun the archeological excavation. It was already becoming overgrown, a tangle of rotting string and new plants, just a shallow depression. He wanted to show Wanda the entrance to the underground chambers, but the brush that he had piled there a year ago was gone and the hole had apparently been repaired and covered. He thought that he remembered the pile of brush that covered it having been there three weeks ago.

"Wanda," Russell said, "I just have this feeling that I was up here Wednesday night. I can't explain why I think that, but I just have this deep impression, not really a memory, but more like some shadows projected before my mind."

"Was that pile of logs here that last time you remember being up here?" Wanda asked.

"No, that part I remember clearly. I was here Saturday three weeks ago. The logs – that whole construction – definitely were not here. It reminds me of some sort of altar. Somebody built that since I was here last and put these yew branches here on top of them."

"What are you going to do with all that," Wanda said, pointing at the stack of logs. "I know that you've always told me that you like to keep this area undisturbed, natural."

Russell chuckled, "Well, except for a ring of eleven upright stones, yeah, as natural as possible. I'll just leave this stuff here, let it rot away and become just another part of the forest. It can become a habitat for some of the animals or birds."

Russell had returned only once after that. It was the day after the winter solstice, December 22nd, and he wanted to see whether the mysterious group had returned. There had been a light snow the night before, and there were no footprints or other signs on the ground. Everything looked totally undisturbed. Before going back down the mountain, Russell had heard birds overhead in the yew. They were large, like ravens, but probably only just big grackles.

Standing by the twisted, rough trunk, Russell remembered a voice from the Lost Day, one that he hadn't remembered before: *Just stay quiet and all will be well*. He was certain now that he had heard that voice that Lost Day. Now he heard it again, clearly not muffled like before. *Just stay quiet and all will be well.* It sounded like the voice of the old man in the old-fashioned blue coat whom he encountered that sleepy afternoon last summer.

Russell looked around. He walked all around the outside of the stone circle, peering into the forest. He had that strong sense that he had felt sometimes before on the mountain, that someone or something was close, watching him, moving with him; but, as always, he saw nothing.

During November and December, Wanda would sometimes gently ask him whether he remembered anything more from That Day, as she called it. She seemed to refuse to call it the Lost Day, as Russell did. At first, Russell would try to summon some trace of any memory; he didn't really care if it was real or false. All he wanted was something that at least looked real. But he usually would just smile, shrug, and shake his head. Before long Wanda stopped asking. "Give it time," was the most that she would say.

Wanda left two days before Christmas to visit her sister in Florida. They celebrated an early Christmas at Wanda's house, sharing the cooking together. When she answered the door, Russell was standing beside two cardboard boxes. He held two smaller boxes, one on top of the other, in his hands.

"What's all this?" Wanda asked.

"Well, these are your Christmas presents," Russell said, handing Wanda the two boxes he was carrying. He picked up the two larger boxes and took them through the front door, as Wanda stood aside.

"And I am returning these," he said, setting the two large boxes inside the door.

Wanda glanced at the two boxes on the floor. "Russell, does this mean," she paused, setting down the two smaller boxes on the small table by the door. "Does this mean that Jack's work is done?"

"Wanda," Russell said quietly, "Jack's work will never be done, because he set out to record something that will never end. But this is the best that I could do with it for now." He picked up the larger of the two boxes from the table, took off the lid, and handed it to Wanda.

"*The Sangman's Ghost,*" he said quietly.

Wanda said nothing. She took the box into the living room, sat in Jack's old chair, and removed the manuscript from the box. Russell saw her shoulders trembling over the stack of typed pages and heard her almost soundless sobs.

Russell quietly picked up the other box from the table by the door and withdrew to the kitchen. He sat at the table and stared out the window, hoping that he had done justice to Jack's work over the years and his sacrifice at the end.

About ten minutes later, Wanda came into the kitchen. Her face looked composed. She smiled as she sat down beside Russell and showed him the single sheet of paper in her hand. It was blank except for these words:

For Wanda

"Russell," she said, "I knew this day would come, but now that it's here –"

"There's nothing that you need to say, Wanda." Russell said, reaching across and taking her hand.

"But Russell, you brought Jack – Jack's work – back to life. You worked so hard and so long, and your name is nowhere in the book."

"And it never should be, Wanda. This is Jack's work and yours, not mine."

"But, Russell."

"Please, Wanda, not another word. I want you to take your time over the next few weeks – take as much time as you want – to read this and tell me whether there are any changes, any additions or deletions or corrections, that I need to make to make this even more like Jack. Then, with your permission, I will send it to Penn State, Pitt, Temple University, and the University of Pennsylvania, if that's okay with you. I have some connections at all four places, and they each have expressed some preliminary interest. It will be a scholarly work, not just a bunch of ghost stories. Jack deserves that respect."

"Oh, Russell," Wanda responded. She said nothing else.

"Do you want me to take those boxes up to the attic?" Russell asked.

"No, never," Wanda said. "Leave them here. I'm going to unpack them and keep the notebooks and journals down here, where people can see them."

"Goodness," she then exclaimed, "we have to finish dinner."

Wanda and Russell focused on preparing a simple Christmas dinner. Later, over coffee, they exchanged gifts.

Wanda gave Russell a Pelikan fountain pen and a bottle of German blue-black ink, "to be used only in your writing," she said. He promised that they would occupy a central place in the only clear spot on his desk, one which he kept perpetually free of clutter, almost like a shrine.

"Well, I still have a lot of writing to do," Russell said.

"Another book? What is it? Tell me." Wanda said. Russell noticed excitement in her voice for the first time that day.

"Well," Russell said, "first I need to finish the Braddock book."

"It's not finished? What happened? Oh Russell, I never wanted you to sacrifice –" Wanda interrupted.

"Don't worry, Wanda. Two things: First, the day that you gave me those boxes, *The Sangman's Ghost* became a priority."

"Not because of me, I hope," Wanda said.

"No," Russell said, not entirely convinced that it was the truth.

"Second," he continued, "I have finished the first draft of the Braddock book, but there still are some points that I am not satisfied with, that need some more research and some better writing. But I'll finish it soon and start my next project."

"Which is?" Wanda asked.

"I don't know for sure," Russell said. "But it's out there, somewhere in the mountains of my mind. I just have to find it."

Russell gave Wanda an old silver tray with the Echo Rapids in Western Pennsylvania engraved on it. "It was my mother's. It was one of her favorite places" was all he could say, hardly able to speak and forcing back tears, when he handed it to her. As much as he wanted to, he couldn't tell her that it also was where she died.

Wanda returned in January, three weeks later, complaining about how her sister and her "monsters" were worse than ever and vowing "never again." Several days later, when Wanda had come over for coffee on her way out to make her Welcome Wagon rounds, Russell asked her how it was going.

"Well, it's strange, Russell," she replied. "Ever since November, there have been a lot of folks moving away from around here, more so than usual for this time of year. Usually we don't see a lot of turnover until late April or May. Maybe I should go into business as the Farewell Lady."

"For example," Wanda continued, "as you know, the Kaisers left in September. I understand that they sold their store to a couple of investors from Scranton. And Connie and Dick Graybill just up and left right before Thanksgiving."

"I wondered why I hadn't heard anything from them. Where'd they go?" Russell asked. "What happened?"

"Well," Wanda said, "it seems that Connie was offered a job as the head of the Anthropology Department at West Virginia University, but they needed her to start immediately."

"So, you spoke with her before she left?" Russell asked.

"No," Wanda replied, "I didn't see her or hear from her after the strange dinner you and I had with them at their place. I found all this out, just a couple days ago, from one of my real estate buddies in town. I didn't even know they were gone.

"She called and asked if I knew of anyone who wanted to buy their place, because she had a couple of 'motivated sellers,' as she described Dick and Connie. My friend said that Connie moved to Morgantown in November and the place had been empty ever since. Connie apparently commuted back and forth until the end of the semester, so that she could finish her courses at Mansfield, but she stayed at a motel over there."

"And what about Dick?" Russell asked. "Did he stay and finish the semester or just move to West Virginia?"

"I don't know," Wanda said. "I sort of got a sense from my friend that Dick stayed here to finish the semester at Mansfield and then moved away. Maybe he and Connie had split up, but she didn't tell me any details, and I didn't feel comfortable asking. I don't want people to think that I've become an old gossip."

Soon after Wanda told him about Connie, he received a telephone call from Susan Kline at the *Wellsboro Bulletin.* It was a cold morning at the end of February. As Russell looked out the window in his study, every tree was sheathed in ice, sparkling like blue crystal in the early morning sun.

"Russell, it's Susan. From the *Bulletin,* remember?"

"Of course, I remember you." Russell was annoyed by the question.

"Oh, I'm sorry," Susan said. "Did I say something wrong?"

"No, no," Russell assured her. "No, my mind was on something else when you called. I was just –" he paused, "just trying to remember where I left my car keys."

"Oh, that happens to me all the time."

"What can I do for you, Susan?"

"Nothing, but I thought you'd be interested in knowing some news about someone we know, Clay Collins – you know, the guy who ran the cougar center, the guy you consulted with about Jack. Well, he has been found."

"Found?"

Susan explained that Clay had been reported missing around the first of November. Apparently, from some notes on his desk, he had gone to an appointment on October 24th or 25th – the dates were written together with a slash – and never returned home. His cleaning lady found the door locked when she came for her weekly visits and noticed the mail piling up higher at his doorstep. The lights had been on in his house all the time. Two weeks later, when she hadn't heard from him, she filed a missing person report with the local police.

"Is he okay?"

"No, as a matter of fact, he's dead. And the ironic part is that it looks like a cougar attacked him, a big one."

"*The* big one," Russell responded.

"Huh?"

"There's a panther up in the forest, Susan. Folks have been talking about it and reporting it for over a hundred years. Clay knew about it. He once told me that he couldn't prove it, but he knew it was real."

"Guess it found him before he found it," Susan said.

"Were they sure it was a cougar?"

"Yes, Russell. Clay had been dead for at least three months, and in the water for some of that time, but there was enough of him left so they could be sure. Being in the cold water all that time helped. The cops and the Coroner didn't screw it up this time, like they did with Jack Abrams. They identified Clay from cards in his wallet and his dental records."

"Where did they find him?"

"That's the odd part," Susan said. "He was found floating face down in the Tioga Reservoir. Something or someone – maybe the cat – dragged him out of the forest and into the water. They think that his body might have floated down the river from somewhere around Mansfield, but they couldn't be sure. But the cause of death was definitely massive bleeding caused by the attack. He was dead before he went into the water.

"It turns out that the poor guy had no friends, at least none that would come forward. He had a sister, who had lived temporarily with him about eight or nine months ago, but she had disappeared, supposedly moved out west somewhere. Finally, right before his body was to be moved from the morgue to be cremated and his ashes buried somewhere, the folks at the Mountain View Chapel came forward and took care of him, gave him a funeral with full military honors, and buried him in the old cemetery up the road from their church."

"You really investigated this then, didn't you Susan?"

"Well, Russell, I was going to do a human-interest piece on Clay. He was really quite an interesting guy: former Marine, a lawyer like you, one of the top experts, it appears, about the Eastern mountain lion, even a little into cryptozoology."

"What happened to the things at his house? He had a lot of material about cougars there."

"Nobody knows," Susan said. "That's a strange part of this story. After about two weeks, Clay's cleaning lady filed the missing person report, but, as is usual in these cases, the cops really don't do any looking for the person. About two weeks after that – so this would be about a month after Clay disappeared – they received an anonymous report that his place had been burglarized. When the police went to investigate, they found the front door unlocked and the place had been stripped clean, not a stick of furniture left. I understand that whoever cleaned the place out even took the nameplate that had been screwed to the front door."

"And who did this?" Russell asked.

"Nobody has any idea. His sister Margaret would be an obvious suspect, but nobody has seen or heard of her since she moved out west last summer. I understand from one of my sources that they could find no trace of her and that she might have even left the country. But I'm not sure that they looked very hard."

"But you said that you *were* going to do a piece on Clay. What happened?" Russell asked. "Aren't you going to publish it? It sounds interesting."

"Well, the *Bulletin* isn't going to publish it. Greg Paxton – you remember, the publisher – told me that it's too gruesome for a family newspaper. The Philly *Daily News* said that they might pick it up. I've also put out some feelers to the *National Enquirer.*"

The following Friday afternoon, when Russell was in Wellsboro, he stopped by the *Bulletin* office on the chance that Susan would be interested in having a cup of coffee and talking more about Clay. The receptionist said that she had quit the previous day to take a job in Philadelphia with the *Daily News.* The receptionist gave Russell Susan's forwarding address at the *Daily News.* It bothered Russell that she hadn't said goodbye, but that was so much like Susan Kline and her transactional approach to life.

The First Day of Spring

Patches of old snow still hid beneath the mountain laurel, but the March sun was warm that afternoon. It was the first day of spring. Russell Poe sat on the pile of logs in front of the old yew tree, looking back up the slope across the Indian Rocks. Spots of purple and yellow – crocuses, buttercups, and the very first wild violets – already dotted the center of the circle of rocks. Russell thought that he could see the first hints of buds on the branches overhead. He hoped that it would be an early summer this year.

Russell thought about how he had stayed away from the Rocks since his last visit in December. What had he been trying to avoid all those weeks? He would tell himself that the weather was too bad, or that he had other things that he needed to do. At the same time, he knew that he was lying to himself. He still took his hikes up into the mountains and along the old Indian trail, and sometimes over the ridge and east down to the river or turning north to wander through the State Game Lands. But he avoided the Rocks. Even when he passed along the trail near them, he would look away. Even thinking about the Rocks brought back the frustration of the Lost Day, and this cause-and-effect relationship only reinforced his unprovable feeling that he had been there and that something so horrible had happened that he had blocked it out, short-term amnesia or not.

Russell looked around the circle. "So, why am I here now?" Russell asked aloud. He supposed that it was a combination of the beautiful early spring weather and the letter that he received that morning that brought him – summoned him? – to the Rocks. Russell had returned late last night from a day trip to Philadelphia and decided to wait until morning to retrieve his mail. Walking back up his drive from the mailbox, he noticed the envelope with the return address of the Mountain View Chapel.

He had a feeling that the letter was about Bill Paxton, who had disappeared in late October. Officer Passarelli telephoned him when she was investigating the missing person report. Russell's last contact with Bill was when he gave Bill the books from Bill's childhood, in late September. He had wondered why Bill had not been in contact with him since, but he was unable to provide any information.

For some reason that he could not articulate, Russell felt that it might be better – somehow more fitting – for him to read the letter from Bill's church at the Rocks. Sitting on the pile of logs by the yew tree, he opened the envelope and read:

Dear Mr. Poe:

As you know, our Pastor, Rev. William Paxton, disappeared almost six months ago. After much soul searching and prayer, the Board of Deacons of this congregation has decided to declare the pastorate vacant and seek a new shepherd for our flock.

We rejoice that our search has been successful. The Lord has led us to a minister of the Gospel who has accepted our call to him to be our new Pastor. As he will be installed later this month, it therefore becomes our sad duty to remove Pastor Paxton's personal effects from the Manse and entrust them to someone for safekeeping until such time as, God willing, he returns to us. If, after a reasonable time, we are denied that blessing, you may dispose of them as you please.

As you may know, Pastor Paxton's only known relative is Mr. Gregory Paxton, of Wilkes-Barre, Pa. Mr. Paxton has told us that he would prefer not to assume this responsibility. We therefore now turn to you, whom some of us know to have been one of Pastor Paxton's close personal friends in the Wellsboro area. Indeed, Pastor Paxton mentioned on many occasions the interests that the two of you shared, and how much he enjoyed your visits together.

If you find yourself in a position to assume custody of Pastor Paxton's personal belongings, which consist of pieces of family furniture, as well as his personal books and papers, which we have boxed up for your convenience, please contact the undersigned at your earliest convenience, preferably before the end of this month.

Confident that the Lord will encourage your favorable response, we thank you in advance for your kind assistance in this matter.

Sincerely,
Sarah Wasilenko
Chairperson

Russell set the letter beside him on the yew branches, still green after so many months after having been cut. He reached into his leather bag and pulled out a half bottle of Pinot Noir, a plastic cup, and a piece of cheese. He looked around the clearing. He tried to picture it with people there, performing ceremonies in the night. He took a deep sip of the wine, closed his eyes, and stretched his neck back against the top log in the pile behind him. He soaked in the sun.

How could he say no to this request? He would have to put aside his suspicions about Bill. Even now, there were some things about Bill Paxton that he liked, even admired. He was willing to trust that Ms. Wasilenko and her colleagues did not know the dark doubts that lingered. It was just a simple request to help the church dispose of some unwanted property, which might have some things of interest for Russell, like the old photographs. It meant nothing more. He would sell most of it, except possibly the rocking chair and the old photography, and give the proceeds to charity.

Russell heard a rustle in the brush. He was a little surprised at how he had become more sensitive to the sounds of the forest. A moment later Whitey Wentworth's lanky form strode into the clearing. He was wearing camouflage coveralls and an ancient green baseball cap and carrying a knapsack slung over one shoulder.

"Afternoon, Russell. I sort of thought I'd find you here today. I figured it would be too nice a day for you to stay cooped up down in the house."

"What brings you up here? I haven't seen you since –" Russell calculated. Since before the Lost Day, he thought.

"Oh, yeah, I am truly sorry about bugging out on you when I know we had a lot of work to do, getting things ready for winter and all. But I got a good steady job over near Towanda and more or less spent the whole winter over there. I meant to call, but you know how it is."

"Yeah, I know how it is," Russell murmured. A thousand voices whispered: *Do not trust this man.*

"Actually," Whitey said, "I was just passing through, taking a short cut, so to speak, and I said to myself, 'I wonder if old Russell Poe would be up here sitting in his favorite spot at the Rocks, enjoying this first day of spring.' So, I came down from the trail and there you were.

"Well, like I said, Russell, I'm just passing through. I heard tell of a patch of old sang – you know the really good stuff – a couple of ridges over and thought I'd check it out."

"When did you become a sangman, Whitey?"

"Always was, Russell, always was, although I didn't know it at the time. Just following in Daddy and Granddaddy's footsteps, I suppose."

"Want a bit of cheese and some wine before you go? I've got plenty." Russell reached in the sack and pulled out another plastic cup, the spare that he always carried in case one got cracked.

Whitey frowned momentarily at the wine, but his voice was cheerful. "Why thank you, Mr. Poe. That's mighty kind."

"Not at all, Mr. Wentworth. Sorry I can't offer you anything a bit stronger."

Whitey dropped his knapsack on the ground. As he did an old leather case, about four inches by eight inches fell out. The top flap fell open, revealing one or two folded sheets of old paper, yellow fading to brown at the edges. Whitey quickly scooped up the case and stuffed it back in his sack.

The two men sat silently eating their cheese and sipping their wine as they each looked off into the forest. After a couple of minutes, Russell said, "Whitey, I've been meaning to ask you –"

"Fire away, Russell. I probably don't know the answer, but I can make up a good one."

"Well, do you remember a night back just before Halloween, when there were some strange things going on up here: campfires and possibly some gunshots?"

"Oh, yeah. I think Sandy – that's my lady friend – I think Sandy told me something about that. Her dad's the police chief down in Wellsboro, you know."

"You weren't up here in this area by any chance?"

Whitey laughed, "With a bunch of goofy hippies prancing around naked up here in the woods? Oh, that's a good one, Russell."

"Well," Russell said, "the Richmond police had gotten some reports of fires and gunshots from somewhere up here, and the police – Chief Verona from the township and Chief Davis from Wellsboro – came out the next morning and asked to look around. They told me that they found some stuff up here, but no evidence of any gunshots."

"No, it wasn't me making any ruckus up here. I was probably sound asleep in my trailer over there in Towanda. I start work at seven thirty every morning. Needed my beauty rest."

"Yeah, me too," Russell said.

Whitey got to his feet and slung his knapsack over his shoulder.

"Well, I got to be going if I'm going to find that stand of sang before nightfall. Thanks very much for the snack. Always a pleasure to see you, Russell."

As Whitey started to walk down the hill, toward the river, Russell called out, "I'm going to need you for a couple of projects. How do I get in touch with you?'

"You can't, Russell. But know this, Russell: You will always be my friend." He gave Russell a funny kind of salute, and a moment later he had vanished into the forest.

Russell looked up the hill, past the tall upright stones. He closed his eyes and let the sunlight warm his face. The afternoon breeze carried the distant sound of an old man, singing a funny little tune with no words. As he opened his eyes, he saw it for just a moment up on the ridgeline: a flash of blue cloth moving – no, dancing – through the forest, carrying a long rifle. He heard the voice again, the voice of an ageless old man: *Just stay quiet and all will be well.*

He remembered the song that Bill Paxton sang for him. He closed his eyes and sang it loudly, wanting it to reverberate forever off the mountains, singing it for John Bard, and for Simon Poe, and for Whitey's father and grandfather, and for Jack Abrams, and yes, even for Bill Paxton and his family, all of whom were long gone:

His blue soldier's coat a-flashin' in the forest
Runnin' the ridges, singin' his song,
A-laughin' as he roams through the endless mountains
Askin' you kindly to come along

Would he be the last person ever to sing that song? He opened his eyes again. The figure in the long blue coat was still up there, standing where the path from the Rocks met the old Indian trail along the ridge, a hazy, incomplete silhouette against the low afternoon sun.

Russell got up slowly and started up the path on his way home.

Made in the USA
Monee, IL
14 June 2024

59775595R00403